A
Garland Series

VICTORIAN
FICTION

NOVELS OF FAITH
AND DOUBT

*A collection of 121 novels
in 92 volumes, selected by
Professor Robert Lee Wolff,
Harvard University,
with a separate introductory volume
written by him
especially for this series.*

ROBERT FALCONER

George MacDonald

Three volumes in one

Garland Publishing, Inc., New York & London

1975

Bibliographical note:

this facsimile has been made from a copy in the
Beinecke Library of Yale University
(Ip.M145.868R)

Library of Congress Cataloging in Publication Data

Macdonald, George, 1824-1905.
  Robert Falconer.

  (Victorian fiction : Novels of faith and doubt ;
v. 60)
  Reprint of the 1868 ed. published by Hurst and
Blackett, London.
  I. Title. II. Series.
PZ3.M144Ro9 [PR4967]   823'.8   75-1510
ISBN 0-8240-1584-3

Printed in the United States of America

ROBERT FALCONER

BY

GEORGE MAC DONALD LL.D.

AUTHOR OF

" ALEC FORBES OF HOWGLEN,"

" DAVID ELGINBROD,"

&c. &c.

Countrymen,
My heart doth joy that yet, in all my life.
I found no man but he was true to me.
BRUTUS in *Julius Cæsar.*

IN THREE VOLUMES

VOL. I.

LONDON:
HURST AND BLACKETT, PUBLISHERS,
13, GREAT MARLBOROUGH STREET.
1868.

*** The author desires to have it understood that not a single poem in this tale is of his own composition. The poems are, however, his property, and appear for the first time in print. The careless work of a friend of his boyhood, he has not even trimmed them.

TO

THE MEMORY

OF THE MAN WHO

STANDS HIGHEST IN THE ORATORY

OF MY MEMORY,

ALEXANDER JOHN SCOTT,

I, DARING, PRESUME TO DEDICATE THIS BOOK.

CONTENTS

OF

THE FIRST VOLUME.

———

PART I.—HIS BOYHOOD.

CHAPTER		PAGE
I.	A Recollection	1
II.	A Visitor	5
III.	The Boar's Head	17
IV.	Shargar	25
V.	The Symposium	36
VI.	Mrs. Falconer	61
VII.	Robert to the Rescue	76
VIII.	The Angel Unawares	85
IX.	A Discovery	94
X.	Another Discovery in the Garret	105
XI.	Private Interviews	129
XII.	Robert's Plan of Salvation	150
XIII.	Robert's Mother	172
XIV.	Mary St. John	183
XV.	Eric Ericson	189
XVI.	Mr. Lammie's Farm	202
XVII.	Adventures	219

CHAPTER   PAGE
XVIII. Nature puts in a Claim   237
  XIX. Robert Steals his own   247
   XX. Jessie Hewson   265
  XXI. The Dragon   279
 XXII. Dr. Anderson   285
XXIII. An auto da fé   290
XXIV. Boot for Bale   309
 XXV. The Gates of Paradise   318

ROBERT FALCONER.

PART I.—HIS BOYHOOD.

CHAPTER I.

A RECOLLECTION.

ROBERT FALCONER, schoolboy, aged fourteen, thought he had never seen his father;
that is, thought he had no recollection of having
ever seen him. But the moment when my story
begins, he had begun to doubt whether his belief
in the matter was correct. And, as he went on
thinking, he became more and more assured that
he had seen his father somewhere about six years
before, as near as a thoughtful boy of his age
could judge of the lapse of a period that would
form half of that portion of his existence which
was bound into one by the reticulations of memory.

For there dawned upon his mind the vision of
one Sunday afternoon. Betty had gone to

church, and he was alone with his grandmother,
reading the *Pilgrim's Progress* to her, when, just
as Christian knocked at the wicket-gate, a tap
came to the street door, and he went to open it.
There he saw a tall, somewhat haggard-looking
man, in a shabby black coat (the vision gradually dawned upon him till it reached the minuteness of all these particulars), his hat pulled down
on to his projecting eyebrows, and his shoes
very dusty, as with a long journey on foot—it
was a hot Sunday, he remembered that—who
looked at him very strangely, and without a
word pushed him aside, and went straight into
his grandmother's parlour, shutting the door behind him. He followed, not doubting that the
man must have a right to go there, but questioning very much his right to shut him out.
When he reached the door, however, he found it
bolted; and outside he had to stay all alone, in
the desolate remainder of the house, till Betty
came home from church.

He could even recall, as he thought about it,
how drearily the afternoon had passed. First
he had opened the street door, and stood in it.
There was nothing alive to be seen, except a
sparrow picking up crumbs, and he would not
stop till he was tired of him. The "Royal Oak,"
down the street to the right, had not even a
horseless gig or cart standing before it; and
King Charles, grinning awfully in its branches on

the signboard, was invisible from the distance at which he stood. In at the other end of the empty street, looked the distant uplands, whose waving corn and grass were likewise invisible, and beyond them rose one blue truncated peak in the distance, all of them wearily at rest this weary Sabbath day. However, there was one thing than which this was better, and that was being at church, which, to this boy at least, was the very fifth essence of dreariness.

He closed the door and went into the kitchen. That was nearly as bad. The kettle was on the fire, to be sure, in anticipation of tea; but the coals under it were black on the top, and it made only faint efforts, after immeasurable intervals of silence, to break into a song, giving a hum like that of a bee a mile off, and then relapsing into hopeless inactivity. Having just had his dinner he was not hungry enough to find any resource in the drawer where the oatcakes lay, and, unfortunately, the old wooden clock in the corner was going, else there would have been some amusement in trying to torment it into demonstrations of life, as he had often done in less desperate circumstances than the present. At last he went upstairs to the very room in which he now was, and sat down upon the floor, just as he was sitting now. He had not even brought his *Pilgrim's Progress* with him from his grandmother's room. But, searching about in all holes and corners, he at length found Klopstock's *Messiah* translated into English, and took refuge there till Betty came home. Nor did he go down till she called him to tea, when, expecting to join his grandmother and the stranger, he found, on the contrary, that he was to have his tea with Betty in the kitchen, after which he again took refuge with Klopstock in the garret, and remained there till it grew dark, when Betty came in search of him, and put him to bed in the gable-room, and not in his usual chamber. In the morning, every trace of the visitor had vanished, even to the thorn stick which he had set down behind the door as he entered.

All this Robert Falconer saw slowly revive on the palimpsest of his memory, as he washed it with the vivifying waters of recollection.

CHAPTER II.

A VISITOR.

IT was a very bare little room in which the boy
sat, but it was his favourite retreat. Behind
the door, in a recess, stood an empty bedstead,
without even a mattress upon it. This was the
only piece of furniture in the room, unless some
shelves crowded with papers tied up in bundles,
and a cupboard in the wall, likewise filled with
papers, could be called furniture. There was no
carpet on the floor, no windows in the walls.
The only light came from the door, and from a
small skylight in the sloping roof, which showed that it was a garret room. Nor did much
light come from the open door, for there was no
window on the walled stair to which it opened ;
only opposite the door a few steps led up into
another garret, larger, but with a lower roof, un-
ceiled, and perforated with two or three holes,
the panes of glass filling which were no larger
than the small blue slates which covered the

roof: from these panes a little dim brown light
tumbled into the room where the boy sat on the
floor, with his head almost between his knees,
thinking.

But there was less light than usual in the
room now, though it was only half-past two
o'clock, and the sun would not set for more than
half an hour yet; for if Robert had lifted his
head and looked up, it would have been at, not
through, the skylight.   No sky was to be seen.
A thick covering of snow lay over the glass. A
partial thaw, followed by frost, had fixed it there
—a mass of imperfect cells and confused crystals.   It was a cold place to sit in, but the boy
had some faculty for enduring cold when it was
the price to be paid for solitude.   And besides,
when he fell into one of his thinking moods, he
forgot, for a season, cold and everything else
but what he was thinking about—a faculty for
which he was to be envied.

If he had gone down the stair, which described half the turn of a screw in its descent, and
had crossed the landing to which it brought him,
he could have entered another bedroom, called
the gable or rather ga'le room, equally at his
service for retirement; but, though carpeted and
comfortably furnished, and having two windows
at right angles, commanding two streets, for it
was a corner house, the boy preferred the garret-
room—he could not tell why.   Possibly, win-

dows to the streets were not congenial to the
meditations in which, even now, as I have said,
the boy indulged.

These meditations, however, though sometimes
as abstruse, if not so continuous, as those of a me-
taphysician—for boys are not unfrequently more
given to metaphysics than older people are able
or, perhaps, willing to believe—were not by any
means confined to such subjects : castle-building
had its full share in the occupation of those lonely hours ; and for this exercise of the construct-
ive faculty, what he knew, or rather what he
did not know, of his own history gave him scope
enough, nor was his brain slow in supplying
him with material corresponding in quantity to
the space afforded.   His mother had been dead
for so many years that he had only the vaguest
recollections of her tenderness, and none of her
person.   All he was told of his father was that
he had gone abroad.   His grandmother would
never talk about him, although he was her own
son.   When the boy ventured to ask a question
about where he was, or when he would return,
she always replied—" Bairns suld haud their
tongues."   Nor would she vouchsafe another
answer to any question that seemed to her from
the farthest distance to bear down upon that
subject.   " Bairns maun learn to haud their
tongues," was the sole variation of which the
response admitted.   And the boy did learn to

hold his tongue. Perhaps he would have thought less about his father if he had had brothers or sisters, or even if the nature of his grandmother had been such as to admit of their relationship being drawn closer—into personal confidence, or some measure of familiarity. How they stood with regard to each other will soon appear.

Whether the visions vanished from his brain because of the thickening of his blood with cold, or he merely acted from one of those undefined and inexplicable impulses which occasion not a few of our actions, I cannot tell, but all at once Robert started to his feet and hurried from the room. At the foot of the garret stair, between it and the door of the gable-room already mentioned, stood another door at right angles to both, of the existence of which the boy was scarcely aware, simply because he had seen it all his life and had never seen it open. Turning his back on this last door, which he took for a blind one, he went down a short broad stair, at the foot of which was a window. He then turned to the left into a long flagged passage or *transe*, passed the kitchen door on the one hand, and the double-leaved street-door on the other; but, instead of going into the parlour, the door of which closed the transe, he stopped at the passage-window on the right, and there stood looking out.

What might be seen from this window certainly

could not be called a very pleasant prospect. A broad street with low houses of cold gray stone is perhaps as uninteresting a form of street as any to be found in the world, and such was the street Robert looked out upon. Not a single member of the animal creation was to be seen in it, not a pair of eyes to be discovered looking out at any of the windows opposite. The sole motion was the occasional drift of a vapour-like film of white powder, which the wind would lift like dust from the snowy carpet that covered the street, and wafting it along for a few yards, drop again to its repose, till another stronger gust, prelusiveof the wind about to rise at sundown,—a wind cold and bitter as death—would rush over the street, and raise a denser cloud of the white water-dust to sting the face of any improbable person who might meet it in its passage. It was a keen, knife-edged frost, even in the house, and what Robert saw to make him stand at the desolate window, I do not know, and I believe he could not himself have told. There he did stand, however, for the space of five minutes or so, with nothing better filling his outer eyes at least than a bald spot on the crown of the street, whence the wind had swept away the snow, leaving it brown and bare, a spot of March in the middle of January.

He heard the town-drummer in the distance, and let the sound invade his passive ears, till it crossed the opening of the street, and vanished " down the town."

" There's Dooble Sanny," he said to himself— " wi' siccan cauld han's, 'at he's playin' upo' the drum-heid as gin he was loupin' in a bowie (*leaping in a cask*)."

Then he stood silent once more, with a look as if anything would be welcome to break the monotony.

While he stood a gentle timorous tap came to the door, so gentle indeed that Betty in the kitchen did not hear it, or she, tall and Roman-nosed as she was, would have answered it before the long-legged dreamer could have reached the door, though he was not above three yards from it. In lack of anything better to do, Robert stalked to the summons. As he opened the door, these words greeted him :

" Is Robert at——eh ! it's Bob himsel' ! Bob, I'm byous (*exceedingly*) cauld."

" What for dinna ye gang hame, than ?"

" What for wasna ye at the schuil the day ?"

" I spier ae queston at you, and ye answer me wi' anither."

" Weel, I hae nae hame to gang till."

" Weel, and I had a sair heid *(a headache)*. But whaur's yer hame gane till than ?"

" The hoose is there a' richt, but whaur my mither is I dinna ken. The door's lockit, an' Jeames Jaup, they tell me 's tane awa' the key.

I doobt my mither's awa' upo' the tramp again,
and what's to come o' me, the Lord kens."

"What's this o' 't ?" interposed a severe but
not unmelodious voice, breaking into the conversation between the two boys ; for the parlour
door had opened without Robert's hearing it, and
Mrs. Falconer, his grandmother, had drawn near
to the speakers.

"What's this o' 't ?" she asked again. "Wha's
that ye're conversin' wi' at the door, Robert ?
Gin it be ony decent laddie, tell him to come in,
and no stan' at the door in sic a day 's this."

As Robert hesitated with his reply, she looked
round the open half of the door, but no sooner
saw with whom he was talking than her tone
changed. By this time Betty, wiping her hands
in her apron, had completed the group by taking
her stand in the kitchen door.

"Na, na," said Mrs. Falconer. "We want
nane sic-like here. What does he want wi' you,
Robert ? Gie him a piece, Betty, and lat him
gang.—Eh, sirs ! the callant hasna a stockin'-fit
upo' 'im—and in sic weather ! "

For, before she had finished her speech, the
visitor, as if in terror of her nearer approach, had
turned his back, and literally showed her, if not
a clean pair of heels, yet a pair of naked heels
from between the soles and uppers of his shoes:
if he had any stockings at all, they ceased before they reached his ankles.

" What ails him at me?" continued Mrs. Falconer, " that he rins as gin I war a boodie? But it's nae wonner he canna bide the sicht o' a decent body, for he 's no used till't. What does he want wi' you, Robert?"

But Robert had a reason for not telling his grandmother what the boy had told him: he thought the news about his mother would only make her disapprove of him the more. In this he judged wrong. He did not know his grandmother yet.

" He 's in my class at the schuil," said Robert, evasively.

" Him? What class, noo?"

Robert hesitated one moment, but, compelled to give some answer, said, with confidence,

" The Bible-class."

" I thocht as muckle! What gars ye play at hide and seek wi' me? Do ye think I dinna ken weel eneuch there's no a lad or a lass at the schuil but 's i' the Bible-class? What wants he here?"

" Ye hardly gae him time to tell me, grannie. Ye frichtit him."

" Me fricht him! What for suld I fricht him, laddie? I 'm no sic ferlie *(wonder)* that onybody needs be frichtit at me."

The old lady turned with visible, though by no means profound offence upon her calm forehead, and walking back into her parlour,

where Robert could see the fire burning right
cheerily, shut the door, and left him and Betty
standing together in the transe. The latter returned to the kitchen, to resume the washing of
the dinner-dishes; and the former returned to
his post at the window. He had not stood more
than half a minute, thinking what was to be
done with his schoolfellow deserted of his mother, when the sound of a coach-horn drew his
attention to the right, down the street, where
he could see part of the other street which
crossed it at right angles, and in which the
gable of the house stood. A minute after, the
mail came in sight—scarlet, spotted with snow
—and disappeared, going up the hill towards
the chief hostelry of the town, as fast as four
horses tired with the bad footing they had had
through the whole of the stage, could draw it
after them. By this time the twilight was falling;
for though the sun had not yet set, miles of
frozen vapour came between him and this part
of the world, and his light was never very
powerful so far north at this season of the year.

Robert turned into the kitchen, and began to
put on his shoes. He had made up his mind
what to do.

"Ye're never gaein' oot, Robert?" said Betty,
in a hoarse tone of expostulation.

"'Deed am I, Betty. What for no?"

"You 'at's been in a' day wi' a sair heid!

I'll jist gang benn the hoose and tell the mistress, and syne we'll see what she'll please to say till't."

" Ye'll do naething o' the kin', Betty. Are ye gaein' to turn clash-pyet (*tell-tale*) at *your* age?"

" What ken ye aboot my age? There's never a man-body i' the toon kens aught aboot my age."

"It's ower muckle for onybody to min' upo' (*remember*), is 't, Betty?"

" Dinna be ill-tongued, Robert, or I'll jist gang benn the hoose to the mistress."

"Betty, wha began wi' bein' ill-tongued? Gin ye tell my grandmither that I gaed oot the nicht, I'll gang to the schuilmaister o' Muckledrum, and get a sicht o' the kirstenin' buik; an' gin yer name binna there, I'll tell ilkabody I meet 'at oor Betty was never kirstened; and that'll be a sair affront, Betty."

"Hoot! was there ever sic a laddie!" said Betty, attempting to laugh it off. " Be sure ye be back afore tay-time, 'cause yer grannie 'ill be speirin' efter ye, and ye wadna hae me lee aboot ye?"

"I wad hae naebody lee about me. Ye jist needna lat on 'at ye hear her. Ye can be deif eneuch when ye like, Betty. But I s' be back afore tay-time, or come on the waur."

Betty, who was in far greater fear of her age being discovered than of being unchristianized

in the search, though the fact was that she
knew nothing certain about the matter, and had
no desire to be enlightened, feeling as if she was
thus left at liberty to hint what she pleased,—
Betty, I say, never had any intention of going
"benn the hoose to the mistress." For the
threat was merely the rod of terror which she
thought it convenient to hold over the back of
the boy, whom she always supposed to be about
some mischief except he were in her own presence and visibly reading a book: if he were
reading aloud, so much the better. But Robert
likewise kept a rod for his defence, and that was
Betty's age, which he had discovered to be such
a precious secret that one would have thought
her virtue depended in some cabalistic manner
upon the concealment of it. And, certainly,
nature herself seemed to favour Betty's weakness, casting such a mist about the number of
her years as the goddesses of old were wont to
cast about a wounded favourite; for some said
Betty was forty, others said she was sixty-five,
and, in fact, almost everybody who knew her
had a different belief on the matter.

By this time Robert had conquered the difficulty of induing boots as hard as a thorough
wetting and as thorough a drying could make
them, and now stood prepared to go. His object in setting out was to find the boy whom his
grandmother had driven from the door with a

hastier and more abject flight than she had in the
least intended.　But, if his grandmother should
miss him, as Betty suggested, and inquire where
he had been, what was he to say?　He did not
mind misleading his grannie, but he had a great
objection to telling her a lie.　His grandmother
herself delivered him from this difficulty.

"Robert, come here," she called from the parlour door.　And Robert obeyed.

"Is 't dingin' on, Robert?" she asked.

"No, grannie; it's only a starnie o' drift."

The meaning of this was that there was no
fresh snow falling, or *beating on*, only a little surface snow blowing about.

"Weel, jist pit yer shune on, man, and rin up
to Miss Naper's upo' the Squaur, and say to Miss
Naper, wi' my compliments, that I wad be sair
obleeged tili her gin she wad len' me that fine
receipt o' hers for crappit heids, and I'll sen' 't
back safe the morn's mornin'.　Rin, noo."

This commission fell in admirably with Robert's plans, and he started at once.

CHAPTER III.

THE BOAR'S HEAD.

MISS NAPIER was the eldest of three maiden sisters who kept the principal hostelry of Rothieden, called The Boar's Head; from which, as Robert reached the square in the dusk, the mail-coach was moving away with a fresh quaternion of horses. He found a good many boxes standing upon the pavement close by the archway that led to the inn-yard, and around them had gathered a group of loungers, not too cold to be interested. These were looking towards the windows of the inn, where the owner of the boxes had evidently disappeared.

" Saw ye ever sic a sicht in oor toon afore !" said *Dooble Sanny*, as people generally called him, his name being Alexander Alexander, pronounced, by those who chose to speak of him with the ordinary respect due from one mortal to another, Sandy Elshender. Double Sandy was a soutar, or shoemaker, remarkable for his love of sweet sounds and whisky. He was, besides, the town-crier, who went about with a drum at certain hours of the morning and evening, like a perambulating clock, and also made public announcements of sales, losses, &c.; for the rest—a fierce, fighting fellow when in anger or in drink, which latter included the former.

"What's the sicht, Sandy?" asked Robert, coming up with his hands in the pockets of his trowsers.

"Sic a sicht as ye never saw, man," returned Sandy; "the bonniest leddy ever man set his ee upo'. I culd na hae thocht there had been sic a woman i' this warl'."

"Hoot, Sandy!" said Robert, "a body wad think she was tint *(lost)* and ye had the cryin' o' her. Speyk laicher, man; she'll maybe hear ye. Is she i' the inn there?"

"Ay is she," answered Sandy. "See sic a warl' o' kists as she's brocht wi' her," he continued, pointing towards the pile of luggage. "Saw ye ever sic a bourach *(heap)*? It jist blecks *(beats)* me to think what ae body can du wi' sae mony kists. For I mayna doobt but there's something or ither in ilka ane o' them. Naebody wad carry aboot toom *(empty)* kists wi' them. I can*not* mak' it oot."

The boxes might well surprise Sandy, if we may draw any conclusions from the fact that the sole implement of personal adornment which he possessed was two inches of a broken comb, for

which he had to search when he happened to
want it, in the drawer of his stool, among awls,
lumps of rosin for his violin, masses of the same
substance wrought into shoemaker's wax for his
ends, and packets of boar's bristles, commonly
called *birse*, for the same.

"Are thae a' ae body's?" asked Robert.

"Troth are they. They're a' hers, I wat.
Ye wad hae thocht she had been gaein' to The
Bothie; but gin she had been that, there wad
hae been a cairriage to meet her," said Crookit
Caumil, the ostler.

The Bothie was the name facetiously given by
Alexander, Baron Rothie, son of the Marquis of
Boarshead, to a house he had built in the neighbourhood, chiefly for the accommodation of his
bachelor friends from London during the shoot-
ing-season.

"Haud yer tongue, Caumil," said the shoemaker. "She's nae sic cattle, yon."

"Haud up the bit bowat (*stable-lantern*), man,
and lat Robert here see the direction upo' them.
Maybe he'll mak' something o't. He's a fine
scholar, ye ken," said another of the bystanders.

The ostler held the lantern to the card upon
one of the boxes, but Robert found only an M.,
followed by something not very definite, and a
J., which might have been an I., Rothieden,
Driftshire, Scotland.

As he was not immediate with his answer,

c 2

Peter Lumley, one of the group, a lazy ne'er-do-weel, who had known better days, but never better manners, and was seldom quite drunk, and seldomer still quite sober, struck in with,

" Ye dinna ken a' thing yet, ye see, Robbie."

From Sandy this would have been nothing but a good-humoured attempt at facetiousness. From Lumley it meant spite, because Robert's praise was in his ears.

" I dinna preten' to ken ae hair mair than ye do yersel', Mr. Lumley; and that's nae sayin' muckle, surely," returned Robert, irritated at his tone more than at his words.

The bystanders laughed, and Lumley flew in a rage.

" Haud yer ill tongue, ye brat," he said. " Wha' are ye to mak' sic remarks upo' yer betters ? A'body kens yer gran'father was naething but the blin' piper o' Portcloddie."

This was news to Robert—probably false, considering the quarter whence it came. But his mother-wit did not forsake him.

" Weel, Mr. Lumley," he answered, "didna he pipe weel ? Daur ye tell me 'at he didna pipe weel ?—as weel's ye cud hae dune't yersel', noo, Mr. Lumley ?"

The laugh again rose at Lumley's expense, who was well known to have tried his hand at most things, and succeeded in nothing. Dooble Sanny was especially delighted.

" De'il hae ye for a de'il's brat! 'At I suld sweer!" was all Lumley's reply, as he sought to conceal his mortification by attempting to join in the laugh against himself. Robert seized the opportunity of turning away and entering the house.

" That ane's no to be droont or brunt aither," said Lumley, as he disappeared.

" He'll no be hang't for closin' *your* mou', Mr. Lumley," said the shoemaker.

Thereupon Lumley turned and followed Robert into the inn.

Robert had delivered his message to Miss Napier, who sat in an arm-chair by the fire, in a little comfortable parlour, held sacred by all about the house. She was paralytic, and unable to attend to her guests further than by giving orders when anything especial was referred to her decision. She was an old lady— nearly as old as Mrs. Falconer—and wore glasses, but they could not conceal the kindness of her kindly eyes. Probably from giving less heed to a systematic theology, she had nothing of that sternness which first struck a stranger on seeing Robert's grandmother. But then she did not know what it was to be contradicted; and if she had been married, and had had sons, perhaps a sternness not dissimilar might have shown itself in her nature.

" Noo ye maunna gang awa' till ye get something," she said, after taking the receipt in request from a drawer within her reach, and laying it upon the table. But ere she could ring the bell which stood by her side, one of her servants came in.

"Please, mem," she said, "Miss Letty and Miss Lizzy's seein' efter the bonny leddy; and sae I maun come to you."

"Is she a' that bonny, Meg?" asked her mistress.

"Na, na, she's nae sae fearsome bonny; but Miss Letty's unco ta'en wi' her, ye ken. An' we a' say as Miss Letty says i' this hoose. But that's no the pint. Mr. Lumley's here, seekin' a gill: is he to hae't?"

"Has he had eneuch, already, do ye think, Meg?"

"I dinna ken aboot eneuch, mem; that's ill to mizzer; but I dinna think he's had ower muckle."

"Weel, lat him tak it. But dinna lat him sit doon."

"Verra weel, mem," said Meg, and departed.

"What gars Mr. Lumley say 'at my gran'father was the blin' piper o' Portcloddie? Can ye tell me, Miss Naper?" asked Robert.

"Whan said he that, Robert?"

"Jist as I cam in."

Miss Napier rang the bell. Another maid appeared.

"Sen' Meg here direckly."

Meg came, her eyes full of interrogation.

" Dinna gie Lumley a drap. Set him up to insult a young gentleman at my door-cheek! He s' no hae a drap here the nicht. He s' *had* ower muckle, Meg, already, an' ye oucht to hae seen that."

" 'Deed, mem, he 's had mair than ower muckle, than ; for there's anither gill ower the thrapple o' 'm. I div my best, mem, but, never tastin' mysel', I canna aye tell hoo muckle 's i' the wame o' a' body 'at comes in."

"Ye're no fit for the place, Meg; that's a fac'."

At this charge Meg took no offence, for she had been in the place for twenty years. And both mistress and maid laughed the moment they parted company.

" Wha's this 'at's come the nicht, Miss Naper, 'at they're sae ta'en wi'?" asked Robert.

"Atweel, I dinna ken yet. She's ower bonnie by a' accoonts to be gaein' about her lane *(alone)*. It's a mercy the baron's no at hame. I wad hae to lock her up wi' the forks and spunes."

" What for that?" asked Robert.

But Miss Napier vouchsafed no further explanation. She stuffed his pockets with sweet biscuits instead, dismissed him in haste, and rang the bell.

" Meg, whaur hae they putten the stranger-leddy ?"

" She's no gaein' to bide at our hoose, mem."

" *What* say ye, lass? She's never gaein' ower to Lucky Happit's, is she?"

" Ow na, mem. She's a leddy, ilka inch o' her. But she's some sib (*relation*) to the auld captain, and she's gaein' doon the street as sune's Caumil's ready to tak' her bit boxies i' the barrow. But I doobt there'll be maist three barrowfu's o' them."

" Atweel. Ye can gang."

CHAPTER IV.

SHARGAR.

ROBERT went out into the thin drift, and again crossing the wide desolate-looking square, turned down an entry leading to a kind of court, which had once been inhabited by a well-to-do class of the townspeople, but had now fallen in estimation. Upon a stone at the door of what seemed an outhouse he discovered the object of his search.

"What are ye sittin' there for, Shargar?"

Shargar is a word of Gaelic origin, applied, with some sense of the ridiculous, to a thin, wasted, dried-up creature. In the present case it was the nickname by which the boy was known at school; and, indeed, where he was known at all.

"What are ye sittin' there for, Shargar? Did naebody offer to tak ye in?"

"Na, nane o' them. I think they maun be a' i' their beds. I'm most dreidfu' cauld."

The fact was, that Shargar's character, whe-

ther by imputation from his mother, or derived
from his own actions, was none of the best.
The consequence was, that although scarcely
one of the neighbours would have allowed him
to sit there all night, each was willing to wait
yet a while, in the hope that somebody else's
humanity would give in first, and save her from
the necessity of offering him a seat by the fireside, and a share of the oatmeal porridge which
probably would be scanty enough for her own
household. For it must be borne in mind that
all the houses in the place were occupied by
poor people, with whom the one virtue, Charity,
was, in a measure, at home, and amidst many
sins, cardinal and other, managed to live in even
some degree of comfort.

" Get up, than, Shargar, ye lazy beggar ! Or
are ye frozen to the door-stane ? I s' awa' for a
kettle o' bilin' water to lowse ye."

" Na, na, Bob. I'm no stucken. I'm only
some stiff wi' the cauld; for wow, but I *am*
cauld !" said Shargar, rising with difficulty.
" Gie 's a haud o' yer han', Bob."

Robert gave him his hand, and Shargar was
straightway upon his feet.

"Come awa' noo, as fest and as quaiet 's ye
can."

" What are ye gaein' to du wi' me, Bob ?"

" What's that to you, Shargar ?"

" Naything. Only I wad like to ken."

" Hae patience, and ye will ken. Only mind ye do as I tell ye, and dinna speik a word."

Shargar followed in silence.

On the way Robert remembered that Miss Napier had not, after all, given him the receipt for which his grandmother had sent him. So he returned to The Boar's Head, and, while he went in, left Shargar in the archway, to shiver, and try in vain to warm his hands by the alternate plans of slapping them on the opposite arms, and hiding them under them.

When Robert came out, he saw a man talking to him under the lamp. The moment his eyes fell upon the two, he was struck by a resemblance between them. Shargar was right under the lamp, the man to the side of it, so that Shargar was shadowed by its frame, and the man was in its full light. The latter turned away, and passing Robert, went into the inn.

" Wha's that ?" asked Robert.

"I dinna ken," answered Shargar. " He spak to me or ever I kent he was there, and garred my hert gie sic a loup 'at it maist fell into my breeks."

"And what said he to ye ?"

" He said was the deevil at my lug, that I did naething but caw my han's to bits upo' my shoothers."

"And what said ye to that ?"

" I said I wissed he was, for he wad aiblins

hae some spare heat aboot him, an' I hadna freely *(quite)* eneuch."

"Weel dune, Shargar! What said he to that?"

" He leuch, and speirt gin I wad list, and gae me a shillin'."

" Ye didna tak it, Shargar ? " asked Robert in some alarm.

"Ay did I. Catch me no takin' a shillin' !"

" But they'll haud ye till 't."

" Na, na. I'm ower shochlin' *(in-kneed)* for a sodger. But that man was nae sodger."

" And what mair said he ?"

" He speirt what I wad do wi' the shillin'."

" And what said ye ?"

" Ow! syne ye cam' oot, and he gaed awa'."

" And ye dinna ken wha it was ?" repeated Robert.

" It was some like my brither, Lord Sandy ; " but I dinna ken," said Shargar.

By this time they had arrived at Yule the baker's shop.

" Bide ye here," said Robert, who happened to possess a few coppers, "till I gang into Eel's."

Shargar stood again and shivered at the door, till Robert came out with a penny loaf in one hand, and a twopenny loaf in the other.

" Gie's a bit, Bob," said Shargar. "I'm as hungry as I am cauld."

" Bide ye still," returned Robert. " There's a

time for a'thing, and your time 's no come to forgather wi' this loaf yet. Does na it smell fine? It's new frae the bakehoose no ten minutes ago. I ken by the fin' *(feel)* o' 't."

"Lat me fin' 't," said Shargar, stretching out one hand, and feeling his shilling with the other.

"Na. Yer han's canna be clean. And fowk suld aye eat clean, whether they gang clean or no."

"I'll awa' in an' buy ane oot o' my ain shillin'," said Shargar, in a tone of resolute eagerness.

"Ye 'll do naething o' the kin'," returned Robert, darting his hand at his collar. "Gie *me* the shillin'. Ye'll want it a' or lang."

Shargar yielded the coin and slunk behind, while Robert again led the way till they came to his grandmother's door.

"Gang to the ga'le o' the hoose there, Shargar, and jist keek roon' the neuk at me; and gin I whustle upo' ye, come up as quaiet 's ye can. Gin I dinna, bide till I come to ye."

Robert opened the door cautiously. It was never locked except at night, or when Betty had gone to the well for water, or to the butcher's or baker's, or the prayer-meeting, upon which occasions she put the key in her pocket, and left her mistress a prisoner. He looked first to the right, along the passage, and saw that his grandmother's door was shut; then across the passage to the left, and saw that the kitchen-door was

likewise shut, because of the cold, for its normal
position was against the wall. Thereupon, closing
the door, but keeping the handle in his hand, and
the bolt drawn back, he turned to the street and
whistled soft and low. Shargar had, in a moment, dragged his heavy feet, ready to part
company with their shoes at any instant, to Robert's side. He bent his ear to Robert's whisper.

" Gang in there, and creep like a moose to the
fit o' the stair. I maun close the door ahin' 's,"
said he, opening the door as he spoke.

" I'm fleyt *(frightened)*, Robert."

" Dinna be a fule. Grannie winna bite aff yer
heid. She had ane till her denner, the day, an'
it was ill sung *(singed)*."

" What ane o' ?"

" A sheep's heid, ye gowk *(fool)*. Gang in
direckly."

Shargar persisted no longer, but, taking about
four steps a minute, slunk past the kitchen
like a thief—not so carefully, however, but that
one of his soles yet looser than the other, gave
one clap upon the flagged passage, when Betty
straightway stood in the kitchen-door, a fierce
picture in a deal-frame. By this time Robert
had closed the outer door, and was following at
Shargar's heels.

" What's this ?" she cried, but not so loud as
to reach the ears of Mrs. Falconer ; for, with true
Scotch foresight, she would not willingly call in

another power before the situation clearly demanded it. " Whaur's Shargar gaein' that gait?"

" Wi' me. Dinna ye see me wi' him ? I'm nae a thief, nor yet's Shargar."

" There may be twa opingons upo' that, Robert. I s' jist awa' benn to the mistress. I s' hae nae sic doin's i' *my* hoose."

" It's nae your hoose, Betty. Dinna lee."

" Weel, I s' hae nae sic things gang by my kitchie-door. There, Robert! what 'll ye mak' o' that ? There 's nae offence, there, I houp, gin it suldna be a'thegither my ain hoose. Tak Shargar oot o' that, or I s' awa' benn the hoose, as I tell ye."

Meantime Shargar was standing on the stones, looking like a terrified white rabbit, and shaking from head to foot with cold and fright combined.

" I 'll tak him oot o' this, but it 's up the stair, Betty. An' gin ye gang benn the hoose aboot it, I sweir to ye, as sure 's death, I'll gang doon to Muckledrum upo' Setterday i' the efternune."

" Gang awa' wi' yer havers. Only gin the mistress speirs onything aboot it, what am I to say ?"

" Bide till she speirs. Auld Spunkie says, ' Ready-made answers are aye to seek.' And I say, Betty, hae ye a cauld pitawta *(potato)* ?"

" I 'll luik and see. Wadna ye like it het up?"

" Ow ay, gin ye binna lang aboot it."

Suddenly a bell rang, shrill and peremptory, right above Shargar's head, causing in him a responsive increase of trembling.

"Haud oot o' my gait. There's the mistess's bell," said Betty.

"Jist bide till we 're roon' the neuk and on to the stair," said Robert, now leading the way.

Betty watched them safe round the corner before she made for the parlour, little thinking to what she had become an unwilling accomplice, for she never imagined that more than an evening's visit was intended by Shargar, which in itself seemed to her strange and improper enough even for such an eccentric boy as Robert to encourage.

Shargar followed in mortal terror, for, like Christian in the *Pilgrim's Progress*, he had no armour to his back. Once round the corner, two strides of three steps each took them to the top of the first stair, Shargar knocking his head in the darkness against the never-opened door. Again three strides brought them to the top of the second flight; and turning once more, still to the right, Robert led Shargar up the few steps into the higher of the two garrets.

Here there was just glimmer enough from the sky to discover the hollow of a close bedstead, built in under the sloping roof, which served it for a tester, while the two ends and most of the front were boarded up to the roof. This bedstead fortunately was not so bare as the one in the other room, although it had not been used for many years, for an old mattress covered the boards with which it was bottomed.

" Gang in there, Shargar. Ye 'll be warmer there than upo' the door-step ony gait. Pit aff yer shune."

Shargar obeyed, full of delight at finding himself in such good quarters. Robert went to a forsaken press in the room, and brought out an ancient cloak of tartan, of the same form as what is now called an Inverness cape, a blue dress-coat, with plain gilt buttons, which shone even now in the all but darkness, and several other garments, amongst them a kilt, and heaped them over Shargar as he lay on the mattress. He then handed him the twopenny and the penny loaves, which were all his stock had reached to the purchase of, and left him, saying,—

"I maun awa' to my tay, Shargar. I'll fess ye a cauld tawtie het again, gin Betty has ony. Lie still, and whatever ye do, dinna come oot o' that."

The last injunction was entirely unnecessary.

" Eh, Bob, I'm jist in haven!" said the poor creature, for his skin began to feel the precious possibility of reviving warmth in the distance.

Now that he had gained a new burrow, the human animal soon recovered from his fears as well. It seemed to him, in the novelty of the place,

that he had made so many doublings to reach it,
that there could be no danger of even the mistress of the house finding him out, for she could
hardly be supposed to look after such a remote
corner of her dominions.   And then he was
boxed in with the bed, and covered with no end
of warm garments, while the friendly darkness
closed him and his shelter all round.   Except
the faintest blue gleam from one of the panes in
the roof, there was soon no hint of light anywhere; and this was only sufficient to make the
darkness visible, and thus add artistic effect to
the operation of it upon Shargar's imagination
—a faculty certainly uneducated in Shargar,
but far, very far from being therefore non-
existent.   It was, indeed, actively operative,
although, like that of many a fine lady and
gentleman, only in relation to such primary
questions as : " What shall we eat ?   And what
shall we drink ?   And wherewithal shall we be
clothed ?"   But as he lay and devoured the new
" white breid," his satisfaction—the bare delight
of his animal existence—reached a pitch such as
even this imagination, stinted with poverty, and
frost-bitten with maternal oppression, had never
conceived possible.   The power of enjoying the
present without anticipation of the future or regard of the past, is the especial privilege of the
animal nature, and of the human nature in proportion as it has not been developed beyond

the animal. Herein lies the happiness of cab
horses and of tramps: to them the gift of forgetfulness is of worth inestimable. Shargar's
heaven was for the present gained.

CHAPTER V.

THE SYMPOSIUM.

ROBERT had scarcely turned out of the square on his way to find Shargar, when a horseman entered it. His horse and he were both apparently black on one side and grey on the other, from the snow-drift settling to windward. The animal looked tired, but the rider sat as easy as if he were riding to cover. The reins hung loose, and the horse went in a straight line for The Boar's Head, stopping under the archway only when his master drew bridle at the door of the inn.

At that moment Miss Letty was standing at the back of Miss Napier's chair, leaning her arms upon it as she talked to her. This was her way of resting as often as occasion arose for a chat with her elder sister. Miss Letty's hair was gathered in a great knot at the top of her head, and little ringlets hung like tendrils down the sides of her face, the benevolence of which was less immediately striking than that of her sister's, because of the constant play of humour upon it, especially about the mouth. If a spirit of satire could be supposed converted into something Christian by an infusion of the tenderest loving-kindness and humanity, remaining still recognizable notwithstanding that all its bitterness was gone, such was the expression of Miss Letty's mouth. It was always half puckered as if in resistance to a comic smile, which showed itself at the windows of the keen grey eyes, however the mouth might be able to keep it within doors. She was neatly dressed in black silk, with a lace collar. Her hands were small and white.

The moment the traveller stopped at the door, Miss Napier started.

"Letty," she said, "wha's that? I could amaist sweir to Black Geordie's fit."

"A' four o' them, I think," returned Miss Letty, as the horse, notwithstanding, or perhaps in consequence of his fatigue, began to paw and move about on the stones impatiently.

The rider had not yet spoken.

"He'll be efter some o' 's deevil-ma'-care sculduddery. But jist rin to the door, Letty, or Lizzy 'll be there afore ye, and maybe she wadna be ower ceevil. What can he be efter noo?"

"What wad the grew (*grayhound*) be efter but maukin (*hare*)?" returned Miss Letty.

" Hoot! nonsense! He kens naething aboot her. Gang to the door, lassie."

Miss Letty obeyed.

" Wha's there ?" she asked, somewhat sharply, as she opened it, " that neither chaps (*knocks*) nor ca's ?—Preserve 's a'! is't you, my lord ?"

" Hoo ken ye me, Miss Letty, withoot seein' my face ?"

"A'body at the Boar's Heid kens Black Geordie as weel 's yer lordship's ain sel'. But whaur comes yer lordship frae in sic a nicht as this ?"

" From Russia. Never dismounted between Moscow and Aberdeen. The ice is bearing to-night."

And the baron laughed inside the upturned collar of his cloak, for he knew that strangely exaggerated stories were current about his feats in the saddle.

" That's a lang ride, my lord, and a sliddery. And what's yer lordship's wull ?"

" Muckle ye care aboot my lordship to stand jawin' there in a night like this! Is nobody going to take my horse ?"

" I beg yer lordship's pardon. Caumil!—Yer lordship never said ye wanted yer lordship's horse ta'en. I thocht ye micht be gaein' on to The Bothie.—Tak Black Geordie here, Caumil. —Come in to the parlour, my lord."

" How d'ye do, Miss Naper ?" said Lord Rothie, as he entered the room. " Here's this jade of a sister of yours asking me why I don't go home to The Bothie, when I choose to stop and water here."

" What'll ye tak, my lord?—Letty, fess the brandy."

" Oh ! damn your brandy ! Bring me a gill of good Glendronach."

" Rin, Letty. His lordship's cauld.—I canna rise to offer ye the airm-cheir, my lord."

" I can get one for myself, thank heaven !"

" Lang may yer lordship return sic thanks."

" For I'm only new begun, ye think, Miss Naper. Well, I don't often trouble heaven with my affairs. By Jove ! I ought to be heard when I do."

" Nae doobt ye will, my lord, whan ye seek onything that's fit to be gien ye."

" True. Heaven's gifts are seldom much worth the asking."

" Haud yer tongue, my lord, and dinna bring doon a judgment upo' my hoose, for it wad be missed oot o' Rothieden."

" You're right there, Miss Naper. And here comes the whisky to stop my mouth."

The Baron of Rothie sat for a few minutes with his feet on the fender before Miss Letty's blazing fire, without speaking, while he sipped the whisky neat from a wine-glass. He was a man about the middle height, rather full-figured, muscular and active, with a small head, and an eye whose brightness had not yet been dimmed by the sensuality which might be read in the condition rather than frame of his countenance. But while he spoke so pleasantly to the Miss Napiers, and his forehead spread broad and smooth over the twinkle of his hazel eye, there was a sharp curve on each side of his upper lip, half-way between the corner and the middle, which reminded one of the same curves in the lip of his ancestral boar's-head, where it was lifted up by the protruding tusks. These curves disappeared, of course, when he smiled, and his smile, being a lord's, was generally pronounced irresistible. He was good-natured, and nowise inclined to stand upon his rank, so long as he had his own way.

"Any customers by the mail to-night, Miss Naper?" he asked, in a careless tone.

"Naebody particlar, my lord."

"I thought ye never let anybody in that wasn't particularly particular. No foot-passengers—eh?"

"Hoot, my lord! that's twa year ago. Gin I had jaloosed him to be a frien' o' yer lordship's, forby bein' a lord himsel', ye ken as weel 's I du that I wadna hae sent him ower the gait to Luckie Happit's, whaur he wadna even be ower sure o' gettin' clean sheets. But gin lords an' lords' sons will walk afit like ither fowk, wha 's to ken them frae ither fowk?"

" Well, Miss Naper, he was no lord at all. He was nothing but a factor-body doon frae Glenbucket."

" There was sma' hairm dune than, my lord. I 'm glaid to hear 't. But what 'll yer lordship hae to yer supper ?"

" I would like a dish o' your chits and nears *(sweetbreads and kidneys)*."

" Noo, think o' that !" returned the landlady, laughing. " You great fowk wad hae the verra coorse o' natur' turned upside doon to shuit yersels. Wha ever heard o' caure *(calves)* at this time o' the year ?"

" Well, anything you like. Who was it came by the mail, did you say ?"

" I said naebody particlar, my lord."

" Well, I 'll just go and have a look at Black Geordie."

" Verra weel, my lord.—Letty, rin an' luik efter him ; and as sune 's he 's roon' the neuk, tell Lizzie no to say a word aboot the leddy. As sure 's deith he 's efter her. Whaur cud he hae heard tell o' her."

Lord Rothie came, a moment after, sauntering into the bar-parlour, where Lizzie, the third Miss Napier, a red-haired, round-eyed, white-toothed woman of forty, was making entries in a book.

" She 's a bonnie lassie that, that came in the coach to-night, they say, Miss Lizzie."

" As ugly's sin, my lord," answered Lizzie.

" I hae seen some sin 'at was nane sae ugly, Miss Lizzie."

" She wad hae clean scunnert (*disgusted*) ye, my lord. It's a mercy ye didna see her."

" If she be as ugly as all that, I would just like to see her."

Miss Lizzie saw she had gone too far.

" Ow, deed! gin yer lordship wants to see her, ye may see her at yer wull. I s' gang and tell her."

And she rose as if to go.

" No, no. Nothing of the sort, Miss Lizzie. Only I heard that she was bonnie, and I wanted to see her. You know I like to look at a pretty girl."

" That's ower weel kent, my lord."

" Well, there's no harm in that, Miss Lizzie."

" There's no harm in *that*, my lord, though yer lordship says 't."

The facts were that his lordship had been to the county-town some forty miles off, and Black Geordie had been sent to Hillknow to meet him; for in any weather that would let him sit, he preferred horseback to every other mode of tra- velling, though he seldom would be followed by a groom. He had posted to Hillknow, and had dined with a friend at the inn. The coach stopping to change horses, he had caught a glimpse of a pretty face, as he thought, from its window, and had hoped to overtake the coach before it reached Rothieden. But stopping to drink another bottle, he had failed; and it was on the merest chance of seeing that pretty face, that he stopped at the Boar's Head. In all probability, had the marquis seen the lady, he would not have thought her at all such a beauty as she appeared in the eyes of Dooble Sanny; nor, I venture to think, had he thought as the shoemaker did, would he yet have dared to address her in other than the words of such respect as he could still feel in the presence of that which was more noble than himself.

Whether or not on his visit to the stable he found anything amiss with Black Geordie, I cannot tell, but he now begged Miss Lizzie to have a bedroom prepared for him.

It happened to be the evening of Friday, one devoted by some of the townspeople to a symposium. To this, knowing that the talk will throw a glimmer on several matters, I will now introduce my reader, as a spectator through the reversed telescope of my history.

A few of the more influential of the inhabitants had grown, rather than formed themselves, into a kind of club, which met weekly at the Boar's Head. Although they had no exclusive right to the room in which they sat, they generally managed to retain exclusive possession of it; for if any supposed objectionable person entered, they always got rid of him, sometimes without his being aware of how they had contrived to make him so uncomfortable. They began to gather about seven o'clock, when it was expected that boiling water would be in readiness for the compound generally called *toddy*, sometimes *punch*. As soon as six were assembled, one was always voted into the chair.

On the present occasion, Mr. Innes, the schoolmaster, was unanimously elected to that honour. He was a hard-featured, sententious, snuffy individual, of some learning, and great respectability.

I omit the political talk with which their intercommunications began ; for however interesting at the time is the scaffolding by which existing institutions arise, the poles and beams when gathered again in the builder's yard are scarcely a subject for the artist.

The first to lead the way towards matters of nearer personality was William MacGregor, the linen manufacturer, a man who possessed a score of hand-looms or so—half of which, from the advance of cotton and the decline of linen-wear, now stood idle—but who had already a sufficient deposit in the hands of Mr. Thomson the banker—agent, that is, for the county-bank—to secure him against any necessity for taking to cotton shirts himself, which were an abomination and offence unpardonable in his eyes.

"Can ye tell me, Mr. Cocker," he said, "what mak's Sandy, Lord Rothie, or Wrathy, or what suld he be ca'd?—tak' to The Bothie at a time like this, whan there's neither huntin', nor fishin', nor shutin', nor onything o' the kin' aboot han' to be playacks till him, the bonnie bairn—'cep' it be otters an' sic like?"

William was a shrunken old man, with white whiskers and a black wig, a keen black eye, always in search of the ludicrous in other people, and a mouth ever on the move, as if masticating something comical.

"You know just as well as I do," answered Mr. Cocker, the Marquis of Boarshead's factor for the surrounding estate. "He never was in the way of giving a reason for anything, least of all for his own movements."

"Somebody was sayin' to me," resumed MacGregor, who, in all probability, invented the story at the moment, "that the prince took him kissin' ane o' his servan' lasses, and kickit him oot o' Carlton Hoose into the street, and he canna win' ower the disgrace o' 't."

"'Deed for the kissin'," said Mr. Thomson, a portly, comfortable-looking man, "that's neither here nor there, though it micht hae been a duchess or twa; but for the kickin', my word! but Lord Sandy was mair likly to kick oot the prince. Do ye min' hoo he did whan the Markis taxed him wi'—— ?"

"Haud a quaiet sough," interposed Mr. Cruickshank, the solicitor; "there's a drap i' the hoose."

This was a phrase well understood by the company, indicating the presence of some one unknown, or unfit to be trusted.

As he spoke he looked towards the farther end of the room, which lay in obscurity; for it was a large room, lighted only by the four candles on the table at which the company sat.

"Whaur, Mr. Cruickshank?" asked the Dominie in a whisper.

"There," answered Sampson Peddie, the bookseller, who seized the opportunity of saying something, and pointed furtively where the solicitor had only looked.

A dim figure was descried at a table in the farthest corner of the room, and they proceeded to carry out the plan they generally adopted to get rid of a stranger.

"Ye made use o' a curious auld Scots phrase this moment, Mr. Curshank : can ye explain hoo it comes to beir the meanin' that it's weel kent to beir?" said the manufacturer.

"Not I, Mr. MacGregor," answered the solicitor. "I'm no philologist or antiquarian. Ask the chairman."

"Gentlemen," responded Mr. Innes, taking a

huge pinch of snuff after the word, and then, passing the box to Mr. Cocker, a sip from his glass before he went on: " the phrase, gentlemen, 'a drap i' the hoose,' no doobt refers to an undesirable presence, for ye're weel awaur that it's a most unpleasin' discovery, in winter especially, to find a drop o' water hangin' from yer ceiling ; a something, in short, whaur it has no business to be, and is not accordingly looked for, or prepared against."

"It seems to me, Mr. Innes," said MacGregor, "that ye hae hit the nail, but no upo' the heid. What mak' ye o' the phrase, no confined to the Scots tongue, I believe, o' an *eaves-drapper?* The whilk, no doobt, represents a body that hings aboot yer winnock, like a drap hangin' ower abune it frae the eaves—therefore called an eaves-dropper? But the sort of whilk we noo speak, are a waur sort a'thegither ; for they come to the inside o' yer hoose, o' yer verra chaumer, an' hing oot their lang lugs to hear what ye carena to be hard save by a dooce frien' or twa ower a het tum'ler."

At the same moment the door opened, and a man entered, who was received with unusual welcome.

" Bless my sowl ! " said the president, rising ; " it's Mr. Lammie !—Come awa', Mr. Lammie. Sit doon ; sit doon. Whaur hae ye been this mony a day, like a pelican o' the wilderness ?"

Mr. Lammie was a large, mild man, with florid cheeks, no whiskers, and a prominent black eye. He was characterized by a certain simple alacrity, a gentle, but outspeaking readiness, which made him a favourite.

" I dinna richtly mak oot wha ye are," he answered. " Ye hae unco little licht here! Hoo are ye a', gentlemen? I s' discover ye by degrees, and pay my respecks accordin'."

And he drew a chair to the table.

" 'Deed I wuss ye wad," returned MacGregor, in a voice pretentiously hushed, but none the less audible.—" There's a drap in yon en' o' the hoose, Mr. Lammie."

" Hoot! never min' the man," said Lammie, looking round in the direction indicated. " I s' warran' he cares as little aboot hiz as we care aboot him. There's nae treason noo-a-days. I carena wha hears what I say."

" For my pairt," said Mr. Peddie, " I canna help wonnerin' gin it cud be oor auld frien' Mr. Faukener."

" Speyk o' the de'il——" said Mr. Lammie.

" Hoot! na," returned Peddie, interrupting. " He wasna a'thegither the de'il."

" Haud the tongue o' ye," retorted Lammie. " Dinna ye ken a proverb whan ye hear 't? De'il hae ye! ye're as sharpset as a missionar'. I was only gaun to say that I'm doobtin' Andrew's deid."

"Ay! ay!" commenced a chorus of questioning.

"Mhm!"

"Aaay!"

"What gars ye think that?"

"And sae he's deid!"

"He was a great favourite, Anerew!"

"Whaur dee'd he?"

"Aye some upsettin' though!"

"Ay. He was aye to be somebody wi' his tale."

"A gude-hertit crater, but ye cudna lippen till him."

"Speyk nae ill o' the deid. Maybe they'll hear ye, and turn roon' i' their coffins, and that'll whumle you i' your beds," said MacGregor, with a twinkle in his eye.

"Ring the bell for anither tum'ler, Sampson," said the chairman.

"What'll be dune wi' that factory place, noo? It'll be i' the market?"

"It's been i' the market for mony a year. But it's no his ava. It belangs to the auld leddy, his mither," said the weaver.

"Why don't you buy it, Mr. MacGregor, and set up a cotton mill? There's not much doing with the linen now," said Mr. Cocker.

"Me!" returned MacGregor, with indignation. "The Lord forgie ye for mintin' *(hinting)* at sic a thing, Mr. Cocker! Me tak to coaton! I wad as sune spin the hair frae Sawtan's hurdies. Short fushionless dirt, that canna grow straucht oot o' the halesome yird, like the bonnie lint-bells, but maun stick itsel' upo' a buss!—set it up! Coorse vulgar stuff, 'at naebody wad weir but loup-coonter lads that wad fain luik like gentlemen by means o' the collars and ruffles—an' a' comin' frae the auld loom! They may weel affoord se'enteen hunner linen to set it aff wi' 'at has naething but coaton inside the breeks o' them."

"But Dr. Wagstaff says it's healthier," interposed Peddie.

"I'll wag a staff till him. De'il a bit o' t' 's healthier! an' that he kens. It's nae sae healthy, an' sae it mak's him mair wark wi' 's poothers an' his drauchts, an' ither stinkin' stuff. Healthier! What neist?"

"Somebody tellt me," said the bookseller, inwardly conscious of offence, "'at hoo Lord Sandy himsel' weirs cotton."

"Ow 'deed, maybe. And he sets mony a worthy example furbye. Hoo mony, can ye tell me, Mr. Peddie, has he pulled doon frae honest, if no frae high estate, and sent oot to seek their livin' as he taucht them? Hoo mony—— ?"

"Hoot, hoot! Mr. MacGregor, his lordship hasn't a cotton shirt in his possession, I'll be bound," said Mr. Cocker. "And, besides, you have not to wash his dirty linen—or cotton either."

"That's as muckle as to say, accordin' to

Cocker, that I'm no to speik a word against him.
But I'll say what I like. He's no *my* maister,"
said MacGregor, who could drink very little
without suffering in his temper and manners ;
and who, besides, had a certain shrewd suspicion as to the person who still sat in the dark end
of the room, possibly because the entrance of
Mr. Lammie had interrupted the exorcism.

The chairman interposed with soothing words ;
and the whole company, Cocker included, did its
best to pacify the manufacturer ; for they all
knew what would be the penalty if they failed.

A good deal of talk followed, and a good deal
of whisky was drunk. They were waited upon
by Meg, who, without their being aware of it,
cast a keen parting glance at them every time
she left the room. At length the conversation
had turned again to Andrew Falconer's death.

"Whaur said ye he dee'd, Mr. Lammie ?"

"I never said he was deid. I said I was feared 'at he was deid."

"An' what gars ye say that ? It micht be o'
consequence to hae't correck," said the solicitor.

"I had a letter frae my auld frien' and his,
Dr. Anderson. Ye min' upo' him, Mr. Innes,
dunna ye ? He's heid o' the medical boord at
Calcutta noo. He says naething but that he
doobts he's gane. He gaed up the country, and
he hasna hard o' him for sae lang. We hae
keepit up a correspondence for mony a year

noo, Dr. Anderson an' me. He was a relation o'
Anerew's, ye ken—a second cousin, or something.   He'll be hame or lang, I'm thinkin', wi'
a fine pension."

" He winna weir a cotton sark, I'll be boon',"
said MacGregor.

" What's the auld leddy gaein' to du wi' that
lang-leggit oye (*grandson*) o' hers, Anerew's
son?" asked Sampson.

"Ow! he'll be gaein' to the college, I'm
thinkin'.   He's a fine lad, and a clever, they tell
me," said Mr. Thomson.

" Indeed, he's all that, and more too," said the
schoolmaster.

" There's naething 'ull du but the college noo!"
said MacGregor, whom nobody heeded, for fear
of again rousing his anger.

" Hoo 'ill she manage that, honest woman?
She maun hae but little to spare frae the cleed-
in' o' 'm."

" She's a gude manager, Mistress Faukner.
And, ye see, she has the bleachgreen yet."

" *She* doesna weir cotton sarks," growled Mac-
Gregor. " Mony's the wob o' mine she's bleached
and boucht tu!"

Nobody heeding him yet, he began to feel in-
sulted, and broke in upon the conversation with
intent.

" Ye haena telt's yet, Cocker," he said, " what
that maister o' yours is duin' here at this time

o' the year. I wad ken that, gin ye please."

"How should I know, Mr. MacGregor?" returned the factor, taking no notice of the offensive manner in which the question was put.

"He's no a hair better nor ane o' thae Algerine pirates 'at Lord Exmooth's het the hips o'—and that's my opingon."

"He's nae amo' your feet, MacGregor," said the banker. "Ye micht jist lat him lie."

"Gin I had him doon, faith gin I wadna lat him lie! I'll jist tell ye ae thing, gentlemen, that cam' to my knowledge no a hunner year ago. An' it's a' as true's gospel, though I hae aye held my tongue aboot it till this verra nicht. Ay! ye'll a' hearken noo; but it's no lauchin', though there was sculduddery eneuch, nae doobt, afore it cam' that len'th. And mony a het drap did the puir lassie greet, I can tell ye. Faith! it was no lauchin' to her. She was a servan' o' oors, an' a ticht bonnie lass she was. They ca'd her the weyver's bonny Mary—that's the name she gaed by. Weel, ye see——"

MacGregor was interrupted by a sound from the further end of the room. The stranger, whom most of them had by this time forgotten, had risen, and was approaching the table where they sat.

"Guid guide us!" interrupted several under their breaths, as all rose, "it's Lord Sandy himsel'!"

"I thank you, gentlemen," he said, with a mixture of irony and contempt, "for the interest you take in my private history. I should have thought it had been as little to the taste as it is to the honour of *some* of you to listen to such a farrago of lies."

"Lees! my lord," said MacGregor, starting to his feet. Mr. Cocker looked dismayed, and Mr. Lammie sheepish—all of them dazed and dumbfounded, except the old weaver, who, as his lordship turned to leave the room, added:

"Lang lugs *(ears)* suld be made o' leather, my lord, for fear they grow het wi' what they hear."

Lord Rothie turned in a rage. He too had been drinking.

"Kick that toad into the street, or, by heaven! it's the last drop any of you drink in this house!" he cried.

"The taed may tell the poddock *(frog)* what the rottan *(rat)* did i' the taed's hole, my lord," said MacGregor, whom independence, honesty, bile, and drink combined to render fearless.

Lord Sandy left the room without another word. His factor took his hat and followed him. The rest dropped into their seats in silence. Mr. Lammie was the first to speak.

"There's a pliskie!" he said.

"I cud jist say the word efter auld Simeon," said MacGregor. "I never thocht to be sae favoured! Eh! but I hae langed, and noo I hae spoken!" with which words he sat down, contented.

When Mr. Cocker overtook his master, as MacGregor had not unfitly styled him, he only got a damning for his pains, and went home considerably crestfallen.

Lord Rothie returned to the landlady in her parlour.

"What's the maitter wi' ye, my lord? What's vexed ye?" asked Miss Napier, with a twinkle in her eyes, for she thought, from the Baron's mortification, he must have received some rebuff, and now that the *bonnie leddy* was safe at Captain Forsyth's, enjoyed the idea of it.

" Ye keep an ill-tongued hoose, Miss Naper," answered his lordship.

Miss Napier guessed at the truth at once— that he had overheard some free remarks on his well-known licence of behaviour.

"Weel, my lord, I do my best. A body canna keep an inn and speir the carritchis (*catechism*) at the door o' 't. But I believe ye're i' the richt, my lord; for I heard an awfu' aff-gang o' sweirin' i' the yard, jist afore yer lordship cam' in. An' noo 'at I think o' 't, it wasna that on-like yer lordship's ain word."

Lord Sandy broke into a loud laugh. He could enjoy a joke against himself when it came from a woman, and was founded on such a trifle as a personal vice.

"I think I'll go to bed," he said when his

laugh was over. "I believe it's the only safe place from your tongue, Miss Naper."

"Letty," cried Miss Napier, "fess a can'le, and show his lordship to the reid room."

Till Miss Letty appeared, the Baron sat and stretched himself. He then rose and followed her into the archway, and up an outside stair to a door which opened immediately upon a handsome old-fashioned room, where a blazing fire lighted up the red hangings. Miss Letty set down the candle, and bidding his lordship good night, turned and left the room, shutting the door, and locking it behind her—a proceeding of which his lordship took no notice, for, however especially suitable it might be in his case, it was only, from whatever ancient source derived, the custom of the house in regard to this particular room and a corresponding chamber on the opposite side of the archway.

Meantime the consternation amongst the members of the club was not so great as not to be talked over, or to prevent the call for more whisky and hot water. All but MacGregor, however, regretted what had occurred. He was so elevated with his victory and a sense of courage and prowess, that he became more and more facetious and overbearing.

"It's all very well for you, Mr. MacGregor," said the dominie, with dignity: "you have nothing to lose."

"Troth! he canna brak the bank—eh, Mr. Tamson?"

"He may give me a hint to make you withdraw your money, though, Mr. MacGregor."

"De'il care gin I do!" returned the weaver. "I can mak' better o' 't ony day."

"But there's yer hoose an' kail-yard," suggested Peddie.

"They're ma ain!—a' ma ain! He canna lay 's finger on onything o' mine but my servan' lass," cried the weaver, slapping his thigh-bone —for there was little else to slap.

Meg, at the moment, was taking her exitglance. She went straight to Miss Napier.

"Willie MacGregor's had eneuch, mem, an' a drappy ower."

"Sen' Caumil doon to Mrs. MacGregor, to say wi' my compliments that she wad do weel to sen' for him," was the response.

Meantime he grew more than troublesome. Ever on the outlook, when sober, after the foibles of others, he laid himself open to endless ridicule when in drink, which, to tell the truth, was a rare occurrence. He was in the midst of a prophetic denunciation of the vices of the nobility, and especially of Lord Rothie, when Meg entering the room, went quietly behind his chair and whispered:

"Maister MacGregor, there's a lassie come for ye."

"I'm nae in," he answered, magnificently.

"But it's the mistress 'at's sent for ye. Somebody's wantin' ye."

"Somebody maun want me, than.—As I was sayin', Mr. Cheerman and gentlemen——"

"Mistress MacGregor 'll be efter ye hersel', gin ye dinna gang," said Meg.

"Lat her come. Duv ye think I'm fleyt at her? De'il a step 'll I gang till I please. Tell her that, Meg."

Meg left the room, with a broad grin on her good-humoured face.

"What's the bitch lauchin' at?" exclaimed MacGregor, starting to his feet.

The whole company rose likewise, using their endeavour to persuade him to go home.

"Duv ye think I'm drunk, sirs? I'll lat ye ken I'm no drunk. I hae a wull o' mine ain yet. Am I to gang hame wi' a lassie to haud me oot o' the gutters? Gin ye daur to alloo that I'm drunk, ye ken hoo ye'll fare, for de'il a fit 'll I gang oot o' this till I hae anither tum'ler."

"I'm thinkin' there's mair o' 's jist want ane mair," said Peddie.

A confirmatory murmur arose as each looked into the bottom of his tumbler, and the bell was instantly rung. But it only brought Meg back with the message that it was time for them all to go home. Every eye turned upon MacGregor reproachfully.

" Ye needna luik at me that gait, sirs. I'm no fou," said he.

" 'Deed no. Naebody taks ye to be," answered the chairman. " Meggie, there's naebody's had ower muckle yet, and twa or three o' 's hasna had freely eneuch. Jist gang an' fess a mutchkin mair. An' there 'll be a shillin' to yersel', lass."

Meg retired, but straightway returned.

" Miss Naper says there's no a drap mair drink to be had i' this hoose the nicht."

" Here, Meggie," said the chairman, " there's yer shillin'; and ye jist gang to Miss Lettie, and gie her my compliments, and say that Mr. Lammie's here, and we haena seen him for a lang time. And "—the rest was spoken in a whisper—" I'll sweir to ye, Meggie, the weyver body sanna hae ae drap o' 't."

Meg withdrew once more, and returned.

" Miss Letty's compliments, sir, and Miss Naper has the keys, and she's gane till her bed, and we maunna disturb her. And it's time 'at a' honest fowk was in their beds tu. And gin Mr. Lammie wants a bed i' this hoose, he maun gang till 't. An' here's his can'le. Gude nicht to ye a', gentlemen."

So saying, Meg set the lighted candle on the sideboard, and finally vanished. The good-tempered, who formed the greater part of the company, smiled to each other, and emptied the last drops of their toddy first into their glasses, and thence into their mouths. The ill-tempered, numbering but one more than Mac-Gregor, growled and swore a little, the former declaring that he would not go home. But the rest walked out and left him, and at last, appalled by the silence, he rose with his wig awry, and trotted—he always trotted when he was tipsy—home to his wife.

CHAPTER VI.

MRS. FALCONER

MEANTIME Robert was seated in the parlour
at the little dark mahogany table, in
which the lamp, shaded towards his grandmother's side, shone brilliantly reflected. Her face
being thus hidden both by the light and the
shadow, he could not observe the keen look of
stern benevolence with which, knowing that he
could not see her, she regarded him as he ate his
thick oat cake of Betty's skilled manufacture,
well loaded with the sweetest butter, and drank
the tea which she had poured out and sugared
for him with liberal hand. It was a comfortable little room, though its inlaid mahogany
chairs and ancient sofa, covered with horsehair,
had a certain look of hardness, no doubt. A
shepherdess and lamb, worked in silks whose
brilliance had now faded halfway to neutrality,
hung in a black frame, with brass rosettes at
the corners, over the chimney-piece—the sole

approach to the luxury of art in the homely little
place. Besides the muslin stretched across the
lower part of the window, it was undefended by
curtains. There was no cat in the room, nor
was there one in the kitchen even; for Mrs.
Falconer had such a respect for humanity that
she grudged every morsel consumed by the
lower creation. She sat in one of the arm-
chairs belonging to the hairy set, leaning back
in contemplation of her grandson, as she took
her tea.

She was a handsome old lady—little, but had
once been taller, for she was more than seventy
now. She wore a plain cap of muslin, lying
close to her face, and bordered a little way
from the edge with a broad black ribbon, which
went round her face, and then, turning at right
angles, went round the back of her neck. Her
grey hair peeped a little way from under this
cap. A clear but short-sighted eye of a light
hazel shone under a smooth thoughtful forehead; a straight and well-elevated, but rather
short nose, which left the firm upper lip long
and capable of expressing a world of dignified
offence, rose over a well-formed mouth, revealing more moral than temperamental sweetness;
while the chin was rather deficient than otherwise, and took little share in indicating the remarkable character possessed by the old lady.

After gazing at Robert for some time, she

took a piece of oat cake from a plate by her side, the only luxury in which she indulged, for it was made with cream instead of water—it was very little she ate of anything—and held it out to Robert in a hand white, soft, and smooth, but with square finger tips, and squat though pearly nails. " Ha'e, Robert," she said; and Robert received it with a " thank you, grannie;" but when he thought she did not see him, slipped it under the table and into his pocket. She saw him well enough, however, and although she would not condescend to ask him why he put it away instead of eating it, the endeavour to discover what could have been his reason for so doing cost her two hours of sleep that night. She would always be at the bottom of a thing if reflection could reach it, but she generally declined taking the most ordinary measures to expedite the process.

When Robert had finished his tea, instead of rising to get his books and betake himself to his lessons, in regard to which his grandmother had seldom any cause to complain, although she would have considered herself guilty of high treason against the boy's future if she had allowed herself once to acknowledge as much, he drew his chair towards the fire, and said:

" Grandmamma."

" He's gaein' to tell me something," said Mrs. Falconer to herself. " Will 't be aboot the puir

barfut crater they ca' Shargar, or will 't be aboot
the piece he pat intil 's pooch ?"

" Weel, laddie ?" she said aloud, willing to
encourage him.

" Is 't true that my gran'father was the blin'
piper o' Portcloddie ?"

" Ay, laddie ; true eneuch. Hoots na ; nae
yer grandfather, but yer father's grandfather,
laddie—my husband's father."

" Hoo cam that aboot ? "

" Weel, ye see, he was oot i' the Forty-five ;
and efter the battle o' Culloden, he had to rin
for 't. He wasna wi' his ain clan at the battle,
for his father had broucht him to the Lawlands
whan he was a lad ; but he played the pipes
till a reg'ment raised by the Laird o' Portcloddie. And for ooks (*weeks*) he had to hide amo'
the rocks. And they tuik a' his property frae
him. It wasna muckle—a wheen hooses, and a
kailyard or twa, wi' a bit fairmy on the tap o' a
cauld hill near the seashore ; but it was eneuch
and to spare ; and whan they tuik it frae him,
he had naething left i' the warl' but his sons.
Yer grandfather was born the verra day o' the
battle, and the verra day 'at the news cam, the
mother deed. But yer great-grandfather wasna
lang or he merried anither wife. He was sic a
man as ony woman micht hae been prood to
merry. She was the dother (*daughter*) o' an
episcopalian minister, and she keepit a school in

Portcloddie. I saw him first mysel' whan I was aboot twenty—that was jist the year afore I was merried. He was a gey (*considerably*) auld man than, but as straucht as an ellwand, and jist pooerfu' beyon' belief. His shackle-bane (*wrist*) was as thick as baith mine; and years and years efter that, whan he tuik his son, my husband, and his grandson, my Anerew——"

"What ails ye, grannie? What for dinna ye gang on wi' the story?"

After a somewhat lengthened pause, Mrs. Falconer resumed as if she had not stopped at all.

"Ane in ilka han', jist for the fun o' 't, he kneipit their heids thegither, as gin they hed been twa carldoddies (*stalks of rib-grass*). But maybe it was the lauchin' o' the twa lads, for they thocht it unco fun. They were maist killed wi' lauchin'. But the last time he did it, the puir auld màn hostit (*coughed*) sair efterhin, and had to gang and lie doon. He didna live lang efter that. But it wasna that 'at killed him, ye ken."

"But hoo cam he to play the pipes?"

"He likit the pipes. And yer grandfather, he tuik to the fiddle."

"But what for did they ca' him the blin' piper o' Portcloddie?"

"Because he turned blin' lang afore his en' cam, and there was naething ither he cud do. And he wad aye mak an honest baubee whan he cud; for siller was fell scarce at that time o'

day amo' the Falconers. Sae he gaed throu
the toon at five o'clock ilka mornin' playin' his
pipes, to lat them 'at war up ken they war up in
time, and them 'at warna, that it was time to
rise. And syne he played them again aboot
aucht o'clock at night, to lat them ken 'at it was
time for dacent fowk to gang to their beds. Ye
see, there wasna sae mony clocks and watches by
half than as there is noo."

" Was he a guid piper, grannie ? "

" What for speir ye that ?"

" Because I tauld that sunk, Lumley——"

" Ca' naebody names, Robert. But what richt
had ye to be speikin' to a man like that ?"

" He spak to me first."

" Whaur saw ye him ?"

" At the Boar's Heid."

" And what richt had ye to gang stan'in'
aboot ? Ye oucht to ha' gane in at ance."

" There was a half-dizzen o' fowk stan'in'
aboot, and I bude (*behoved*) to speik whan I was
spoken till."

" But ye budena stop an' mak ae fule mair."

" Isna that ca'in' names, grannie ?"

" 'Deed, laddie, I doobt ye hae me there. But
what said the fallow Lumley to ye ?"

" He cast up to me that my grandfather was
naething but a blin' piper."

" And what said ye ?"

" I daured him to say 'at he didna pipe weel."

" Weel dune, laddie ! And ye micht say 't wi'
a gude conscience, for he wadna hae been piper
till 's regiment at the battle o' Culloden gin he
hadna pipit weel. Yon's his kilt hingin' up i'
the press i' the garret. Ye'll hae to grow, Robert, my man, afore ye fill that."

" And whase was that blue coat wi' the bonny
gowd buttons upo' 't?" asked Robert, who
thought he had discovered a new approach to an
impregnable hold, which he would gladly storm
if he could.

" Lat the coat sit. What has that to do wi'
the kilt? A blue coat and a tartan kilt gang na
weel thegither."

" Excep' in an auld press whaur naebody sees
them. Ye wadna care, grannie, wad ye, gin I
was to cut aff the bonnie buttons?"

" Dinna lay a finger upo' them. Ye wad be
gaein' playin' at pitch and toss or ither sic ploys
wi' them. Na, na, lat them sit."

" I wad only niffer them for bools (*exchange
them for marbles*)."

" I daur ye to touch the coat or onything 'ither
that's i' that press."

" Weel, weel, grannie. I s' gang and get my
lessons for the morn."

" It's time, laddie. Ye hae been jabberin'
ower muckle. Tell Betty to come and tak' awa'
the taythings."

Robert went to the kitchen, got a couple of

hot potatoes and a candle, and carried them up
stairs to Shargar, who was fast asleep. But
the moment the light shone upon his face, he
started up, with his eyes, if not his senses, wide
awake.

"It wasna me, mither! I tell ye it wasna
me!"

And he covered his head with both arms, as if
to defend it from a shower of blows.

"Haud yer tongue, Shargar. It's me."

But before Shargar could come to his senses,
the light of the candle falling upon the blue coat
made the buttons flash confused suspicions into
his mind.

"Mither, mither," he said, "ye hae gane ower
far this time. There's ower mony o' them, and
they're no the safe colour. We'll be baith hangt,
as sure's there's a deevil in hell."

As he said thus, he went on trying to pick
the buttons from the coat, taking them for sovereigns, though how he could have seen a sovereign at that time in Scotland I can only conjecture. But Robert caught him by the shoulders, and shook him awake with no gentle hands,
upon which he began to rub his eyes, and mut-
ter sleepily:

"Is that you, Bob? I hae been dreamin', I
doobt."

"Gin ye dinna learn to dream quaieter, ye'll
get you and me tu into mair trouble nor I

care to hae aboot ye, ye rascal. Haud the tongue o' ye, and eat this tawtie, gin ye want onything mair. And here's a bit o' reamy cakes tu ye. Ye winna get that in ilka hoose i' the toon. It's my grannie's especial."

Robert felt relieved after this, for he had eaten all the cakes Miss Napier had given him, and had had a pain in his conscience ever since.

"Hoo got ye a haud o' 't?" asked Shargar, evidently supposing he had stolen it.

"She gies me a bit noo and than."

"And ye didna eat it yersel'? Eh, Bob!"

Shargar was somewhat overpowered at this fresh proof of Robert's friendship. But Robert was still more ashamed of what he had not done.

He took the blue coat carefully from the bed, and hung it in its place again, satisfied now, from the way his grannie had spoken, or, rather, declined to speak, about it, that it had belonged to his father.

"Am I to rise?" asked Shargar, not understanding the action.

"Na, na, lie still. Ye'll be warm eneuch wantin' thae sovereigns. I'll lat ye oot i' the mornin' afore grannie's up. And ye maun mak' the best o't efter that till it's dark again. We'll sattle a' aboot it at the schuil the morn. Only we maun be circumspec', ye ken."

"Ye cudna lay yer han's upo' a drap o' whusky, cud ye, Bob?"

Robert stared in horror. A boy like that asking for whisky! and in his grandmother's house, too!

"Shargar," he said solemnly, "there's no a drap o' whusky i' this hoose. It's awfu' to hear ye mention sic a thing. My grannie wad smell the verra name o' 't a mile awa'. I doobt that's her fit upo' the stair a'ready."

Robert crept to the door, and Shargar sat staring with horror, his eyes looking from the gloom of the bed like those of a half-strangled dog. But it was a false alarm, as Robert presently returned to announce.

"Gin ever ye sae muckle as mention whusky again, no to say drink ae drap o' 't, you and me pairt company, and that I tell *you*, Shargar," said he, emphatically.

"I'll never luik at it; I'll never mint at dreamin' o' 't," answered Shargar, coweringly. "Gin she pits 't intil my moo', I'll spit it oot. But gin *ye* strive wi' me, Bob, I'll cut my throat —I will; an' that 'll be seen and heard tell o'."

All this time, save during the alarm of Mrs. Falconer's approach, when he sat with a mouthful of hot potato, unable to move his jaws for terror, and the remnant arrested half way in its progress from his mouth after the bite—all this time Shargar had been devouring the provisions

Robert had brought him, as if he had not seen
food that day. As soon as they were finished,
he begged for a drink of water, which Robert
managed to procure for him. He then left him
for the night, for his longer absence might
have brought his grandmother after him, who
had perhaps only too good reasons for being
doubtful, if not suspicious, about boys in general, though certainly not about Robert in particular. He carried with him his books from
the other garret room where he kept them, and
sat down at the table by his grandmother, preparing his latin and geography by her lamp,
while she sat knitting a white stocking with
fingers as rapid as thought, never looking at her
work, but staring into the fire, and seeing visions
there which Robert would have given everything he could call his own to see, and then
would have given his life to blot out of the
world if he had seen them. Quietly the evening passed, by the peaceful lamp and the cheerful fire, with the Latin on the one side of the
table, and the stocking on the other, as if ripe
and purified old age and hopeful unstained
youth had been the only extremes of humanity
known to the world. But the bitter wind was
howling by fits in the chimney, and the offspring
of a nobleman and a gipsy lay asleep in the
garret, covered with the cloak of an old Highland rebel.

At nine o'clock, Mrs. Falconer rang the bell for Betty, and they had *worship*. Robert read a chapter, and his grandmother prayed an extempore prayer, in which they that looked at the wine when it was red in the cup, and they that worshipped the woman clothed in scarlet and seated upon the seven hills, came in for a strange mixture, in which the vengeance yielded only to the pity.

"Lord, lead them to see the error of their ways," she cried. "Let the rod of thy wrath awake the worm of their conscience, that they may know verily that there is a God that ruleth in the earth. Dinna lat them gang to hell, O Lord, we beseech thee."

As soon as prayers were over, Robert had a tumbler of milk and some more oatcake, and was sent to bed; after which it was impossible for him to hold any further communication with Shargar. For his grandmother, little as one might suspect it who entered the parlour in the daytime, always slept in that same room, in a bed closed in with doors like those of a large press in the wall, while Robert slept in a little closet, looking into a garden at the back of the house, the door of which opened from the parlour close to the head of his grandmother's bed. It was just large enough to hold a good-sized bed with curtains, a chest of drawers, a bureau, a large eight-day clock, and one chair, leaving in the centre about five feet square for him to move about in. There was more room as well as more comfort in the bed. He was never allowed a candle, for light enough came through from the parlour, his grandmother thought; so he was soon extended between the whitest of cold sheets, with his knees up to his chin, and his thoughts following his lost father over all spaces of the earth with which his geography-book had made him acquainted.

He was in the habit of leaving his closet and creeping through his grandmother's room before she was awake—or at least before she had given any signs to the small household that she was restored to consciousness, and that the life of the house must proceed. He therefore found no difficulty in liberating Sharger from his prison, except what arose from the boy's own unwillingness to forsake his comfortable quarters for the fierce encounter of the January blast which awaited him. But Robert did not turn him out before the last moment of safety had arrived; for, by the aid of signs known to himself, he watched the progress of his grandmother's dressing—an operation which did not consume much of the morning, scrupulous as she was with regard to neatness and cleanliness —until Betty was called in to give her careful assistance to the final disposition of the *mutch*, when Shargar's exit could be delayed no lon-

ger. Then he mounted to the foot of the second
stair, and called in a keen whisper,

" Noo, Shargar, cut for the life o' ye."

And down came the poor fellow, with long
gliding steps, ragged and reluctant, and, without a word or a look, launched himself out into
the cold, and sped away he knew not whither.
As he left the door, the only suspicion of light
was the dull and doubtful shimmer of the snow
that covered the street, keen particles of which
were blown in his face by the wind, which, having been up all night, had grown very cold,
and seemed delighted to find one unprotected
human being whom it might badger at its own
bitter will. Outcast Shargar! Where he spent
the interval between Mrs. Falconer's door and
that of the school, I do not know. There was
a report amongst his school-fellows that he had
been found by Scroggie, the fish-cadger, lying
at full length upon the back of his old horse,
which, either from compassion or indifference,
had not cared to rise up under the burden.
They said likewise that, when accused by
Scroggie of housebreaking, though nothing had
to be broken to get in, only a string with a peculiar knot, on the invention of which the cad-
ger prided himself, to be undone, all that Shargar had to say in his self-defence was, that he
had a terrible sair wame, and that the horse
was warmer nor the stanes i' the yard ; and he

had dune him nae ill, nae even drawn a hair
frae his tale—which would have been a difficult
feat, seeing the horse's tail was as bare as his
hoof.

CHAPTER VII.

ROBERT TO THE RESCUE !

THAT Shargar was a parish scholar—
which means that the parish paid his fees,
although, indeed, they were hardly worth paying—made very little difference to his position amongst his school-fellows. Nor did the
fact of his being ragged and dirty affect his
social reception to his discomfort. But the accumulated facts of the oddity of his personal
appearance, his supposed imbecility, and the bad
character borne by his mother, placed him in a
very unenviable relation to the tyrannical and
vulgar-minded amongst them. Concerning his
person, he was long, and, as his name implied,
lean, with pale-red hair, reddish eyes, no visible
eyebrows or eyelashes, and very pale face—in
fact, he was half way to an Albino. His arms
and legs seemed of equal length, both exceedingly long. The handsomeness of his mother
appeared only in his nose and mouth, which

were regular and good, though expressionless: and the birth of his father only in his small delicate hands and feet, of which any girl who cared only for smallness, and heeded neither character nor strength, might have been proud. His feet, however, were supposed to be enormous, from the difficulty with which he dragged after him the huge shoes in which in winter they were generally encased.

The imbecility, like the large feet, was only imputed. He certainly was not brilliant, but neither did he make a fool of himself in any of the few branches of learning of which the parish-scholar came in for a share. That which gained him the imputation was the fact that his nature was without a particle of the aggressive, and all its defensive of as purely negative a character as was possible. Had he been a dog, he would never have thought of doing anything for his own protection beyond turning up his four legs in silent appeal to the mercy of the heavens. He was an absolute sepulchre in the swallowing of oppression and ill-usage. It vanished in him. There was no echo of complaint, no murmur of resentment from the hollows of that soul. The blows that fell upon him resounded not, and no one but God remembered them.

His mother made her living as she herself best knew, with occasional well-begrudged as-

sistance from the parish. Her chief resource
was no doubt begging from house to house for
the handful of oatmeal which was the recognized,
and, in the court of custom-taught conscience,
the legalized dole upon which every beggar had
a claim ; and if she picked up at the same time
a chicken, or a boy's rabbit, or any other stray
luxury, she was only following the general rule
of society, that your first duty is to take care of
yourself. She was generally regarded as a
gipsy, but I doubt if she had any gipsy blood
in her veins. She was simply a tramper, with
occasional fits of localization. Her worst fault
was the way she treated her son, whom she
starved apparently that she might continue able
to beat him.

The particular occasion which led to the recognition of the growing relation between Robert and Shargar was the following. Upon a
certain Saturday—some sidereal power inimical
to boys must have been in the ascendant—a
Saturday of brilliant but intermittent sunshine,
the white clouds seen from the school windows
indicating by their rapid transit across those fields
of vision that fresh breezes friendly to kites, or
draigons, as they were called at Rothieden, were
frolicking in the upper regions—nearly a dozen
boys were *kept in* for not being able to pay down
from memory the usual instalment of Shorter
Catechism always due at the close of the week.

Amongst these boys were Robert and Shargar.
Sky-revealing windows and locked door were
too painful; and in proportion as the feeling of
having nothing to do increased, the more uneasy did the active element in the boys become,
and the more ready to break out into some abnormal manifestation. Everything—sun, wind,
clouds—was busy out of doors, and calling to
them to come and join the fun; and activity at
the same moment excited and restrained naturally turns to mischief. Most of them had already learned the obnoxious task—one quarter
of an hour was enough for that—and now what
should they do next? The eyes of three or four
of the eldest of them fell simultaneously upon
Shargar.

Robert was sitting plunged in one of his day-
dreams, for he, too, had learned his catechism,
when he was roused from his reverie by a question from a pale-faced little boy, who looked up
to him as a great authority.

"What for 's 't ca'd the *Shorter* Carritchis,
Bob?"

"'Cause it's no fully sae lang's the Bible," answered Robert, without giving the question the
consideration due to it, and was proceeding to
turn the matter over in his mind, when the mental process was arrested by a shout of laughter.
The other boys had tied Shargar's feet to the
desk at which he sat—likewise his hands, at full

stretch; then, having attached about a dozen
strings to as many elf-locks of his pale-red hair,
which was never cut or trimmed, had tied them
to various pegs in the wall behind him, so that
the poor fellow could not stir.   They were now
crushing up pieces of waste paper, not a few
leaves of stray school-books being regarded in
that light, into bullets, dipping them in ink and
aiming them at Shargar's face.

For some time Shargar did not utter a word;
and Robert, although somewhat indignant at
the treatment he was receiving, felt as yet no
impulse to interfere, for success was doubtful.
But, indeed, he was not very easily roused to
action of any kind; for he was as yet mostly in
the larva-condition of character, when everything
is transacted inside.   But the fun grew more
furious, and spot after spot of ink gloomed upon
Shargar's white face.   Still Robert took no notice, for they did not seem to be hurting him
much.   But when he saw the tears stealing down
his patient cheeks, making channels through
the ink which now nearly covered them, he could
bear it no longer.   He took out his knife, and
under pretence of joining in the sport, drew
near to Shargar, and, with rapid hand, cut the
cords—all but those that bound his feet, which
were less easy to reach without exposing himself defenceless.

The boys of course turned upon Robert.   But

ere they came to more than abusive words a di-
version took place.

Mrs. Innes, the schoolmaster's wife—a stout,
kind-hearted woman, the fine condition of whose
temperament was clearly the result of her physical prosperity—appeared at the door which
led to the dwelling-house above, bearing in her
hands a huge tureen of potato-soup, for her
motherly heart could not longer endure the
thought of dinnerless boys. Her husband being
engaged at a parish meeting, she had a chance
of interfering with success.

But ere Nancy, the servant, could follow with
the spoons and plates, Wattie Morrison had
taken the tureen, and out of spite at Robert,
had emptied its contents on the head of Shargar, who was still tied by the feet, with the
words: "Shargar, I anoint thee king over us,
and here is thy crown," giving the tureen, as
he said so, a push on to his head, where it remained.

Shargar did not move, and for one moment
could not speak, but the next he gave a shriek
that made Robert think he was far worse scald-
ed than turned out to be the case. He darted
to him in rage, took the tureen from his head,
and, his blood being fairly up now, flung it with
all his force at Morrison, and felled him to the
earth. At the same moment the master entered
by the street-door and his wife by the house-

door, which was directly opposite. In the middle of the room the prisoners surrounded the fallen tyrant—Robert, with the red face of wrath, and Shargar, with a complexion the mingled result of tears, ink, and soup, which latter clothed him from head to foot besides, standing on the outskirts of the group. I need not follow the story farther. Both Robert and Morrison *got a lickin'* ; and if Mr. Innes had been like some schoolmasters of those times, Shargar would not have escaped his share of the evil things going.

From that day Robert assumed the acknowledged position of Shargar's defender. And if there was pride and a sense of propriety mingled with his advocacy of Shargar's rights, nay, even if the relation was not altogether free from some amount of show-off on Robert's part, I cannot yet help thinking that it had its share in that development of the character of Falconer which has chiefly attracted me to the office of his biographer. There may have been in it the exercise of some patronage ; probably it was not pure from the pride of beneficence ; but at least it was a loving patronage and a vigorous beneficence ; and, under the reaction of these, the good which in Robert's nature was as yet only in a state of solution, began to crystallize into character.

But the effect of the new relation was far more

remarkable on Shargar. As incapable of self-defence as ever, he was yet in a moment roused to fury by any attack upon the person or the dignity of Robert: so that, indeed, it became a new and favourite mode of teasing Shargar to heap abuse, real or pretended, upon his friend. From the day when Robert thus espoused his part, Shargar was Robert's dog. That very evening, when she went to take a parting peep at the external before locking the door for the night, Betty found him sitting upon the doorstep, only, however, to send him off, as she described it, "wi' a flech* in 's lug (*a flea in his ear*)." For the character of the mother was always associated with the boy, and avenged upon him. I must, however, allow that those delicate dirty fingers of his could not with safety be warranted from occasional picking and stealing.

At this period of my story, Robert himself was rather a grotesque-looking animal, very tall and lanky, with especially long arms, which excess of length they retained after he was full-grown. In this respect Shargar and he were alike; but the long legs of Shargar were unmatched in Robert, for at this time his body was peculiarly long. He had large black eyes, deep

* In Scotch the *ch* and *gh* are almost always guttural. The *gh* according to Mr. Alexander Ellis, the sole authority in the past pronunciation of the country, was guttural in England in the time of Shakspere.

sunk even then, and a Roman nose, the size of which in a boy of his years looked portentous. For the rest, he was dark-complexioned, with dark hair, destined to grow darker still, with hands and feet well modelled, but which would have made four feet and four hands such as Shargar's.

When his mind was not oppressed with the consideration of any important metaphysical question, he learned his lessons well; when such was present, the Latin grammar, with all its attendant servilities, was driven from the presence of the lordly need. That once satisfied in spite of pandies and imprisonments, he returned with fresh zest, and, indeed, with some ephemeral ardour, to the rules of syntax or prosody, though the latter, in the mode in which it was then and there taught, was almost as useless as the task set himself by a worthy lay-preacher in the neighbourhood—of learning the first nine chapters of the first Book of the Chronicles, in atonement for having, in an evil hour of freedom of spirit, ventured to suggest that such lists of names, even although forming a portion of Holy Writ, could scarcely be reckoned of equally divine authority with St. Paul's Epistle to the Romans.

CHAPTER VIII.

THE ANGEL UNAWARES.

ALTHOUGH Betty seemed to hold little communication with the outer world, she yet
contrived somehow or other to bring home what
gossip was going to the ears of her mistress,
who had very few visitors; for, while her neighbours held Mrs. Falconer in great and evident
respect, she was not the sort of person to sit
down and have a *news* with. There was a certain sedate self-contained dignity about her
which the common mind felt to be chilling and
repellent; and from any gossip of a personal
nature—what Betty brought her always excepted—she would turn away, generally with the
words, "Hoots! I canna bide clashes."

On the evening following that of Shargar's
introduction to Mrs. Falconer's house, Betty
came home from the butcher's—for it was
Saturday night, and she had gone to fetch
the beef for their Sunday's broth—with the
news that the people next door, that is, round

the corner in the next street, had a visitor.

The house in question had been built by Robert's father, and was, compared with Mrs. Falconer's one-story-house, large and handsome. Robert had been born, and had spent a few years of his life in it, but could recall nothing of the facts of those early days. Some time before the period at which my history commences it had passed into other hands, and it was now quite strange to him. It had been bought by a retired naval officer, who lived in it with his wife—the only Englishwoman in the place, until the arrival, at the Boar's Head, of the lady so much admired by Dooble Sanny.

Robert was up stairs when Betty emptied her news-bag, and so heard nothing of this bit of gossip. He had just assured Shargar that as soon as his grandmother was asleep he would look about for what he could find, and carry it up to him in the garret. As yet he had confined the expenditure out of Shargar's shilling to two-pence.

The household always retired early—earlier on Saturday night in preparation for the Sabbath— and by ten o'clock grannie and Betty were in bed. Robert, indeed, was in bed too; but he had lain down in his clothes, waiting for such time as might afford reasonable hope of his grandmother being asleep, when he might both ease Shargar's hunger and get to sleep himself.

Several times he got up, resolved to make his attempt; but as often his courage failed and he lay down again, sure that grannie could not be asleep yet. When the clock beside him struck eleven, he could bear it no longer, and finally rose to do his endeavour.

Opening the door of the closet slowly and softly, he crept upon his hands and knees into the middle of the parlour, feeling very much like a thief, as, indeed, in a measure he was, though from a blameless motive. But just as he had accomplished half the distance to the door, he was arrested and fixed with terror; for a deep sigh came from grannie's bed, followed by the voice of words. He thought at first that she had heard him, but he soon found that he was mistaken. Still, the fear of discovery held him there on all fours, like a chained animal. A dull red gleam, faint and dull, from the embers of the fire, was the sole light in the room. Everything so common to his eyes in the daylight seemed now strange and *eerie* in the dying coals, and at what was to the boy the unearthly hour of the night.

He felt that he ought not to listen to grannie, but terror made him unable to move.

"Och hone! och hone!" said grannie from the bed. "I've a sair, sair hert. I've a sair hert i' my breist, O Lord! thoo knowest. My ain Anerew! To think o' my bairnie that I cairriet

i' my ain body, that sookit my breists, and leuch
i' my face—to think o' 'im bein' a reprobate! O
Lord! cudna he be eleckit yet? Is there *nae*
turning' o' thy decrees? Na, na; that wadna
do at a'. But while there's life there's houp.
But wha kens whether he be alive or no? Naebody can tell. Glaidly wad I luik upon 's deid
face gin I cud believe that his sowl wasna amang
the lost. But eh! the torments o' that place!
and the reik that gangs up for ever an' ever,
smorin' *(smothering)* the stars! And my Anerew
doon i' the hert o' 't cryin'! And me no able to
win till him! O Lord! I *canna* say thy will be
done. But dinna lay 't to my chairge; for gin
ye was a mither yersel' ye wadna pit him there.
O Lord! I'm verra ill-fashioned. I beg yer
pardon. I'm near oot o' my min'. Forgie me,
O Lord! for I hardly ken what I'm sayin'. He
was my ain babe, my ain Anerew, and ye gae
him to me yersel'. And noo he's for the finger
o' scorn to pint at; an ootcast an' a wan'erer
frae his ain country, an' daurna come within sicht
o' 't for them 'at wad tak' the law o' 'm. An' it's
a' drink—drink an' ill company! He wad hae
dune weel eneuch gin they wad only hae latten
him be. What for maun men be aye drink-
drinkin' at something or ither? *I* never want
it. Eh! gin I war as young as whan he was
born, I wad be up an' awa' this verra nicht to
luik for him. But it's no use me tryin' 't. O

God! ance mair I pray thee to turn him frae the error o' 's ways afore he goes hence an' isna more. And O dinna lat Robert gang efter him, as he's like eneuch to do. Gie me grace to haud him ticht, that he may be to the praise o' thy glory for ever an' ever. Amen."

Whether it was that the weary woman here fell asleep, or that she was too exhausted for further speech, Robert heard no more, though he remained there frozen with horror for some minutes after his grandmother had ceased. This, then, was the reason why she would never speak about his father! She kept all her thoughts about him for the silence of the night, and loneliness with the God who never sleeps, but watches the wicked all through the dark. And his father was one of the wicked! And God was against him! And when he died he would go to hell! But he was not dead yet: Robert was sure of that. And when he grew a man, he would go and seek him, and beg him on his knees to repent and come back to God, who would forgive him then, and take him to heaven when he died. And there he would be good, and good people would love him.

Something like this passed through the boy's mind ere he moved to creep from the room, for his was one of those natures which are active in the generation of hope. He had almost forgotten what he came there for; and had it not

been that he had promised Shargar, he would
have crept back to his bed and left him to bear his
hunger as best he could. But now, first his right
hand, then his left knee, like any other quadru-
ped, he crawled to the door, rose only to his
knees to open it, took almost a minute to the
operation, then dropped and crawled again, till
he had passed out, turned, and drawn the door
to, leaving it slightly ajar. Then it struck him
awfully that the same terrible passage must be
gone through again. But he rose to his feet,
for he had no shoes on, and there was little
danger of making any noise, although it was
pitch dark—he knew the house so well. With
gathering courage, he felt his way to the kitchen, and there groped about; but he could find
nothing beyond a few *quarters* of oat-cake, which,
with a mug of water, he proceeded to carry up
to Shargar in the garret.

When he reached the kitchen-door, he was
struck with amazement and for a moment with
fresh fear. A light was shining into the *transe*
from the stair which went up at right angles from
the end of it. He knew it could not be grannie, and
he heard Betty snoring in her own den, which
opened from the kitchen. He thought it must be
Shargar who had grown impatient; but how he
had got hold of a light he could not think. As soon
as he turned the corner, however, the doubt was
changed into mystery. At the top of the broad

low stair, stood a woman-form with a candle in her hand, gazing about her as if wondering which way to go. The light fell full upon her face, the beauty of which was such that, with her dress, which was white—being, in fact, a nightgown—and her hair, which was hanging loose about her shoulders and down to her waist, it led Robert at once to the conclusion (his reasoning faculties already shaken by the events of the night) that she was an angel come down to comfort his grannie; and he kneeled involuntarily at the foot of the stair, and gazed up at her, with the cakes in one hand, and the mug of water in the other, like a meat-and-drink offering. Whether he had closed his eyes or bowed his head, he could not say; but he became suddenly aware that the angel had vanished—he knew not when, how, or whither. This for a time confirmed his assurance that it was an angel. And although he was undeceived before long, the impression made upon him that night was never effaced. But, indeed, whatever Falconer heard or saw was something more to him than it would have been to anybody else.

Elated, though awed, by the vision, he felt his way up the stair in the new darkness, as if walking in a holy dream, trod as if upon sacred ground as he crossed the landing where the angel had stood—went up and up, and found Shargar wide awake with expectant hunger.

He, too, had caught a glimmer of the light. But
Robert did not tell him what he had seen. That
was too sacred a subject to enter upon with
Shargar, and he was intent enough upon his
supper not to be inquisitive.

Robert left him to finish it at his leisure, and
returned to cross his grandmother's room once
more, half expecting to find the angel standing
by her bedside. But all was dark and still.
Creeping back as he had come, he heard her
quiet, though deep, breathing, and his mind was
at ease about her for the night. What if the
angel he had surprised had only come to appear
to grannie in her sleep? Why not? There were
such stories in the Bible, and grannie was certainly as good as some of the people in the Bible
that saw angels—Sarah, for instance. And if the
angels came to see grannie, why should they not
have some care over his father as well? It
might be—who could tell?

It is perhaps necessary to explain Robert's
vision. The angel was the owner of the boxes
he had seen at the Boar's Head. Looking around
her room before going to bed, she had seen a
trap in the floor near the wall, and, raising it,
had discovered a few steps of a stair leading
down to a door. Curiosity naturally led her to
examine it. The key was in the lock. It opened
outwards, and there she found herself, to her
surprise, in the heart of another dwelling, of

lowlier aspect. She never saw Robert; for while he approached with shoeless feet, she had been glancing through the open door of the gable-room, and when he knelt, the light which she held in her hand had, I presume, hidden him from her. He, on his part, had not observed that the moveless door stood open at last.

I have already said that the house adjoining had been built by Robert's father. The lady's room was that which he had occupied with his wife, and in it Robert had been born. The door, with its trap-stair, was a natural invention for uniting the levels of the two houses, and a desirable one in not a few of the forms which the weather assumed in that region. When the larger house passed into other hands, it had never entered the minds of the simple people who occupied the contiguous dwellings, to build up the doorway between.

CHAPTER IX.

A DISCOVERY.

THE friendship of Robert had gained Shargar the favourable notice of others of the school-public. These were chiefly of those who came from the country, ready to follow an example set them by a town boy. When his desertion was known, moved both by their compassion for him, and their respect for Robert, they began to give him some portion of the dinner they brought with them; and never in his life had Shargar fared so well as for the first week after he had been cast upon the world. But in proportion as their interest faded with the novelty, so their appetites reasserted former claims of use and wont, and Shargar began once more to feel the pangs of hunger. For all that Robert could manage to procure for him without attracting the attention he was so anxious to avoid, was little more than sufficient to keep his hunger alive, Shargar being gifted with a great appetite, and Robert having no allowance of pocket-money from his grandmother. The three pence he had been able to spend on him were what remained of sixpence Mr. Innes had given him for an exercise which he wrote in blank verse instead of in prose—an achievement of which the schoolmaster was proud, both from his reverence for Milton, and from his inability to compose a metrical line himself. And how and when he should ever possess another penny was even unimaginable. Shargar's shilling was likewise spent. So Robert could but go on pocketing instead of eating all that he dared, watching anxiously for opportunity of evading the eyes of his grandmother. On her dimness of sight, however, he depended too confidently after all; for either she was not so blind as he thought she was, or she made up for the defect of her vision by the keenness of her observation. She saw enough to cause her considerable annoyance, though it suggested nothing inconsistent with rectitude on the part of the boy, further than that there was something underhand going on. One supposition after another arose in the old lady's brain, and one after another was dismissed as improbable. First, she tried to persuade herself that he wanted to take the provisions to school with him, and eat them there—a proceeding of which she certainly did not approve, but for the reproof of which she was unwilling to betray the loopholes of her eyes. Next she concluded, for half a day, that he must have a pair of rabbits hidden away in some nook or other—possibly in the little strip of garden belonging to the house. And so conjecture followed conjecture for a whole week, during which, strange to say, not even Betty knew that Shargar slept in the house. For so careful and watchful were the two boys, that although she could not help suspecting something from the expression and behaviour of Robert, what that something might be she could not imagine; nor had she and her mistress as yet exchanged confidences on the subject. Her observation coincided with that of her mistress as to the disappearance of odds and ends of eatables—potatoes, cold porridge, bits of oatcake; and even, on one occasion, when Shargar happened to be especially ravenous, a yellow, or cured and half-dried, haddock, which the lad devoured raw, vanished from her domain. He went to school in the morning smelling so strong in consequence, that they told him he must have been passing the night in Scroggie's cart, and not on his horse's back this time.

The boys kept their secret well.

One evening, towards the end of the week, Robert, after seeing Shargar disposed of for the night, proceeded to carry out a project which had grown in his brain within the last two days, in consequence of an occurrence with which his relation to Shargar had had something to do. It was this:

The housing of Shargar in the garret had led Robert to make a close acquaintance with the place. He was familiar with all the outs and ins of the little room which he considered his own, for that was a civilized, being a plastered, ceiled, and comparatively well-lighted little room, but not with the other, which was three times its size, very badly lighted, and showing the naked couples from roof-tree to floor. Besides, it contained no end of dark corners, with which his childish imagination had associated undefined horrors, assuming now one shape, now another. Also there were several closets in it, constructed in the angles of the place, and several chests—two of which he had ventured to peep into. But although he had found them filled, not with bones, as he had expected, but one with papers, and one with garments, he had yet dared to carry his researches no further. One evening, however, when Betty was out, and he had got hold of her candle, and gone up to keep Shargar company for a few minutes, a sudden impulse seized him to have a peep into all the closets. One of them he knew a little about, as containing, amongst other things, his father's coat with the gilt buttons, and his great-grandfather's kilt, as well as other garments useful to Shargar: now he would see what was in the rest. He did not find anything very interesting, however, till he arrived at the last. Out of it he drew a long queer-shaped box into the light of Betty's dip.

"Luik here, Shargar!" he said under his breath, for they never dared to speak aloud in these precincts—luik here! What can there be in this box? Is 't a bairnie's coffin, duv ye think? Luik at it."

In this case Shargar, having roamed the country a good deal more than Robert, and having been present at some merrymakings with his mother, of which there were comparatively few in that country-side, was better informed than his friend.

"Eh! Bob, duvna ye ken what that is? I thocht ye kent a' thing. That's a fiddle."

"That's buff an' styte *(stuff and nonsense)*, Shargar. Do ye think I dinna ken a fiddle whan I see ane, wi' its guts ootside o' 'ts wame, an' the thoomacks to screw them up wi' an' gar 't skirl?"

"Buff an' styte yersel'!" cried Shargar, in indignation, from the bed. "Gie's a haud o' 't."

Robert handed him the case. Shargar undid the hooks in a moment, and revealed the creature lying in its shell like a boiled bivalve.

"I tellt ye sae!" he exclaimed triumphantly. "Maybe ye'll lippen to me *(trust me)* neist time."

"An' I tellt *you*," retorted Robert, with an

equivocation altogether unworthy of his growing honesty. " I was cocksure that cudna be
a fiddle. There's the fiddle i' the hert o' 't!
Losh! I min' noo. It maun be my grandfather's fiddle 'at I hae heard tell o'."

" No to ken a fiddle-case !" reflected Shargar,
with as much of contempt as it was possible for
him to show.

" I tell ye what, Shargar," returned Robert, in-
dignantly; " ye may ken the box o' a fiddle better
nor I do, but de'il hae me gin I dinna ken the
fiddle itsel' raither better nor ye do in a fortnicht
frae this time. I s' tak it to Dooble Sanny; he
can play the fiddle fine. An' I'll play 't too, or
the de'il s' be in't."

" Eh, man, that 'll be gran' !" cried Shargar,
incapable of jealousy. " We can gang to a' the
markets thegither and gaither baubees (*halfpence*)."

To this anticipation Robert returned no reply,
for, hearing Betty come in, he judged it time to
restore the violin to its case, and Betty's candle
to the kitchen, lest she should invade the upper
regions in search of it. But that very night he
managed to have an interview with *Dooble Sanny*,
the shoemaker, and it was arranged between
them that Robert should bring his violin on the
evening at which my story has now arrived.

Whatever motive he had for seeking to com-
mence the study of music, it holds even in

more important matters that, if the thing pursued
be good, there is a hope of the pursuit purifying
the motive.   And Robert no sooner heard the
fiddle utter a few mournful sounds in the hands
of the soutar, who was no contemptible performer,
than he longed to establish such a relation between himself and the strange instrument, that,
dumb and deaf as it had been to him hitherto,
it would respond to his touch also, and tell him
the secrets of its queerly-twisted skull, full of
sweet sounds instead of brains.   From that
moment he would be a musician for music's own
sake, and forgot utterly what had appeared to
him, though I doubt if it was, the sole motive of
his desire to learn—namely, the necessity of re-
taining his superiority over Shargar.

What added considerably to the excitement of
his feelings on the occasion, was the expression
of reverence, almost of awe, with which the shoemaker took the instrument from its case, and the
tenderness with which he handled it.   The fact
was that he had not had a violin in his hands for
nearly a year, having been compelled to pawn
his own in order to alleviate the sickness brought
on his wife by his own ill-treatment of her, once
that he came home drunk from a wedding.   It
was strange to think that such dirty hands should
be able to bring such sounds out of the instrument
the moment he got it safely cuddled under his
cheek.   So dirty were they, that it was said

Dooble Sanny never required to carry any rosin with him for fiddler's need, his own fingers having always enough upon them for one bow at least. Yet the points of those fingers never lost the delicacy of their touch. Some people thought this was in virtue of their being washed only once a week—a custom Alexander justified on the ground that, in a trade like his, it was of no use to wash oftener, for he would be just as dirty again before night.

The moment he began to play, the face of the soutar grew ecstatic. He stopped at the very first note, notwithstanding, let fall his arms, the one with the bow, the other with the violin, at his sides, and said, with deep-drawn respiration and lengthened utterance:

"Eh !"

Then after a pause, during which he stood motionless:

"The crater maun be a Cry Moany ! Hear till her !" he added, drawing another long note.

Then, after another pause:

"She's a Straddle Vawrious at least! Hear till her ! I never had sic a combination o' timmer and catgut atween my cleuks (*claws*) afore."

As to its being a Stradivarius, or even a Cremona at all, the testimony of Dooble Sanny was not worth much on the point. But the shoemaker's admiration roused in the boy's mind a reverence for the individual instrument which he never lost.

From that day the two were friends.

Suddenly the soutar started off at full speed in a strathspey, which was soon lost in the wail of a Highland psalm-tune, giving place in its turn to " Sic a wife as Willie had !" And on he went without pause, till Robert dared not stop any longer. The fiddle had bewitched the fiddler.

" Come as aften 's ye like, Robert, gin ye fess this leddy wi' ye," said the soutar.

And he stroked the back of the violin tenderly with his open palm.

" But wad ye hae ony objection to lat it lie aside ye, and lat me come whan I can ?"

" Objection, laddie ?   I wad as sune objeck to lattin my ain wife lie aside me."

" Ay," said Robert, seized with some anxiety about the violin as he remembered the fate of the wife, " but ye ken Elspet comes aff a' the waur sometimes."

Softened by the proximity of the wonderful violin, and stung afresh by the boy's words as his conscience had often stung him before, for he loved his wife dearly save when the demon of drink possessed him, the tears rose in Elshender's eyes. He held out the violin to Robert, saying, with unsteady voice :

" Hae, tak her awa'. I dinna deserve to hae sic a thing i' *my* hoose. But hear me, Robert, and lat hearin' be believin'. I never was sae drunk but I cud tune my fiddle. Mair by token,

ance they fand me lyin' o' my back i' the Corrie,
an' the watter, they say, was ower a' but the
mou' o' me; but I was haudin' my fiddle up
abune my heid, and de'il a spark o' watter was
upo' *her*."

"It's a pity yer wife wasna yer fiddle, than,
Sanny," said Robert, with more presumption
than wit.

"'Deed ye're i' the richt, there, Robert. Hae,
tak yer fiddle."

"Deed no," returned Robert. " I maun jist
lippen (*trust*) to ye, Sanders. I canna bide
langer the nicht; but maybe ye'll tell me hoo to
haud her the neist time 'at I come—will ye?"

"That I *wull*, Robert, come whan ye like.
An' gin ye come o' ane 'at cud play this fiddle
as this fiddle deserves to be playt, ye'll do me
credit."

"Ye min' what that sumph Lumley said to me
the ither nicht, Sanders, aboot my grandfather?"

"Ay, weel eneuch. A dish o' drucken havers!"

"It was true eneuch aboot my great-grandfather, though."

"No! Was't railly?"

"Ay. He was the best piper in 's regiment
at Culloden. Gin they had a' fouchten as he
pipit, there wad hae been anither tale to tell.
And he was toon-piper forby, jist like you, Sanders, efter they took frae him a' 'at he had."

"Na! heard ye ever the like o' that! Weel,

wha wad hae thocht it? Faith! we maun hae
you fiddle as weel as yer lucky-daiddy pipit.—
But here's the King o' Bashan comin' efter his
butes, an' them no half dune yet!" exclaimed
Dooble Sanny, settling in haste to his awl and
his *lingel* (Fr. *ligneul*). He'll be roarin' mair like
a bull o' the country than the king o' 't."

‚As Robert departed, Peter Ogg came in, and
as he passed the window, he heard the shoemaker averring:

"I haena risen frae my stule sin' ane o'clock;
but there's a sicht to be dune to them, Mr. Ogg."

Indeed, *Alexander ab Alexandro*, as Mr. Innes
facetiously styled him, was in more ways than
one worthy of the name of *Dooble*. There
seemed to be two natures in the man, which all
his music had not yet been able to blend.

CHAPTER X.

ANOTHER DISCOVERY IN THE GARRET.

LITTLE did Robert dream of the reception that awaited him at home. Almost as soon as he had left the house, the following events began to take place.

The mistress's bell rang, and Betty "gaed benn the hoose to see what she cud be wantin'," whereupon a conversation ensued.

"Wha was that at the door, Betty?" asked Mrs. Falconer; for Robert had not shut the door so carefully as he ought, seeing that the deafness of his grandmother was of much the same faculty as her blindness.

Had Robert not had a hold of Betty by the forelock of her years, he would have been unable to steal any liberty at all. Still Betty had a conscience, and although she would not offend Robert if she could help it, yet she would not lie.

" 'Deed, mem, I canna jist distinckly say 'at I heard the door," she answered.

"Whaur's Robert?" was her next question.

"He's generally up the stair aboot this hoor, mem—that is, whan he's no i' the parlour at 's lessons."

"What gangs he sae muckle up the stair for, Betty, do ye ken? It's something by ordinar' wi' 'm."

"'Deed I dinna ken, mem. I never tuik it into my heid to gang considerin' aboot it. He'll hae some ploy o' 's ain, nae doobt. Laddies will be laddies, ye ken, mem."

"I doobt, Betty, ye'll be aidin' an' abettin'. An' it disna become yer years, Betty."

"My years are no to fin' faut wi', mem. They're weel eneuch."

"That's naething to the pint, Betty. What's the laddie aboot?"

"Do ye mean whan he gangs up the stair, mem?"

"Ay. Ye ken weel eneuch what I mean."

"Weel, mem, I tell ye I dinna ken. An' ye never heard me tell ye a lee sin' ever I was i' yer service, mem."

"Na, nae doonricht. Ye gang aboot it an' aboot it, an' at last ye come sae near leein' that gin ye spak anither word, ye wad be at it; and it jist fleys (*frights*) me frae speirin' ae ither queston at ye. An' that's hoo ye win oot o' 't. But noo 'at it's aboot my ain oye (*grandson*), I'm no gaein' to tyne (*lose*) him to save a woman o'

your years, wha oucht to ken better ; an' sae I'll
speir at ye, though ye suld be driven to lee like
Sawtan himsel'.—What's he aboot whan he
gangs up the stair? Noo!"

"Weel, as sure's deith, I dinna ken. Ye drive
me to sweirin', mem, an' no to leein'."

"I carena. Hae ye no idea aboot it, than,
Betty?"

"Weel, mem, I think sometimes he canna be
weel, and maun hae a tod (*fox*) in's stamack, or
something o' that nater. For what he eats is
awfu'. An' I think whiles he jist gangs up the
stair to eat at 's ain wull."

"That jumps wi' my ain observations, Betty.
Do ye think he micht hae a rabbit, or maybe a
pair o' them, in some boxie i' the garret, noo?"

"And what for no, gin he had, mem?"

"What for no? Nesty stinkin' things! But
that's no the pint. I aye hae to haud ye to the
pint, Betty. The pint is, whether he has rabbits or no?"

"Or guinea-pigs," suggested Betty.

"Weel."

"Or maybe a pup or twa. Or I kent a laddie ance 'at keepit a haill faimily o' kittlins. Or
maybe he micht hae a bit lammie. There was
an uncle o' min' ain——"

"Haud yer tongue, Betty! Ye hae ower
muckle to say for a' the sense there's intil 't."

"Weel, mem, ye speirt questons at me."

"Weel, I hae had eneuch o' yer answers, Betty. Gang and tell Robert to come here di-reckly."

Betty went, knowing perfectly that Robert had gone out, and returned with the information. Her mistress searched her face with a keen eye.

"That maun hae been himsel' efter a' whan ye thocht ye hard the door gang," said Betty.

"It's a strange thing that I suld hear him benn here wi' the door steekit, an' your door open at the verra door-cheek o' the ither, an' you no hear him, Betty. And me sae deif as weel!"

"'Deed, mem," retorted Betty, losing her temper a little, "I can be as deif's ither fowk mysel' whiles."

When Betty grew angry, Mrs. Falconer inva-riably grew calm, or, at least, put her temper out of sight. She was silent now, and continued silent till Betty moved to return to her kitchen, when she said, in the tone of one who had just arrived at an important resolution:

"Betty, we'll jist awa' up the stair an' luik."

"Weel, mem, I hae nae objections."

"Nae objections! What for suld you or ony ither body hae ony objections to me gaein' whaur I like i' my ain hoose? Umph!" ex-claimed Mrs. Falconer, turning and facing her maid.

" In coorse, mem. I only meant I had nae objections to gang wi' ye."

" And what for suld you or ony ither woman that I paid twa pun' five i' the half-year till, daur to hae objections to gaein' whaur I wantit ye to gang i' my ain hoose !"

" Hoot, mem ! it was but a slip o' the tongue —naething mair."

" Slip me nae sic slips, or ye'll come by a fa' at last, I doobt, Betty," concluded Mrs. Falconer, in a mollified tone, as she turned and led the way from the room.

They got a candle in the kitchen and proceeded up stairs, Mrs. Falconer still leading, and Betty following. They did not even look into the ga'le-room, not doubting that the dignity of the best bed-room was in no danger of being violated even by Robert, but took their way upwards to the room in which he kept his school-books—almost the only articles of property which the boy possessed. Here they found nothing suspicious. All was even in the best possible order—not a very wonderful fact, seeing a few books and a slate were the only things there besides the papers on the shelves.

What the feelings of Shargar must have been when he heard the steps and voices, and saw the light approaching his place of refuge, we will not change our point of view to inquire. He certainly was as little to be envied at that moment as at any moment during the whole of his existence.

The first sense Mrs. Falconer made use of in the search after possible animals lay in her nose. She kept snuffing constantly, but, beyond the usual musty smell of neglected apartments, had as yet discovered nothing. The moment she entered the upper garret, however—

"There's an ill-faured smell here, Betty," she said, believing that they had at last found the trail of the mystery; "but it's no like the smell o' rabbits. Jist luik i' the nuik there ahin' the door."

"There's naething here," responded Betty.

"Roon the en' o' that kist there. I s' luik into the press."

As Betty rose from her search behind the chest and turned towards her mistress, her eyes crossed the cavernous opening of the bed. There, to her horror, she beheld a face like that of a galvanized corpse staring at her from the darkness. Shargar was in a sitting posture, paralysed with terror, waiting, like a fascinated bird, till Mrs. Falconer and Betty should make the final spring upon him, and do whatever was equivalent to devouring him upon the spot. He had sat up to listen to the noise of their ascending footsteps, and fear had so overmastered him, that he either could not, or forgot that he could lie down and cover his head with some of the many garments scattered around him.

"I didna say *whusky*, did I?" he kept repeating to himself, in utter imbecility of fear.

"The Lord preserve 's!" exclaimed Betty, the moment she could speak; for during the first few seconds, having caught the infection of Shargar's expression, she stood equally paralysed. "The Lord preserve 's!" she repeated.

"Ance is eneuch," said Mrs. Falconer, sharply, turning round to see what the cause of Betty's ejaculation might be.

I have said that she was dim-sighted. The candle they had was little better than a penny dip. The bed was darker than the rest of the room. Shargar's face had none of the more distinctive characteristics of manhood upon it.

"Gude preserve 's!" exclaimed Mrs. Falconer in her turn: "it's a wumman."

Poor deluded Shargar, thinking himself safer under any form than that which he actually bore, attempted no protest against the mistake. But, indeed, he was incapable of speech. The two women flew upon him to drag him out of the bed. Then first recovering his powers of motion, he sprung up in an agony of terror, and darted out between them, overturning Betty in his course.

"Ye rouch limmer!" cried Betty, from the floor. "Ye lang-leggit jaud!" she added, as she rose—and at the same moment Shargar

banged the street-door behind him in his terror
—" I wat ye dinna carry yer coats ower syde
(*too long*)!"

For Shargar, having discovered that the way
to get the most warmth from Robert's great-
grandfather's kilt was to wear it in the manner
for which it had been fabricated, was in the
habit of fastening it round his waist before he
got into bed; and the eye of Betty, as she fell,
had caught the swing of this portion of his attire.

But poor Mrs. Falconer, with sunken head,
walked out of the garret in the silence of despair. She went slowly down the steep stair,
supporting herself against the wall, her round-
toed shoes creaking solemnly as she went, took
refuge in the ga'le-room, and burst into a violent fit of weeping. For such depravity she
was not prepared. What a terrible curse hung
over her family! Surely they were all reprobate from the womb, not one elected for salvation from the guilt of Adam's fall, and therefore
abandoned to Satan as his natural prey, to be
led captive of him at his will. She threw herself on her knees at the side of the bed, and
prayed heart-brokenly. Betty heard her as she
limped past the door on her way back to her
kitchen.

Meantime Shargar had rushed across the
next street on his bare feet into the Crookit

Wynd, terrifying poor old Kirstan Peerie, the divisions betwixt the compartments of whose memory had broken down, into the exclamation to her next neighbour, Tam Rhin, with whom she was trying to gossip:

"Eh, Tammas! that 'll be ane o' the slauchtert at Culloden."

He never stopped till he reached his mother's deserted abode—strange instinct! There he ran to earth like a hunted fox. Rushing at the door, forgetful of everything but refuge, he found it unlocked, and closing it behind him, stood panting like the hart that has found the water-brooks. The owner had looked in one day to see whether the place was worth repairing, for it was a mere outhouse, and had forgotten to turn the key when he left it. Poor Shargar! Was it more or less of a refuge that the mother that bore him was not there either to curse or welcome his return? Less—if we may judge from a remark he once made in my hearing many long years after:

"For, ye see," he said, "a mither's a mither, be she the verra de'il."

Searching about in the dark, he found the one article unsold by the landlord, a stool, with but two of its natural three legs. On this he balanced himself and waited—simply for what Robert would do; for his faith in Robert was unbounded, and he had no other hope on earth.

But Shargar was not miserable. In that wretched hovel, his bare feet clasping the clay floor in constant search of a wavering equilibrium, with pitch darkness around him, and incapable of the simplest philosophical or religious reflection, he yet found life good. *For it had interest.* Nay, more, it had hope. I doubt, however, whether there is any interest at all without hope.

While he sat there, Robert, thinking him snug in the garret, was walking quietly home from the shoemaker's; and his first impulse on entering was to run up and recount the particulars of his interview with Alexander. Arrived in the dark garret, he called Shargar, as usual, in a whisper—received no reply—thought he was asleep—called louder (for he had had a penny from his grandmother that day for bringing home two pails of water for Betty, and had just spent it upon a loaf for him)—but no Shargar replied. Thereupon he went to the bed to lay hold of him and shake him. But his searching hands found no Shargar. Becoming alarmed, he ran down stairs to beg a light from Betty.

When he reached the kitchen, he found Betty's nose as much in the air as its construction would permit. For a hook-nosed animal, she certainly was the most harmless and ovine creature in the world, but this was a case in which feminine modesty was both concerned and aggrieved. She showed her resentment no further, however, than by simply returning no answer in syllable, or sound, or motion, to Robert's request. She was washing up the tea-things, and went on with her work as if she had been in absolute solitude, saving that her countenance could hardly have kept up that expression of injured dignity had such been the case. Robert plainly saw, to his great concern, that his secret had been discovered in his absence, and that Shargar had been expelled with contumely. But, with an instinct of facing the worst at once which accompanied him through life, he went straight to his grandmother's parlour.

"Well, grandmamma," he said, trying to speak as cheerfully as he could.

Grannie's prayers had softened her a little, else she would have been as silent as Betty; for it was from her mistress that Betty had learned this mode of torturing a criminal. So she was just able to return his greeting in the words, "Weel, Robert," pronounced with a finality of tone that indicated she had done her utmost, and had nothing to add.

"Here's a browst (*brewage*)!" thought Robert to himself; and, still on the principle of flying at the first of mischief he saw—the best mode of meeting it, no doubt—addressed his grand-

mother at once. The effort necessary gave a
tone of defiance to his words.

"What for willna ye speik to me, grannie?"
he said. "I'm no a haithen, nor yet a papist."

"Ye're waur nor baith in ane, Robert."

"Hoots! ye winna say baith, grannie," returned Robert, who, even at the age of fourteen,
when once compelled to assert himself, assumed
a modest superiority.

"Nane o' sic impidence!" retorted Mrs. Falconer. "I wonner whaur ye learn that. But
it's nae wonner. Evil communications corrupt
gude mainners. Ye're a lost prodigal, Robert,
like yer father afore ye. I hae jist been sittin'
here thinkin' wi' mysel' whether it wadna be
better for baith o' 's to lat ye gang an' reap the
fruit o' yer doin's at ance; for the hard ways is
the best road for transgressors. I'm no bund to
keep ye."

"Weel, weel, I s' awa' to Shargar. Him and
me 'ill haud on thegither better nor you an' me,
grannie. He's a puir cratur, but he can stick
till a body."

"What are ye haverin' aboot Shargar for, ye
heepocreet loon? Ye'll no gang to Shargar, I s'
warran'! Ye'll be efter that vile limmer that's
turnt my honest hoose intil a sty this last fortnicht."

"Grannie, I dinna ken what ye mean."

"*She* kens, than. I sent her aff like ane o'

Samson's foxes, wi' a firebrand at her tail.   It's
a pity it wasna tied atween the twa o' ye."

"Preserve 's, grannie! Is 't possible ye hae
ta'en Shargar for ane o' wumman-kin'?"

"I ken naething aboot Shargar, I tell ye.   I
ken that Betty an' me tuik an ill-faured dame i'
the bed i' the garret."

"Cud it be his mither?" thought Robert in
bewilderment; but he recovered himself in a
moment, and answered,

"Shargar *may* be a quean efter a', for onything 'at I ken to the contrary; but I aye tuik
him for a loon. Faith, sic a quean as he'd mak!"

And careless to resist the ludicrousness of the
idea, he burst into a loud fit of laughter, which
did more to reassure his grannie than any
amount of protestation could have done, however she pretended to take offence at his ill-
timed merriment.

Seeing his grandmother staggered, Robert
gathered courage to assume the offensive.

"But, granny! hoo ever Betty, no to say you,
cud hae driven oot a puir half-stervit cratur like
Shargar, even supposin' he oucht to hae been in
coaties, and no in troosers—and the mither o'
him run awa' an' left him—it's mair nor I can
unnerstan'.   I misdoobt me sair but he's gane
and droont himsel'."

Robert knew well enough that Shargar would
not drown himself without at least bidding him

good-bye; but he knew, too, that his grandmother could be wrought upon. Her conscience
was more tender than her feelings; and this peculiarity occasioned part of the mutual non-
understanding rather than misunderstanding
between her grandson and herself. The first
relation she bore to most that came near her
was one of severity and rebuke; but underneath
her cold outside lay a warm heart, to which conscience acted the part of a somewhat capricious
stoker, now quenching its heat with the cold
water of duty, now stirring it up with the poker
of reproach, and ever treating it as an inferior
and a slave. But her conscience was, on the
whole, a better friend to her race than her
heart; and, indeed, the conscience is always a
better friend than a heart whose motions are
undirected by it. From Falconer's account of
her, however, I cannot help thinking that she
not unfrequently took refuge in severity of tone
and manner from the threatened ebullition of a
feeling which she could not otherwise control,
and which she was ashamed to manifest. Possibly conscience had spoken more and more
gently as its behests were more and more readily obeyed, until the heart began to gather courage, and at last, as in many old people, took
the upper hand, which was outwardly inconve-
nient to one of Mrs. Falconer's temperament.
Hence, in doing the kindest thing in the world,

she would speak in a tone of command, even of rebuke, as if she were compelling the performance of the most unpleasant duty in the person who received the kindness. But the human heart is hard to analyse, and, indeed, will not submit quietly to the operation, however gently performed. Nor is the result at all easy to put into words. It is best shown in actions.

Again, it may appear rather strange that Robert should be able to talk in such an easy manner to his grandmother, seeing he had been guilty of concealment, if not of deception. But she had never been so actively severe towards Robert as she had been towards her own children. To him she was wonderfully gentle for her nature, and sought to exercise the saving harshness which she still believed necessary, solely in keeping from him every enjoyment of life which the narrowest theories as to the rule and will of God could set down as worldly. Frivolity, of which there was little in this sober boy, was in her eyes a vice; loud laughter almost a crime; cards, and *novelles*, as she called them, were such in her estimation, as to be beyond my powers of characterization. Her commonest injunction was, "Noo be *douce*,"—that is, *sober*—uttered to the soberest boy she could ever have known. But Robert was a large-hearted boy, else this life would never have had to be written; and so, through all this, his

deepest nature came into unconscious contact
with that of his noble old grandmother.   There
was nothing small about either of them.   Hence
Robert was not afraid of her.   He had got more
of her nature in him than of her son's.   She
and his own mother had more share in him than
his father, though from him he inherited good
qualities likewise.

He had concealed his doings with Shargar
simply because he believed that they could not
be done if his grandmother knew of his plans.
Herein he did her less than justice.   But so unpleasant was concealment to his nature, and so
much did the dread of discovery press upon
him, that the moment he saw the thing had
come out into the daylight of her knowledge,
such a reaction of relief took place as, operating
along with his deep natural humour and the
comical circumstance of the case, gave him an
ease and freedom of communication which he
had never before enjoyed with her.   Likewise
there was a certain courage in the boy which, if
his own natural disposition had not been so
quiet that he felt the negations of her rule the
less, might have resulted in underhand doings
of a very different kind, possibly, from those of
benevolence.

He must have been a strange being to look
at, I always think, at this point of his development, with his huge nose, his black eyes, his

lanky figure, and his sober countenance, on which a smile was rarely visible, but from which burst occasional *guffaws* of laughter.

At the words "droont himsel'," Mrs. Falconer started.

"Rin, laddie, rin," she said, "an' fess him back direckly! Betty! Betty! gang wi' Robert and help him to luik for Shargar. Ye auld, blin', doited body, 'at says ye can see, and canna tell a lad frae a lass!"

"Na, na, grannie. I'm no gaein' oot wi' a dame like her trailin' at my fut. She wad be a sair hinnerance to me. Gin Shargar be to be gotten—that is, gin he be in life—I s' get him wantin' Betty. And gin ye dinna ken him for the crater ye fand i' the garret, he maun be sair changed sin' I left him there."

"Weel, weel, Robert, gang yer wa's. But gin ye be deceivin' me, may the Lord——forgie ye, Robert, for sair ye'll need it."

"Nae fear o' that, grannie," returned Robert, from the street-door, and vanished.

Mrs. Falconer stalked——No, I will not use that word of the gait of a woman like my friend's grandmother. "Stately stept she butt the hoose" to Betty. She felt strangely soft at the heart, Robert not being *yet* proved a reprobate; but she was not therefore prepared to drop one atom of the dignity of her relation to her servant.

" Betty," she said, " ye hae made a mistak."

" What's that, mem?" returned Betty.

" It wasna a lass ava: it was that crater Shargar."

" Ye said it was a lass yersel' first, mem."

" Ye ken weel eneuch that I'm short-sichtit, an' hae been frae the day o' my birth."

" I'm no auld eneuch to min' upo' that, mem," returned Betty revengefully, but in an undertone, as if she did not intend her mistress to hear. And although she heard well enough, her mistress adopted the subterfuge. " But I'll sweir the crater *I* saw was in cwytes (*petticoats*)."

" Sweir not at all, Betty. Ye hae made a mistak ony gait."

" Wha says that, mem?"

" Robert."

" Aweel, gin he be tellin' the trowth——"

" Daur ye mint (*insinuate*) to me that a son o' mine wad tell onything but the trowth?"

" Na, na, mem. But gin that wasna a quean, ye canna deny but she luikit unco like ane, and no a blate (*bashful*) ane eyther."

" Gin he was a loon, he wadna luik like a *blate* lass, ony gait, Betty. And *there* ye're wrang."

" Weel, weel, mem, hae 't yer ain gait," muttered Betty.

" I wull hae 't my ain gait," retorted her mistress, " because it's the richt gait, Betty. An'

noo ye maun jist gang up the stair, an' get the
place cleant oot an' put in order."

"I wull do that, mem."

"Ay wull ye. An' luik weel aboot, Betty,
you that can see sae weel, in case there suld be
ony cattle aboot; for he's nane o' the cleanest,
yon dame !"

"I wull do that, mem."

"An' gang direckly, afore he comes back."

"Wha comes back?"

"Robert, of coorse."

"What for that?"

"'Cause he 's comin' wi' 'im."

"What *he* 's comin' wi' 'im ?"

"Ca' 't *she*, gin ye like. It's Shargar."

"Wha says that?" exclaimed Betty, sniffing
and starting at once.

"*I* say that. An' ye gang an' du what I tell
ye, this minute."

Betty obeyed instantly; for the tone in which
the last words were spoken was one she was
not accustomed to dispute. She only muttered
as she went, "It 'll a' come upo' me as usual."

Betty's job was long ended before Robert returned. Never dreaming that Shargar could
have gone back to the old haunt, he had looked
for him everywhere before that occurred to him
as a last chance. Nor would he have found
him even then, for he would not have thought
of his being inside the deserted house, had

not Shargar heard his footsteps in the street.

He started up from his stool saying, "That's Bob!" but was not sure enough to go to the door: he might be mistaken; it might be the landlord. He heard the feet stop and did not move; but when he heard them begin to go away again, he rushed to the door, and bawled on the chance at the top of his voice, "Bob! Bob!"

"Eh! ye crater!" said Robert, "*ir* ye there efter a'?"

"Eh! Bob," exclaimed Shargar, and burst into tears. "I thocht ye wad come efter me."

"Of coorse," answered Robert, coolly. "Come awa' hame."

"Whaur til?" asked Shargar, in dismay."

"Hame to yer ain bed at my grannie's."

"Na, na," said Shargar, hurriedly, retreating within the door of the hovel. "Na, na, Bob, lad, I s' no du that. She's an awfu' wuman, that grannie o' yours. I canna think hoo ye can bide wi' her. I'm weel oot o' her grups, *I* can tell ye."

It required a good deal of persuasion, but at last Robert prevailed upon Shargar to return. For was not Robert his tower of strength? And if Robert was not frightened at his grannie, or at Betty, why should he be? At length they entered Mrs. Falconer's parlour, Robert dragging in Shargar after him, having failed altogether

in encouraging him to enter after a more dignified fashion.

It must be remembered that although Shargar
was still kilted, he was not the less trowsered,
such as the trowsers were. It makes my heart
ache to think of those trowsers—not believing
trowsers essential to blessedness either, but
knowing the superiority of the old Roman costume of the kilt.

No sooner had Mrs. Falconer cast her eyes
upon him than she could not but be convinced
of the truth of Robert's averment.

"Here he is, grannie; and gin ye bena saitis-
feed yet——"

"Haud yer tongue, laddie. Ye hae gi'en me
nae cause to doobt yer word."

Indeed, during Robert's absence, his grandmother had had leisure to perceive of what an
absurd folly she had been guilty. She had also
had time to make up her mind as to her duty
with regard to Shargar; and the more she
thought about it, the more she admired the conduct of her grandson, and the better she saw
that it would be right to follow his example.
No doubt she was the more inclined to this benevolence that she had as it were received her
grandson back from the jaws of death.

When the two lads entered, from her arm-
chair Mrs. Falconer examined Shargar from head
to foot with the eye of a queen on her throne,

and a countenance immoveable in stern gentleness, till Shargar would gladly have sunk into the shelter of the voluminous kilt from the gaze of those quiet hazel eyes.

At length she spoke :

" Robert, tak him awa'."

" Whaur'll I tak him till, grannie ?"

" Tak him up to the garret. Betty 'ill ha' ta'en a tub o' het water up there 'gen this time, and ye maun see that he washes himsel' frae heid to fut, or he s' no bide an 'oor i' my hoose. Gang awa' an' see till 't this minute."

But she detained them yet awhile with various directions in regard of cleansing, for the carrying out of which Robert was only too glad to give his word. She dismissed them at last, and Shargar by and by found himself in bed, clean, and, for the first time in his life, between a pair of linen sheets—not altogether to his satisfaction, for mere order and comfort were substituted for adventure and success.

But greater trials awaited him. In the morning he was visited by Brodie, the tailor, and Elshender, the shoemaker, both of whom he held in awe as his superiors in the social scale, and by them handled and measured from head to feet, the latter included ; after which he had to lie in bed for three days, till his clothes came home ; for Betty had carefully committed every article of his former dress to the kitchen fire,

not without a sense of pollution to the bottom
of her kettle. Nor would he have got them for
double the time, had not Robert haunted the
tailor, as well as the soutar, like an evil conscience, till they had finished them. Thus griev-
ous was Shargar's introduction to the comforts
of respectability. Nor did he like it much better
when he was dressed, and able to go about ; for
not only was he uncomfortable in his new clothes,
which, after the very easy fit of the old ones,
felt like a suit of plate-armour, but he was liable
to be sent for at any moment by the awful
sovereignty in whose dominions he found himself,
and which, of course, proceeded to instruct him
not merely in his own religious duties, but in the
religious theories of his ancestors, if, indeed,
Shargar's ancestors ever had any. And now the
Shorter Catechism seemed likely to be changed
into the Longer Catechism ; for he had it Sundays as well as Saturdays, besides Alleine's
Alarm to the Unconverted, Baxter's *Saint's Rest*,
Erskine's *Gospel Sonnets*, and other books of a
like kind. Nor was it any relief to Shargar that
the gloom was broken by the incomparable
Pilgrim's Progress and the *Holy War*, for he
cared for none of these things. Indeed, so
dreary did he find it all, that his love to Robert
was never put to such a severe test. But for
that, he would have run for it. Twenty times a
day was he so tempted.

At school, though it was better, yet it was bad.
For he was ten times as much laughed at for his
new clothes, though they were of the plainest,
as he had been for his old rags. Still he bore
all the pangs of unwelcome advancement without a grumble, for the sake of his friend alone,
whose dog he remained as much as ever. But
his past life of cold and neglect, and hunger and
blows, and homelessness and rags, began to
glimmer as in the distance of a vaporous sunset,
and the loveless freedom he had then enjoyed
gave it a bloom as of summer-roses.

I wonder whether there may not have been
in some unknown corner of the old lady's mind
this lingering remnant of paganism, that, in re-
claiming the outcast from the error of his ways,
she was making an offering acceptable to that
God whom her mere prayers could not move to
look with favour upon her prodigal son Andrew.
Nor from her own acknowledged religious belief
as a background would it have stuck so fiery off
either. Indeed, it might have been a partial
corrective of some yet more dreadful articles of
her creed.—which she held, be it remembered,
because she could not help it.

CHAPTER XI.

PRIVATE INTERVIEWS.

THE winter passed slowly away. Robert and Shargar went to school together, and learned their lessons together at Mrs. Falconer's table. Shargar soon learned to behave with tolerable propriety; was obedient, as far as eye-service went; looked as queer as ever; did what he pleased, which was nowise very wicked, the moment he was out of the old lady's sight; was well fed and well cared for; and when he was asked how he was, gave the invariable answer: "Middlin'." He was not very happy.

There was little communication in words between the two boys, for the one had not much to say, and the pondering fits of the other grew rather than relaxed in frequency and intensity. Yet amongst chance acquaintances in the town Robert had the character of a wag, of which he was totally unaware himself. Indeed, although he had more than the ordinary share of humour, I suspect it was not so much his fun as his earnest that got him the character; for he would say such altogether unheard-of and strange things, that the only way they were capable of accounting for him was as a humorist.

"Eh!" he said once to Elshender, during a pause common to a thunder-storm and a lesson on the violin, "eh! wadna ye like to be up in that clood wi' a spaud, turnin' ower the divots and catchin the flashes lyin' aneath them like lang reid fiery worms?"

"Ay, man, but gin ye luik up to the cloods that gait, ye'll never be muckle o' a fiddler."

This was merely an outbreak of that insolence of advice so often shown to the young from no vantage-ground but that of age and faithlessness, reminding one of the "jigging fool" who interfered between Brutus and Cassius on the sole ground that he had seen more years than they. As if ever a fiddler that did not look up to the clouds would be anything but a catgut-scraper! Even Elshender's fiddle was the one angel that held back the heavy curtain of his gross nature, and let the sky shine through. He ought to have been set fiddling every Sunday morning, and from his fiddling dragged straight to church. It was the only thing man could have done for his conversion, for then his heart was open. But I fear the prayers would have closed it before the sermon came. He should rather have been compelled to take his fiddle to church with him,

and have a gentle scrape at it in the pauses of
the service; only there are no such pauses in the
service, alas! And Dooble Sanny, though not
too religious to get drunk occasionally, was a
great deal too religious to play his fiddle on
the Sabbath: he would not willingly anger the
powers above; but it was sometimes a sore
temptation, especially after he got possession of
old Mr. Falconer's wonderful instrument.

"Hoots, man!" he would say to Robert;
"dinna han'le her as gin she war an egg-box.
Tak haud o' her as gin she war a leevin' crater.
Ye maun jist straik her canny, an' wile the
music oot o' her; for she's like ither women: gin
ye be rouch wi' her, ye winna get a word oot o'
her. An' dinna han'le her that gait. She canna
bide to be contred an' pu'd this gait and that
gait.—Come to me, my bonny leddy. Ye'll tell
me yer story, winna ye, my dauty (*pet*)?"

And with every gesture as if he were humouring a shy and invalid girl, he would, as he said,
wile the music out of her in sobs and wailing,
till the instrument, gathering courage in his
embrace, grew gently merry in its confidence,
and broke at last into airy laughter. He always
spoke, and apparently thought, of his violin as
a woman, just as a sailor does of his craft. But
there was nothing about him, except his love for
music and its instruments, to suggest other than
a most uncivilized nature. That which was fine

in him was constantly checked and held down
by the gross; the merely animal overpowered
the spiritual; and it was only upon occasion
that his heavenly companion, the violin, could
raise him a few feet above the mire and the clay.
She never succeeded in setting his feet on a
rock; while, on the contrary, he often dragged
her with him into the mire of questionable company and circumstances. Worthy Mr. Falconer
would have been horrified to see his umquhile
modest companion in such society as that into
which she was now introduced at times. But
nevertheless the soutar was a good and patient
teacher; and although it took Robert *rather* more
than a fortnight to redeem his pledge to Shargar, he did make progress. It could not, however, be rapid, seeing that an hour at a time,
two evenings in the week, was all that he could
give to the violin. Even with this moderation,
the risk of his absence exciting his grandmother's suspicion and inquiry was far from small.

And now, were those really faded old memories of his grandfather and his merry kindness,
all so different from the solemn benevolence of
his grandmother, which seemed to revive in his
bosom with the revivification of the violin?
The instrument had surely laid up a story in its
hollow breast, had been dreaming over it all the
time it lay hidden away in the closet, and was
now telling out its dreams about the old times

in the ear of the listening boy. To him also it began to assume something of that mystery and life which had such a softening, and, for the moment at least, elevating influence on his master.

At length the love of the violin had grown upon him so, that he could not but cast about how he might enjoy more of its company. It would not do, for many reasons, to go oftener to the shoemaker's, especially now that the days were getting longer. Nor was that what he wanted. He wanted opportunity for practice. He wanted to be alone with the creature, to see if she would not say something more to him than she had ever said yet. Wafts and odours of melodies began to steal upon him ere he was aware in the half lights between sleeping and waking: if he could only entice them to creep out of the violin, and once "bless his humble ears" with the bodily hearing of them! Perhaps he might —who could tell? But how? But where?

There was a building in Rothieden not old, yet so deserted that its very history seemed to have come to a standstill, and the dust that filled it to have fallen from the plumes of passing centuries. It was the property of Mrs. Falconer, left her by her husband. Trade had gradually ebbed away from the town till the thread-factory stood unoccupied, with all its machinery rusting and mouldering, just as the work-people had risen and left it one hot, midsummer day, when

they were told that their services were no longer
required. Some of the thread even remained
upon the spools, and in the hollows of some of
the sockets the oil had as yet dried only into a
paste ; although to Robert the desertion of the
place appeared immemorial. It stood at a fur-
long's distance from the house, on the outskirt of
the town. There was a large, neglected garden
behind it, with some good fruit-trees, and plenty
of the bushes which boys love for the sake of
their berries. After grannie's jam-pots were
properly filled, the remnant of these, a gleaning
far greater than the gathering, was at the disposal of Robert, and, philosopher although in
some measure he was already, he appreciated
the privilege. Haunting this garden in the previous summer, he had for the first time made acquaintance with the interior of the deserted factory. The door to the road was always kept
locked, and the key of it lay in one of grannie's
drawers ; but he had then discovered a back entrance less securely fastened, and with a strange
mingling of fear and curiosity had from time to
time extended his rambles over what seemed to
him the huge desolation of the place. Half
of it was well built of stone and lime, but of
the other half the upper part was built of wood,
which now showed signs of considerable decay.
One room opened into another through the length
of the place, revealing a vista of machines, stand-

ing with an air of the last folding of the wings of silence over them, and the sense of a deeper and deeper sinking into the soundless abyss. But their activity was not so far vanished but that by degrees Robert came to fancy that he had some time or other seen a woman seated at each of those silent powers, whose single hand set the whole frame in motion, with its numberless spindles and spools rapidly revolving—a vague mystery of endless threads in orderly complication, out of which came some desired, to him unknown, result, so that the whole place was full of a bewildering tumult of work, every little reel contributing its share, as the water-drops clashing together make the roar of a tempest. Now all was still as the church on a week-day, still as the school on a Saturday afternoon. Nay, the silence seemed to have settled down like the dust, and grown old and thick, so dead and old that the ghost of the ancient noise had arisen to haunt the place.

Thither would Robert carry his violin, and there would he woo her.

"I'm thinkin' I maun tak her wi' me the nicht, Sanders," he said, holding the fiddle lovingly to his bosom, after he had finished his next lesson.

The shoemaker looked blank.

"Ye're no gaein' to desert me, are ye?"

"Na, weel I wat!" returned Robert. "But I

want to try her at hame. I maun get used till her a bittie, ye ken, afore I can du onything wi' her."

"I wiss ye had na brought her here ava. What I *am* to du wantin' her!"

"What for dinna ye get yer ain back?"

"I haena the siller, man. And, forbye, I doobt I wadna be that sair content wi' her noo gin I had her. I used to think her gran'. But I'm clean oot o' conceit o' her. That bonnie leddy's ta'en 't clean oot o' me."

"But ye canna hae her aye, ye ken, Sanders. She's no mine. She's my grannie's, ye ken."

"What's the use o' her to *her?* She pits nae vailue upon her. Eh, man, gin she wad gie her to me, I wad haud her i' the best o' shune a' the lave o' her days."

"That wadna be muckle, Sanders, for she hasna had a new pair sin' ever I mind."

"But I wad haud Betty in shune as weel."

"Betty pays for her ain shune, I reckon."

"Weel, I wad haud *you* in shune, and yer bairns, and yer bairns' bairns," cried the soutar, with enthusiasm.

"Hoot, toot, man! Lang or that ye'll be fiddlin' i' the new Jerooslem."

"Eh, man!" said Alexander, looking up—he had just cracked the *roset-ends* off his hands, for he had the upper leather of a boot in the grasp of the clams, and his right hand hung arrested on its blind way to the awl—"duv ye think there 'll be fiddles there? I thocht they war a' hairps, a thing 'at I never saw, but it canna be up till a fiddle."

"I dinna ken," answered Robert; "but ye suld mak a pint o' seein' for yersel'.

"Gin I thoucht there wad be fiddles there, faith I wad hae a try. It wadna be muckle o' a Jeroozlem to me wantin' my fiddle. But gin there be fiddles, I daursay they 'll be gran' anes. I daursay they wad gi' me a new ane—I mean ane as auld as Noah's 'at he played i' the ark whan the de'il cam' in by to hearken. I wad fain hae a try. Ye ken a' aboot it wi' that grannie o' yours: hoo's a body to begin?"

"By giein' up the drink, man."

"Ay—ay—ay—I reckon ye're richt. Weel, I'll think aboot it whan ance I'm throu wi' this job. That 'll be neist ook, or thereabouts, or aiblins twa days efter. I'll hae some leiser than."

Before he had finished speaking he had caught up his awl and begun to work vigorously, boring his holes as if the nerves of feeling were continued to the point of the tool, inserting the bristles that served him for needles with a delicacy worthy of soft-skinned fingers, drawing through the rosined threads with a whisk, and untwining them with a crack from the leather that guarded his hands.

"Gude nicht to ye," said Robert, with the fiddle-case under his arm.

The shoemaker looked up, with his hands bound in his threads.

"Ye're no gaein' to tak her frae me the nicht?"

"Ay am I, but I'll fess her back again. I'm no gaein' to Jericho wi' her."

"Gang to Hecklebirnie wi' her, and that's three mile ayont hell."

"Na; we maun win farther nor that. There canna be muckle fiddlin' there."

"Weel, tak her to the new Jeroozlem. I s' gang doon to Lucky Leary's, and fill mysel' roarin' fou, an' it 'll be a' your wyte *(blame)*."

"I doobt *ye*'ll get the straiks *(blows)* though. Or maybe ye think Bell 'ill tak them for ye."

Dooble Sanny caught up a huge boot, the sole of which was filled with broad-headed nails as thick as they could be driven, and, in a rage, threw it at Robert as he darted out. Through its clang against the *door-cheek*, the shoemaker heard a cry from the instrument. He cast everything from him and sprang after Robert. But Robert was down the wynd like a long-legged grayhound, and Elshender could only follow like a fierce mastiff. It was love and grief, though, and apprehension and remorse, not vengeance, that winged his heels. He soon saw that pursuit was vain.

" Robert ! Robert !" he cried ; " I canna win
up wi' ye. Stop, for God's sake ! Is she hurtit ?"

Robert stopped at once.

" Ye hae made a bonny leddy o' her—a la-
meter (*cripple*) I doobt, like yer wife," he answered, with indignation.

"Dinna be aye flingin' a man's fau'ts in 's
face. It jist maks him 'at he canna bide himsel'
or you eyther. Lat's see the bonny crater."

Robert complied, for he too was anxious.
They were now standing in the space in front
of Shargar's old abode, and there was no one to
be seen. Elshender took the box, opened it
carefully, and peeped in with a face of great
apprehension.

"I thocht that was a'!" he said with some
satisfaction. " I kent the string whan I heard it.
But we 'll sune get a new thairm till her," he
added, in a tone of sorrowful commiseration and
condolence, as he took the violin from the case,
tenderly as if it had been a hurt child.

One touch of the bow, drawing out a *goul* of
grief, satisfied him that *she* was uninjured. Next
a hurried inspection showed him that there was
enough of the catgut twisted round the peg to
make up for the part that was broken off. In a moment he had fastened it to the tail-piece, tightened and tuned it. Forthwith he took the bow from
the case-lid, and in jubilant guise he expatiated
upon the wrong he had done his bonny leddy,

till the doors and windows around were crowded
with heads peering through the dark to see
whence the sounds came, and a little child tod-
dled across from one of the lowliest houses with
a ha'penny for the fiddler.   Gladly would Robert
have restored it with interest, but, alas! there
was no interest in his bank, for not a ha'-
penny had he in the world.   The incident recalled Sandy to Rothieden and its cares.   He
restored the violin to its case, and while Robert
was fearing he would take it under his arm
and walk away with it, handed it back with a
humble sigh and a "Praise be thankit;" then
without another word, turned and went to his
lonely stool and home " untreasured of its mistress."   Robert went home too, and stole like a
thief to his room.

The next day was a Saturday, which, indeed,
was the real old Sabbath, or at least the half of
it, to the schoolboys of Rothieden.   Even
Robert's grannie was Jew enough, or rather
Christian enough, to respect this remnant of the
fourth commandment—divine antidote to the rest
of the godless money-making and soul-saving
week—and he had the half-day to himself.   So
as soon as he had had his dinner, he managed
to give Shargar the slip, left him to the inroads
of a desolate despondency, and stole away to
the old factory-garden.   The key of that he had
managed to purloin from the kitchen where it

hung ; nor was there much danger of its absence being discovered, seeing that in winter no one thought of the garden. The smuggling of the violin out of the house was the " dearest danger " —the more so that he would not run the risk of carrying her out unprotected, and it was altogether a bulky venture with the case. But by spying and speeding he managed it, and soon found himself safe within the high walls of the garden.

It was early spring. There had been a heavy fall of sleet in the morning, and now the wind blew gustfully about the place. The neglected trees shook showers upon him as he passed under them, trampling down the rank growth of the grass-walks. The long twigs of the wall-trees, which had never been nailed up, or had been torn down by the snow and the blasts of winter, went trailing away in the moan of the fitful wind, and swung back as it sunk to a sigh. The currant and gooseberry bushes, bare and leafless, and "shivering all for cold," neither reminded him of the feasts of the past summer, nor gave him any hope for the next. He strode careless through it all to gain the door at the bottom. It yielded to a push, and the long grass streamed in over the threshold as he entered. He mounted by a broad stair in the main part of the house, passing the silent clock in one of its corners, now expiating in motionlessness the false accusations it had brought against the work-people, and turned into the chaos of machinery.

I fear that my readers will expect, from the minuteness with which I recount these particulars, that, after all, I am going to describe a rendezvous with a lady, or a ghost at least. I will not plead in excuse that I, too, have been infected with Sandy's mode of regarding *her*, but I plead that in the mind of Robert the proceeding was involved in something of that awe and mystery with which a youth approaches the woman he loves. He had not yet arrived at the period when the feminine assumes its paramount influence, combining in itself all that music, colour, form, odour, can suggest, with something infinitely higher and more divine; but he had begun to be haunted with some vague aspirations towards the infinite, of which his attempts on the violin were the outcome. And now that he was to be alone, for the first time, with this wonderful realizer of dreams and awakener of visions, to do with her as he would, to hint by gentle touches at the thoughts that were fluttering in his soul, and listen for her voice that by the echoes in which she strove to respond he might know that she understood him, it was no wonder if he felt an etherial foretaste of the expectation that haunts the approach of souls.

But I am not even going to describe his first *tête-à-tête* with his violin. Perhaps he returned from it somewhat disappointed. Probably he found her coy, unready to acknowledge his demands on her attention. But not the less willingly did he return with her to the solitude of the ruinous factory. On every safe occasion, becoming more and more frequent as the days grew longer, he repaired thither, and every time returned more capable of drawing the coherence of melody from that matrix of sweet sounds.

At length the people about began to say that the factory was haunted; that the ghost of old Mr. Falconer, unable to repose while neglect was ruining the precious results of his industry, visited the place night after night, and solaced his disappointment by renewing on his favourite violin strains not yet forgotten by him in his grave, and remembered well by those who had been in his service, not a few of whom lived in the neighbourhood of the forsaken building.

One gusty afternoon, like the first, but late in the spring, Robert repaired as usual to this his secret haunt. He had played for some time, and now, from a sudden pause of impulse, had ceased, and begun to look around him. The only light came from two long pale cracks in the rain-clouds of the west. The wind was blowing through the broken windows, which stretched away on either hand. A dreary, windy gloom, therefore, pervaded the desolate place; and in the dusk, and their settled order, the machines looked multitudinous. An *eerie* sense of discomfort came over him as he gazed, and he lifted his violin to dispel the strange unpleasant feeling that grew upon him. But at the first long stroke across the strings, an awful sound arose in a further room; a sound that made him all but drop the bow, and cling to his violin. It went on. It was the old, all but forgotten whirr of bobbins, mingled with the gentle groans of the revolving horizontal wheel, but magnified in the silence of the place, and the echoing imagination of the boy, into something preternaturally awful. Yielding for a moment to the growth of goose-skin, and the insurrection of hair, he recovered himself by a violent effort, and walked to the door that connected the two compartments. Was it more or less fearful that the jenny was not going of itself? that the figure of an old woman sat solemnly turning and turning the hand-wheel? Not without calling in the jury of his senses, however, would he yield to the special plea of his imagination, but went nearer, half expecting to find that the *mutch*, with its big flapping borders, glimmering white in the gloom across many a machine, surrounded the face of a skull. But he was soon satisfied that it was only a blind woman everybody knew—so old that she had become childish. She had heard the reports of the factory being haunted, and, groping about with her half-withered brain full of them, had found the garden and the back door open, and had climbed to the first-floor by a farther stair, well known to her when she used to work that very machine. She had seated herself instinctively, according to ancient wont, and had set it in motion once more.

Yielding to an impulse of experiment, Robert began to play again. Thereupon her disordered ideas broke out in words. And Robert soon began to feel that it could hardly be more ghastly to look upon a ghost than to be taken for one.

"Ay, ay, sir," said the old woman, in a tone of commiseration, "it maun be sair to bide. I dinna wonner 'at ye canna lie still. But what gars ye gang daunerin aboot *this* place? It's no yours ony langer. Ye ken whan fowk's deid, they tyne the grip (*lose hold*). Ye suld gang hame to yer wife. She micht say a word to quaiet yer auld banes, for she's a douce an' a wice woman—the mistress."

Then followed a pause. There was a horror about the old woman's voice, already half dissolved by death, in the desolate place, that almost took from Robert the power of motion. But his violin sent forth an accidental twang, and that set her going again.

"Ye was aye a douce honest gentleman yersel', an' I dinna wonner ye canna bide it. But
I wad hae thoucht glory micht hae hauden ye
in. But yer ain son! Eh ay! And a braw
lad and a bonnie! It's a sod thing he bude to
gang the wrang gait; and it's no wonner, as I
say, that ye lea' the worms to come an' luik
efter him. I doobt—I doobt it winna be to you
he'll gang at the lang last. There winna be
room for him aside ye in Awbrahawm's boasom.
And syne to behave sae ill to that winsome wife
o' his! I dinna wonner 'at ye maun be up! Eh
na! But, sir, sin ye are up, I wish ye wad
speyk to John Thamson no to tak' aff the day
'at I was awa' last ook, for 'deed I was verra
unweel, and bude to keep my bed."

Robert was beginning to feel uneasy as to
how he should get rid of her, when she rose,
and saying, "Ay, ay, I ken it 's sax o'clock,"
went out as she had come in. Robert followed,
and saw her safe out of the garden, but did not
return to the factory.

So his father had behaved ill to his mother
too!

"But what for hearken to the havers o' a
dottled auld wife?" he said to himself, pondering as he walked home.

Old Janet told a strange story of how she had
seen the ghost, and had had a long talk with
him, and of what he said, and of how he groaned

and played the fiddle between. And finding that the report had reached his grandmother's ears, Robert thought it prudent, much to his discontent, to intermit his visits to the factory. Mrs. Falconer, of course, received the rumour with indignant scorn, and peremptorily refused to allow any examination of the premises.

But how have the violin by him and not hear her speak? One evening the longing after her voice grew upon him till he could resist it no longer. He shut the door of his garret-room, and, with Shargar by him, took her out and began to play softly, gently—oh so softly, so gently! Shargar was enraptured. Robert went on playing.

Suddenly the door opened, and his grannie stood awfully revealed before them. Betty had heard the violin, and had flown to the parlour in the belief that, unable to get any one to heed him at the factory, the ghost had taken Janet's advice, and come home. But his wife smiled a smile of contempt, went with Betty to the kitchen—over which Robert's room lay—heard the sounds, put off her creaking shoes, stole up-stairs on her soft white lambswool stockings, and caught the pair. The violin was seized, put in its case, and carried off; and Mrs. Falconer rejoiced to think she had broken a gin set by Satan for the unwary feet of her poor Robert. Little she knew the wonder of that violin—

how it had kept the soul of her husband alive!
Little she knew how dangerous it is to shut an
open door, with ever so narrow a peep into the
eternal, in the face of a son of Adam! And
little she knew how determinedly and restlessly
a nature like Robert's would search for another,
to open one possibly which she might consider
ten times more dangerous than that which she
had closed.

When Alexander heard of the affair, he was
at first overwhelmed with the misfortune; but
gathering a little heart at last, he set to "working," as he said himself, "like a verra deevil;"
and as he was the best shoemaker in the town,
and for the time abstained utterly from whisky,
and all sorts of drink but well-water, he soon
managed to save the money necessary, and redeem the old fiddle. But whether it was from
fancy, or habit, or what, even Robert's inexperienced ear could not accommodate itself, save
under protest, to the instrument which once
his teacher had considered all but perfect; and
it needed the master's finest touch to make its
tone other than painful to the sense of the neo-
phyte.

No one can estimate too highly the value of
such a resource to a man like the shoemaker, or
a boy like Robert. Whatever it be that keeps
the finer faculties of the mind awake, wonder
alive, and the interest above mere eating and

drinking, money-making and money-saving; whatever it be that gives gladness, or sorrow, or hope—this, be it violin, pencil, pen, or, highest of all, the love of woman, is simply a divine gift of holy influence for the salvation of that being to whom it comes, for the lifting of him out of the mire and up on the rock. For it keeps a way open for the entrance of deeper, holier, grander influences, emanating from the same riches of the Godhead. And though many have genius that have no grace, they will only be so much the worse, so much the nearer to the brute, if you take from them that which corresponds to Dooble Sanny's fiddle.

CHAPTER XII.

ROBERT'S PLAN OF SALVATION.

FOR some time after the loss of his friend, Robert went loitering and mooning about, quite neglecting the lessons to which he had not, it must be confessed, paid much attention for many weeks. Even when seated at his grannie's table, he could do no more than fix his eyes on his book: to learn was impossible; it was even disgusting to him. But his was a nature which, foiled in one direction, must, absolutely helpless against its own vitality, straightway send out its searching roots in another. Of all forces, that of growth is the one irresistible, for it is the creating power of God, the law of life and of being. Therefore no accumulation of refusals, and checks, and turnings, and forbiddings, from all the good old grannies in the world, could have prevented Robert from striking root downward, and bearing fruit upward, though, as in all higher natures, the fruit was a long way off yet. But his soul was only sad and hungry. He was not unhappy, for he had been guilty of nothing that weighed on his conscience. He had been doing many things of late, it is true, without asking leave of his grandmother, but wherever prayer is felt to be of no avail, there cannot be the sense of obligation save on compulsion. Even direct disobedience in such case will generally leave little soreness, except the thing forbidden should be in its own nature wrong, and then, indeed, " Don Worm, the conscience," may begin to bite. But Robert felt nothing immoral in playing upon his grandfather's violin, nor even in taking liberties with a piece of lumber for which nobody cared but possibly the dead; therefore he was not unhappy, only much disappointed, very empty, and somewhat gloomy. There was nothing to look forward to now, no secret full of riches and endless in hope—in short, no violin.

To feel the full force of his loss, my reader must remember that around the childhood of Robert, which he was fast leaving behind him, there had gathered no tenderness—none at least by him recognizable as such. All the women he came in contact with were his grandmother and Betty. He had no recollection of having ever been kissed. From the darkness and negation of such an embryo-existence, his nature had been unconsciously striving to escape—struggling to get from below ground into the sunlit

air—sighing after a freedom he could not have
defined, the freedom that comes, not of independence, but of love—not of lawlessness, but of the
perfection of law.   Of this beauty of life, with
its wonder and its deepness, this unknown glory,
his fiddle had been the type.   It had been the
ark that held, if not the tables of the covenant,
yet the golden pot of angel's food, and the rod
that budded in death.   And now that it was
gone, the gloomier aspect of things began to lay
hold upon him; his soul turned itself away from
the sun, and entered into the shadow of the
under-world.   Like the white-horsed twins of
lake Regillus, like Phœbe, the queen of skyey
plain and earthly forest, every boy and girl,
every man and woman, that lives at all, has to
divide many a year between Tartarus and
Olympus.

For now arose within him, not without ulti-
mate good, the evil phantasms of a theology
which would explain all God's doings by low con-
ceptions, low I mean for humanity even, of right,
and law, and justice, then only taking refuge in
the fact of the incapacity of the human understanding when its own inventions are impugned
as undivine.   In such a system, hell is invariably the deepest truth, and the love of God is
not so deep as hell.   Hence, as foundations
must be laid in the deepest, the system is
founded in hell, and the first article in the creed

that Robert Falconer learned was, " I believe in hell." Practically, I mean, it was so ; else how should it be that as often as a thought of religious duty arose in his mind, it appeared in the form of escaping hell, of fleeing from the wrath to come? For his very nature was hell, being not born *in* sin and brought forth in iniquity, but born sin and brought forth iniquity. And yet God made him. He must believe that. And he must believe, too, that God was just, awfully just, punishing with fearful pains those who did not go through a certain process of mind which it was utterly impossible they should go through without a help which he would give to some, and withhold from others, the reason of the difference not being such, to say the least of it, as to come within the reach of the persons concerned. And this God they said was love. It was logically absurd, of course, yet, thank God, they did say that God was love ; and many of them succeeded in believing it, too, and in ordering their ways as if the first article of their creed had been " I believe in God ;" whence, in truth, we are bound to say it was the first in power and reality, if not in order; for what are we to say a man believes, if not what he acts upon? Still the former article was the one they brought chiefly to bear upon their children. This mortar, probably they thought, threw the shell straighter than any of the other field-pieces of the church-

militant. Hence it was even in justification of
God himself that a party arose to say that a man
could believe without the help of God at all, and
after believing only began to receive God's help—
a heresy all but as dreary and barren as the former. Not one dreamed of saying—at least such
a glad word of prophecy never reached Rothieden—that, while nobody can do without the
help of the Father any more than a new-born
babe could of itself live and grow to a man, yet
that in the giving of that help the very fatherhood of the Father finds its one gladsome labour; that for that the Lord came; for that the
world was made; for that we were born into it;
for that God lives and loves like the most loving man or woman on earth, only infinitely more,
and in other ways and kinds besides, which we
cannot understand; and that therefore to be a
man is the soul of eternal jubilation.

Robert consequently began to take fits of soul-
saving, a most rational exercise, worldly wise
and prudent—right too on the principles he had
received, but not in the least Christian in its nature, or even God-fearing. His imagination began to busy itself in representing the dire consequences of not entering into the one refuge
of faith. He made many frantic efforts to believe
that he believed; took to keeping the Sabbath
very carefully—that is, by going to church three
times, and to Sunday-school as well; by never

walking a step save to or from church; by
never saying a word upon any subject uncon-
nected with religion, chiefly theoretical; by
never reading any but religious books; by never
whistling; by never thinking of his lost fiddle,
and so on—all the time feeling that God was
ready to pounce upon him if he failed once; till
again and again the intensity of his efforts utterly defeated their object by destroying for the
time the desire to prosecute them with the power
to will them. But through the horrible vapours
of these vain endeavours, which denied God altogether as the maker of the world, and the former of his soul and heart and brain, and sought
to worship him as a capricious demon, there
broke a little light, a little soothing, soft twilight, from the dim windows of such literature as
came in his way. Besides *The Pilgrim's Progress*
there were several books which shone moon-like
on his darkness, and lifted something of the
weight of that Egyptian gloom off his spirit. One
of these, strange to say, was Defoe's *Religious
Courtship*, and one, Young's *Night Thoughts*. But
there was another which deserves particular notice, inasmuch as it did far more than merely interest or amuse him, raising a deep question in
his mind, and one worthy to be asked.   This
book was the translation of Klopstock's *Messiah*, to which I have already referred. It was not
one of his grandmother's books, but had probab-

ly belonged to his father: he had found it in his
little garret room.   But as often as she saw him
reading it, she seemed rather pleased, he thought.
As to the book itself, its florid expatiation
could neither offend nor injure a boy like Robert,
while its representation of our Lord was to him
a wonderful relief from that given in the pulpit,
and in all the religious books he knew. But the
point for the sake of which I refer to it in particular is this: Amongst the rebel angels who are
of the actors in the story, one of the principal is
a cherub who repents of making his choice with
Satan, mourns over his apostasy, haunts unseen
the steps of our Saviour, wheels lamenting about
the cross, and would gladly return to his lost
duties in heaven, if only he might—a doubt
which I believe is left unsolved in the volume,
and naturally enough remained unsolved in Robert's mind:—Would poor Abaddon be forgiven
and taken home again? For although naturally, that is, to judge by his own instincts, there
could be no question of his forgiveness, according to what he had been taught there could be no
question of his perdition. Having no one to talk
to, he divided himself and went to buffets on
the subject, siding, of course, with the better
half of himself which supported the merciful
view of the matter; for all his efforts at keeping
the Sabbath, had in his own honest judgment
failed so entirely, that he had no ground for be-

lieving himself one of the elect.   Had he succeeded in persuading himself that he was, there
is no saying to what lengths of indifference
about others the chosen prig might have advanced by this time.

He made one attempt to open the subject
with Shargar.

"Shargar, what think ye?" he said suddenly,
one day.   "Gin a de'il war to repent, wad God
forgie him?"

"There's no sayin' what fowk wad du ance
they're tried," returned Shargar, cautiously.

Robert did not care to resume the question
with one who so circumspectly refused to
take a metaphysical or *a priori* view of the
matter.

He made an attempt with his grandmother.

One Sunday, his thoughts, after trying for a
time to revolve in due orbit around the mind of
the Rev. Hugh MacCleary, as projected in a sermon which he had botched up out of a commen-
tary, failed at last and flew off into what the
said gentleman would have pronounced " very
dangerous speculation, seeing no man is to go
beyond what is written in the Bible, which con-
tains not only the truth, but the whole truth,
and nothing but the truth, for this time and for
all future time—both here and in the world to
come."   Some such sentence, at least, was in
his sermon that day, and the preacher no doubt

supposed St. Matthew, not St. Matthew Henry,
accountable for its origination.   In the Limbo
into which Robert's then spirit flew, it had been
sorely exercised about the substitution of the
sufferings of Christ for those which humanity
must else have endured while ages rolled on—
mere ripples on the ocean of eternity.

" Noo, be douce," said Mrs. Falconer, solemnly, as Robert, a trifle lighter at heart from the
result of his cogitations than usual, sat down to
dinner : he had happened to smile across the
table to Shargar. And he was douce, and smiled
no more.

They ate their broth, or, more properly, *supped* it, with horn spoons, in absolute silence ;
after which Mrs. Falconer put a large piece of
meat on the plate of each, with the same for-
mula :

" Hae. Ye s' get nae mair."

The allowance was ample in the extreme,
bearing a relation to her words similar to that
which her practice bore to her theology. A
piece of cheese, because it was the Sabbath, followed, and dinner was over.

When the table had been cleared by Betty,
they drew their chairs to the fire, and Robert
had to read to his grandmother, while Shargar
sat listening. He had not read long, however,
before he looked up from his Bible and began
the following conversation :—

" Wasna it an ill trick o' Joseph, gran'mither, to put that cup, an' a siller ane tu, into the mou' o' Benjamin's seck ?"

" What for that, laddie ? He wanted to gar them come back again, ye ken."

" But he needna hae gane aboot it in sic a play-actor-like gait. He needna hae latten them awa' ohn tellt *(without telling)* them that he was their brither."

" They had behaved verra ill till him."

" He used to clype *(tell tales)* upo' them, though."

" Laddie, tak ye care what ye say aboot Joseph, for he was a teep o' Christ."

" Hoo was that, gran'mither ?"

" They sellt him to the Ishmeleets for siller, as Judas did Him."

" Did he beir the sins o' them 'at sellt him ?"

" Ye may say, in a mainner, 'at he did ; for he was sair afflickit afore he wan up to be the King's richt han' ; an' syne he keepit a hantle o' ill aff o' 's brithren."

" Sae, gran'mither, ither fowk nor Christ micht suffer for the sins o' their neebors ?"

" Ay, laddie, mony a ane has to do that. But no to mak atonement, ye 'ken. Naething but the sufferin' o' the spotless cud du that. The Lord wadna be saitisfeet wi' less nor that. It maun be the innocent to suffer for the guilty."

" I unnerstan' that," said Robert, who had

heard it so often that he had not yet thought of
trying to understand it. " But gin we gang to
the gude place, we'll be a' innocent, willna we,
grannie ?"

" Ay, that we will—washed spotless, and pure,
and clean, and dressed i' the weddin' garment,
and set doon at the table wi' Him and wi his
Father. That's them 'at believes in him, ye ken."

" Of coorse, grannie.—Weel, ye see, I hae been
thinkin' o' a plan for maist han' toomin' (*almost
emptying*) hell."

" What's i' the bairn's heid noo ? Troth, ye're
no blate, meddlin' wi' sic subjecks, laddie !"

" I didna want to say onything to vex ye,
grannie. I s' gang on wi' the chapter."

" Ow, say awa'. Ye sanna say muckle 'at's
wrang afore I cry *haud*," said Mrs. Falconer,
curious to know what had been moving in the
boy's mind, but watching him like a cat, ready
to spring upon the first visible hair of the old
Adam.

And Robert, recalling the outbreak of terrible
grief which he had heard on that memorable
night, really thought that his project would
bring comfort to a mind burdened with such care,
and went on with the exposition of his plan.

" A' them 'at sits doon to the supper o' the
Lamb 'll sit there because Christ suffert the punishment due to their sins—winna they, grannie ?"

" Doobtless, laddie."

"But it 'll be some sair upo' them to sit there aitin' an' drinkin' an' talkin' awa', an' enjoyin' themsel's, whan ilka noo an' than there 'll come a sough o' wailin' up frae the ill place, an' a smell o' burnin' ill to bide."

"What put that i' yer heid, laddie? There's no rizzon to think 'at hell's sae near haven as a' that. The Lord forbid it !"

"Weel, but, grannie, they'll ken't a' the same, whether they smell 't or no. An' I canna help thinkin' that the farrer awa' I thoucht they war, the waur I wad like to think upo' them. 'Deed it wad be waur."

"What are ye drivin' at, laddie? I canna unnerstan' ye," said Mrs. Falconer, feeling very uncomfortable, and yet curious, almost anxious, to hear what would come next. "I trust we winna hae to think muckle——"

But here, I presume, the thought of the added desolation of her Andrew if she, too, were to forget him, as well as his Father in heaven, checked the flow of her words. She paused, and Robert took up his parable and went on, first with yet another question.

"Duv ye think, grannie, that a body wad be allooed to speik a word i' public, like, there—at the lang table, like, I mean ?"

"What for no, gin it was dune wi' moedesty, and for a guid rizzon? But railly, laddie, I doobt ye're haverin' a'thegither. Ye hard naething like that, I'm sure, the day, frae Mr. Mac-cleary."

"Na, na; he said naething aboot it. But maybe I'll gang and speir at him, though."

"What aboot ?"

"What I'm gaein' to tell ye, grannie."

"Weel, tell awa', and hae dune wi' 't. I'm growin' tired o' 't."

It was something else than tired she was growing.

"Weel, I'm gaein' to try a' that I can to win in there."

"I houp ye will. Strive and pray. Resist the deevil. Walk i' the licht. Lippen not to yersel', but trust in Christ and his salvation."

"Ay, ay, grannie.—Weel——"

"Are ye no dune yet ?"

"Na. I 'm but jist beginnin'."

"Beginnin' are ye ? Humph !"

"Weel, gin I win in there, the verra first nicht I sit doon wi' the lave o' them, I'm gaein' to rise up an' say—that is, gin the Maister, at the heid o' the table, disna bid me sit doon—an' say : 'Brithers an' sisters, the haill o' ye, hearken to me for ae minute; an', O Lord! gin I say wrang, jist tak the speech frae me, and I'll sit doon dumb an' rebukit. We're a' here by grace and no by merit, save His, as ye a' ken better nor I can tell ye, for ye hae been langer here nor me. But it's jist ruggin' an' rivin' at my hert to think o' them 'at 's doon there. Maybe ye can hear them. I canna. Noo, we hae nae merit, an' they hae nae merit, an' what for are we here and them there? But we're washed clean and innocent noo; and noo, whan there's no wyte lying upo' oursel's, it seems to me that we micht beir some o' the sins o' them 'at hae ower mony. I call upo' ilk' ane o' ye 'at has a frien' or a nee-bor down yonner, to rise up an' taste nor bite nor sup mair till we gang up a'thegither to the fut o' the throne, and pray the Lord to lat's gang and du as the Maister did afore's, and bier their griefs, and cairry their sorrows doon in hell there; gin it maybe that they may repent and get remission o' their sins, an' come up here wi' us at the lang last, and sit doon wi' 's at this table, a' throuw the merits o' oor Saviour Jesus Christ, at the heid o' the table there. Amen.'"

Half ashamed of his long speech, half over-come by the feelings fighting within him, and altogether bewildered, Robert burst out crying like a baby, and ran out of the room—up to his own place of meditation, where he threw himself on the floor. Shargar, who had made neither head nor tail of it all, as he said afterwards, sat staring at Mrs. Falconer. She rose, and going into Robert's little bed-room, closed the door, and what she did there is not far to seek.

When she came out, she rang the bell for tea, and sent Shargar to look for Robert. When he appeared, she was so gentle to him that it woke quite a new sensation in him. But after tea was over, she said,—

"Noo, Robert, lat's hae nae mair o' this. Ye ken as weel's I du that them 'at gangs *there* their doom is fixed, and noething *can* alter 't. An' we're not to alloo oor ain fancies to cairry 's ayont the Scripter. We hae oor ain salvation to work oot wi' fear an' trimlin'. We hae naething to do wi' what's hidden. Luik ye till 't 'at ye win in yersel'. That's eneuch for you to min'. —Shargar, ye can gang to the kirk. Robert 's to bide wi' me the nicht."

Mrs. Falconer very rarely went to church, for she could not hear a word, and found it irksome.

When Robert and she were alone together,

"Laddie," she said, "be ye waure o' judgin' the Almichty. What luiks to you a' wrang may be a' richt. But it's true eneuch 'at we dinna ken a'thing; an' he's no deid yet—I dinna believe 'at he is—and he'll maybe win in yet."

Here her voice failed her. And Robert had nothing to say now. He had said all his say before.

"Pray, Robert, pray for yer father, laddie," she resumed; "for we hae muckle rizzon to be anxious aboot 'im. Pray while there's life an' houp. Gie the Lord no rist. Pray till 'im day an' nicht, as I du, that he wad lead 'im to see the error o' his ways, an' turn to the Lord, wha 's ready to pardon. Gin yer mother had lived, I wad hae had mair houp, I confess, for she was a braw leddy and a bonny, and *that* sweet-tongued! She cud hae wiled a maukin frae its lair wi' her bonnie Hielan' speech. I never likit to hear nane o' them speyk the Erse *(Irish,* that is *Gaelic),* it was aye sae gloggie and baneless; and I cudna unnerstan' ae word o' 't. Nae mair cud yer father—hoot! yer gran'father, I mean—though his father cud speyk it weel. But to hear yer mother—mamma, as ye used to ca' her aye, efter the new fashion—to hear her speyk English, that was sweet to the ear; for the braid Scotch she kent as little o' as I do o' the Erse. It was hert's care aboot him that shortent her days. And a' that 'll be laid upo' him. He'll hae 't a' to beir an' accoont for. Och hone! Och hone! Eh! Robert, my man, be a guid lad, an' serve the Lord wi' a' yer hert, an' sowl, an' stren'th, an' min'; for gin ye gang wrang, yer ain father 'll hae to beir naebody kens hoo muckle o' the wyte o' 't, for he's dune naething to bring ye up i' the way ye suld gang, an' haud ye oot o' the ill gait. For the sake o' yer puir father, haud ye to the richt road. It may spare him a pang or twa i' the ill place. Eh, gin the Lord wad only tak me, and lat him gang!"

Involuntarily and unconsciously the mother's love was adopting the hope which she had denounced in her grandson. And Robert saw it, but he was never the man when I knew him to push a victory. He said nothing. Only a tear or two at the memory of the wayworn man, his recollection of whose visit I have already recorded, rolled down his cheeks. He was at such a distance from him!—such an impassable gulf yawned between them!—that was the grief! Not the gulf of death, nor the gulf that divides hell from heaven, but the gulf of abjuration by the good because of his evil ways. His grandmother, herself weeping fast and silently, with scarce altered countenance, took her neatly-folded handkerchief from her pocket, and wiped her grandson's fresh cheeks, then wiped her own withered face; and from that moment Robert knew that he loved her.

Then followed the Sabbath-evening prayer that she always offered with the boy, whichever he was, who kept her company. They knelt down together, side by side, in a certain corner of the room, the same, I doubt not, in which she knelt at her private devotions, before going to bed. There she uttered a long extempore prayer, rapid in speech, full of divinity and scripture-phrases, but not the less earnest and simple, for it flowed from a heart of faith. Then Robert had to pray after her, loud in her ear, that she might hear him thoroughly, so that he often felt as if he were praying to her, and not to God at all.

She had begun to teach him to pray so early

that the custom reached beyond the confines of his memory. At first he had had to repeat the words after her; but soon she made him construct his own utterances, now and then giving him a suggestion in the form of a petition when he seemed likely to break down, or putting a phrase into what she considered more suitable language. But all such assistance she had given up long ago.

On the present occasion, after she had ended her petitions with those for Jews and pagans, and especially for the "Pop' o' Rom'," in whom with a rare liberality she took the kindest interest, always praying God to give him a good wife, though she knew perfectly well the marriage creed of the priesthood, for her faith in the hearer of prayer scorned every theory but that in which she had herself been born and bred, she turned to Robert with the usual "Noo, Robert," and Robert began. But after he had gone on for some time with the ordinary phrases, he turned all at once into a new track, and instead of praying in general terms for "those that would not walk in the right way," said,

"O Lord! save my father," and there paused.

"If it be thy will," suggested his grandmother.

But Robert continued silent. His grandmother repeated the subjunctive clause.

"I'm tryin', grandmother," said Robert, "but I canna say 't. I daurna say an *if* aboot it. It wad be like giein' in till 's damnation. We *maun hae* him saved, grannie!"

"Laddie! laddie! haud yer tongue!" said Mrs. Falconer, in a tone of distressed awe. "O Lord, forgie 'im. He's young and disna ken better yet. He canna unnerstan' thy ways, nor, for that maitter, can I preten' to unnerstan' them mysel'. But thoo art a' licht, and in thee is no darkness at all. And thy licht comes into oor blin' een, and mak's them blinner yet. But, O Lord, gin it wad please thee to hear oor prayer . . . . eh! hoo we wad praise thee! And my Andrew wad praise thee mair nor ninety and nine o' them 'at need nae repentance."

A long pause followed. And then the only words that would come were: "For Christ's sake. Amen."

When she said that God was light, instead of concluding therefrom that he could not do the deeds of darkness, she was driven, from a faith in the teaching of Jonathan Edwards as implicit as that of "any lay papist of Loretto," to doubt whether the deeds of darkness were not after all deeds of light, or at least to conclude that their character depended not on their own nature, but on who did them.

They rose from their knees, and Mrs. Falconer sat down by her fire, with her feet on her little wooden stool, and began, as was her wont in that household twilight, ere the lamp was lighted, to review her past life, and follow her lost son through all conditions and circumstances to her imaginable. And when the world to come arose before her, clad in all the glories which her fancy, chilled by education and years, could supply, it was but to vanish in the gloom of the remembrance of him with whom she dared not hope to share its blessedness. This at least was how Falconer afterwards interpreted the sudden changes from gladness to gloom which he saw at such times on her countenance.

But while such a small portion of the universe of thought was enlightened by the glowworm lamp of the theories she had been taught, she was not limited for light to that feeble source. While she walked on her way, the moon, unseen herself behind the clouds, was illuminating the whole landscape so gently and evenly, that the glowworm being the only visible point of radiance, to it she attributed all the light. But she felt bound to go on believing as she had been taught; for sometimes the most original mind has the strongest sense of law upon it, and will, in default of a better, obey a beggarly one—only till the higher law that swallows it up manifests itself. Obedience was as essential an element of her creed as of that of any

purest-minded monk; neither being sufficiently
impressed with this: that, while obedience is
the law of the kingdom, it is of considerable
importance that that which is obeyed should be
in very truth the will of God. It is one thing,
and a good thing, to do for God's sake that
which is not his will: it is another thing, and
altogether a better thing—how much better, no
words can tell—to do for God's sake that which
is his will. Mrs. Falconer's submission and
obedience led her to accept as the will of God,
lest she should be guilty of opposition to him,
that which it was anything but giving him
honour to accept as such. Therefore her love
to God was too like the love of the slave or the
dog; too little like the love of the child, with
whose obedience the Father cannot be satisfied
until he cares for His reason as the highest form
of His will. True, the child who most faithfully desires to know the inward will or reason of
the Father, will be the most ready to obey
without it; only for this obedience it is essential that the apparent command at least be such
as he can suppose attributable to the Father.
Of his own self he is bound to judge what is
right, as the Lord said. Had Abraham doubted
whether it was in any case right to slay his
son, he would have been justified in doubting
whether God really required it of him, and
would have been bound to delay action until the

arrival of more light. True, the will of God can never be other than good; but I doubt if any man can ever be sure that a thing is the will of God, save by seeing into its nature and character, and beholding its goodness. Whatever God does must be right, but are we sure that we know what he does? That which men say he does may be very wrong indeed.

This burden she in her turn laid upon Robert —not unkindly, but as needful for his training towards well-being. Her way with him was shaped after that which she recognized as God's way with her. "Speir nae questons, but gang an' du as ye're tellt." And it was anything but a bad lesson for the boy. It was one of the best he could have had—that of authority. It is a grand thing to obey without asking questions, so long as there is nothing evil in what is commanded. Only Grannie concealed her reasons without reason; and God *makes* no secrets. Hence she seemed more stern and less sympathetic than she really was.

She sat with her feet on the little wooden stool, and Robert sat beside her staring into the fire, till they heard the outer door open, and Shargar and Betty come in from church.

CHAPTER XIII.

ROBERT'S MOTHER.

EARLY on the following morning, while Mrs.
Falconer, Robert, and Shargar were at
breakfast, Mr. Lammie came. He had delayed
communicating the intelligence he had received
till he should be more certain of its truth.
Older than Andrew, he had been a great friend
of his father, and likewise of some of Mrs. Falconer's own family. Therefore he was received
with a kindly welcome. But there was a cloud
on his brow which in a moment revealed that
his errand was not a pleasant one.

"I haena seen ye for a lang time, Mr. Lammie. Gae butt the hoose, lads. Or I'm thinkin' it maun be schule-time. Sit ye doon, Mr.
Lammie, and lat 's hear yer news."

"I cam frae Aberdeen last nicht, Mistress
Faukner," he began.

"Ye haena been hame sin' syne?" she rejoined.

"Na. I sleepit at the Boar's Heid."

"What for did ye that? What gart ye be at that expense, whan ye kent I had a bed i' the ga'le-room?"

"Weel, ye see, they're auld frien's o' mine, and I like to gang to them whan I'm i' the gait o' 't."

"Weel, they're a fine faimily, the Miss Napers. And, I wat, sin' they maun sell drink, they du 't wi' discretion. That's weel kent."

Possibly Mr. Lammie, remembering what then occurred, may have thought the discretion a little in excess of the drink, but he had other matters to occupy him now. For a few moments both were silent.

"There's been some ill news, they tell me, Mrs. Faukner," he said at length, when the silence had grown painful.

"Humph!" returned the old lady, her face becoming stony with the effort to suppress all emotion. "Nae aboot Anerew?"

"'Deed is 't, mem. An' ill news, I'm sorry to say."

"Is he ta'en?"

"Ay is he—by a jyler that winna tyne the grup."

"He's no deid, John Lammie? Dinna say 't."

"I maun say 't, Mrs. Faukner. I had it frae Dr. Anderson, yer ain cousin. He hintit at it afore, but his last letter leaves nae room to doobt upo' the subjeck. I'm unco sorry to be the beirer o' sic ill news, Mrs. Faukner, but I had nae chice."

" Ohone! Ohone! the day o' grace is by at last! My puir Anerew!" exclaimed Mrs. Falconer, and sat dumb thereafter.

Mr. Lammie tried to comfort her with some of the usual comfortless commonplaces. She neither wept nor replied, but sat with stony face staring into her lap, till, seeing that she was as one that heareth not, he rose and left her alone with her grief. A few minutes after he was gone, she rang the bell, and told Betty in her usual voice to send Robert to her.

" He's gane to the schule, mem."

" Rin efter him, an' tell him to come hame."

When Robert appeared, wondering what his grandmother could want with him, she said :

" Close the door, Robert. I canna lat ye gang to the schule the day. We maun lea' him oot noo."

" Lea' wha oot, grannie?"

" Him, him—Anerew. Yer father, laddie. I think my hert 'll brak."

" Lea' him oot o' what, grannie? I dinna unnerstan' ye."

" Lea' him oot o' oor prayers, laddie, and I canna bide it."

" What for that?"

" He's deid."

" Are ye sure?"

" Ay, ower sure—ower sure, laddie."

" Weel, I dinna believe 't."

" What for that?"

" 'Cause I winna believe 't. I'm no bund to believe 't, am I?"

" What's the gude o' that? What for no believe 't? Dr. Anderson's sent hame word o' 't to John Lammie. Och hone! och hone!"

" I tell ye I winna believe 't, grannie, 'cep' God himsel' tells me. As lang 's I dinna believe 'at he's deid, I can keep him i' my prayers. I'm no gaein' to lea' him oot, I tell ye, grannie."

" Well, laddie, I canna argue wi' ye. I hae nae hert till 't. I doobt I maun greit. Come awa'."

She took him by the hand and rose, then let him go again, saying,

" Sneck the door, laddie."

Robert bolted the door, and his grandmother again taking his hand, led him to the usual corner. There they knelt down together, and the old woman's prayer was one great and bitter cry for submission to the divine will. She rose a little strengthened, if not comforted, saying:

" Ye maun pray yer lane, laddie. But oh be a guid lad, for ye're a' that I hae left; and gin ye gang wrang tu, ye'll bring doon my gray hairs wi' sorrow to the grave. They're gray eneuch, and they're near eneuch to the grave, but gin ye turn oot weel, I'll maybe haud up my heid a bit yet. But O Anerew! my son! my son! Would God I had died for thee!"

And the words of her brother in grief, the king of Israel, opened the floodgates of her heart, and she wept. Robert left her weeping, and closed the door quietly as if his dead father had been lying in the room.

He took his way up to his own garret, closed that door too, and sat down upon the floor, with his back against the empty bedstead.

There were no more castles to build now. It was all very well to say that he would not believe the news and would pray for his father, but he did believe them—enough at least to spoil the praying. His favourite employment, seated there, had hitherto been to imagine how he would grow a great man, and set out to seek his father, and find him, and stand by him, and be his son and servant. Oh! to have the man stroke his head and pat his cheek, and love him! One moment he imagined himself his indignant defender, the next he would be climbing on his knee, as if he were still a little child, and laying his head on his shoulder. For he had had no fondling his life long, and his heart yearned for it. But all this was gone now. A dreary time lay before him, with nobody to please, nobody to serve; with nobody to praise him. Grannie never praised him. She must have thought praise something wicked. And his father was in misery, for ever and ever! Only somehow that thought was not quite thinkable. It was more the vanishing of hope from his own life than a sense of his father's fate that oppressed him.

He cast his eyes, as in a hungry despair, around the empty room—or, rather, I should have said, in that faintness which makes food at once essential and loathsome; for despair has no proper hunger in it. The room seemed as empty as his life. There was nothing for his eyes to rest upon but those bundles and bundles of dust-browned papers on the shelves before him. What were they all about? He understood that they were his father's: now that he was dead, it would be no sacrilege to look at them. Nobody cared about them. He would see at least what they were. It would be something to do in this dreariness.

Bills and receipts, and everything ephemeral —to feel the interest of which, a man must be a poet indeed—was all that met his view. Bundle after bundle he tried, with no better success. But as he drew near the middle of the second shelf, upon which they lay several rows deep, he saw something dark behind, hurriedly displaced the packets between, and drew forth a small work-box. His heart beat like that of the prince in the fairy-tale, when he comes to the door of the Sleeping Beauty. This at least

must have been hers.   It was a common little
thing, probably a childish possession, and kept
to hold trifles worth more than they looked to
be.   He opened it with bated breath.   The first
thing he saw was a half-finished reel of cotton—
a *pirn*, he called it.   Beside it was a gold
thimble.   He lifted the tray.   A lovely face in
miniature, with dark hair and blue eyes, lay
looking earnestly upward.   At the lid of this
coffin those eyes had looked for so many years!
The picture was set all round with pearls in an
oval ring.   How Robert knew them to be pearls,
he could not tell, for he did not know that he
had ever seen any pearls before, but he knew
they were pearls, and that pearls had something
to do with the New Jerusalem.   But the sadness of it all at length overpowered him, and he
burst out crying.   For it was awfully sad that
his mother's portrait should be in his own mother's box.

He took a bit of red tape off a bundle of the
papers, put it through the eye of the setting,
and hung the picture round his neck, inside his
clothes, for grannie must not see it.   She would
take that away as she had taken his fiddle.   He
had a nameless something now for which he had
been longing for years.

Looking again in the box, he found a little
bit of paper, discoloured with antiquity, as it
seemed to him, though it was not so old as him-

self. Unfolding it he found written upon it a well-known hymn, and at the bottom of the hymn, the words: "O Lord! my heart is very sore."—The treasure upon Robert's bosom was no longer the symbol of a mother's love, but of a woman's sadness, which he could not reach to comfort. In that hour, the boy made a great stride towards manhood. Doubtless his mother's grief had been the same as grannie's—the fear that she would lose her husband for ever. The hourly fresh griefs from neglect and wrong did not occur to him; only the *never never more.* He looked no farther, took the portrait from his neck and replaced it with the paper, put the box back, and walled it up in solitude once more with the dusty bundles. Then he went down to his grandmother, sadder and more desolate than ever.

He found her seated in her usual place. Her New Testament, a large-print-octavo, lay on the table beside her unopened; for where within those boards could she find comfort for a grief like hers? That it was the will of God might well comfort any suffering of her own, but would it comfort Andrew? and if there was no comfort for Andrew, how was Andrew's mother to be comforted?

Yet God had given his first-born to save his brethren: how could he be pleased that she should dry her tears and be comforted? True,

N 2

some awful unknown force of a necessity with which God could not cope came in to explain it; but this did not make God more kind, for he knew it all every time he made a man; nor man less sorrowful, for God would have his very mother forget him, or, worse still, remember him and be happy.

"Read a chapter till me, laddie," she said.

Robert opened and read till he came to the words: "I pray not for the world."

"*He* was o' the world," said the old woman; "and gin Christ wadna pray for him, what for suld I?"

Already, so soon after her son's death, would her theology begin to harden her heart. The strife which results from believing that the higher love demands the suppression of the lower, is the most fearful of all discords, the absolute love slaying love—the house divided against itself; one moment all given up for the will of Him, the next the human tenderness rushing back in a flood. Mrs. Falconer burst into a very agony of weeping. From that day for many years, the name of her lost Andrew never passed her lips in the hearing of her grandson, and certainly in that of no one else.

But in a few weeks she was more cheerful. It is one of the mysteries of humanity that mothers in her circumstances, and holding her creed, do regain not merely the faculty of going

on with the business of life, but, in most cases,
even cheerfulness. The infinite Truth, the Love
of the universe, supports them beyond their
consciousness, coming to them like sleep from
the roots of their being, and having nothing to
do with their opinions or beliefs. And hence
spring those comforting subterfuges of hope to
which they all fly. Not being able to trust the
Father entirely, they yet say: " Who can tell
what took place at the last moment? Who can
tell whether God did not please to grant them
saving faith at the eleventh hour?"—that so
they might pass from the very gates of hell,
the only place for which their life had fitted
them, into the bosom of love and purity! This
God could do for all : this for the son beloved
of his mother perhaps he might do !

O rebellious mother heart! dearer to God
than that which beats laboriously solemn under
Genevan gown or Lutheran surplice! if thou
wouldst read by thine own large light, instead
of the glimmer from the phosphorescent brains
of theologians, thou mightst even be able to understand such a simple word as that of the
Saviour, when, wishing his disciples to know
that he had a nearer regard for them as his
brethren in holier danger, than those who had
not yet partaken of his light, and therefore
praying for them not merely as human beings,
but as the human beings they were, he said to

his Father in their hearing: "I pray not for the world, but for them,"—not for the world now, but for them—a meaningless utterance, if he never prayed for the world; a word of small meaning, if it was not his very wont and custom to pray for the world—for men as men. Lord Christ! not alone from the pains of hell, or of conscience—not alone from the outer darkness of self and all that is mean and poor and low, do we fly to thee; but from the anger that arises within us at the wretched words spoken in thy name, at the degradation of thee and of thy Father in the mouths of those that claim especially to have found thee, do we seek thy feet. Pray thou for them also, for they know not what they do.

CHAPTER XIV.

MARY ST. JOHN.

AFTER this, day followed day in calm, dull, progress. Robert did not care for the games through which his schoolfellows forgot the little they had to forget, and had therefore few in any sense his companions. So he passed his time out of school in the society of his grandmother and Shargar, except that spent in the garret, and the few hours a week occupied by the lessons of the shoemaker. For he went on, though half-heartedly, with those lessons, given now upon Sandy's redeemed violin which he called his *old wife*, and made a little progress even, as we sometimes do when we least think it.

He took more and more to brooding in the garret; and as more questions presented themselves for solution, he became more anxious to arrive at the solution, and more uneasy as he failed in satisfying himself that he had arrived at it; so that his brain, which needed quiet for the true formation of its substance, as a cooling liquefaction or an evaporating solution for the just formation of its crystals, became in danger of settling into an abnormal arrangement of the cellular deposits.

I believe that even the new-born infant is, in some of his moods, already grappling with the deepest metaphysical problems, in forms infinitely too rudimental for the understanding of the grown philosopher—as far, in fact, removed from his ken on the one side, that of intelligential beginning, the germinal subjective, as his abstrusest speculations are from the final solutions of absolute entity on the other. If this be the case, it is no wonder that at Robert's age the deepest questions of his coming manhood should be in active operation, although so surrounded with the yolk of common belief and the shell of accredited authority, that the embryo faith, which, in minds like his, always takes the form of doubt, could not be defined any more than its existence could be disproved. I have given a hint at the tendency of his mind already, in the fact that one of the most definite inquiries to which he had yet turned his thoughts was, whether God would have mercy upon a repentant devil. An ordinary puzzle had been—if his father were to marry again, and it should turn out after all that his mother was not dead, what was his father to do? But this was over now. A third was, why, when he came out of church,

sunshine always made him miserable, and he
felt better able to be good when it rained or
snowed hard. I might mention the inquiry
whether it was not possible somehow to elude
the omniscience of God; but that is a common
question with thoughtful children, and indicates
little that is characteristic of the individual.
That he puzzled himself about the perpetual
motion may pass for little likewise; but one
thing which is worth mentioning, for indeed it
caused him considerable distress, was, that, in
reading the *Paradise Lost,* he could not help
sympathizing with Satan, and feeling—I do not
say thinking—that the Almighty was pompous,
scarcely reasonable, and somewhat revengeful.

He was recognized amongst his schoolfellows
as remarkable for his love of fair play; so much
so, that he was their constant referee. Add to
this that, notwithstanding his sympathy with
Satan, he almost invariably sided with his master, in regard of any angry reflection or sedi-
tious movement, and even when unjustly pun-
ished himself, the occasional result of a certain
backwardness in self-defence, never showed any
resentment—a most improbable statement, I
admit, but nevertheless true—and I think the
rest of his character may be left to the gradual
dawn of its historical manifestation.

He had long ere this discovered who the angel was that had appeared to him at the top of

the stair upon that memorable night; but he could hardly yet say that he had seen her; for, except one dim glimpse he had had of her at the window as he passed in the street, she had not appeared to him save in the vision of that night. During the whole winter she scarcely left the house, partly from the state of her health, affected by the sudden change to a northern climate, partly from the attention required by her aunt, to aid in nursing whom she had left the warmer south. Indeed, it was only to return the visits of a few of Mrs. Forsyth's chosen, that she had crossed the threshold at all; and those visits were paid at a time when all such half-grown inhabitants as Robert were gathered under the leathery wing of Mr. Innes.

But long before the winter was over, Rothieden had discovered that the stranger, the English lady, Mary St. John, outlandish, almost heathenish as her lovely name sounded in its ears, had a power as altogether strange and new as her name. For she was not only an admirable performer on the pianoforte, but such a simple enthusiast in music, that the man must have had no music or little heart in him in whom her playing did not move all that there was of the deepest.

Occasionally there would be quite a small crowd gathered at night by the window of Mrs. Forsyth's drawing-room, which was on the ground-floor, listening to music such as had never before been heard in Rothieden. More than once, when Robert had not found Sandy Elshender at home on the lesson-night, and had gone to seek him, he had discovered him lying in wait, like a fowler, to catch the sweet sounds that flew from the opened cage of her instrument. He leaned against the wall with his ear laid over the edge, and as near the window as he dared to put it, his rough face, gnarled and blotched, and hirsute with the stubble of neglected beard—his whole ursine face transfigured by the passage of the sweet sounds through his chaotic brain, which they swept like the wind of God, when of old it moved on the face of the waters that clothed the void and formless world.

"Haud yer tongue!" he would say in a hoarse whisper, when Robert sought to attract his attion; "hand yer tongue, man, and hearken. Gin yon bonny leddy 'at yer grannie keeps lockit up i' the aumry war to tak to the piano, that's jist hoo she wad play. Lord, man! pit yer sowl i' yer lugs, an' hearken."

The soutar was all wrong in this; for if old Mr. Falconer's violin had taken woman-shape, it would have been that of a slight, worn, swarthy creature, with wild black eyes, great and restless, a voice like a bird's, and thin fingers that clawed the music out of the wires like the quills of the old harpsichord; not that of Mary St. John,

who was tall, and could not help being stately,
was large and well-fashioned, as full of repose
as Handel's music, with a contralto voice to
make you weep, and eyes that would have
seemed but for their maidenliness, to be always
ready to fold you in their lucid gray depths.

Robert stared at the soutar, doubting at first
whether he had not been drinking.   But the in-
toxication of music produces such a different
expression from that of drink, that Robert saw
at once that if he had indeed been drinking, at
least the music had got above the drink.   As
long as the playing went on, Elshender was not
to be moved from the window.

But to many of the people of Rothieden the
music did not recommend the musician; for
every sort of music, except the most unmusical
of psalm-singing, was in their minds of a piece
with " dancin' an' play-actin', an' ither warldly
vainities an' abominations."   And Robert, being
as yet more capable of melody than harmony,
grudged to lose a lesson on Sandy's " auld wife
o' a fiddle " for any amount of Miss St. John's
playing.

CHAPTER XV.

ERIC ERICSON.

ONE gusty evening—it was of the last day in March—Robert well remembered both the date and the day—a bleak wind was driving up the long street of the town, and Robert was standing looking out of one of the windows in the gable-room. The evening was closing into night. He hardly knew how he came to be there, but when he thought about it he found it was play-Wednesday, and that he had been all the half-holiday trying one thing after another to interest himself withal, but in vain. He knew nothing about east winds; but not the less did this dreary wind of the dreary March world prove itself upon his soul. For such a wind has a shadow wind along with it, that blows in the minds of men. There was nothing genial, no growth in it. It killed, and killed most dogmatically. But it is an ill wind that blows nobody good. Even an east wind must bear some blessing on its ugly wings. And as Robert looked down from the gable, the wind was blowing up the street before it half a dozen footfaring students from Aberdeen, on their way home at the close of the session, probably to the farmlabours of the spring.

This was a glad sight, as that of the returning storks in Denmark. Robert knew where they would put up, sought his cap, and went out. His grandmother never objected to his going to see Miss Napier : it was in her house that the weary men would this night rest.

It was not without reason that Lord Rothie had teased his hostess about receiving foot-passengers, for to such it was her invariable custom to make some civil excuse, sending Meg or Peggy to show them over the way to the hostelry next in rank, a proceeding recognized by the inferior hostess as both just and friendly, for the good woman never thought of measuring The Star against the Boar's Head. More than one comical story had been the result of this law of the Boar's Head, unalterable almost as that of the Medes and Persians. I say *almost*, for to one class of the footfaring community the official ice about the hearts of the three women did thaw, yielding passage to a full river of hospitality and generosity; and that was the class to which these wayfarers belonged.

Well may Scotland rejoice in her universities,

for whatever may be said against their system—I have no complaint to make—they are divine in their freedom: men who follow the plough in the spring and reap the harvest in the autumn, may, and often do, frequent their sacred precincts when the winter comes—so fierce, yet so welcome—so severe, yet so blessed—opening for them the doors to yet harder toil and yet poorer fare. I fear, however, that of such there will be fewer and fewer, seeing one class which supplied a portion of them has almost vanished from the country—that class which was its truest, simplest, and noblest strength—that class which at one time rendered it something far other than a ridicule to say that Scotland was pre-eminently a God-fearing nation—I mean the class of cottars.

Of this class were some of the footfaring company. But there were others of more means than the men of this lowly origin, who either could not afford to travel by the expensive coaches, or could find none to accommodate them. Possibly some preferred to walk. However this may have been, the various groups which at the beginning and close of the session passed through Rothieden weary and footsore, were sure of a hearty welcome at the Boar's Head. And much the men needed it. Some of them would have walked between one and two hundred miles before completing their journey.

Robert made a circuit, and fleet of foot, was in Miss Napier's parlour before the travellers made their appearance on the square. When they knocked at the door, Miss Letty herself went and opened it.

"Can ye tak 's in, mem?" was on the lips of their spokesman, but Miss Letty had the first word.

"Come in, come in, gentlemen. This is the first o' ye, and ye're the mair welcome. It's like seein' the first o' the swallows. An' sic a day as ye hae had for yer lang traivel!" she went on, leading the way to her sister's parlour, and followed by all the students, of whom the one that came hindmost was the most remarkable of the group—at the same time the most weary and downcast.

Miss Napier gave them a similar welcome, shaking hands with every one of them. She knew them all but the last. To him she involuntarily showed a more formal respect, partly from his appearance, and partly that she had never seen him before. The whisky-bottle was brought out, and all partook, save still the last. Miss Lizzie went to order their supper.

"Noo, gentlemen," said Miss Letty, "wad ony o' ye like to gang an' change yer hose, and pit on a pair o' slippers?"

Several declined, saying they would wait until they had had their supper; the roads had been quite dry, &c., &c. One said he would, and another said his feet were blistered.

"Hoot awa'!"* exclaimed Miss Letty.—"Here, Peggy!" she cried, going to the door; "tak a pail o' het watter up to the chackit room. Jist ye gang up, Mr. Cameron, and Peggy 'ill see to yer feet.—Noo, sir, will *ye* gang to yer room an' mak yersel' comfortable?—jist as gin ye war at hame, for sae ye are."

She addressed the stranger thus. He replied in a low indifferent tone:

"No, thank you; I must be off again directly."

He was from Caithness, and talked no Scotch.

"'Deed, sir, ye'll do naething o' the kin'. Here ye s' bide, tho' I suld lock the door."

"Come, come, Ericson, none o' your nonsense!" said one of his fellows. "Ye ken yer feet are sae blistered ye can hardly put ane by the ither.—It was a' we cud du, mem, to get him alang the last mile."

"That s' be my business, than," concluded Miss Letty.

She left the room, and returning in a few minutes, said, as a matter of course, but with authority,

"Mr. Ericson, ye maun come wi' me."

Then she hesitated a little. Was it maiden-

* An exclamation of pitiful sympathy, inexplicable to the understanding. Thus the author covers his philological ignorance of the cross-breeding of the phrase.

liness in the waning woman of five and forty ?
It was, I believe; for how can a woman always
remember how old she is ?   If ever there was a
young soul in God's world, it was Letty Napier.
And the young man was tall and stately as a
Scandinavian chief, with a look of command,
tempered with patient endurance, in his eagle
face, for he was more like an eagle than any
other creature, and in his countenance signs of
suffering. Miss Letty seeing this, was moved,
and her heart swelled, and she grew conscious
and shy, and turning to Robert, said,

"Come up the stair wi' 's, Robert; I may
want ye."

Robert jumped to his feet.   His heart too had
been yearning towards the stranger.

As if yielding to the inevitable, Ericson rose
and followed Miss Letty.   But when they had
reached the room, and the door was shut behind
them, and Miss Letty pointed to a chair beside
which stood a little wooden tub full of hot water,
saying, "Sit ye doon there, Mr. Ericson," he
drew himself up, all but his graciously-bowed
head, and said:

"Ma'am, I must tell you that I followed the
rest in here from the very stupidity of weariness.
I have not a shilling in my pocket."

"God bless me !" said Miss Letty—and God
did bless her, I am sure—" we maun see to the
feet first.   What wad ye du wi' a shillin' gin ye

had it? Wad ye clap ane upo' ilka blister?"

Ericson burst out laughing, and sat down. But still he hesitated.

"Aff wi' yer shune, sir. Duv ye think I can wash yer feet throu ben' leather?" said Miss Letty, not disdaining to advance her fingers to a shoe-tie.

"But I'm ashamed. My stockings are all in holes."

"Weel, ye s' get a clean pair to put on the morn, an' I'll darn them 'at ye hae on, gin they be worth darnin', afore ye gang—an' what are ye sae camstairie (*unmanageable*) for? A body wad think ye had a clo'en fit in ilk ane o' thae bits o' shune o' yours. I winna promise to please yer mither wi' my darnin' though."

"I have no mother to find fault with it," said Ericson.

"Weel, a sister's waur."

"I have no sister, either."

This was too much for Miss Letty. She could keep up the bravado of humour no longer. She fairly burst out crying. In a moment more the shoes and stockings were off, and the blisters in the hot water. Miss Letty's tears dropped into the tub, and the salt in them did not hurt the feet with which she busied herself, more than was necessary, to hide them.

But no sooner had she recovered herself than she resumed her former tone.

" A shillin'! said ye? An' a' thae greedy gleds
(*kites*) o' professors to pay, that live upo' the verra
blude and banes o' sair-vroucht students! Hoo
cud ye hae a shillin' ower? Troth, it's nae wonner
ye haena ane left. An' a' the merchan's there
jist leevin' upo' ye! Lord hae a care o' 's! sic
bonnie feet!—Wi' blisters I mean. I never saw
sic a sicht o' raw puddin's in my life. Ye're no
fit to come doon the stair again."

All the time she was tenderly washing and
bathing the weary feet. When she had dressed
them and tied them up, she took the tub of water
and carried it away, but turned at the door.

" Ye'll jist mak up yer min' to bide a twa
three days," she said; " for thae feet cudna bide
to be carried, no to say to carry a weicht like you.
There's naebody to luik for ye, ye ken. An'
ye're no to come doon the nicht. I'll sen' up yer
supper. And Robert there 'll bide and keep ye
company."

She vanished; and a moment after, Peggy
appeared with a *salamander*—that is a huge poker,
ending not in a point, but a red-hot ace of spades
—which she thrust between the bars of the grate,
into the heart of a nest of brushwood. Presently
a cheerful fire illuminated the room.

Ericson was seated on one chair, with his feet
on another, his head sunk on his bosom, and his
eyes thinking. There was something about him
almost as powerfully attractive to Robert as it had

been to Miss Letty. So he sat gazing at him, and longing for a chance of doing something for him. He had reverence already, and some love, but he had never felt at all as he felt towards this man. Nor was it as the Chinese puzzlers called Scotch metaphysicians, might have represented it—a combination of love and reverence. It was the recognition of the eternal brotherhood between him and one nobler than himself—hence a lovely eager worship.

Seeing Ericson look about him as if he wanted something, Robert started to his feet.

"Is there onything ye want, Mr. Ericson?" he said, with service standing in his eyes.

"A small bundle I think I brought up with me," replied the youth.

It was not there. Robert rushed down stairs, and returned with it—a nightshirt and a hairbrush or so, tied up in a blue cotton handkerchief. This was all that Robert was able to do for Ericson that evening.

He went home and dreamed about him. He called at the Boar's Head the next morning before going to school, but Ericson was not yet up. When he called again as soon as morning-school was over, he found that they had persuaded him to keep his bed, but Miss Letty took him up to his room. He looked better, was pleased to see Robert, and spoke to him kindly. Twice yet Robert called to inquire after him that day, and once more he saw him, for he took his tea up to him.

The next day Ericson was much better, received Robert with a smile, and went out with him for a stroll, for all his companions were gone, and of some students who had arrived since, he did not know any. Robert took him to his grandmother, who received him with stately kindness. Then they went out again, and passed the windows of Captain Forsyth's house. Mary St. John was playing. They stood for a moment, almost involuntarily, to listen. She ceased.

"That's the music of the spheres," said Ericson, in a low voice, as they moved on.

"Will you tell me what that means?" asked Robert. "I 've come upon 't ower an' ower in Milton."

Thereupon Ericson explained to him what Pythagoras had taught about the stars moving in their great orbits with sounds of awful harmony, too grandly loud for the human organ to vibrate in response to their music—hence unheard of men. And Ericson spoke as if he believed it. But after he had spoken, his face grew sadder than ever ; and, as if to change the subject, he said, abruptly,—

"What a fine old lady your grandmother is, Robert !"

"Is she ?" returned Robert.

"I don't mean to say she's like Miss Letty," said Ericson. " *She's* an angel !"

A long pause followed. Robert's thoughts went roaming in their usual haunts.

"Do you think, Mr. Ericson," he said, at length, taking up the old question still floating unanswered in his mind, " do you think if a devil was to repent, God would forgive him ?"

Ericson turned and looked at him. Their eyes met. The youth wondered at the boy. He had recognized in him a younger brother, one who had begun to ask questions, calling them out into the deaf and dumb abyss of the universe.

"If God was as good as I would like him to be, the devils themselves would repent," he said, turning away.

Then he turned again, and looking down upon Robert like a sorrowful eagle from a crag over its *harried* nest, said :

"If I only knew that God was as good as— that woman, I should die content."

Robert heard words of blasphemy from the mouth of an angel, but his respect for Ericson compelled a reply.

"What woman, Mr. Ericson ?" he asked.

"I mean Miss Letty, of course."

"But surely ye dinna think God's nae as guid as she is ? Surely he 's as good as he can be. He *is* good, ye ken."

"Oh, yes. They *say* so. And then they tell you something about him that isn't good, and go on calling him good all the same. But calling anybody good doesn't make him good, you know."

"Then ye dinna believe 'at God *is* good, Mr. Ericson?" said Robert, choking with a strange mingling of horror and hope.

"I didn't say that, my boy. But to know that God was good, and fair, and kind—heartily, I mean, not half-ways, and with *ifs* and *buts*— my boy, there would be nothing left to be miserable about."

In a momentary flash of thought, Robert wondered whether this might not be his old friend, the repentant angel, sent to earth as a man, that he might have a share in the redemption, and work out his own salvation. And from this very moment the thoughts about God that had hitherto been moving in formless solution in his mind began slowly to crystallize.

The next day, Eric Ericson, not without a *piece in ae pouch* and money in another, took his way home, if home it could be called where neither father, mother, brother, nor sister awaited his return. For a season Robert saw him no more.

As often as his name was mentioned, Miss Letty's eyes would grow hazy, and as often she would make some comical remark.

"Puir fallow!" she would say, "he was ower lang-leggit for this warld."

Or again:

"Ay, he was a braw chield. But he canna live. His feet's ower sma'."

Or yet again:

"Saw ye ever sic a gowk, to mak sic a wark aboot sittin' doon an' haein' his feet washed, as gin that cost a body onything!"

CHAPTER XVI.

MR. LAMMIE'S FARM.

ONE of the first warm mornings in the beginning of summer, the boy woke early, and
lay awake, as was his custom, thinking. The
sun, in all the indescribable purity of its morning
light, had kindled a spot of brilliance just about
where his grannie's head must be lying asleep
in its sad thoughts, on the opposite side of the
partition.

He lay looking at the light. There came a
gentle tapping at his window. A long streamer
of honeysuckle, not yet in blossom, but alive
with the life of the summer, was blown by the
air of the morning against his window-pane, as
if calling him to get up and look out. He did
get up and look out.

But he started back in such haste that he fell
against the side of his bed. Within a few yards
of his window, bending over a bush, was the
loveliest face he had ever seen—the only face,
in fact, he had ever yet felt to be beautiful. For

the window looked directly into the garden of the next house : its honeysuckle tapped at his window, its sweet-peas grew against his window-sill. It was the face of the angel of that night ; but how different when illuminated by the morning sun from then, when lighted up by a chamber-candle ! The first thought that came to him was the half-ludicrous, all-fantastic idea of the shoemaker about his grandfather's violin being a woman. A vaguest dream-vision of her having escaped from his grandmother's aumrie (*store-closet*), and wandering free amidst the wind and among the flowers, crossed his mind before he had recovered sufficiently from his surprise to prevent Fancy from cutting any more of those too ridiculous capers in which she indulged at will in sleep, and as often besides as she can get away from the spectacles of old Grannie Judgment.

But the music of her revelation was not that of the violin ; and Robert vaguely felt this, though he searched no further for a fitting instrument to represent her. If he had heard the organ indeed !—but he knew no instrument save the violin : the piano he had only heard through the window. For a few moments her face brooded over the bush, and her long finely-modelled fingers travelled about it as if they were creating a flower upon it—probably they were assisting the birth or blowing of some beauty

—and then she raised herself with a lingering look, and vanished from the field of the window.

But ever after this, when the evening grew dark, Robert would steal out of the house, leaving his book open by his grannie's lamp, that its patient expansion might seem to say, "He will come back presently," and dart round the corner with quick quiet step, to hear if Miss St. John was playing. If she was not, he would return to the Sabbath stillness of the parlour, where his grandmother sat meditating or reading, and Shargar sat brooding over the freedom of the old days ere Mrs. Falconer had begun to reclaim him. There he would seat himself once more at his book—to rise again ere another hour had gone by, and hearken yet again at her window whether the stream might not be flowing now. If he found her at her instrument he would stand listening in earnest delight, until the fear of being missed drove him in : this secret too might be discovered, and this enchantress too sent, by the decree of his grandmother, into the limbo of vanities. Thus strangely did his evening life oscillate between the too peaceful negations of grannie's parlour, and the vital gladness of the unknown lady's window. And skilfully did he manage his retreats and returns, curtailing his absences with such moderation that, for a long time, they awoke no suspicion in the mind of his grandmother.

I suspect myself that the old lady thought he had gone to his prayers in the garret. And I believe she thought that he was praying for his dead father; with which most papistical, and, therefore, most unchristian observance, she yet dared not interfere, because she expected Robert to defend himself triumphantly with the simple assertion that he did not believe his father was dead. Possibly the mother was not sorry that her poor son should be prayed for, in case he might be alive after all, though she could no longer do so herself—not merely *dared not*, but persuaded herself that she *would not*. Robert, however, was convinced enough, and hopeless enough, by this time, and had even less temptation to break the twentieth commandent by praying for the dead, than his grandmother had; for with all his imaginative outgoings after his father, his love to him was as yet, compared to that father's mother's, "as moonlight unto sunlight, and as water unto wine."

Shargar would glance up at him with a queer look as he came in from these excursions, drop his head over his task again, look busy and miserable, and all would glide on as before.

When the first really summer weather came, Mr. Lammie one day paid Mrs. Falconer a second visit. He had not been able to get over the remembrance of the desolation in which he had left her. But he could do nothing for her, he thought, till it was warm weather. He was accompanied by his daughter, a woman approaching the further verge of youth, bulky and florid, and as full of tenderness as her large frame could hold. After much, and, for a long time, apparently useless persuasion, they at last believed they had prevailed upon her to pay them a visit for a fortnight. But she had only retreated within another of her defences.

"I canna leave thae twa laddies alane. They wad be up to a' mischeef."

"There's Betty to luik efter them," suggested Miss Lammie.

"Betty!" returned Mrs. Falconer, with scorn. "Betty's naething but a bairn hersel'—muckler and waur faured (*worse favoured*)."

"But what for shouldna ye fess the lads wi' ye?" suggested Mr. Lammie.

"I hae no richt to burden you wi' them."

"Weel, I hae aften wonnert what gart ye burden yersel' wi' that Shargar, as I understan' they ca' him," said Mr. Lammie.

"Jist naething but a bit o' greed," returned the old lady, with the nearest approach to a smile that had shown itself upon her face since Mr. Lammie's last visit.

"I dinna understan' that, Mistress Faukner," said Miss Lammie.

"I'm sae sure o' haein' 't back again, ye ken, —wi' interest," returned Mrs. Falconer.

"Hoo's that? His father winna con ye ony thanks for haudin' him in life."

"He that giveth to the poor lendeth to the Lord, ye ken, Miss Lammie."

"Atweel, gin ye like to lippen to that bank, nae doobt ae way or anither it 'll gang to yer accoont," said Miss Lammie.

"It wad ill become us, ony gait," said her father, "nae to gie him shelter for your sake, Mrs. Faukner, no to mention ither names, sin' it's yer wull to mak the puir lad ane o' the faimily.—They say his ain mither's run awa' an' left him."

"'Deed she's dune that."

"Can ye mak onything o' 'im?"

"He's douce eneuch. An' Robert says he does nae that ill at the schuil."

"Weel, jist fess him wi' ye. We'll hae some place or ither to put him intil, gin it suld be only a shak'-doon upo' the flure."

"Na, na. There's the schuilin'—what's to be dune wi' that?"

"They can gang i' the mornin', and get their denner wi' Betty here; and syne come hame to their fower-hoors (*four o'clock tea*) whan the schule's ower i' the efternune. 'Deed, mem, ye maun jist come for the sake o' the auld frien'-ship atween the faimilies."

"Weel, gin it maun be sae, it maun be sae," yielded Mrs. Falconer, with a sigh.

She had not left her own house for a single night for ten years. Nor is it likely she would have now given in, for immovableness was one of the most marked of her characteristics, had she not been so broken by mental suffering, that she did not care much about anything, least of all about herself.

Innumerable were the instructions in propriety of behaviour which she gave the boys in prospect of this visit. The probability being that they would behave just as well as at home, these instructions were considerably unnecessary, for Mrs. Falconer was a strict enforcer of all social rules. Scarcely less unnecessary were the directions she gave as to the conduct of Betty, who received them all in erect submission, with her hands under her apron. She ought to have been a young girl instead of an elderly woman, if there was any propriety in the way her mistress spoke to her. It proved at least her own belief in the description she had given of her to Miss Lammie.

"Noo, Betty, ye maun be dooce. An' dinna stan' at the door i' the gloamin'. An' dinna stan' claikin' an' jawin' wi' the ither lasses whan ye gang to the wall for watter. An' whan ye gang intil a chop, dinna hae them sayin' ahint yer back, as sune's yer oot again, 'She's her ain mistress by way o',' or sic like. An' min' ye hae worship wi' yersel', whan I'm nae here to

hae 't wi' ye. Ye can come benn to the parlour
gin ye like. An' there's my muckle Testament.
And dinna gie the lads a' thing they want. Gie
them plenty to ait, but no ower muckle. Fowk
suld aye lea' aff wi' an eppiteet."

Mr. Lammie brought his gig at last, and took
grannie away to Bodyfauld. When the boys
returned from school at the dinner-hour, it was
to exult in a freedom which Robert had never
imagined before. But even he could not know
what a relief it was to Shargar to eat without
the awfully calm eyes of Mrs. Falconer watching, as it seemed to him, the progress of every
mouthful down that capacious throat of his.
The old lady would have been shocked to learn
how the imagination of the ill-mothered lad interpreted her care over him, but she would not
have been surprised to know that the two were
merry in her absence. She knew that, in some
of her own moods, it would be a relief to think
that that awful eye of God was not upon her.
But she little thought that even in the lawless
proceedings about to follow, her Robert, who
now felt such a relief in her absence, would be
walking straight on, though blindly, towards a
sunrise of faith, in which he would know that
for the eye of his God to turn away from him
for one moment would be the horror of the outer
darkness.

Merriment, however, was not in Robert's

thoughts, and still less was mischief. For the
latter, whatever his grandmother might think,
he had no capacity. The world was already
too serious, and was soon to be too beautiful
for mischief. After that, it would be too sad,
and then, finally, until death, too solemn glad.
The moment he heard of his grandmother's intended visit, one wild hope and desire and intent had arisen within him.

When Betty came to the parlour-door to lay
the cloth for their dinner, she found it locked.

"Open the door!" she cried, but cried in vain.
From impatience she passed to passion; but it
was of no avail: there came no more response
than from the shrine of the deaf Baal. For to
the boys it was an opportunity not at any risk
to be lost. Dull Betty never suspected what
they were about. They were ranging the place
like two tiger-cats whose whelps had been carried off in their absence—questing, with nose to
earth and tail in air, for the scent of their enemy. My simile has carried me too far: it was
only a dead old gentleman's violin that a couple
of boys was after—but with what eagerness,
and, on the part of Robert, what alternations of
hope and fear! And Shargar was always the
reflex of Robert, so far as Shargar could reflect
Robert. Sometimes Robert would stop, stand
still in the middle of the room, cast a mathematical glance of survey over its cubic contents,

and then dart off in another inwardly suggested direction of search. Shargar, on the other hand, appeared to rummage blindly without a notion of casting the illumination of thought upon the field of search. Yet to him fell the success. When hope was growing dim, after an hour and a half of vain endeavour, a scream of utter discordance heralded the resurrection of the lady of harmony. Taught by his experience of his wild mother's habits to guess at those of *douce* Mrs. Falconer, Shargar had found the instrument in her bed at the foot, between the feathers and the mattress. For one happy moment Shargar was the benefactor, and Robert the grateful recipient of favour. Nor, I do believe, was this thread of the still thickening cable that bound them ever forgotten : broken it could not be.

Robert drew the recovered treasure from its concealment, opened the case with trembling eagerness, and was stooping, with one hand on the neck of the violin, and the other on the bow, to lift them from it, when Shargar stopped him.

His success had given him such dignity, that for once he dared to act from himself.

" Betty 'ill hear ye," he said.

" What care I for Betty ? She daurna tell. I ken hoo to manage her."

" But wadna 't be better 'at she didna ken ?"

" She's sure to fin' oot whan she mak's the

bed. She turns't ower and ower jist like a muckle tyke (*dog*) worryin' a rottan *(rat)*."

" De'il a bit o' her s' be a hair wiser ! Ye dinna play tunes upo' the boxie, man."

Robert caught at the idea. He lifted the " bonny leddy " from her coffin ; and while he was absorbed in the contemplation of her risen beauty, Shargar laid his hands on Boston's *Four-fold State*, the torment of his life on the Sunday evenings which it was his turn to spend with Mrs. Falconer, and threw it as an offering to the powers of Hades into the case, which he then buried carefully, with the feather-bed for mould, the blankets for sod, and the counterpane studiously arranged for stone, over it. He took heed, however, not to let Robert know of the substitution of Boston for the fiddle, because he knew Robert could not tell a lie. Therefore, when he murmured over the volume some of its own words which he had read the preceding Sunday, it was in a quite inaudible whisper : " Now is it good for nothing but to cumber the ground, and furnish fuel for Tophet."

Robert must now hide the violin better than his grannie had done, while at the same time it was a more delicate necessity, seeing it had lost its shell, and he shrunk from putting her in the power of the shoemaker again. It cost him much trouble to fix on the place that was least unsuitable. First he put it into the well of the clock-case, but instantly bethought him what the awful consequence would be if one of the weights should fall from the gradual decay of its cord. He had heard of such a thing happening. Then he would put it into his own place of dreams and meditations. But what if Betty should take a fancy to change her bed? or some friend of his grannie's should come to spend the night? How would the bonny leddy like it? What a risk she would run! If he put her under the bed, the mice would get at her strings—nay, perhaps knaw a hole right through her beautiful body. On the top of the clock, the brass eagle with outspread wings might scratch her, and there was not space to conceal her. At length he concluded—wrapped her in a piece of paper, and placed her on the top of the chintz tester of his bed, where there was just room between it and the ceiling: that would serve till he bore her to some better sanctuary. In the meantime she was safe, and the boy was the blessedest boy in creation.

These things done, they were just in the humour to have a lark with Betty. So they unbolted the door, rang the bell, and when Betty appeared, red-faced and wrathful, asked her very gravely and politely whether they were not going to have some dinner before they went back to school: they had now but twenty minutes left. Betty was so *dumfoundered* with

their impudence that she could not say a word.
She did make haste with the dinner, though,
and revealed her indignation only in her manner of putting the things on the table. As the
boys left her, Robert contented himself with the
single hint:

"Betty, Bodyfauld's i' the perris o' Kettle-
drum. Min' ye that."

Betty *glowered* and said nothing.

But the delight of the walk of three miles
over hill and dale and moor and farm to Mr.
Lammie's! The boys, if not as wild as colts—
that is, as wild as most boys would have been
—were only the more deeply excited. That
first summer walk, with a goal before them, in
all the freshness of the perfecting year, was
something which to remember in after days
was to Falconer nothing short of ecstasy. The
westering sun threw long shadows before them
as they trudged away eastward, lightly laden
with the books needful for the morrow's lessons. Once beyond the immediate purlieus of
the town and the various plots of land occupied
by its inhabitants, they crossed a small river,
and entered upon a region of little hills, some
covered to the top with trees, chiefly larch,
others cultivated, and some bearing only
heather, now nursing in secret its purple flame
for the outburst of the autumn. The road
wound between, now swampy and worn into

deep ruts, now sandy and broken with large
stones. Down to its edge would come the
dwarfed oak, or the mountain ash, or the silver
birch, single and small, but lovely and fresh;
and now green fields, fenced with walls of
earth as green as themselves, or of stones overgrown with moss, would stretch away on both
sides, sprinkled with busily feeding cattle. Now
they would pass through a farm-steading, per-
fumed with the breath of cows, and the odour
of burning peat—so fragrant! though not yet
so grateful to the inner sense as it would be
when encountered in after years and in foreign
lands. For the smell of burning and the smell
of earth are the deepest underlying sensuous
bonds of the earth's unity, and the common
brotherhood of them that dwell thereon. Now
the scent of the larches would steal from the
hill, or the wind would waft the odour of the
white clover, beloved of his grandmother, to
Robert's nostrils, and he would turn aside to
pull her a handful. Then they clomb a high
ridge, on the top of which spread a moorland,
dreary and desolate, brightened by nothing
save " the canna's hoary beard " waving in the
wind, and making it look even more desolate
from the sympathy they felt with the forsaken
grass. This crossed, they descended between
young plantations of firs and rowan-trees and
birches, till they reached a warm house on the

side of the slope, with farm-offices and ricks of
corn and hay all about it, the front overgrown
with roses and honeysuckle, and a white-flower-
ing plant unseen of their eyes hitherto, and
therefore full of mystery. From the open kitchen-door came the smell of something good.
But beyond all to Robert was the welcome of
Miss Lammie, whose small fat hand closed upon
his like a very love-pudding, after partaking of
which even his grandmother's stately reception,
followed immediately by the words "Noo be
dooce," could not chill the warmth in his bosom.

I know but one writer whose pen would have
been able worthily to set forth the delights of
the first few days at Bodyfauld—Jean Paul.
Nor would he have disdained to make the gladness of a country school-boy the theme of that
pen. Indeed, often has he done so. If the
writer has any higher purpose than the amusement of other boys, he will find the life of a
country boy richer for his ends than that of a
town boy. For example, he has a deeper sense
of the marvel of nature, a tenderer feeling of
her feminality. I do not mean that the other
cannot develope this sense, but it is generally
feeble, and there is consequently less chance of
its surviving. As far as my experience goes,
town girls and country boys love nature most.
I have known town girls love her as passionately as country boys. Town boys have too

many books and pictures. They see Nature in
mirrors—invaluable privilege *after they know herself, not before.* They have greater opportunity
of observing human nature; but here also *the
books* are too many and various. They are
cleverer than country boys, but they are less
profound; their observation may be quicker;
their perception is shallower. They know better
what to do on an emergency; they know worse
how to order their ways. Of course, in this, as
in a thousand other matters, Nature will burst
out laughing in the face of the would-be philosopher, and bringing forward her town boy,
will say, " Look here !" For the town boys are
Nature's boys after all, at least so long as doc-
trines of self-preservation and ambition have not
turned them from children of the kingdom into
dirt-worms. But I must stop, for I am getting
up to the neck in a bog of discrimination. As
if I did not know the nobility of some townspeople, compared with the worldliness of some
country folk ! I give it up. We are all good
and all bad. God mend all. Nothing will do
for Jew or Gentile, Frenchman or Englishman,
Negro or Circassian, town boy or country boy,
but the kingdom of heaven which is within him,
and must come thence to the outside of him.

To a boy like Robert the changes of every
day, from country to town with the gay morning, from town to country with the sober even-

ing—for country as Rothieden might be to Edinburgh, much more was Bodyfauld country to Rothieden—were a source of boundless delight. Instead of houses, he saw the horizon; instead of streets or walled gardens, he roamed over fields bathed in sunlight and wind. Here it was good to get up before the sun, for then he could see the sun get up. And of all things those evening shadows lengthening out over the grassy wildernesses—for fields of a very moderate size appeared such to an imagination ever ready at the smallest hint to ascend its solemn throne—were a deepening marvel. Town to country is what a ceiling is to a cælum.

CHAPTER XVII.

ADVENTURES.

GRANNIE'S first action every evening, the moment the boys entered the room, was to glance up at the clock, that she might see whether they had arrived in reasonable time. This was not pleasant, because it admonished Robert how impossible it was for him to have a lesson on his own violin so long as the visit to Bodyfauld lasted. If they had only been allowed to sleep at Rothieden, what a universe of freedom would have been theirs! As it was, he had but two hours to himself, pared at both ends, in the middle of the day. Dooble Sanny might have given him a lesson at that time, but he did not dare to carry his instrument through the streets of Rothieden, for the proceeding would be certain to come to his grandmother's ears. Several days passed indeed before he made up his mind as to how he was to reap any immediate benefit from the recovery of the violin. For after he had made up his mind to

run the risk of successive mid-day *solos* in the
old factory—he was not prepared to carry the
instrument through the streets, or be seen entering the place with it.

But the factory lay at the opposite corner of
a quadrangle of gardens, the largest of which
belonged to itself; and the corner of this garden
touched the corner of Captain Forsyth's, which
had formerly belonged to Andrew Falconer:
he had had a door made in the walls at the
point of junction, so that he could go from his
house to his business across his own property:
if this door were not locked, and Robert could
pass without offence, what a north-west passage
it would be for him! The little garden belonging to his grandmother's house had only a slight
wooden fence to divide it from the other, and
even in this fence there was a little gate: he
would only have to run along Captain Forsyth's
top-walk to reach the door. The blessed
thought came to him as he lay in bed at Bodyfauld: he would attempt the passage the very
next day.

With his violin in its paper under his arm, he
sped like a hare from gate to door, found it not
even latched, only pushed-to and rusted into
such rest as it was dangerous to the hinges to
disturb. He opened it, however, without any
accident, and passed through; then closing it
behind him, took his way more leisurely through

the tangled grass of his grandmother's property.
When he reached the factory, he judged it prudent to search out a more secret nook, one more
full of silence, that is, whence the sounds would
be less certain to reach the ears of the passers-
by, and came upon a small room, near the top,
which had been the manager's bedroom, and
which, as he judged from what seemed the signs
of ancient occupation, a cloak hanging on the
wall, and the ashes of a fire lying in the grate,
nobody had entered for years : it was the safest
place in the world. He undid his instrument
carefully, tuned its strings tenderly, and soon
found that his former facility, such as it was,
had not ebbed away beyond recovery. Hasten-
ing back as he came, he was just in time for his
dinner, and narrowly escaped encountering
Betty in the transe. He had been tempted to
leave the instrument, but no one could tell what
might happen, and to doubt would be to be
miserable with anxiety.

He did the same for several days without in-
terruption—not, however, without observation.
When, returning from his fourth visit, he opened
the door between the gardens, he started back
in dismay, for there stood the beautiful lady.

Robert hesitated for a moment whether to fly
or speak. He was a Lowland country boy, and
therefore rude of speech, but he was three parts
a Celt, and those who know the address of the

Irish or of the Highlanders, know how much that involves as to manners and bearing. He advanced the next instant and spoke.

"I beg yer pardon, mem. I thoucht naebody wad see me. I haena dune nae ill."

"I had not the least suspicion of it, I assure you," returned Miss St. John. "But, tell me, what makes you go through here always at the same hour with the same parcel under your arm?"

"Ye winna tell naebody—will ye, mem, gin I tell you?"

Miss St. John, amused, and interested besides in the contrast between the boy's oddly noble face and good bearing on the one hand, and on the other the drawl of his bluntly articulated speech and the coarseness of his tone, both seeming to her in the extreme of provincialism, promised; and Robert, entranced by all the qualities of her voice and speech, and nothing disenchanted by the nearer view of her lovely face, confided in her at once.

"Ye see, mem," he said, "I cam upo' my grandfather's fiddle. But my grandmither thinks the fiddle's no gude. And sae she tuik an' she hed it. But I faun' 't again. An' I daurna play i' the hoose, though my grannie 's i' the country, for Betty hearin' me and tellin' her. And sae I gang to the auld fact'ry there. It belangs to my grannie, and sae does the yaird

(*garden*). An' this hoose an' yaird was ance my
father's, and sae he had that door throu, they
tell me. An' I thocht gin it suld be open, it wad
be a fine thing for me, to haud fowk ohn seen me.
But it was verra ill-bred to you, mem, I ken, to
to come throu your yaird ohn speirt leave. I
beg yer pardon, mem, an' I'll jist gang back, an'
roon' by the ro'd. This is my fiddle I hae
aneath my airm. We bude to pit back the case
o' 't whaur it was afore, i' my grannie's bed,
to haud her ohn kent 'at she had tint the grup
o' 't."

Certainly Miss St. John could not have understood the half of the words Robert used, but she
understood his story notwithstanding. Herself
an enthusiast in music, her sympathies were at
once engaged for the awkward boy who was
thus trying to steal an entrance into the fairy
halls of sound. But she forbore any further allusion to the violin for the present, and contented herself with assuring Robert that he was
heartily welcome to go through the garden as
often as he pleased. She accompanied her words
with a smile that made Robert feel not only
that she was the most beautiful of all princesses
in fairy-tales, but that she had presented him
with something beyond price in the most self-
denying manner. He took off his cap, thanked
her with much heartiness, if not with much
polish, and hastened to the gate of his grand-

mother's little garden. A few years later such an encounter might have spoiled his dinner : I have to record no such evil result of the adventure.

With Miss St. John, music was the highest form of human expression, as must often be the case with those whose feeling is much in advance of their thought, and to whom, therefore, what may be called mental sensation is the highest known condition. Music to such is poetry in solution, and generates that infinite atmosphere, common to both musician and poet, which the latter fills with shining worlds.—But if my reader wishes to follow out for himself the idea herein suggested, he must be careful to make no confusion between those who feel musically or think poetically, and the musician or the poet. One who can only play the music of others, however exquisitely, is not a musician, any more than one who can read verse to the satisfaction, or even expound it to the enlightenment of the poet himself, is therefore a poet.—When Miss St. John would worship God, it was in music that she found the chariot of fire in which to ascend heavenward. Hence music was the divine thing in the world for her; and to find any one loving music humbly and faithfully was to find a brother or sister believer. But she had been so often disappointed in her expectations from those she took to be such, that of late she had become less sanguine. Still there was something about this boy that roused once more her musical hopes ; and, however she may have restrained herself from the full indulgence of them, certain it is that the next day, when she saw Robert pass, this time leisurely, along the top of the garden, she put on her bonnet and shawl, and, allowing him time to reach his den, followed him, in the hope of finding out whether or not he could play. I do not know what proficiency the boy had attained, very likely not much, for a man can feel the music of his own bow, or of his own lines, long before any one else can discover it. He had already made a path, not exactly worn one, but trampled one, through the neglected grass, and Miss St. John had no difficulty in finding his entrance to the factory.

She felt a little *eerie*, as Robert would have called it, when she passed into the waste silent place ; for besides the wasteness and the silence, motionless machines have a look of death about them, at least when they bear such signs of disuse as those that filled these rooms. Hearing no violin, she waited for a while in the ground-floor of the building ; but still hearing nothing, she ascended to the first-floor. Here, likewise, all was silence. She hesitated, but at length ventured up the next stair, beginning, however, to feel a little troubled as well as *eerie*, the silence

was so obstinately persistent. Was it possible
that there was no violin in that brown paper?
But that boy could not be a liar. Passing shelves
piled-up with stores of old thread, she still went
on, led by a curiosity stronger than her gathering fear. At last she came to a little room, the
door of which was open, and there she saw
Robert lying on the floor with his head in a pool
of blood.

Now Mary St. John was both brave and kind;
and, therefore, though not insensible to the fact
that she too must be in danger where violence
had been used to a boy, she set about assisting
him at once. His face was deathlike, but she
did not think he was dead. She drew him out
into the passage, for the room was close, and
did all she could to recover him; but for some
time he did not even breathe. At last his lips
moved, and he murmured:

"Sandy, Sandy, ye've broken my bonnie
leddy."

Then he opened his eyes, and seeing a face to
dream about bending in kind consternation over
him, closed them again with a smile and a sigh,
as if to prolong his dream.

The blood now came fast into his forsaken
cheeks, and began to flow again from the wound
in his head. The lady bound it up with her
handkerchief. After a little he rose, though
with difficulty, and stared wildly about him, say-

ing, with imperfect articulation, "Father! father!" Then he looked at Miss St. John with a kind of dazed inquiry in his eyes, tried several times to speak, and could not.

"Can you walk at all?" asked Miss St. John, supporting him, for she was anxious to leave the place.

"Yes, mem, weel eneuch," he answered.

"Come along, then. I will help you home."

"Na, na," he said as if he had just recalled something. "Dinna min' me. Rin hame, mem, or he'll see ye!"

"Who will see me?"

Robert stared more wildly, put his hand to his head, and made no reply. She half led, half supported him down the stair, as far as the first landing, when he cried out in a tone of anguish:

"My bonnny leddy!"

"What is it?" asked Miss St. John, thinking he meant her.

"My fiddle! my fiddle! She'll be a' in bits," he answered, and turned to go up again.

"Sit down here," said Miss St. John, "and I'll fetch it."

Though not without some tremor, she darted back to the room. Then she turned faint for the first time, but determinedly supporting herself, she looked about, saw a brown-paper parcel on a shelf, took it, and hurried out with a shudder.

Q 2

Robert stood leaning against the wall. He stretched out his hands eagerly.

"Gie me her. Gie me her."

"You had better let me carry it. You are not able."

"Na, na, mem. Ye dinna ken hoo easy she is to hurt."

"Oh, yes, I do!" returned Miss St. John, smiling, and Robert could not withstand the smile.

"Weel, tak care o' her, as ye wad o' yer ain sel', mem," he said, yielding.

He was now much better, and before he had been two minutes in the open air, insisted that he was quite well. When they reached Captain Forsyth's garden he again held out his hands for his violin.

"No, no," said his new friend. "You wouldn't have Betty see you like that, would you?"

"No, mem; but I'll put in the fiddle at my ain window, and she sanna hae a chance o' seein' 't," answered Robert, not understanding her; for though he felt a good deal of pain, he had no idea what a dreadful appearance he presented.

"Don't you know that you have a wound on your head?" asked Miss St. John.

"Na! hev I?" said Robert, putting up his hand. "But I maun gang—there's nae help for 't," he added.—"Gin I cud only win to my ain room ohn Betty seen me!—Eh! mem, I hae blaudit (*spoiled*) a' yer bonny goon. That's a sair vex."

"Never mind it," returned Miss St. John, smiling. "It is of no consequence. But you must come with me. I must see what I can do for your head. Poor boy!"

"Eh, mem! but ye *are* kin'! Gin ye speik like that ye'll gar me greit. Naebody ever spak' to me like that afore. Maybe ye kent my mamma. Ye 're sae like her."

This word *mamma* was the only remnant of her that lingered in his speech. Had she lived he would have spoken very differently. They were now walking towards the house.

"No, I did not know your mamma. Is she dead?"

"Lang syne, mem. And sae they tell me is yours."

"Yes; and my father too. Your father is alive, I hope?"

Robert made no answer. Miss St. John turned.

The boy had a strange look, and seemed struggling with something in his throat. She thought he was going to faint again, and hurried him into the drawing-room. Her aunt had not yet left her room, and her uncle was out.

"Sit down," she said—so kindly—and Robert sat down on the edge of a chair. Then she left the room, but presently returned with a little brandy. "There," she said, offering the glass, "that will do you good."

"What is 't, mem?"

"Brandy. There's water in it, of course."

"I daurna touch 't. Granrfie cudna bide me to touch 't."

So determined was he, that Miss St. John was forced to yield. Perhaps she wondered that the boy who would deceive his grandmother about a violin should be so immovable in regarding her pleasure in the matter of a needful medicine. But in this fact I begin to see the very Falconer of my manhood's worship.

"Eh, mem! gin ye wad play something upo' *her*," he resumed, pointing to the piano, which, although he had never seen one before, he at once recognized, by some hidden mental operation, as the source of the sweet sounds heard at the window, "it wad du me mair guid than a haill bottle o' brandy, or whusky either."

"How do you know that?" asked Miss St. John, proceeding to sponge the wound.

"'Cause mony's the time I hae stud oot there i' the street, hearkenin'. Dooble Sanny says 'at ye play jist as gin ye war my gran'father's fiddle hersel', turned into the bonniest cratur ever God made."

"How did you get such a terrible cut?"

She had removed the hair, and found that the injury was severe.

The boy was silent. She glanced round in his face. He was staring as if he saw nothing, heard nothing. She would try again.

"Did you fall? Or how did you cut your head?"

"Yes, yes, mem, I fell," he answered, hastily, with an air of relief, and possibly with some tone of gratitude for the suggestion of a true answer.

"What made you fall?"

Utter silence again. She felt a kind of *turn*— I do not know another word to express what I mean: the boy must have fits, and either could not tell, or was ashamed to tell, what had befallen him. Thereafter she too was silent, and Robert thought she was offended. Possibly he felt a change in the touch of her fingers.

"Mem, I *wad* like to tell ye," he said, "but I daurna."

"Oh! never mind," she returned kindly.

"Wad ye promise nae to tell *nae*body?"

"I don't want to know," she answered, confirmed in her suspicion, and at the same time ashamed of the alteration of feeling which the discovery had occasioned.

An uncomfortable silence followed, broken by Robert.

"Gin ye binna pleased wi' me, mem," he said, "I canna bide ye to gang on wi' siccan a job 's that."

How Miss St. John could have understood him, I cannot think ; but she did.

"Oh! very well," she answered smiling. " Just as you please. Perhaps you had better take this piece of plaster to Betty, and ask her to finish the dressing for you."

Robert took the plaster mechanically, and, sick at heart and speechless, rose to go, forgetting even his *bonny leddy* in his grief.

" You had better take your violin with you," said Miss St. John, urged to the cruel experiment by a strong desire to see what the strange boy would do.

He turned. The tears were streaming down his odd face. They went to her heart, and she was bitterly ashamed of herself.

" Come along. Do sit down again. I only wanted to see what you would do. I am very sorry," she said, in a tone of kindness such as Robert had never imagined.

He sat down instantly, saying :

" Eh, mem! it's sair to bide ;" meaning, no doubt, the conflict between his inclination to tell her all, and his duty to be silent.

The dressing was soon finished, his hair combed down over it, and Robert looking once more respectable.

" Now, I think that will do," said his nurse.

"Eh, thank ye, mem!" answered Robert, rising. "Whan I'm able to play upo' the fiddle as weel 's ye play upo' the piana, I'll come and play at yer window ilka nicht, as lang 's ye like to hearken."

She smiled, and he was satisfied. He did not dare again ask her to play to him. But she said of herself, "Now I will play something to you, if you like," and he resumed his seat devoutly.

When she had finished a lovely little air, which sounded to Robert like the touch of her hands, and her breath on his forehead, she looked round, and was satisfied, from the rapt expression of the boy's countenance, that at least he had plenty of musical sensibility. As if despoiled of volition, he stood motionless till she said:

"Now you had better go, or Betty will miss you."

Then he made her a bow in which awkwardness and grace were curiously mingled, and taking up his precious parcel, and holding it to his bosom as if it had been a child for whom he felt an access of tenderness, he slowly left the room and the house.

Not even to Shargar did he communicate his adventure. And he went no more to the deserted factory to play there. Fate had again interposed between him and his bonny leddy.

When he reached Bodyfauld he fancied his grandmother's eyes more watchful of him than

usual, and he strove the more to resist the weariness, and even faintness, that urged him to go
to bed.   Whether he was able to hide as well a
certain trouble that clouded his spirit I doubt.
His wound he did manage to keep a secret,
thanks to the care of Miss St. John, who had
dressed it with court-plaster.

When he woke the next morning, it was with
the consciousness of having seen something
strange the night before, and only when he
found that he was not in his own room at his
grandmother's, was he convinced that it must
have been a dream and no vision.   For in the
night, he had awaked there as he thought, and
the moon was shining with such clearness, that
although it did not shine into his room, he could
see the face of the clock, and that the hands
were both together at the top.   Close by the
clock stood the bureau, with its end against the
partition forming the head of his grannie's bed.

All at once he saw a tall man, in a blue coat
and bright buttons, about to open the lid of the
bureau. The same moment he saw a little elderly man in a brown coat and a brown wig, by his
side, who sought to remove his hand from the
lock.   Next appeared a huge stalwart figure, in
shabby old tartans, and laid his hand·on the
head of each.   But the wonder widened and
grew; for now came a stately Highlander with
his broadsword by his side, and an eagle's

feather in his bonnet, who laid his hand on the other Highlander's arm.

When Robert looked in the direction whence this last had appeared, the head of his grannie's bed had vanished, and a wild hill-side, covered with stones and heather, sloped away into the distance. Over it passed man after man, each with an ancestral air, while on the gray sea to the left, gallies covered with Norsemen, tore up the white foam, and dashed one after the other up to the strand. How long he gazed, he did not know, but when he withdrew his eyes from the extended scene, there stood the figure of his father, still trying to open the lid of the bureau, his grandfather resisting him, the blind piper with his hand on the head of both, and the stately chief with his hand on the piper's arm. Then a mist of forgetfulness gathered over the whole, till at last he awoke and found himself in the little wooden chamber at Bodyfauld, and not in the visioned room. Doubtless his loss of blood the day before had something to do with the dream or vision, whichever the reader may choose to consider it. He rose, and after a good breakfast, found himself very little the worse, and forgot all about his dream, till a circumstance which took place not long after recalled it vividly to his mind.

The enchantment of Bodyfauld soon wore off. The boys had no time to enter into the full enjoy-

ment of country ways, because of those weary
lessons, over the *getting* of which Mrs. Falconer
kept as strict a watch as ever; while to Robert
the evening journey, his violin and Miss St. John
left at Rothieden, grew more than tame. The
return was almost as happy an event to him as
the first going. Now he could resume his lessons with the soutar.

With Shargar it was otherwise. The freedom
for so much longer from Mrs. Falconer's eyes
was in itself so much of a positive pleasure, that
the walk twice a day, the fresh air, and the
scents and sounds of the country, only came in
as supplementary. But I do not believe the boy
even then had so much happiness as when he
was beaten and starved by his own mother. And
Robert, growing more and more absorbed in his
own thoughts and pursuits, paid him less and
less attention as the weeks went on, till Shargar at length judged it for a time an evil day
on which he first had slept under old Ronald
Falconer's kilt.

CHAPTER XVIII.

NATURE PUTS IN A CLAIM.

BEFORE the day of return arrived, Robert had taken care to remove the violin from his bedroom, and carry it once more to its old retreat in Shargar's garret. The very first evening, however, that grannie again spent in her own armchair, he hied from the house as soon as it grew dusk, and made his way with his brown-paper parcel to Sandy Elshender's.

Entering the narrow passage from which his shop door opened, and hearing him hammering away at a sole, he stood and unfolded his treasure, then drew a low sigh from her with his bow, and awaited the result. He heard the lapstone fall thundering on the floor, and, like a spider from his cavern, Dooble Sandy appeared in the door, with the *bend*-leather in one hand, and the hammer in the other.

" Lordsake, man ! hae ye gotten her again ? Gie's a grup o' her !" he cried, dropping leather and hammer.

" Na, na," returned Robert, retreating towards the outer door. " Ye maun sweir upo' *her* that, whan I want her, I sall hae her ohn demur, or I sanna lat ye lay roset upo' her."

" I swear 't, Robert; I sweir 't upo' *her*," said the soutar hurriedly, stretching out both his hands as if to receive some human being into his embrace.

Robert placed the violin in those grimy hands. A look of heavenly delight dawned over the hirsute and dirt-besmeared countenance, which drooped into tenderness as he drew the bow across the instrument, and wiled from her a thin wail as of sorrow at their long separation. He then retreated into his den, and was soon sunk in a trance, deaf to everything but the violin, from which no entreaties of Robert, who longed for a lesson, could rouse him; so that he had to go home grievously disappointed, and unrewarded for the risk he had run in venturing the stolen visit.

Next time, however, he fared better; and he contrived so well that, from the middle of June to the end of August, he had two lessons a week, mostly upon the afternoons of holidays. For these his master thought himself well paid by the use of the instrument between. And Robert made great progress.

Occasionally he saw Miss St. John in the garden, and once or twice met her in the town; but

her desire to find in him a pupil had been greatly quenched by her unfortunate conjecture as to
the cause of his accident. She had, however,
gone so far as to mention the subject to her
aunt, who assured her that old Mrs. Falconer
would as soon consent to his being taught gam-
bling as music. The idea, therefore, passed
away; and beyond a kind word or two when she
met him, there was no further communication
between them. But Robert would often dream
of waking from a swoon, and finding his head
lying on her lap, and her lovely face bending
over him full of kindness and concern.

By the way, Robert cared nothing for poetry.
Virgil was too troublesome to be enjoyed; and
in English he had met with nothing but the
dried leaves and gum-flowers of the last century.
Miss Letty once lent him *The Lady of the Lake*;
but before he had read the first canto through,
his grandmother laid her hands upon it, and,
without saying a word, dropped it behind a
loose skirting-board in the pantry, where the
mice soon made it a ruin sad to behold. For Miss
Letty, having heard from the woful Robert of
its strange disappearance, and guessing its
cause, applied to Mrs. Falconer for the volume;
who forthwith, the tongs aiding, extracted it
from its hole, and, without shade of embarrassment, held it up like a drowned kitten before the
eyes of Miss Letty, intending thereby, no doubt,

to impress her with the fate of all seducing
spirits that should attempt an entrance into her
kingdom : Miss Letty only burst into merry
laughter over its fate. So the lode of poetry failed for the present from Robert's life. Nor did it
matter much ; for had he not his violin ?

I have, I think, already indicated that his
grandfather had been a linen manufacturer. Although that trade had ceased, his family had still
retained the bleachery belonging to it, commonly called the *bleachfield*, devoting it now to the
service of those large calico manufactures which
had ruined the trade in linen, and to the whiten-
ing of such yarn as the country housewives still
spun at home, and the webs they got woven of it
in private looms. To Robert and Shargar it was
a wondrous pleasure when the pile of linen which
the week had accumulated at the office under
the gale-room, was on Saturday heaped high upon
the base of a broad-wheeled cart, to get up on it
and be carried to the said bleachfield, which lay
along the bank of the river. Soft-laid and high-
borne, gazing into the blue sky, they traversed
the streets in a holiday triumph ; and although,
once arrived, the manager did not fail to get
some labour out of them, yet the store of amusement was endless. The great wheel, which drove
the whole machinery ; the plash-mill, or, more
properly, wauk-mill—a word Robert derived
from the resemblance of the mallets to two huge

feet, and of their motion to walking—with the water plashing and squirting from the blows of their heels; the beatles thundering in *arpeggio* upon the huge cylinder round which the white cloth was wound—each was haunted in its turn and season. The pleasure of the water itself was inexhaustible. Here sweeping in a mass along the race; there divided into branches and hurrying through the walls of the various houses; here sliding through a wooden channel across the floor to fall into the river in a half-concealed cataract, there bubbling up through the bottom of a huge wooden cave or vat, there resting placid in another; here gurgling along a spout; there flowing in a narrow canal through the green expanse of the well-mown bleachfield, or lifted from it in narrow curved wooden scoops, like fairy canoes with long handles, and flung in showers over the outspread yarn—the water was an endless delight.

It is strange how some individual broidery or figure upon nature's garment will delight a boy long before he has ever looked nature in the face, or begun to love herself. But Robert was soon to become dimly conscious of a life within these things—a life not the less real that its operations on his mind had been long unrecognized.

On the grassy bank of the gently-flowing river, at the other edge of whose level the little canal squabbled along, and on the grassy brae

which rose immediately from the canal, were
stretched, close beside each other, with scarce a
stripe of green betwixt, the long white webs of
linen, fastened down to the soft mossy ground
with wooden pegs, whose tops were twisted into
their edges. Strangely would they billow in the
wind sometimes, like sea-waves, frozen and enchanted flat, seeking to rise and wallow in the
wind with conscious depth and whelming mass.
But generally they lay supine, saturated with
light and its cleansing power.   Falconer's jubilation in the white and green of a little boat, as
we lay, one bright morning, on the banks of the
Thames between Richmond and Twickenham,
led to such a description of the bleachfield that
I can write about it as if I had known it myself.

One Saturday afternoon in the end of July,
when the westering sun was hotter than at mid-
day, he went down to the lower end of the field,
where the river was confined by a dam, and
plunged from the bank into deep water. After
a swim of half an hour, he ascended the higher
part of the field, and lay down upon a broad
web to bask in the sun.   In his ears was the
hush rather than rush of the water over the dam,
the occasional murmur of a belt of trees that
skirted the border of the field, and the dull
continuous sound of the beatles at their work
below, like a persistent growl of thunder on the
horizon.

Had Robert possessed a copy of *Robinson Crusoe,* or had his grandmother not cast the *Lady of the Lake,* mistaking it for an idol, if not to the moles and the bats, yet to the mice and the black-beetles, he might have been lying reading it, blind and deaf to the face and the voice of nature, and years might have passed before a response awoke in his heart. It is good that children of faculty, as distinguished from capacity, should not have too many books to read, or too much of early lessoning. The increase of examinations in our country will increase its capacity and diminish its faculty. We shall have more compilers and reducers, and fewer thinkers; more modifiers and completers, and fewer inventors.

He lay gazing up into the depth of the sky, rendered deeper and bluer by the masses of white cloud that hung almost motionless below it, until he felt a kind of bodily fear lest he should fall off the face of the round earth into the abyss. A gentle wind, laden with pine-odours from the sun-heated trees behind him, flapped its light wing in his face: the humanity of the world smote his heart; the great sky towered up over him, and its divinity entered his soul; a strange longing after something "he knew not nor could name" awoke within him, followed by the pang of a sudden fear that there was no such thing as that which he sought, that it was

all a fancy of his own spirit; and then the voice
of Shargar broke the spell, calling to him from
afar to come and see a great salmon that lay
by a stone in the water. But once aroused, the
feeling was never stilled; the desire never left
him; sometimes growing even to a passion that
was relieved only by a flood of tears.

Strange as it may sound to those who have
never thought of such things save in connection
with Sundays and Bibles and churches and ser-
mons, that which was now working in Falconer's
mind was the first dull and faint movement of
the greatest need that the human heart possesses
—the need of the God-Man. There must be
truth in the scent of that pine wood: some one
must mean it. There must be a glory in those
heavens that depends not upon our imagination:
some power greater than they must dwell in
them. Some spirit must move in that wind
that haunts us with a kind of human sorrow;
some soul must look up to us from the eye of
that starry flower. It must be something human, else not to us divine.

Little did Robert think that such was his
need—that his soul was searching after One
whose form was constantly presented to him,
but as constantly obscured and made unlovely
by the words without knowledge spoken in the
religious assemblies of the land; that he was
longing without knowing it on the Saturday for

that from which on the Sunday he would be repelled without knowing it. Years passed before he drew nigh to the knowledge of what he
sought.

For weeks the mood broken by the voice
of his companion did not return, though the
forms of nature were henceforth full of a pleasure he had never known before. He loved the
grass; the water was more gracious to him;
he would leave his bed early, that he might
gaze on the clouds of the east, with their borders gold-blasted with sunrise; he would linger
in the fields that the amber and purple, and
green and red, of the sunset, might not escape
after the sun unseen. And as long as he felt
the mystery, the revelation of the mystery lay
before and not behind him.

And Shargar—had he any soul for such
things? Doubtless; but how could he be other
than lives behind Robert? For the latter had
ancestors—that is, he came of people with a
mental and spiritual history; while the former had
been born the birth of an animal; of a *noble* sire,
whose family had for generations filled the
earth with fire, famine, slaughter, and licentious-
ness; and of a wandering outcast mother, who
blindly loved the fields and woods, but retained
her affection for her offspring scarcely beyond
the period while she suckled them. The love
of freedom and of wild animals that she had

given him, however, was far more precious than
any share his male ancestor had born in his
mental constitution. After his fashion he as
well as Robert enjoyed the sun and the wind
and the water and the sky ; but he had sympathies with the salmon and the rooks and the
wild rabbits even stronger than those of Robert.

CHAPTER XIX.

ROBERT STEALS HIS OWN.

THE period of the *hairst-play*, that is, of the harvest holiday time, drew near, and over the north of Scotland thousands of half-grown hearts were beating with glad anticipation. Of the usual devices of boys to cheat themselves into the half-belief of expediting a blessed approach by marking its rate, Robert knew nothing: even the notching of sticks was unknown at Rothieden; but he had a mode notwithstanding. Although indifferent to the games of his schoolfellows, there was one amusement, a solitary one nearly, and *therein* not so good as most amusements, into which he entered with the whole energy of his nature: it was kite-flying. The moment that the *hairst-play* approached near enough to strike its image through the eyes of his mind, Robert proceeded to make his kite, or *draigon*, as he called it. Of how many pleasures does pocket-money deprive the unfortunate possessor! What is the going into a

shop and buying what you want, compared with
the gentle delight of hours and days filled with
gaining effort after the attainment of your end?
Never boy that bought his kite, even if the
adornment thereafter lay in his own hands, and
the pictures were gorgeous with colour and gilding, could have half the enjoyment of Robert
from the moment he went to the coopers to ask
for an old gird, or hoop, to the moment when
he said, " Noo, Shargar !" and the kite rose
slowly from the depth of the aërial flood. The
hoop was carefully examined, the best portion
cut away from it, that pared to a light strength,
its ends confined to the proper curve by a string,
and then away went Robert to the *wright's* shop.
There a slip of wood, of proper length and
thickness, was readily granted to his request,
free as the daisies of the field. Oh! those horrid town conditions, where nothing is given for
the asking, but all sold for money! In Robert's
kite the only thing that cost money was the
string to fly it with, and that the grandmother
willingly provided, for not even her ingenuity
could discover any evil, direct or implicated, in
kite-flying. Indeed, I believe the old lady felt
not a little sympathy with the exultation of the
boy when he saw his kite far aloft, diminished
to a speck in the vast blue ; a sympathy, it may
be, rooted in the religious aspirations which she
did so much at once to rouse and to suppress in

the bosom of her grandchild. But I have not yet reached the kite-flying, for I have said nothing of the kite's tail, for the sake of which principally I began to describe the process of its growth.

As soon as the body of the dragon was completed, Robert attached to its spine the string which was to take the place of its caudal elongation, and at a proper distance from the body joined to the string the first of the cross-pieces of folded paper which in this animal represent the continued vertebral processes. Every morning, the moment he issued from his chamber, he proceeded to the garret where the monster lay, to add yet another joint to his tail, until at length the day should arrive when, the lessons over for a blessed eternity of five or six weeks, he would tip the whole with a piece of wood, to which grass, *quantum suff.*, might be added from the happy fields.

Upon this occasion the dragon was a monster one. With a little help from Shargar, he had laid the skeleton of a six-foot specimen, and had carried the body to a satisfactory completion.

The tail was still growing, having as yet only sixteen joints, when Mr. Lammie called with an invitation for the boys to spend their holidays with him. It was fortunate for Robert that he was in the room when Mr. Lammie presented his petition, otherwise he would never have heard of it till the day of departure arrived, and would thus have lost all the delights of anticipation. In frantic effort to control his ecstasy, he sped to the garret, and with trembling hands tied the second joint of the day to the tail of the dragon—the first time he had ever broken the law of its accretion. Once broken, that law was henceforth an object of scorn, and the tail grew with frightful rapidity. It was indeed a great dragon. And none of the paltry fields about Rothieden should be honoured with its first flight, but from Bodyfauld should the majestic child of earth ascend into the regions of upper air.

My reader may here be tempted to remind me that Robert had been only too glad to return to Rothieden from his former visit. But I must in my turn remind him that the circumstances were changed. In the first place, the fiddle was substituted for grannie; and in the second, the dragon for the school.

The making of this dragon was a happy thing for Shargar, and a yet happier thing for Robert, in that it introduced again for a time some community of interest between them. Shargar was happier than he had been for many a day because Robert used him; and Robert was yet happier than Shargar in that his conscience, which had reproached him for his neglect of him, was now silent. But not even his dragon

had turned aside his attentions from his violin;
and many were the consultations between the
boys as to how best she might be transported
to Bodyfaud, where endless opportunities of
holding communion with her would not be wanting. The difficulty was only how to get her
clear of Rothieden.

The play commenced on a Saturday; but not
till the Monday were they to be set at liberty.
Wearily the hours of mental labour and bodily
torpidity which the Scotch called the Sabbath
passed away, and at length the millennial morning dawned. Robert and Shargar were up before the sun. But strenuous were the efforts
they made to suppress all indications of excitement, lest grannie, fearing the immoral influence
of gladness, should give orders to delay their
departure for an awfully indefinite period, which
might be an hour, a day, or even a week. Horrible conception! Their behaviour was so de-
corous that not even a hinted threat escaped
the lips of Mrs. Falconer.

They set out three hours before noon, carrying the great kite, and Robert's school-bag, of
green baize, full of sundries: a cart from Bodyfauld was to fetch their luggage later in the
day. As soon as they were clear of the houses,
Shargar lay down behind a dyke with the kite,
and Robert set off at full speed for Dooble Sanny's shop, making a half-circuit of the town to

avoid the chance of being seen by granny or
Betty. Having given due warning before, he
found the brown paper parcel ready for him,
and carried it off in fearful triumph. He joined
Shargar in safety, and they set out on their
journey as rich and happy a pair of tramps as
ever tramped, having six weeks of their own in
their pockets to spend and not spare.

A hearty welcome awaited them, and they
were soon revelling in the glories of the place,
the first instalment of which was in the shape of
curds and cream, with oatcake and butter, as
much as they liked. After this they would
"e'en to it like French falconers" with their kite,
for the wind had been blowing bravely all the
morning, having business to do with the harvest. The season of stubble not yet arrived,
they were limited to the pasturage and moorland, which, however, large as their kite was,
were spacious enough. Slowly the great-headed
creature arose from the hands of Shargar, and
ascended about twenty feet, when, as if seized
with a sudden fit of wrath or fierce indignation,
it turned right round and dashed itself with
headlong fury to the earth, as if sooner than
submit to such influences a moment longer it
would beat out its brains at once.

"It hasna half tail eneuch," cried Robert.
"It's queer 'at things winna gang up ohn hauden
them doon. Pu' a guid han'fu' o' clover, Shar-

gar. She's had her fa', an' noo she'll gang up
a' richt. She's nane the waur o' 't."

Upon the next attempt, the kite rose triumphantly. But just as it reached the length of
the string it shot into a faster current of air,
and Robert found himself first dragged along
in spite of his efforts, and then lifted from his
feet. After carrying him a few yards, the dragon
broke its string, dropped him in a ditch, and,
drifting away, went fluttering and waggling
downwards in the distance.

"Luik whaur she gangs, Shargar," cried Robert, from the ditch.

Experience coming to his aid, Shargar took
landmarks of the direction in which it went; and
ere long they found it with its tail entangled in
the topmost branches of a hawthorn-tree, and its
head beating the ground at its foot. It was at
once agreed that they would not fly it again till
they got some stronger string.

Having heard the adventure, Mr. Lammie
produced a shilling from the pocket of his cordu-
roys, and gave it to Robert to spend upon the
needful string. He resolved to go to the town
the next morning and make a grand purchase
of the same. During the afternoon he roamed
about the farm with his hands in his pockets,
revolving if not many memories, yet many questions, while Shargar followed like a pup at the
heels of Miss Lammie, to whom, during his for-

mer visit, he had become greatly attached.

In the evening, resolved to make a confidant
of Mr. Lammie, and indeed to cast himself upon
the kindness of the household generally, Robert
went up to his room to release his violin from
its prison of brown paper. What was his dismay to find—not his bonny leddy, but her poor
cousin, the soutar's auld wife ! It was too bad.
Dooble Sanny indeed !

He first stared, then went into a rage, and
then came out of it to go into a resolution. He
replaced the unwelcome fiddle in the parcel, and
came down stairs gloomy and still wrathful, but
silent. The evening passed over, and the inhabitants of the farmhouse went early to bed.
Robert tossed about fuming on his. He had not
undressed.

About eleven o'clock, after all had been still
for more than an hour, he took his shoes in one
hand and the brown parcel in the other, and
descending the stairs like a thief, undid the
quiet wooden bar that secured the door, and let
himself out. All was darkness, for the moon
was not yet up, and he felt a strange sensation
of ghostliness in himself—awake and out of
doors, when he ought to be asleep and unconscious in bed. He had never been out so late
before, and felt as if walking in the region of the
dead, existing when and where he had no business to exist. For it was the time Nature kept

for her own quiet, and having once put her children to bed—hidden them away with the world wiped out of them—enclosed them in her ebony box, as George Herbert says—she did not expect to have her hours of undress and meditation intruded upon by a venturesome school-boy. Yet she let him pass. He put on his shoes and hurried to the road. He heard a horse stamp in the stable, and saw a cat dart across the corn-yard as he went through. Those were all the signs of life about the place.

It was a cloudy night and still. Nothing was to be heard but his own footsteps. The cattle in the fields were all asleep. The larch and spruce-trees on the top of the hill by the foot of which his road wound were still as clouds. He could just see the sky through their stems. It was washed with the faintest of light, for the moon, far below, was yet climbing towards the horizon. A star or two sparkled where the clouds broke, but so little light was there, that, until he had passed the moorland on the hill, he could not get the horror of moss-holes, and deep springs covered with treacherous green, out of his head. But he never thought of turning. When the fears of the way at length fell back and allowed his own thoughts to rise, the sense of a presence, or of something that might grow to a presence, was the first to awake in him. The stillness seemed to be thinking all around his head. But the way grew so dark, where it lay through a corner of the pine-wood, that he had to feel the edge of the road with his foot to make sure that he was keeping upon it, and the sense of the silence vanished. Then he passed a farm, and the motions of horses came through the dark, and a doubtful crow from a young inexperienced cock, who did not yet know the moon from the sun. Then a sleepy low in his ear startled him, and made him quicken his pace involuntarily.

By the time he reached Rothieden all the lights were out, and this was just what he wanted.

The economy of Dooble Sanny's abode was this: the outer door was always left on the latch at night, because several families lived in the house; the soutar's workshop opened from the passage, close to the outer door, therefore its door was locked; but the key hung on a nail just inside the soutar's bedroom. All this Robert knew.

Arrived at the house, he lifted the latch, closed the door behind him, took off his shoes once more, like a housebreaker, as indeed he was, although a righteous one, and felt his way to and up the stair to the bed-room. There was a sound of snoring within. The door was a little ajar. He reached the key and descended, his heart beating more and more wildly as he ap-

proached the realization of his hopes. Gently
as he could he turned it in the lock. In a moment more he had his hands on the spot where
the shoemaker always laid his violin. But his
heart sank within him: there was no violin
there. A blank of dismay held him both motionless and thoughtless; nor had he recovered his
senses before he heard footsteps, which he well
knew, approaching in the street. He slunk at
once into a corner. Elshender entered, feeling
his way carefully, and muttering at his wife.
He was tipsy, most likely, but that had never
yet interfered with the safety of his fiddle: Robert heard its faint echo as he laid it gently
down. Nor was he too tipsy to lock the door
behind him, leaving Robert incarcerated amongst
the old boots and leather and rosin.

For one moment only did the boy's heart fail
him. The next he was in action, for a happy thought
had already struck him. Hastily, that he might
forestall sleep in the brain of the soutar, he undid his parcel, and after carefully enveloping his
own violin in the paper, took the old wife of the
soutar, and proceeded to perform upon her a
trick which in a merry moment his master had
taught him, and which, not without some feeling
of irreverence, he had occasionally practised upon
his own bonny lady.

The shoemaker's room was overhead; its thin
floor of planks was the ceiling of the workshop.

Ere Dooble Sanny was well laid by the side of
his sleeping wife, he heard a frightful sound
from below, as of some one tearing his beloved
violin to pieces. No sound of rending coffin-
planks or rising dead would have been so horrible in the ears of the soutar. He sprang from
his bed with a haste that shook the crazy tene-
ment to its foundation.

The moment Robert heard that, he put the
violin in its place, and took his station by the
door-cheek. The soutar came tumbling down the
stair, and rushed at the door, but found that he
had to go back for the key. When, with uncertain hand, he had opened at length, he went
straight to the nest of his treasure, and Robert
slipping out noiselessly, was in the next street
before Dooble Sanny, having found the fiddle
uninjured, and not discovering the substitution,
had finished concluding that the whisky and his
imagination had played him a very discourteous
trick between them, and retired once more to bed.
And not till Robert had cut his foot badly with
a piece of glass, did he discover that he had left
his shoes behind him. He tied it up with his
handkerchief, and limped home the three miles,
too happy to think of consequences.

Before he had gone far, the moon floated up
on the horizon, large, and shaped like the broad-
side of a barrel. She stared at him in amazement to see him out at such a time of the night.

But he grasped his violin and went on. He had
no fear now, even when he passed again over
the desolate moss, although he saw the stag-
nant pools glimmering about him in the moonlight. And ever after this he had a fancy for
roaming at night. He reached home in safety,
found the door as he had left it, and ascended
to his bed, triumphant in his fiddle.

In the morning bloody prints were discovered
on the stair, and traced to the door of his room.
Miss Lammie entered in some alarm, and found
him fast asleep on his bed, still dressed, with a
brown-paper parcel in his arms, and one of his
feet evidently enough the source of the frightful
stain. She was too kind to wake him, and inquiry was postponed till they met at breakfast,
to which he descended bare-footed, save for a
handkerchief on the injured foot.

"Robert, my lad," said Mr. Lammie, kindly,
"hoo cam ye by that bluidy fut?"

Robert began the story, and, guided by a few
questions from his host, at length told the tale
of the violin from beginning to end, omitting
only his adventure in the factory. Many a
guffaw from Mr. Lammie greeted its progress,
and Miss Lammie laughed till the tears rolled
unheeded down her cheeks, especially when
Shargar, emboldened by the admiration Robert
had awakened, imparted his private share in the
comedy, namely, the entombment of Boston in

s 2

a fifth-fold state; for the Lammies were none of the *unco guid* to be censorious upon such exploits. The whole business advanced the boys in favour at Bodyfauld; and the entreaties of Robert that nothing should reach his grandmother's ears were entirely unnecessary.

After breakfast Miss Lammie dressed the wounded foot. But what was to be done for shoes, for Robert's Sunday pair had been left at home? Under ordinary circumstances it would have been no great hardship to him to go barefoot for the rest of the autumn, but the cut was rather a serious one. So his feet were cased in a pair of Mr. Lammie's Sunday boots, which, from their size, made it so difficult for him to get along, that he did not go far from the doors, but revelled in the company of his violin in the corn-yard amongst last year's ricks, in the barn, and in the hayloft, playing all the tunes he knew, and trying over one or two more from a very dirty old book of Scotch airs, which his teacher had lent him.

In the evening, as they sat together after supper, Mr. Lammie said:

"Weel, Robert hoo 's the fiddle?"

"Fine, I thank ye, sir," answered Robert.

"Lat 's hear what ye can do wi' 't."

Robert fetched the instrument and complied.

"That's no that ill," remarked the farmer. "But eh! man, ye suld hae heard yer gran'-fa-

ther han'le the bow. That *was* something to
hear—ance in a body's life. Ye wad hae jist
thoucht the strings had been drawn frae his ain
inside, he kent them sae weel, and han'led them
sae fine. He jist fan' *(felt)* them like wi' 's fingers throu' the bow an' the horsehair an' a', an'
a' the time he was drawin' the soun' like the
sowl frae them, an' they jist did onything 'at he
likit. Eh! to hear him play the Flooers o' the
Forest wad hae garred ye greit."

"Cud my father play?" asked Robert.

"Ay, weel eneuch for *him.* He could du onything he likit to try, better nor middlin'. I
never saw sic a man. He played upo' the bag-
pipes, an' the flute, an' the bugle, an' I kenna
what a'; but a'thegither they cam na within
sicht o' his father upo' the auld fiddle. Lat 's
hae a luik at her."

He took the instrument in his hands reverent-
ly, turned it over and over, and said:

"Ay, ay; it's the same auld mull, an' I wat
it grun' *(ground)* bonny meal.—That sma' crater
noo 'ill be worth a hunner poun', I s' warran',"
he added, as he restored it carefully into Robert's hands, to whom it was honey and spice
to hear his bonny lady paid her due honours.
"Can ye play the Flooers o' the Forest, no?" he
added yet again.

"Ay can I," answered Robert, with some
pride, and laid the bow on the violin, and play-

ed the air through without blundering a single
note.

" Weel, that 's verra weel," said Mr. Lammie.
" But it 's nae mair like as yer gran'father played it, than gin there war twa sawyers at it, ane
at ilka lug o' the bow, wi' the fiddle atween
them in a saw-pit."

Robert's heart sank within him; but Mr. Lammie went on :

" To hear the bow croudin' *(cooing)*, an wailin', an' greitin' ower the strings, wad hae jist
garred ye see the lands o' braid Scotlan' wi' a'
the lasses greitin' for the lads that lay upo' reid
Flodden side ; lasses to cut, and lasses to gether,
and lasses to bin', and lasses to stook, and lasses
to lead, and no a lad amo' them a'. It 's jist
the murnin' o' women, doin' men's wark as
weel 's their ain, for the men that suld hae been
there to du 't ; and I s' warran' ye, no a word
to the orra *(exceptional, over-all)* lad that didna
gang wi' the lave *(rest)*."

Robert had not hitherto understood it—this
wail of a pastoral and ploughing people over
those who had left their side to return no more
from the field of battle.   But Mr. Lammie's description of his grandfather's rendering laid hold
of his heart.

" I wad raither be grutten for nor kissed,"
said he, simply.

" Haud ye to that, my lad," returned Mr.

Lammie. " Lat the lasses greit for ye gin they
like; but haud oot ower frae the kissin'. I wadna mell wi' 't."

" Hoot, father, dinna put sic nonsense i' the
bairns' heids," said Miss Lammie.

" Whilk 's the nonsense, Aggy ?" asked her
father, slily. " But I doobt," he added, " he'll
never play the Flooers o' the Forest as it suld
be playt, till he's had a taste o' the kissin', lass."

" Weel, it's a queer instructor o' yowth, 'at
says an' onsays i' the same breith."

" Never ye min'. I haena contradickit mysel'
yet; for I hae *said* naething. But, Robert, my
man, ye maun pit mair sowl into yer fiddlin'.
Ye canna play the fiddle till ye can gar 't greit.
It's unco ready to that o' 'ts ain sel'; an' it's my
opingon that there's no anither instrument but
the fiddle fit to play the Flooers o' the Forest
upo', for that very rizzon, in a' his Maijesty's
dominions.—My father playt the fiddle, but no
like your gran'father."

Robert was silent. He spent the whole of
the next morning in reiterated attempts to alter
his style of playing the air in question, but in
vain—as far at least as any satisfaction to himself was the result. He laid the instrument
down in despair, and sat for an hour disconsolate upon the bedside. His visit had not as yet
been at all so fertile in pleasure as he had anti-
cipated. He could not fly his kite; he could

not walk.; he had lost his shoes; Mr. Lammie had not approved of his playing; and, although he had his will of the fiddle, he could not get his will out of it. He could never play so as to please Miss St. John. Nothing but manly pride kept him from crying. He was sorely disappointed and dissatisfied; and the world might be dreary even at Bodyfauld.

Few men can wait *upon* the bright day in the midst of the dull one. Nor can many men even wait *for* it.

CHAPTER XX.

JESSIE HEWSON.

THE wound on Robert's foot festered, and had not yet healed when the sickle was first put to the barley. He hobbled out, however, to the reapers, for he could not bear to be left alone with his violin, so dreadfully oppressive was the knowledge that he could not use it after its nature. He began to think whether his incapacity was not a judgment upon him for taking it away from the soutar, who could do so much more with it, and to whom, consequently, it was so much more valuable. The pain in his foot, likewise, had been very depressing; and but for the kindness of his friends, especially of Miss Lammie, he would have been altogether "a weary wight forlorn."

Shargar was happier than ever he had been in his life. His white face hung on Miss Lammie's looks, and haunted her steps from spence (*store-room, as in Devonshire*) to milk-house, and from milk-house to chessel, surmounted by the

glory of his red hair, which a farm-servant de-
clared he had once mistaken for a fun-buss
(*whin-bush*) on fire. This day she had gone to
the field to see the first handful of barley cut,
and Shargar was there, of course.

It was a glorious day of blue and gold, with
just wind enough to set the barley-heads a talking. But, whether from the heat of the sun, or
the pain of his foot operating on the general discouragement under which he laboured,
Robert turned faint all at once, and dragged
himself away to a cottage on the edge of the
field.

It was the dwelling of a cottar, whose family
had been settled upon the farm of Bodyfauld
from time immemorial. They were, indeed,
like other cottars, a kind of feudal dependents,
occupying an acre or two of the land, in return
for which they performed certain stipulated labour, called *cottar-wark*. The greater part of
the family was employed in the work of the
farm, at the regular wages.

Alas for Scotland that such families are now
to seek! Would that the parliaments of our
country held such a proportion of noble-minded
men as was once to be found in the clay huts
on a hill-side, or grouped about a central farm,
huts whose wretched look would move the pity
of many a man as inferior to their occupants as
a King Charles's lap-dog is to a shepherd's col-

ley. The utensils of their life were mean enough:
the life itself was often *elixir vitœ*—a true family life, looking up to the high, divine life.
But well for the world that such life has been
scattered over it, east and west, the seed of
fresh growth in new lands. Out of offence to
the individual, God brings good to the whole; for
he pets no nation, but trains it for the perfect
globular life of all nations—of his world—of his
universe. As he makes families mingle, to redeem each from its family selfishness, so will he
make nations mingle, and love and correct and
reform and develop each other, till the planet-
world shall go singing through space one harmony to the God of the whole earth. The excellence must vanish from one portion, that it
may be diffused through the whole. The seed
ripens on one favoured mound, and is scattered
over the plain. We console ourselves with the
higher thought, that if Scotland is worse, the
world is better. Yea, even they by whom the
offence came, and who have first to reap the
woe of that offence, because they did the will of
God to satisfy their own avarice in laying land
to land and house to house, shall not reap their
punishment in having their own will, and
standing therefore alone in the earth when the
good of their evil deeds returns upon it; but
the tears of men that ascended to heaven in the
heat of their burning dwellings shall descend in

the dew of blessing even on the hearts of them
that kindled the fire.—" Something too much of
this."

Robert lifted the latch, and walked into the
cottage. It was not quite so strange to him as
it would be to most of my readers; still, he had
not been in such a place before. A girl who
was stooping by the small peat fire on the
hearth looked up, and, seeing that he was lame,
came across the heights and hollows of the clay
floor to meet him. Robert spoke so faintly that
she could not hear.

" What's yer wull?" she asked; then, changing her tone—" Eh! ye're no weel," she said.
" Come in to the fire. Tak' a haud o' me, and
come yer wa's butt."

She was a pretty, indeed graceful girl of
about eighteen, with the elasticity rather than
undulation of movement which distinguishes
the peasant from the city girl. She led him to
the chimla-lug (*the ear of the chimney*), carefully
levelled a wooden chair to the inequalities of
the floor, and said:

" Sit ye doon. Will I fess a drappy o' milk?"

" Gie me a drink o' water, gin ye please," said
Robert.

She brought it. He drank, and felt better.
A baby woke in a cradle on the other side of
the fire, and began to cry. The girl went and
took him up; and then Robert saw what she

was like. Light-brown hair clustered about a delicately-coloured face and hazel eyes. Later in the harvest her cheeks would be ruddy—now they were peach-coloured. A white neck rose above a pink print jacket, called a wrapper; and the rest of her visible dress was a blue petticoat. She ended in pretty, brown bare feet. Robert liked her, and began to talk. If his imagination had not been already filled, he would have fallen in love with her, I dare say, at once; for, except Miss St. John, he had never seen anything he thought so beautiful. The baby cried now and then.

"What ails the bairnie?" he asked.

"Ow, it's jist cuttin' it's teeth. Gin it greits muckle, I maun jist tak' it oot to my mither. She'll sune quaiet it. Are ye haudin' better?"

"Hoot ay. I'm a' richt noo. Is yer mither shearin'?"

"Na. She's gatherin'. The shearin' 's some sair wark for her e'en noo. I suld hae been shearin', but my mither wad fain hae a day o' the hairst. She thocht it wad du her gude. But I s' warran' a day o' 't 'll sair (*satisfy*) her, and I s' be at it the morn. She's been unco dowie (*ailing*) a' the summer; and sae has the bairnie."

"Ye maun hae had a sair time o' 't, than."

"Ay, some. But I aye got some sleep. I jist tuik the towie (*string*) into the bed wi' me, and whan the bairnie grat, I waukit, an' rockit it till 't fell asleep again. But whiles naething wad du but tak him till 's mammie."

All the time she was hushing and fondling the child, who went on fretting when not actually crying.

"Is he yer brither, than?" asked Robert.

"Ay, what ither? I maun tak him, I see. But ye can sit there as lang 's ye like; and gin ye gang afore I come back, jist turn the key i' the door to lat onybody ken that there's naebody i' the hoose."

Robert thanked her, and remained in the shadow by the chimney, which was formed of two smoke-browned planks fastened up the wall, one on each side, and an inverted wooden funnel above to conduct the smoke through the roof. He sat for some time gloomily gazing at a spot of sunlight which burned on the brown clay floor. All was still as death. And he felt the white-washed walls even more desolate than if they had been smoke-begrimed.

Looking about him, he found over his head something which he did not understand. It was as big as the stump of a great tree. Apparently it belonged to the structure of the cottage, but he could not, in the imperfect light, and the dazzling of the sun-spot at which he had been staring, make out what it was, or how it came to be up there—unsupported as far as he could see. He rose to examine it, lifted a bit of tarpaulin which hung before it, and found a rickety box, suspended by a rope from a great nail in the wall. It had two shelves in it full of books.

Now, although there were more books in Mr. Lammie's house than in his grandmother's, the only one he had found that in the least enticed him to read, was a translation of George Buchanan's *History of Scotland*. This he had begun to read faithfully, believing every word of it, but had at last broken down at the fiftieth king or so. Imagine, then, the moon that arose on the boy when, having pulled a ragged and thumb-worn book from among those of James Hewson the cottar, he, for the first time, found himself in the midst of the *Arabian Nights*. I shrink from all attempt to set forth in words the rainbow-coloured delight that coruscated in his brain. When Jessie Hewson returned, she found him seated where she had left him, so buried in his volume that he did not lift his head when she entered.

" Ye hae gotten a buik," she said.

" Ay have I," answered Robert decisively.

"It's a fine buik, that. Did ye ever see 't afore?"

" Na, never."

" There's three wolums o' 't about, here and there," said Jessie ; and with the child on one arm, she proceeded with the other hand to search for them in the *crap o' the wa'*, that is, on the top of the wall where the rafters rest.

There she found two or three books, which, after examining them, she placed on the dresser beside Robert.

"There's nane o' them there," she said; "but maybe ye wad like to luik at that anes."

Robert thanked her, but was too busy to feel the least curiosity about any book in the world but the one he was reading. He read on, heart and soul and mind absorbed in the marvels of the eastern skald; the stories told in the streets of Cairo, amidst gorgeous costumes, and camels, and white-veiled women, vibrating here in the heart of a Scotch boy, in the darkest corner of a mud cottage, at the foot of a hill of cold-loving pines, with a barefooted girl and a baby for his companions.

But the pleasure he had been having was of a sort rather to expedite than to delay the subjective arrival of dinner-time. There was, however, happily no occasion to go home in order to appease his hunger; he had but to join the men and women in the barley-field: there was sure to be enough, for Miss Lammie was at the head of the commissariat.

When he had had as much milk-porridge as he could eat, and a good slice of swack (*elastic*) cheese with a cap (*wooden bowl*) of ale, all of which he consumed as if the good of them lay in the haste of their appropriation, he hurried back to the cottage, and sat there reading the

Arabian Nights, till the sun went down in the orange-hued west, and the gloamin' came, and with it the reapers, John and Elspet Hewson, and their son George, to their supper and early bed.

John was a cheerful, rough, Roman-nosed, black-eyed man, who took snuff largely, and was not careful to remove the traces of the habit. He had a loud voice, and an original way of regarding things, which, with his vivacity, made every remark sound like the proclamation of a discovery.

" Are ye there, Robert ?" said he, as he entered. Robert rose, absorbed and silent.

"He's been here a'day, readin' like a colliginer," said Jessie.

"What are ye readin' sae eident *(diligent),* man?" asked John.

" A buik o' stories, here," answered Robert, carelessly, shy of being supposed so much engrossed with them as he really was.

I should never expect much of a young poet who was not rather ashamed of the distinction which yet he chiefly coveted. There is a modesty in all young delight. It is wild and shy, and would hide itself, like a boy's or maiden's first love, from the gaze of the people. Something like this was Robert's feeling over the *Arabian Nights.*

"Ay," said John, taking snuff from a small

bone spoon, "it's a gran' buik that. But my son Charley, him 'at 's deid an' gane hame, wad hae tellt ye it was idle time readin' that, wi' sic a buik as that ither lyin' at yer elbuck."

He pointed to one of the books Jessie had taken from the *crap o' the wa'* and laid down beside him on the well-scoured dresser. Robert took up the volume and opened it. There was no title-page.

"*The Tempest?*" he said. "What is 't? Poetry?"

"Ay is 't. It's Shackspear."

"I hae heard o' *him*," said Robert. "What was he?"

"A player kin' o' a chiel', wi' an unco sicht o' brains," answered John. "He cudna hae had muckle time to gang skelpin' and sornin' aboot the country like maist o' thae cattle, gin he vrote a' that, I'm thinkin'."

"Whaur did he bide?"

"Awa' in Englan'—maistly aboot Lonnon, I'm thinkin'. That's the place for a' by-ordinar fowk, they tell me."

"Hoo lang is 't sin he deid?"

"I dinna ken. A hunner year or twa, I s' warran'. It's a lang time. But I'm thinkin' fowk than was jist something like what they are noo. But I ken unco little aboot him, for the prent 's some sma', and I'm some ill for losin' my characters, and sae I dinna win that far benn wi' him. Geordie there 'll tell ye mair aboot him."

But George Hewson had not much to communicate, for he had but lately landed in Shakspere's country, and had got but a little way inland yet. Nor did Robert much care, for his head was full of the *Arabian Nights*. This, however, was his first introduction to Shakspere.

Finding himself much at home, he stopped yet a while, shared in the supper, and resumed his seat in the corner when the book was brought out for worship. The iron lamp, with its wick of rush-pith, which hung against the side of the chimney, was lighted, and John sat down to read. But as his eyes and the print, too, had grown a little dim with years, the lamp was not enough, and he asked for a " fir-can'le." A splint of fir dug from the peat-bog was handed to him. He lighted it at the lamp, and held it in his hand over the page. Its clear resinous flame enabled him to read a short psalm. Then they sang a most wailful tune, and John prayed. If I were to give the prayer as he uttered it, I might make my reader laugh, therefore I abstain, assuring him only that, although full of long words—amongst the rest, *aspiration* and *ravishment*—the prayer of the cheerful, joke-loving cottar contained evidence of a degree of religious development rare, I doubt, amongst bishops.

When Robert left the cottage, he found the sky

partly clouded and the air cold. The nearest way home was across the barley-stubble of the day's reaping, which lay under a little hill covered with various species of the pine. His own soul, after the restful day he had spent, and under the reaction from the new excitement of the stories he had been reading, was like a quiet, moonless night. The thought of his mother came back upon him, and her written words, "O Lord, my heart is very sore;" and the thought of his father followed that, and he limped slowly home, laden with mournfulness. As he reached the middle of the field, the wind was suddenly there with a low *sough* from out of the north-west. The heads of barley in the sheaves leaned away with a soft rustling from before it; and Robert felt for the first time the sadness of a harvest-field. Then the wind swept away to the pine-covered hill, and raised a rushing and a wailing amongst its thin-clad branches, and to the ear of Robert the trees were singing over again in their night solitudes the air sung by the cottar's family. When he looked to the north-west, whence the wind came, he saw nothing but a pale cleft in the sky. The meaning, the music of the night awoke in his soul; he forgot his lame foot, and the weight of Mr. Lammie's great boots, ran home and up the stair to his own room, seized his violin with eager haste, nor laid it down again till he could draw from it, at will, a sound like the moaning of the wind over the stubble-field. Then he knew that he could play the Flowers of the Forest. The Wind that Shakes the Barley cannot have been named from the barley after it was cut, but while it stood in the field : the Flowers of the Forest was of the gathered harvest.

He tried the air once over in the dark, and then carried his violin down to the room where Mr. and Miss Lammie sat.

"I think I can play 't noo, Mr. Lammie," he said abruptly.

" Play what, callant ?" asked his host.

" The Flooers o' the Forest."

" Play awa' than."

And Robert played—not so well as he had hoped. I daresay it was a humble enough performance, but he gave something at least of the expression Mr. Lammie desired. For, the moment the tune was over, he exclaimed,

" Weel dune, Robert man ! ye 'll be a fiddler some day yet !"

And Robert was well satisfied with the praise.

" I wish yer mother had been alive," the farmer went on. "She wad hae been rael prood to hear ye play like that. Eh ! she likit the fiddle weel. And she culd play bonny upo' the piana hersel'. It was something to hear the twa o' them playin' thegither, him on the fiddle

—that verra fiddle o' 's father's 'at ye hae i' yer han'—and her on the piana. Eh! but she was a bonnie wuman as ever I saw, an' that quaiet! It's my belief she never thocht aboot her ain beowty frae week's en' to week's en', and that's no sayin' little—is 't, Aggy ?"

"I never preten't ony richt to think aboot sic," returned Miss Lammie, with a mild indignation.

"That's richt, lass. Od, ye're aye i' the richt —though I say 't 'at sudna."

Miss Lammie must indeed have been goodnatured, to answer only with a genuine laugh. Shargar looked explosive with anger. But Robert would fain hear more of his mother.

"What was my mother like, Mr. Lammie ?" he asked.

"Eh, my man! ye suld hae seen her upon a bonnie bay mere that yer father gae her. Faith! she sat as straught as a rash, wi' jist a hing i' the heid o' her, like the heid o' a halm o' wild aits."

"My father wasna that ill till her than ?" suggested Robert.

"Wha ever daured say sic a thing ?" returned Mr. Lammie, but in a tone so far from satisfactory to Robert, that he inquired no more in that direction.

I need hardly say that from that night Robert was more than ever diligent with his violin.

CHAPTER XXI.

THE DRAGON.

NEXT day, his foot was so much better, that he sent Shargar to Rothieden to buy the string, taking with him Robert's school-bag, in which to carry off his Sunday shoes; for as to those left at Dooble Sanny's, they judged it unsafe to go in quest of them: the soutar could hardly be in a humour fit to be intruded upon.

Having procured the string, Shargar went to Mrs. Falconer's. Anxious not to encounter her, but, if possible, to bag the boots quietly, he opened the door, peeped in, and seeing no one, made his way towards the kitchen. He was arrested, however, as he crossed the passage by the voice of Mrs. Falconer calling, "Wha's that?" There she was at the parlour door. It paralysed him. His first impulse was to make a rush and escape. But the boots—he could not go without at least an attempt upon them. So he turned and faced her with inward trembling.

"Wha 's that ?" repeated the old lady, regarding him fixedly. " Ow, it's you! What duv *ye* want? Ye camna to see *me*, I'm thinkin'! What hae ye i' that bag ?"

"I cam to coff (*buy*) twine for the draigon," answered Shargar.

"Ye had twine eneuch afore!"

"It bruik. It wasna strang eneuch."

"Whaur got ye the siller to buy mair? Lat 's see 't ?"

Shargar took the string from the bag.

"Sic a sicht o' twine! What paid ye for 't."

"A shillin'."

"Whaur got ye the shillin' ?"

"Mr. Lammie gae 't to Robert."

"I winna hae ye tak siller frae naebody. It's ill mainners. Hae!" said the old lady, putting her hand in her pocket, and taking out a shilling. "Hae," she said. "Gie Mr. Lammie back his shillin', an' tell 'im 'at I wadna hae ye learn sic ill customs as tak siller. It's eneuch to gang sornin' upon 'im (*exacting free quarters*) as ye du, ohn beggit for siller. Are they a' weel ?"

"Ay, brawly," answered Shargar, putting the shilling in his pocket.

In another moment Shargar had, without a word of adieu, embezzled the shoes, and escaped from the house without seeing Betty. He went straight to the shop he had just left, and bought another shilling's worth of string.

When he got home, he concealed nothing from Robert, whom he found seated in the barn, with his fiddle, waiting his return.

Robert started to his feet. He could appropriate his grandfather's violin, to which, possibly, he might have shown as good a right as his grandmother—certainly his grandfather would have accorded it him—but her money was sacred.

"Shargar, ye vratch!" he cried, "fess that shillin' here direckly. Tak the twine wi' ye, and gar them gie ye back the shillin'."

"They winna brak the bargain," cried Shargar, beginning almost to whimper, for a savoury smell of dinner was coming across the yard.

"Tell them it's stown siller, and they'll be in het watter aboot it gin they dinna gie ye 't back."

"I maun hae my denner first," remonstrated Shargar.

But the spirit of his grandmother was strong in Robert, and in a matter of rectitude there must be no temporizing. Therein he could be as tyrannical as the old lady herself.

"De'il a bite or a sup s' gang ower your thrapple till I see that shillin'."

There was no help for it. Six hungry miles must be trudged by Shargar ere he got a morsel

to eat.   Two hours and a half passed before he
re-appeared.   But he brought the shilling.   As
to how he recovered it, Robert questioned him
in vain.   Shargar, in his turn, was obstinate.

" She's a some camstairy (*unmanageable*) wife,
that grannie o' yours," said Mr. Lammie, when
Robert returned the shilling with Mrs. Falconer's
message, " but I reckon I maun pit it i' my pooch,
for she *will* hae her ain gait, an' I dinna want
to strive wi' her.   But gin ony o' ye be in want
o' a shillin' ony day, lads, as lang's I'm abune
the yird—this ane 'll be grown twa, or maybe
mair, 'gen that time."

So saying, the farmer put the shilling in his
pocket, and buttoned it up.

The dragon flew splendidly now, and its
strength was mighty.   It was Robert's custom
to drive a stake in the ground, slanting against
the wind, and thereby tether the animal as if it
were up there grazing in its own natural region.   Then he would lie down by the stake and
read the *Arabian Nights*, every now and then casting a glance upward at the creature alone in the
waste air, yet all in his power by the string at his
side.   Somehow the high-flown dragon was a
bond between him and the blue; he seemed
nearer to the sky while it flew, or at least the
heaven seemed less far away and inaccessible.
While he lay there gazing, all at once he would
find that his soul was up with the dragon,

feeling as it felt, tossing about with it in the torrents of the air. Out at his eyes it would go, traverse the dim stairless space, and sport with the wind-blown monster. Sometimes, to aid his aspiration, he would take a bit of paper, make a hole in it, pass the end of the string through the hole, and send the messenger scudding along the line athwart the depth of the wind. If it stuck by the way, he would get a telescope of Mr. Lammie's, and therewith watch its struggles till it broke loose, then follow it careering up to the kite. Away with each successive paper his imagination would fly, and a sense of air, and height, and freedom, settled from his play into his very soul, a germ to sprout hereafter, and enrich the forms of his aspirations. And all his after-memories of kite-flying were mingled with pictures of eastern magnificence, for from the airy height of the dragon his eyes always came down upon the enchanted pages of John Hewson's book.

Sometimes, again, he would throw down his book, and sitting up with his back against the stake, lift his bonny leddy from his side, and play as he had never played in Rothieden, playing to the dragon aloft, to keep him strong in his soaring, and fierce in his battling with the winds of heaven. Then he fancied that the monster swooped and swept in arcs, and swayed curving to and fro, in rhythmic response to the music floating up through the wind.

What a full globated symbolism lay then around the heart of the boy in his book, his violin, his kite!

CHAPTER XXII.

DR. ANDERSON.

ONE afternoon, as they were sitting at their tea, a footstep in the garden approached the house, and then a figure passed the window. Mr. Lammie started to his feet.

"Bless my sowl, Aggy! that's Anderson!" he cried, and hurried to the door.

His daughter followed. The boys kept their seats. A loud and hearty salutation reached their ears; but the voice of the farmer was all they heard. Presently he returned bringing with him the tallest and slenderest man Robert had ever seen. He was considerably over six feet, with a small head, and delicate, if not fine features, a gentle look in his blue eyes, and a slow clear voice, which sounded as if it were thinking about every word it uttered. The hot sun of India seemed to have burned out everything self-assertive, leaving him quietly and rather sadly contemplative.

"Come in, come in," repeated Mr. Lammie,
overflowing with glad welcome.   "What 'll ye
hae?   There's a frien' o' yer ain," he continued,
pointing to Robert, "an' a fine lad."   Then lower-
ing his voice, he added: "A son o' poor Anerew's, ye ken, Doctor."

The boys rose, and Dr. Anderson stretching
his long arms across the table, shook hands kindly with Robert and Shargar.   Then he sat down
and began to help himself to the cakes (*oat-
cake*) at which Robert wondered, seeing there
was " white breid " on the table.   Miss Lammie
presently came in with the tea-pot and some
additional dainties, and the boys took the
opportunity of beginning at the beginning
again.

Dr. Anderson remained for a few days at
Bodyfauld, sending Shargar to Rothieden for
some necessaries from the Boar's Head, where
he had left his servant and luggage.   During
this time Mr. Lammie was much occupied with
his farm affairs, anxious to get his harvest in as
quickly as possible, because a change of weather
was to be dreaded; so the doctor was left a good
deal to himself.   He was fond of wandering
about, but, thoughtful as he was, did not object
to the companionship which Robert implicitly offered him: before many hours were over, the
two were friends.

Various things attracted Robert to the doctor.

First, he was a relation of his own, older than himself, the first he had known except his father, and Robert's heart was one of the most dutiful. Second, or perhaps I ought to have put this first, he was the only *gentleman*, except Eric Ericson, whose acquaintance he had yet made. Third, he was kind to him, and gentle to him, and, above all, respectful to him; and to be respected was a new sensation to Robert altogether. And lastly, he could tell stories of elephants and tiger-hunts, and all *The Arabian Nights* of India. He did not volunteer much talk, but Robert soon found that he could draw him out.

But what attracted the man to the boy?

" Ah! Robert," said the doctor, one day sadly, "it's a sore thing to come home after being thirty years away."

He looked up at the sky, then all round at the hills: the face of nature alone remained the same. Then his glance fell on Robert, and he saw a pair of black eyes looking up at him, brimful of tears. And thus the man was drawn to the boy.

Robert worshipped Dr. Anderson. As long as he remained their visitor, kite and violin and all were forgotten, and he followed him like a dog. To have such a gentleman for a relation, was grand indeed. What could he do for him? He ministered to him in all manner of trifles —a little to the amusement of Dr. Anderson,

but more to his pleasure, for he saw that the boy
was both large-hearted and lowly-minded: Dr.
Anderson had learned to read character, else he
would never have been the honour to his profession that he was.

But all the time Robert could not get him to
speak about his father.   He steadily avoided the
subject.

When he went away, the two boys walked
with him to the Boar's Head, caught a glimpse
of his Hindoo attendant, much to their wonder-
ment, received from the Doctor a sovereign
apiece and a kind good-bye, and returned to
Bodyfauld.

Dr. Anderson remained a few days longer at
Rothieden, and amongst others visited Mrs. Falconer, who was his first cousin.   What passed
between them Robert never heard, nor did his
grandmother even allude to the visit.   He went
by the mail-coach from Rothieden to Aberdeen,
and whether he should ever see him again Robert did not know.

He flew his kite no more for a while, but betook himself to the work of the harvest-field, in
which he was now able for a share.   But his
violin was no longer neglected.

Day after day passed in the delights of labour,
broken for Robert by *The Arabian Nights*, and
the violin, and for Shargar by attendance upon
Miss Lammie, till the fields lay bare of their

harvest, and the night-wind of autumn moaned everywhere over the vanished glory of the country, and it was time to go back to school.

CHAPTER XXIII.

AN AUTO DA FÉ.

THE morning at length arrived when Robert and Shargar must return to Rothieden. A keen autumnal wind was blowing far-off feathery clouds across a sky of pale blue ; the cold freshened the spirits of the boys, and tightened their nerves and muscles, till they were like bowstrings. No doubt the winter was coming, but the sun, although his day's work was short and slack, was still as clear as ever. So gladsome was the world, that the boys received the day as a fresh holiday, and strenuously forgot to-morrow. The wind blew straight from Rothieden, and between sun and wind a bright thought awoke in Robert. The dragon should not be carried—he should fly home.

After they had said farewell, in which Shargar seemed to suffer more than Robert, and had turned the corner of the stable, they heard the good farmer shouting after them,

"There'll be anither hairst neist year, boys,"

which wonderfully restored their spirits. When they reached the open road, Robert laid his violin carefully into a broom-bush. Then the tail was unrolled, and the dragon ascended steady as an angel whose work is done. Shargar took the stick at the end of the string, and Robert resumed his violin. But the creature was hard to lead in such a wind; so they made a loop on the string, and passed it round Shargar's chest, and he tugged the dragon home. Robert longed to take his share in the struggle, but he could not trust his violin to Shargar, and so had to walk beside ingloriously. On the way they laid their plans for the accommodation of the dragon. But the violin was the greater difficulty. Robert would not hear of the factory, for reasons best known to himself, and there were serious objections to taking it to Dooble Sanny. It was resolved that the only way was to seize the right moment, and creep upstairs with it before presenting themselves to Mrs. Falconer. Their intended manœuvres with the kite would favour the concealment of this stroke.

Before they entered the town they drew in the kite a little way, and cut off a dozen yards of the string, which Robert put in his pocket, with a stone tied to the end. When they reached the house, Shargar went into the little garden and tied the string of the kite to the paling between that and Captain Forsyth's. Robert open-

ed the street-door, and having turned his head
on all sides like a thief, darted with his violin
up the stairs. Having laid his treasure in one
of the presses in Shargar's garret, he went to his
own, and from the skylight threw the stone
down into the captain's garden, fastening the
other end of the string to the bedstead. . Escaping as cautiously as he had entered, he passed hurriedly into their neighbour's garden, found
the stone, and joined Shargar. The ends were
soon united, and the kite let go. It sunk for a
moment, then, arrested by the bedstead, towered
again to its former "pride of place," sailing over
Rothieden, grand and unconcerned, in the wastes
of air.

But the end of its tether was in Robert's garret. And that was to him a sense of power, a
thought of glad mystery. There was henceforth,
while the dragon flew, a relation between the
desolate little chamber, in that lowly house
buried among so many more aspiring abodes,
and the unmeasured depths and spaces, the stars,
and the unknown heavens. And in the next
chamber, lay the fiddle free once more,—yet another magical power whereby his spirit could
forsake the earth and mount heavenwards.

All that night, all the next day, all the next
night, the dragon flew.

Not one smile broke over the face of the old
lady as she received them. Was it because she

did not know what acts of disobedience, what breaches of the moral law, the two children of possible perdition might have committed while they were beyond her care, and she must not run the risk of smiling upon iniquity? I think it was rather that there was no smile in her religion, which, while it developed the power of a darkened conscience, over-laid and half-smothered all the lovelier impulses of her grand nature. How could she smile? Did not the world lie under the wrath and curse of God? Was not her own son in hell for ever? Had not the blood of the Son of God been shed for him in vain? Had not God meant that it should be in vain? For by the gift of his spirit could he not have enabled him to accept the offered pardon? And for anything she knew, was not Robert going after him to the place of misery? How could she smile?

"Noo be dooce," she said, the moment she had shaken hands with them, with her cold hands, so clean and soft and smooth. With a volcanic heart of love, her outside was always so still and cold!—snow on the mountain-sides, hot vein-coursing lava within. For her highest duty was submission to the will of God. Ah! if she had only known the God who claimed her submission! But there is time enough for every heart to know him.

"Noo be dooce," she repeated "an' sit doon,

and tell me aboot the fowk at Bodyfauld. I
houpe ye thankit them, or ye left, for their
muckle kindness to ye."

The boys were silent.

" Didna ye thank them ?"

" No, grannie; I dinna think 'at we did."

" Weel, that was ill-faured o' ye. Eh! but
the hert is deceitfu' aboon a' thing, and desperately wicked. Who can know it? Come
awa'. Come awa'. Robert festen the door."

And she led them to the corner for prayer,
and poured forth a confession of sin for them
and for herself, such as left little that could have
been added by her own profligate son, had he
joined in the prayer. Either there are no degrees in guilt, or the Scotch language was equal
only to the confession of children and holy
women, and could provide no more awful words
for the contrition of the prodigal or the hypocrite. But the words did little harm, for Robert's
mind was full of the kite and the violin, and
was probably nearer God thereby than if he had
been trying to feel as wicked as his grandmother told God that he was. Shargar was
even more divinely employed at the time than
either; for though he had not had the manners to thank his benefactor, his heart had all
the way home been full of tender thoughts of
Miss Lammie's kindness; and now, instead of
confessing sins that were not his, he was loving

her over and over, and wishing to be back with her instead of with this awfully good woman, in whose presence there was no peace, for all the atmosphere of silence and calm in which she sat.

Confession over, and the boys at liberty again, a new anxiety seized them. Grannie must find out that Robert's shoes were missing, and what account was to be given of the misfortune, for Robert would not, or could not lie? In the midst of their discussion a bright idea flashed upon Shargar, which, however, he kept to himself: he would steal them, and bring them home in triumph, emulating thus Robert's exploit in delivering his bonny leddy.

The shoemaker sat behind his door to be out of the draught: Shargar might see a great part of the workshop without being seen, and he could pick Robert's shoes from among a hundred. Probably they lay just where Robert had laid them, for Dooble Sanny paid attention to any job only in proportion to the persecution accompanying it.

So the next day Shargar contrived to slip out of school just as the writing lesson began, for he had great skill in conveying himself unseen, and, with his book-bag, slunk barefooted into the soutar's entry.

The shop door was a little way open, and the red eyes of Shargar had only the corner next it

to go peering about in. But there he saw the
shoes. He got down on his hands and knees,
and crept nearer. Yes, they were beyond a
doubt Robert's shoes. He made a long arm like
a beast of prey, seized them, and, losing his presence of mind upon possession, drew them too
hastily towards him. The shoemaker saw them
as they vanished through the door, and darted
after them. Shargar was off at full speed, and
Sandy followed with hue and cry. Every idle
person in the street joined in the pursuit, and
all who were too busy or too respectable to run
crowded to door and windows. Shargar made
instinctively for his mother's old lair; but bethinking himself when he reached the door, he
turned, and, knowing nowhere else to go, fled in
terror to Mrs. Falconer's, still, however, holding
fast by the shoes, for they were Robert's.

As Robert came home from school, wondering
what could have become of his companion, he
saw a crowd about his grandmother's door, and
pushing his way through it in some dismay,
found Dooble Sanny and Shargar confronting
each other before the stern justice of Mrs. Falconer.

"Ye're a leear," the soutar was panting out.
"I haena had a pair o' shune o' Robert's i' my
han's this three month. Thae shune—lat me see
them—they're—— Here's Robert himsel'. Are
thae shune yours, noo, Robert?"

"Ay are they. Ye made them yersel'."

"Hoo cam they in my chop, than?"

"Speir nae mair quest'ons nor 's worth answer-in'," said Robert, with a look meant to be significant. "They 're my shune, and I'll keep them. Aiblins ye dinna aye ken wha's shune ye hae, or whan they cam in to ye."

"What for didna Shargar come an' speir efter them, than, in place o' makin' a thief o' himsel' that gait?"

"*Ye* may haud yer tongue," returned Robert, with yet more significance.

"I was aye a gowk (*idiot*)," said Shargar, in apologetic reflection, looking awfully white, and afraid to lift an eye to Mrs. Falconer, yet reassured a little by Robert's presence.

Some glimmering seemed now to have dawned upon the soutar, for he began to prepare a retreat. Meantime Mrs. Falconer sat silent, allowing no word that passed to escape her. She wanted to be at the bottom of the mysterious affair, and therefore held her peace.

"Weel, I'm sure, Robert, ye never tellt me aboot the shune," said Alexander. "I s' jist tak' them back wi' me, and du what's wantit to them. And I'm sorry that I hae gien ye this tribble, Mistress Faukner; but it was a' that fule's wite there. I didna even ken it was him, till we war near-han' the hoose."

"Lat me see the shune," said Mrs. Falconer,

speaking almost for the first time. " What's the maitter wi' them ?"

Examining the shoes, she saw they were in a perfectly sound state, and this confirmed her suspicion that there was more in the affair than had yet come out. Had she taken the straight-forward measure of examining Robert, she would soon have arrived at the truth. But she had such a dread of causing a lie to be told, that she would adopt any roundabout way rather than ask a plain question of a suspected culprit. So she laid the shoes down beside her, saying to the soutar :

" There's naething amiss wi' the shune. Ye can lea' them."

Thereupon Alexander went away, and Robert and Shargar would have given more than their dinner to follow him. Grannie neither asked any questions, however, nor made a single remark on what had passed. Dinner was served and eaten, and the boys returned to their after-noon school.

No sooner was she certain that they were safe under the school-master's eye than the old lady put on her black silk bonnet and her black wollen shawl, took her green cotton umbrella, which served her for a staff, and, refusing Betty's proffered assistance, set out for Dooble Sanny's shop.

As she drew near she heard the sounds of his

violin. When she entered, he laid his *auld wife* carefully aside, and stood in an expectant attitude.

"Mr. Elshender, I want to be at the boddom o' this," said Mrs. Falconer.

"Weel, mem, gang to the boddom o' 't," returned Dooble Sanny, dropping on his stool, and taking his stone upon his lap and stroking it, as if it had been some quadrupedal pet. Full of rough but real politeness to women when in good humour, he lost all his manners along with his temper upon the slightest provocation, and her tone irritated him.

"Hoo cam Robert's shune to be i' your shop?"

"Somebody bude till hae brocht them, mem. In a' my expairience, and that's no sma', I never kent pair o' shune gang ohn a pair o' feet i' the wame o' them."

"Hoots! what kin' o' gait 's that to speyk till a body? Whase feet was inside the shune?"

"De'il a bit o' me kens, mem."

"Dinna sweir, whatever ye du."

"De'il but I *will* sweir, mem; an' gin ye anger me, I'll jist sweir awfu'."

"I'm sure I hae nae wuss to anger ye, man! Canna ye help a body to win at the boddom o' a thing ohn angert an' sworn?"

"Weel, I kenna wha brocht the shune, as I tellt ye a'ready."

"But they wantit nae men'in'."

"I micht hae men't them an' forgotten 't, mem."

"Noo ye're leein'."

"Gin ye gang on that gait, mem, I winna speyk a word o' trowth frae this moment foret."

" Jist tell me what ye ken aboot thae shune, an' I'll no say anither word."

" Weel, mem, I'll tell ye the trowth. The de'il brocht them in ae day in a lang taings; and says he, 'Elshender, men' thae shune for puir Robby Faukner; an' dooble-sole them for the life o' ye; for that auld luckie-minnie o' his 'ill sune hae him doon oor gait, and the grun''s het i' the noo; an' I dinna want to be ower sair upon him, for he's a fine chield, an' 'll mak a fine fiddler gin he live lang eneuch.'"

Mrs. Falconer left the shop without another word, but with an awful suspicion which the last heedless words of the shoemaker had aroused in her bosom. She left him bursting with laughter over his lapstone. He caught up his fiddle and played "The de'il's i' the women" lustily and with expression. But he little thought what he had done.

As soon as she reached her own room, she went straight to her bed and *disinterred* the bonny leddy's coffin. She was gone; and in her stead, horror of horrors! lay in the unhallowed chest that body of divinity known as Boston's *Fourfold State.* Vexation, anger, dis-

appointment, and grief, possessed themselves of
the old woman's mind. She ranged the house
like the "questing beast" of the Round Table,
but failed in finding the violin before the return
of the boys. Not a word did she say all that
evening, and their oppressed hearts foreboded
ill. They felt that there was thunder in the
clouds, a sleeping storm in the air; but how or
when it would break they had no idea.

Robert came home to dinner the next day a
few minutes before Shargar. As he entered his
grandmother's parlour, a strange odour greeted
his sense. A moment more, and he stood rooted
with horror, and his hair began to rise on his
head. His violin lay on its back on the fire, and
a yellow tongue of flame was licking the red lips
of a hole in its belly. All its strings were shrivelled
up save one, which burst as he gazed. And beside,
stern as a Druidess, sat his grandmother in her
chair, feeding her eyes with grim satisfaction on
the detestable sacrifice. At length the rigidity
of Robert's whole being relaxed in an involuntary
howl like that of a wild beast, and he turned and
rushed from the house in a helpless agony of
horror. Where he was going he knew not, only
a blind instinct of modesty drove him to hide
his passion from the eyes of men.

From her window Miss St. John saw him
tearing like one demented along the top walk
of the captain's garden, and watched for his re-

turn. He came far sooner than she expected.

Before he arrived at the factory, Robert began to hear strange sounds in the desolate place. When he reached the upper floor, he found men with axe and hammer destroying the old woodwork, breaking the old jennies, pitching the balls of lead into baskets, and throwing the spools into crates. Was there nothing but destruction in the world? There, most horrible! his "bonny leddy" dying of flames, and here, the temple of his refuge torn to pieces by unhallowed hands! What could it mean? Was his grandmother's vengeance here too? But he did not care. He only felt like the dove sent from the ark, that there was no rest for the sole of his foot, that there was no place to hide his head in his agony—that he was naked to the universe; and like a heartless wild thing hunted till its brain is of no more use, he turned and rushed back again upon his track. At one end was the burning idol, at the other the desecrated temple.

No sooner had he entered the captain's garden than Miss St. John met him.

"What is the matter with you, Robert?" she asked, kindly.

"Oh, mem!" gasped Robert, and burst into a very storm of weeping.

It was long before he could speak. He cowered before Miss St. John as if conscious of an unfriendly presence, and seeking to shelter himself by her tall figure from his grandmother's eyes. For who could tell but at the moment she might be gazing upon him from some window, or even from the blue vault above? There was no escaping her. She was the all-seeing eye personified—the eye of the God of the theologians of his country, always searching out the evil, and refusing to acknowledge the good. Yet so gentle and faithful was the heart of Robert, that he never thought of her as cruel. He took it for granted that somehow or other she must be right. Only what a terrible thing such righteousness was! He stood and wept before the lady.

Her heart was sore for the despairing boy. She drew him to a little summer-seat. He entered with her, and sat down, weeping still. She did her best to soothe him. At last, sorely interrupted by sobs, he managed to let her know the fate of his "bonny leddy." But when he came to the words, "She's burnin' in there upo' granny's fire," he broke out once more with that wild howl of despair, and then, ashamed of himself, ceased weeping altogether, though he could not help the intrusion of certain chokes and sobs upon his otherwise even, though low and sad speech.

Knowing nothing of Mrs. Falconer's character, Miss St. John set her down as a cruel and heartless as well as tyrannical and bigoted old woman, and took the mental position of enmity towards her. In a gush of motherly indignation she kissed Robert on the forehead.

From that chrism he arose a king.

He dried his eyes; not another sob even broke from him; he gave one look, but no word of gratitude to Miss St. John; bade her good-bye; and walked composedly into his grandmother's parlour, where the neck of the violin yet lay upon the fire only half consumed. The rest had vanished utterly.

"What are they duin' doon at the fact'ry, grannie?" he asked.

"What's wha duin', laddie?" returned his grandmother, curtly.

"They're takin' 't doon."

"Takin' what doon?" she returned, with raised voice.

"Takin' doon the hoose."

The old woman rose.

"Robert, ye may hae spite in yer hert for what I hae dune this mornin', but I cud do no ither. An' it's an ill thing to tak sic amen's o' me, as gin I had dune wrang, by garrin' me troo 'at yer grandfather's property was to gang the gait o' 's auld, useless, ill-mainnert scraich o' a fiddle."

"She was the bonniest fiddle i' the country-side, grannie. And she never gae a scraich in

her life 'cep' whan she was han'let in a mainner
unbecomin'. But we s' say nae mair aboot her,
for she's gane, an' no by a fair strae-deith (*death
on one's own straw*) either. She had nae blude
to cry for vengeance; but the snappin' o' her
strings an' the crackin' o' her banes may hae
made a cry to gang far eneuch notwithstand-
in'."

The old woman seemed for one moment re-
buked under her grandson's eloquence. He had
made a great stride towards manhood since the
morning.

" The fiddle's my ain," she said in a defensive
tone. " And sae is the fact'ry," she added, as if
she had not quite reassured herself concerning
it.

" The fiddle's yours nae mair, grannie. And
for the fact'ry—ye winna believe me : gang and
see yersel'."

Therewith Robert retreated to his garret.

When he opened the door of it, the first thing
he saw was the string of his kite, which, strange
to tell, so steady had been the wind, was still
up in the air—still tugging at the bed-post.
Whether it was from the stinging thought that
the true sky-soarer, the violin, having been devoured by the jaws of the fire-devil, there was
no longer any significance in the outward and
visible sign of the dragon, or from a dim feeling
that the time of kites was gone by and man-

hood on the threshold, I cannot tell; but he drew his knife from his pocket, and with one down-stroke cut the string in twain. Away went the dragon, free, like a prodigal, to his ruin. And with the dragon, afar into the past, flew the childhood of Robert Falconer. He made one remorseful dart after the string as it swept out of the skylight, but it was gone beyond remeid. And never more, save in twilight dreams, did he lay hold on his childhood again. But he knew better and better, as the years rolled on, that he approached a deeper and holier childhood, of which that had been but the feeble and necessarily vanishing type.

As the kite sank in the distance, Mrs. Falconer issued from the house, and went down the street towards the factory.

Before she came back the cloth was laid for dinner, and Robert and Shargar were both in the parlour awaiting her return. She entered heated and dismayed, went into Robert's bedroom, and shut the door hastily. They heard her open the old bureau. In a moment after she came out with a more luminous expression upon her face than Robert had ever seen it bear. It was as still as ever, but there was a strange light in her eyes, which was not confined to her eyes, but shone in a measure from her colourless forehead and cheeks as well. It was long before Robert was able to interpret that change in her look, and that increase of kindness towards himself and Shargar, apparently such a contrast with the holocaust of the morning. Had they both been Benjamins they could not have had more abundant platefuls than she gave them that day. And when they left her to return to school, instead of the usual "Noo be douce," she said in gentle, almost loving tones, "Noo, be good lads, baith o' ye."

The conclusion at which Falconer did arrive was that his grandmother had hurried home to see whether the title-deeds of the factory were still in her possession, and had found that they were gone—taken, doubtless, by her son Andrew. At whatever period he had appropriated them, he must have parted with them but recently. And the hope rose luminous that her son had not yet passed into the region "where all life dies, death lives." Terrible consolation! Terrible creed which made the hope that he was still on this side of the grave working wickedness, light up the face of the mother, and open her hand in kindness. Is it suffering, or is it wickedness, that is the awful thing? "Ah! but they are both combined in the other world." And in this world too, I answer; only, according to Mrs. Falconer's creed, in the other world God, for the sake of the suffering, renders the wickedness eternal!

The old factory was in part pulled down, and

out of its remains a granary constructed. Nor
did the old lady interpose a word to arrest the
alienation of her property.

CHAPTER XXIV.

MARY ST. JOHN was the orphan daughter
of an English clergyman, who had left her
money enough to make her at least independ-
ent. Mrs. Forsyth, hearing that her niece was
left alone in the world, had concluded that her
society would be a pleasure to herself and a relief to the housekeeping. Even before her father's death, Miss St. John, having met with a
disappointment, and concluded herself dead to
the world, had been looking about for some way
of doing good. The prospect of retirement,
therefore, and of being useful to her sick aunt,
had drawn her northwards.

She was now about six-and-twenty, filled
with two passions—one for justice, the other for
music. Her griefs had not made her selfish,
nor had her music degenerated into sentiment.
The gentle style of the instruction she had received had never begotten a diseased self-con-
sciousness; and if her religion lacked something

of the intensity without which a character like hers could not be evenly balanced, its force was not spent on the combating of unholy doubts and selfish fears, but rose on the wings of her music in gentle thanksgiving. Tears had changed her bright-hued hopes into a dove-coloured submission, through which her mind was passing towards a rainbow dawn such as she had never dreamed of. To her as yet the Book of Common Prayer contained all the prayers that human heart had need to offer; what things lay beyond its scope must lie beyond the scope of religion. All such things must be parted with one day, and if they had been taken from her very soon, she was the sooner free from the painful necessity of watching lest earthly love should remove any of the old landmarks dividing what was God's from what was only man's. She had now retired within the pale of religion, and left the rest of her being, as she thought, "to dull forgetfulness a prey."

She had little comfort in the society of her aunt. Indeed, she felt strongly tempted to return again to England the same month, and seek a divine service elsewhere. But it was not at all so easy then as it is now for a woman to find the opportunity of being helpful in the world of suffering.

Mrs. Forsyth was one of those women who

get their own way by the very *vis inertiæ* of their silliness. No argument could tell upon her. She was so incapable of seeing anything noble that her perfect satisfaction with everything she herself thought, said, or did, remained unchallenged. She had just illness enough to swell her feeling of importance. She looked down upon Mrs. Falconer from such an immeasurable height that she could not be indignant with her for anything; she only vouchsafed a laugh now and then at her oddities, holding no further communication with her than a condescending bend of the neck when they happened to meet, which was not once a year. But, indeed, she would have patronized the angel Gabriel, if she had had a chance, and no doubt given him a hint or two upon the proper way of praising God. For the rest, she was good-tempered, looked comfortable, and quarrelled with nobody but her rough honest old bear of a husband, whom, in his seventieth year, she was always trying to teach good manners, with the frequent result of a storm of swearing.

But now Mary St. John was thoroughly interested in the strange boy whose growing musical pinions were ever being clipped by the shears of unsympathetic age and crabbed religion, and the idea of doing something for him to make up for the injustice of his grandmother awoke in her a slight glow of that interest in

life which she sought only in doing good. But
although ere long she came to love the boy very
truly, and although Shargar's life was bound up
in the favour of Robert, yet neither stooping
angel nor foot-following dog ever loved the lad
with the love of that old grannmother, who
would for him have given herself to the fire to
which she had doomed his greatest delight.

For some days Robert worked hard at his lessons, for he had nothing else to do. Life was
very gloomy now. If he could only go to sea,
or away to keep sheep on the stormy mountains!
If there were only some war going on, that he
might *list* ! Any fighting with the elements, or
with the oppressors of the nations, would make
life worth having, a man worth being. But God
did not heed. He leaned over the world, a dark
care, an immovable fate, bearing down with the
weight of his presence all aspiration, all budding
delights of children and young persons: all must
crouch before him, and uphold his glory with
the sacrificial death of every impulse, every admiration, every lightness of heart, every bubble
of laughter. Or—which to a mind like Robert's
was as bad—if he did not punish for these things,
it was because they came not within the sphere
of his condescension, were not worth his notice :
of sympathy could be no question.

But this gloom did not last long. When
souls like Robert's have been ill-taught about

God, the true God will not let them gaze too long upon the Moloch which men have set up to represent him. He will turn away their minds from that which men call Him, and fill them with some of his own lovely thoughts or works, such as may by degrees prepare the way for a vision of the Father.

One afternoon Robert was passing the soutar's shop. He had never gone near him since his return. But now, almost mechanically, he went in at the open door.

"Weel, Robert, ye *are* a stranger. But what's the maitter wi' ye? Faith! yon was an ill plisky ye played me to brak into my chop an' steal the bonnie leddy."

"Sandy," said Robert, solemnly, "ye dinna ken what ye hae dune by that trick ye played me. Dinna ever mention *her* again i' *my* hearin'."

"The auld witch hasna gotten a grup o' her again?" cried the shoemaker, starting half up in alarm. "She cam here to me aboot the shune, but I reckon I sortet her!"

"I winna speir what ye said," returned Robert. "It's no maitter noo."

And the tears rose to his eyes. His bonny lady!

"The Lord guide 's!" exclaimed the soutar. "What *is* the maitter wi' the bonny leddy?"

"There's nae bonnie leddy ony mair. I saw her brunt to death afore my verra ain een."

The shoemaker sprang to his feet and caught up his paring knife.

"For God's sake, say 'at yer leein'!" he cried.

"I wish I war leein'," returned Robert.

The soutar uttered a terrible oath, and swore—

"I'll murder the auld ——." The epithet he ended with is too ugly to write.

"Daur to say sic a word in ae breath wi' my grannie," cried Robert, snatching up the lapstone, "an' I'll brain ye upo' yer ain shop-flure."

Sandy threw the knife on his stool, and sat down beside it. Robert dropped the lapstone. Sanny took it up and burst into tears, which before they were half down his face, turned into tar with the blackness of the same.

"I'm an awfu' sinner," he said, "and vengeance has owerta'en me. Gang oot o' my chop! I wasna worthy o' her. Gang oot, I say, or I'll kill ye."

Robert went. Close by the door he met Miss St. John. He pulled off his cap, and would have passed her. But she stopped him.

"I am going for a walk a little way," she said. "Will you go with me?"

She had come out in the hope of finding him, for she had seen him go up the street.

"That I wull," returned Robert, and they walked on together.

When they were beyond the last house, Miss St. John said:

"Would you like to play on the piano, Robert?"

"Eh, mem!" said Robert, with a deep suspiration. Then, after a pause: "But duv ye think I cud?"

"There's no fear of that. Let me see your hands."

"They're some black, I doobt, mem," he remarked, rubbing them hard upon his trowsers before he showed them; "for I was amaist cawin' oot the brains o' Dooble Sanny wi' his ain lapstane. He's an ill-tongued chield. But eh! mem, ye suld hear him play upo' the fiddle! He's greitin' his een oot e'en noo for the bonny leddy."

Not discouraged by her inspection of his hands, black as they were, Miss St. John continued.

"But what would your grandmother say?" she asked.

"She maun ken naething aboot it, mem. I can-*not* tell her a'thing. She wad greit an' pray awfu', an' lock me up, I daursay. Ye see, she thinks a' kin' o' music 'cep' psalm-singin' comes o' the deevil himsel'. An' I canna believe that. For aye whan I see onything by ordinar bonny, sic like as the mune was last nicht, it aye gars me greit for my brunt fiddle."

"Well, you must come to me every day for half an hour at least, and I will give you a lesson on my piano. But you can't learn by that. And my aunt could never bear to hear you practising. So I'll tell you what you must do. I have a small piano in my own room. Do you know there is a door from your house into my room?"

"Ay?" said Robert; "That hoose *was* my father's afore your uncle bought it. My father biggit it."

"Is it long since your father died?"

"I dinna ken."

"Where did he die?"

"I dinna ken."

"Do you remember it?"

"No, mem."

"Well, if you will come to my room, you shall practise there. I shall be down stairs with my aunt. But perhaps I may look up now and then, to see how you are getting on. I will leave the door unlocked, so that you can come in when you like. If I don't want you, I will lock the door. You understand? You mustn't be handling things, you know."

"'Deed, mem, ye may lippen (*trust*) to me. But I'm jist feared to lat ye hear me lay a finger upo' the piana, for it's little I cud do wi' my fiddle, an', for the piana! I'm feart I'll jist scunner (*disgust*) ye."

"If you really want to learn, there will be no fear of that," returned Miss St. John, guessing

at the meaning of the word *scunner*. "I don't
think I am doing anything wrong," she added,
half to herself, in a somewhat doubtful tone.

"'Deed no, mem. Ye're jist an angel una-
awares. For I maist think sometimes that my
grannie 'ill drive me wud (*mad*); for there's naething to read but guid buiks, an' naething to
sing but psalms; an' there's nae fun aboot the
hoose but Betty; an' puir Shargar's nearhan'
dementit wi' 't. An' we maun pray till her
whether we will or no. An' there's no comfort
i' the place but plenty to ate; an' that canna be
guid for onybody. She likes flooers, though,
an' wad like me to gar them grow; but I dinna
care aboot it: they tak sic a time afore they
come to onything."

Then Miss St. John inquired about Shargar,
and began to feel rather differently towards the
old lady when she had heard the story. But
how she laughed at the tale, and how light-
hearted Robert went home, are neither to be told.

The next Sunday, the first time for many
years, Dooble Sanny was at church with his
wife, though how much good he got by going
would be a serious question to discuss.

CHAPTER XXV.

THE GATES OF PARADISE.

ROBERT had his first lesson the next Saturday afternoon. Eager and undismayed by the presence of Mrs. Forsyth, good-natured and contemptuous—for had he not a protecting angel by him?—he hearkened for every word of Miss St. John, combated every fault, and undermined every awkwardness with earnest patience. Nothing delighted Robert so much as to give himself up to one greater. His mistress was thoroughly pleased, and even Mrs. Forsyth gave him two of her soft finger tips to do something or other with—Robert did not know what, and let them go.

About eight o'clock that same evening, his heart beating like a captured bird's, he crept from grannie's parlour, past the kitchen, and up the low stair to the mysterious door. He had been trying for an hour to summon up courage to rise, feeling as if his grandmother must suspect where he was going. Arrived at

the barrier, twice his courage failed him ; twice
he turned and sped back to the parlour. A
third time he made the essay, a third time
stood at the wondrous door—so long as blank
as a wall to his careless eyes, now like the door
of the magic *Sesame* that led to the treasure-
cave of Ali Baba. He laid his hand on the
knob, withdrew it, thought he heard some one
in the transe, rushed up the garret stair, and
stood listening, hastened down, and with a sudden influx of determination opened the door,
saw that the trap was raised, closed the door
behind him, and standing with his head on the
level of the floor, gazed into the paradise of
Miss St. John's room. To have one peep into
such a room was a kind of salvation to the half-
starved nature of the boy. All before him was
elegance, richness, mystery. Womanhood radiated from everything. A fire blazed in the
chimney. A rug of long white wool lay before
it. A little way off stood the piano. Ornaments sparkled and shone upon the dressing-
table. The door of a wardrobe had swung a
little open, and discovered the sombre shimmer
of a black silk dress. Something gorgeously
red, a China crape shawl, hung glowing beyond
it. He dared not gaze any longer. He had
already been guilty of an immodesty. He hastened to ascend, and seated himself at the piano.

Let my reader aid me for a moment with his

imagination—reflecting what it was to a boy
like Robert, and in Robert's misery, to open a
door in his own meagre dwelling and gaze into
such a room—free to him.   If he will aid me so,
then let him aid himself by thinking that the
house of his own soul has such a door into the
infinite beauty, whether he has yet found it or
not.

" Just think," Robert said to himself, " o' *me*
in sic a place ! It's a pailace. It's a fairy pailace.
And that angel o' a leddy bides here, and sleeps
there !   I wonner gin she ever dreams aboot
onything as bonny 's hersel' !"

Then his thoughts took another turn.

" I wonner gin the room was onything like
this whan my mamma sleepit in't ?   *I* cudna
hae been born in sic a gran' place.   But my
mamma micht hae weel lien here."

The face of the miniature, and the sad words
written below the hymn, came back upon him,
and he bowed his head upon his hands.   He
was sitting thus when Miss St. John came behind him, and heard him murmur the one word
Mamma ! She laid her hand on his shoulder.
He started and rose.

" I beg yer pardon, mem.   I hae no business
to be here, excep' to play.   But I cudna help
thinkin' aboot my mother ; for I was born in
this room, mem.   Will I gang awa' again ? "

He turned towards the door.

"No, no," said Miss St. John. "I only came to see if you were here. I cannot stop now; but to-morrow you must tell me about your mother. Sit down, and don't lose any more time. Your grandmother will miss you. And then what would come of it ?"

Thus was this rough diamond of a Scotch boy, rude in speech, but full of delicate thought, gathered under the modelling influences of the finished, refined, tender, sweet-tongued, and sweet-thoughted Englishwoman, who, if she had been less of a woman, would have been repelled by his uncouthness; if she had been less of a lady, would have mistaken his commonness for vulgarity. But she was just, like the type of womankind, a virgin-mother. She saw the nobility of his nature through its homely garments, and had been, indeed, sent to carry on the work from which his mother had been too early taken away.

"There's jist ae thing, mem, that vexes me a wee, an' I dinna ken what to think aboot it," said Robert, as Miss St. John was leaving the room. "Maybe ye cud bide ae minute till I tell ye."

"Yes, I can. What is it ?"

"I'm nearhan' sure that whan I lea' the parlour, grannie 'ill think I'm awa' to my prayers; and sae she'll think better o' me nor I deserve. An' I canna bide that."

Y

" What should make you suppose that she will think so ?"

" Fowk kens what ane anither's aboot, ye ken, mem."

"Then she'll know you are not at your prayers."

" Na. For sometimes I div gang to my prayers for a whilie like, but nae for lang, for I'm nae like ane o' them 'at He wad care to hear sayin' a lang screed o' a prayer till 'im. I hae but ae thing to pray aboot."

" And what's that, Robert ?"

One of his silences had seized him. He looked confused, and turned away.

" Never mind," said Miss St. John, anxious to relieve him, and establish a comfortable relation between them ; " you will tell me another time."

" I doobt no, mem," answered Robert, with what most people would think an excess of honesty.

But Miss St. John made a better conjecture as to his apparent closeness.

" At all events," she said, " don't mind what your grannie may think, so long as you have no wish to make her think it. Good night."

Had she been indeed an angel from heaven, Robert could not have worshipped her more. And why should he ? Was she less God's messenger that she had beautiful arms instead of less beautiful wings ?

He practised his scales till his unaccustomed
fingers were stiff, then shut the piano with reverence, and departed, carefully peeping into
the disenchanted region without the gates to
see that no enemy lay in wait for him as he
passed beyond them. He closed the door gently; and in one moment the rich lovely room
and the beautiful lady were behind him, and
before him the bare stair between two white-
washed walls, and the long flagged transe that
led to his silent grandmother seated in her arm-
chair, gazing into the red coals—for somehow
grannie's fire always glowed, and never blazed
—with her round-toed shoes pointed at them
from the top of her little wooden stool. He
traversed the stair and the transe, entered the
parlour, and sat down to his open book as
though nothing had happened. But his grandmother saw the light in his face, and did think
he had just come from his prayers. And she
blessed God that he had put it in her heart to
burn the fiddle.

The next night Robert took with him the
miniature of his mother, and showed it to Miss
St. John, who saw at once that, whatever might
be his present surroundings, his mother must
have been a lady. A certain fancied resemblance in it to her own mother likewise drew
her heart to the boy. Then Robert took from
his pocket the gold thimble, and said,

"This thimmel was my mamma's. Will ye tak it, mem, for ye ken it's o' nae use to me."

Miss St. John hesitated for a moment.

"I will keep it for you, if you like," she said, for she could not bear to refuse it.

"Na, mem; I want ye to keep it to yersel'; for I'm sure my mamma wad hae likit you to hae 't better nor ony ither body."

"Well, I will use it sometimes for your sake. But mind, I will not take it from you; I will only keep it for you."

"Weel, weel, mem; gin ye 'll keep it till I speir for 't, that'll du weel eneuch," answered Robert, with a smile.

He laboured diligently; and his progress corresponded to his labour. It was more than intellect that guided him: Falconer had genius for whatever he cared for.

Meantime the love he bore his teacher, and the influence of her beauty, began to mould him, in his kind and degree, after her likeness, so that he grew nice in his person and dress, and smoothed the roughness and moderated the broadness of his speech with the amenities of the English which she made so sweet upon her tongue. He became still more obedient to his grandmother, and more diligent at school; gathered to himself golden opinions without knowing it, and was gradually developing into a rustic gentleman.

Nor did the piano absorb all his faculties. Every divine influence tends to the rounded perfection of the whole. His love of nature grew more rapidly. Hitherto it was only in summer that he had felt the presence of a power in her and yet above her: in winter, now, the sky was true and deep, though the world was waste and sad; and the tones of the wind that roared at night about the goddess-haunted house, and moaned in the chimneys of the lowly dwelling that nestled against it, woke harmonies within him which already he tried to spell out falteringly. Miss St. John began to find that he put expressions of his own into the simple things she gave him to play, and even dreamed a little at his own will when alone with the passive instrument. Little did Mrs. Falconer think into what a seventh heaven of accursed music she had driven her boy.

But not yet did he tell his friend, much as he loved and much as he trusted her, the little he knew of his mother's sorrows and his father's sins, or whose the hand that had struck him when she found him lying in the waste factory.

For a time almost all his trouble about God went from him. Nor do I think that this was only because he rarely thought of him at all: God gave him of Himself in Miss St. John. But words dropped now and then from off the shelves where his old difficulties lay, and they fell like seeds upon the heart of Miss St. John, took root, and rose in thoughts : in the heart of a true woman the talk of a child even will take life.

One evening Robert rose from the table, not unwatched of his grandmother, and sped swiftly and silently through the dark, as was his custom, to enter the chamber of enchantment. Never before had his hand failed to alight, sure as a lark on its nest, upon the brass handle of the door that admitted him to his paradise.　It missed it now, and fell on something damp, and rough, and repellent instead.　Horrible, but true suspicion !　While he was at school that day, his grandmother, moved by what doubt or by what certainty she never revealed, had had the doorway walled up.　He felt the place all over. It was to his hands the living tomb of his mother's vicar on earth.

He returned to his book, pale as death, but said never a word.　The next day the stones were plastered over.

Thus the door of bliss vanished from the earth. And neither the boy nor his grandmother ever said that it had been.

END OF THE FIRST VOLUME.

LONDON:　PRINTED BY MACDONALD AND TUGWELL, BLENHEIM HOUSE

ROBERT FALCONER

BY

GEORGE MAC DONALD LL.D.

AUTHOR OF

" ALEC FORBES OF HOWGLEN,"

" DAVID ELGINBROD,"

&c. &c.

> Countrymen.
> My heart doth joy that yet, in all my life,
> I found no man but he was true to me.
> > BRUTUS in *Julius Cæsar.*

IN THREE VOLUMES.

VOL. II.

LONDON:

HURST AND BLACKETT, PUBLISHERS,

13, GREAT MARLBOROUGH STREET.

1868.

The right of Translation is reserved.

LONDON :

PRINTED BY MACDONALD AND TUGWELL,

BLENHEIM HOUSE.

CONTENTS

OF

THE SECOND VOLUME.

———

PART II.—HIS YOUTH.

CHAPTER		PAGE
I.	ROBERT KNOCKS—AND THE DOOR IS NOT OPENED	1
II.	THE STROKE	16
III.	THE END CROWNS ALL	28
IV.	THE ABERDEEN GARRET	42
V.	THE COMPETITION	53
VI.	DR. ANDERSON AGAIN	60
VII.	ERIC ERICSON	68
VIII.	A HUMAN PROVIDENCE	89
IX.	A HUMAN SOUL	98
X.	A FATHER AND A DAUGHTER	116
XI.	ROBERT'S VOW	127
XII.	THE GRANITE CHURCH	133
XIII.	SHARGAR'S ARM	147
XIV.	MYSIE'S FACE	154
XV.	THE LAST OF THE COALS	176
XVI.	A STRANGE NIGHT	191
XVII.	HOME AGAIN	208

CHAPTER		PAGE
XVIII.	A Grave Opened	218
XIX.	Robert Mediates	224
XX.	Ericson Loses to Win	242
XXI.	Shargar Aspires	249
XXII.	Robert in Action	263
XXIII.	Robert finds a New Instrument	280
XXIV.	Death	286
XXV.	In Memoriam	293

ROBERT FALCONER.

PART II.—HIS YOUTH.

CHAPTER I.

ROBERT KNOCKS—AND THE DOOR IS NOT OPENED.

THE remainder of that winter was dreary indeed. Every time Robert went up the
stair to his garret, he passed the door of a tomb.
With that gray mortar Mary St. John was walled up, like the nun he had read of in the *Mar-
mion* she had lent him. He might have rung the
bell at the street door, and been admitted into
the temple of his goddess, but a certain vague
terror of his grannie, combined with equally
vague qualms of conscience for having deceived
her, and the approach in the far distance of a
ghastly suspicion that violins, pianos, moonlight, and lovely women were distasteful to the
over-ruling Fate, and obnoxious to the venge-

ance stored in the gray cloud of his providence, drove him from the awful entrance of the temple of his Isis.

Nor did Miss St. John dare to make any advances to the dreadful old lady. She would wait. For Mrs. Forsyth, she cared nothing about the whole affair. It only gave her fresh opportunity for smiling condescensions about " poor Mrs. Falconer." So Paradise was over and gone.

But though the loss of Miss St. John and the piano was the last blow, his sorrow did not rest there, but returned to brood over his bonny lady. She was scattered to the winds. Would any of her ashes ever rise in the corn, and moan in the ripening wind of autum ? Might not some atoms of the *bonny leddy* creep into the pines on the hill, whose " soft and soul-like sounds " had taught him to play the Flowers of the Forest on those strings which, like the nerves of an amputated limb, yet thrilled through his being ? Or might not some particle find its way by winds and waters to sycamore forest of Italy, there creep up through the channels of its life to some finely-rounded curve of noble tree, on the side that ever looks sunwards, and be chosen once again by the violin-hunter, to be wrought into a new and fame-gathering instrument ?

Could it be that his bonny lady had learned her wondrous music in those forests, from the shine of the sun, and the sighing of the winds

through the sycamores and pines ? For Robert
knew that the broad-leaved sycamore, and the
sharp, needle-leaved pine, had each its share in
the violin. Only as the wild innocence of human
nature, uncorrupted by wrong, untaught by suffering, is to that nature struggling out of darkness into light, such and so different is the
living wood, with its sweetest tones of obedient
impulse, answering only to the wind which
bloweth where it listeth, to that wood, chosen,
separated, individualized, tortured into strange,
almost vital shape, after a law to us nearly unknown, strung with strings from animal organiza-
tions, and put into the hands of man to utter the
feelings of a soul that has passed through a like
history. This Robert could not yet think, and
had to grow able to think it by being himself
made an instrument of God's music.

What he could think was that the glorious
mystery of his bonny leddy was gone for ever
—and alas! she had no soul. Here was an
eternal sorrow. He could never meet her again.
His affections, which must live for ever, were
set upon that which had passed away. But the
child that weeps because his mutilated doll will
not rise from the dead, shall yet find relief from
his sorrow, a true relief, both human and divine.
He shall know that that which in the doll made
him love the doll, has not passed away. And
Robert must yet be comforted for the loss of his

bonny leddy. If she had had a soul, nothing but
her own self could ever satisfy him. As she had
no soul, another body might take her place, nor
accasion reproach of inconstancy.

But, in the meantime, the shears of Fate having cut the string of the sky-soaring kite of his
imagination, had left him with the stick in his
hand.   And thus the rest of that winter was
dreary enough. The glow was out of his heart ;
the glow was out of the world. The bleak, kind-
less wind was hissing through those pines that
clothed the hill above Bodyfauld, and over the
dead garden, where in the summer time the rose
had looked down so lovingly on the heartsease.
If he had stood once more at gloaming in that
barley-stubble, not even the wail of Flodden-
field would have found him there, but a keen
sense of personal misery and hopeless cold. Was
the summer a lie ?

Not so. The winter restrains, that the summer
may have the needful time to do its work well ;
for the winter is but the sleep of summer.

Now in the winter of his discontent, and in
Nature finding no help, Robert was driven in-
wards—into his garret, into his soul. There, the
door of his paradise being walled up, he began,
vaguely, blindly, to knock against other doors
—sometimes against stone-walls and rocks, taking them for doors—as travel-worn, and hence
brain-sick men have done in a desert of moun-

tains. A door, out or in, he must find, or perish.

It fell, too, that Miss St. John went to visit some friends who lived in a coast town twenty miles off; and a season of heavy snow followed by frost setting in, she was absent for six weeks, during which time, without a single care to trouble him from without, Robert was in the very desert of desolation. His spirits sank fearfully. He would pass his old music-master in the street with scarce a recognition, as if the bond of their relation had been utterly broken, had vanished in the smoke of the martyred violin, and all their affection had gone into the dust-heap of the past.

Dooble Sanny's character did not improve. He took more and more whisky, his bouts of drinking alternating as before with fits of hopeless repentance. His work was more neglected than ever, and his wife having no money to spend even upon necessaries, applied in desperation to her husband's bottle for comfort. This comfort, to do him justice, he never grudged her; and sometimes before midday they would both be drunk—a condition expedited by the lack of food. When they began to recover, they would quarrel fiercely; and at last they became a nuisance to the whole street. Little did the whisky-hating old lady know to what god she had really offered up that violin—if the consequences of the holocaust can be admitted as indicating the power which had accepted it.

But now began to appear in Robert the first signs of a practical outcome of such truth as his grandmother had taught him, operating upon the necessities of a simple and earnest nature. Reality, however lapt in vanity, or even in falsehood, cannot lose its power. It *is*—the other is not. She had taught him to look up—that there was a God. He would put it to the test. Not that he doubted it yet: he only doubted whether there was a hearing God. But was not that worse? It was, I think. For it is of far more consequence what kind of a God, than whether a God or no. Let not my reader suppose I think it possible there could be other than a perfect God—perfect—even to the vision of his creatures, the faith that supplies the lack of vision being yet faithful to that vision. I speak from Robert's point of outlook. But, indeed, whether better or worse is no great matter, so long as he would see it or what there was. He had no comfort, and, without reasoning about it, he felt that life ought to have comfort—from which point he began to conclude that the only thing left was to try whether the God in whom his grandmother believed might not help him. If the God would but hear him, it was all he had yet learned to require of his Godhood. And that must ever be the first thing to require.

More demands would come, and greater answers
he would find. But now—if God would but hear
him ! If he spoke to him but one kind word,
it would be the very soul of comfort; he could
no more be lonely. A fountain of glad imaginations gushed up in his heart at the thought.
What if from the cold winter of his life, he
had but to open the door of his garret-room,
and, kneeling by the bare bedstead, enter into
the summer of God's presence ! What if God
spoke to him face to face ! He had so spoken to
Moses. He sought him from no fear of the future, but from present desolation; and if God
came near to him, it would not be with storm
and tempest, but with the voice of a friend.
And surely, if there was a God at all, that is, not
a power greater than man, but a power by
whose power man was, he must hear the voice
of the creature whom he had made, a voice that
came crying out of the very need which he had
created. Younger people than Robert are capable of such divine metaphysics. Hence he
continued to disappear from his grandmother's
parlour at much the same hour as before. In the
cold, desolate garret, he knelt and cried out
into that which lay beyond the thought that
cried, the unknowable infinite, after the God
that may be known as surely as a little child
knows his mysterious mother. And from behind him, the pale-blue, star-crowded sky shone

upon his head, through the window that looked upwards only.

Mrs. Falconer saw that he still went away as he had been wont, and instituted observations, the result of which was the knowledge that he went to his own room. Her heart smote her, and she saw that the boy looked sad and troubled. There was scarce room in her heart for increase of love, but much for increase of kindness, and she did increase it. In truth, he needed the smallest crumb of comfort that might drop from the table of God's "feastful friends."

Night after night he returned to the parlour cold to the very heart. God was not to be found, he said then. He said afterwards that even then " God was with him though he knew it not."

For the very first night, the moment that he knelt and cried, " O Father in heaven, hear me, and let thy face shine upon me "—like a flash of burning fire the words shot from the door of his heart: "I dinna care for him to love me, gin he doesna love ilka body;" and no more prayer went from the desolate boy that night, although he knelt an hour of agony in the freezing dark. Loyal to what he had been taught, he struggled hard to reduce his rebellious will to what he supposed to be the will of God. It was all in vain. Ever a voice within him—surely the voice of that God

who he thought was not hearing—told him
that what he wanted was the love belonging to
his human nature, his human needs—not the
preference of a court-favourite. He had a dim
consciousness that he would be a traitor to his
race if he accepted a love, even from God, given
him as an exception from his kind. But he did
not care to have such a love. It was not what
his heart yearned for. It was not *love*. He could
not love such a love. Yet he strove against it
all—fought for religion against right as he
could; struggled to reduce his rebellious feelings, to love that which was unlovely, to choose
that which was abhorrent, until nature almost
gave way under the effort. Often would he
sink moaning on the floor, or stretch himself
like a corpse, save that it was face downwards,
on the boards of the bedstead. Night after
night he returned to the battle, but with no per-
manent *success*. What a success that would have
been ! Night after night he came pale and
worn from the conflict, found his grandmother
and Shargar composed, and in the quietness of
despair, sat down beside them to his Latin version.

He little thought, that every night, at the moment when he stirred to leave the upper room, a
pale-faced, red-eyed figure rose from its seat on
the top of the stair by the door, and sped with
long-legged noiselessness to resume its seat by

the grandmother before he should enter. Shargar
saw that Robert was unhappy, and the nearest
he could come to the sharing of his unhappiness
was to take his place outside the door within
which he had retreated.   Little, too, did Shargar on his part, think that Robert, without knowing it, was pleading for him inside—pleading
for him and for all his race in the weeping that
would not be comforted.

Robert had not the vaguest fancy that God
was with him—the spirit of the Father groaning
with the spirit of the boy in intercession that
could not be uttered. If God had come to him
then and comforted him with the assurance of
individual favour—but the very supposition is
a taking of his name in vain—Had Robert
found comfort in the fancied assurance that God
was his friend in especial, that some private
favour was granted to his prayers, that, indeed,
would have been to be left to his own inventions, to bring forth not fruits meet for repentance, but fruits for which repentance alone is
meet.   But God *was* with him, and was indeed
victorious in the boy when he rose from his
knees, for the last time, as he thought, saying,
" I cannot yield—I will pray no more."—With
a burst of bitter tears he sat down on the bedside till the loudest of the storm was over, then
dried his dull eyes, in which the old outlook had
withered away, and trod unknowingly in the

silent footsteps of Shargar, who was ever one corner in advance of him, down to the dreary lessons and unheeded prayers; but, thank God, not to the sleepless night, for some griefs bring sleep the sooner.

My reader must not mistake my use of the words *especial* and *private*, or suppose that I do not believe in an *individual* relation between every man and God, yes, a *peculiar* relation, differing from the relation between every other man and God! But this very individuality and peculiarity can only be founded on the broadest truths of the Godhood and the manhood.

Mrs. Falconer, ere she went to sleep, gave thanks that the boys had been at their prayers together. And so, in a very deep sense, they had.

And well they might have been; for Shargar was nearly as desolate as Robert, and would certainly, had his mother claimed him now, have gone on the tramp with her again. Wherein could this civilized life show itself to him better than that to which he had been born? For clothing he cared little, and he had always managed to kill his hunger or thirst, if at longer intervals, then with greater satisfaction. Wherein is the life of that man who merely does his eating and drinking and clothing after a civilized fashion better than that of the gipsy or tramp? If the civilized man is honest to boot,

and gives good work in return for the bread or
turtle on which he dines, and the gipsy, on the
other hand, steals his dinner, I recognize the
importance of the difference; but if the rich
man plunders the community by exorbitant
profits, or speculation with other people's money,
while the gipsy adds a fowl or two to the produce of his tinkering; or, once again, if the gipsy
is as honest as the honest citizen, which is not
so rare a case by any means as people imagine,
I return to my question: Wherein, I say, is the
warm house, the windows hung with purple,
and the table covered with fine linen, more
divine than the tent or the blue sky, and the
dipping in the dish? Why should not Shargar
prefer a life with the mother God had given him
to a life with Mrs. Falconer? Why should he
prefer geography to rambling, or Latin to Ro-
many? His purposelessness and his love for
Robert alone kept him where he was.

The next evening, having given up his praying, Robert sat with his Sallust before him.
But the fount of tears began to swell, and the
more he tried to keep it down, the more it went
on swelling till his throat was filled with a lump
of pain. He rose and left the room. But he
could not go near the garret. That door too
was closed. He opened the house door instead,
and went out into the street. There, nothing
was to be seen but faint blue air full of moon-

light, solid houses, and shining snow. Bare-headed he wandered round the corner of the house to the window whence first he had heard the sweet sounds of the piano-forte. The fire within lighted up the crimson curtains, but no voice of music came forth. The window was as dumb as the pale, faintly befogged moon over-head, itself seeming but a skylight through which shone the sickly light of the passionless world of the dead. Not a form was in the street. The eyes of the houses gleamed here and there upon the snow. He leaned his elbow on the window-sill behind which stood that sealed fountain of lovely sound, looked up at the moon, careless of her or of aught else in heaven or on earth, and sunk into a reverie, in which nothing was consciously present but a stream of fog-smoke that flowed slowly, list-lessly across the face of the moon, like the ghost of a dead cataract. All at once a wailful sound arose in his head. He did not think for some time whether it was born in his brain, or en-tered it from without. At length he recognized the Flowers of the Forest, played as only the soutar could play it. But alas! the cry re-sponsive to his bow came only from the auld wife—no more from the bonny leddy! Then he remembered that there had been a humble wedding that morning on the opposite side of the way; in the street department of the jollity

of which Shargar had taken a small share by
firing a brass cannon, subsequently confiscated
by Mrs. Falconer.   But this was a strange tune
to play at a wedding!   The soutar half way to
his goal of drunkenness, had begun to repent
for the fiftieth time that year, had with his repentance mingled the memory of the bonny
leddy ruthlessly tortured to death for his wrong,
and had glided from a strathspey into that
sorrowful moaning.   The lament interpreted itself to his disconsolate pupil as he had never
understood it before, not even in the stubble-
field; for it now spoke his own feelings of waste
misery, forsaken loneliness. Indeed Robert learned more of music in those few minutes of the
foggy winter night and open street, shut out of
all doors, with the tones of an ancient grief and
lamentation floating through the blotted moonlight over his ever present sorrow, than he could
have learned from many lessons even of Miss St.
John.   He was cold to the heart, yet went in a
little comforted.

Things had gone ill with him.   Outside of
Paradise, deserted of his angel, in the frost and
the snow, the voice of the despised violin once
more the source of a sad comfort!   But there is
no better discipline than an occasional descent
from what we count well being, to a former
despised or less happy condition.   One of the
results of this taste of damnation in Robert was,

that when he was in bed that night, his heart began to turn gently towards his old master. How much did he not owe him, after all! Had he not acted ill and ungratefully in deserting him? His own vessel filled to the brim with grief, had he not let the waters of its bitterness overflow into the heart of the soutar? The wail of that violin echoed now in Robert's heart, not for Flodden, not for himself, but for the debased nature that drew forth the plaint. Comrades in misery, why should they part? What right had he to forsake an old friend and benefactor because he himself was unhappy? He would go and see him the very next night. And he would make friends once more with the much "suffering instrument" he had so wrongfully despised.

CHAPTER II.

THE STROKE.

THE following night, he left his books on the table, and the house itself behind him, and sped like a grayhound to Dooble Sanny's shop, lifted the latch, and entered.

By the light of a single dip set on a chair, he saw the shoemaker seated on his stool, one hand lying on the lap of his leathern apron, his other hand hanging down by his side, and the fiddle on the ground at his feet. His wife stood behind him, wiping her eyes with her blue apron. Through all its accumulated dirt, the face of the soutar looked ghastly, and they were eyes of despair that he lifted to the face of the youth as he stood holding the latch in his hand. Mrs. Alexander moved towards Robert, drew him in, and gently closed the door behind him, resuming her station like a sculptured mourner behind her motionless husband.

" What on airth's the maitter wi' ye, Sandy ?" said Robert.

" Eh, Robert !" returned the shoemaker, and a tone of affection tinged the mournfulness with which he uttered the strange words—" eh, Robert ! the Almichty *will* gang his ain gait, and I'm in his grup noo."

" He 's had a stroke," said his wife, without removing her apron from her eyes.

" I hae gotten my pecks (*blows*)," resumed the soutar, in a despairing voice, which gave yet more effect to the fantastic eccentricity of conscience which from the midst of so many grave faults chose such a one as especially bringing the divine displeasure upon him : " I hae gotten my pecks for cryin' doon my ain auld wife to set up your bonny leddy. The tane 's gane a' to aise an' stew (*ashes and dust*), an' frae the tither," he went on, looking down on the violin at his feet as if it had been something dead in its youth—" an' frae the tither I canna draw a cheep, for my richt han' has forgotten her cunnin'. Man, Robert, I canna lift it frae my side."

" Ye maun gang to yer bed," said Robert, greatly concerned.

" Ow, ay, I maun gang to my bed, and syne to the kirkyaird, and syne to hell, I ken that weel eneuch. Robert, I lea' my fiddle to you. Be guid to the auld wife, man—better nor I hae been. An auld wife 's better nor nae fiddle."

He stooped, lifted the violin with his left hand, gave it to Robert, rose, and made for the door. They helped him up the creaking stair, got him half-undressed, and laid him in his bed. Robert put the violin on the top of a press within sight of the sufferer, left him groaning, and ran for the doctor. Having seen him set out for the patient's dwelling, he ran home to his grandmother.

Now while Robert was absent, occasion had arisen to look for him : unusual occurrence, a visitor had appeared, no less a person than Mr. Innes, the schoolmaster. Shargar had been banished in consequence from the parlour, and had seated himself outside Robert's room, never doubting that Robert was inside. Presently he heard the bell ring, and then Betty came up the stair, and said Robert was wanted. Thereupon Shargar knocked at the door, and as there was neither voice nor hearing, opened it, and found, with a well-known horror, that he had been watching an empty room. He made no haste to communicate the fact. Robert might return in a moment, and his absence from the house not be discovered. He sat down on the bedstead and waited. But Betty came up again, and before Shargar could prevent her, walked into the room with her candle in her hand. In vain did Shargar intreat her to go and say that Robert was coming. Betty would not risk the danger of discovery in connivance, and descended to open afresh the fountain of the old lady's anxiety. She did not, however, betray her disquietude to Mr. Innes.

She had asked the schoolmaster to visit her, in order that she might consult him about Robert's future. Mr. Innes expressed a high opinion of the boy's faculties and attainments, and strongly urged that he should be sent to college. Mrs. Falconer inwardly shuddered at the temptations to which this course would expose him; but he must leave home or be apprentice to some trade. She would have chosen the latter, I believe, but for religion towards the boy's parents, who would never have thought of other than a profession for him. While the schoolmaster was dwelling on the argument that he was pretty sure to gain a good *bursary,* and she would thus be relieved for four years, probably for ever, from further expense on his account, Robert entered.

" Whaur hae ye been, Robert?" asked Mrs. Falconer.

" At Dooble Sanny's," answered the boy.

" What hae ye been at there ?"

" Helpin' him till's bed."

" What's come ower him ?"

" A stroke."

" That's what comes o' playin' the fiddle."

" I never heard o' a stroke comin' frae a fiddle, grannie. It comes oot o' a clood whiles. Gin he had hauden till 's fiddle, he wad hae been playin' her the nicht, in place o' 's airm lyin' at 's side like a lang lingel *(ligneul—shoemaker's thread)*."

" Hm !" said his grandmother, concealing her indignation at this freedom of speech, " ye dinna believe in God's judgments !"

" Nae upo' fiddles," returned Robert.

Mr. Innes sat and said nothing, with difficulty concealing his amusement at this passage of arms.

It was but within the last few days that Robert had become capable of speaking thus. His nature had at length arrived at the point of so far casting off the incubus of his grandmother's authority as to assert some measure of freedom and act openly. His very hopelessness of a hearing in heaven had made him indifferent to things on earth, and therefore bolder. Thus, strange as it may seem, the blessing of God descended on him in the despair which enabled him to speak out and free his soul from the weight of concealment. But it was not despair alone that gave him strength. On his way home from the shoemaker's, he had been thinking what he could do for him; and had resolved, come of it what might, that he would visit him every evening, and try whether he could not comfort him a little by playing upon his violin.

So that it was loving kindness towards man, as well as despair towards God, that gave him strength to resolve that between him and his grandmother all should be above-board from henceforth.

"Nae upo' fiddles," Robert had said.

"But upo' them 'at plays them," returned his grandmother.

"Na ; nor upo' them 'at burns them," retorted Robert—impudently it must be confessed ; for every man is open to commit the fault of which he is least capable.

But Mrs. Falconer had too much regard to her own dignity to indulge her feelings. Possibly too her sense of justice, which Falconer always said was stronger than that of any other woman he had ever known, as well as some movement of her conscience interfered. She was silent, and Robert rushed into the breach which his last discharge had effected.

"An' I want to tell ye, grannie, that I mean to gang an' play the fiddle to puir Sanny ilka nicht for the best pairt o' an hoor ; an' excep' ye lock the door an' hide the key, I *will* gang. The puir sinner sanna be desertit by God an' man baith."

He scarcely knew what he was saying before it was out of his mouth ; and as if to cover it up, he hurried on.

"An' there's mair in 't.—Dr. Anderson gae

Shargar an' me a sovereign the piece. An' Doo-ble Sanny s' hae them, to haud him ohn deid o' hunger an' cauld."

" What for didna ye tell me 'at Dr. Anderson had gien ye sic a sicht o' siller? It was ill-faured o' ye—an' him as weel."

" 'Cause ye wad hae sent it back till 'im; an' Shargar and me we thocht we wad raither keep it."

" Considerin' 'at I'm at sae muckle expense wi' ye baith, it wadna hae been ill-contrived to hae brocht the siller to me, an' latten me du wi' 't as I thocht fit.—Gang na awa', laddie," she added, as she saw Robert about to leave the room.

" I'll be back in a minute, grannie," returned Robert.

" He's a fine lad, that!" said Mr. Innes; " an' guid 'll come o' 'm, and that 'll be heard tell o'."

" Gin he had but the grace o' God, there wadna be muckle to compleen o'," acquiesced his grandmother.

" There's time eneuch for that, Mrs. Faukner. Ye canna get auld heids upo' young shoothers, ye ken."

" 'Deed for that maitter, ye may get mony an auld heid upo' auld shoothers, and nae a spark o' grace in 't to lat it see hoo to lay itsel' doon i' the grave."

Robert returned before Mr. Innes had made up his mind as to whether the old lady intended a personal rebuke.

"Hae, grannie," he said, going up to her, and putting the two sovereigns in her white palm.

He had found some difficulty in making Shargar give up his, else he would have returned sooner.

"What's this o' 't, laddie?" said Mrs. Falconer. "Hoots! I'm nae gaein' to tak yer siller. Lat the puir soutar-craturs hae 't. But dinna gie them mair nor a shillin' or twa at ance—jist to haud them in life. They deserve nae mair. But they maunna sterve. And jist ye tell them, laddie, at gin they spen' ae saxpence o' 't upo' whusky, they s' get nae mair."

"Ay, ay, grannie," responded Robert, with a glimmer of gladness in his heart. "And what aboot the fiddlin', grannie?" he added, half playfully, hoping for some kind concession therein as well.

But he had gone too far. She vouchsafed no reply, and her face grew stern with offence. It was one thing to give bread to eat, another to give music and gladness. No music but that which sprung from effectual calling and the perseverance of the saints could be lawful in a world that was under the wrath and curse of God.   Robert waited in vain for a reply.

" Gang yer wa's," she said at length.   " Mr.
Innes and me has some business to mak an en'
o', an' we want nae assistance."

Robert rejoined Shargar, who was still be-
moaning the loss of his sovereign.   His face
brightened when he saw its well-known yellow
shine once more, but darkened again as soon
as Robert told him to what service it was now
devoted.

" It's my ain," he said, with a suppressed ex-
postulatory growl.

Robert threw the coin on the floor.

" Tak yer filthy lucre !" he exclaimed with
contempt, and turned to leave Shargar alone in
the garret with his sovereign.

" Bob !" Shargar almost screamed, " tak it, or
I'll cut my throat."

This was his constant threat when he was
thoroughly in earnest.

" Cut it, an' hae dune wi' 't," said Robert,
cruelly.

Shargar burst out crying.

" Len' me yer knife, than, Bob," he sobbed,
holding out his hand.

Robert burst into a roar of laughter, caught
up the sovereign from the floor, sped with it
to the baker's, who refused to change it because
he had no knowledge of anything representing
the sum of twenty shillings except a pound-

note, succeeded in getting silver for it at the
bank, and then ran to the soutar's.

After he left the parlour, the discussion of his
fate was resumed and finally settled between
his grandmother and the schoolmaster. The
former, in regard of the boy's determination to
befriend the shoemaker in the matter of music
as well as of money, would now have sent him
at once to the grammar-school in Old Aberdeen,
to prepare for the *competition* in the month of
November; but the latter persuaded her that if
the boy gave his whole attention to Latin till
the next summer, and then went to the grammar-school for three months or so, he would
have an excellent chance of success. As to the
violin, the schoolmaster said, wisely enough :—

"He that *will* to Cupar *maun* to Cupar; and
gin ye kep *(intercept)* him upo' the shore-road,
he'll tak to the hill-road; an' I s' warran' a
braw lad like Robert 'll get mony a ane in Eb-
berdeen 'll be ready eneuch to gie him a lift wi'
the fiddle, and maybe tak him into waur company nor the puir bed-ridden soutar; an' wi'
you an' me to hing on to the tail o' 'im like, he
canna gang ower the scar *(cliff)* afore he learns
wit."

"Hm!" was the old lady's comprehensive response.

It was further arranged that Robert should
be informed of their conclusion, and so roused

to effort in anticipation of the trial upon which his course in life must depend.

Nothing could have been better for Robert than the prospect of a college education. But his first thought at the news was not of the delights of learning nor of the honourable course that would ensue, but of Eric Ericson, the poverty-stricken, friendless descendant of yarls and sea-rovers. He would see *him*—the only man that understood him! Not until the passion of this thought had abated, did he begin to perceive the other advantages before him. But so practical and thorough was he in all his proposals and means, that ere half an hour was gone, he had begun to go over his Rudiments again. He now wrote a version, or translation from English into Latin, five times a week, and read Cæsar, Virgil, or Tacitus, every day. He gained permission from his grandmother to remove his bed to his own garret, and there, from the bedstead at which he no longer kneeled, he would often rise at four in the morning, even when the snow lay a foot thick on the skylight, kindle his lamp by means of a tinder-box and a splinter of wood dipped in sulphur, and sitting down in the keen cold, turn half a page of Addison into something as near Ciceronian Latin as he could effect. This would take him from an hour and a half to two hours, when he would tumble again into bed, blue and stiff, and sleep

till it was time to get up and go to the morning school before breakfast. His health was
excellent, else it could never have stood such
treatment.

CHAPTER III.

"THE END CROWNS ALL."

HIS sole relaxation almost lay in the visit he paid every evening to the soutar and his wife. Their home was a wretched place; but notwithstanding the poverty in which they were now sunk, Robert soon began to see a change, like the dawning of light, an *alba*, as the Italians call the dawn, in the appearance of something white here and there about the room. Robert's visits had set the poor woman trying to make the place look decent. It soon became at least clean, and there is a very real sense in which cleanliness is next to godliness. If the people who want to do good among the poor would give up patronizing them, would cease from trying to convert them before they have gained the smallest personal influence with them, would visit them as those who have just as good a right to be here as they have, it would be all the better for both, perhaps chiefly for themselves.

For the first week or so, Alexander, unable either to work or play, and deprived of his usual consolation of drink, was very testy and unmanageable. If Robert, who strove to do his best, in the hope of alleviating the poor fellow's sufferings—chiefly those of the mind—happened to mistake the time or to draw a false note from the violin, Sandy would swear as if he had been the Grand Turk and Robert one of his slaves. But Robert was too vexed with himself, when he gave occasion to such an outburst, to mind the outburst itself. And invariably when such had taken place, the shoemaker would ask forgiveness before he went. Holding out his left hand, from which nothing could efface the stains of rosin and lamp-black and heel-ball, save the sweet cleansing of mother-earth, he would say :

"Robert, ye'll jist pit the sweirin' doon wi' the lave *(rest)*, an' score 't oot a'thegither. I'm an ill-tongued vratch, an' I'm beginnin' to see 't. But, man, ye 're jist behavin' to me like God himsel', an' gin it warna for you, I wad jist lie here roarin' an' greitin' an' damnin' frae mornin' to nicht.—Ye *will* be in the morn's night—willna ye?" he would always end by asking with some anxiety.

"Of coorse I will," Robert would answer.

"Gude nicht, than, gude nicht.—I'll try and get a sicht o' my sins ance mair," he added, one evening. "Gin I could only be a wee bit sorry for them, I reckon He wad forgie me. Dinna ye think he wad, Robert?"

"Nae doobt, nae doobt," answered Robert, hurriedly. "They a' say 'at gin a man repents the richt gait, he'll forgie him."

He could not say more than "They say," for his own horizon was all dark, and even in saying this much he felt like a hypocrite. A terrible waste, heaped thick with the potsherds of hope, lay outside that door of prayer which he had, as he thought, nailed up for ever.

"An' what *is* the richt gait?" asked the soutar.

"'Deed, that's mair nor I ken, Sandy," answered Robert mournfully.

"Weel, gin *ye* dinna ken, what's to come o' *me?*" said Alexander anxiously.

"Ye maun speir at Himsel'," returned Robert, "an' jist tell him 'at ye dinna ken, but ye'll do onything 'at he likes."

With these words he took his leave hurriedly, somewhat amazed to find that he had given the soutar the strange advice to try just what he had tried so unavailingly himself. And stranger still, he found himself, before he reached home, praying once more in his heart—both for Dooble Sanny and for himself. From that hour a faint hope was within him that some day he might try again, though he dared not yet encounter such effort and agony.

All this time he had never doubted that there was God; nor had he ventured to say within himself that perhaps God was not good; he had simply come to the conclusion that for him there was no approach to the fountain of his being.

In the course of a fortnight or so, when his system had covered over its craving after whisky, the irritability of the shoemaker almost vanished. It might have been feared that his conscience would then likewise relax its activity; but it was not so: it grew yet more tender. He now began to give Robert some praise, and make allowances for his faults, and Robert dared more in consequence, and played with more spirit. I do not say that his style could have grown fine under such a master, but at least he learned the difference between slovenliness and accuracy, and between accuracy and expression, which last is all of original that the best mere performer can claim.

One evening he was scraping away at Tullochgorum when Mr. Maccleary walked in. Robert ceased. The minister gave him one searching glance, and sat down by the bedside. Robert would have left the room.

"Dinna gang, Robert," said Sandy, and Robert remained.

The clergyman talked very faithfully as far as the shoemaker was concerned; though whether he was equally faithful towards God might be questioned. He was one of those prudent men, who are afraid of dealing out the truth freely lest it should fall on thorns or stony places. Hence of course the good ground came in for a scanty share too. Believing that a certain precise condition of mind was necessary for its proper reception, he would endeavour to bring about that condition first. He did not know that the truth makes its own nest in the ready heart, and that the heart may be ready for it before the priest can perceive the fact, seeing that the imposition of hands confers, now-a-days at least, neither love nor common sense. He therefore dwelt upon the sins of the soutar, magnifying them and making them hideous, in the idea that thus he magnified the law, and made it honourable, while of the special tenderness of God to the sinner he said not a word. Robert was offended, he scarcely knew why, with the minister's mode of treating his friend; and after Mr. Maccleary had taken a far kinder leave of them than God could approve, if he resembled his representation, Robert sat still, oppressed with darkness.

"It's a' true," said the soutar; "but, man Robert, dinna ye think the minister was some sair upo' me?"

"I duv think it," answered Robert.

"Something beirs 't in upo' me 'at He wadna be sae sair upo' me himsel'. There's something i' the New Testament, some gait, 'at's pitten 't into my heid; though, faith, I dinna ken whaur to luik for 't. Canna ye help me oot wi' 't, man ?"

Robert could think of nothing but the parable of the prodigal son. Mrs. Alexander got him the New Testament and he read it. She sat at the foot of the bed listening.

" There !" cried the soutar, triumphantly, " I telled ye sae ! Not ae word aboot the puir lad's sins ! It was a' a hurry an' a scurry to get the new shune upo' 'im, an' win at the calfie an' the fiddlin' an' the dancin'.—O Lord," he broke out, " I'm comin' hame as fest 's I can; but my sins are jist like muckle bauchles *(shoes down at heel)* upo' my feet and winna lat me. I expec' nae ring and nae robe, but I wad fain hae a fiddle i' my grup when the neist prodigal comes hame; an' gin I dinna fiddle weel, it s' no be my wyte. —Eh, man ! but that is what I ca' gude, an' a' the minister said—honest man—'s jist blether till 't.—O Lord, I sweir gin ever I win up again, I'll put in ilka steek *(stitch)* as gin the shune war for the feet o' the prodigal himsel'. It sall be gude wark, O Lord. An' I'll never lat taste o' whusky intil my mou'—nor smell o' whusky intil my nose, gin sae be 'at I can help it—I sweir 't, O Lord. An' gin I binna raised up again——"

Here his voice trembled and ceased, and

silence endured for a short minute. Then he called his wife.

"Come here, Bell. Gie me a kiss, my bonny lass. I hae been an ill man to you."

"Na, na, Sandy. Ye hae aye been gude to me—better nor I deserved. Ye hae been naebody's enemy but yer ain."

"Haud yer tongue. Ye 're speykin' waur blethers nor the minister, honest man ! I tell ye I hae been a damned scoon'rel to ye. I haena even hauden my han's aff o' ye. And eh ! ye war a bonny lass whan I married ye. I hae blaudit (*spoiled*) ye a'thegither. But gin I war up, see gin I wadna gie ye a new goon, an' that wad be something to make ye like yersel' again. I'm affrontet wi' mysel' 'at I had been sic a brute o' a man to ye. But ye maun forgie me noo, for I do believe i' my hert 'at the Lord's forgien me. Gie me anither kiss, lass. God be praised, and mony thanks to *you!* Ye micht hae run awa' frae me lang or noo, an' a'body wad hae said ye did richt.—Robert, play a spring."

Absorbed in his own thoughts, Robert began to play The Ewie wi' the Crookit Horn.

"Hoots ! hoots !" cried Sandy angrily. "What are ye aboot. Nae mair o' that. I hae dune wi' that. What's i' the heid o' ye, man ?"

"What 'll I play than, Sandy ?" asked Robert meekly.

"Play The Lan' o' the Leal, or My Nannie's

awa', or something o' that kin'. I'll be leal to ye
noo, Bell. An' we winna pree o' the whusky
nae mair, lass."

"I canna bide the smell o' 't," cried Bell, sobbing.

Robert struck in with The Lan' o' the Leal.
When he had played it over two or three times,
he laid the fiddle in its place, and departed—
able just to see, by the light of the neglected
candle, that Bell sat on the bedside stroking the
rosiny hand of her husband, the rhinoceros-hide
of which was yet delicate enough to let the love
through to his heart.

After this the soutar never called his fiddle
his *auld wife*.

Robert walked home with his head sunk on
his breast. Dooble Sanny, the drinking, ranting,
swearing soutar, was inside the wicket-gate; and
he was left outside for all his prayers, with the
arrows from the castle of Beelzebub sticking in
his back. He would have another try some day
—but not yet—he dared not yet.

Henceforth Robert had more to do in reading the New Testament than in playing the fiddle to the soutar, though they never parted
without an air or two. Sandy continued hopeful and generally cheerful, with alternations which
the reading generally fixed on the right side for
the night. Robert never attempted any com-
ments, but left him to take from the word what

nourishment he could. There was no return of strength to the helpless arm, and his constitution was gradually yielding.

The rumour got abroad that he was a " changed character,"—how is not far to seek, for Mr. Maccleary fancied himself the honoured instrument of his conversion, whereas paralysis and the New Testament were the chief agents, and even the violin had more share in it than the minister. For the spirit of God lies all about the spirit of man like a mighty sea, ready to rush in at the smallest chink in the walls that shut him out from his own—walls which even the tone of a violin afloat on the wind of that spirit is sometimes enough to rend from battlement to base, as the blast of the rams' horns rent the walls of Jericho. And now to the day of his death, the shoemaker had need of nothing. Food, wine, and delicacies were sent him by many who, while they considered him outside of the kingdom, would have troubled themselves in no way about him. What with visits of condolence and flattery, inquiries into his experience, and long prayers by his bedside, they now did their best to send him back among the swine. The soutar's humour, however, aided by his violin, was a strong antidote against these evil influences.

" I doobt I'm gaein' to dee, Robert," he said at length one evening as the lad sat by his bedside.

"Weel, that winna do ye nae ill," answered Robert, adding with just a touch of bitterness— "ye needna care aboot that."

"I do *not* care aboot the deein' o' 't. But I jist want to live lang eneuch to lat the Lord ken 'at I'm in doonricht earnest aboot it. I hae nae chance o' drinkin' as lang 's I'm lyin' here."

"Never ye fash yer heid aboot that. Ye can lippen (*trust*) that to him, for it's his ain business. He'll see 'at ye 're a' richt. Dinna ye think 'at he 'll lat ye aff."

"The Lord forbid," responded the soutar, earnestly. "It maun be a' pitten richt. It wad be dreidfu' to be latten aff. I wadna hae him content wi' cobbler's wark.—I hae 't," he resumed, after a few minutes' pause: "the Lord's easy pleased, but ill to saitisfee. I'm sair pleased wi' your playin', Robert, but it's naething like the richt thing yet. It does me gude to hear ye, though, for a' that."

The very next night he found him evidently sinking fast. Robert took the violin, and was about to play, but the soutar stretched out his one left hand, and took it from him, laid it across his chest and his arm over it, for a few moments, as if he were bidding it farewell, then held it out to Robert, saying,

"Hae, Robert. She's yours.—Death's a sair divorce.—Maybe they 'll hae an orra* fiddle

* Extra—over all—ower a'—orra—one more than is wanted.

whaur I'm gaein', though. Think o' a Rothieden soutar playin' afore his grace!"

Robert saw that his mind was wandering, and mingled the paltry honours of earth with the grand simplicities of heaven. He began to play the Land o' the Leal. For a little while Sandy seemed to follow and comprehend the tones, but by slow degrees the light departed from his face. At length his jaw fell, and with a sigh, the body parted from Dooble Sanny, and he went to God.

His wife closed mouth and eyes without a word, laid the two arms, equally powerless now, straight by his sides, then seating herself on the edge of the bed, said,

"Dinna bide, Robert. It's a' ower noo. He's gane hame. Gin I war only wi' 'im wherever he is!"

She burst into tears, but dried her eyes a moment after, and seeing that Robert still lingered, said,

"Gang, Robert, an' sen' Mistress Downie to me. Dinna greit—there's a gude lad; but tak yer fiddle an' gang. Ye can be no more use."

Robert obeyed. With his violin in his hand, he went home; and, with his violin still in his hand, walked into his grandmother's parlour.

"Hoo daur ye bring sic a thing into my hoose?" she said, roused by the apparent defiance of her grandson. "Hoo daur ye, efter what's come an' gane?"

"'Cause Dooble Sanny's come and gane, grannie, and left naething but this ahint him. And this ane's mine, whase ever the ither micht be. His wife's left wi'oot a plack, an' I s' warran' the gude fowk o' Rothieden winna mak sae muckle o' her noo 'at her man's awa'; for she never was sic a randy as he was, an' the triumph o' grace in her 's but sma', therefore. Sae I maun mak the best 'at I can o' the fiddle for her. An' ye maunna touch this ane, grannie; for though ye may think it richt to burn fiddles, ither fowk disna; and this has to do wi' ither fowk, grannie; it's no atween you an' me, ye ken," Robert went on, fearful lest she might consider herself divinely commissioned to extirpate the whole race of stringed instruments,—"for I maun sell 't for her."

"Tak it oot o' my sicht," said Mrs. Falconer, and said no more.

He carried the instrument up to his room, laid it on his bed, locked his door, put the key in his pocket, and descended to the parlour.

"He's deid, is he?" said his grandmother, as he re-entered.

"Ay is he, grannie," answered Robert. "He deid a repentant man."

"An' a believin'?" asked Mrs. Falconer.

"Weel, grannie, I canna say 'at he believed a'

thing 'at ever was, for a body michtna ken a' thing."

"Toots, laddie! Was 't savin' faith?"

"I dinna richtly ken what ye mean by that; but I'm thinkin' it was muckle the same kin' o' faith 'at the prodigal had; for they baith rase an' gaed hame."

"'Deed, maybe ye 're richt, laddie," returned Mrs. Falconer, after a moment's thought. "We'll houp the best."

All the remainder of the evening she sat motionless, with her eyes fixed on the rug before her, thinking, no doubt, of the repentance and salvation of the fiddler, and what hope there might yet be for her own lost son.

The next day being Saturday, Robert set out for Bodyfauld, taking the violin with him. He went alone, for he was in no mood for Shargar's company. It was a fine spring day, the woods were budding, and the fragrance of the larches floated across his way. There was a lovely sadness in the sky, and in the motions of the air, and in the scent of the earth—as if they all knew that fine things were at hand which never could be so beautiful as those that had gone away. And Robert wondered how it was that everything should look so different. Even Bodyfauld seemed to have lost its enchantment, though his friends were as kind as ever. Mr. Lammie went into a rage at the story of the lost violin, and Miss Lammie cried from sympathy with Robert's distress at the fate of his bonny leddy. Then he came to the occasion of his visit, which was to beg Mr. Lammie, when next he went to Aberdeen, to take the soutar's fiddle, and get what he could for it, to help his widow.

"Poor Sanny!" said Robert, "it never cam' intil 's heid to sell her, nae mair nor gin she had been the auld wife 'at he ca'd her."

Mr. Lammie undertook the commission; and the next time he saw Robert, handed him ten pounds as the result of the negotiation. It was all Robert could do, however, to get the poor woman to take the money. She looked at it with repugnance, almost as if it had been the price of blood. But Robert having succeeded in overcoming her scruples, she did take it, and therewith provide a store of *sweeties*, and reels of cotton, and tobacco, for sale in Sandy's workshop. She certainly did not make money by her merchandise, for her anxiety to be honest rose to the absurd; but she contrived to live without being reduced to prey upon her own gingerbread and rock.

CHAPTER IV.

THE ABERDEEN GARRET.

MISS ST. JOHN had long since returned
from her visit, but having heard how
much Robert was taken up with his dying
friend, she judged it better to leave her intended
proposal of renewing her lessons alone for the
present. Meeting him, however, soon after
Alexander's death, she introduced the subject,
and Robert was enraptured at the prospect of
the re-opening of the gates of his paradise. If
he did not inform his grandmother of the fact,
neither did he attempt to conceal it; but she
took no notice, thinking probably that the
whole affair would be effectually disposed of by
his departure. Till that period arrived, he had
a lesson almost every evening, and Miss St.
John was surprised to find how the boy had
grown since the door was built up. Robert's
gratitude grew into a kind of worship.

The evening before his departure for Bodyfauld—whence his grandmother had arranged

that he should start for Aberdeen, in order that
he might have the company of Mr. Lammie,
whom business drew thither about the same
time—as he was having his last lesson, Mrs.
Forsyth left the room. Thereupon Robert, who
had been dejected all day at the thought of the
separation from Miss St. John, found his heart
beating so violently that he could hardly
breathe. Probably she saw his emotion, for
she put her hand on the keys, as if to cover it
by showing him how some movement was to be
better effected. He seized her hand and lifted
it to his lips. But when he found that instead
of snatching it away, she yielded it, nay gently
pressed it to his face, he burst into tears, and
dropped on his knees, as if before a goddess.

"Hush, Robert! Don't be foolish," she said,
quietly and tenderly. "Here is my aunt coming."

The same moment he was at the piano again,
playing My Bonny Lady Ann, so as to aston-
ish Miss St. John, and himself as well. Then
he rose, bade her a hasty good night, and hurried away.

A strange conflict arose in his mind at the
prospect of leaving the old place, on every house
of whose streets, on every swell of whose surrounding hills he left the clinging shadows of
thought and feeling. A faintly purpled mist
arose, and enwrapped all the past, changing

even his grayest troubles into tales of fairyland,
and his deepest griefs into songs of a sad
music. Then he thought of Shargar, and what
was to become of him after he was gone. The
lad was paler and his eyes were redder than
ever, for he had been weeping in secret. He
went to his grandmother and begged that Shargar might accompany him to Bodyfauld.

" He maun bide at hame an' min' his beuks,"
she answered; "for he winna hae them that
muckle langer. He maun be doin' something
for himsel'."

So the next morning the boys parted—Shargar to school, and Robert to Bodyfauld—Shargar left behind with his desolation, his sun gone
down in a west that was not even stormy, only
gray and hopeless, and Robert moving towards
an east which reflected, like a faint prophecy,
the west behind him tinged with love, death,
and music, but mingled the colours with its own
saffron of coming dawn.

When he reached Bodyfauld he marvelled to
find that all its glory had returned. He found
Miss Lammie busy among the rich yellow pools
in her dairy, and went out into the garden,
now in the height of its summer. Great cab-
bage roses hung heavy-headed splendours towards purple-black heartseases, and thin-filmed
silvery pods of honesty; tall white lilies mingled
with the blossoms of currant bushes, and at their

feet the narcissi of old classic legend pressed their
warm-hearted paleness into the plebeian thicket
of the many-striped gardener's garters. It was
a lovely type of a commonwealth indeed, of the
garden and kingdom of God. His whole mind
was flooded with a sense of sunny wealth. The
farmer's neglected garden blossomed into higher
glory in his soul. The bloom and the richness
and the use were all there; but instead of each
flower was a delicate ethereal sense or feeling
about that flower. Of these how gladly would
he have gathered a posy to offer Miss St. John!
but, alas! he was no poet; or rather he had but
the half of the poet's inheritance—he could see:
he could not say. But even if he had been full
of poetic speech, he would yet have found that
the half of his posy remained ungathered, for
although we have speech enough now to be
" cousin to the deed," as Chaucer says it must
always be, we have not yet enough speech to
cousin the tenth part of our feelings. Let him
who doubts recall one of his own vain attempts
to convey that which made the oddest of dreams
entrancing in loveliness—to convey that aroma
of thought, the conscious absence of which made
him a fool in his own eyes when he spoke such
silly words as alone presented themselves for
the service. I can no more describe the emotion aroused in my mind by a gray cloud parting over a gray stone, by the smell of a sweet

pea, by the sight of one of those long upright
pennons of striped grass with the homely name,
than I can tell what the glory of God is who
made these things. The man whose poetry is
like nature in this, that it produces individual,
incommunicable moods and conditions of mind,
—a sense of elevated, tender, marvellous, and
evanescent existence, must be a poet indeed.
Every dawn of such a feeling is a light-brushed
bubble rendering visible for a moment the dark
unknown sea of our being which lies beyond the
lights of our consciousness, and is the stuff and
the region of our eternal growth. But think
what language must become before it will tell
dreams!—before it will convey the delicate
shades of fancy that come and go in the brain
of a child!—before it will let a man know
wherein one face differeth from another face in
glory! I suspect, however, that for such purposes it is rather music than articulation that is
needful—that, with a hope of these finer results, the language must rather be turned into
music than logically extended.

The next morning he awoke at early dawn,
hearing the birds at his window. He rose and
went out. The air was clear and fresh as a new-
made soul. Bars of mottled cloud were bent
across the eastern quarter of the sky, which lay
like a great ethereal ocean ready for the launch
of the ship of glory that was now gliding to-

wards its edge. Everything was waiting to
conduct him across the far horizon to the south,
where lay the stored-up wonder of his coming
life. The lark sang of something greater than
he could tell; the wind got up, whispered at it,
and lay down to sleep again; the sun was at
hand to bathe the world in the light and gladness alone fit to typify the radiance of Robert's
thoughts. The clouds that formed the shore of
the upper sea were already burning from saffron
into gold. A moment more and the first insup-
portable sting of light would shoot from behind
the edge of that low blue hill, and the first day
of his new life would be begun. He watched,
and it came. The well-spring of day, fresh and
exuberant as if now first from the holy will of
the Father of Lights, gushed into the basin of
the world, and the world was more glad than
tongue or pen can tell. The supernal light alone,
dawning upon the human heart, can exceed the
marvel of such a sunrise.

And shall life itself be less beautiful than one
of its days? Do not believe it, young brother.
Men call the shadow, thrown upon the universe
where their own dusky souls come between it
and the eternal sun, life, and then mourn that it
should be less bright than the hopes of their
childhood. Keep thou thy soul translucent,
that thou mayest never see its shadow; at least
never abuse thyself with the philosophy which

calls that shadow life.   Or, rather would I say,
become thou pure in heart, and thou shalt see
God, whose vision alone is life.

Just as the sun rushed across the horizon he
heard the tramp of a heavy horse in the yard,
passing from the stable to the cart that was to
carry his trunk to the turnpike road, three miles
off, where the coach would pass.   Then Miss
Lammie came and called him to breakfast, and
there sat the farmer in his Sunday suit of black,
already busy.   Robert was almost too happy to
eat; yet he had not swallowed two mouthfuls
before the sun rose unheeded, the lark sang unheeded, and the roses sparkled with the dew that
bowed yet lower their heavy heads, all unheeded.
By the time they had finished, Mr. Lammie's gig
was at the door, and they mounted and followed
the cart.   Not even the recurring doubt and
fear that hollowness was at the heart of it all,
for that God could not mean such reinless gladness, prevented the truth of the present joy
from sinking deep into the lad's heart.   In his
mind he saw a boat moored to a rock, with no
one on board, heaving on the waters of a rising
tide, and waiting to bear him out on the sea of
the unknown.   The picture arose of itself: there
was no paradise of the west in his imagination,
as in that of a boy of the sixteenth century, to
authorize its appearance.   It rose again and
again; the dew glittered as if the light were its

own; the sun shone as he had never seen him shine before; the very mare that sped them along held up her head and stepped out as if she felt it the finest of mornings. Had she also a future, poor old mare? Might there not be a paradise somewhere? and if in the furthest star instead of next-door America, why, so much the more might the Atlantis of the nineteenth century surpass Manoa the golden of the seventeenth!

The gig and the cart reached the road together. One of the men who had accompanied the cart took the gig; and they were left on the road-side with Robert's trunk and box—the latter a present from Miss Lammie.

Their places had been secured, and the guard knew where he had to take them up. Long before the coach appeared, the notes of his horn, as like the colour of his red coat as the blindest of men could imagine, came echoing from the side of the heathery, stony hill under which they stood, so that Robert turned wondering, as if the chariot of his desires had been coming over the top of Drumsnaig, to carry him into a heaven where all labour was delight. But round the corner in front came the four-in-hand red mail instead. *She* pulled up gallantly; the wheelers lay on their hind quarters, and the leaders parted theirs from the pole; the boxes were hoisted up; Mr. Lammie climbed, and Robert

scrambled to his seat; the horn blew; the
coachman spake oracularly; the horses obeyed;
and away went the gorgeous symbol of sovereignty careering through the submissive region.
Nor did Robert's delight abate during the
journey—certainly not when he saw the blue
line of the sea in the distance, a marvel and
yet a fact.

Mrs. Falconer had consulted the Misses Napier,
who had many acquaintances in Aberdeen, as to
a place proper for Robert, and suitable to her
means. Upon this point Miss Letty, not without a certain touch of design, as may appear
in the course of my story, had been able to
satisfy her. In a small house of two floors and
a garret, in the old town, Mr. Lammie took leave
of Robert.

It was from a garret window still, but a storm-
window now, that Robert looked—eastward
across fields and sand-hills, to the blue expanse
of waters—not blue like southern seas, but slaty
blue, like the eyes of northmen. It was rather
dreary; the sun was shining from overhead
now, casting short shadows and much heat; the
dew was gone up, and the lark had come down;
he was alone; the end of his journey was come,
and was not anything very remarkable. His
landlady interrupted his gaze to know what he
would have for dinner, but he declined to use
any discretion in the matter. When she left

the room he did not return to the window, but sat down upon his box. His eye fell upon the other, a big wooden cube. Of its contents he knew nothing. He would amuse himself by making inquisition. It was nailed up. He borrowed a screw-driver and opened it. At the top lay a linen bag full of oatmeal; underneath that was a thick layer of oat cake; underneath that two cheeses, a pound of butter, and six pots of jam, which ought to have tasted of roses, for it came from the old garden where the roses lived in such sweet companionship with the currant bushes; underneath that, &c.; and underneath &c., a box which strangely recalled Shargar's garret, and one of the closets therein. With beating heart he opened it, and lo, to his marvel, and the restoration of all the fair day, there was the violin which Dooble Sanny had left him when he forsook her for—some one or other of the queer instruments of Fra Angelico's angels?

In a flutter of delight he sat down on his trunk again and played the most mournful of tunes. Two white pigeons, which had been talking to each other in the heat on the roof, came one on each side of the window and peeped into the room; and out between them, as he played, Robert saw the sea, and the blue sky above it. Is it any wonder that, instead of turning to the lying pages and contorted sentences of the Livy which he had already unpacked from his box, he

forgot all about school, and college, and bursary,
and went on playing till his landlady brought
up his dinner, which he swallowed hastily that
he might return to the spells of his enchantress!

CHAPTER V.

THE COMPETITION.

I COULD linger with gladness even over this part of my hero's history. If the school work was dry it was thorough. If that academy had no sweetly shadowing trees; if it did stand within a parallellogram of low stone walls, containing a roughly-gravelled court; if all the region about suggested hot stones and sand— beyond still was the sea and the sky; and that court, morning and afternoon, was filled with the shouts of eager boys, kicking the football with mad rushings to and fro, and sometimes with wounds and faintings—fit symbol of the equally resultless ambition with which many of them would follow the game of life in the years to come. Shock-headed Highland colts, and rough Lowland steers as many of them were, out of that group, out of the roughest of them, would emerge in time a few gentlemen—not of the type of your trim, self-contained, clerical exquisite—but large-hearted, courteous gentle-

men, for whom a man may thank God. And if
the master was stern and hard, he was true; if
the pupils feared him, they yet cared to please
him; if there might be found not a few more
widely-read scholars than he, it would be hard
to find a better teacher.

Robert leaned to the collar and laboured, not
greatly moved by ambition, but much by the
hope of the bursary and the college life in the
near distance. Not unfrequently he would rush
into the thick of the football game, fight like a
maniac for one short burst, and then retire and
look on. He oftener regarded than mingled.
He seldom joined his fellows after school hours,
for his work lay both upon his conscience and
his hopes; but if he formed no very deep friend-
ships amongst them, at least he made no ene-
mies, for he was not selfish, and in virtue of the
Celtic blood in him was invariably courteous.
His habits were in some things altogether ir-
regular. He never went out for a walk; but
sometimes, looking up from his Virgil or his
Latin version, and seeing the blue expanse in
the distance breaking into white under the viewless wing of the summer wind, he would fling
down his dictionary or his pen, rush from his
garret, and fly in a straight line, like a sea-gull
weary of lake and river, down to the waste
shore of the great deep. This was all that stood
for the Arabian Nights of moon-blossomed

marvel; all the rest was Aberdeen days of Latin
and labour.

Slowly the hours went, and yet the dreaded,
hoped-for day came quickly. The quadrangle
of the stone-crowned college grew more awful
in its silence and emptiness every time Robert
passed it; and the professors' houses looked like
the sentry-boxes of the angels of learning, soon
to come forth and judge the feeble mortals who
dared present a claim to their recognition. October faded softly by, with its keen fresh mornings, and cold memorial green-horisoned evenings, whose stars fell like the stray blossoms of
a more heavenly world, from some ghostly wind
of space that had caught them up on its awful
shoreless sweep. November came, " chill and
drear," with its heartless, hopeless nothingness;
but as if to mock the poor competitors, rose,
after three days of Scotch mist, in a lovely
" halcyon day " of " St. Martin's summer,"
through whose long shadows anxious young
faces gathered in the quadrangle, or under the
arcade, each with his Ainsworth's Dictionary,
the sole book allowed, under his arm. But when
the sacrist appeared and unlocked the public
school, and the black-gowned professors walked
into the room, and the door was left open for
the candidates to follow, then indeed a great
awe fell upon the assembly, and the lads crept
into their seats as if to a trial for life before a

bench of the incorruptible. They took their places; a portion of Robertson's *History of Scotland* was given them to turn into Latin; and soon there was nothing to be heard in the assembly but the turning of the leaves of dictionaries, and the scratching of pens constructing the first rough copy of the Latinized theme.

It was done. Four weary hours, nearly five, one or two of which passed like minutes, the others as if each minute had been an hour, went by, and Robert in a kind of desperation, after a final reading of the Latin, gave in his paper, and left the room. When he got home, he asked his landlady to get him some tea. Till it was ready he would take his violin. But even the violin had grown dull, and would not speak freely. He returned to the torture—took out his first copy, and went over it once more. Horror of horrors! a *maxie!*—that is a *maximus error*. Mary Queen of Scots had been left so far behind in the beginning of the paper, that she forgot the rights of her sex in the middle of it, and in the accusative of a future participle passive—I do not know if more modern grammarians have a different name for the growth— had submitted to be *dum*, and her rightful *dam* was henceforth and for ever debarred.

He rose, rushed out of the house, down through the garden, across two fields and a wide road, across the links, and so to the moan-

ing lip of the sea—for it was moaning that
night. From the last bulwark of the sandhills
he dropt upon the wet sands, and there he
paced up and down—how long, God only, who
was watching him, knew—with the low limitless
form of the murmuring lip lying out and out
into the sinking sky like the life that lay low
and hopeless before him, for the want at most
of twenty pounds a year (that was the highest
bursary then) to lift him into a region of possible well-being. Suddenly a strange phenomenon appeared within him. The subject hitherto
became the object to a new birth of consciousness. He began to look at himself. " There's
a sair bit in there," he said, as if his own bosom
had been that of another mortal. " What's to
be dune wi' 't ? I doobt it maun bide it. Weel,
the crater had better bide it quaietly, and no
cry oot. Lie doon, an' haud yer tongue. *Soror
tua haud meretrix est*, ye brute !" He burst out
laughing, after a doubtful and ululant fashion, I
daresay ; but he went home, took up his *auld
wife*, and played " Tullochgorum " some fifty
times over, with extemporized variations.

The next day he had to translate a passage
from Tacitus ; after executing which somewhat
heartlessly, he did not open a Latin book for a
whole week. The very sight of one was disgusting to him. He wandered about the New
Town, along Union Street, and up and down

the stairs that led to the lower parts, haunted
the quay, watched the vessels, learned their
forms, their parts and capacities, made friends
with a certain Dutch captain whom he heard
playing the violin in his cabin, and on the
whole, notwithstanding the wretched prospect
before him, contrived to spend the week with
considerable enjoyment. Nor does an occasional episode of lounging hurt a life with any
true claims to the epic form.

The day of decision at length arrived. Again
the black-robed powers assembled, and again
the hoping, fearing lads—some of them not lads,
men, and mere boys—gathered to hear their
fate. Name after name was called out;—a
twenty pound bursary to the first, one of seven-
teen to the next, three or four of fifteen and fourteen, and so on, for about twenty, and still no
Robert Falconer. At last, lagging wearily in
the rear, he heard his name, went up listlessly,
and was awarded five pounds. He crept home,
wrote to his grandmother, and awaited her reply. It was not long in coming; for although
the carrier was generally the medium of communication, Miss Letty had contrived to send
the answer by coach. It was to the effect that
his grandmother was sorry that he had not been
more successful, but that Mr. Innes thought it
would be quite worth while to try again, and he
must therefore come home for another year.

This was mortifying enough, though not so bad as it might have been. Robert began to pack his box. But before he had finished it he shut the lid and sat upon it. To meet Miss St. John thus disgraced, was more than he could bear. If he remained, he had a chance of winning prizes at the end of the session, and that would more than repair his honour. The five pound bursars were privileged in paying half fees; and if he could only get some teaching, he could manage. But who would employ a *bejan* when a *magistrand* might be had for next to nothing? Besides, who would recommend him? The thought of Dr. Anderson flashed into his mind, and he rushed from the house without even knowing where he lived.

CHAPTER VI.

DR. ANDERSON AGAIN.

AT the Post Office he procured the desired
information at once. Dr. Anderson lived
in Union Street, towards the western end of it.

Away went Robert to find the house. That
was easy. What a grand house of smooth granite and wide approach it was! The great
door was opened by a man-servant, who looked
at the country boy from head to foot.

" Is the doctor in ?" asked Robert.

" Yes."

" I wad like to see him."

" Wha will I say wants him ?"

" Say the laddie he saw at Bodyfauld."

The man left Robert in the hall, which was
spread with tiger and leopard skins, and had a
bright fire burning in a large stove. Returning
presently, he led him through noiseless swing-
doors covered with cloth into a large library.
Never had Robert conceived such luxury.
What with Turkey carpet, crimson curtains,

easy chairs, grandly-bound books and morocco-covered writing-table, it seemed the very ideal of comfort. But Robert liked the grandeur too much to be abashed by it.

"Sit ye doon there," said the servant, "and the doctor 'ill be wi' ye in ae minute."

He was hardly out of the room before a door opened in the middle of the books, and the doctor appeared in a long dressing-gown. He looked inquiringly at Robert for one moment, then made two long strides like a pair of eager compasses, holding out his hand.

"I'm Robert Faukner," said the boy. "Ye'll min', maybe, Doctor, 'at ye war verra kin' to me ance, and tellt me lots o' stories—at Body-fauld, ye ken."

"I'm very glad to see you, Robert," said Dr. Anderson. "Of course I remember you perfect-ly; but my servant did not bring your name, and I did not know but it might be the other boy—I forget his name."

"Ye mean Shargar, sir. It's no him."

"I can see that," said the doctor laughing, "although you are altered. You have grown quite a man! I am very glad to see you," he repeated, shaking hands with him again. "When did you come to town?"

"I hae been at the grammer school i' the auld toon for the last three months," said Robert.

"Three months!" exclaimed Dr. Anderson. "And never came to see me till now! That was too bad of you, Robert."

"Weel, ye see, sir, I didna ken better. An' I had a heap to do, an' a' for naething, efter a'. But gin I had kent 'at ye wad like to see me, I wad hae likit weel to come to ye."

"I have been away most of the summer," said the doctor; "but I have been at home for the last month. You haven't had your dinner, have you?"

"Weel, I dinna exackly ken what to say, sir. Ye see, I wasna that sharp-set the day, sae I had jist a mou'fu' o' breid and cheese. I'm turnin' hungry, noo, I maun confess."

The doctor rang the bell.

"You must stop and dine with me.—Johnston," he continued as his servant entered, "tell the cook that I have a gentleman to dinner with me to-day, and she must be liberal."

"Guidsake, sir!" said Robert, "dinna set the woman agen me."

He had no intention of saying anything humorous, but Dr. Anderson laughed heartily.

"Come into my room till dinner-time," he said, opening the door by which he had entered.

To Robert's astonishment, he found himself in a room bare as that of the poorest cottage. A small square window, small as the window in

John Hewson's, looked out upon a garden neatly kept, but now "having no adorning but cleanliness." The place was just the *benn end* of a cottage. The walls were whitewashed, the ceiling was of bare boards, and the floor was sprinkled with a little white sand. The table and chairs were of common deal, white and clean, save that the former was spotted with ink. A greater contrast to the soft, large, richly-coloured room they had left could hardly be imagined. A few bookshelves on the wall were filled with old books. A fire blazed cheerily in the little grate. A bed with snow-white coverlet stood in a recess.

"This is the nicest room in the house, Robert," said the doctor. "When I was a student like you——"

Robert shook his head.

"I'm nae student yet," he said; but the doctor went on:

"I had the benn end of my father's cottage to study in, for he treated me like a stranger-gentleman when I came home from college. The father respected the son for whose advantage he was working like a slave from morning till night. My heart is sometimes sore with the gratitude I feel to him. Though he's been dead for thirty years—would you believe it, Robert? —well, I can't talk more about him now. I made this room as like my father's benn end as

I could, and I am happier here than anywhere in the world."

By this time Robert was perfectly at home. Before the dinner was ready he had not only told Dr. Anderson his present difficulty, but his whole story as far back as he could remember. The good man listened eagerly, gazed at the boy with more and more of interest, which deepened till his eyes glistened as he gazed, and when a ludicrous passage intervened, welcomed the laughter as an excuse for wiping them. When dinner was announced, he rose without a word and led the way to the dining-room. Robert followed, and they sat down to a meal simple enough for such a house, but which to Robert seemed a feast followed by a banquet. For after they had done eating, on the doctor's part a very meagre performance—they retired to his room again, and then Robert found the table covered with a snowy cloth, and wine and fruits arranged upon it.

It was far into the night before he rose to go home. As he passed through a thick rain of pin-point drops, he felt that although those cold granite houses, with glimmering dead face, stood like rows of sepulchres, he was in reality walking through an avenue of homes. Wet to the skin long before he reached Mrs. Fyvie's in the *auld toon*, he was notwithstanding as warm as the under side of a bird's wing. For he had to sit down and write to his grandmother informing her that Dr. Anderson had employed him to copy for the printers a book of his upon the Medical Boards of India, and that as he was going to pay him for that and other work at a rate which would secure him ten shillings a week, it would be a pity to lose a year for the chance of getting a bursary next winter.

The doctor did want the manuscript copied; and he knew that the only chance of getting Mrs. Falconer's consent to Robert's receiving any assistance from him, was to make some business arrangement of the sort. He wrote to her the same night, and after mentioning the unexpected pleasure of Robert's visit, not only explained the advantage to himself of the arrangement he had proposed, but set forth the greater advantage to Robert, inasmuch as he would thus be able in some measure to keep a hold of him. He judged that although Mrs. Falconer had no great opinion of his religion, she would yet consider his influence rather on the side of good than otherwise in the case of a boy else abandoned to his own resources.

The end of it all was that his grandmother yielded, and Robert was straightway a Bejan, or Yellow-beak.

Three days had he been clothed in the red gown of the Aberdeen student, and had attended the Humanity and Greek class-rooms. On

the evening of the third day he was seated at
his table preparing his Virgil for the next, when
he found himself growing very weary, and no
wonder, for, except the walk of a few hundred
yards to and from the college, he had had no
open air for those three days. It was raining
in a persistent November fashion, and he
thought of the sea, away through the dark and
the rain, tossing uneasily. Should he pay it a
visit? He sat for a moment,

This way and that dividing the swift mind,*

when his eye fell on his violin. He had been
so full of his new position and its requirements,
that he had not touched it since the session
opened. Now it was just what he wanted. He
caught it up eagerly, and began to play. The
power of the music seized upon him, and he
went on playing, forgetful of everything else,
till a string broke. It was all too short for further use. Regardless of the rain or the depth
of darkness to be traversed before he could find
a music-shop, he caught up his cap, and went
to rush from the house.

His door opened immediately on the top step
of the stair, without any landing. There was a
door opposite, to which likewise a few steps led

* Tennyson's *Morte d'Arthur.*
  Atque animum nunc huc celerem, nunc dividit illuc.
  Æneid: IV. 285.

immediately up. The stairs from the two doors united a little below. So near were the doors that one might stride across the fork. The opposite door was open, and in it stood Eric Ericson.

CHAPTER VII.

ERIC ERICSON.

ROBERT sprang across the dividing chasm,
clasped Ericson's hand in both of his,
looked up into his face, and stood speechless.
Ericson returned the salute with a still kindness
—tender and still. His face was like a gray
morning sky of summer from whose level cloud-
fields rain will fall before noon.

"So it was you," he said, "playing the violin
so well?"

"I was doin' my best," answered Robert.
"But eh! Mr. Ericson, I wad hae dune better
gin I had kent ye was hearkenin'."

"You couldn't do better than your best," returned Eric, smiling.

"Ay, but yer best micht aye grow better, ye
ken," persisted Robert.

"Come into my room," said Ericson. "This
is Friday night, and there is nothing but chapel
to-morrow. So we'll have talk instead of work."

In another moment they were seated by a

tiny coal fire in a room one side of which was the slope of the roof, with a large, low skylight in it looking seawards. The sound of the distant waves, unheard in Robert's room, beat upon the drum of the skylight, through all the world of mist that lay between it and them—dimly, vaguely—but ever and again with a swell of gathered force, that made the distant tumult doubtful no more.

"I am sorry I have nothing to offer you," said Ericson.

"You remind me of Peter and John at the Beautiful Gate of the temple," returned Robert, attempting to speak English like the Northerner, but breaking down as his heart got the better of him. "Eh! Mr. Ericson, gin ye kent what it is to me to see the face o' ye, ye wadna speyk like that. Jist lat me sit an' leuk at ye. I want nae mair."

A smile broke up the cold, sad, gray light of the young eagle-face. Stern at once and gentle when in repose, its smile was as the summer of some lovely land where neither the heat nor the sun shall smite them. The youth laid his hand upon the boy's head, then withdrew it hastily, and the smile vanished like the sun behind a cloud. Robert saw it, and as if he had been David before Saul, rose instinctively and said,

"I'll gang for my fiddle.—Hoots! I hae broken ane o' the strings. We maun bide till the morn.

But I want nae fiddle mysel' whan I hear the great water oot there."

"You're young yet, my boy, or you might hear voices in that water—! I've lived in the sound of it all my days. When I can't rest at night, I hear a moaning and crying in the dark, and I lie and listen till I can't tell whether I'm a man or some God-forsaken sea in the sunless north."

"Sometimes I believe in naething but my fiddle," answered Robert.

"Yes, yes. But when it comes *into* you, my boy! You won't hear much music in the cry of the sea after that. As long as you've got it at arm's length, it's all very well. It's interesting then, and you can talk to your fiddle about it, and make poetry about it," said Ericson, with a smile of self-contempt. "But as soon as the real earnest comes that is all over. The sea-moan is the cry of a tortured world then. Its hollow bed is the cup of the world's pain, ever rolling from side to side and dashing over its lip. Of all that might be, ought to be, nothing to be had!—I could get music out of it once. Look here. I could trifle like that once."

He half rose, then dropped on his chair. But Robert's believing eyes justified confidence, and Ericson had never had any one to talk to. He rose again, opened a cupboard at his side, took out some papers, threw them on the table, and, taking his hat, walked towards the door.

"Which of your strings is broken?" he asked.

"The third," answered Robert.

"I will get you one," said Ericson; and before Robert could reply he was down the stair. Robert heard him cough, then the door shut, and he was gone in the rain and fog.

Bewildered, unhappy, ready to fly after him, yet irresolute, Robert almost mechanically turned over the papers upon the little deal table. He was soon arrested by the following verses, headed

A NOONDAY MELODY.

Everything goes to its rest;
  The hills are asleep in the noon;
And life is as still in its nest
  As the moon when she looks on a moon
In the depths of a calm river's breast
  As it steals through a midnight in June.

The streams have forgotten the sea
  In the dream of their musical sound;
The sunlight is thick on the tree,
  And the shadows lie warm on the ground—
So still, you may watch them and see
  Every breath that awakens around.

The churchyard lies still in the heat,
  With its handful of mouldering bone;
As still as the long stalk of wheat
  In the shadow that sits by the stone,
As still as the grass at my feet
  When I walk in the meadows alone.

The waves are asleep on the main,
　And the ships are asleep on the wave ;
And the thoughts are as still in my brain
　As the echo that sleeps in the cave ;
All rest from their labour and pain—
　Then why should not I in my grave?

His heart ready to burst with a sorrow, admiration, and devotion, which no criticism interfered to qualify, Robert rushed out into the
darkness, and sped, fleet-footed, along the only
path which Ericson could have taken.   He could
not bear to be left in the house while his friend
was out in the rain.

He was sure of joining him before he reached
the new town, for he was fleet-footed, and there
was a path only on one side of the way, so that
there was no danger of passing him in the dark.
As he ran he heard the moaning of the sea.
There must be a storm somewhere, away in the
deep spaces of its dark bosom, and its lips muttered of its far unrest.   When the sun rose it
would be seen misty and gray, tossing about
under the one rain cloud that like a thinner
ocean overspread the heavens—tossing like an
animal that would fain lie down and be at peace
but could not compose its unwieldy strength.

Suddenly Robert slackened his speed, ceased
running, stood, gazed through the darkness at
a figure a few yards before him.

An old wall, bowed out with age and the weight

behind it, flanked the road in this part. Doors
in this wall, with a few steps in front of them
and more behind, led up into gardens upon a
slope, at the top of which stood the houses to
which they belonged. Against one of these doors
the figure stood with its head bowed upon its
hands. When Robert was within a few feet, it
descended and went on.

"Mr. Ericson!" exclaimed Robert. "Ye'll get
yer deith gin ye stan' that gait i' the weet."

"Amen," said Ericson, turning with a smile
that glimmered wan through the misty night.
Then changing his tone, he went on: "What
are you after, Robert?"

"You," answered Robert. "I cudna bide to
be left my lane whan I micht be wi' ye a' the
time—gin ye wad lat me. Ye war oot o' the
hoose afore I weel kent what ye was aboot. It's
no a fit nicht for ye to be oot at a', mair by token
'at ye're no the ablest to stan' cauld an' weet."

"I've stood a great deal of both in my time,"
returned Ericson; "but come along. We'll go
and get that fiddle-string."

"Dinna ye think it wad be fully better to
gang hame?" Robert ventured to suggest.

"What would be the use? I'm in no mood
for Plato to-night," he answered, trying hard
to keep from shivering.

"Ye hae an ill cauld upo' ye," persisted Robert;
"an' ye maun be as weet 's a dishcloot."

Ericson laughed—a strange, hollow laugh.

"Come along," he said. "A walk will do me good. We'll get the string, and then you shall play to me. That will do me more good yet."

Robert ceased opposing him, and they walked together to the new town. Robert bought the string, and they set out, as he thought, to return.

But not yet did Ericson seem inclined to go home. He took the lead, and they emerged upon the quay.

There were not many vessels. One of them was the Antwerp tub, already known to Robert. He recognized her even in the dull light of the quay lamps. Her captain being a prudent and well-to-do Dutchman, never slept on shore; he preferred saving his money; and therefore, as the friends passed, Robert caught sight of him walking his own deck and smoking a long clay pipe before turning in.

" A fine nicht, capt'n," said Robert.

"It does rain," returned the captain. " Will you come on board and have one schnapps before you turn in ?"

"I hae a frien' wi' me here," said Robert, feeling his way.

" Let him come and be welcomed."

Ericson making no objection, they went on board, and down into the neat little cabin, which was all the roomier for the straightness of the vessel's quarter. The captain got out a square, coffin-shouldered bottle, and having respect to the condition of their garments, neither of the young men refused his hospitality, though Robert did feel a little compunction at the thought of the horror it would have caused his grand-mother. Then the Dutchman got out his violin and asked Robert to play a Scotch air. But in the middle of it his eyes fell on Ericson, and he stopped at once. Ericson was sitting on a locker, leaning back against the side of the vessel : his eyes were open and fixed, and he seemed quite unconscious of what was passing. Robert fancied at first that the hollands he had taken had gone to his head, but he saw at the same moment, from his glass, that he had scarcely tasted the spirit. In great alarm they tried to rouse him, and at length succeeded. He closed his eyes, opened them again, rose up, and was going away.

" What's the maitter wi' ye, Mr. Ericson ?" said Robert, in distress.

" Nothing, nothing," answered Ericson, in a strange voice. " I fell asleep I believe. It was very bad manners, captain. I beg your pardon. I believe I am overtired."

The Dutchman was as kind as possible, and begged Ericson to stay the night and occupy his berth. But he insisted on going home, although he was clearly unfit for such a walk.

They bade the skipper good-night, went on shore, and set out, Ericson leaning rather heavily upon Robert's arm. Robert led him up Marischal Street.

The steep ascent was too much for Ericson. He stood still upon the bridge and leaned over the wall of it. Robert stood beside, almost in despair about getting him home.

"Have patience with me, Robert," said Ericson, in his natural voice. "I shall be better presently. I don't know what's come to me. If I had been a Celt now, I should have said I had a touch of the second sight. But I am, as far as I know, pure Northman."

"What did you see?" asked Robert, with a strange feeling that miles of the spirit world, if one may be allowed such a contradiction in words, lay between him and his friend.

Ericson returned no answer. Robert feared he was going to have a relapse; but in a moment more he lifted himself up and bent again to the *brae*.

They got on pretty well till they were about the middle of the Gallowgate.

"I can't," said Ericson feebly, and half leaned half fell against the wall of a house.

"Come into this shop," said Robert. "I ken the man. He'll lat ye sit doon."

He managed to get him in. He was as pale as death. The bookseller got a chair, and he sank into it. Robert was almost at his wit's end. There was no such thing as a cab in Aberdeen for years and years after the date of my story. He was holding a glass of water to Ericson's lips, —when he heard his name, in a low earnest whisper, from the door. There, round the door-cheek, peered the white face and red head of Shargar.

"Robert! Robert!" said Shargar.

"I hear ye," returned Robert coolly: he was too anxious to be surprised at anything. "Haud yer tongue. I'll come to ye in a minute."

Ericson recovered a little, refused the whisky offered by the bookseller, rose, and staggered out.

"If I were only home!" he said. "But where is home?"

"We'll try to mak ane," returned Robert. "Tak a haud o' me. Lay yer weicht upo' me. —Gin it warna for yer len'th, I cud cairry ye weel eneuch. Whaur 's that Shargar?" he muttered to himself, looking up and down the gloomy street.

But no Shargar was to be seen. Robert peered in vain into every dark court they crept past, till at length he all but came to the conclusion that Shargar was only "fantastical."

When they had reached the hollow, and were crossing the canal-bridge by Mount Hooly, Ericson's strength again failed him, and again he leaned upon the bridge. Not had he leaned long before Robert found that he had fainted. In desperation he began to hoist the tall form upon his back, when he heard the quick step of a runner behind him and the words—

" Gie 'im to me, Robert; gie 'im to me. I can cairry 'im fine."

" Haud awa' wi' ye," returned Robert; and again Shargar fell behind.

For a few hundred yards he trudged along manfully; but his strength, more from the nature of his burden than its weight, soon gave way. He stood still to recover. The same moment Shargar was by his side again.

" Noo, Robert," he said, pleadingly.

Robert yielded, and the burden was shifted to Shargar's back.

How they managed it they hardly knew themselves; but after many changes they at last got Ericson home, and up to his own room. He had revived several times, but gone off again. In one of his faints, Robert undressed him and got him into bed. He had so little to cover him, that Robert could not help crying with misery. He himself was well provided, and would gladly have shared with Ericson, but that was hopeless. He could, however, make him warm in bed. Then leaving Shargar in charge, he sped back to the new town to Dr. Anderson. The doctor had his carriage out at once, wrapped

Robert in a plaid and brought him home with him.

Ericson came to himself, and seeing Shargar by his bedside, tried to sit up, asking feebly,

"Where am I?"

"In yer ain bed, Mr. Ericson," answered Shargar.

"And who are you?" asked Ericson again, bewildered.

Shargar's pale face no doubt looked strange under his crown of red hair.

"Ow! I'm naebody."

"You must be somebody, or else my brain's in a bad state," returned Ericson.

"Na, na, I'm naebody. Naething ava (*at all*). Robert 'll be hame in ae meenit.—I'm Robert's tyke (*dog*)," concluded Shargar, with a sudden inspiration.

This answer seemed to satisfy Ericson, for he closed his eyes and lay still; nor did he speak again till Robert arrived with the doctor.

Poor food, scanty clothing, undue exertion in travelling to and from the university, hard mental effort against weakness, disquietude of mind, all borne with an endurance unconscious of itself, had reduced Eric Ericson to his present condition. Strength had given way at last, and he was now lying in the low border wash of a dead sea of fever.

The last of an ancient race of poor men, he

had no relative but a second cousin, and no
means except the little he advanced him, chiefly
in kind, to be paid for when Eric had a profession. This cousin was in the herring trade,
and the chief assistance he gave him was to
send him by sea, from Wick to Aberdeen, a small
barrel of his fish every session. One herring,
with two or three potatoes, formed his dinner as
long as the barrel lasted. But at Aberdeen or
elsewhere no one carried his head more erect than
Eric Ericson—not from pride, but from simplicity and inborn dignity ; and there was not a
man during his curriculum more respected than
he. An excellent classical scholar—as scholar-
ship went in those days—he was almost the
only man at the university who made his knowledge of Latin serve towards an acquaintance
with the Romance languages. He had gained
a small bursary, and gave lessons when he
could.

But having no level channel for the outgoing
of the waters of one of the tenderest hearts that
ever lived, those waters had sought to break a
passage upwards. Herein his experience corresponded in a considerable degree to that of Robert;
only Eric's more fastidious and more instructed
nature bred a thousand difficulties which he
would meet one by one, whereas Robert, less
delicate and more robust, would break through
all the oppositions of theological science falsely

so called, and take the kingdom of heaven by force. But indeed the ruins of the ever falling temple of theology had accumulated far more heavily over Robert's well of life, than over that of Ericson: the obstructions to his faith were those that rolled from the disintegrating mountains of humanity, rather than the rubbish heaped upon it by the careless masons who take the quarry whence they hew the stones for the temple—built without hands eternal in the heavens.

When Dr. Anderson entered, Ericson opened his eyes wide. The doctor approached, and taking his hand began to feel his pulse. Then first Ericson comprehended his visit.

"I can't," he said, withdrawing his hand. "I am not so ill as to need a doctor."

"My dear sir," said Dr. Anderson, courteously, "there will be no occasion to put you to any pain."

"Sir," said Eric, "I have no money."

The doctor laughed.

"And I have more than I know how to make a good use of."

"I would rather be left alone," persisted Ericson, turning his face away.

"Now, my dear sir," said the doctor, with gentle decision, "that is very wrong. With what face can you offer a kindness when your turn comes, if you won't accept one yourself?"

Ericson held out his wrist.   Dr. Anderson
questioned, prescribed, and, having given directions, went home, to call again in the morning.

And now Robert was somewhat in the position of the old woman who "had so many child-
dren she didn't know what to do."   Dr. Anderson ordered nourishment for Ericson, and here
was Shargar upon his hands as well !   Shargar
and he could share, to be sure, and exist : but
for Ericson— ?

Not a word did Robert exchange with Shargar till he had gone to the druggist's and got the
medicine for Ericson, who, after taking it, fell
into a troubled sleep.   Then, leaving the two
doors open, Robert joined Sharger in his own
room.   There he made up a good fire, and they
sat and dried themselves.

"Noo, Shargar," said Robert at length, " hoo
cam *ye* here ? "

His question was too like one of his grandmother's to be pleasant to Shargar.

"Dinna speyk to me that gait, Robert, or I'll
cut my throat," he returned.

"Hoots ! I maun ken a' aboot it," insisted Robert, but with much modified and partly convict-
ed tone.

"Weel, I never said I wadna tell ye a' aboot
it.   The fac' 's this—an' I'm no' up to the leein'
as I used to be, Robert : I hae tried it ower an'
ower, but a lee comes rouch throw my thrap-

ple *(windpipe)* noo. Faith! I cud hae leed ance wi' onybody, barrin' the de'il. I winna lee. I'm nae leein'. The fac' 's jist this: I cudna bide ahin' ye ony langer."

"But what, the muckle lang-tailed deevil! am I to do wi' ye?" returned Robert, in real perplexity, though only pretended displeasure.

"Gie me something to ate, an' I'll tell ye what to do wi' me," answered Shargar. "I dinna care a scart *(scratch)* what it is."

Robert rang the bell and ordered some porridge, and while it was preparing, Shargar told his story—how having heard a rumour of apprenticeship to a tailor, he had the same night dropped from the gable window to the ground, and with three halfpence in his pocket had wandered and begged his way to Aberdeen, arriving with one halfpenny left.

"But what am I to do wi' ye?" said Robert once more, in as much perplexity as ever.

"Bide till I hae tellt ye, as I said I wad," answered Shargar. "Dinna ye think I'm the haveless *(careless and therefore helpless)* crater I used to be. I hae been in Aberdeen three days! Ay, an' I hae seen you ilka day in yer reid goon, an' richt braw it is. Luik ye here!"

He put his hand in his pocket and pulled out what amounted to two or three shillings, chiefly in coppers, which he exposed with triumph on the table.

"Whaur got ye a' that siller, man?" asked Robert.

"Here and there, I kenna whaur; but I hae gien the weicht o' 't for 't a' the same—rinnin' here an' rinnin' there, cairryin' boxes till an' frae the smacks, an' doin' a'thing whether they bade me or no. Yesterday mornin' I got thrippence by hingin' aboot the Royal afore the coches startit. I luikit a' up and doon the street till I saw somebody hine awa wi' a porkmanty. Till 'im I ran, an' he was an auld man, an' maist at the last gasp wi' the weicht o' 't, an' gae me 't to carry. An' wha duv ye think gae me a shillin' the verra first nicht?—Wha but my brither Sandy?"

"Lord Rothie?"

"Ay, faith. I kent him weel eneuch, but little he kent me. There he was upo' Black Geordie. He's turnin' auld noo."

"Yer brither?"

"Na. He's young eneuch for ony mischeef; but Black Geordie. What on earth gars him gang stravaguin' aboot upo' that deevil? I doobt he's a kelpie, or a hell-horse, or something no canny o' that kin'; for faith! brither Sandy's no ower canny himsel', I'm thinkin'. But Geordie—the aulder the waur set (*inclined*). An' sae I'm thinkin' wi' his maister."

"Did ye ever see yer father, Shargar?"

"Na. Nor I dinna want to see 'im. I'm

upo' my mither's side. But that's naething to
the pint. A' that I want o' you 's to lat me
come hame at nicht, an' lie upo' the flure here.
I sweir I'll lie i' the street gin ye dinna lat me.
I'll sleep as soun' 's Peter MacInnes whan Maccleary's preachin'. An' I winna ate muckle—I
hae a dreidfu' pooer o' aitin'—an' a' 'at I gether
I'll fess hame to you, to du wi' 't as ye like.—
Man, I cairriet a heap o' things the day till the
skipper o' that boat 'at ye gaed intil wi' Maister
Ericson the nicht. He's a fine chiel' that skipper !"

Robert was astonished at the change that
had passed upon Shargar. His departure had
cast him upon his own resources, and allowed
the individuality repressed by every event of his
history, even by his worship of Robert, to begin
to develop itself. Miserable for a few weeks, he
had revived in the fancy that to work hard at
school would give him some chance of rejoining
Robert. Thence, too, he had watched to please
Mrs. Falconer, and had indeed begun to buy
golden opinions from all sorts of people. He
had a hope in prospect. But into the midst fell
the whisper of the apprenticeship like a thunder-
bolt out of a clear sky. He fled at once.

" Weel, ye can hae my bed the nicht," said
Robert, " for I maun sit up wi' Mr. Ericson."

" 'Deed I'll hae naething o' the kin'. I'll
sleep upo' the flure, or else upo' the door-stane.

Man, I'm no clean eneuch efter what I've come
throu sin' I drappit frae the window-sill i' the
ga'le-room.   But jist len' me yer plaid, an' I'll
sleep upo' the rug here as gin I war i' Paradees.
An' faith, sae I am, Robert.   Ye maun gang to
yer bed some time the nicht forby (*besides*), or
ye winna be fit for yer wark the morn.   Ye can
jist gie me a kick, an' I'll be up afore ye can gie
me anither."

Their supper arrived from below; and, each on
one side of the fire, they ate the porridge, con-
versing all the while about old times—for the
youngest life has its old times, its golden age—
and old adventures,—Dooble Sanny, Betty, &c.
&c.   There were but two subjects which Robert
avoided—Miss St. John and the Bonnie Leddy.
Shargar was at length deposited upon the little
bit of hearthrug which adorned rather than en-
riched the room, with Robert's plaid of shepherd
tartan around him, and an Ainsworth's dictionary under his head for a pillow.

"Man, I fin' mysel' jist like a muckle colley"
(*sheep-dog*), he said.   "Whan I close my een,
I'm no sure 'at I'm no i' the inside o' yer auld
luckie-daiddie's kilt.   The Lord preserve me frae
ever sic a fricht again as yer grannie an' Betty
gae me the nicht they fand me in 't!   I dinna
believe it's in natur' to hae sic a fricht twise
in ae lifetime.   Sae I'll fa' asleep at ance, an'
say nae mair—but as muckle o' my prayers as I

can min' upo' noo 'at grannie's no at my lug."

"Haud yer impidence, an' yer tongue thegither," said Robert. "Min' 'at my granny's been the best frien' ye ever had."

"'Cep' my ain mither," returned Shargar, with a sleepy doggedness in his tone.

During their conference, Ericson had been slumbering. Robert had visited him from time to time, but he had not awaked. As soon as Shargar was disposed of, he took his candle and sat down by him. He grew more uneasy. Robert guessed that the candle was the cause, and put it out. Ericson was quieter. So Robert sat in the dark.

But the rain had now ceased. Some upper wind had swept the clouds from the sky, and the whole world of stars was radiant over the earth and its griefs.

"O God, where art thou?" he said in his heart, and went to his own room to look out.

There was no curtain, and the blind had not been drawn down, therefore the earth looked in at the storm-window. The sea neither glimmered nor shone. It lay across the horizon like a low level cloud, out of which came a moaning. Was this moaning all of the earth, or was there trouble in the starry places too? thought Robert, as if already he had begun to suspect the truth from afar—that save in the secret place of the Most High, and in the heart that is hid with the Son of Man in the bosom of the Father, there is trouble—a sacred unrest—everywhere —the moaning of a tide setting homewards, even towards the bosom of that Father.

CHAPTER VIII.

A HUMAN PROVIDENCE.

ROBERT kept himself thoroughly awake the whole night, and it was well that he had not to attend classes in the morning. As the gray of the world's reviving consciousness melted in at the window, the things around and within him looked and felt ghastly. Nothing is liker the gray dawn than the soul of one who has been watching by a sick bed all the long hours of the dark, except, indeed, it be the first glimmerings of truth on the mind lost in the dark of a godless life.

Ericson had waked often, and Robert had administered his medicine carefully. But he had been mostly between sleeping and waking, and had murmured strange words, whose passing shadows rather than glimmers roused the imagination of the youth as with messages from regions unknown.

As the light came he found his senses going,

and went to his own room again to get a book
that he might keep himself awake by reading at
the window. To his surprise Shargar was gone,
and for a moment he doubted whether he had
not been dreaming all that had passed between
them the night before. His plaid was folded
up and laid upon a chair, as if it had been there
all night, and his Ainsworth was on the table.
But beside it was the money Shargar had drawn
from his pockets.

About nine o'clock Dr. Anderson arrived,
found Ericson not so much worse as he had expected, comforted Robert, and told him he must
go to bed.

"But I cannot leave Mr. Ericson," said Robert.

"Let your friend—what's his odd name?—
watch him during the day."

"Shargar, you mean, sir. But that's his
nickname. His rale name they say his mither
says, is George Moray—wi' an *o* an' no a *u-r.*—
Do you see, sir?" concluded Robert significantly.

"No, I don't," answered the doctor.

"They say he's a son o' the auld Markis's,
that's it. His mither's a randy wife 'at gangs
aboot the country—a gipsy they say. There's
nae doobt aboot *her.* An' by a' accoonts the father's likly eneuch."

"And how on earth did you come to have
such a questionable companion?"

"Shargar's as fine a crater as ever God made," said Robert warmly. "Ye'll alloo 'at God made him, doctor; though his father an' mither thochtna muckle aboot him or God either whan they got him atween them? An' Shargar couldna help it. It micht ha' been you or me for that maitter, doctor."

"I beg your pardon, Robert," said Dr. Anderson quietly, although delighted with the fervour of his young kinsman: "I only wanted to know how he came to be your companion."

"I beg *your* pardon, doctor—but I thoucht ye was some scunnert at it; an' I canna bide Shargar to be luikit doon upo'. Luik here," he continued, going to his box, and bringing out Shargar's little heap of coppers, in which two sixpences obscurely shone, "he brocht a' that hame last nicht, an' syne sleepit upo' the rug i' my room there. We'll want a' 'at he can mak an' me too afore we get Mr. Ericson up again."

"But ye haena tellt me yet," said the doctor, so pleased with the lad that he relapsed into the dialect of his youth, "hoo ye cam to forgather wi' 'im."

"I tellt ye a' aboot it, doctor. It was a' my granny's doin', God bless her—for weel he may, an' muckle she needs 't."

"Oh! yes; I remember now all your grandmother's part in the story," returned the doctor. "But I still want to know how he came here."

"She was gaein' to mak a taylor o' 'm; an' he jist ran awa', an' cam to me."

"It was too bad of him that—after all she had done for him."

"Ow, 'deed no, doctor. Even whan ye boucht a man an' paid for him, accordin' to the Jewish law, ye cudna mak a slave o' 'im for a'thegither, ohn him seekin' 't himsel'.—Eh! gin she could only get my father hame!" sighed Robert, after a pause.

"What should she want him home for?" asked Dr. Anderson, still making conversation.

"I didna mean hame to Rothieden. I believe she cud bide never seein' 'im again, gin only he wasna i' the ill place. She has awfu' notions aboot burnin' ill sowls for ever an' ever. But it's no hersel'. It's the wyte o' the ministers. Doctor, I do believe she wad gang an' be brunt hersel' wi' a great thanksgivin', gin it wad lat ony puir crater oot o' 't—no to say my father. An' I sair misdoobt gin mony o' them 'at pat it in her heid wad do as muckle. I'm some feared they're like Paul afore he was convertit: he wadna lift a stane himsel', but he likit weel to stan' oot by an' luik on."

A deep sigh, almost a groan, from the bed, reminded them that they were talking too much and too loud for a sick room. It was followed by the words, muttered, but articulate,

" What's the good when you don't know whether there's a God at all ?"

"'Deed, that's verra true, Mr. Ericson," returned Robert. "I wish ye wad fin' oot an' tell me. I wad be blithe to hear what ye had to say anent it—gin it was *ay*, ye ken."

Ericson went on murmuring, but inarticulately now.

" This won't do at all, Robert, my boy," said Dr. Anderson. " You must not talk about such things with him, or indeed about anything. You must keep him as quiet as ever you can."

" I thocht he was comin' till himsel'," returned Robert. " But I will tak care, I assure ye, doctor. Only I'm feared I may fa' asleep the nicht, for I was dooms sleepy this mornin'."

" I will send Johnston as soon as I get home, and you must go to bed when he comes."

"'Deed, doctor, that winna do at a'. It wad be ower mony strange faces a'thegither. We'll get Mistress Fyvie to luik till 'im the day, an' Shargar canna work the morn, bein' Sunday. An' I'll gang to my bed for fear o' doin' waur, though I doobt I winna sleep i' the daylicht."

Dr. Anderson was satisfied, and went home— cogitating much. This boy, this cousin of his, made a vortex of good about him into which whoever came near it was drawn. He seemed at the same time quite unaware of anything worthy in his conduct. The good he did

sprung from some inward necessity, with just
enough in it of the salt of choice to keep it from
losing its savour. To these cogitations of Dr.
Anderson, I add that there was no conscious
exercise of religion in it—for there his mind
was all at sea. Of course I believe notwithstanding that religion had much, I ought to say
everything, to do with it. Robert had not yet
found in God a reason for being true to his fellows; but, if God was leading him to be the
man he became, how could any good results of
this leading be other than religion? All good
is of God. Robert began where he could. The
first table was too high for him; he began with
the second. If a man love his brother whom
he hath seen, the love of God whom he hath
not seen, is not very far off. These results in
Robert were the first outcome of divine facts
and influences—they were the buds of the fruit
hereafter to be gathered in perfect devotion.
God be praised by those who know religion to
be the truth of humanity—its own truth that
sets it free—not binds, and lops, and mutilates
it! who see God to be the father of every human soul—the ideal Father, not an inventor of
schemes, or the upholder of a court etiquette
for whose use he has chosen to desecrate the
name of *justice!*

To return to Dr. Anderson. I have had little
opportunity of knowing his history in India.

He returned from it half-way down the hill of
ife, sad, gentle, kind, and rich. Whence his
sadness came, we need not inquire. Some woman out in that fervid land may have darkened
his story—darkened it wronglessly, it may be,
with coldness, or only with death. But to return home without wife to accompany him or
child to meet him,—to sit by his riches like a
man over a fire of straws in a Siberian frost; to
know that old faces were gone, and old hearts
changed, that the pattern of things in the heavens had melted away from the face of the
earth, that the chill evenings of autumn were
settling down into longer and longer nights,
and that no hope lay any more beyond the
mountains—surely this was enough to make a
gentle-minded man sad, even if the individual
sorrows of his history had gathered into gold
and purple in the west. I say *west* advisedly.
For we are journeying, like our globe, ever towards the east. Death and the west are behind
us—ever behind us, and settling into the un-
changeable.

It was natural that he should be interested in
the fine promise of Robert, in whom he saw revived the hopes of his own youth, but in a nature at once more robust and more ideal.
Where the doctor was refined, Robert was
strong; where the doctor was firm with a firmness he had cultivated, Robert was imperious

with an imperiousness time would mellow;
where the doctor was generous and careful at
once, Robert gave his mite and forgot it. He
was rugged in the simplicity of his truthfulness,
and his speech bewrayed him as altogether of
the people; but the doctor knew the hole of the
pit whence he had been himself digged. All
that would fall away as the spiky shell from the
polished chestnut, and be reabsorbed in the
growth of the grand cone-flowering tree, to
stand up in the sun and wind of the years a
very altar of incense. It is no wonder, I repeat,
that he loved the boy, and longed to further his
plans. But he was too wise to overwhelm him
with a cataract of fortune instead of blessing
him with the merciful dew of progress.

"The fellow will bring me in for no end of
expense," he said, smiling to himself, as he drove
home in his chariot. "The less he means it the
more unconscionable he will be. There's that
Ericson—but that isn't worth thinking of. I
must do something for that queer protégé of
his, though—that Shargar. The fellow is as
good as a dog, and that's saying not a little for
him. I wonder if he can learn—or if he takes
after his father the marquis, who never could
spell. Well, it is a comfort to have something
to do worth doing. I did think of endowing a
hospital; but I'm not sure that it isn't better to
endow a good man than a hospital. I'll think

about it. I won't say anything about Shargar either, till I see how he goes on. I might give him a job, though, now and then. But where to fall in with him—prowling about after jobs?"

He threw himself back in his seat, and laughed with a delight he had rarely felt. He was a providence watching over the boys, who expected nothing of him beyond advice for Ericson! Might there not be a Providence that equally transcended the vision of men, shaping to nobler ends the blocked-out designs of their rough-hewn marbles?

His thoughts wandered back to his friend the Brahmin, who died longing for that absorption into deity which had been the dream of his life : might not the Brahmin find the grand idea shaped to yet finer issues than his aspiration had dared contemplate?—might he not inherit in the purification of his will such an absorption as should intensify his personality?

CHAPTER IX.

A HUMAN SOUL.

ERICSON lay for several weeks, during which
time Robert and Shargar were his only
nurses. They contrived, by abridging both
rest and labour, to give him constant attendance. Shargar went to bed early and got up
early, so as to let Robert have a few hours'
sleep before his classes began. Robert again
slept in the evening, after Shargar came home,
and made up for the time by reading while he
sat by his friend. Mrs. Fyvie's attendance was
in requisition only for the hours when he had
to be at lectures. By the greatest economy of
means, consisting of what Shargar brought in
by jobbing about the quay and the coach-offices,
and what Robert had from Dr. Anderson for
copying his manuscript, they contrived to procure for Ericson all that he wanted. The shopping of the two boys, in their utter ignorance
of such delicacies as the doctor told them to
get for him, the blunders they made as to the

shops at which they were to be bought, and the consultations they held, especially about the preparing of the prescribed nutriment, afforded them many an amusing retrospect in after years. For the house was so full of lodgers, that Robert begged Mrs. Fyvie to give herself no trouble in the matter. Her conscience, however, was uneasy, and she spoke to Dr. Anderson; but he assured her that she might trust the boys. What cooking they could not manage, she undertook cheerfully, and refused to add anything to the rent on Shargar's account.

Dr. Anderson watched everything, the two boys as much as his patient. He allowed them to work on, sending only the wine that was necessary from his own cellar. The moment the supplies should begin to fail, or the boys to look troubled, he was ready to do more. About Robert's perseverance he had no doubt: Shargar's faithfulness he wanted to prove.

Robert wrote to his grandmother to tell her that Shargar was with him, working hard. Her reply was somewhat cold and offended, but was inclosed in a parcel containing all Shargar's garments, and ended with the assurance that as long as he did well she was ready to do what she could.

Few English readers will like Mrs. Falconer; but her grandchild considered her one of the noblest women ever God made; and I, from

his account, am of the same mind. Her care
was fixed

> To fill her odorous lamp with *deeds* of light,
> And hope that reaps not shame.

And if one must choose between the *how* and
the *what*, let me have the *what*, come of the *how*
what may. I know of a man so sensitive, that
he shuts his ears to his sister's griefs, because
it spoils his digestion to think of them.

One evening Robert was sitting by the table
in Ericson's room. Dr. Anderson had not called
that day, and he did not expect to see him now,
for he had never come so late. He was quite
at his ease, therefore, and busy with two things
at once, when the doctor opened the door and
walked in. I think it is possible that he came
up quietly with some design of surprising him.
He found him with a stocking on one hand, a
darning needle in the other, and a Greek
book open before him. Taking no apparent notice of him, he walked up to the bedside, and
Robert put away his work. After his interview
with his patient was over, the doctor signed to
him to follow him to the next room. There
Shargar lay on the rug already snoring. It
was a cold night in December, but he lay in his
under-clothing, with a single blanket round
him.

" Good training for a soldier," said the doctor; "and so was your work a minute ago, Robert."

"Ay," answered Robert, colouring a little; "I was readin' a bit o' the Anabasis."

The doctor smiled a far-off sly smile.

"I think it was rather the Katabasis, if one might venture to judge from the direction of your labours."

"Weel," answered Robert, "what wad ye hae me do? Wad ye hae me lat Mr. Ericson gang wi' holes i' the heels o' 's hose, whan I can mak them a' snod, an' learn my Greek at the same time? Hoots, doctor! dinna lauch at me. I was doin' nae ill. A body may please themsel's —whiles surely, ohn sinned."

"But it's such waste of time! Why don't you buy him new ones?"

"'Deed that's easier said than dune. I hae eneuch ado wi' my siller as 'tis; an' gin it warna for you, doctor, I *do* not ken what wad come o' 's; for ye see I hae no richt to come upo' my grannie for ither fowk. There wad be nae en' to that."

"But I could lend you the money to buy him some stockings."

"An' whan wad I be able to pay ye, do ye think, doctor? In anither warl' maybe, whaur the currency micht be sae different there wad be no possibility o' reckonin' the rate o' exchange. Na, na."

"But I will give you the money if you like."

"Na, na. You hae dune eneuch already, an' mony thanks. Siller's no sae easy come by to be wastit, as lang's a darn 'll do. Forbye, gin ye began wi' *his* claes, ye wadna ken whaur to haud ; for it wad jist be the new claith upo' the auld garment : ye micht as weel new cleed him at ance."

"And why not if I choose, Mr. Falconer ?"

"Speir ye that at *him*, an' see what ye'll get— a luik 'at wad fess a corbie (*carrion crow*) frae the lift (*sky*). I wadna hae ye try that. Some fowk's poverty maun be han'let jist like a sair place, doctor. He canna weel compleen o' a bit darnin'. —He canna tak that ill," repeated Robert, in a tone that showed he yet felt some anxiety on the subject ; "but new anes ! I wadna like to be by whan he fand that oot. Maybe he micht tak them frae a wuman ; but frae a man body ! —na, na ; I maun jist darn awa'. But I'll mak them dacent eneuch afore I hae dune wi' them. A fiddler has fingers."

The doctor smiled a pleased smile ; but when he got into his carriage, again he laughed heartily.

The evening deepened into night. Robert thought Ericson was asleep. But he spoke.

"Who is that at the street door ?" he said.

They were at the top of the house, and there was no window to the street. But Ericson's senses were preternaturally acute, as is often the case in such illnesses.

" I dinna hear onybody," answered Robert.

" There was somebody," returned Ericson.

From that moment he began to be restless, and was more feverish than usual throughout the night.

Up to this time he had spoken little, was depressed with a suffering to which he could give no name—not pain, he said—but such that he could rouse no mental effort to meet it: his endurance was passive altogether. This night his brain was more affected. He did not rave, but often wandered; never spoke nonsense, but many words that would have seemed nonsense to ordinary people: to Robert they seemed inspired. His imagination, which was greater than any other of his fine faculties, was so roused that he talked in verse—probably verse composed before and now recalled. He would even pray sometimes in measured lines, and go on murmuring petitions, till the words of the murmur became undistinguishable, and he fell asleep. But even in his sleep he would speak; and Robert would listen in awe; for such words, falling from such a man, were to him as dim breaks of coloured light from the rainbow walls of the heavenly city.

" If God were *thinking* me," said Ericson, " ah ! But if he be only *dreaming* me, I shall go mad."

Ericson's outside was like his own northern

clime—dark, gentle, and clear, with gray-blue
seas, and a sun that seems to shine out of the
past, and know nothing of the future.   But
within glowed a volcanic angel of aspiration,
fluttering his half grown wings, and ever reaching towards the heights whence all things are
visible, and where all passions are safe because
true, that is divine.   Iceland herself has her
Hecla.

Robert listened with keenest ear.   A mist of
great meaning hung about the words his friend
had spoken.   He might speak more.   For some
minutes he listened in vain, and was turning at
last towards his book in hopelessness, when he
did speak yet again : Robert's ear soon detected
the rhythmic motion of his speech.

> " Come in the glory of thine excellence ;
>   Rive the dense gloom with wedges of clear light ;
>   And let the shimmer of thy chariot wheels
>   Burn through the cracks of night.—So slowly, Lord,
>   To lift myself to thee with hands of toil,
>   Climbing the slippery cliff of unheard prayer !
>   Lift up a hand among my idle days—
>   One beckoning finger.   I will cast aside
>   The clogs of earthly circumstance, and run
>   Up the broad highways where the countless worlds
>   Sit ripening in the summer of thy love."

Breathless for fear of losing a word, Robert
yet remembered that he had seen something like
these words in the papers Ericson had given him

to read on the night when his illness began. When he had fallen asleep and silent, he searched and found the poem from which I give the following extracts. He had not looked at the papers since that night.

A PRAYER.

O Lord, my God, how long
Shall my poor heart pant for a boundless joy?
How long, O mighty Spirit, shall I hear
The murmur of Truth's crystal waters slide
From the deep caverns of their endless being,
But my lips taste not, and the grosser air
Choke each pure inspiration of thy will?
. . . .

I would be a wind,
Whose smallest atom is a viewless wing,
All busy with the pulsing life that throbs
To do thy bidding; yea, or the meanest thing
That has relation to a changeless truth,
Could I but be instinct with thee—each thought
The lightning of a pure intelligence,
And every act as the loud thunder-clap
Of currents warring for a vacuum.
. . . .

Lord, clothe me with thy truth as with a robe.
Purge me with sorrow. I will bend my head,
And let the nations of thy waves pass over,
Bathing me in thy consecrated strength.
And let the many-voiced and silver winds
Pass through my frame with their clear influence.
O save me—I am blind; lo! thwarting shapes
Wall up the void before, and thrusting out

Lean arms of unshaped expectation, beckon
Down to the night of all unholy thoughts.

.   .   .   .

I have seen
Unholy shapes lop off my shining thoughts,
Which I had thought nursed in thine emerald light ;
And they have lent me leathern wings of fear,
Of baffled pride and harrowing distrust ;
And Godhead with its crown of many stars,
Its pinnacles of flaming holiness,
And voice of leaves in the green summer-time,
Has seemed the shadowed image of a self.
Then my soul blackened ; and I rose to find
And grasp my doom, and cleave the arching deeps
Of desolation.

.   .   .   .

O Lord, my soul is a forgotten well ;
Clad round with its own rank luxuriance ;
A fountain a kind sunbeam searches for,
Sinking the lustre of its arrowy finger
Through the long grass its own strange virtue *
Hath blinded up its crystal eye withal :
Make me a broad strong river coming down
With shouts from its high hills, whose rocky hearts
Throb forth the joy of their stability
In watery pulses from their inmost deeps,
And I shall be a vein upon thy world,
Circling perpetual from the parent deep.
O First and Last, O glorious all in all,
In vain my faltering human tongue would seek

* This line is one of many instances in which my reader
will see both the carelessness of Ericson, and my religion
towards his remains.

To shape the vesture of the boundless thought,
Summing all causes in one burning word;
Give me the spirit's living tongue of fire,
Whose only voice is in an attitude
Of keenest tension, bent back on itself
With a strong upward force; even as thy bow
Of bended colour stands against the north,
And, in an attitude to spring to heaven,
Lays hold of the kindled hills.

     Most mighty One,
Confirm and multiply my thoughts of good;
Help me to wall each sacred treasure round
With the firm battlements of special action.
Alas my holy, happy thoughts of thee
Make not perpetual nest within my soul,
But like strange birds of dazzling colours stoop
The trailing glories of their sunward speed,
For one glad moment filling my blasted boughs
With the sunshine of their wings.

     Make me a forest
Of gladdest life, wherein perpetual spring
Lifts up her leafy tresses in the wind.

     Lo! now I see
Thy trembling starlight sit among my pines,
And thy young moon slide down my arching boughs
With a soft sound of restless eloquence.
And I can feel a joy as when thy hosts
Of trampling winds, gathering in maddened bands,
Roar upward through the blue and flashing day
Round my still depths of uncleft solitude.

     Hear me, O Lord,
When the black night draws down upon my soul,
And voices of temptation darken down

The misty wind, slamming thy starry doors,
With bitter jests.   " Thou fool !" they seem to say,
" Thou hast no seed of goodness in thee ; all
Thy nature hath been stung right through and through.
Thy sin hath blasted thee, and made thee old.
Thou hadst a will, but thou hast killed it—dead—
And with the fulsome garniture of life
Built out the loathsome corpse.   Thou art a child
Of night and death, even lower than a worm.
Gather the skirts up of thy shadowy self,
And with what resolution thou hast left,
Fall on the damned spikes of doom."

                    O take me like a child,
If thou hast made me for thyself, my God,
And lead me up thy hills : I shall not fear
So thou wilt make me pure, and beat back sin
With the terrors of thine eye.

          .   .   .   .

                    Lord, hast thou sent
Thy moons to mock us with perpetual hope?
Lighted within our breasts the love of love,
To make us ripen for despair, my God?
   Oh, dost thou hold each individual soul
Strung clear upon thy flaming rods of purpose?
Or does thine inextinguishable will
Stand on the steeps of night with lifted hand,
Filling the yawning wells of monstrous space
With mixing thought—drinking up single life
As in a cup? and from the rending folds
Of glimmering purpose, do all thy navied stars
Slide through the gloom with mystic melody,
Like wishes on a brow?   Oh, is my soul,
Hung like a dew-drop in thy grassy ways,
Drawn up again into the rack of change,

Even through the lustre which created it?
O mighty one, thou wilt not smite me through
With scorching wrath, because my spirit stands
Bewildered in thy circling mysteries.

．　　．　　．　　．　　．　　．　　．　　．

Here came the passage Robert had heard him
repeat, and then the following paragraph:

Lord, thy strange mysteries come thickening down
Upon my head like snow-flakes, shutting out
The happy upper fields with chilly vapour.
Shall I content my soul with a weak sense
Of safety? or feed my ravenous hunger with
Sore-purged hopes, that are not hopes, but fears
Clad in white raiment?
I know not but some thin and vaporous fog,
Fed with the rank excesses of the soul,
Mocks the devouring hunger of my life
With satisfaction: lo! the noxious gas
Feeds the lank ribs of gaunt and ghastly death
With double emptiness, like a balloon,
Borne by its lightness o'er the shining lands,
A wonder and a laughter.
　　The creeds lie in the hollow of men's hearts
Like festering pools glassing their own corruption;
The slimy eyes stare up with dull approval,
And answer not when thy bright starry feet
Move on the watery floors.

．　　．　　．　　．　　．　　．　　．　　．

O wilt thou hear me when I cry to thee?
I am a child lost in a mighty forest;
The air is thick with voices, and strange hands
Reach through the dusk and pluck me by the skirts.
There is a voice which sounds like words from home,

But, as I stumble on to reach it, seems
To leap from rock to rock.   Oh! if it is
Willing obliquity of sense, descend,
Heal all my wanderings, take me by the hand,
And lead me homeward through the shadows.

   Let me not by my wilful acts of pride
Block up the windows of thy truth, and grow
A wasted, withered thing, that stumbles on
Down to the grave with folded hands of sloth
And leaden confidence.

.   .   .   -   .   .   .   .

There was more of it, as my type indicates.
Full of faults, I have given so much to my reader,
just as it stood upon Ericson's blotted papers,
the utterance of a true soul " crying for the
light." But I give also another of his poems,
which Robert read at the same time, revealing
another of his moods when some one of the
clouds of holy doubt and questioning love which
so often darkened his sky, did at length

    Turn forth her silver lining on the night:

SONG.

They are blind and they are dead :
  We will wake them as we go ;
There are words have not been said ;
   There are sounds they do not know.
    We will pipe and we will sing—
    With the music and the spring,
    Set their hearts a wondering.

They are tired of what is old :
 We will give it voices new ;
For the half hath not been told
 Of the Beautiful and True.
  Drowsy eyelids shut and sleeping !
  Heavy eyes oppressed with weeping !
  Flashes through the lashes leaping !

Ye that have a pleasant voice,
 Hither come without delay ;
Ye will never have a choice
 Like to that ye have to-day :
  Round the wide world we will go,
  Singing through the frost and snow,
  Till the daisies are in blow.

Ye that cannot pipe or sing,
 Ye must also come with speed ;
Ye must come and with you bring
 Weighty words and weightier deed :
  Helping hands and loving eyes,
  These will make them truly wise—
  Then will be our Paradise.

As Robert read, the sweetness of the rhythm seized upon him, and, almost unconsciously, he read the last stanza aloud. Looking up from the paper with a sigh of wonder and delight—there was the pale face of Ericson gazing at him from the bed! He had risen on one arm, looking like a dead man called to life against his will, who found the world he had left already stranger to him than the one into which he had but peeped.

"Yes," he murmured; "I could say that once. It's all gone now. Our world is but our moods."

He fell back on his pillow. After a little, he murmured again:

"I might fool myself with faith again. So it is better not. I would not be fooled. To believe the false and be happy is the very belly of misery. To believe the true and be miserable, is to be true—and miserable. If there is no God, let me know it. I will not be fooled. I will not believe in a God that does not exist. Better be miserable because I *am*, and cannot help it.— O God!"

Yet in his misery, he cried upon God.

These words came upon Robert with such a shock of sympathy, that they destroyed his consciousness for the moment, and when he *thought* about them, he almost doubted if he had heard them. He rose and approached the bed. Ericson lay with his eyes closed, and his face contorted as by inward pain. Robert put a spoonful of wine to his lips. He swallowed it, opened his eyes, gazed at the boy as if he did not know him, closed them again, and lay still.

Some people take comfort from the true eyes of a dog—and a precious thing to the loving heart is the love of even a dumb animal.* What

* Why should Sir Walter Scott, who felt the death of

comfort then must not such a boy as Robert have been to such a man as Ericson? Often and often when he was lying asleep as Robert thought, he was watching the face of his watcher. When the human soul is not yet able to receive the vision of the God-Man, God sometimes— might I not say always?—reveals himself, or at least gives himself, in some human being whose face, whose hands are the ministering angels of his unacknowledged presence, to keep alive the fire of love on the altar of the heart, until God hath provided the sacrifice—that is, until the soul is strong enough to draw it from the concealing thicket. Here were two, each thinking that God had forsaken him, or was not to be found by him, and each the very love of God, commissioned to tend the other's heart. In each was he present to the other. The one thought himself the happiest of mortals in waiting upon his big brother, whose least smile was joy enough for one day; the other wondered at the unconscious goodness of the boy, and while he gazed at his ruddy-brown face, believed in God.

Camp, his bull-terrier, so much that he declined a dinner engagement in consequence, say on the death of his next favourite, a grayhound bitch—"Rest her body, since I dare not say soul!"? Where did he get that *dare not*? Is it well that the daring of genius should be circumscribed by an unbelief so common-place as to be capable only of subscription?

For some time after Ericson was taken ill, he was too depressed and miserable to ask how he was cared for. But by slow degrees it dawned upon him that a heart deep and gracious, like that of a woman, watched over him. True, Robert was uncouth, but his uncouthness was that of a half-fledged angel. The heart of the man and the heart of the boy were drawn close together. Long before Ericson was well he loved Robert enough to be willing to be indebted to him, and would lie pondering—not how to repay him, but how to return his kindness.

How much Robert's ambition to stand well in the eyes of Miss St John contributed to his progress I can only imagine; but certainly his ministrations to Ericson did not interfere with his Latin and Greek. I venture to think that they advanced them, for difficulty adds to result, as the ramming of the powder sends the bullet the further. I have heard, indeed, that when a carrier wants to help his horse up hill, he sets a boy on his back.

Ericson made little direct acknowledgment to Robert: his tones, his gestures, his looks, all thanked him ; but he shrunk from words, with the maidenly shamefacedness that belongs to true feeling. He would even assume the authoritative, and send him away to his studies, but Robert knew how to hold his own. The relation of elder brother and younger was already established between them. Shargar likewise took his share in the love and the fellowship, worshipping in that he believed.

CHAPTER X.

A FATHER AND A DAUGHTER.

THE presence at the street door of which Ericson's over-acute sense had been aware on a past evening, was that of Mr. Lindsay, walking home with bowed back and bowed head from the college library, where he was privileged to sit after hours as long as he pleased over books too big to be comfortably carried home to his cottage. He had called to inquire after Ericson, whose acquaintance he had made in the library, and cultivated until almost any Friday evening Ericson was to be found seated by Mr. Lindsay's parlour-fire.

As he entered the room that same evening, a young girl raised herself from a low seat by the fire to meet him. There was a faint rosy flush on her cheek, and she held a volume in her hand as she approached her father. They did not kiss: kisses were not a legal tender in Scotland then: possibly there has been a depreciation in the value of them since they were.

"I've been to ask after Mr. Ericson," said Mr. Lindsay.

"And how is he?" asked the girl.

"Very poorly indeed," answered her father.

"I am sorry. You'll miss him, papa."

"Yes, my dear. Tell Jenny to bring my lamp."

"Won't you have your tea first, papa?"

"Oh yes, if it's ready."

"The kettle has been boiling for a long time, but I wouldn't make the tea till you came in."

Mr. Lindsay was an hour later than usual, but Mysie was quite unaware of that: she had been absorbed in her book, too much absorbed even to ring for better light than the fire afforded. When her father went to put off his long, bifurcated greatcoat, she returned to her seat by the fire, and forgot to make the tea. It was a warm, snug room, full of dark, old-fashioned, spider-legged furniture; low-pitched, with a bay-window, open like an ear to the cries of the German Ocean at night, and like an eye during the day to look out upon its wide expanse. This ear or eye was now curtained with dark crimson, and the room, in the firelight, with the young girl for a soul to it, affected one like an ancient book in which he reads his own latest thought.

Mysie was nothing over the middle height— delicately fashioned, at once slender and round, with extremities neat as buds. Her complexion was fair, and her face pale, except when a flush, like that of a white rose, overspread it. Her cheek was lovelily curved, and her face rather short. But at first one could see nothing for her eyes. They were the largest eyes; and their motion reminded one of those of Sordello in the Purgatorio:

E nel muover degli occhi onesta e tarda :

they seemed too large to move otherwise than with a slow turning like that of the heavens. At first they looked black, but if one ventured inquiry, which was as dangerous as to gaze from the battlements of Elsinore, he found them a not very dark brown. In her face, however, especially when flushed, they had all the effect of what Milton describes as

Quel sereno fulgor d'amabil nero.

A wise observer would have been a little troubled in regarding her mouth. The sadness of a morbid sensibility hovered about it—the sign of an imagination wrought upon from the centre of self. Her lips were neither thin nor compressed—they closed lightly, and were richly curved; but there was a mobility almost tremulous about the upper lip that gave sign of the possibility of such an oscillation of feeling as might cause the whole fabric of her nature to rock dangerously.

The moment her father re-entered, she started from her stool on the rug, and proceeded to make the tea. Her father took no notice of her neglect, but drew a chair to the table, helped himself to a piece of oat-cake, hastily loaded it with as much butter as it could well carry, and while eating it forgot it and everything else in the absorption of a volume he had brought in with him from his study, in which he was tracing out some genealogical thread of which he fancied he had got a hold. Mysie was very active now, and lost the expression of *far-off-ness* which had hitherto characterized her countenance; till, having poured out the tea, she too plunged at once into her novel, and, like her father, forgot everything and everybody near her.

Mr. Lindsay was a mild, gentle man, whose face and hair seemed to have grown gray together. He was very tall, and stooped much. He had a mouth of much sensibility, and clear blue eyes, whose light was rarely shed upon any one within reach except his daughter—they were so constantly bent downwards, either on the road as he walked, or on his book as he sat. He had been educated for the church, but had never risen above the position of a parish schoolmaster. He had little or no impulse to utterance, was shy, genial, and, save in reading, indolent. Ten years before this point of my history he had been taken up by an active lawyer

in Edinburgh, from information accidentally
supplied by Mr. Lindsay himself, as the next
heir to a property to which claim was laid by
the head of a county family of wealth. Proba-
bilities were altogether in his favour, when he
gave up the contest upon the offer of a comfortable annuity from the disputant. To leave his
schooling and his possible estate together, and
sit down comfortably by his own fireside, with
the means of buying books, and within reach of
a good old library—that of King's College by
preference—was to him the sum of all that was
desirable. The income offered him was such
that he had no fear of laying aside enough for
his only child, Mysie; but both were so ill-fitted
for saving, he from looking into the past, she
from looking into—what shall I call it? I can
only think of negatives—what was neither past,
present, nor future, neither material nor eternal, neither imaginative in any true sense, nor
actual in any sense, that up to the present hour
there was nothing in the bank, and only the
money for impending needs in the house. He
could not be called a man of learning; he was
only a great bookworm; for his reading lay all
in the nebulous regions of history. Old family
records, wherever he could lay hold upon them,
were his favourite dishes; old, musty books, that
looked as if they knew something everybody
else had forgotten, made his eyes gleam, and

his white taper-fingered hand tremble with eagerness. With such a book in his grasp he saw something ever beckoning him on, a dimly precious discovery, a wonderful fact just the shape of some missing fragment in the mosaic of one of his pictures of the past. To tell the truth, however, his discoveries seldom rounded themselves into pictures, though many fragments of the minutely dissected map would find their places, whereupon he rejoiced like a mild giant refreshed with soda-water. But I have already said more about him than his place justifies; therefore, although I could gladly linger over the portrait, I will leave it. He had taught his daughter next to nothing. Being his child, he had the vague feeling that she inherited his wisdom, and that what he knew she knew. So she sat reading novels, generally trashy ones, while he knew no more of what was passing in her mind than of what the Admirable Crichton might, at the moment, be disputing with the angels.

I would not have my reader suppose that Mysie's mind was corrupted. It was so simple and childlike, leaning to what was pure, and looking up to what was noble, that anything directly bad in the books she happened—for it was all hap-hazard—to read, glided over her as a black cloud may glide over a landscape, leaving it sunny as before.

I cannot therefore say, however, that she was nothing the worse. If the darkening of the sun keep the fruits of the earth from growing, the earth is surely the worse, though it be blackened by no deposit of smoke. And where good things do not grow, the wild and possibly noxious will grow more freely. There may be no harm in the yellow tanzie—there is much beauty in the red poppy; but they are not good for food. The result in Mysie's case would be this—not that she would call evil good and good evil, but that she would take the beautiful for the true and the outer shows of goodness for goodness itself—not the worst result, but bad enough, and involving an awful amount of suffering and possibly of defilement. He who thinks to climb the hill of happiness thus, will find himself floundering in the blackest bog that lies at the foot of its precipices. I say *he*, not *she*, advisedly. All will acknowledge it of the woman: it is as true of the man, though he may get out easier. Will he? I say, checking myself. I doubt it much. In the world's eye, yes; but in God's? Let the question remain unanswered.

When he had eaten his toast, and drunk his tea, apparently without any enjoyment, Mr. Lindsay rose with his book in his hand, and withdrew to his study.

He had not long left the room when Mysie

was startled by a loud knock at the back door, which opened on a lane, leading along the top of the hill. But she had almost forgotten it again, when the door of the room opened, and a gentleman entered without any announcement—for Jennie had never heard of the custom. When she saw him, Mysie started from her seat, and stood in visible embarrassment. The colour went and came on her lovely face, and her eyelids grew very heavy. She had never seen the visitor before: whether he had ever seen her before, I cannot certainly say. She felt herself trembling in his presence, while he advanced with perfect composure. He was a man no longer young, but in the full strength and show of manhood—the Baron of Rothie. Since the time of my first description of him, he had grown a moustache, which improved his countenance greatly, by concealing his upper lip with its tusky curves. On a girl like Mysie, with an imagination so cultivated, and with no opportunity of comparing its fancies with reality, such a man would make an instant impression.

"I beg your pardon, Miss—Lindsay, I presume?—for intruding upon you so abruptly. I expected to see your father—not one of the graces."

She blushed all the colour of her blood now. The baron was quite enough like the hero of whom she had just been reading to admit of her imagination jumbling the two. Her book fell. He lifted it and laid it on the table. She could not speak even to thank him. Poor Mysie was scarcely more than sixteen.

"May I wait here till your father is informed of my visit?" he asked.

Her only answer was to drop again upon her low stool.

Now Jenny had left it to Mysie to acquaint her father with the fact of the baron's presence; but before she had time to think of the necessity of doing something, he had managed to draw her into conversation. He was as great a hypocrite as ever walked the earth, although he flattered himself that he was none, because he never pretended to cultivate that which he despised—namely, religion. But he was a hypocrite nevertheless; for the falser he knew himself, the more honour he judged it to persuade women of his truth.

It is unnecessary to record the slight, graceful, marrowless talk into which he drew Mysie, and by which he both bewildered and bewitched her. But at length she rose, admonished by her inborn divinity, to seek her father. As she passed him, the baron took her hand and kissed it. She might well tremble. Even such contact was terrible. Why? Because there was no love in it. When the sense of beauty which God had given him that he might worship, awoke in Lord Rothie, he did not worship, but devoured, that he might, as he thought, possess! The poison of asps was under those lips. His kiss was as a kiss from the grave's mouth, for his throat was an open sepulchre. This was all in the past, reader. Baron Rothie was a foam-flake of the court of the Prince Regent. There are no such men now-a-days! It is a shame to speak of such, *and therefore they are not!* Decency has gone so far to abolish virtue. Would to God that a writer could be decent *and honest!* St. Paul counted it a shame to speak of some things, and yet he did speak of them—because those to whom he spoke *did* them.

Lord Rothie had, in five minutes, so deeply interested Mr. Lindsay in a question of genealogy, that he begged his lordship to call again in a few days, when he hoped to have some result of research to communicate.

One of the antiquarian's weaknesses, cause and result both of his favourite pursuits, was an excessive reverence for rank. Had its claims been founded on mediated revelation, he could not have honoured it more. Hence when he communicated to his daughter the name of their visitor, it was "with bated breath and whispering humbleness," which deepened greatly the impression made upon her by the presence and conversation of the baron. Mysie was in danger.

Shargar was late that evening, for he had a job that detained him. As he handed over his money to Robert, he said,

"I saw Black Geordie the nicht again, stan'in' at a back door, an' Jock Mitchell, upo' Reid Rorie, haudin' him."

"Wha's Jock Mitchell?" asked Robert.

"My brither Sandy's ill-faured groom," answered Shargar. "Whatever mischeef Sandy's up till, Jock comes in i' the heid or tail o' 't."

"I wonner what he's up till noo."

"Faith! nae guid. But I aye like waur to meet Sandy by himsel' upo' that reekit deevil o' his. Man, it's awfu' whan Black Geordie turns the white o' 's ee, an' the white o' 's teeth upo' ye. It's a' the white 'at there is about 'im."

"Wasna yer brither i' the airmy, Shargar?"

"Ow, 'deed ay. They tell me he was at Watterloo. He's a cornel, or something like that."

"Wha tellt ye a' that?"

"My mither whiles," answered Shargar.

CHAPTER XI.

ROBERT'S VOW.

ERICSON was recovering slowly. He could sit up in bed the greater part of the day, and talk about getting out of it. He was able to give Robert an occasional help with his Greek, and to listen with pleasure to his violin. The night-watching grew less needful, and Ericson would have dispensed with it willingly, but Robert would not yet consent.

But Ericson had seasons of great depression, during which he could not away with music, or listen to the words of the New Testament. During one of these Robert had begun to read a chapter to him, in the faint hope that he might draw some comfort from it.

"Shut the book," he said. "If it were the word of God to men, it would have brought its own proof with it."

"Are ye sure it hasna?" asked Robert.

"No," answered Ericson. "But why should a fellow that would give his life—that's not

much, but it's all *I've* got—to believe in God,
not be able? Only I confess *that* God in the
New Testament wouldn't satisfy me. There's no
help. I must just die, and go and see.—She'll
be left without anybody. What does it matter?
She would not mind a word I said. And the
God they talk about will just let her take her
own way. He always does."

He had closed his eyes and forgotten that
Robert heard him. He opened them now, and
fixed them on him with an expression that
seemed to ask, " Have I been saying anything I
ought not ?"

Robert knelt by the bedside, and said, slowly,
with strongly repressed emotion.

" Mr. Ericson, I sweir by God, gin there *be* ane,
that gin ye dee, I'll tak up what ye lea' ahin'
ye. Gin there be onybody ye want luikit efter,
I'll luik efter her. I'll do what I can for her to
the best o' my abeelity, sae help me God—aye
savin' what I maun do for my ain father, gin he
be in life, to fess *(bring)* him back to the richt
gait, gin there be a richt gait. Sae ye can think
aboot whether there's onything ye wad like to
lippen till me."

A something grew in Ericson's eyes as Robert
spoke. Before he had finished, they beamed on
the boy.

" I think there must be a God somewhere after
all," he said, half soliloquizing. " I should be

sorry you hadn't a God, Robert. Why should I wish it for your sake? How could I want one for myself if there never was one? If a God had nothing to do with my making, why should I feel that nobody but God can set things right? Ah! but he must be such a God as I could imagine—altogether, absolutely true and good. If we came out of nothing, we could not invent the idea of a God—could we, Robert? Nothing would be our God. If we come from God, nothing is more natural, nothing *so* natural, as to want him, and when we haven't got him, to try to find him.—What if he should be in us after all, and working in us this way? just this very way of crying out after him?"

"Mr. Ericson," cried Robert, "dinna say ony mair 'at ye dinna believe in God. Ye *duo* believe in 'im—mair, I'm thinkin', nor onybody 'at I ken, 'cep', maybe, my grannie—only hers is a some queer kin' o' a God to believe in. I dinna think I cud ever manage to believe in *him* mysel'."

Ericson sighed and was silent. Robert remained kneeling by his bedside, happier, clearer-headed, and more hopeful than he had ever been. What if all was right at the heart of things—right, even as a man, if he could understand, would say was right; right, so that a man who understood in part could believe it to be ten times more right than he did understand!

Vaguely, dimly, yet joyfully, Robert saw something like this in the possibility of things.   His heart was full, and the tears filled his eyes. Ericson spoke again.

"I have felt like that often for a few moments," he said; "but always something would come and blow it away. I remember one spring morning—but if you will bring me that bundle of papers, I will show you what, if I can find it, will let you understand—"

Robert rose, went to the cupboard, and brought the pile of loose leaves. Ericson turned them over, and, Robert was glad to see, now and then sorted them a little.   At length he drew out a sheet, carelessly written, carelessly corrected, and hard to read.

"It is not finished, or likely to be," he said, as he put the paper in Robert's hand.

"Won't you read it to me yourself, Mr. Ericson?" suggested Robert.

"I would sooner put it in the fire," he answered—"it's fate, anyhow. I don't know why I haven't burnt them all long ago.—Rubbish, and diseased rubbish ! Read it yourself, or leave it."

Eagerly Robert took it, and read. The following was the best he could make of it:

> Oh that a wind would call
> From the depths of the leafless wood !
> Oh that a voice would fall
> On the ear of my solitude !

Far away is the sea,
With its sound and its spirit-tone :
Over it white clouds flee,
But I am alone, alone.

Straight and steady and tall
The trees stand on their feet ;
Fast by the old stone wall
The moss grows green and sweet ;
But my heart is full of fears,
For the sun shines far away ;
And they look in my face through tears,
And the light of a dying day.

My heart was glad last night,
As I pressed it with my palm ;
Its throb was airy and light
As it sang some spirit-psalm ;
But it died away in my breast
As I wandered forth to-day—
As a bird sat dead on its nest,
While others sang on the spray.

O weary heart of mine,
Is there ever a truth for thee ?
Will ever a sun outshine
But the sun that shines on me ?
Away, away through the air
The clouds and the leaves are blown ;
And my heart hath need of prayer,
For it sitteth alone, alone.

And Robert looked with sad reverence at Ericson,—nor ever thought that there was one who, in the face of the fact, and in recognition of it, had dared say, " Not a sparrow shall fall on the ground without your Father." The sparrow does fall—but he who sees it is yet the Father.

And we know only the fall, and not the sparrow.

CHAPTER XII.

THE GRANITE CHURCH.

THE next day was Sunday. Robert sat, after breakfast, by his friend's bed.

"You haven't been to church for a long time, Robert: wouldn't you like to go to-day?" said Ericson.

"I dinna want to lea' you, Mr. Ericson; I can bide wi' ye a' day the day, an' that's better nor goin' to a' the kirks in Aberdeen."

"I should like you to go to-day, though; and see if, after all, there may not be a message for us. If the church be the house of God, as they call it, there should be, now and then at least, some sign of a pillar of fire about it, some indication of the presence of God whose house it is. I wish you would go and see. I haven't been to church for a long time, except to the college-chapel, and I never saw anything more than a fog there."

"Michtna the fog be the torn-edge like, o' the cloody pillar?" suggested Robert.

" Very likely," assented Ericson; " for, whatever truth there may be in christianity, I'm pretty sure the mass of our clergy have never got beyond Judaism. They hang on about the skirts of that cloud for ever."

" Ye see, they think as lang 's they see the fog, they hae a grup o' something.   But they canna get a grup o' the glory that excelleth, for *it's* not to luik at, but to lat ye see a' thing."

Ericson regarded him with some surprise. Robert hastened to be honest.

" It's no that I ken onything aboot it, Mr. Ericson.   I was only bletherin' (*talking nonsense*) —rizzonin' frae the twa symbols o' the cloud an' the fire—kennin' nothing aboot the thing itsel'. I'll awa' to the kirk, an' see what it's like. Will I gie ye a buik afore I gang?"

" No, thank you.   I'll just lie quiet till you come back—if I can."

Robert instructed Shargar to watch for the slightest sound from the sick-room, and went to church.

As he approached the granite cathedral, the only one in the world, I presume, its stern solidity, so like the country and its men, laid hold of his imagination for the first time.   No doubt the necessity imposed by the unyielding material had its share, and that a large one, in the character of the building : whence else that simplest of west windows, six lofty, narrow

slits of light, parted by granite shafts of equal
width, filling the space between the corner but-
tresses of the nave, and reaching from door to
roof? whence else the absence of tracery in
the windows—except the severely gracious
curves into which the mullions divide?—But this
cause could not have determined those towers,
so strong that they might have borne their
granite weight soaring aloft, yet content with
the depth of their foundation, and aspiring not.
The whole aspect of the building is an outcome,
an absolute blossom of the northern nature.

There is but the nave of the church remaining. About 1680, more than a century
after the Reformation, the great tower fell, destroying the choir, chancel, and transept, which
have never been rebuilt. May the reviving faith
of the nation in its own history, and God at the
heart of it, lead to the restoration of this grand
old monument of the belief of their fathers. De-
formed as the interior then was with galleries,
and with Gavin Dunbar's flat ceiling, an awe fell
upon Robert as he entered it. When in after
years he looked down from between the pillars
of the gallery, that creeps round the church
through the thickness of the wall, like an artery,
and recalled the service of this Sunday morning,
he felt more strongly than ever that such a faith
had not reared that cathedral. The service was
like the church only as a dead body is like a

man.   There was no fervour in it, no aspiration.
The great central tower was gone.

That morning prayers and sermon were philoso-
phically dull, and respectable as any after-dinner
speech.   Nor could it well be otherwise : one of
the favourite sayings of its minister was, that a
clergyman is nothing but a moral policeman.
As such, however, he more resembled one of
Dogberry's watch.   He could not even preach
hell with any vigour ; for as a gentleman he re-
coiled from the vulgarity of the doctrine, yielding only a few feeble words on the subject as a
sop to the Cerberus that watches over the dues
of the Bible—quite unaware that his notion of
the doctrine had been drawn from the Æneid,
and not from the Bible.

"Well, have you got anything, Robert?" asked Ericson, as he entered his room.

"Nothing," answered Robert.

"What was the sermon about?"

"It was all to prove that God is a benevo-
lent being."

"Not a devil, that is," answered Ericson.
"Small consolation that."

"Sma' eneuch," responded Robert. "I cudna
help thinkin' I kent mony a tyke *(dog)* that God
had made wi' mair o' what I wad ca' the divine
natur' in him nor a' that Dr. Soulis made oot to
be in God himsel'.   He had no ill intentions wi'
us—it amuntit to that.   He wasna ill-willy, as

the bairns say. But the doctor had some sair
wark, I thoucht, to mak that oot, seein' we war
a' the children o' wrath, accordin' to him, born
in sin, and inheritin' the guilt o' Adam's first
trespass. I dinna think Dr. Soulis cud say that
God had dune the best he cud for 's. But he
never tried to say onything like that. He jist
made oot that he was a verra respectable kin' o'
a God, though maybe no a'thing we micht
wuss. We oucht to be thankfu' that he gae's
a wee blink o' a chance o' no bein' brunt to a'
eternity, wi' nae chance ava. I dinna say that
he *said* that, but that's what it a' seemed to me
to come till. He said a hantle aboot the care o'
Providence, but a' the gude that he did seemed
to me to be but a haudin' aff o' something ill
that he had made as weel. Ye wad hae thocht
the deevil had made the warl', and syne God
had pitten us intil't, and jist gied a bit wag o' 's
han' whiles to haud the deevil aff o' 's whan
he was like to destroy the breed a'thegither.
For the grace that he spak aboot, that was less
nor the nature an' the providence. I cud see
unco little o' grace intil 't."

Here Ericson broke in—fearful, apparently,
lest his boy-friend should be actually about to
deny the God in whom he did not himself believe.

"Robert," he said solemnly, " one thing is
certain: if there be a God at all, he is not like

that. If there be a God at all, we shall know him by his perfection—his grand perfect truth, fairness, love—a love to make life an absolute good—not a mere accommodation of difficulties, not a mere preponderance of the balance on the side of well-being. Love only could have been able to create. But they don't seem jealous for the glory of God, those men. They don't mind a speck, or even a blot, here and there upon him. The world doesn't make them miserable. They can get over the misery of their fellow-men without being troubled about them, or about the God that could let such things be.* They represent a God who does wonderfully well, on the whole, after a middling fashion.

* Amongst Ericson's papers I find the following sonnets, which belong to the mood here embodied :

Oft, as I rest in quiet peace, am I
Thrust out at sudden doors, and madly driven
Through desert solitudes, and thunder-riven
Black passages which have not any sky.
The scourge is on me now, with all the cry
Of ancient life that hath with murder striven.
How many an anguish hath gone up to heaven !
How many a hand in prayer been lifted high
When the black fate came onward with the rush
Of whirlwind, avalanche, or fiery spume !
Even at my feet is cleft a shivering tomb
Beneath the waves ; or else with solemn hush
The graveyard opens, and I feel a crush
As if we were all huddled in one doom.

I want a God who loves perfectly. He may kill; he may torture even ; but if it be for love's sake, Lord, here am I. Do with me as thou wilt."

Had Ericson forgotten that he had no proof of such a God ? The next moment the intellectual demon was awake.

" But what's the good of it all ?" he said. " I don't even know that there *is* anything outside of me."

" Ye ken that I'm here, Mr. Ericson," suggested Robert.

" I know nothing of the sort. You may be another phantom—only clearer."

" Ye speik to me as gin ye thocht me somebody."

" So does the man to his phantoms, and you call him mad. It is but a yielding to the pres-

Comes there, O Earth, no breathing time for thee ?
No pause upon thy many-chequered lands ?
Now resting on my bed with listless hands,
I mourn thee resting not. Continually
Hear I the plashing borders of the sea
Answer each other from the rocks and sands.
Troop all the rivers seawards ; nothing stands,
But with strange noises hasteth terribly.
Loam-eared hyenas go a moaning by.
Howls to each other all the bloody crew
Of Afric's tigers. But, O men, from you
Comes this perpetual sound more loud and high
Than aught that vexes air. I hear the cry
Of infant generations rising too.

sure of constant suggestion. I do not know —I cannot know if there is anything outside of me."

"But gin there warna, there wad be naebody for ye to love, Mr. Ericson."

"Of course not."

"Nor naebody to love you, Mr. Ericson."

"Of course not."

"Syne ye wad be yer ain God, Mr. Ericson."

"Yes. That would follow."

"I canna imagine a waur hell—closed in amo' naething—wi' naething a' aboot ye, luikin' something a' the time—kennin' 'at it 's a' a lee, and nae able to win clear o' 't."

"It is hell, my boy, or anything worse you can call it."

"What for suld ye believe that, than, Mr. Ericson? I wadna believe sic an ill thing as that. I dinna think I cud believe 't, gin ye war to pruv 't to me."

"I don't believe it. Nobody could prove that either, even if it were so. I am only miserable that I can't prove the contrary."

"Suppose there war a God, Mr. Ericson, do ye think ye bude (*behoved*) to be able to pruv that? Do ye think God cud stan' to be pruved as gin he war something sma' eneuch to be turned roon' and roon', and luikit at upo' ilka side? Gin there war a God, wadna it jist be sae—that we cudna prove him to be, I mean?"

"Perhaps. That is something. I have often thought of that. But then you can't prove *any-thing* about it."

"I canna help thinkin o' what Mr. Innes said to me ance. I was but a laddie, but I never forgot it. I plaguit him sair wi' wantin' to unnerstan' ilka thing afore I wad gang on wi' my questons (*sums*). Says he, ae day, 'Robert, my man, gin ye *will* aye unnerstan' afore ye du as ye're tellt, ye'll never unnerstan' onything. But gin ye du the thing I tell ye, ye'll be i' the mids o' 't afore ye ken 'at ye're gaein' intil 't.' I jist thocht I wad try him. It was at lang division that I boglet maist. Weel, I gaed on, and I cud du the thing weel eneuch, ohn made ae mistak. And aye I thocht the maister was wrang, for I never kent the rizzon o' a' that be-ginnin' at the wrang en', an' takin' doon an' substrackin', an' a' that. Ye wad hardly believe me, Mr. Ericson: it was only this verra day, as I was sittin' i' the kirk—it was a lang psalm they war singin'—that ane wi' the foxes i' the tail o' 't —lang division came into my heid again; and first aye bit glimmerin' o' licht cam in, and syne anither, an' afore the psalm was dune I saw throu' the haill process o' 't. But ye see, gin I hadna dune as I was tauld, and learnt a' aboot hoo it was dune aforehan', I wad hae had nae-thing to gang rizzonin' aboot, an' wad hae fun' oot naething."

"That's good, Robert. But when a man is dying for food, he can't wait."

"He micht try to get up and luik, though. He needna bide in 's bed till somebody comes an' sweirs till him 'at he saw a haddie *(haddock)* i' the press."

"I have been looking, Robert—for years."

"Maybe, like me, only for the *rizzon* o' 't, Mr. Ericson—gin ye'll forgie my impidence."

"But what's to be done in this case, Robert? Where's the work that you can do in order to understand? Where's your long division, man?"

"Ye're ayont me noo. I canna tell that, Mr. Ericson. It canna be gaein' to the kirk, surely. Maybe it micht be sayin' yer prayers and readin' yer Bible."

Ericson did not reply, and the conversation dropped. Is it strange that neither of these disciples should have thought of turning to the story of Jesus, finding some word that he had spoken, and beginning to do that as a first step towards a knowledge of the doctrine that Jesus was the incarnate God, come to visit his people —a very unlikely thing to man's wisdom, yet an idea that has notwithstanding ascended above man's horizon, and shown itself the grandest idea in his firmament?

In the evening Ericson asked again for his papers, from which he handed Robert the following poem :—

WORDS IN THE NIGHT.

I woke at midnight, and my heart,
My beating heart said this to me:
Thou seest the moon how calm and bright,
The world is fair by day and night,
But what is that to thee?
One touch to me—down dips the light
Over the land and sea.
All is mine, all is my own!
Toss the purple fountain high!
The breast of man is a vat of stone;
I am alive, I, only I!

One little touch and all is dark;
The winter with its sparkling moons,
The spring with all her violets,
The crimson dawns and rich sunsets,
The autumn's yellowing noons.
I only toss my purple jets,
And thou art one that swoons
Upon a night of gust and roar,
Shipwrecked among the waves, and seems
Across the purple hills to roam;
Sweet odours touch him from the foam,
And downward sinking still he dreams
He walks the clover field at home,
And hears the rattling teams.
All is mine; all is my own!
Toss the purple fountain high!
The breast of man is a vat of stone;
I am alive, I, only I!

Thou hast beheld a throated fountain spout
Full in the air, and in the downward spray
A hovering Iris span the marble tank,

Which as the wind came, ever rose and sank
Violet and red ; so my continual play
Makes beauty for the Gods with many a prank
Of human excellence, while they,
Weary of all the noon, in shadows sweet
Supine and heavy-eyed rest in the boundless heat :
Let the world's fountain play !
Beauty is pleasant in the eyes of Jove ;
Betwixt the wavering shadows where he lies
He marks the dancing column with his eyes
Celestial, and amid his inmost grove
Upgathers all his limbs, serenely blest,
Lulled by the mellow noise of the great world's unrest.

One heart beats in all nature, differing
But in the work it works ; its doubts and clamours
Are but the waste and brunt of instruments
Wherewith a work is done ; or as the hammers
On forge Cyclopean plied beneath the rents
Of lowest Etna, conquering into shape
The hard and scattered ore :
Choose thou narcotics, and the dizzy grape
Outworking passion, lest with horrid crash
Thy life go from thee in a night of pain.
So tutoring thy vision, shall the flash
Of dove white-breasted be to thee no more
Than a white stone heavy upon the plain.

Hark the cock crows loud !
And without, all ghastly and ill,
Like a man uplift in his shroud,
The white white morn is propped on the hill ;
And adown from the eaves, pointed and chill,
The icicles 'gin to glitter ;
And the birds with a warble short and shrill,
Pass by the chamber-window still—

With a quick uneasy twitter.
Let me pump warm blood, for the cold is bitter;
And wearily, wearily, one by one,
Men awake with the weary sun.
Life is a phantom shut in thee;
I am the master and keep the key;
So let me toss thee the days of old,
Crimson and orange and green and gold;
So let me fill thee yet again
With a rush of dreams from my spout amain;
For all is mine; all is my own;
Toss the purple fountain high!
The breast of man is a vat of stone;
And I am alive, I, only I.

Robert having read, sat and wept in silence. Ericson saw him, and said tenderly,

"Robert, my boy, I'm not always so bad as that. Read this one—though I never feel like it now. Perhaps it may come again some day, though. I may once more deceive myself and be happy."

"Dinna say that, Mr. Ericson. That's waur than despair. That's flat unbelief. Ye no more ken that ye're deceivin' yersel' than ye ken that ye're no doin' 't."

Ericson did not reply; and Robert read the following sonnet aloud, feeling his way delicately through its mazes :—

Lie down upon the ground, thou hopeless one!
Press thy face in the grass, and do not speak.
Dost feel the green globe whirl? Seven times a week

Climbeth she out of darkness to the sun,
Which is her god ; seven times she doth not shun
Awful eclipse, laying her patient cheek
Upon a pillow ghost-beset with shriek
Of voices utterless which rave and run
Through all the star-penumbra, craving light
And tidings of the dawn from East and West.
Calmly she sleepeth, and her sleep is blest
With heavenly visions, and the joy of Night
Treading aloft with moons.   Nor hath she fright
Though cloudy tempests beat upon her breast.

Ericson turned his face to the wall, and Robert withdrew to his own chamber.

CHAPTER XIII.

SHARGAR'S ARM.

NOT many weeks passed before Shargar knew Aberdeen better than most Aberdonians. From the Pier-head to the Rubislaw Road, he knew, if not every court, yet every thoroughfare and short cut. And Aberdeen began to know him. He was very soon recognized as trustworthy, and had pretty nearly as much to do as he could manage. Shargar, therefore, was all over the city like a cracker, and could have told at almost any hour where Dr. Anderson was to be found—generally in the lower parts of it, for the good man visited much among the poor, giving them almost exclusively the benefit of his large experience. Shargar delighted in keeping an eye upon the doctor, carefully avoiding to show himself.

One day as he was hurrying through the Green (*a non rirendo*) on a mission from the Rothieden carrier, he came upon the doctor's chariot standing in one of the narrowest streets, and, as usual, paused to contemplate the equipage and get a peep of the owner. The morning was very sharp. There was no snow, but a cold fog, like vaporized hoar-frost, filled the air. It was weather in which the East Indian could not venture out on foot, else he could have reached the place by a stair from Union Street far sooner than he could drive thither. His horses apparently liked the cold as little as himself. They had been moving about restlessly for some time before the doctor made his appearance. The moment he got in and shut the door, one of them reared, while the other began to haul on his traces, eager for a gallop. Something about the chain gave way, the pole swerved round under the rearing horse, and great confusion and danger would have ensued, had not Shargar rushed from his coign of vantage, sprung at the bit of the rearing horse, and dragged him off the pole, over which he was just casting his near leg. As soon as his feet touched the ground he too pulled, and away went the chariot and down went Shargar. But in a moment more several men had laid hold of the horses' heads, and stopped them.

"Oh Lord!" cried Shargar, as he rose with his arm dangling by his side, " what will Donal' Joss say? I'm like to swarf (*faint*). Haud awa' frae that basket, ye wuddyfous (*withyfowls, gallows-birds*)," he cried, darting towards the hamper he had left in the entry of a court, round which a few ragged urchins had gathered; but just as he reached it he staggered and fell. Nor did he know anything more till he found the carriage stopping with himself and the hamper inside it.

As soon as the coachman had got his harness put to rights, the doctor had driven back to see how the lad had fared, for he had felt the carriage go over something. They had found him lying beside his hamper, had secured both, and as a preliminary measure were proceeding to deliver the latter.

" Whaur am I? whaur the deevil am I?" cried Shargar, jumping up and falling back again.

" Don't you know me, Moray?" said the doctor, for he felt shy of calling the poor boy by his nickname: *he* had no right to do so.

"Na, I dinna ken ye. Lat me awa'.—I beg yer pardon, doctor: I thocht ye was ane o' thae wuddyfous rinnin' awa' wi' Donal' Joss's basket. Eh me! sic a stoun' i' my airm! But naebody ca's me Moray. They a' ca' me Shargar. What richt hae *I* to be ca'd *Moray?*" added the poor boy, feeling, I almost believe for the first time, the stain upon his birth. Yet he had as good a right before God to be called *Moray* as any other son of that worthy sire, the Baron of Rothie included. Possibly the trumpet-blowing angels did call him Moray, or some better name.

"The coachman will deliver your parcel, Moray," said the doctor, this time repeating the name with emphasis.

"Deil a bit o' 't!" cried Shargar. "He daurna lea' his box wi' thae deevils o' horses. What gars ye keep sic horses, doctor? They'll play some mischeef some day."

"Indeed, they've played enough already, my poor boy. They've broken your arm."

"Never min' that. That's no muckle. Ye're welcome, doctor, to my twa airms for what ye hae dune for Robert an' that lang-leggit frien' o' his—the Lord forgie me—Mr. Ericson. But ye maun jist pay him what I canna mak for a day or twa, till 't jines again—to haud them gaein', ye ken.—It winna be muckle to you, doctor," added Shargar, beseechingly.

"Trust me for that, Moray," returned Dr. Anderson. "I owe you a good deal more than that. My brains might have been out by this time."

"The Lord be praised!" said Shargar, making about his first profession of Christianity. "Robert 'ill think something o' me noo."

During this conversation the coachman sat expecting some one to appear from the shop, and longing to pitch into the "camstary" horse, but not daring to lift his whip beyond its natural angle. No one came. All at once Shargar knew where he was.

"Guid be here! we're at Donal's door! Guid day to ye, doctor; an' I'm muckle obleeged to ye. Maybe, gin ye war comin' oor gait, the morn, or the neist day, to see Maister Ericson, ye wad tie up my airm, for it gangs wallopin' aboot, an' that canna be guid for the stickin' o' 't thegither again."

"My poor boy! you don't think I'm going to leave you here, do you?" said the doctor, proceeding to open the carriage-door.

"But whaur's the hamper?" said Shargar, looking about him in dismay.

"The coachman has got it on the box," answered the doctor.

"Eh! that 'll never do. Gin thae rampaugin' brutes war to tak a start again, what wad come o' the bit basket? I maun get it doon direckly."

"Sit still. I will get it down, and deliver it myself." As he spoke the doctor got out.

"Tak care o' 't, sir; tak care o' 't. William Walker said there was a jar o' drained hinney i' the basket; an' the bairns wad miss 't sair gin 't war spult."

"I will take good care of it," responded the doctor.

He delivered the basket, returned to the carriage, and told the coachman to drive home.

"Whaur are ye takin' me till?" exclaimed Shargar. "Willie hasna payed me for the parcel."

"Never mind Willie. I'll pay you," said the doctor.

"But Robert wadna like me to tak siller whaur I did nae wark for 't," objected Shargar. "He's some pernickety (*precise*)—Robert. But I'll jist say 'at ye garred me, doctor. Maybe that 'll saitisfee him. An' faith! I'm queer aboot my left fin here."

" We'll soon set it all right," said the doctor.

When they reached his house he led the way to his surgery, and there put the broken limb in splints. He then told Johnston to help the patient to bed.

"I maun gang hame," objected Shargar. " What wad Robert think?"

" I will tell him all about it," said the doctor.

" Yersel, sir?" stipulated Shargar.

" Yes, myself."

" Afore nicht?"

"Directly," answered the doctor, and Shargar yielded.

"But what *will* Robert say?" were his last words, as he fell asleep, appreciating, no doubt, the superiority of the bed to his usual lair upon the hearthrug.

Robert was delighted to hear how well Shargar had acquitted himself. Followed a small consultation about him; for the accident had ripened the doctor's intentions concerning the outcast.

"As soon as his arm is sound again, he shall go to the grammar-school," he said.

"An' the college?" asked Robert.

"I hope so," answered the doctor. "Do you think he will do well? He has plenty of courage, at all events, and that is a fine thing."

"Ow ay," answered Robert; "he's no ill aff for smeddum (*spirit*)—that is, gin it be for ony ither body. He wad never lift a han' for himsel'; an' that's what garred me tak till him sae muckle. He's a fine crater. He canna gang him lane, but he'll gang wi' onybody—and haud up wi' him."

"What do you think him fit for, then?"

Now Robert had been building castles for Shargar out of the hopes which the doctor's friendliness had given him. Therefore he was ready with his answer.

"Gin ye cud ensure him no bein' made a general o', he wad mak a gran' sojer. Set 's face foret, and say 'quick mairch,' an' he'll ca his bagonet throu auld Hornie. But lay nae consequences upo' him, for he cudna stan' unner them."

Dr. Anderson laughed, but thought none the less, and went home to see how his patient was getting on.

CHAPTER XIV.

MYSIE'S FACE.

MEANTIME Ericson grew better. A space of hard, clear weather, in which everything sparkled with frost and sunshine, did him good. But not yet could he use his brain. He turned with dislike even from his friend Plato. He would sit in bed or on his chair by the fireside for hours, with his hands folded before him, and his eyelids drooping, and let his thoughts flow, for he could not think. And that these thoughts flowed not always with other than sweet sounds over the stones of question, the curves of his lip would testify to the friendly-furtive glance of the watchful Robert. None but the troubled mind knows its own consolations ; and I believe the saddest life has its own presence—however it may be unrecognized as such—of the upholding Deity. Doth God care for the hairs that perish from our heads ? To a mind like Ericson's the remembered scent, the recurring vision of a flower loved in childhood, is enough to sustain anxiety with beauty, for the lovely is itself healing and hope-giving, because it is the form and presence of the true. To have such a presence is *to be;* and while a mind exists in any high consciousness, the intellectual trouble that springs from the desire to know its own life, to be assured of its rounded law and security, ceases, for the desire itself falls into abeyance.

But although Ericson was so weak, he was always able and ready to help Robert in any difficulty not unfrequently springing from his imperfect preparation in Greek; for while Mr. Innes was an excellent Latin scholar, his knowledge of Greek was too limited either to compel learning or inspire enthusiasm. And with the keen instinct he possessed in everything immediate between man and man, Robert would sometimes search for a difficulty in order to request its solution; for then Ericson would rouse himself to explain as few men could have explained: where a clear view was to be had of anything, Ericson either had it or knew that he had it not. Hence Robert's progress was good; for one word from a wise helper will clear off a whole atmosphere of obstructions.

At length one day when Robert came home he found him seated at the table, with his slate, working away at the Differential Calculus.

After this he recovered more rapidly, and ere another week was over began to attend one class a day. He had been so far in advance before, that though he could not expect prizes, there was no fear of his *passing*.

One morning, Robert, coming out from a lecture, saw Ericson in the quadrangle talking to an elderly gentleman. When they met in the afternoon Ericson told him that that was Mr. Lindsay, and that he had asked them both to spend the evening at his house. Robert would go anywhere to be with his friend.

He got out his Sunday clothes, and dressed himself with anxiety : he had visited scarcely at all, and was shy and doubtful. He then sat down to his books, till Ericson came to his door —dressed, and hence in Robert's eyes ceremonial —a stately, graceful gentleman. Renewed awe came upon him at the sight, and renewed gratitude. There was a flush on Ericson's cheek, and a fire in his eye. Robert had never seen him look so grand. But there was a something about him that rendered him uneasy—a look that made Ericson seem strange, as if his life lay in some far-off region.

" I want you to take your violin with you, Robert," he said.

" Hoots !" returned Robert, "hoo can I do that ? To tak her wi' me the first time I gang to a strange hoose, as gin I thocht a'body wad

think as muckle o' my auld wife as I do mysel'!
That wadna be mainners—wad it noo, Mr. Ericson?"

"But I told Mr. Lindsay that you could play
well. The old gentleman is fond of Scotch
tunes, and you will please him if you take it."

"That maks a' the differ," answered Robert.

"Thank you," said Erison, as Robert went towards his instrument; and, turning, would have
walked from the house without any additional
protection.

"Whaur are ye gaein' that gait, Mr. Ericson? Tak yer plaid, or ye'll be laid up again,
as sure's ye live."

"I'm warm enough," returned Ericson.

"That's naething. The cauld 's jist lyin' i'
the street like a verra deevil to get a grup o' ye.
Gin ye dinna pit on yer plaid, I winna tak my
fiddle."

Ericson yielded; and they set out together.

I will account for Ericson's request about the
violin.

He went to the episcopal church on Sundays,
and sat where he could see Mysie—sat longing
and thirsting ever till the music returned. Yet
the music he never heard; he watched only its
transmutation into form, never taking his eyes
off Mysie's face. Reflected thence in a metamorphosed echo, he followed all its changes.
Never was one powerless to produce it more

strangely responsive to its influence. She had no voice; she had never been taught the use of any instrument. A world of musical feeling was pent up in her, and music raised the suddener storms in her mobile nature, that she was unable to give that feeling utterance. The waves of her soul dashed the more wildly against their shores, inasmuch as those shores were precipitous, and yielded no outlet to the swelling waters. It was that his soul might hover like a bird of Paradise over the lovely changes of her countenance, changes more lovely and frequent than those of an English May, that Ericson persuaded Robert to take his violin.

The last of the sunlight was departing, and a large full moon was growing through the fog on the horizon. The sky was almost clear of clouds, and the air was cold and penetrating. Robert drew Eric's plaid closer over his chest. Eric thanked him lightly, but his voice sounded eager; and it was with a long hasty stride that he went up the hill through the gathering of the light frosty mist. He stopped at the stair upon which Robert had found him that memorable night. They went up. The door had been left on the latch for their entrance. They went up more steps between rocky walls. When in after years he read the *Purgatorio*, as often as he came to one of its ascents, Robert saw this stair with his inward eye. At the top of the stair was the garden, still ascending, and at the top of the garden shone the glow of Mr. Lindsay's parlour through the red-curtained window. To Robert it shone a refuge for Ericson from the night air; to Ericson it shone the casket of the richest jewel of the universe. Well might the ruddy glow stream forth to meet him! Only in glowing red could such beauty be rightly closed. With trembling hand he knocked at the door.

They were shown at once into the parlour. Mysie was putting away her book as they entered, and her back was towards them. When she turned, it seemed even to Robert as if all the light in the room came only from her eyes. But that light had been all gathered out of the novel she had just laid down. She held out her hand to Eric, and her sweet voice was yet more gentle than wont, for he had been ill. His face flushed at the tone. But although she spoke kindly, he could hardly have fancied that she showed him special favour.

Robert stood with his violin under his arm, feeling as awkward as if he had never handled anything more delicate than a pitchfork. But Mysie sat down to the table, and began to pour out the tea, and he came to himself again. Presently her father entered. His greeting was warm and mild and sleepy. He had come from poring over Spotiswood, in search of some Will

o' the wisp or other, and had grown stupid
from want of success. But he revived after a
cup of tea, and began to talk about northern
genealogies; and Ericson did his best to listen.
Robert wondered at the knowledge he displayed:
he had been tutor the foregoing summer in one
of the oldest and poorest, and therefore proudest families in Caithness. But all the time his
host talked Ericson's eyes hovered about Mysie,
who sat gazing before her with look distraught,
with wide eyes and scarce-moving eyelids, beholding something neither on sea or shore; and
Mr. Lindsay would now and then correct Ericson
in some egregious blunder; while Mysie would
now and then start awake and ask Robert or
Ericson to take another cup of tea. Before the
sentence was finished, however, she would let it
die away, speaking the last words mechanically,
as her consciousness relapsed into dreamland.
Had not Robert been with Ericson, he would
have found it wearisome enough; and except
things took a turn, Ericson could hardly be
satisfied with the pleasure of the evening.
Things did take a turn.

"Robert has brought his fiddle," said Ericson,
as the tea was removed.

"I hope he will be kind enough to play something," said Mr. Lindsay.

"I'll do that," answered Robert, with alacrity.
"But ye maunna expec' ower muckle, for I'm but

a prentice-han'," he added, as he got the instrument ready.

Before he had drawn the bow once across it, attention awoke in Mysie's eyes; and before he had finished playing, Ericson must have had quite as much of the " beauty born of murmuring sound " as was good for him. Little did Mysie think of the sky of love, alive with silent thoughts, that arched over her. The earth teems with love that is unloved. The universe itself is one sea of infinite love, from whose consort of harmonies if a stray note steal across the sense, it starts bewildered.

Robert played better than usual. His touch grew intense, and put on all its delicacy, till it was like that of the spider, which, as Pope so admirably says,

Feels at each thread, and lives along the line.

And while Ericson watched its shadows, the music must have taken hold of him too; for when Robert ceased, he sang a wild ballad of the northern sea, to a tune strange as itself. It was the only time Robert ever heard him sing. Mysie's eyes grew wider and wider as she listened. When it was over,

" Did ye write that sang yersel', Mr. Ericson ?" asked Robert.

" No," answered Ericson. " An old shepherd up in our parts used to say it to me when I was a boy."

" Didna he sing 't ?" Robert questioned further.

" No, he didn't. But I heard an old woman crooning it to a child in a solitary cottage on the shore of Stroma, near the Swalchie whirlpool, and that was the tune she sang it to, if singing it could be called."

" I don't quite understand it, Mr. Ericson," said Mysie. " What does it mean ?"

" There was once a beautiful woman lived there-away," began Ericson.—But I have not room to give the story as he told it, embellishing it, no doubt, as with such a mere tale was lawful enough, from his own imagination. The substance was that a young man fell in love with a beautiful witch, who let him go on loving her till he cared for nothing but her, and then began to kill him by laughing at him. For no witch can fall in love herself, however much she may like to be loved. She mocked him till he drowned himself in a pool on the seashore. Now the witch did not know that; but as she walked along the shore, looking for things, she saw his hand lying over the edge of a rocky basin. Nothing is more useful to a witch than the hand of a man, so she went to pick it up. When she found it fast to an arm, she would have chopped it off, but seeing whose it was, she would, for some reason or other best known to a witch, draw off his ring first. For it was an enchanted ring which she had given him to be-

witch his love, and now she wanted both it and
the hand to draw to herself the lover of a young
maiden whom she hated. But the dead hand
closed its fingers upon hers, and her power was
powerless against the dead. And the tide came
rushing up, and the dead hand held her till she
was drowned. She lies with her lover to this
day at the bottom of the Swalchie whirlpool;
and when a storm is at hand, strange moanings
rise from the pool, for the youth is praying the
witch lady for her love, and she is praying him
to let go her hand.

While Ericson told the story the room still
glimmered about Robert as if all its light came
from Mysie's face, upon which the flickering firelight alone played. Mr. Lindsay sat a little
back from the rest, with an amused expression :
legends of such sort did not come within the
scope of his antiquarian reach, though he was
ready enough to believe whatever tempted his
own taste, let it be as destitute of likelihood as
the story of the dead hand. When Ericson
ceased, Mysie gave a deep sigh, and looked full
of thought, though I daresay it was only feeling. Mr. Lindsay followed with an old tale of
the Sinclairs, of which he said Ericson's reminded him, though the sole association was that
the foregoing was a Caithness story, and the
Sinclairs are a Caithness family. As soon as it
was over, Mysie, who could not hide all her

impatience during its lingering progress, asked
Robert to play again. He took up his violin,
and with great expression gave the air of Ericson's ballad two or three times over, and then
laid down the instrument. He saw indeed that
it was too much for Mysie, affecting her more,
thus presented after the story, than the singing
of the ballad itself. Thereupon Ericson, whose
spirits had risen greatly at finding that he could
himself secure Mysie's attention, and produce
the play of soul in feature which he so much delighted to watch, offered another story; and
the distant rush of the sea, borne occasionally
into the " grateful gloom" upon the cold sweep
of a February wind, mingled with one tale after
another, with which he entranced two of his
audience, while the third listened mildly content.

The last of the tales Ericson told was as follows :—

"One evening-twilight in spring, a young English student, who had wandered northwards as
far as the outlying fragments of Scotland called
the Orkney and Shetland islands, found himself
on a small island of the latter group, caught in
a storm of wind and hail, which had come on
suddenly. It was in vain to look about for any
shelter; for not only did the storm entirely ob-
scure the landscape, but there was nothing around
him save a desert moss.

" At length, however, as he walked on for mere

walking's sake, he found himself on the verge of a cliff, and saw, over the brow of it, a few feet below him, a ledge of rock, where he might find some shelter from the blast, which blew from behind. Letting himself down by his hands, he alighted upon something that crunched beneath his tread, and found the bones of many small animals scattered about in front of a little cave in the rock, offering the refuge he sought. He went in, and sat upon a stone. The storm increased in violence, and as the darkness grew he became uneasy, for he did not relish the thought of spending the night in the cave. He had parted from his companions on the opposite side of the island, and it added to his uneasiness that they must be full of apprehension about him. At last there came a lull in the storm, and the same instant he heard a footfall, stealthy and light as that of a wild beast, upon the bones at the mouth of the cave. He started up in some fear, though the least thought might have satisfied him that there could be no very dangerous animals upon the island. Before he had time to think, however, the face of a woman appeared in the opening. Eagerly the wanderer spoke. She started at the sound of his voice. He could not see her well, because she was turned towards the darkness of the cave.

" 'Will you tell me how to find my way across the moor to Shielness?' he asked.

" ' You cannot find it to-night,' she answered, in a sweet tone, and with a smile that bewitched him, revealing the whitest of teeth.

" ' What am I to do, then ?' he asked.

" ' My mother will give you shelter, but that is all she has to offer.'

" ' And that is far more than I expected a minute ago,' he replied. 'I shall be most grateful.'

" She turned in silence and left the cave. The youth followed.

" She was barefooted, and her pretty brown feet went catlike over the sharp stones, as she led the way down a rocky path to the shore. Her garments were scanty and torn, and her hair blew tangled in the wind. She seemed about five and twenty, lithe and small. Her long fingers kept clutching and pulling nervously at her skirts as she went. Her face was very gray in complexion, and very worn, but delicately formed, and smooth-skinned. Her thin nostrils were tremulous as eyelids, and her lips, whose curves were faultless, had no colour to give sign of indwelling blood. What her eyes were like he could not see, for she had never lifted the delicate films of her eyelids.

" At the foot of the cliff they came upon a little hut leaning against it, and having for its inner apartment a natural hollow within it. Smoke was spreading over the face of the rock, and the grateful odour of food gave hope to the hungry student. His guide opened the door of the cottage ; he followed her in, and saw a woman bending over a fire in the middle of the floor. On the fire lay a large fish boiling. The daughter spoke a few words, and the mother turned and welcomed the stranger. She had an old and very wrinkled, but honest face, and looked troubled. She dusted the only chair in the cottage, and placed it for him by the side of the fire, opposite the one window, whence he saw a little patch of yellow sand over which the spent waves spread themselves out listlessly. Under this window there was a bench, upon which the daughter threw herself in an unusual posture, resting her chin upon her hand. A moment after the youth caught the first glimpse of her blue eyes. They were fixed upon him with a strange look of greed, amounting to craving, but as if aware that they belied or betrayed her, she dropped them instantly. The moment she veiled them, her face, notwithstanding its colourless complexion, was almost beautiful.

" When the fish was ready, the old woman wiped the deal table, steadied it upon the uneven floor, and covered it with a piece of fine table-linen. She then laid the fish on a wooden platter, and invited the guest to help himself. Seeing no other provision, he pulled from his pocket a hunting knife, and divided a portion from the fish, offering it to the mother first.

" ' Come, my lamb,' said the old woman ; and the daughter approached the table.   But her nostrils and mouth quivered with disgust.

" The next moment she turned and hurried from the hut.

" ' She doesn't like fish,' said the old woman, ' and I haven't anything else to give her.'

" ' She does not seem in good health,' he rejoined.

" The woman answered only with a sigh, and they ate their fish with the help of a little ryebread. As they finished their supper, the youth heard the sound as of the pattering of a dog's feet upon the sand close to the door; but ere he had time to look out of the window, the door opened and the young woman entered.   She looked better, perhaps from having just washed her face.   She drew a stool to the corner of the fire opposite him.   But as she sat down, to his bewilderment, and even horror, the student spied a single drop of blood on her white skin within her torn dress. The woman brought out a jar of whisky, put a rusty old kettle on the fire, and took her place in front of it. As soon as the water boiled, she proceeded to make some toddy in a wooden bowl.

" Meantime the youth could not take his eyes off the young woman, so that at length he found himself fascinated, or rather bewitched.   She kept her eyes for the most part veiled with the loveliest eyelids fringed with darkest lashes, and he gazed entranced; for the red glow of the little oil-lamp covered all the strangeness of her complexion. But as soon as he met a stolen glance out of those eyes unveiled, his soul shuddered within him. Lovely face and craving eyes alternated fascination and repulsion.

"The mother placed the bowl in his hands. He drank sparingly, and passed it to the girl. She lifted it to her lips, and as she tasted—only tasted it—looked at him. He thought the drink must have been drugged and have affected his brain. Her hair smoothed itself back, and drew her forehead backwards with it; while the lower part of her face projected towards the bowl, revealing, ere she sipped, her dazzling teeth in strange prominence. But the same moment the vision vanished; she returned the vessel to her mother, and rising, hurried out of the cottage.

"Then the old woman pointed to a bed of heather in one corner with a murmured apology; and the student, wearied both with the fatigues of the day and the strangeness of the night, threw himself upon it, wrapped in his cloak. The moment he lay down, the storm began afresh, and the wind blew so keenly through the crannies of the hut, that it was only by

drawing his cloak over his head that he could
protect himself from its currents. Unable to
sleep, he lay listening to the uproar which grew
in violence, till the spray was dashing against
the window. At length the door opened, and
the young woman came in, made up the fire,
drew the bench before it, and lay down in the
same strange posture, with her chin propped on
her hand and elbow, and her face turned towards the youth. He moved a little; she
dropped her head, and lay on her face, with her
arms crossed beneath her forehead. The mother
had disappeared.

" Drowsiness crept over him. A movement of
the bench roused him, and he fancied he saw
some four-footed creature as tall as a large dog
trot quietly out of the door. He was sure he
felt a rush of cold wind. Gazing fixedly
through the darkness, he thought he saw the
eyes of the damsel encountering his, but a glow
from the falling together of the remnants of the
fire, revealed clearly enough that the bench was
vacant. Wondering what could have made her
go out in such a storm, he fell fast asleep.

" In the middle of the night he felt a pain in
his shoulder, came broad awake, and saw the
gleaming eyes and grinning teeth of some animal close to his face. Its claws were in his
shoulder, and its mouth in the act of seeking
his throat. Before it had fixed its fangs, how-

ever, he had its throat in one hand, and sought his knife with the other. A terrible struggle followed; but regardless of the tearing claws, he found and opened his knife. He had made one futile stab, and was drawing it for a surer, when, with a spring of the whole body, and one wildly-contorted effort, the creature twisted its neck from his hold, and with something betwixt a scream and a howl, darted from him. Again he heard the door open; again the wind blew in upon him, and it continued blowing; a sheet of spray dashed across the floor, and over his face. He sprung from his couch and bounded to the door.

"It was a wild night—dark, but for the flash of whiteness from the waves as they broke within a few yards of the cottage; the wind was raving, and the rain pouring down the air. A gruesome sound as of mingled weeping and howling came from somewhere in the dark. He turned again into the hut and closed the door, but could find no way of securing it.

"The lamp was nearly out, and he could not be certain whether the form of the young woman was upon the bench or not. Overcoming a strong repugnance, he approached it, and put out his hands—there was nothing there. He sat down and waited for the daylight: he dared not sleep any more.

"When the day dawned at length, he went out

yet again, and looked around. The morning was dim and gusty and gray. The wind had fallen, but the waves were tossing wildly. He wandered up and down the little strand, longing for more light.

"At length he heard a movement in the cottage. By and by the voice of the old woman called to him from the door.

"'You're up early, sir. I doubt you didn't sleep well.'

"'Not very well,' he answered. 'But where is your daughter?'

"'She's not awake yet,' said the mother. 'I'm afraid I have but a poor breakfast for you. But you'll take a dram and a bit of fish. It's all I've got.'

"Unwilling to hurt her, though hardly in good appetite, he sat down at the table. While they were eating the daughter came in, but turned her face away and went to the further end of the hut. When she came forward after a minute or two, the youth saw that her hair was drenched, and her face whiter than before. She looked ill and faint, and when she raised her eyes, all their fierceness had vanished, and sadness had taken its place. Her neck was now covered with a cotton handkerchief. She was modestly attentive to him, and no longer shunned his gaze. He was gradually yielding to the temptation of braving another night in the hut, and seeing what would follow, when the old woman spoke.

" 'The weather will be broken all day, sir,' she said. 'You had better be going, or your friends will leave without you.'

" Ere he could answer, he saw such a beseeching glance on the face of the girl, that he hesitated, confused. Glancing at the mother, he saw the flash of wrath in her face. She rose and approached her daughter, with her hand lifted to strike her. The young woman stooped her head with a cry. He darted round the table to interpose between them. But the mother had caught hold of her ; the handkerchief had fallen from her neck ; and the youth saw five blue bruises on her lovely throat—the marks of the four fingers and the thumb of a left hand. With a cry of horror he darted from the house, but as he reached the door he turned. His hostess was lying motionless on the floor, and a huge gray wolf came bounding after him."

An involuntary cry from Mysie interrupted the story-teller. He changed his tone at once.

" I beg your pardon, Miss Lindsay, for telling you such a horrid tale. Do forgive me. I didn't mean to frighten you more than a little."

" Only a case of lycanthropia," remarked Mr. Lindsay, as coolly as if that settled everything about it and lycanthropia, horror and all, at once.

Mysie tried to laugh, but succeeded badly. Robert took his violin, and its tones had soon swept all the fear from her face, leaving in its stead a trouble that has no name—the trouble of wanting one knows not what—or how to seek it.

It was now time to go home. Mysie gave each an equally warm good-night and thanks, Mr. Lindsay accompanied them to the door, and the students stepped into the moonlight. Across the links the sound of the sea came with a swell.

As they went down the garden, Ericson stopped. Robert thought he was looking back to the house, and went on. When Ericson joined him, he was pale as death.

" What *is* the maitter wi' ye, Mr. Ericson?" he asked in terror.

" Look there !" said Ericson, pointing, not to the house, but to the sky.

Robert looked up. Close about the moon were a few white clouds. Upon these white clouds, right over the moon, and near as the eyebrow to an eye, hung part of an opalescent halo, bent into the rude, but unavoidable suggestion of an eyebrow ; while, close around the edge of the moon, clung another, a pale storm-halo. To this pale iris and faint-hued eyebrow the full moon itself formed the white pupil: the whole was a perfect eye of ghastly death, staring out of the winter heaven. The vision may never have been before, may never have been again, but this Ericson and Robert saw that night.

CHAPTER XV.

THE LAST OF THE COALS.

THE next Sunday Robert went with Ericson
to the episcopal chapel, and for the first
time in his life heard the epic music of the organ.   It was a new starting point in his life.
The worshipping instrument flooded his soul
with sound, and he stooped beneath it as a
bather on the shore stoops beneath the broad
wave rushing up the land.   But I will not
linger over this portion of his history.   It is
enough to say that he sought the friendship of
the organist, was admitted to the instrument;
touched, trembled, exulted; grew dissatisfied,
fastidious, despairing; gathered hope and tried
again, and yet again; till at last, with constantly recurring fits of self-despite, he could
not leave the grand creature alone.   It became
a rival even to his violin.   And once before the
end of March, when the organist was ill, and
another was not to be had, he ventured to oc-

cupy his place both at morning and evening service.

Dr. Anderson kept George Moray in bed for a few days, after which he went about for a while with his arm in a sling. But the season of bearing material burdens was over for him now. Dr. Anderson had an interview with the master of the grammar-school; a class was assigned to Moray, and with a delight, resting chiefly on his social approximation to Robert, which in one week elevated the whole character of his person and countenance and bearing. George Moray bent himself to the task of mental growth. Having good helpers at home, and his late-developed energy turning itself entirely into the new channel, he got on admirably. As there was no other room to be had in Mrs. Fyvie's house, he continued for the rest of the session to sleep upon the rug, for he would not hear of going to another house. The doctor had advised Robert to drop the nickname as much as possible; but the first time he called him Moray, Shargar threatened to cut his throat, and so between the two the name remained.

I presume that by this time Doctor Anderson had made up his mind to leave his money to Robert, but thought it better to say nothing about it, and let the boy mature his independence. He had him often to his house. Ericson frequently accompanied him; and as there

was a good deal of original similarity between
the doctor and Ericson, the latter soon felt his
obligation no longer a burden. Shargar likewise, though more occasionally, made one of
the party, and soon began, in his new circumstances, to develop the manners of a gentleman.
I say *develop* advisedly, for Shargar had a deep
humanity in him, as abundantly testified by his
devotion to Robert, and humanity is the body
of which true manners is the skin and ordinary
manifestation : true manners are the polish
which lets the internal humanity shine through,
just as the polish on marble reveals its veined
beauty. Many talks did the elderly man hold
with the three youths, and his experience of life
taught Ericson and Robert much, especially
what he told them about his Brahmin friend in
India. Moray, on the other hand, was chiefly
interested in his tales of adventure when on
service in the Indian army, or engaged in the
field sports of that region so prolific in mon-
sters. His gipsy blood and lawless childhood,
spent in wandering familiarity with houseless
nature, rendered him more responsive to these
than the others, and his kindled eye and perti-
nent remarks raised in the doctor's mind an
early question whether a commission in India
might not be his best start in life.

Between Ericson and Robert, as the former
recovered his health, communication from the

deeper strata of human need became less frequent. Ericson had to work hard to recover something of his leeway ; Robert had to work hard that prizes might witness for him to his grandmother and Miss St. John. To the latter especially, as I think I have said before, he was anxious to show well, wiping out the blot, as he considered it, of his all but failure in the matter of a bursary. For he looked up to her as to a goddess who just came near enough to the earth to be worshipped by him who dwelt upon it.

The end of the session came nigh. Ericson passed his examinations with honour. Robert gained the first Greek and third Latin prize. The evening of the last day arrived, and on the morrow the students would be gone—some to their homes of comfort and idleness, others to hard labour in the fields ; some to steady reading, perhaps to school again to prepare for the next session, and others to be tutors all the summer months, and return to the wintry city as to freedom and life. Shargar was to remain at the grammar-school.

That last evening Robert sat with Ericson in his room. It was a cold night—the night of the last day of March. A bitter wind blew about the house, aud dropped spiky hailstones upon the skylight. The friends were to leave on the morrow, but to leave together ; for they

had already sent their boxes, one by the carrier
to Rothieden, the other by a sailing vessel to
Wick, and had agreed to walk together as far
as Robert's home, where he was in hopes of in-
ducing his friend to remain for a few days if he
found his grandmother agreeable to the plan.
Shargar was asleep on the rug for the last time,
and Robert had brought his coal-scuttle into
Ericson's room to combine their scanty remains
of well-saved fuel in a common glow, over which
they now sat.

"I wonder what my grannie 'ill say to me,"
said Robert.

"She'll be very glad to see you, whatever she
may say," remarked Ericson.

"She'll say 'Noo, be dooce,' the minute I hae
shacken hands wi' her," said Robert.

"Robert," returned Ericson solemnly, "if I
had a grandmother to go home to, she might
box my ears if she liked—I wouldn't care. You
do not know what it is not to have a soul belonging to you on the face of the earth. It is
so cold and so lonely!"

"But you have a cousin, haven't you?" suggested Robert.

Ericson laughed, but good-naturedly.

"Yes," he answered, "a little man with a
fishy smell, in a blue tail-coat with brass buttons, and a red and black nightcap."

"But," Robert ventured to hint, "he might

go in a kilt and top-boots, like Satan in my grannie's copy o' the *Paradise Lost*, for anything I would care."

" Yes, but he's just like his looks. The first thing he'll do the next morning after I go *home*, will be to take me into his office, or shop, as he calls it, and get down his books, and show me how many barrels of herring I owe him, with the price of each. To do him justice, he only charges me wholesale."

" What 'll he do that for ?"

" To urge on me the necessity of diligence, and the choice of a profession," answered Ericson, with a smile of mingled sadness and irresolution. "He will set forth what a loss the interest of the money is, even if I should pay the principal ; and remind me that although he has stood my friend, his duty to his own family imposes limits. And he has at least a couple of thousand pounds in the county bank. I don't believe he would do anything for me but for the honour it will be to the family to have a professional man in it. And yet my father was the making of him."

" Tell me about your father. What was he ?"

" A gentle-minded man, who thought much and said little. He farmed the property that had been his father's own, and is now leased by my fishy cousin afore mentioned."

" And your mother ?"

" She died just after I was born, and my father never got over it."

" And you have no brothers or sisters ?"

" No, not one. Thank God for your grandmother, and do all you can to please her."

A silence followed, during which Robert's heart swelled and heaved with devotion to Ericson ; for notwithstanding his openness, there was a certain sad coldness about him that restrained Robert from letting out all the tide of his love. The silence became painful, and he broke it abruptly.

" What are you going to be, Mr. Ericson ?"

" I wish you could tell me, Robert. What would you have me to be ? Come now."

Robert thought for a moment.

" Weel, ye canna be a minister, Mr. Ericson, 'cause ye dinna believe in God, ye ken," he said, simply.

" Don't say that, Robert," Ericson returned, in a tone of pain with which no displeasure was mingled. " But you are right. At best I only hope in God ; I don't believe in him."

" I'm thinkin' there canna be muckle differ atween houp an' faith," said Robert. " Mony a ane 'at says they believe in God has unco little houp o' onything frae 's han', I'm thinkin'."

My reader may have observed a little change for the better in Robert's speech. Dr. Anderson had urged upon him the necessity of being

able at least to speak English; and he had
been trying to modify the antique Saxon dialect they used at Rothieden with the newer and
more refined English. But even when I knew
him, he would upon occasion, especially when
the subject was religion or music, fall back into
the broadest Scotch. It was as if his heart
could not issue freely by any other gate than
that of his grandmother tongue.

Fearful of having his last remark contradicted
—for he had an instinctive desire that it should
lie undisturbed where he had cast it in the field
of Ericson's mind, he hurried to another question.

"What for shouldna ye be a doctor?"

"Now you'll think me a fool, Robert, if I tell
you why."

"Far be it frae me to daur think sic a word,
Mr. Ericson!" said Robert devoutly.

"Well, I'll tell you, whether or not," returned
Ericson. "I could, I believe, amputate a living
limb with considerable coolness; but put a knife
in a dead body I could not."

"I think I know what you mean. Then you
must be a lawyer."

"A lawyer! O Lord!" said Ericson.

"Why not?" asked Robert, in some wonder-
ment; for he could not imagine Ericson acting
from mere popular prejudice or fancy.

"Just think of spending one's life in an atmosphere of squabbles. It's all very well when one gets to be a judge and dispense justice; but— well, it's not for me. I *could* not do the best for my clients. And a lawyer has nothing to do with the kingdom of heaven—only with his clients. He *must* be a party-man. He must secure for one so often at the loss of the rest. My duty and my conscience would always be at strife."

"Then what *will* you be, Mr. Ericson?"

"To tell the truth, I would rather be a watchmaker than anything else I know. I might make one watch that would go right, I suppose, if I lived long enough. But no one would take an apprentice of my age. So I suppose I must be a tutor, knocked about from one house to another, patronized by ex-pupils, and smiled upon as harmless by mammas and sisters to the end of the chapter. And then something of a pauper's burial, I suppose. *Che sara sara.*"

Ericson had sunk into one of his worst moods. But when he saw Robert looking unhappy, he changed his tone, and would be—what he could not be—merry.

"But what's the use of talking about it?" he said. "Get your fiddle, man, and play The Wind that shakes the Barley."

"No, Mr. Ericson," answered Robert; "I have no heart for the fiddle. I would rather have some poetry."

"Oh!—Poetry!" returned Ericson, in a tone of contempt—yet not very hearty contempt.

"We're gaein' awa', Mr. Ericson," said Robert; "an' the Lord 'at we ken naething aboot alane kens whether we'll ever meet again i' this place. And sae——"

"True enough, my boy," interrupted Ericson. "I have no need to trouble myself about the future. I believe that is the real secret of it after all. I shall never want a profession or anything else."

"What do you mean, Mr. Ericson?" asked Robert, in half-defined terror.

"I mean, my boy, that I shall not live long. I know that—thank God!"

"How do you know it?"

"My father died at thirty, and my mother at six-and-twenty, both of the same disease. But that's not how I know it."

"How do you know it then?"

Ericson returned no answer. He only said—

"Death will be better than life. One thing I don't like about it though," he added, "is the coming on of unconsciousness. I cannot bear to lose my consciousness even in sleep. It is such a terrible thing!"

"I suppose that's ane o' the reasons that we canna be content withoot a God," responded Robert. "It's dreidfu' to think even o' fa'in' asleep withoot some ane greater an' nearer than the *me* watchin' ower't. But I'm jist sayin' ower again what I hae read in ane o' your papers, Mr. Ericson. Jist lat me luik."

Venturing more than he had ever yet ventured, Robert rose and went to the cupboard where Ericson's papers lay. His friend did not check him. On the contrary, he took the papers from his hand, and searched for the poem indicated.

" I'm not in the way of doing this sort of thing, Robert," he said.

" I know that," answered Robert.

And Ericson read.

SLEEP.

Oh, is it Death that comes
To have a foretaste of the whole?
  To-night the planets and the stars
  Will glimmer through my window-bars,
But will not shine upon my soul.

For I shall lie as dead,
Though yet I am above the ground;
  All passionless, with scarce a breath,
  With hands of rest and eyes of death,
I shall be carried swiftly round.

Or if my life should break
The idle night with doubtful gleams,
  Through mossy arches will I go,
  Through arches ruinous and low,
And chase the true and false in dreams.

Why should I fall asleep?
When I am still upon my bed,

The moon will shine, the winds will rise,
  And all around and through the skies
The light clouds travel o'er my head.

O, busy, busy things!
Ye mock me with your ceaseless life;
    For all the hidden springs will flow,
    And all the blades of grass will grow,
When I have neither peace nor strife.

And all the long night through,
The restless streams will hurry by;
    And round the lands, with endless roar,
    The white waves fall upon the shore,
And bit by bit devour the dry.

Even thus, but silently,
Eternity, thy tide shall flow—
    And side by side with every star
    Thy long-drawn swell shall bear me far,
An idle boat with none to row.

My senses fail with sleep;
My heart beats thick; the night is noon;
    And faintly through its misty folds
    I hear a drowsy clock that holds
Its converse with the waning moon.

Oh, solemn mystery!
That I should be so closely bound
    With neither terror nor constraint,
    Without a murmur of complaint,
And lose myself upon such ground!

"Rubbish!" said Ericson, as he threw down
the sheets, disgusted with his own work, which
so often disappoints the writer, especially if he

is by any chance betrayed into reading it aloud.

"Dinna say that, Mr. Ericson," returned Robert. "Ye maunna say that. Ye hae nae richt to lauch at honest wark, whether it be yer ain or ony ither body's. The poem noo——"

"Don't call it a poem," interrupted Ericson. "It's not worthy of the name."

"I *will* ca' 't a poem," persisted Robert; "for it's a poem to me, whatever it may be to you. An' hoo I ken 'at it's a poem is jist this: it opens my een like music to something I never saw afore."

"What is that?" asked Ericson, not sorry to be persuaded that there might after all be some merit in the productions painfully despised of himself.

"Jist this: it's only whan ye dinna want to fa' asleep 'at it luiks fearsome to ye. An' maybe the fear o' death comes i' the same way: we're feared at it 'cause we're no a'thegither ready for 't; but whan the richt time comes, it'll be as nat'ral as fa'in' asleep whan we're doonricht sleepy. Gin there be a God to ca' oor Father in heaven, I'm no thinkin' that he wad to sae mony bonny tunes pit a scraich for the hinder end. I'm thinkin', gin there be onything in 't ava—ye ken I'm no sayin', for I dinna ken—we maun jist lippen till him to dee dacent an' bonny, an' nae sic strange awfu' fash aboot it as some fowk wad mak a religion o' expeckin'."

Ericson looked at Robert with admiration mingled with something akin to merriment.

"One would think it was your grandfather holding forth, Robert," he said. "How came you to think of such things at your age?"

"I'm thinkin'," answered Robert, "ye warna muckle aulder nor mysel' whan ye took to sic things, Mr. Ericson. But 'deed, maybe my luckie-daddie *(grandfather)* pat them i' my heid, for I had a heap ado wi' his fiddle for a while. She's deid noo."

Not understanding him, Ericson began to question, and out came the story of the violins. They talked on till the last of their coals was burnt out, and then they went to bed.

Shargar had undertaken to rouse them early, that they might set out on their long walk with a long day before them. But Robert was awake before Shargar. The all but soulless light of the dreary season awoke him, and he rose and looked out. Aurora, as aged now as her loved Tithonus, peered, gray-haired and desolate, over the edge of the tossing sea, with hardly enough of light in her dim eyes to show the broken crests of the waves that rushed shorewards before the wind of her rising. Such an east wind was the right breath to issue from such a pale mouth of hopeless revelation as that which opened with dead lips across the troubled sea on the far horizon. While he gazed, the east darkened; a cloud of hail rushed against the window; and Robert retreated to his bed. But ere he had fallen asleep, Ericson was beside him; and before he was dressed, Ericson appeared again, with his stick in his hand. They left Shargar still asleep, and descended the stairs, thinking to leave the house undisturbed. But Mrs. Fyvie was watching for them, and insisted on their taking the breakfast she had prepared. They then set out on their journey of forty miles, with half a loaf in their pockets, and money enough to get bread and cheese, and a bottle of the poorest ale, at the far-parted roadside inns.

When Shargar awoke, he wept in desolation, then crept into Robert's bed, and fell fast asleep again.

CHAPTER XVI.

A STRANGE NIGHT.

THE youths had not left the city a mile behind, when a thick snowstorm came on. It
did not last long, however, and they fought
their way through it into a glimpse of sun. To
Robert, healthy, powerful, and except at rare
times, hopeful, it added to the pleasure of the
journey to contend with the storm, and there
was a certain steely indifference about Ericson
that carried him through. They trudged on
steadily for three hours along a good turnpike
road, with great black masses of cloud sweeping
across the sky, which now sent them a glimmer
of sunlight, and now a sharp shower of hail.
The country was very dreary—a succession of
undulations rising into bleak moorlands, and hills
whose heather would in autumn flush the land
with glorious purple, but which now looked black
and cheerless, as if no sunshiue could ever warm
them. Now and then the moorland would sweep
down to the edge of the road, diversified with

dark holes from which peats were dug, and an occasional quarry of gray granite. At one moment endless pools would be shining in the sunlight, and the next the hail would be dancing a mad fantastic dance all about them: they pulled their caps over their brows, bent their heads, and struggled on.

At length they reached their first stage, and after a meal of bread and cheese and an offered glass of whisky, started again on their journey. They did not talk much, for their force was spent on their progress.

After some consultation whether to keep the road or take a certain short cut across the moors, which would lead them into it again with a saving of several miles, the sun shining out with a little stronger promise than he had yet given, they resolved upon the latter. But in the middle of the moorland the wind and the hail came on with increased violence, and they were glad to tack from one to another of the huge stones that lay about, and take a short breathing time under the lee of each; so that when they recovered the road, they had lost as many miles in time and strength as they had saved in distance. They did not give in, however, but after another rest and a little more refreshment, started again.

The evening was now growing dusk around them, and the fatigue of the day was telling so severely on Ericson, that when in the twilight they heard the blast of a horn behind them, and turning saw the two flaming eyes of a well-known four-horse coach come fluctuating towards them, Robert insisted on their getting up and riding the rest of the way.

" But I can't afford it," said Ericson.

" But I can," said Robert.

"I don't doubt it," returned Ericson. " But I owe you too much already."

" Gin ever we win hame—I mean to the heart o' hame—ye can pay me there."

" There will be no need then."

" Whaur's the need than to mak sic a wark aboot a saxpence or twa atween this and that? I thocht ye cared for naething that time or space or sense could grip or measure. Mr. Ericson, ye're no half sic a philosopher as ye wad set up for.—Hillo !"

Ericson laughed a weary laugh, and as the coach stopped in obedience to Robert's hail, he scrambled up behind.

The guard knew Robert, was pitiful over the condition of the travellers, would have put them inside, but that there was a lady there, and their clothes were wet, got out a great horse-rug and wrapped Robert in it, put a spare coat of his own, about an inch thick, upon Ericson, drew out a flask, took a pull at it, handed it to his new passengers, and blew a vigorous blast on his long horn, for they were approaching a desolate

shed where they had to change their weary
horses for four fresh thorough-breds.

Away they went once more, careering through
the gathering darkness.   It was delightful indeed to have to urge one weary leg past the
other no more, but be borne along towards food,
fire, and bed.   But their adventures were not
so nearly over as they imagined.   Once more
the hail fell furiously—huge hailstones, each
made of many, half-melted and welded together
into solid lumps of ice.   The coachman could
scarcely hold his face to the shower, and the
blows they received on their faces and legs,
drove the thin-skinned, high-spirited horses nearly mad. At length they would face it no longer.
At a turn in the road, where it crossed a brook
by a bridge with a low stone wall, the wind met
them right in the face with redoubled vehe-
mence; the leaders swerved from it, and were
just rising to jump over the parapet, when the
coachman, whose hands were nearly insensible
with cold, threw his leg over the reins, and pulled them up.   One of the leaders reared, and
fell backwards; one of the wheelers kicked vigorously; a few moments, and in spite of the guard
at their heads, all was one struggling mass of
bodies and legs, with a broken pole in the midst.
The few passengers got down; and Robert,
fearing that yet worse might happen and remembering the lady, opened the door. He found

her quite composed. As he helped her out,

"What is the matter?" asked the voice dearest to him in the world—the voice of Miss St. John.

He gave a cry of delight. Wrapped in the horse-cloth, Miss St. John did not know him.

"What is the matter?" she repeated.

"Ow, naething, mem—naething. Only I doobt we winna get ye hame the nicht."

"Is it you, Robert?" she said, gladly recognizing his voice.

"Ay, it's me, and Mr. Ericson. "We'll tak care o' ye, mem."

"But surely we shall get home!"

Robert had heard the crack of the breaking pole.

"'Deed, I doobt no."

"What are we to do then?"

"Come into the lythe (shelter) o' the bank here, oot o' the gait o' thae brutes o' horses," said Robert, taking off his horse-cloth and wrapping her in it.

The storm hissed and smote all around them. She took Robert's arm. Followed by Ericson, they left the coach and the struggling horses, and withdrew to a bank that overhung the road. As soon as they were out of the wind, Robert, who had made up his mind, said,

"We canna be mony yairds frae the auld hoose o' Bogbonnie. We micht win throu the

o 2

nicht there weel eneuch. I'll speir at the gaird, the minute the horses are clear. We war 'maist ower the brig, I heard the coachman say."

"I know quite well where the old house is," said Ericson. "I went in the last time I walked this way."

"Was the door open?" asked Robert.

"I don't know," answered Ericson. "I found one of the windows open in the basement."

"We'll get the len' o' ane o' the lanterns, an' gang direckly. It canna be mair nor the breedth o' a rig or twa frae the burn."

"I can take you by the road," said Ericson.

"It will be very cold," said Miss St. John,—already shivering, partly from disquietude.

"There's timmer eneuch there to haud 's warm for a twalmonth," said Robert.

He went back to the coach. By this time the horses were nearly extricated. Two of them stood steaming in the lamplight, with their sides going at twenty bellows' speed. The guard would not let him have one of the coach lamps, but gave him a small lantern of his own. When he returned with it, he found Ericson and Miss St. John talking together.

Ericson led the way, and the others followed.

"Whaur are ye gaein', gentlemen?" asked the guard, as they passed the coach.

"To the auld hoose," answered Robert.

"Ye canna do better. I maun bide wi' the

coch till the lave gang back to Drumheid wi' the horses, on' fess anither pole. Faith, it 'ill be weel into the mornin' or we win oot o' this. Tak care hoo ye gang. There's holes i' the auld hoose, I doobt."

"We'll tak gude care, ye may be sure, Hector," said Robert, as they left the bridge.

The house to which Ericson was leading them was in the midst of a field. There was just light enough to show a huge mass standing in the dark, without a tree or shelter of any sort. When they reached it, all that Miss St. John could distinguish was a wide broken stair leading up to the door, with glimpses of a large, plain, ugly, square front. The stones of the stair sloped and hung in several directions; but it was plain to a glance that the place was dilapidated through extraordinary neglect, rather than by the usual wear of time. In fact, it belonged only to the beginning of the preceding century, somewhere in Queen Anne's time. There was a heavy door to it, but fortunately for Miss St. John, who would not quite have relished getting in at the window of which Ericson had spoken, it stood a little ajar. The wind roared in the gap and echoed in the empty hall into which they now entered. Certainly Robert was right: there was wood enough to keep them warm; for that hall, and every room into which they went, from top to bottom of the huge house, was lined with pine. No paint-brush had ever passed upon it. Neither was there a spot to be seen upon the grain of the wood : it was clean as the day when the house was finished, only it had grown much browner. A close gallery, with window frames which had never been glazed, at one story's height, leading across from the one side of the first floor to the other, looked down into the great echoing hall, which rose in the centre of the building to the height of two stories; but this was unrecognizable in the poor light of the guard's lantern. All the rooms on every floor opened each into the other; —but why should I give such a minute description, making my reader expect a ghost story, or at least a nocturnal adventure? I only want him to feel something of what our party felt as they entered this desolate building, which, though some hundred and twenty years old, bore not a single mark upon the smooth floors or spotless walls to indicate that article of furniture had ever stood in it, or human being ever inhabited it. There was a strange and unusual horror about the place—a feeling quite different from that belonging to an ancient house, however haunted it might be. It was like a body that had never had a human soul in it. There was no sense of a human history about it. Miss St. John's feeling of *eeriness* rose to the height when, in wandering through the many rooms in search of one where the windows were less broken, she came upon one spot in the floor. It was only a hole worn down through floor after floor, from top to bottom, by the drip of the rains from the broken roof: it looked like the disease of the desolate place and she shuddered.

Here they must pass the night, with the wind roaring awfully through the echoing emptiness, and every now and then the hail clashing against what glass remained in the windows. They found one room with the window well boarded up, for until lately some care had been taken of the place to keep it from the weather. There Robert left his companions, who presently heard the sounds of tearing and breaking below, necessity justifying him in the appropriation of some of the wood-work for their own behoof. He tore a panel or two from the walls, and returning with them, lighted a fire on the empty hearth, where, from the look of the stone and mortar, certainly never fire had blazed before. The wood was dry as a bone, and burnt up gloriously.

Then first Robert bethought himself that they had nothing to eat. He himself was full of merriment, and cared nothing about eating; for had he not Miss St. John and Ericson there? but for them something must be provided. He took his lantern and went back though the storm. The hail had ceased, but the wind blew tremendously. The coach stood upon the bridge like a stranded vessel, its two lamps holding doubtful battle with the wind, now flaring out triumphantly, now almost yielding up the ghost. Inside, the guard was snoring in defiance of the pother o'er his head.

" Hector! Hector!" cried Robert.

" Ay, ay," answered Hector. "It's no time to wauken yet."

"Hae ye nae basket, Hector, wi' something to eat in 't—naething gaein' to Rothieden 'at a a body micht say *by yer leave* till?"

"Ow! it's you, is 't?" returned Hector, rousing himself. " Na. Deil ane. An' gin I had, I daurna gie ye 't."

" I wad mak free to steal 't, though, an' tak my chance," said Robert. " But ye say ye hae nane?"

"Nane, I tell ye. Ye winna hunger afore the mornin', man."

" I'll stan' hunger as weel 's you ony day, Hector. It's no for mysel'. There's Miss St. John."

" Hoots!" said Hector, peevishly, for he wanted to go to sleep again, "gang and mak luve till her. Nae lass 'll think o' meat as lang 's ye do that. That 'll haud her ohn hungert."

The words were like blasphemy in Robert's ear. He make love to Miss St. John! He turned from the coach-door in disgust. But

there was no place he knew of where anything could be had, and he must return empty-
handed.

The light of the fire shone through a little
hole in the boards that closed the window. His
lamp had gone out, but, guided by that, he
found the road again, and felt his way up the
stairs. When he entered the room he saw Miss
St. John sitting on the floor, for there was nowhere else to sit, with the guard's coat under
her. She had taken off her bonnet. Her back
leaned against the side of the chimney, and her
eyes were bent thoughtfully on the ground. In
their shine Robert read instinctively that Ericson had said something that had set her thinking. He lay on the floor at some distance, leaning on his elbow, and his eye had the flash in
it that indicates one who has just ceased speaking. They had not found his absence awkward
at least.

"I hae been efter something to eat," said
Robert ; "but I canna fa' in wi' onything. We
maun jist tell stories or sing sangs, as fowk do
in buiks, or else Miss St. John 'ill think lang."

They did sing songs, and they did tell stories.
I will not trouble my reader with more than the
sketch of one which Robert told—the story
of the old house wherein they sat—a house
without a history, save the story of its no history. It had been built for the jointure-house

of a young countess, whose husband was an old
man. A lover to whom she had turned a deaf
ear had left the country, begging ere he went
her acceptance of a lovely Italian grayhound.
She was weak enough to receive the animal.
Her husband died the same year, and before the
end of it the dog went mad, and bit her. According to the awful custom of the time they
smothered her between two feather-beds, just
as the house of Bogbonnie was ready to receive
her furniture, and become her future dwelling.
No one had ever occupied it.

If Miss St. John listened to story and song
without as much show of feeling as Mysie Lindsay would have manifested, it was not that she
entered into them less deeply. It was that she
was more, not felt less.

Listening at her window once with Robert,
Eric Ericson had heard Mary St. John play:
this was their first meeting. Full as his mind
was of Mysie, he could not fail to feel the charm
of a noble, stately womanhood that could give
support, instead of rousing sympathy for helplessness. There was in the dignified simplicity
of Mary St. John that which made every good
man remember his mother; and a good man
will think this grand praise, though a fast girl
will take it for a doubtful compliment.

Seeing her begin to look weary, the young
men spread a couch for her as best they could,

made up the fire, and telling her they would be
in the hall below, retired, kindled another fire,
and sat down to wait for the morning. They
held a long talk. At length Robert fell asleep
on the floor.

Ericson rose. One of his fits ot impatient
doubt was upon him. In the dying embers of
the fire he strode up and down the waste hall,
with the storm raving around it. He was destined to an early death; he would leave no one
of his kin to mourn for him; the girl whose fair
face had possessed his imagination, would not
give one sigh to his memory, wandering on
through the regions of fancy all the same; and
the death-struggle over, he might awake in a
godless void, where, having no creative power
in himself, he must be tossed about, a conscious
yet helpless atom, to eternity. It was not anni-
hilation he feared, although he did shrink from
the thought of unconsciousness; it was life without law that he dreaded, existence without the
bonds of a holy necessity, thought without faith,
being without God.

For all her fatigue Miss St. John could not
sleep. The house quivered in the wind which
howled more and more madly through its long
passages and empty rooms; and she thought
she heard cries in the midst of the howling. In
vain she reasoned with herself: she could not
rest. She rose and opened the door of her room,

with a vague notion of being nearer to the
young men.

It opened upon the narrow gallery, already
mentioned as leading from one side of the first
floor to the other at mid-height along the end
of the hall. The fire below shone into this
gallery, for it was divided from the hall only by
a screen of crossing bars of wood, like unglazed
window-frames, possibly intended to hold glass.
Of the relation of the passage to the hall Mary
St. John knew nothing, till, approaching the
light, she found herself looking down into the
red dusk below. She stood rivetted; for in the
centre of the hall, with his hands clasped over
his head like the solitary arch of a ruined Gothic
aisle, stood Ericson.

His agony had grown within him—the agony
of the silence that brooded immovable throughout the infinite, whose sea would ripple to no
breath of the feeble tempest of his prayers.   At
length it broke from him in low but sharp sounds
of words.

"O God," he said, "if thou art, why dost thou
not speak? If I am thy handiwork—dost thou
forget that which thou hast made?"

He paused, motionless, then cried again:

"There can be no God, or he would hear."

"God has heard *me*!" said a full-toned voice
of feminine tenderness somewhere in the air.
Looking up, Eriscon saw the dim form of Mary

St. John half way up the side of the lofty hall.
The same moment she vanished—trembling at
the sound of her own voice.

Thus to Ericson as to Robert had she appeared
as an angel.

And was she less of a divine messenger because she had a human body, whose path lay
not through the air? The storm of misery
folded its wings in Eric's bosom, and, at the
sound of her voice, there was a great calm.
Nor if we inquire into the matter shall we find
that such an effect indicated anything derogatory
to the depth of his feelings or the strength of
his judgment. It is not through the judgment
that a troubled heart can be set at rest. It
needs a revelation, a vision; a something for the
higher nature that breeds and infolds the intellect, to recognize as of its own, and lay hold
of by faithful hope. And what fitter messenger
of such hope than the harmonious presence of
a woman, whose form itself tells of highest law,
and concord, and uplifting obedience; such a
one whose beauty walks the upper air of noble
loveliness; whose voice, even in speech, is one
of the "sphere-born harmonious sisters"? The
very presence of such a being gives Unbelief the
lie, deep as the throat of her lying. Harmony,
which is beauty and law, works necessary faith
in the region capable of truth. It needs the intervention of no reasoning. It is beheld. This

visible Peace, with that voice of woman's truth,
said, " God has heard *me !*"   What better testimony could an angel have brought him ?   Or
why should an angel's testimony weigh more
than such a woman's ?   The mere understanding of a man like Ericson would only have demanded of an angel proof that he was an angel,
proof that angels knew better than he did in
the matter in question, proof that they were
not easy-going creatures that took for granted
the rumours of heaven.   The best that a miracle
can do is to give hope; of the objects of faith it
can give no proof; one spiritual testimony is worth
a thousand of them.   For to gain the sole proof
of which these truths admit, a man must grow
into harmony with them.   If there are no such
things he cannot become conscious of a harmony
that has no existence; he cannot thus deceive
himself; if there are, they must yet remain
doubtful until the harmony between them and
his own willing nature is established.   The perception of this harmony is their only and incommunicable proof.   For this process time is
needful; and therefore we are saved by hope.
Hence it is no wonder that before another half-
hour was over, Ericson was asleep by Robert's
side.

They were aroused in the cold gray light of
the morning by the blast of Hector's horn.   Miss
St. John was ready in a moment.   The coach

was waiting for them at the end of the grassy
road that led from the house.   Hector put them
all inside.   Before they reached Rothieden the
events of the night began to wear the doubtful
aspect of a dream.   No allusion was made to
what had occurred while Robert slept ; but all
the journey Ericson felt towards Miss St. John
as Wordsworth felt towards the leech-gatherer,
who, he says, was

> like a man from some far region sent,
> To give me human strength, by apt admonishment.

And Robert saw a certain light in her eyes which
reminded him of how she looked when, having
repented of her momentary hardness towards
him, she was ministering to his wounded head.

CHAPTER XVII.

HOME AGAIN.

WHEN Robert opened the door of his grand-mother's parlour, he found the old lady seated at breakfast. She rose, pushed back her chair, and met him in the middle of the room; put her old arms round him, offered her smooth white cheek to him, and wept. Robert wondered that she did not look older; for the time he had been away seemed an age, although in truth only eight months.

"Hoo are ye, laddie?" she said. "I'm richt glaid, for I hae been thinkin' lang to see ye. Sit ye doon."

Betty rushed in, drying her hands on her apron. She had not heard him enter.

"Eh losh!" she cried, and put her wet apron to her eyes. "Sic a man as ye 're grown, Ro-bert! A puir body like me maunna be speykin' to ye noo."

"There's nae odds in me, Betty," returned Robert.

" 'Deed but there is. Ye 're sax feet an' a hairy ower, I s' warran'."

" I said there was nae odds i' me, Betty," persisted Robert, laughing.

" I kenna what may be in ye," retorted Betty; " but there's an unco' odds upo' ye."

" Haud yer tongue, Betty," said her mistress. " Ye oucht to ken better nor stan' jawin' wi' young men. Fess mair o' the creamy cakes."

" Maybe Robert wad like a drappy o' parritch."

" Onything, Betty," said Robert. " I'm at deith's door wi' hunger."

" Rin, Betty, for the cakes. An' fess a loaf o' white breid; we canna bide for the parritch."

Robert fell to his breakfast, and while he ate —somewhat ravenously—he told his grandmother the adventures of the night, and introduced the question whether he might not ask Ericson to stay a few days with him.

" Ony frien' o' yours, laddie," she replied, qualifying her words only with the addition— " gin he be a frien'.—Whaur is he noo?"

" He's up at Miss Naper's."

" Hoots! What for didna ye fess him in wi' ye?—Betty!"

" Na, na, grannie. The Napers are frien's o' his. We maunna interfere wi' them. I'll gang up mysel' ance I hae had my brakfast."

" Weel, weel, laddie. Eh! I'm blythe to see ye! Hae ye gotten ony prizes noo?"

" Ay have I. I'm sorry they 're nae baith o'
them the first. But I hae the first o' ane an' the
third o' the ither."

" I *am* pleased at that, Robert. Ye'll be a man
some day gin ye haud frae drink an' frae—frae
leein'."

" I never tellt a lee i' my life, grannie."

" Na. I dinna think 'at ever ye did.—An'
what's that crater Shargar aboot ?"

" Ow, jist gaein' to be a croon o' glory to ye,
grannie. He vroucht like a horse till Dr. Anderson took him by the han', an' sent him to the
schuil. An' he's gaein' to mak something o' 'im,
or a' be dune. He's a fine crater, Shargar."

" He tuik a munelicht flittin' frae here," rejoined the old lady, in a tone of offence. " He
micht hae said gude day to me, I think."

" Ye see he was feart at ye, grannie."

" Feart at *me*, laddie! Wha ever was feart at
me? I never feart onybody i' my life."

So little did the dear old lady know that she
was a terror to her neighbourhood !—simply because, being a law to herself, she would therefore be a law to other people,—a conclusion that
cannot be concluded.

Mrs. Falconer's courtesy did not fail. Her
grandson had ceased to be a child; her responsibility had in so far ceased; her conscience
was relieved at being rid of it; and the humanity of her great heart came out to greet the

youth. She received Ericson with perfect hospitality, made him at home as far as the stately respect she showed him would admit of his being so, and confirmed in him the impression of her which Robert had given him. They held many talks together; and such was the circumspection of Ericson that, not saying a word he did not believe, he so said what he did believe, or so avoided the points upon which they would have differed seriously, that although his theology was of course far from satisfying her, she yet affirmed her conviction that the root of the matter was in him. This distressed Ericson, however, for he feared he must have been deceitful, if not hypocritical.

It was with some grumbling that the Napiers, especially Miss Letty, parted with him to Mrs. Falconer. The hearts of all three had so taken to the youth, that he found himself more at home in that hostelry than anywhere else in the world. Miss Letty was the only one that spoke lightly of him—she even went so far as to make good-natured game of him sometimes—all because she loved him more than the others—more indeed than she cared to show, for fear of exposing " an old woman's ridiculous fancy," as she called her predilection.—" A lang-leggit, prood, landless laird," she would say, with a moist glimmer in her loving eyes, " wi' the maist ridiculous feet ye ever saw—hardly room for the five taes atween the twa! Losh!"

When Robert went forth into the streets, he was surprised to find how friendly every one was. Even old William MacGregor shook him kindly by the hand, inquired after his health, told him not to study too hard, informed him that he had a copy of a queer old book that he would like to see, &c., &c. Upon reflection Robert discovered the cause: though he had scarcely gained a bursary, he had gained prizes; and in a little place like Rothieden—long may there be such places!—everybody with any brains at all took a share in the distinction he had merited.

Ericson stayed only a few days. He went back to the twilight of the north, his fishy cousin, and his tutorship at Sir Olaf Petersen's. Robert accompanied him ten miles on his journey, and would have gone further, but that he was to play on his violin before Miss St. John the next day for the first time.

When he told his grandmother of the appointment he had made, she only remarked, in a tone of some satisfaction,

" Weel, she's a fine lass, Miss St. John; and gin ye tak to ane anither, ye canna do better."

But Robert's thoughts were so different from Mrs. Falconer's that he did not even suspect what she meant. He no more dreamed of marrying Miss St John than of marrying his forbidden grandmother. Yet she was no less at this period the ruling influence of his life ; and if it had not been for the benediction of her presence and power, this part of his history too would have been torn by inward troubles. It is not good that a man should batter day and night at the gate of heaven. Sometimes he can do nothing else, and then nothing else is worth doing; but the very noise of the siege will sometimes drown the still small voice that calls from the open postern. There is a door wide to the jewelled wall not far from any one of us, even when he least can find it.

Robert, however, notwithstanding the pedestal upon which Miss St. John stood in his worshipping regard, began to be aware that his feeling towards her was losing something of its placid flow, and I doubt whether Miss St. John did not now and then see that in his face which made her tremble a little, and doubt whether she stood on safe ground with a youth just waking into manhood—tremble a little, not for herself, but for him. Her fear would have found itself more than justified, if she had surprised him kissing her glove, and then replacing it where he had found it, with the air of one consciously guilty of presumption.

Possibly also Miss St. John may have had to confess to herself that had she not had her history already, and been ten years his senior, she

might have found no little attraction in the noble
bearing and handsome face of young Falconer.
The rest of his features had now grown into
complete harmony of relation with his whilom
premature and therefore portentous nose; his
eyes glowed and gleamed with humanity,
and his whole countenance bore self-evident
witness of being a true face and no mask, a revelation of his individul being, and not a mere
inheritance from a fine breed of fathers and mothers. As it was, she could admire and love
him without danger of falling in love with him;
but not without fear lest he should not assume
the correlative position. She saw no way of
prevention, however, without running a risk of
worse. She shrunk altogether from *putting on*
anything; she abhorred tact, and pretence was
impracticable with Mary St. John. She resolved
that if she saw any definite ground for uneasiness she would return to England, and leave
any impression she might have made to wear
out in her absence and silence. Things did not
seem to render this necessary yet.

Meantime the violin of the dead shoemaker
blended its wails with the rich harmonies of
Mary St. John's piano, and the soul of Robert
went forth upon the level of the sound and hovered about the beauty of his friend. Oftener
than she approved was she drawn by Robert's
eagerness into these *consorts.*

But the heart of the king is in the hands of the Lord.

While Robert thus once more for a season stood behind the cherub with the flaming sword, Ericson was teaching two stiff-necked youths in a dreary house in the midst of one of the moors of Caithness. One day he had a slight attack of blood-spitting, and welcomed it as a sign from what heaven there might be beyond the grave.

He had not received the consolation of Miss St. John without, although unconsciously, leaving something in her mind in return. No human being has ever been allowed to occupy the position of a pure benefactor. The receiver has his turn, and becomes the giver. From her talk with Ericson, and even more from the influence of his sad holy doubt, a fresh touch of the actinism of the solar truth fell upon the living seed in her heart, and her life burst forth afresh, began to bud in new questions that needed answers, and new prayers that sought them.

But she never dreamed that Robert was capable of sympathy with such thoughts and feelings : he was but a boy. Nor in power of dealing with truth was he at all on the same level with her, for however poor he might have considered her theories, she had led a life hitherto, had passed through sorrow without bitterness,

had done her duty without pride, had hoped
without conceit of favour, had, as she believed,
heard the voice of God saying, "This is the
way." Hence she was not afraid when the mists
of prejudice began to rise from around her path,
and reveal a country very different from what
she had fancied it. She was soon able to perceive
that it was far more lovely and full of righteousness and peace than she had supposed. But
this anticipates; only I shall have less occasion
to speak of Miss St. John by the time she has
come into this purer air of the uphill road.

Robert was happier than he ever could have
expected to be in his grandmother's house.
She treated him like an honoured guest, let him
do as he would, and go where he pleased.
Betty kept the gable room in the best of order
for him, and, pattern of housemaids, dusted his
table without disturbing his papers. For he
began to have papers; nor were they occupied
only with the mathematics to which he was
now giving his chief attention, preparing, with
the occasional help of Mr. Innes, for his second
session.

He had fits of wandering, though; visited
all the old places; spent a week or two more
than once at Bodyfauld; rode Mr. Lammie's
half-broke filly; revelled in the glories of the
summer once more; went out to tea occasionally, or supped with the schoolmaster; and, ex-

cept going to church on Sunday, which was a weariness to every inch of flesh upon his bones, enjoyed everything.

CHAPTER XVIII.

A GRAVE OPENED.

ONE thing that troubled Robert on this his first return home, was the discovery that the surroundings of his childhood had deserted him. There they were, as of yore, but they seemed to have nothing to say to him—no remembrance of him. It was not that everything looked small and narrow; it was not that the streets he saw from his new quarters, the gable-room, were awfully still after the roar of Aberdeen, and a passing cart seemed to shudder at the loneliness of the noise itself made; it was that everything seemed to be conscious only of the past and care nothing for him now. The very chairs with their inlaid backs had an embalmed look, and stood as in a dream. He could pass even the walled-up door without emotion, for all the feeling that had been gathered about the knob that admitted him to Mary St. John, had transferred itself to the brass bell-pull at her street-door.

But one day, after standing for a while at the window, looking down on the street where he had first seen the beloved form of Ericson, a certain old mood began to revive in him. He had been working at quadratic equations all the morning; he had been foiled in the attempt to find the true algebraic statement of a very tough question involving various ratios; and, vexed with himself, he had risen to look out, as the only available *zeitvertreib*. It was one of those rainy days of spring which it needs a hopeful mood to distinguish from autumnal ones —dull, depressing, persistent: there might be sunshine in Mercury or Venus—but on the earth could be none, from his right hand round by India and America to his left; and certainly there was none between—a mood to which all sensitive people are liable who have not yet learned by faith in the everlasting to rule their own spirits. Naturally enough his thoughts turned to the place where he had suffered most—his old room in the garret. Hitherto he had shrunk from visiting it ; but now he turned away from the window, went up the steep stairs, with their one sharp corkscrew curve, pushed the door, which clung unwillingly to the floor, and entered. It was a nothing of a place—with a window that looked only to heaven. There was the empty bedstead against the wall, where he had so often kneeled, sending forth vain prayers to a deaf heaven! Had they indeed been vain prayers, and to a deaf heaven? or had they been prayers which a hearing God must answer not according to the haste of the praying child, but according to the calm course of his own infinite law of love?

Here, somehow or other, the things about him did not seem so much absorbed in the past, notwithstanding those untroubled rows of papers bundled in red tape. True, they looked almost awful in their lack of interest and their non-humanity, for there is scarcely anything that absolutely loses interest save the records of money; but his mother's workbox lay behind them. And, strange to say, the side of that bed drew him to kneel down: he did not yet believe that prayer was in vain. If God had not answered him before, that gave no certainty that he would not answer him now. It was, he found, still as rational as it had ever been to hope that God would answer the man that cried to him. This came, I think, from the fact that God had been answering him all the time, although he had not recognized his gifts as answers. Had he not given him Erio-son, his intercourse with whom and his familiarity with whose doubts had done anything but quench his thirst after the higher life? For Ericson's, like his own, were true and good and reverent doubts, not merely consistent with but in a great measure springing from devoutness and aspiration. Surely such doubts are far more precious in the sight of God than many beliefs?

He kneeled and sent forth one cry after the Father, arose, and turned towards the shelves, removed some of the bundles of letters, and drew out his mother's little box.

There lay the miniature, still and open-eyed as he had left it. There too lay the bit of paper, brown and dry, with the hymn and the few words of sorrow written thereon. He looked at the portrait, but did not open the folded paper. Then first he thought whether there might not be something more in the box: what he had taken for the bottom seemed to be a tray. He lifted it by two little ears of ribbon, and there, underneath, lay a letter addressed to his father, in the same old-fashioned handwriting as the hymn. It was sealed with brown wax, full of spangles, impressed with a bush of something—he could not tell whether rushes or reeds or flags. Of course he dared not open it. His holy mother's words to his erring father must be sacred even from the eyes of their son. But what other or fitter messenger than himself could bear it to its destination? It was for this that he had been guided to it.

For years he had regarded the finding of his father as the first duty of his manhood : it was as if his mother had now given her sanction to the quest, with this letter to carry to the husband who, however he might have erred, was yet dear to her. He replaced it in the box, but the box no more on the forsaken shelf with its dreary barricade of soulless records. He carried it with him, and laid it in the bottom of his box, which henceforth he kept carefully locked: there lay as it were the pledge of his father's salvation, and his mother's redemption from an eternal grief.

He turned to his equation: it had cleared itself up; he worked it out in five minutes. Betty came to tell him that the dinner was ready, and he went down, peaceful and hopeful, to his grandmother.

While at home he never worked in the evenings: it was bad enough to have to do so at college. Hence nature had a chance with him again. Blessings on the wintry blasts that broke into the first youth of Summer! They made him feel what summer was! Blessings on the cheerless days of rain, and even of sleet and hail, that would shove the reluctant year back into January. The fair face of Spring, with her tears dropping upon her quenchless smiles, peeped in suppressed triumph from behind the growing corn and the budding sallows on the river-bank. Nay, even when the snow came once more in defiance of calendars, it was but a back-ground from which the near genesis should " stick fiery off."

In general he had a lonely walk after his lesson with Miss St. John was over: there was no one at Rothieden to whom his heart and intellect both were sufficiently drawn to make a close friendship possible. He had companions, however: Ericson had left his papers with him. The influence of these led him into yet closer sympathy with Nature and all her moods; a sympathy which, even in the stony heart of London, he not only did not lose but never ceased to feel. Even there a breath of wind would not only breathe upon him, it would breathe into him; and a sunset seen from the Strand was lovely as if it had hung over rainbow seas. On his way home he would often go into one of the shops where the neighbours congregated in the evenings, and hold a little talk; and although, with Miss St. John filling his heart, his friend's poems his imagination, and geometry and algebra his intellect, great was the contrast between his own inner mood and the words by which he kept up human relations with his townsfolk, yet in after years he counted it one of the greatest blessings of a lowly birth and education that he knew hearts and feelings which to understand one must have been young amongst them. He would not have had a chance of knowing such as these if he had been the son of Dr. Anderson and born in Aberdeen.

CHAPTER XIX.

ROBERT MEDIATES.

ONE lovely evening in the first of the summer Miss St. John had dismissed him earlier than usual, and he had wandered out for a walk. After a round of a couple of miles, he returned by a fir-wood, through which went a pathway. He had heard Mary St. John say that she was going to see the wife of a labourer who lived at the end of this path. In the heart of the trees it was growing very dusky; but when he came to a spot where they stood away from each other a little space, and the blue sky looked in from above with one cloud floating in it from which the rose of the sunset was fading, he seated himself on a little mound of moss that had gathered over an ancient stump by the footpath, and drew out his friend's papers. Absorbed in his reading, he was not aware of an approach till the rustle of silk startled him. He lifted up his eyes, and saw Miss St. John a few yards from him on the pathway. He rose.

"It's almost too dark to read now, isn't it, Robert?" she said.

"Ah!" said Robert, "I know this writing so well that I could read it by moonlight. I wish I might read some of it to you. You *would* like it."

"May I ask whose it is, then? Poetry, too!"

"It's Mr. Ericson's. But I'm feared he wouldna like me to read it to anybody but myself. And yet——"

"I don't think he would mind me," returned Miss St. John. "I do know him a little. It is not as if I were *quite* a stranger, you know. Did he tell you not?"

"No. But then he never thought of such a thing. I don't know if it's fair, for they are carelessly written, and there are words and lines here and there that I am sure he would alter if he cared for them ae hair."

"Then if he doesn't care for them, he won't mind my hearing them. There!" she said, seating herself on the stump. "You sit down on the grass and read me—one at least."

"You'll remember they were never intended to be read?" urged Robert, not knowing what he was doing, and so fulfilling his destiny.

"I will be as jealous of his honour as ever you can wish," answered Miss St. John gaily.

Robert laid himself on the grass at her feet, and read:—

VOL. II.

Q

MY TWO GENIUSES.

One is a slow and melancholy maid :
I know not if she cometh from the skies,
Or from the sleepy gulfs, but she will rise
Often before me in the twilight shade
Holding a bunch of poppies, and a blade
Of springing wheat : prostrate my body lies
Before her on the turf, the while she ties
A fillet of the weed about my head ;
And in the gaps of sleep I seem to hear
A gentle rustle like the stir of corn,
And words like odours thronging to my ear :
" Lie still, beloved, still until the morn ;
Lie still with me upon this rolling sphere,
Still till the judgment—thou art faint and worn."

The other meets me in the public throng :
Her hair streams backward from her loose attire ;
She hath a trumpet and an eye of fire ;
She points me downward steadily and long—
" There is thy grave—arise, my son, be strong !
Hands are upon thy crown ; awake, aspire
To immortality ; heed not the lyre
Of the enchantress, nor her poppy-song ;
But in the stillness of the summer calm,
Tremble for what is godlike in thy being.
Listen awhile, and thou shalt hear the psalm
Of victory sung by creatures past thy seeing ;
And from far battle-fields there comes the neighing
Of dreadful onset, though the air is balm."

Maid with the poppies, must I let thee go?
Alas ! I may not ; thou art likewise dear ;
I am but human, and thou hast a tear,
When she hath nought but splendour, and the glow

Of a wild energy that mocks the flow
Of the poor sympathies which keep us here.
Lay past thy poppies, and come twice as near,
And I will teach thee, and thou too shalt grow ;
And thou shalt walk with me in open day
Through the rough thoroughfares with quiet grace ;
And the wild-visaged maid shall lead the way,
Timing her footsteps to a gentler pace,
As her great orbs turn ever on thy face,
Drinking in draughts of loving help alway.

Miss St. John did not speak.

"War ye able to follow him?" asked Robert.

"Quite, I assure you," she answered, with a tremulousness in her voice which delighted Robert as evidence of his friend's success.

"But they're nae a' so easy to follow, I can tell ye, mem. Just hearken to this," he said, with some excitement.

When the storm was proudest,
And the wind was loudest,
I heard the hollow caverns drinking down below ;
When the stars were bright,
And the ground was white,
I heard the grasses springing underneath the snow.

Many voices spake—
The river to the lake,
The iron-ribbed sky was talking to the sea ;
And every starry spark
Made music with the dark,
And said how bright and beautiful everything must be.

Q 2

"That line, mem," remarked Robert, "'s only jist scrattit in, as gin he had no intention o' leavin' 't, an' only set it there to keep room for anither. But we'll jist gang on wi' the lave o' 't. I ouchtna to hae interruppit it.

When the sun was setting,
All the clouds were getting
Beautiful and silvery in the rising moon;
Beneath the leafless trees
Wrangling in the breeze,
I could hardly see them for the leaves of June.

When the day had ended,
And the night descended,
I heard the sound of streams that I heard not through the day,
And every peak afar,
Was ready for a star,
And they climbed and rolled around until the morning gray.

Then slumber soft and holy
Came down upon me slowly;
And I went I know not whither, and I lived I know not how;
My glory had been banished,
For when I woke it vanished,
But I waited on its coming, and I am waiting now.

"*There!*" said Robert, ending, "can ye mak onything o' that, Miss St. John?"

"I don't say I can in words," she answered; "but I think I could put it all into music."

"But surely ye maun hae some notion o' what it's aboot afore you can do that."

"Yes; but I have some notion of what it's about, I think. Just lend it to me; and by the time we have our next lesson, you will see whether I'm not able to show you I understand it. I shall take good care of it," she added, with a smile, seeing Robert's reluctance to part with it. "It doesn't matter my having it, you know, now that you've read it to me. I want to make you do it justice.—But it's quite time I were going home. Besides, I really don't think you can see to read any more."

"Weel, it's better no to try, though I hae them maistly upo' my tongue: I might blunder, and that wad blaud them.—Will you let me go home with you?" he added, in pure tremulous English.

"Certainly, if you like," she answered; and they walked towards the town.

Robert opened the fountain of his love for Ericson, and let it gush like a river from a hillside. He talked on and on about him, with admiration, gratitude, devotion. And Miss St. John was glad of the veil of the twilight over her face as she listened, for the boy's enthusiasm trembled through her as the wind through an Æolian harp. Poor Robert! He did not know, I say, what he was doing, and so was fulfilling his sacred destiny.

"Bring your manuscripts when you come next," she said, as they walked along—gently adding,

" I admire your friend's verses very much, and should like to hear more of them."

" I'll be sure an' do that," answered Robert, in delight that he had found one to sympathize with him in his worship of Ericson, and that one his other idol.

When they reached the town, Miss St. John, calling to mind its natural propensity to gossip, especially on the evening of a market-day, when the shopkeepers, their labours over, would be standing in a speculative mood at their doors, surrounded by groups of friends and neighbours, felt shy of showing herself on the square with Robert, and proposed that they should part, giving as a by-the-by reason that she had a little shopping to do as she went home. Too simple to suspect the real reason, but with a heart that delighted in obedience, Robert bade her good night at once, and took another way.

As he passed the door of Merson the haberdasher's shop, there stood William MacGregor, the weaver, looking at nothing and doing nothing. We have seen something of him before: he was a remarkable compound of good nature and bad temper. People were generally afraid of him, because he had a biting satire at his command, amounting even to wit, which found vent in verse—not altogether despicable even from a literary point of view. The only person he, on his part, was afraid of, was his own wife; for upon her, from lack of apprehension, his keenest irony fell, as he said, like water on a duck's back, and in respect of her he had, therefore, no weapon of offence to strike terror withal. Her dulness was her defence. He liked Robert. When he saw him, he wakened up, laid hold of him by the button, and drew him in.

"Come in, lad," he said, "an' tak a pinch. I'm waitin' for Merson." As he spoke he took from his pocket his *mull*, made of the end of a ram's horn, and presented it to Robert, who accepted the pledge of friendship. While he was partaking, MacGregor drew himself with some effort upon the counter, saying in a half-comical, half-admonitory tone,

"Weel, and hoo's the mathematics, Robert?"

"Thrivin'," answered Robert, falling into his humour.

"Weel, that's verra weel. Duv ye min', Robert, hoo, whan ye was aboot the age o' aucht year aul', ye cam' to me ance at my shop aboot something yer gran'mither, honest woman, wantit, an' I, by way o' takin' my fun o' ye, said to ye, 'Robert, ye hae grown desperate; ye're a man clean; ye hae gotten the breeks on.' An' says ye, 'Ay, Mr. MacGregor, I want naething noo but a watch an' a wife?'"

"I doobt I've forgotten a' aboot it, Mr. Mac-
Gregor," answered Robert. "But I've made
some progress, accordin' to your story, for Dr.
Anderson, afore I cam hame, gae me a watch.
An' a fine crater it is, for it aye does its best,
an' sae I excuse its shortcomin's."

"There's just ae thing, an' nae anither," returned the manufacturer, "that I can*not* excuse
in a watch. Gin a watch gangs ower fest, ye
fin' 't oot. Gin she gangs ower slow, ye fin' 't
oot, an' ye can aye calculate upo' 't correck
eneuch for maitters sublunairy, as Mr. Maccleary
says. An' gin a watch stops a'thegither, ye
ken it's failin', an' ye ken whaur it sticks, an' a'
'at ye say 's 'Tut, tut, de'il hae 't for a watch!'
But there's ae thing that God nor man canna
bide in a watch, an' that's whan it stan's still
for a bittock, an' syne gangs on again. Ay,
ay! tic, tic, tic! wi' a fair face and a leein' hert.
It wad gar ye believe it was a' richt, and time
for anither tum'ler, whan it's twal o'clock, an'
the kirkyaird fowk thinkin' aboot risin'. Fegs,
I had a watch o' my father's, an' I regairdit it
wi' a reverence mair like a human bein': the
second time it played me that pliskie, I dang
oot its guts upo' the loupin'-on-stane at the
door o' the chop. But lat the watch sit: whaur's
the wife? Ye canna be a man yet wantin' the
wife—by yer ain statement."

"The watch cam unsoucht, Mr. MacGregor,

an' I'm thinkin' sae maun the wife," answered Robert, laughing.

" Preserve me for ane frae a wife that comes unsoucht," returned the weaver. " But, my lad, there may be some wives that winna come whan they *are* soucht. Preserve me frae them too!—Noo, maybe ye dinna ken what I mean— *but tak ye tent what ye're aboot.* Dinna ye think 'at ilka bonnie lass 'at may like to haud a wark wi' ye 's jist ready to mairry ye aff han' whan ye say, ' Noo, my dawtie.'—An' ae word mair, Robert: Young men, especially braw lads like yersel', 's unco ready to fa' in love wi' women fit to be their mithers. An' sae ye see——"

He was interrupted by the entrance of a girl. She had a shawl over her head, notwithstanding it was summer weather, and crept in hesitatingly, as if she were not quite at one with herself as to her coming purchase. Approaching a boy behind the counter on the opposite side of the shop, she asked for something, and he proceeded to serve her. Robert could not help thinking, from the one glimpse of her face he had got through the dusk, that he had seen her before. Suddenly the vision of an earthen floor with a pool of brown sunlight upon it, bare feet, brown hair, and soft eyes, mingled with a musk odour wafted from Arabian fairyland, rose before him : it was Jessie Hewson.

" I ken that lassie," he said, and moved to

get down from the counter on which he too had seated himself.

"Na, na," whispered the manufacturer, laying, like the Ancient Mariner, a brown skinny hand of restraint upon Robert's arm—" na, na, never heed her. Ye maunna speyk to ilka lass 'at ye ken.—Poor thing! she's been doin' something wrang, to gang slinkin' aboot i' the gloamin' like a baukie (*bat*), wi' her plaid ower her heid. Dinna fash wi' her."

" Nonsense !" returned Robert, with indignation. " What for shouldna I speik till her ? She's a decent lassie—a dochter o' James Hewson, the cottar at Bodyfauld. I ken her fine."

He said this in a whisper ; but the girl seemed to hear it, for she left the shop with a perturbation which the dimness of the late twilight could not conceal. Robert hesitated no longer, but followed her, heedless of the louder expostulations of MacGregor. She was speeding away down the street, but he took longer strides than she, and was almost up with her, when she drew her shawl closer about her head, and increased her pace.

" Jessie !" said Robert, in a tone of expostulation. But she made no answer. Her head sunk lower on her bosom, and she hurried yet faster. He gave a long stride or two and laid his hand on her shoulder. She stood still, trembling.

" Jessie, dinna ye ken me—Robert Faukner ? Dinna be feart at me. What's the maitter wi' ye, 'at ye winna speik till a body ? Hoo's a' the fowk at hame ?"

She burst out crying, cast one look into Robert's face, and fled. What a change was in that face ! The peach-colour was gone from her cheek ; it was pale and thin. Her eyes were hollow, with dark shadows under them, the shadows of a sad sunset. A foreboding of the truth arose in his heart, and the tears rushed up into his eyes. The next moment the eidolon of Mary St. John, moving gracious and strong, clothed in worship and the dignity which is its own defence, appeared beside that of Jessie Hewson, her bowed head shaken with sobs, and her weak limbs urged to ungraceful flight. As if walking in the vision of an eternal truth, he went straight to Captain Forsyth's door.

" I want to speak to Miss St. John, Isie," said Robert.

" She'll be doon in a minit."

" But isna yer mistress i' the drawin'-room ? —I dinna want to see her."

" Ow, weel," said the girl, who was almost fresh from the country, " jist rin up the stair, an' chap at the door o' her room."

With the simplicity of a child, for what a girl told him to do must be right, Robert sped up the stair, his heart going like a fire-engine. He had never approached Mary's room from this side, but instinct or something else led him straight to her door. He knocked.

"Come in," she said, never doubting it was the maid, and Robert entered.

She was brushing her hair by the light of a chamber candle. Robert was seized with awe, and his limbs trembled. He could have kneeled before her—not to beg forgiveness, he did not think of that—but to worship, as a man may worship a woman. It is only a strong, pure heart like Robert's that ever can feel all the inroad of the divine mystery of womanhood. But he did not kneel. He had a duty to perform. A flush rose in Miss St. John's face, and sank away, leaving it pale. It was not that she thought once of her own condition, with her hair loose on her shoulders, but, able only to .conjecture what had brought him thither, she could not but regard Robert's presence with dismay. She stood with her ivory brush in her right hand uplifted, and a great handful of hair in her left. She was soon relieved, however, although, what with his contemplated intercession, the dim vision of Mary's lovely face between the masses of her hair, and the lavender odour that filled the room—perhaps also a faint suspicion of impropriety sufficient to give force to the rest—Robert was thrown back into the abyss of his mother-tongue, and out of this abyss talked like a Behemoth.

"Robert!" said Mary, in a tone which, had he not been so eager after his end, he might have interpreted as one of displeasure.

"Ye maun hearken till me, mem.—Whan I was oot at Bodyfauld," he began methodically, and Mary, bewildered, gave one hasty brush to her handful of hair and again stood still: she could imagine no connection between this meeting and their late parting— "Whan I was oot at Bodyfauld ae simmer, I grew acquant wi' a bonnie lassie there, the dochter o' Jeames Hewson, an honest cottar, wi' Shakspeare an' the Arabian Nichts upo' a skelf i' the hoose wi' 'im. 1 gaed in ae day whan I wasna weel; an' she jist ministert to me, as nane ever did but yersel', mem. An' she was that kin' an' mither-like to the wee bit greitin' bairnie 'at she had to tak care o' 'cause her mither was oot wi' the lave shearin'! Her face was jist like a simmer day, an' weel I likit the luik o' the lassie!—I met her again the nicht. Ye never saw sic a change. A white face, an' nothing but greitin' to come oot o' her. She ran frae me as gin I had been the de'il himsel'. An' the thocht o' you, sae bonnie an' straucht an' gran' cam ower me."

Yielding to a masterful impulse, Robert did kneel now. As if sinner, and not mediator, he pressed the hem of her garment to his lips.

" Dinna be angry at me, Miss St. John," he pleaded, " but be mercifu' to the lassie. Wha's to help her that can no more luik a man i' the face, but the clear-e'ed lass that wad luik the sun himsel' oot o' the lift gin he daured to say a word against her. It's ae woman that can uphaud anither. Ye ken what I mean, an' I needna say mair."

He rose and turned to leave the room.

Bewildered and doubtful, Miss St. John did not know what to answer, but felt that she must make some reply.

" You haven't told me where to find the girl, or what you want me to do with her."

" I'll fin' oot whaur she bides," he said, moving again towards the door.

" But what am I to do with her, Robert ?"

" That's your pairt. Ye maun fin' oot what to do wi' her. I canna tell ye that. But gin I was you, I wad gie her a kiss to begin wi'. She's nane o' yer brazen-faced hizzies, yon. A kiss wad be the savin' o' her."

" But you may be—But I have nothing to go upon. She would resent my interference."

" She's past resentin' onything. She was gaein' aboot the toon like ane o' the deid 'at hae naething to say to onybody, an' naebody onything to say to them. Gin she gangs on like that she'll no be alive lang."

That night Jessie Hewson disappeared. A mile or two up the river under a high bank, from which the main current had receded, lay an awful, swampy place—full of reeds, except in the middle where was one round space full of dark water and mud. Near this Jessie Hewson was seen about an hour after Robert had thus pled for her with his angel.

The event made a deep impression upon Robert. The last time that he saw them, James and his wife were as cheerful as usual, and gave him a hearty welcome. Jessie was in service, and doing well, they said. The next time he opened the door of the cottage it was like the entrance to a haunted tomb. Not a smile was in the place. James's cheeriness was all gone. He was sitting at the table with his head leaning on his hand. His bible was open before him, but he was not reading a word. His wife was moving lislessly about. They looked just as Jessie had looked that night—as if they had died long ago, but somehow or other could not get into their graves and be at rest. The child Jessie had nursed with such care was toddling about, looking rueful with loss. George had gone to America, and the whole of that family's joy had vanished from the earth.

The subject was not resumed between Miss St. John and Robert. The next time he saw her, he knew by her pale troubled face that she had heard the report that filled the town ; and she knew by his silence that it had indeed reference to the same girl of whom he had spoken to her. The music would not go right that evening. Mary was *distraite*, and Robert was troubled. It was a week or two before there came a change. When the turn did come, over his being love rushed up like a spring-tide from the ocean of the Infinite.

He was accompanying her piano with his violin. He made blunders, and her playing was out of heart. They stopped as by consent, and a moment's silence followed. All at once she broke out with something Robert had never heard before. He soon found that it was a fantasy upon Ericson's poem. Ever through a troubled harmony ran a silver thread of melody from far away. It was the caverns drinking from the tempest overhead, the grasses growing under the snow, the stars making music with the dark, the streams filling the night with the sounds the day had quenched, the whispering call of the dreams left behind in " the fields of sleep,"—in a word, the central life pulsing in aeonian peace through the outer ephemeral storms. At length her voice took up the theme. The silvery thread became song, and through all the opposing, supporting harmonies she led it to the solution of a close in which the only sorrow was in the music itself, for its very life

is an "endless ending." She found Robert
kneeling by her side. As she turned from the
instrument his head drooped over her knee.
She laid her hand on his clustering curls, bethought herself, and left the room. Robert
wandered out as in a dream. At midnight he
found himself on a solitary hill-top, seated in
the heather, with a few tiny fir-trees about him,
and the sounds of a wind, ethereal as the stars
overhead, flowing through their branches: he
heard the sound of it, but it did not touch him.

Where was God?

In him and his question.

CHAPTER XX.

ERICSON LOSES TO WIN.

IF Mary St. John had been an ordinary woman, and if, notwithstanding, Robert had been in love with her, he would have done very little in preparation for the coming session. But although she now *possessed* him, although at times he only knew himself as loving her, there was such a mountain air of calm about her, such an outgoing divinity of peace, such a largely moulded harmony of being, that he could not love her otherwise than grandly. For her sake, weary with loving her, he would yet turn to his work, and, to be worthy of her, or rather, for he never dreamed of being worthy of her, to be worthy of leave to love her, would forget her enough to lay hold of some abstract truth of lines, angles, or symbols. A strange way of being in love, reader? You think so? I would there were more love like it: the world would be centuries nearer its redemption if a millionth part of the love in it were of the sort. All I insist, however, on my reader's believing is, that it showed, in a youth like Robert, not less but more love that he could go against love's sweetness for the sake of love's greatness. Literally, not figuratively, Robert would kiss the place where her foot had trod; but I know that once he rose from such a kiss "to trace the hyperbola by means of a string."

It had been arranged between Ericson and Robert, in Miss Napier's parlour, the old lady knitting beside, that Ericson should start, if possible, a week earlier than usual, and spend the difference with Robert at Rothieden. But then the old lady had opened her mouth and spoken. And I firmly believe, though little sign of tenderness passed between them, it was with an elder sister's feeling for Letty's admiration of the "lan'less laird," that she said as follows:—

"Dinna ye think, Mr. Ericson, it wad be but fair to come to us neist time? Mistress Faukner, honest lady, an' lang hae I kent her, 's no sae auld a frien' to you, Mr. Ericson, as oorsel's—nae offence to her, ye ken. A'body canna be frien's to a'body, ane as lang 's anither, ye ken."

"'Deed I maun alloo, Miss Naper," interposed Robert, "it's only fair. Ye see, Mr. Ericson, I cud see as muckle o' ye almost, the tae way as the tither. Miss Naper maks me welcome as weel's you."

"An' I *will* mak ye welcome, Robert, as lang's ye're a gude lad, as ye are, and gang na efter— nae ill gait.   But lat me hear o' yer doin' as sae mony young gentlemen do, especially whan they're ta'en up by their rich relations, an', pub- lic-hoose as this is, I'll close the door o' 't i' yer face."

" Bless me, Miss Naper !" said Robert, " what hae I dune to set ye at me that gait?   Faith, I dinna ken what ye mean."

" Nae mair do I, laddie.   I hae naething against ye whatever.   Only ye see auld fowk luiks aheid, an' wad fain be as sure o' what's to come as o' what's gane."

" Ye maun bide for that, I doobt," said Robert.

" Laddie," retorted Miss Napier, " ye hae mair sense nor ye hae ony richt till.   Haud the tongue o' ye.   Mr. Ericson 's to come here neist."

And the old lady laughed such good humour into her stocking-sole, that the foot destined to wear it ought never to have been cold while it lasted. So it was then settled; and a week before Robert was to start for Aberdeen, Ericson walked into The Boar's Head.   Half an hour after that, Crookit Caumill was shown into the ga'le room with the message to Maister Robert that Maister Ericson was come, and wanted to see him.

Robert pitched Hutton's Mathematics into the grate, sprung to his feet, all but embraced Crookit Caumill on the spot, and was deterred only by the perturbed look the man wore. Crookit Caumill was a very human creature, and hadn't a fault but the drink, Miss Napier said. And very little of that he would have had if she had been as active as she was willing.

"What's the maitter, Caumill?" asked Robert, in considerable alarm.

"Ow, naething, sir," returned Campbell.

"What gars ye look like that, than?" insisted Robert.

"Ow, naething. But whan Miss Letty cried doon the close upo' me, she had her awpron till her een, an' I thocht something bude to be wrang; but I hadna the hert to speir."

Robert darted to the door, and rushed to the inn, leaving Caumill describing *iambi* on the road behind him.

When he reached The Boar's Head there was nobody to be seen. He darted up the stair to the room where he had first waited upon Ericson.

Three or four maids stood at the door. He asked no question, but went in, a dreadful fear at his heart. Two of the sisters and Dr. Gow stood by the bed.

Ericson lay upon it, clear-eyed, and still. His cheek was flushed. The doctor looked round as Robert entered.

"Robert," he said, "you must keep your friend here quiet. He's broken a blood-vessel—walked too much, I suppose. He'll be all right soon, I hope; but we can't be too careful. Keep him quiet—that's the main thing. He mustn't speak a word."

So saying he took his leave.

Ericson held out his thin hand. Robert grasped it. Ericson's lips moved as if he would speak.

"Dinna speik, Mr. Ericson," said Miss Letty, whose tears were flowing unheeded down her cheeks, "dinna speik. We a' ken what ye mean an' what ye want wi'oot that."

Then she turned to Robert, and said in a whisper,

"Dr. Gow wadna hae ye sent for; but I kent weel eneuch 'at he wad be a' the quaieter gin ye war here. Jist gie a chap upo' the flure gin ye want onything, an' I'll be wi' ye in twa seconds."

The sisters went away. Robert drew a chair beside the bed, and once more was nurse to his friend. The doctor had already bled him at the arm: such was the ordinary mode of treatment then.

Scarcely was he seated, when Ericson spoke —a smile flickering over his worn face.

"Robert, my boy," he said.

"Dinna speak," said Robert, in alarm; "dinna speak, Mr. Ericson."

"Nonsense," returned Ericson, feebly. "They're making a work about nothing. I've done as much twenty times since I saw you last, and I'm not dead yet. But I think it's coming."

"What's coming?" asked Robert, rising in alarm.

"Nothing," answered Ericson, soothingly,— "only death.—I should like to see Miss St. John once before I die. Do you think she would come and see me if I were really dying?"

"I'm sure she wad. But gin ye speik like this, Miss Letty winna lat *me* come near ye, no to say *her*. Oh, Mr. Ericson! gin ye dee, I sanna care to live."

Bethinking himself that such was not the way to keep Ericson quiet, he repressed his emotion, sat down behind the curtain, and was silent. Ericson fell fast asleep. Robert crept from the room, and telling Miss Letty that he would return presently, went to Miss St. John.

"How can I go to Aberdeen without him!" he thought as he walked down the street.

Neither was a guide to the other; but the questioning of two may give just the needful points by which the parallax of a truth may be gained.

"Mr. Ericson's here, Miss St. John," he said, the moment he was shown into her presence.

Her face flushed. Robert had never seen her look so beautiful.

"He's verra ill," he added.

Her face grew pale—very pale.

"He asked if I thought you would go and see him—that is if he were going to die."

A sunset flush, but faint as on the clouds of the east, rose over her pallor.

"I will go at once," she said, rising.

"Na, na," returned Robert, hastily. "It has to be managed. It's no to be dune a' in a hurry. For ae thing, there's Dr. Gow says he maunna speak ae word; and for anither, there's Miss Letty 'ill jist be like a watch-dog to haud a'body oot ower frae 'im. We maun bide oor time. But gin ye say ye'll gang, that 'll content him i' the meantime. I'll tell him."

"I will go any moment," she said. "Is he very ill?"

"I'm afraid he is. I doobt I'll hae to gang to Aberdeen withoot him."

A week after, though he was better, his going was out of the question. Robert wanted to stay with him, but he would not hear of it. He would follow in a week or so, he said, and Robert must start fair with the rest of the *semies*.

But all the removal he was ever able to bear was to the "red room," the best in the house, opening, as I have already mentioned, from an outside stair in the archway. They put up a great screen inside the door, and there the lan'-less laird lay like a lord.

CHAPTER XXI.

SHARGAR ASPIRES.

ROBERT'S heart was dreary when he got on the box-seat of the mail-coach at Rothieden—it was yet drearier when he got down at the Royal Hotel in the street of Bon Accord—and it was dreariest of all when he turned his back on Ericson's, and entered his own room at Mrs. Fyvie's.

Shargar had met him at the coach. Robert had scarcely a word to say to him. And Shargar felt as dreary as Robert when he saw him sit down, and lay his head on the table without a word.

"What's the maitter wi' ye, Robert?" he faltered out at last. "Gin ye dinna speyk to me, I'll cut my throat. I will, faith!"

"Haud yer tongue wi' yer nonsense, Shargar. Mr. Ericson's deein'."

"O lord!" said Shargar, and said nothing more for the space of ten minutes.

Then he spoke again—slowly and sententiously.

"He hadna you to tak' care o' him, Robert. Whaur is he?"

"At the Boar's Heid."

"That's weel. He'll be luikit efter there."

"A body wad like to hae their ain han' in 't, Shargar."

"Ay. I wiss we had him here again."

The ice of trouble thus broken, the stream of talk flowed more freely.

"Hoo are ye gettin' on at the schule, man?" asked Robert.

"Nae that ill," answered Shargar. "I was at the heid o' my class yesterday for five meenits."

"An' hoo did ye like it?"

"Man, it was fine. I thocht I was a gentleman a' at ance."

"Haud ye at it, man," said Robert, as if from the heights of age and experience, "and maybe ye *will* be a gentleman some day."

"Is 't poassible, Robert? A crater like me grow intil a gentleman?" said Shargar, with wide eyes.

"What for no?" returned Robert.

"Eh, man!" said Shargar.

He stood up, sat down again, and was silent.

"For ae thing," resumed Robert, after a pause, during which he had been pondering upon the possibilities of Shargar's future—"for ae thing, I doobt whether Dr. Anderson wad hae ta'en

ony fash aboot ye, gin he hadna thocht ye had
the makin' o' a gentleman i' ye."

" Eh, man!" said Shargar.

He stood up again, sat down again, and was
finally silent.

Next day Robert went to see Dr. Anderson,
and told him about Ericson. The doctor shook
his head, as doctors have done in such cases
from Æsculapius downwards. Robert pressed
no further questions.

" Will he be taken care of where he is?" asked
the doctor.

" Guid care o'," answered Robert.

" Has he any money, do you think?"

" I hae nae doobt he has some, for he's been
teachin' a' the summer. The like o' him maun
an' will work whether they're fit or no."

" Well at all events, you write, Robert, and
give him the hint that he's not to fash himself
about money, for I have more than he'll want.
And you may just take the hint yourself at the
same time, Robert, my boy," he added in, if possible, a yet kinder tone.

Robert's way of showing gratitude was the
best way of all. He returned kindness with faith.

" Gin I be in ony want, doctor, I'll jist rin
to ye at ance. An' gin I want ower muckle ye
maun jist say *na*."

" That's a good fellow. You take things as a
body means them."

"But hae ye naething ye wad like me to do for ye this session, sir?"

"No. I won't have you do anything but your own work. You have more to do than you had last year. Mind your work; and as often as you get tired over you books, shut them up and come to me. You may bring Shargar with you sometimes, but we must take care and not make too much of him all at once."

"Ay, ay, Doctor. But he's a fine crater, Shargar, an' I dinna think he'll be that easy to blaud. What do you think he's turnin' ower i' that reid heid o' his noo?"

"I can't tell that. But there's something to come out of the red head, I do believe. What is he thinking of?"

"Whether it be possible for him ever to be a gentleman. Noo I tak that for a good sign i' the likes o' him."

"No doubt of it. What did you say to him?"

"I tellt him 'at hoo I didna think ye wad hae ta'en sae muckle fash gin ye hadna had some houps o' the kin' aboot him."

"You said well. Tell him from me that I expect him to be a gentleman. And by the way, Robert, do try a little, as I think I said to you once before, to speak English. I don't mean that you should give up Scotch, you know."

"Weel, sir, I *hae* been tryin'; but what am I

to do whan ye speyk to me as gin ye war my ain father. I canna min' upo' a word o' English whan ye do that."

Dr. Anderson laughed, but his eyes glittered.

Robert found Shargar busy over his Latin version. With a " Weel, Shargar," he took his books and sat down. A few moments after, Shargar lifted his head, stared a while at Robert, and then said,

" Duv you railly think it, Robert ?"

" Think what ? What are ye haverin' at, ye gowk ?"

" Duv ye think 'at I ever *could* grow intil a gentleman ?"

" Dr. Anderson says he expecs 't o' ye."

" Eh, man !"

A long pause followed, and Shargar spoke again.

" Hoo am I to begin, Robert ?"

" Begin what ?"

" To be a gentleman."

Robert scratched his head, like Brutus, and at length became oracular.

" Speyk the truth," he said.

" I'll do that. But what aboot—my father ?"

" Naebody 'ill cast up yer *father* to ye. Ye need hae nae fear o' that."

" My mither, than ?" suggested Shargar, with hesitation.

" Ye maun haud yer face to the fac'."

"Ay, ay. But gin they said onything, ye ken
—aboot *her*."

"Gin ony man-body says a word agen yer
mither, ye maun jist knock him doon upo' the
spot."

"But I michtna be able."

"Ye could try, ony gait."

"He micht knock *me* down, ye ken."

"Weel, gae doon than."

"Ay."

This was all the instruction Robert ever gave
Shargar in the duties of a gentleman. And I
doubt whether Shargar sought further enlightenment by direct question of any one. He worked
harder than ever; grew cleanly in his person,
even to fastidiousness; tried to speak English;
and a wonderful change gradually, but rapidly,
passed over his outer man. He grew taller and
stronger, and as he grew stronger, his legs grew
straighter, till the defect of approximating knees,
the consequence of hardship, all but vanished.
His hair became darker, and the albino look less
remarkable, though still he would remind one of
a vegetable grown in a cellar.

Dr. Anderson thought it well that he should
have another year at the grammar school before
going to college.—Robert now occupied Ericson's room, and left his own to Shargar.

Robert heard every week from Miss St. John
about Ericson. Her reports varied much; but

on the whole he got a little better as the winter went on. She said that the good women at the Boar's Head paid him every attention : she did not say that almost the only way to get him to eat was to carry him delicacies which she had prepared with her own hands.

She had soon overcome the jealousy with which Miss Letty regarded her interest in their guest, and before many days had passed she would walk into the archway and go up to his room without seeing any one, except the sister whom she generally found there. By what gradations their intimacy grew I cannot inform my reader, for on the events lying upon the boundary of my story, I have received very insufficient enlightenment; but the result it is easy to imagine. I have already hinted at an early disappointment of Miss St. John. She had grown greatly since, and her estimate of what she had lost had altered considerably in consequence. But the change was more rapid after she became acquainted with Ericson. She would most likely have found the young man she thought she was in love with in the days gone by a very commonplace person now. The heart which she had considered dead to the world had, even before that stormy night in the old house, begun to expostulate against its owner's mistake, by asserting a fair indifference to that portion of its past history. And now, to her large nature the simplicity, the suffering, the patience, the imagination, the grand poverty of Ericson, were irresistibly attractive. Add to this that she became his nurse, and soon saw that he was not indifferent to her—and if she fell in love with him as only a full-grown woman can love, without Ericson's *lips* saying anything that might not by Love's jealousy be interpreted as only of grateful affection, why should she not?

And what of Marjory Lindsay? Ericson had not forgotten her. But the brightest star must grow pale as the sun draws near; and on Ericson there were two suns rising at once on the low sea-shore of life whereon he had been pacing up and down moodily for three-and-twenty years, listening evermore to the unprogressive rise and fall of the tidal waves, all talking of the eternal, all unable to reveal it—the sun of love and the sun of death. Mysie and he had never met. She pleased his imagination; she touched his heart with her helplessness; but she gave him no welcome to the shrine of her beauty: he loved through admiration and pity. He broke no faith to her; for he had never offered her any save in looks, and she had not accepted it. She was but a sickly plant grown in a hot-house. On his death-bed he found a woman a hiding-place from the wind, a covert from the tempest, the shadow of a great rock in a weary land! A strong she-angel with mighty wings, Mary St. John came behind him as he fainted out of life, tempered the burning heat of the Sun of Death, and laid him to sleep in the cool twilight of her glorious shadow. In the stead of trouble about a wilful, thoughtless girl, he found repose and protection and motherhood in a great-hearted woman.

For Ericson's sake, Robert made some effort to preserve the acquaintance of Mr. Lindsay and his daughter. But he could hardly keep up a conversation with Mr. Lindsay, and Mysie showed herself utterly indifferent to him even in the way of common friendship. He told her of Ericson's illness: she said she was sorry to hear it, and looked miles away. He could never get within a certain atmosphere of—what shall I call it? *avertedness* that surrounded her. She had always lived in a dream of unrealities; and the dream had almost devoured her life.

One evening Shargar was later than usual in coming home from the walk, or ramble rather, without which he never could settle down to his work. He knocked at Robert's door.

" Whaur do ye think I've been, Robert?"

" Hoo suld I ken, Shargar?" answered Robert, puzzling over a problem.

" I've been haein' a glaiss wi' Jock Mitchell."

" Wha's Jock Mitchell?"

" My brither Sandy's groom, as I tellt ye afore."

" Ye dinna think I can min' a' your havers,
Shargar. Whaur was the comin' gentleman
whan ye gaed to drink wi' a chield like that,
wha, gin my memory serves me, ye tauld me
yersel' was i' the mids o' a' his maister's deevilry ?"

" Yer memory serves ye weel eneuch to be
doon upo' me," said Shargar. " But there's a
bit wordy 'at they read at the cathedral kirk the
last Sunday 'at's stucken to me as gin there was
something by ordinar' in 't."

" What's that ?" asked Robert, pretending to
go on with his calculations all the time.

" Ow, nae muckle; only this : 'Judge not, that
ye be not judged '.—I took a lesson frae Jeck
the giant-killer, wi' the Welsh giant—was 't
Blunderbore they ca'd him ?—an' poored the
maist o' my glaiss doon my breist. It wasna
like ink ; it wadna du my sark ony ill."

" But what garred ye gang wi' 'im at a' ? He
wasna fit company for a gentleman."

" A gentleman 's some saft gin he be ony the
waur o' the company he gangs in till. There may be
rizzons, ye ken. Ye needna du as they du. Jock
Mitchell was airin' Reid Rorie an' Black Geordie.
An' says I—for I wantit to ken whether I was
sic a breme-buss (*broom-bush*) as I used to be—
says I, 'Hoo are ye, Jock Mitchell?' An' says
Jock, 'Brawly. Wha the deevil are ye?' An'
says I, ' Nae mair o' a deevil nor yersel', Jock

Mitchell, or Alexander, Baron Rothie, either—
though maybe that's no little o' ane.' 'Preserve
me!' cried Jock, 'it's Shargar.'—'Nae mair o'
that, Jock,' says I. 'Gin I bena a gentleman, or
a' be dune,'—an' there I stack, for I saw I was
a muckle fule to lat oot onything o' the kin' to
Jock. And sae he seemed to think, too, for he
brak oot wi' a great guffaw; an' to win ower 't,
I jined, an' leuch as gin naething was farrer aff
frae my thochts than ever bein' a gentleman.
'Whaur do ye pit up, Jock?' I said. 'Oot by
here,' he answert, 'at Luckie Maitlan's.'—'That's
a queer place for a baron to put up, Jock,' says
I. 'There's rizzons,' says he, an' lays his fore-
finger upo' the side o' 's nose, o' whilk there was
hardly eneuch to haud it ohn gane intil the op-
posit ee. 'We're no far frae there,' says I—
an' deed I can hardly tell ye, Robert, what garred
me say sae, but I jist wantit to ken what that
gentleman-brither o' mine was efter; 'tak the
horse hame,' says I—'I'll jist loup upo' Black
Geordie—an' we'll hae a glaiss thegither. I'll
stan' treat.' Sae he gae me the bridle, an' I
lap on. The deevil tried to get a moufu' o' my
hip, but, faith! I was ower swack for 'im; an'
awa we rade."

"I didna ken 'at ye cud ride, Shargar."

"Hoots! I cudna help it. I was aye takin'
the horse to the watter at The Boar's Heid, or
The Royal Oak, or Lucky Happit's, or The

Aucht an' Furty. That's hoo I cam to ken
Jock sae weel. We war guid eneuch frien's
whan I didna care for leein' or sweirin,' an' sic
like."

" And what on earth did ye want wi' 'im noo ?"

" I tell ye I wantit to ken what that ne'er-do-
weel brither o' mine was efter. I had seen the
horses stan'in' aboot twa or three times i' the
gloamin'; an' Sandy maun be aboot ill gin he
be aboot onything."

" What can 't maitter to you, Shargar, what a
man like him 's aboot ?"

" Weel, ye see, Robert, my mither aye broucht
me up to ken a' 'at fowk was aboot, for she said
ye cud never tell whan it micht turn oot to the
weelfaur o' yer advantage—gran' words !—I
wonner whaur she forgathert wi' them. But
she was a terrible wuman, my mither, an' kent
a heap o' things—mair nor 't was gude to ken,
maybe. She gaed aboot the country sae muckle,
an' they say the gipsies she gaed amang 's a
dreadfu' auld fowk, an' hae the wisdom o' the
Egyptians 'at Moses wad hae naething to do
wi'."

" Whaur is she noo ?"

" I dinna ken. She may turn up ony day."

" There's ae thing, though, Shargar : gin ye
want to be a gentleman, ye maunna gang keekin'
that gate intil ither fowk's affairs."

" Weel, I maun gie 't up. I winna say a word

o' what Jock Mitchell tellt me aboot Lord Sandy."

" Ow, say awa'."

"Na, na; ye wadna like to hear aboot ither fowk's affairs. My mither tellt me he did verra ill efter Watterloo till a fremt (*stranger*) lass at Brussels. But that's neither here nor there. I maun set aboot my version, or I winna get it dune the nicht."

" What is Lord Sandy after? What did the rascal tell you? Why do you make such a mystery of it?" said Robert, authoritatively, and in his best English.

" 'Deed I cudna mak naething o' 'm. He winkit an' he mintit (*hinted*) an' he gae me to unnerstan' 'at the deevil was efter some lass or ither, but wha—my lad was as dumb 's the graveyard about that. Gin I cud only win at that, maybe I cud play him a plisky. But he coupit ower three glasses o' whusky, an' the mair he drank the less he wad say. An' sae I left him."

" Well, take care what you're about, Shargar. I don't think Dr. Anderson would like you to be in such company," said Robert; and Shargar departed to his own room and his version.

Towards the end of the session Miss St. John's reports of Ericson were worse. Yet he was very hopeful himself, and thought he was getting better fast. Every relapse he regarded as tem-

porary; and when he got a little better, thought
he had recovered his original position. It was
some relief to Miss St. John to communicate her
anxiety to Robert.

After the distribution of the prizes, of which
he gained three, Robert went the same evening
to visit Dr. Anderson, intending to go home the
next day. The doctor gave him five golden
sovereigns—a rare sight in Scotland. Robert
little thought in what service he was about to
spend them.

CHAPTER XXII.

ROBERT IN ACTION.

IT was late when he left his friend. As he walked through the Gallowgate, an ancient narrow street, full of low courts, some one touched him upon the arm. He looked round. It was a young woman. He turned again to walk on.

"Mr. Faukner," she said, in a trembling voice, which Robert thought he had heard before.

He stopped.

"I don't know you," he said. "I can't see your face. Tell me who you are."

She returned no answer, but stood with her head aside. He could see that her hands shook.

"What do you want with me—if you won't say who you are?"

"I want to tell you something," she said; "but I canna speyk here. Come wi' me."

"I won't go with you without knowing who you are or where you're going to take me."

" Dinna ye ken me ?" she said pitifully, turning a little towards the light of the gas-lamp, and looking up in his face.

" It canna be Jessie Hewson ?" said Robert, his heart swelling at the sight of the pale worn countenance of the girl.

" I was Jessie Hewson ance," she said, " but naebody here kens me by that name but yersel'. Will ye come in ? There's no a crater i' the hoose but mysel'."

Robert turned at once.   " Go on," he said.

She led the way up a narrow stone stair between two houses. A door high up in the gable admitted them.   The boards bent so much under his weight that Robert feared the floor would fall.

" Bide ye there, sir, till I fess a licht," she said.

This was Robert's first introduction to a phase of human life with which he became familiar afterwards.

" Mind hoo ye gang, sir," she resumed, returning with a candle. " There's nae flurin' there.   Haud i' the middle efter me, or ye'll gang throu."

She led him into a room, with nothing in it but a bed, a table, and a chair. On the table was a half-made shirt. In the bed lay a tiny baby, fast asleep. It had been locked up alone in the dreary garret. Robert approached to

look at the child, for his heart felt very warm
to poor Jessie.

"A bonnie bairnie," he said.

"Isna he, sir? Think o' 'im comin' to me!
Nobody can tell the mercy o' 't. Isna it strange
that the verra sin suld bring an angel frae haven
upo' the back o' 't to uphaud an' restore the
sinner? Fowk thinks it's a punishment; but eh
me! it's a mercifu' ane. It's a wonner he didna
think shame to come to me. But he cam to beir
my shame."

Robert wondered at her words. She talked
of her sin with such a meek openness! She
looked her shame in the face, and acknowledged
it hers. Had she been less weak and worn,
perhaps she could not have spoken thus.

"But what am I aboot!" she said, checking
herself. "I didna fess ye here to speyk aboot
mysel'. He's efter mair mischeef, and gin onything cud be dune to haud him frae 't——"

"Wha's efter mischeef, Jessie?" interrupted
Robert.

"Lord Rothie. He's gaein' aff the nicht in
Skipper Hornbeck's boat to Antwerp, I think
they ca' 't, an' a bonnie young leddy wi' 'im.
They war to sail wi' the first o' the munelicht.
—Surely I'm nae ower late," she added, going to the window. "Na, the mune canna be
up yet."

"Na," said Robert; "I dinna think she rises

muckle afore twa o'clock the nicht. But hoo
ken ye? Are ye sure o' 't? It's an awfu' thing
to think o'."

"To convence ye, I maun jist tell ye the
trowth. The hoose we're in hasna a gude character. We're middlin' dacent up here; but
the lave o' the place is dreadfu'. Eh for the
bonnie leys o' Bodyfauld! Gin ye see my father, tell him I'm nane waur than I was."

"They think ye droont i' the Dyer's Pot, as
they ca' 't."

"There I am again!" she said—"miles awa'
an' nae time to be lost!—My lord has a man
they ca' Mitchell. Ower weel I ken him.
There's a wuman doon the stair 'at he comes to
see whiles; an' twa or three nichts ago, I heard
them lauchin' thegither. Sae I hearkened.
They war baith some fou I'm thinkin'. I cudna
tell ye a' 'at they said. That's a punishment
noo, gin ye like—to see and hear the warst o' yer
ain ill doin's. He tellt the limmer a heap o' his
lord's secrets. Ay, he tellt her aboot me, an'
hoo I had gane and droont mysel'. I could
hear 'maist ilka word 'at he said; for ye see the
flurin' here 's no verra soon', and I was jist 'at
I cudna help hearkenin'. My lord's aff the
nicht, as I tell ye. It's a queer gait, but a quaiet,
he thinks, nae doobt. Gin onybody wad but
tell her hoo mony een the baron's made sair wi'
greitin' !"

" But hoo's that to be dune?" said Robert.

" I dinna ken. But I hae been watchin' to see you ever sin' syne. I hae seen ye gang by mony a time. Ye're the only man I ken 'at I could speyk till aboot it. Ye maun think what ye can do. The warst o' 't is I canna tell wha she is or whaur she bides."

"In that case, I canna see what's to be dune."

" Cudna ye watch them aboord, an' slip a letter intil her han'? Or ye cud gie 't to the skipper to gie her."

" I ken the skipper weel eneuch. He's a respectable man. Gin he kent what the baron was efter, he wadna tak him on boord."

" That wad do little guid. He wad only hae her aff some ither gait."

" Weel," said Robert, rising, " I'll awa' hame, an' think aboot it as I gang.—Wad ye tak a feow shillin's frae an auld frien'?" he added with hesitation, putting his hand in his pocket.

" Na—no a baubee," she answered. " Nobody sall say it was for mysel' I broucht ye here. Come efter me, an' min' whaur ye pit doon yer feet. It's no sicker."

She led him to the door. He bade her good night.

" Tak care ye dinna fa' gaein' doon the stair. It's maist as steep 's a wa'."

As Robert came from between the houses, he caught a glimpse of a man in a groom's dress going in at the street-door of that he had left.

All the natural knighthood in him was roused. But what could he do? To write was a sneaking way. He would confront the baron. The baron and the girl would both laugh at him. The sole conclusion he could arrive at was to consult Shargar.

He lost no time in telling him the story.

"I tauld ye he was up to some deevilry or ither," said Shargar. "I can shaw ye the verra hoose he maun be gaein' to tak her frae."

"Ye vratch! what for didna ye tell me that afore?"

"Ye wadna hear aboot ither fowk's affairs. Na, not you! But some fowk has no richt to consideration. The verra stanes they say 'ill cry oot ill secrets like brither Sandy's."

"Whase hoose is 't?"

"I dinna ken. I only saw him come oot o' 't ance, an' Jock Mitchell was haudin' Black Geordie roon' the neuk. It canna be far frae Mr. Lindsay's 'at you an' Mr. Ericson used to gang till."

"Come an' lat me see 't direckly," cried Robert, starting up, with a terrible foreboding at his heart.

They were in the street in a moment. Shargar led the way by a country lane to the top of the hill on the right, and then turning to the left, brought him to some houses standing well apart from each other. It was a region unknown to Robert. They were the backs of the houses of which Mr. Lindsay's was one.

"This is the hoose," said Shargar.

Robert rushed into action. He knocked at the door. Mr. Lindsay's Jenny opened it.

"Is yer mistress in, Jenny?" he asked at once.

"Na. Ay. The maister's gane to Bors Castle."

"It's Miss Lindsay I want to see."

"She's up in her ain room wi' a sair heid."

Robert looked her hard in the face, and knew she was lying.

"I want to see her verra partic'lar," he said.

"Weel, ye canna see her," returned Jenny angrily. "I'll tell her onything ye like."

Concluding that little was to be gained by longer parley, but quite uncertain whether Mysie was in the house or not, Robert turned to Shargar, took him by the arm, and walked away in silence. When they were beyond earshot of Jenny, who stood looking after them,

"Ye're sure that's the hoose, Shargar?" said Robert quietly.

"As sure's deith, and may be surer, for I saw him come oot wi' my ain een."

"Weel, Shargar, it's grown something awfu' noo. It's Miss Lindsay. Was there iver sic a villain as that Lord Rothie—that brither o'yours!"

"I disoun 'im frae this verra 'oor," said Shargar solemnly.

"Something *maun* be dune. We'll awa' to the quay, an' see what'll turn up. I wonner hoo's the tide."

"The tide's risin'. They'll never try to win oot till it's slack watter—furbye 'at the Amphitrite, for as braid 's she is, and her bows modelled efter the cheeks o' a resurrection cherub upo' a gravestane, draws a heap o' watter: an' the bar they say 's waur to win ower nor usual: it's been gatherin' again."

As they spoke, the boys were making for the new town, eagerly. Just opposite where the Amphitrite lay was a public-house: into that they made up their minds to go, and there to write a letter, which they would give to Miss Lindsay if they could, or, if not, leave with Skipper Hoornbeek. Before they reached the river, a thick rain of minute drops began to fall, rendering the night still darker, so that they could scarcely see the vessels from the pavement on the other side of the quay, along which they were hurrying, to avoid the cables, rings, and stone posts that made its margin dangerous in the dim light. When they came to the Smack Inn they crossed right over to reach the Amphitrite. A growing fear kept them silent as they approached her berth. It was empty. They turned and stared at each other in dismay.

One of those amphibious animals that loiter about the borders of the water was seated on a stone smoking, probably fortified against the rain by the whisky inside him.

" Whaur's the Amphitrite, Alan?" asked Shargar, for Robert was dumb with disappointment and rage.

"Half doon to Stanehive by this time, I'm thinkin'," answered Alan. "For a brewin' tub like her, she fummles awa nae ill wi' a licht win' astarn o' her. But I'm doobtin' afore she win across the herrin-pot her fine passengers 'll win at the boddom o' their stamacks. It's like to blaw a bonnetfu', and she rows awfu' in ony win'. I dinna think she cud capsize, but for wamlin' she's waur nor a bairn with the grips."

In absolute helplessness, the boys had let him talk on: there was nothing more to be done; and Alan was in a talkative mood.

"Fegs! gin 't come on to blaw," he resumed, "I wadna wonner gin they got the skipper to set them ashore at Stanehive. I heard auld Horny say something aboot lyin' to there for a bit, to tak a keg or something aboord."

The boys looked at each other, bade Alan good night, and walked away.

"Hoo far is 't to Stonehaven, Shargar?" said Robert.

"I dinna richtly ken. Maybe frae twal to fifteen mile."

Robert stood still. Shargar saw his face pale as death, and contorted with the effort to control his feelings.

"Shargar," he said, "what *am* I to do? I vowed to Mr. Ericson that, gin he deid, I wad luik efter that bonny lassie. An' noo whan he's lyin' a' but deid, I hae latten her slip throu' my fingers wi' clean carelessness. What *am* I to do? Gin I cud only win to Stonehaven afore the Amphitrite! I cud gang aboord wi' the keg, and gin I cud do naething mair, I wad hae tried to do my best. Gin I do naething, my hert 'll brak wi' the weicht o' my shame."

Shargar burst into a roar of laughter. Robert was on the point of knocking him down, but took him by the throat as a milder proceeding, and shook him.

"Robert! Robert!" gurgled Shargar, as soon as his choking had overcome his merriment, "ye're an awfu' Hielan'man. Hearken to me. I beg—g—g yer pardon. What I was thinkin' o' was——"

Robert relaxed his hold. But Shargar, notwithstanding the lesson Robert had given him, could hardly speak yet for the enjoyment of his own device.

"Gin we could only get rid o' Jock Mitchell!——" he crowed; and burst out again.

"He's wi' a wuman i' the Gallowgate," said Robert.

"Losh, man!" exclaimed Shargar, and started off at full speed.

He was no match for his companion, however.

"Whaur the deevil are ye rinnin' till, ye wir-rycow (*scarecrow*)?" panted Robert, as he laid hold of his collar.

"Lat me gang, Robert," gasped Shargar. "Losh, man! ye'll be on Black Geordie in anither ten meenits, an' me ahin' ye upo' Reid Rorie. An' faith gin we binna at Stanehive afore the Dutch-man wi' 's boddom foremost, it 'll be the faut o' the horse and no o' the men."

Robert's heart gave a bound of hope.

"Hoo 'ill ye get them, Shargar?" he asked eagerly.

"Steal them," answered Shargar, struggling to get away from the grasp still upon his collar.

"We micht be hanged for that."

"Weel, Robert, I'll tak a' the wyte o' 't. Gin it hadna been for you, I micht ha' been hangt by this time for ill doin': for you're sake I'll be hangt for weel doin', an' welcome. Come awa'. To steal a mairch upo' brither Sandy wi' aucht (*eight*) horse-huves o' 's ain! Ha! ha! ha!"

They sped along, now running themselves out of breath, now walking themselves into it again, until they reached a retired hostelry between the two towns. Warning Robert not to show himself, Shargar disappeared round the corner of the house.

Robert grew weary, and then anxious. At length Shargar's face came through the darkness.

"Robert," he whispered, "gie's yer bonnet. I'll be wi' ye in a moment noo."

Robert obeyed, too anxious to question him. In about three minutes more Shargar reappeared, leading what seemed the ghost of a black horse; for Robert could see only his eyes, and his hoofs made scarcely any noise. How he had managed it with a horse of Black Geordie's temper, I do not know, but some horses will let some persons do anything with them: he had drawn his own stockings over his fore feet, and tied their two caps upon his hind hoofs.

"Lead him awa' quaietly up the road till I come to ye," said Shargar, as he took the mufflings off the horse's feet. "An' min' 'at he doesna tak a nip o' ye. He's some ill for bitin'. I'll be efter ye direckly. Rorie's saiddlet an' bridled. He only wants his carpet-shune."

Robert led the horse a few hundred yards, then stopped and waited. Shargar soon joined him, already mounted on Red Roderick.

"Here's yer bonnet, Robert. It's some foul, I doobt. But I cudna help it. Gang on, man. Up wi' ye. Maybe I wad hae better keepit

Geordie mysel'. But ye can ride. Ance ye're on, he canna bite ye."

But Robert needed no encouragement from Shargar. In his present mood he would have mounted a griffin. He was on horseback in a moment. They trotted gently through the streets, and out of the town. Once over the Dee, they gave their horses the rein, and off they went through the dark drizzle. Before they got half way they were wet to the skin; but little did Robert, or Shargar either, care for that. Not many words passed between them.

"Hoo 'ill ye get the horse (*plural*) in again, Shargar?" asked Robert.

"Afore I get them back," answered Shargar, "they'll be tired eneuch to gang hame o' themsel's. Gin we had only had the luck to meet Jock!—that wad hae been gran'."

"What for that?"

"I wad hae cawed Reid Rorie ower the heid o' 'm, an' left him lyin'—the coorse villain!"

The horses never flagged till they drew up in the main street of Stonehaven. Robert ran down to the harbour to make inquiry, and left Shargar to put them up.

The moon had risen, but the air was so full of vapour that she only succeeded in melting the darkness a little. The sea rolled in front, awful in its dreariness, under just light enough to show a something unlike the land. But the rain

had ceased, and the air was clearer. Robert
asked a solitary man, with a telescope in his
hand, whether he was looking out for the Amphitrite. The man asked him gruffly in return
what he knew of her. Possibly the nature of
the keg to be put on board had something to do
with his Scotch reply. Robert told him he was
a friend of the captain, had missed the boat, and
would give any one five shillings to put him on
board. The man went away and returned with
a companion. After some further questioning
and bargaining, they agreed to take him. Robert loitered about the pier full of impatience.
Shargar joined him.

Day began to break over the waves. They
gleamed with a blue-gray leaden sheen. The men
appeared coming along the harbour, and descended by a stair into a little skiff, where a barrel, or something like one lay under a tarpaulin.
Robert bade Shargar good-bye, and followed.
They pushed off, rowed out into the bay, and
lay on their oars waiting for the vessel. The
light grew apace, and Robert fancied he could
distinguish the two horses with one rider against
the sky on the top of the cliffs, moving northwards. Turning his eyes to the sea, he saw the
canvas of the brig, and his heart beat fast. The
men bent to their oars. She drew nearer, and lay
to. When they reached her he caught the rope
the sailors threw, was on board in a moment, and

went aft to the captain. The Dutchman stared.
In a few words Robert made him understand his
object, offering to pay for his passage, but the
good man would not hear of it.   He told him
that the lady and gentleman had come on
board as brother and sister : the baron was too
knowing to run his head into the noose of Scotch
law.

" I cannot throw him over the board," said the
skipper ; " and what am I to do ? I am afraid it
is of no use.   Ah ! poor thing !"

By this time the vessel was under way.   The
wind freshened.   Mysie had been ill ever since
they left the mouth of the river : now she was
much worse.   Before another hour passed, she
was crying to be taken home to her papa.   Still
the wind increased, and the vessel laboured much.

Robert never felt better, and if it had not
been for the cause of his sea-faring, would have
thoroughly enjoyed it.   He put on some sea-
going clothes of the captain's, and set himself to
take his share in working the brig, in which he
was soon proficient enough to be useful. When
the sun rose, they were in a tossing wilderness
of waves.   With the sunrise, Robert began to
think he had been guilty of a great folly.   For
what could he do ?   How was he to prevent
the girl from going off with her lover the moment they landed ? But his poor attempt would
verify his willingness.

The baron came on deck now and then, looking bored. He had not calculated on having to nurse the girl. Had Mysie been well, he could have amused himself with her, for he found her ignorance interesting. As it was, he felt injured, and indeed disgusted at the result of the experiment.

On the third day the wind abated a little; but towards night it blew hard again, and it was not until they reached the smooth waters of the Scheldt that Mysie made her appearance on deck, looking dreadfully ill, and altogether like a miserable, unhappy child. Her beauty was greatly gone, and Lord Rothie did not pay her much attention.

Robert had as yet made no attempt to communicate with her, for there was scarcely a chance of her concealing a letter from the baron. But as soon as they were in smooth water, he wrote one, telling her in the simplest language that the baron was a bad man, who had amused himself by making many women fall in love with him, and then leaving them miserable: he knew one of them himself.

Having finished his letter, he began to look abroad over the smooth water, and the land smooth as the water. He saw tall poplars, the spires of the forest, and rows of round-headed dumpy trees, like domes. And he saw that all the buildings like churches, had either spires like poplars, or low round domes like those other trees. The domes gave an eastern aspect to the country. The spire of Antwerp cathedral especially had the poplar for its model. The pinnacles which rose from the base of each successive start of its narrowing height were just the clinging, upright branches of the poplar —a lovely instance of Art following Nature's suggestion.

CHAPTER XXIII.

ROBERT FINDS A NEW INSTRUMENT.

AT length the vessel lay along side the quay, and as Mysie stepped from its side the skipper found an opportunity of giving her Robert's letter. It was the poorest of chances, but Robert could think of no other. She started on receiving it, but regarding the skipper's significant gestures put it quietly away. She looked anything but happy, for her illness had deprived her of courage, and probably roused her conscience. Robert followed the pair, saw them enter "The Great Labourer"—what could the name mean? could it mean The Good Shepherd?—and turned away helpless, objectless indeed, for he had done all that he could, and that all was of no potency. A world of innocence and beauty was about to be hurled from its orbit of light into the blackness of outer chaos; he knew it, and was unable to speak word or do deed that should frustrate the power of a devil who so loved himself that he counted it an honour to a girl to

have him for her ruin. Her after life had no
significance for him, save as a trophy of his victory. He never perceived that such victory
was not yielded to him; that he gained it by
putting on the garments of light; that if his inward form had appeared in its own ugliness,
not one of the women whose admiration he had
secured would not have turned from him as from
the monster of an old tale.

Robert wandered about till he was so weary
that his head ached with weariness. At length
he came upon the open space before the cathedral, whence the poplar-spire rose aloft into
a blue sky flecked with white clouds. It
was near sunset, and he could not see the
sun, but the upper half of the spire shone glorious in its radiance. From the top his eye
sank to the base. In the base was a little door
half open. Might not that be the lowly narrow
entrance through the shadow up to the sun-
filled air? He drew near with a kind of tremor,
for never before had he gazed upon visible grandeur growing out of the human soul, in the majesty
of everlastingness—a tree of the Lord's planting.
Where had been but an empty space of air and
light and darkness, had risen, and had stood for
ages, a mighty wonder awful to the eye, solid to
the hand. He peeped through the opening of
the door: there was the foot of a stair—marvellous as the ladder of Jacob's dream—turning

away towards the unknown. He pushed the
door and entered. A man appeared and barred
his advance. Robert put his hand in his pocket
and drew out some silver. The man took one
piece—looked at it—turned it over—put it in
his pocket, and led the way up the stair. Robert followed and followed and followed.

He came out of stone walls upon an airy platform whence the spire ascended heavenwards.
His conductor led upward still, and he followed,
winding within a spiral network of stone, through
which all the world looked in. Another platform,
and yet another spire springing from its basement. Still up they went, and at length stood on a
circle of stone surrounding like a coronet the
last base of the spire which lifted its apex un-
trodden. Then Robert turned and looked below.
He grasped the stones before him. The loneliness
was awful.

There was nothing between him and the roofs
of the houses, four hundred feet below, but the
spot where he stood. The whole city, with its
red roofs, lay under him. He stood uplifted on
the genius of the builder, and the town beneath
him was a toy. The all but featureless flat
spread forty miles on every side, and the roofs
of the largest buildings below were as dove-
cots. But the space between was alive with
awe—so vast, so real!

He turned and descended, winding through

the network of stone which was all between
him and space. The object of the architect
must have been to melt away the material from
before the eyes of the spirit. He hung in the
air in a cloud of stone. As he came in his descent within the ornaments of one of the base-
ments, he found himself looking through two
thicknesses of stone lace on the nearing city.
Down there was the beast of prey and his vic-
tim; but for the moment he was above the region of sorrow. His weariness and his headache
had vanished utterly. With his mind tossed
on its own speechless delight, he was slowly
descending still, when he saw on his left hand
a door a-jar. He would look what mystery lay
within. A push opened it. He discovered only
a little chamber lined with wood. In the centre
stood something—a bench-like piece of furniture, plain and worn. He advanced a step;
peered over the top of it; saw keys, white and
black; saw pedals below: it was an organ!
Two strides brought him in front of it. A
wooden stool, polished and hollowed with centuries of use, was before it. But where was
the bellows? That might be down hundreds
of steps below, for he was half-way only to the
ground. He seated himself musingly, and
struck, as he thought, a dumb chord. Responded, up in the air, far overhead, a mighty
booming clang. Startled, almost frightened,

even as if Mary St. John had said she loved
him, Robert sprung from the stool, and, without
knowing why, moved only by the chastity of
delight, flung the door to the post. It banged
and clicked. Almost mad with the joy of the
titanic instrument, he seated himself again at
the keys, and plunged into a tempest of clang-
ing harmony. One hundred bells hang in that
tower of wonder, an instrument for a city, nay,
for a kingdom. Often had Robert dreamed that
he was the galvanic centre of a thunder-cloud
of harmony, flashing off from every finger the
willed lightning tone : such was the unexpected
scale of this instrument—so far aloft in the
sunny air rang the responsive notes, that his
dream appeared almost realized. The music,
like a fountain bursting upwards, drew him up
and bore him aloft. From the resounding cone
of bells overhead he no longer heard their tones
proceed, but saw level-winged forms of light
speeding off with a message to the nations. It
was only his roused phantasy; but a sweet
tone is nevertheless a messenger of God ; and a
right harmony and sequence of such tones is a
little gospel.

At length he found himself following, till
that moment unconsciously, the chain of tunes
he well remembered having played on his violin
the night he went first with Ericson to see
Mysie, ending with his strange chant about

the witch lady and the dead man's hand.

Ere he had finished the last, his passion had begun to fold its wings, and he grew dimly aware of a beating at the door of the solitary chamber in which he sat. He knew nothing of the enormity of which he was guilty—presenting unsought the city of Antwerp with a glorious phantasia. He did not know that only upon grand, solemn, world-wide occasions, such as a king's birthday or a ball at the Hôtel de Ville, was such music on the card. When he flung the door to, it had closed with a spring lock, and for the last quarter of an hour three gens-d'arme, commanded by the sacristan of the tower, had been thundering thereat. He waited only to finish the last notes of the wild Orcadian chant, and opened the door. He was seized by the collar, dragged down the stair into the street, and through a crowd of wondering faces—poor unconscious dreamer! it will not do to think on the house-top even, and you had been dreaming very loud indeed in the church spire—away to the bureau of the police.

CHAPTER XXIV.

DEATH.

I NEED not recount the proceedings of the Belgian police; how they interrogated Robert concerning a letter from Mary St. John which they found in an inner pocket; how they looked doubtful over a copy of Horace that lay in his coat, and put evidently a momentous question about some algebraical calculations on the fly leaf of it. Fortunately or unfortunately —I do not know which—Robert did not understand a word they said to him. He was locked up, and left to fret for nearly a week; though what he could have done had he been at liberty, he knew as little as I know. At last, long after it was useless to make any inquiry about Miss Lindsay, he was set at liberty. He could just pay for a steerage passage to London, whence he wrote to Dr. Anderson for a supply, and was in Aberdeen a few days after.

This was Robert's first cosmopolitan experience. He confided the whole affair to the doc-

tor, who approved of all, saying it could have been
of no use, but he had done right. He advised
him to go home at once, for he had had letters
inquiring after him. Ericson was growing
steadily worse—in fact, he feared Robert might
not see him alive.

If this news struck Robert to the heart, his
pain was yet not without some poor allevia-
tion:—he need not tell Ericson about Mysie,
but might leave him to find out the truth when,
free of a dying body, he would be better able
to bear it. That very night he set off on foot
for Rothieden. There was no coach from Aberdeen till eight the following morning, and before that he would be there.

It was a dreary journey without Ericson.
Every turn of the road reminded him of him.
And Ericson too was going a lonely unknown
way.

Did ever two go together upon that way?
Might not two die together and not lose hold
of each other all the time, even when the sense
of the clasping hands was gone, and the soul
had withdrawn itself from the touch? Happy
they who prefer the will of God to their own
even in this, and would, as the best friend, have
him near who *can* be near—him who made the
fourth in the fiery furnace! Fable or fact,
reader, I do not care. The One I mean *is*, and
in him I hope.

Very weary was Robert when he walked into his grandmother's house.

Betty came out of the kitchen at the sound of his entrance.

"Is Mr. Ericson——?"

"Na; he's nae deid," she answered. "He'll maybe live a day or twa, they say."

"Thank God!" said Robert, and went to his grandmother.

"Eh, laddie!" said Mrs. Falconer, the first greetings over, "ane 's ta'en an' anither 's left! but what for 's mair nor I can faddom. There's that fine young man, Maister Ericson, at deith's door; an' here am I, an auld runklet wife, left to cry upo' deith, an' he winna hear me."

"Cry upo' God, grannie, an' no upo' deith," said Robert, catching at the word as his grandmother herself might have done. He had no such unfair habit when I knew him, and always spoke to one's meaning, not one's words. But then he had a wonderful gift of knowing what what one's meaning was.

He did not sit down, but, tired as he was, went straight to The Boar's Head. He met no one in the archway, and walked up to Ericson's room. When he opened the door, he found the large screen on the other side, and hearing a painful cough, lingered behind it, for he could not control his feelings sufficiently. Then he heard a voice—Ericson's voice; but oh, how changed!

—He had no idea that he ought not to listen.

"Mary," the voice said, "do not look like that. *I* am not suffering. It is only my body. Your arm round me makes me so strong! Let me lay my head on your shoulder."

A brief pause followed.

"But, Eric," said Mary's voice, "there is one that loves you better than I do."

"If there is," returned Ericson, feebly, "he has sent his angel to deliver me."

"But you do believe in him, Eric?"

The voice expressed anxiety no less than love.

"I am going to see. There is no other way. When I find him, I shall believe in him. I shall love him with all my heart, I know. I love the thought of him now."

"But that's not himself, my—darling!" she said.

"No. But I cannot love himself till I find him. Perhaps there is no Jesus."

"Oh, don't say that. I can't bear to hear you talk so."

"But, dear heart, if you're so sure of him, do you think he would turn me away because I don't do what I can't do? I would if I could with all my heart. If I were to say I believed in him, and then didn't trust him, I could understand it. But when it's only that I'm not sure about what I never saw, or had enough of proof to satisfy me of, how can he be vexed at that?

You seem to me to do him great wrong, Mary. Would you now banish me for ever, if I should, when my brain is wrapped in the clouds of death, forget you along with everything else for a moment?"

"No, no, no. Don't talk like that, Eric, dear. There may be reasons, you know."

"I know what they say well enough. But I expect Him, if there is a Him, to be better even than you, my beautiful—and I don't know a fault in you, but that you believe in a God you can't trust. If I believed in a God, wouldn't I trust him just? And I do hope in him. We'll see, my darling. When we meet again I think you'll say I was right."

Robert stood like one turned into marble. Deep called unto deep in his soul. The waves and the billows went over him.

Mary St. John answered not a word. I think she must have been conscience-stricken. Surely the Son of Man saw *nearly* as much faith in Ericson as in her. Only she clung to the word as a bond that the Lord had given her: she would rather have his bond.

Ericson had another fit of coughing. Robert heard the rustling of ministration. But in a moment the dying man again took up the word. He seemed almost as axious about Mary's faith as she was about his.

"There's Robert," he said: "I do believe that

boy would die for me, and I never did anything to deserve it. Now Jesus Christ must be as good as Robert at least. *I* think he must be a great deal better, if he's Jesus Christ at all. Now Robert might be hurt if I didn't believe in *him*. But I've never seen Jesus Christ. It's all in an old book, over which the people that say they believe in it the most, fight like dogs and cats. I beg your pardon, my Mary; but they do, though the words are ugly."

"Ah! but if you had tried it as I've tried it, you would know better, Eric."

"I think I should, dear. But it's too late now. I must just go and see. There's no other way left."

The terrible cough came again. As soon as the fit was over, with a grand despair in his heart, Robert went from behind the screen.

Ericson was on a couch. His head lay on Mary St. John's bosom. Neither saw him.

"Perhaps," said Ericson, panting with death, "a kiss in heaven may be as good as being married on earth, Mary."

She saw Robert and did not answer. Then Eric saw him. He smiled; but Mary grew very pale.

Robert came forward, stooped and kissed Ericson's forehead, kneeled and kissed Mary's hand, rose and went out.

From that moment they were both dead to

him.   *Dead*, I say—not lost, not estranged, but dead—that is, awful and holy.   He wept for Eric.   He did not weep for Mary yet.   But he found a time.

Ericson died two days after.

Here endeth Robert's youth.

CHAPTER XXV.

IN MEMORIAM.

IN memory of Eric Ericson, I add a chapter of sonnets gathered from his papers, almost desiring that those only should read them who turn to the book a second time. How his papers came into my possession, will be explained afterwards.

———

Tumultuous rushing o'er the outstretched plains ;
A wildered maze of comets and of suns ;
The blood of changeless God that ever runs
With quick diastole up the immortal veins ;
A phantom host that moves and works in chains ;
A monstrous ficton which, collapsing, stuns
The mind to stupor and amaze at once ;
A tragedy which that man best explains
Who rushes blindly on his wild career
With trampling hoofs and sound of mailed war,
Who will not nurse a life to win a tear,
But is extinguished like a falling star:—
Such will at times this life appear to me,
Until I learn to read more perfectly.

HOM. IL. v. 403.

If thou art tempted by a thought of ill,
Crave not too soon for victory, nor deem
Thou art a coward if thy safety seem
To spring too little from a righteous will:
For there is nightmare on thee, nor until
Thy soul hath caught the morning's early gleam
Seek thou to analyse the monstrous dream
By painful introversion; rather fill
Thine eye with forms thou knowest to be truth:
But see thou cherish higher hope than this;
A hope hereafter that thou shalt be fit
Calm-eyed to face distortion, and to sit
Transparent among other forms of youth
Who own no impulse save to God and bliss.

And must I ever wake, gray dawn, to know
Thee standing sadly by me like a ghost?
I am perplexed with thee, that thou shouldst cost
This Earth another turning: all a-glow
Thou shouldst have reached me, with a purple show
Along far mountain-tops: and I would post
Over the breadth of seas though I were lost
In the hot phantom-chase for life, if so
Thou camest ever with this numbing sense
Of chilly distance and unlovely light;
Waking this gnawing soul anew to fight
With its perpetual load: I drive thee hence—
I have another mountain-range from whence
Bursteth a sun unutterably bright.

GALILEO.

" And yet it moves !"   Ah, Truth, where wert thou then,
  When all for thee they racked each piteous limb ?
  Wert thou in Heaven, and busy with thy hymn,
  When those poor hands convulsed that held thy pen ?
  Art thou a phantom that deceivest men
  To their undoing ? or dost thou watch him
  Pale, cold, and silent in his dungeon dim ?
  And wilt thou ever speak to him again ?
" It moves, it moves !   Alas, my flesh was weak ;
  That was a hideous dream !   I'll cry aloud
  How the green bulk wheels sunward day by day !
  Ah me ! ah me ! perchance my heart was proud
  That I alone should know that word to speak ;
  And now, sweet Truth, shine upon these, I pray."

If thou wouldst live the Truth in very deed,
Thou hast thy joy, but thou hast more of pain.
Others will live in peace, and thou be fain
To bargain with despair, and in thy need
To make thy meal upon the scantiest weed.
These palaces, for thee they stand in vain ;
Thine is a ruinous hut ; and oft the rain
Shall drench thee in the midnight ; yea the speed
Of earth outstrip thee pilgrim, while thy feet
Move slowly up the heights.   Yet will there come
Through the time-rents about thy moving cell,
An arrow for despair, and oft the hum
Of far-off populous realms where spirits dwell.

TO   * * * *

Speak, Prophet of the Lord ! We may not start
To find thee with us in thine ancient dress,
Haggard and pale from some bleak wilderness,
Empty of all save God and thy loud heart :
Nor with like rugged message quick to dart
Into the hideous fiction mean and base :
But yet, O prophet man, we need not less,
But more of earnest ; though it is thy part
To deal in other words, if thou wouldst smite
The living Mammon, seated, not as then
In bestial quiescence grimly dight,
But thrice as much an idol-god as when
He stared at his own feet from morn to night.*

THE WATCHER.

From out a windy cleft there comes a gaze
Of eyes unearthly which go to and fro
Upon the people's tumult, for below
The nations smite each other : no amaze
Troubles their liquid rolling, or affrays
Their deep-set contemplation : steadily glow
Those ever holier eye-balls, for they grow
Liker unto the eyes of one that prays.
And if those clasped hands tremble, comes a power
As of the might of worlds, and they are holden
Blessing above us in the sunrise golden ;
And they will be uplifted till that hour
Of terrible rolling which shall rise and shake
This conscious nightmare from us and we wake.

---

* This sonnet and the preceding are both one line deficient.

THE BELOVED DISCIPLE.

I

One do I see and twelve ; but second there
Methinks I know thee, thou beloved one ;
Not from thy nobler port, for there are none
More quiet-featured ; some there are who bear
Their message on their brows, while others wear
A look of large commission, nor will shun
The fiery trial, so their work is done :
But thou hast parted with thine eyes in prayer—
Unearthly are they both ; and so thy lips
Seem like the porches of the spirit land ;
For thou hast laid a mighty treasure by,
Unlocked by Him in Nature, and thine eye
Burns with a vision and apocalypse
Thy own sweet soul can hardly understand.

II

A Boanerges too ! Upon my heart
It lay a heavy hour : features like thine
Should glow with other message than the shine
Of the earth-burrowing levin, and the start
That cleaveth horrid gulfs. Awful and swart
A moment stoodest thou, but less divine—
Brawny and clad in ruin !—till with mine
Thy heart made answering signals, and apart
Beamed forth thy two rapt eye-balls doubly clear,
And twice as strong because thou didst thy duty,
And though affianced to immortal Beauty,
Hiddest not weakly underneath her veil
The pest of Sin and Death which maketh pale :
Henceforward be thy spirit doubly dear. *

* To these two sonnets Falconer had appended this note.
"Something I wrote to Ericson concerning these, during my

THE LILY OF THE VALLEY.

There is not any weed but hath its shower,
There is not any pool but hath its star;
And black and muddy though the waters are,
We may not miss the glory of a flower,
And winter moons will give them magic power
To spin in cylinders of diamond spar;
And everything hath beauty near and far,
And keepeth close and waiteth on its hour.
And I when I encounter on my road
A human soul that looketh black and grim,
Shall I more ceremonious be than God?
Shall I refuse to watch one hour with him
Who once beside our deepest woe did bud
A patient watching flower about the brim.

———

'Tis not the violent hands alone that bring
The curse, the ravage, and the downward doom,
Although to these full oft the yawning tomb
Owes deadly surfeit; but a keener sting,
A more immortal agony, will cling
To the half-fashioned sin which would assume
Fair Virtue's garb. The eye that sows the gloom
With quiet seeds of Death henceforth to spring
What time the sun of passion burning fierce
Breaks through the kindly cloud of circumstance;
The bitter word, and the unkindly glance,

first college vacation, produced a reply of which the following
is a passage: 'On writing the first I was not aware that James
and John were the Sons of Thunder. For a time it did
indeed grieve me to think of the spiritual-minded John as
otherwise than a still and passionless lover of Christ.'"

The crust and canker coming with the years,
Are liker Death than arrows, and the lance
Which through the living heart at once doth pierce.

SPOKEN OF SEVERAL PHILOSOPHERS.

I pray you, all ye men, who put your trust
In moulds and systems and well-tackled gear,
Holding that Nature lives from year to year
In one continual round because she must—
Set me not down, I pray you, in the dust
Of all these centuries, like a pot of beer,
A pewter-pot disconsolately clear,
Which holds a potful, as is right and just.
I will grow clamorous—by the rood, I will,
If thus ye use me like a pewter pot.
Good friend, thou art a toper and a sot—
I will not be the lead to hold thy swill,
Nor any lead : I will arise and spill
Thy silly beverage, spill it piping hot.

Nature, to him no message dost thou bear,
Who in thy beauty findeth not the power
To gird himself more strongly for the hour
Of night and darkness. Oh, what colours rare
The woods, the valleys, and the mountains wear
To him who knows thy secret, and in shower
And fog, and ice-cloud, hath a secret bower
Where he may rest until the heavens are fair !
Not with the rest of slumber, but the trance
Of onward movement steady and serene,
Where oft in struggle and in contest keen
His eyes will opened be, and all the dance

Of life break on him, and a wide expanse
Roll upward through the void, sunny and green.

TO JUNE.

Ah, truant, thou art here again, I see !
For in a season of such wretched weather
I thought that thou hadst left us altogether,
Although I could not choose but fancy thee
Skulking about the hill-tops, whence the glee
Of thy blue laughter peeped at times, or rather
Thy bashful awkwardness, as doubtful whether
Thou shouldst be seen in such a company
Of ugly runaways, unshapely heaps
Of ruffian vapour, broken from restraint
Of their slim prison in the ocean deeps.
But yet I may not chide : fall to thy books,
Fall to immediately without complaint—
There they are lying, hills and vales and brooks.

WRITTEN ABOUT THE LONGEST DAY.

Summer, sweet Summer, many-fingered Summer !
We hold thee very dear, as well we may :
It is the kernel of the year to-day—
All hail to thee ! Thou art a welcome comer !
If every insect were a fairy drummer,
And I a fifer that could deftly play,
We'd give the old Earth such a roundelay
That she would cast all thought of labour from her.
Ah ! what is this upon my window-pane ?
Some sulky drooping cloud comes pouting up,
Stamping its glittering feet along the plain !
Well, I will let that idle fancy drop.

Oh, how the spouts are bubbling with the rain !
And all the earth shines like a silver cup !

ON A MIDGE.

Whence do ye come, ye creatures ? Each of you
Is perfect as an angel ; wings and eyes
Stupendous in their beauty—gorgeous dyes
In feathery fields of purple and of blue !
Would God I saw a moment as ye do !
I would become a molecule in size,
Rest with you, hum with you, or slanting rise
Along your one dear sunbeam, could I view
The pearly secret which each tiny fly,
Each tiny fly that hums and bobs and stirs,
Hides in its little breast eternally
From you, ye prickly grim philosophers,
With all your theories that sound so high :
Hark to the buzz a moment, my good sirs !

ON A WATERFALL.

Here stands a giant stone from whose far top
Comes down the sounding water. Let me gaze
Till every sense of man and human ways
Is wrecked and quenched for ever, and I drop
Into the whirl of time, and without stop
Pass downward thus ! Again my eyes I raise
To thee, dark rock ; and though the mist and haze
My strength returns when I behold thy prop
Gleam stern and steady through the wavering wrack.
Surely thy strength is human, and like me
Thou bearest loads of thunder on thy back !
And, lo, a smile upon thy visage black—

A breezy tuft of grass which I can see
Waving serenely from a sunlit crack!

————

Above my head the great pine-branches tower;
Backwards and forwards each to the other bends,
Beckoning the tempest-cloud which hither wends
Like a slow-laboured thought, heavy with power:
Hark to the patter of the coming shower!
Let me be silent while the Almighty sends
His thunder-word along; but when it ends
I will arise and fashion from the hour
Words of stupendous import, fit to guard
High thoughts and purposes, which I may wave,
When the temptation cometh close and hard,
Like fiery brands betwixt me and the grave
Of meaner things—to which I am a slave
If evermore I keep not watch and ward.

————

I do remember how when very young,
I saw the great sea first, and heard its swell
As I drew nearer, caught within the spell
Of its vast size and its mysterious tongue.
How the floor trembled, and the dark boat swung
With a man in it, and a great wave fell
Within a stone's cast! Words may never tell
The passion of the moment, when I flung
All childish records by, and felt arise
A thing that died no more! An awful power
I claimed with trembling hands and eager eyes,
Mine, mine for ever, an immortal dower.—
The noise of waters soundeth to this hour,
When I look seaward through the quiet skies.

ON THE SOURCE OF THE ARVE.

Hear'st thou the dash of water loud and hoarse
With its perpetual tidings upward climb,
Struggling against the wind? Oh, how sublime!
For not in vain from its portentous source,
Thy heart, wild stream, hath yearned for its full force.
But from thine ice-toothed caverns dark as time
At last thou issuest, dancing to the rhyme
Of thy outvolleying freedom! Lo, thy course
Lies straight before thee as the arrow flies,
Right to the ocean-plains. Away, away!
Thy parent waits thee, and her sunset dyes
Are ruffled for thy coming, and the gray
Of all her glittering borders flashes high
Against the glittering rocks : oh, haste, and fly!

END OF THE SECOND VOLUME.

LONDON: PRINTED BY MACDONALD AND TUGWELL, BLENHEIM HOUSE.

ROBERT FALCONER

BY

GEORGE MAC DONALD LL.D.

AUTHOR OF

" ALEC FORBES OF HOWGLEN,"

" DAVID ELGINBROD,"

&c., &c.

> Countrymen.
> My heart doth joy that yet, in all my life,
> I found no man but he was true to me.
> BRUTUS in *Julius Cæsar*.

IN THREE VOLUMES.

VOL. III.

LONDON:
HURST AND BLACKETT, PUBLISHERS,
13, GREAT MARLBOROUGH STREET.
1868.

The right of Translation is reserved

LONDON

PRINTED BY MACDONALD AND TUGWELL, BLENHEIM HOUSE,

BLENHEIM STREET, OXFORD STREET.

CONTENTS

OF

THE THIRD VOLUME.

PART III.—HIS MANHOOD.

CHAPTER						PAGE
I. IN THE DESERT	.	.	.	.	.	1
II. HOME AGAIN	.	.	.	.	.	24
III. A MERE GLIMPSE	.	.	.	.	.	40
IV. THE DOCTOR'S DEATH	.		.	.	.	49
V. A TALK WITH GRANNIE		.	.	.	.	63
VI. SHARGAR'S MOTHER	.	.	.	.	.	77
VII. THE SILK-WEAVER	.	.	.	.	.	89
VIII. MY OWN ACQUAINTANCE		.	.	.	.	104
IX. THE BROTHERS	.	.	.	.	.	139
X. A NEOPHYTE	.	.	.	.	.	156
XI. THE SUICIDE	.	.	.	.	.	177
XII. ANDREW AT LAST	.	.	.	.	.	213
XIII. ANDREW REBELS	.	.	.	.	.	227
XIV. THE BROWN LETTER	.	.	.	.	.	237
XV. FATHER AND SON	.	.	.	.	.	248
XVI. CHANGE OF SCENE	.	.	.	.	.	255
XVII. IN THE COUNTRY	.	.	.	.	.	265
XVIII. THREE GENERATIONS	.	.	.	.	.	287
XIX. THE WHOLE STORY	.	.	.	.	.	291
XX. THE VANISHING	.	.	.	.	.	300

ROBERT FALCONER.

PART III.—HIS MANHOOD.

CHAPTER I.

IN THE DESERT.

A LIFE lay behind Robert Falconer, and a
life lay before him. He stood on a shoal
between.

The life behind him was in its grave. He had
covered it over and turned away. But he knew
it would rise at night.

The life before him was not yet born; and what
should issue from that dull ghastly unrevealing
fog on the horizon, he did not care. Thither
the tide setting eastward would carry him, and
his future must be born. All he cared about was
to leave the empty garments of his dead behind
him—the sky and the fields, the houses and the
gardens which those dead had made alive with

their presence. Travel, motion, ever on, ever away, was the sole impulse in his heart. Nor had the thought of finding his father any share in his restlessness.

He told his grandmother that he was going back to Aberdeen. She looked in his face with surprise, but seeing trouble there, asked no questions. As if walking in a dream, he found himself at Dr. Anderson's door.

"Why, Robert," said the good man, "what has brought you back? Ah! I see. Poor Ericson! I am very sorry, my boy. What can I do for you?"

"I can't go on with my studies now, sir," answered Robert. "I have taken a great longing for travel. Will you give me a little money and let me go?"

"To be sure I will. Where do you want to go?"

"I don't know. Perhaps as I go I shall find myself wanting to go somewhere. You're not afraid to trust me, are you, sir?"

"Not in the least, Robert. I trust you perfectly. You shall do just as you please.—Have you any idea how much money you will want?"

"No. Give me what you are willing I should spend : I will go by that."

"Come along to the bank then. I will give you enough to start with. Write at once when you want more. Don't be too saving. Enjoy yourself as well as you can. I shall not grudge it."

Robert smiled a wan smile at the idea of enjoying himself. His friend saw it, but let it pass. There was no good in persuading a man whose grief was all he had left, that he must ere long part with that too. That would have been in lowest deeps of sorrow to open a yet lower deep of horror. But Robert would have refused, and would have been right in refusing to believe with regard to himself what might be true in regard to most men. He might rise above his grief; he might learn to contain his grief; but lose it, forget it?—never.

He went to bid Shargar farewell. As soon as he had a glimpse of what his friend meant, he burst out in an agony of supplication.

"Tak me wi' ye, Robert," he cried. "Ye're a gentleman noo. I'll be yer man. I'll put on a livery coat, an' gang wi' ye. I'll awa' to Dr. Anderson. He's sure to lat me gang."

"No, Shargar," said Robert, "I can't have you with me. I've come into trouble, Shargar, and I must fight it out alone."

"Ay, ay; I ken. Puir Mr. Ericson!"

"There's nothing the matter with Mr. Ericson. Don't ask me any questions. I've said more to you now than I've said to anybody besides."

"That *is* guid o' you, Robert. But am I never to see ye again?"

" I don't know. Perhaps we may meet some day."

" *Perhaps* is nae muckle to say, Robert," protested Shargar.

" It's more than can be said about everything, Shargar," returned Robert, sadly.

" Weel, I maun jist tak it as 't comes," said Shargar, with a despairing philosophy derived from the days when his mother thrashed him. " But, eh! Robert, gin it had only pleased the Almichty to sen' me into the warl' in a some respectable kin' o' a fashion!"

" Wi' a chance a' gaein' aboot the country like that curst villain yer brither, I suppose?" retorted Robert, rousing himself for a moment.

" Na, na," responded Shargar. " I'll stick to my ain mither. *She* never learned *me* sic tricks."

" Do ye that. Ye canna compleen o' God. It's a' richt as far 's ye're concerned. Gin he dinna mak something o' ye yet, it'll be *your* wyte, no his, I'm thinkin'."

They walked to Dr. Anderson's together, and spent the night there. In the morning Robert got on the coach for Edinburgh.

I cannot, if I would, follow him on his travels. Only at times, when the conversation rose in the dead of night, by some Jacob's ladder of blessed ascent, into regions where the heart of such a man could open as in its own natural clime, would a few words cause the clouds that enveloped this period of his history to dispart, and grant me a peep into the phantasm of his past. I suspect, however, that much of it left upon his mind no recallable impressions. I suspect that much of it looked to himself in the retrospect like a painful dream, with only certain objects and occurrences standing prominent enough to clear the moonlight mist enwrapping the rest.

What the precise nature of his misery was I shall not even attempt to conjecture. That would be to intrude within the holy place of a human heart. One thing alone I will venture to affirm—that bitterness against either of his friends, whose spirits rushed together and left his outside, had no place in that noble nature. His fate lay behind him, like the birth of Shargar, like the death of Ericson, a decree.

I do not even know in what direction he first went. That he had seen many cities and many countries was apparent from glimpses of ancient streets, of mountain-marvels, of strange constellations, of things in heaven and earth which no one could have seen but himself, called up by the magic of his words. A silent man in company, he talked much when his hour of speech arrived. Seldom, however, did he narrate any incident save in connection with some truth of human nature, or fact of the universe.

I do know that the first thing he always

did on reaching any new place was to visit the
church with the loftiest spire; but he never
looked into the church itself until he had left the
earth behind him as far as that church would afford him the possibility of ascent. Breathing the
air of its highest region, he found himself vaguely strengthened, yes comforted.   One peculiar
feeling he had, into which I could enter only
upon happy occasion, of the presence of God
in the wind.   He said the wind up there on the
heights of human aspiration always made him
long and pray.   Asking him one day something
about his going to church so seldom, he answered thus:

"My dear boy, it does me ten times more good
to get outside the spire than to go inside the
church. The spire is the most essential, and consequently the most neglected part of the building.
It symbolizes the aspiration without which no
man's faith can hold its own.   But the effort of
too many of her priests goes to conceal from the
worshippers the fact that there is such a stair,
with a door to it out of the church.   It looks
as if they feared their people would desert them
for heaven.   But I presume it arises generally
from the fact that they know of such an ascent
themselves, only by hearsay.   The knowledge of
God is good, but the church is better!"

"Could it be," I ventured to suggest, "that,

in order to ascend, they must put off the priests' garments ?"

"Good, my boy!" he answered. "All are priests up there, and must be clothed in fine linen, clean and white—the righteousness of saints—not the imputed righteousness of another,—that is a lying doctrine—but their own righteousness which God has wrought in them by Christ."

I never knew a man in whom the inward was so constantly clothed upon by the outward, whose ordinary habits were so symbolic of his spiritual tastes, or whose enjoyment of the sight of his eyes and the hearing of his ears was so much informed by his highest feelings. He regarded all human affairs from the heights of religion, as from their church-spires he looked down on the red roofs of Antwerp, on the black roofs of Cologne, on the gray roofs of Strasburg, or on the brown roofs of Basel—uplifted for the time above them, not in dissociation from them.

On the base of the missing twin-spire at Strasburg, high over the roof of the church, stands a little cottage—how strange its white muslin window-curtains look up there! To the day of his death he cherished the fancy of writing a book in that cottage, with the grand city to which London looks a modern mushroom, its thousand roofs with row upon row of win-

dows in them—often five garret stories, one
above the other, and its thickets of multiform
chimneys, the thrones and procreant cradles of
the storks, marvellous in history, habit, and dignity—all below him.

He was taken ill at Valence, and lay there for
a fortnight, oppressed with some kind of low
fever.   One night he awoke from a refreshing
sleep, but could not sleep again.   It seemed to
him afterwards as if he had lain waiting for
something.   Anyhow something came.   As it
were a faint musical rain had invaded his hearing ; but the night was clear, for the moon was
shining on his window-blind.   The sound came
nearer, and revealed itself a delicate tinkling of
bells.   It drew nearer still and nearer, growing
in sweet fulness as it came, till at length a slow
torrent of tinklings went past his window in the
street below.   It was the flow of a thousand
little currents of sound, a gliding of silvery
threads, like the talking of water-ripples against
the side of a barge in a slow canal—all as soft
as the moonlight, as exquisite as an odour, each
sound tenderly truncated and dull.   A great
multitude of sheep was shifting its quarters
in the night, whence and whither and why he
never knew.   To his heart they were the mes-
sengers of the Most High.   For into that heart,
soothed and attuned by their thin harmony, not
on the wind that floated without breaking their

lovely message, but on the ripples of the wind that bloweth where it listeth, came the words, unlooked for, their coming unheralded by any mental premonition, "My peace I give unto you." The sounds died slowly away in the distance, fainting out of the air, even as they had grown upon it, but the words remained.

In a few moments he was fast asleep, comforted by pleasure into repose; his dreams were of gentle self-consoling griefs; and when he awoke in the morning—"My peace I give unto you," was the first thought of which he was conscious. It may be that the sound of the sheepbells made him think of the shepherds that watched their flocks by night, and they of the multitude of the heavenly host, and they of the song—"On earth peace": I do not know. The important point is not how the words came, but that the words remained—remained until he understood them, and they became to him spirit and life.

He soon recovered strength sufficiently to set out again upon his travels, great part of which he performed on foot. In this way he reached Avignon. Passing from one of its narrow streets into an open place in the midst, all at once he beheld, towering above him, on a height that overlooked the whole city and surrounding country, a great crucifix. The form of the Lord of Life still hung in the face of heaven and earth. He bowed his head involuntarily. No matter that when he drew nearer the power of it vanished. The memory of it remained with its first impression, and it had a share in what followed.

He made his way eastward towards the Alps. As he walked one day about noon over a desolate heath-covered height, reminding him not a little of the country of his childhood, the silence seized upon him. In the midst of the silence arose the crucifix, and once more the words which had often returned upon him sounded in the ears of the inner hearing, "My peace I give unto you." They were words he had known from the earliest memorial time. He had heard them in infancy, in childhood, in boyhood, in youth: now first in manhood it flashed upon him that the Lord did really mean that the peace of his soul should be the peace of their souls; that the peace wherewith his own soul was quiet, the peace at the very heart of the universe, was henceforth theirs—open to them, to all the world, to enter and be still. He fell upon his knees, bowed down in the birth of a great hope, held up his hands towards heaven, and cried, "Lord Christ, give me thy peace."

He said no more, but rose, caught up his stick, and strode forward, thinking.

He had learned what the sentence meant; what that was of which it spoke he had not yet

learned. The peace he had once sought, the
peace that lay in the smiles and tenderness of a
woman, had " overcome him like a summer
cloud," and had passed away. There was surely
a deeper, a wider, a grander peace for him than
that, if indeed it was the same peace wherewith
the king of men regarded his approaching end,
that he had left as a heritage to his brothers.
Suddenly he was aware that the earth had begun to live again. The hum of insects arose
from the heath around him; the odour of its
flowers entered his dulled sense; the wind
kissed him on the forehead; the sky domed up
over his head; and the clouds veiled the distant
mountain tops like the smoke of incense ascending from the altars of the worshipping earth.
All nature began to minister to one who had
begun to lift his head from the baptism of fire.
He had thought that Nature could never more
be anything to him; and she was waiting on
him like a mother. The next moment he was
offended with himself for receiving ministrations
the reaction of whose loveliness might no longer
gather around the form of Mary St. John.
Every wavelet of scent, every toss of a flower's
head in the breeze, came with a sting in its
pleasure—for there was no woman to whom
they belonged. Yet he could not shut them
out, for God and not woman is the heart of the
universe. Would the day ever come when the

loveliness of Mary St. John, felt and acknowledged as never before, would be even to him a
joy and a thanksgiving? If ever, then because
God is the heart of all.

I do not think this mood, wherein all forms of
beauty sped to his soul as to their own needful
centre, could have lasted over many miles of his
journey. But such delicate inward revelations
are none the less precious that they are evanescent. Many feelings are simply too good to
last—using the phrase not in the unbelieving
sense in which it is generally used, expressing
the conviction that God is a hard father, fond of
disappointing his children, but to express the fact
that intensity and endurance cannot yet coexist
in the human economy. But the virtue of a
mood depends by no means on its immediate
presence. Like any other experience, it may be
believed in, and, in the absence which leaves the
mind free to contemplate it, work even more
good than in its presence.

At length he came in sight of the Alpine
regions. Far off, the heads of the great mountains rose into the upper countries of cloud,
where the snows settled on their stony heads,
and the torrents ran out from beneath the frozen
mass to gladden the earth below with the faith
of the lonely hills. The mighty creatures lay
like grotesque animals of a far-off titanic time,
whose dead bodies had been first withered into

stone, then worn away by the storms, and covered with shrouds and palls of snow, till the outlines of their forms were gone, and only rough shapes remained like those just blocked out in the sculptor's marble, vaguely suggesting what the creatures had been, as the corpse under the sheet of death is like a man. He came amongst the valleys at their feet, with their blue-green waters hurrying seawards—from stony heights of air into the mass of " the restless wavy plain ;" with their sides of rock rising in gigantic terrace after terrace up to the heavens; with their scaling pines, erect and slight, cone-head aspiring above cone-head, ambitious to clothe the bare mass with green, till failing at length in their upward efforts, the savage rock shot away and beyond and above them, the white and blue glaciers clinging cold and cruel to their ragged sides, and the dead blank of whiteness covering their final despair. He drew near to the lower glaciers, to find their awful abysses tremulous with liquid blue, a blue tender and profound as if fed from the reservoir of some hidden sky intenser than ours ; he rejoiced over the velvety fields dotted with the toy-like houses of the mountaineers; he sat for hours listening by the side of their streams ; he grew weary, felt oppressed, longed for a wider outlook, and began to climb towards a mountain village of which he had heard from a traveller, to find solitude and freedom in an air as lofty as if he climbed twelve of his beloved cathedral spires piled up in continuous ascent.

After ascending for hours in zigzags through pine woods, where the only sound was of the little streams trotting down to the valley below, or the distant hush of some thin waterfall, he reached a level, and came out of the woods. The path now led along the edge of a precipice descending sheer to the uppermost terrace of the valley he had left. The valley was but a cleft in the mass of the mountain: a little way over sank its other wall, steep as a plumb-line could have made it, of solid rock. On his right lay green fields of clover and strange grasses. Ever and anon from the cleft steamed up great blinding clouds of mist, which now wandered about over the nations of rocks on the mountain side beyond the gulf, now wrapt himself in their bewildering folds. In one moment the whole creation had vanished, and there seemed scarce existence enough left for more than the following footstep; the next, a mighty mountain stood in front, crowned with blinding snow, an awful fact; the lovely heavens were over his head, and the green sod under his feet; the grasshoppers chirped about him, and the gorgeous butterflies flew. From regions far beyond came the bells of the kine and the goats. He reached a little inn, and there took up his quarters.

I am able to be a little minute in my description, because I have since visited the place myself. Great heights rise around it on all sides. It stands as between heaven and hell, suspended between peaks and gulfs. The wind must roar awfully there in the winter; but the mountains stand away with their avalanches, and all the summer long keep the cold off the grassy fields.

The same evening, he was already weary. The next morning it rained. It rained fiercely all day. He would leave the place on the morrow. In the evening it began to clear up. He walked out. The sun was setting. The snowpeaks were faintly tinged with rose, and the ragged masses of vapour that hung lazy and leaden-coloured about the sides of the abyss, were partially dyed a sulky orange red. Then all faded into gray. But as the sunlight vanished, a veil sank from the face of the moon, already halfway to the zenith, and she gathered courage and shone, till the mountain looked lovely as a ghost in the gleam of its snow and the glimmer of its glaciers. "Ah!" thought Falconer, "such a peace at last is all a man can look for—the repose of a spectral Elysium, a world where passion has died away, and only the dim ghost of its memory returns to disturb with a shadowy sorrow the helpless content of its undreaming years. The religion that can do but this much is not a very great or very divine thing. The

human heart cannot invent a better it may be,
but it can imagine grander results.

He did not yet know what the religion was of
which he spoke. As well might a man born
stone-deaf estimate the power of sweet sounds,
or he who knows not a square from a circle pro-
nounce upon the study of mathematics.

The next morning rose brilliant—an ideal
summer day. He would not go yet: he would
spend one day more in the place. He opened
his valise to get some lighter garments. His
eye fell on a New Testament. Dr. Anderson
had put it there. He had never opened it yet,
and now he let it lie. Its time had not yet
come. He went out.

Walking up the edge of the valley, he came
upon a little stream whose talk he had heard
for some hundred yards. It flowed through a
grassy hollow, with steeply sloping sides.
Water is the same all the world over; but there
was more than water here to bring his childhood back to Falconer. For at the spot where
the path led him down to the *burn*, a little crag
stood out from the bank,—a gray stone like
many he knew on the stream that watered the
valley of Rothieden: on the top of the stone
grew a little heather; and beside it, bending
towards the water, was a silver birch. He sat
down on the foot of the rock, shut in by the
high grassy banks from the gaze of the awful

mountains. The sole unrest was the run of the water beside him, and it sounded so homely, that he began to jabber Scotch to it. He forgot that this stream was born in the clouds, far up where that peak rose into the air behind him; he did not know that a couple of hundred yards from where he sat, it tumbled headlong into the valley below: with his country's birch-tree beside him, and the rock crowned with its tuft of heather over his head, the quiet as of a Sabbath afternoon fell upon him—that quiet which is the one altogether lovely thing in the Scotch Sabbath—and once more the words arose in his mind, "My peace I give unto you."

Now he fell a thinking what this peace could be. And it came into his mind as he thought, that Jesus had spoken in another place about giving rest to those that came to him, while here he spoke about "*my* peace." Could this *my* mean a certain *kind* of peace that the Lord himself possessed? Perhaps it was in virtue of that peace, whatever it was, that he was the Prince of Peace. Whatever peace he had must be the highest and best peace—therefore the one peace for a man to seek, if indeed, as the words of the Lord seemed to imply, a man was capable of possessing it. He remembered the New Testament in his box, and, resolving to try whether he could not make something more out of it, went back to the inn quieter in heart than since he left his home. In the evening he returned to the brook, and fell to searching the story, seeking after the peace of Jesus.

He found that the whole passage stood thus:—

"Peace I leave with you, my peace I give unto you: not as the world giveth give I unto you. Let not your heart be troubled, neither let it be afraid."

He did not leave the place for six weeks. Every day he went to the burn, as he called it, with his New Testament; every day tried yet again to make out something more of what the Saviour meant. By the end of the month it had dawned upon him, he hardly knew how, that the peace of Jesus (although, of course, he could not know what it was like till he had it) must have been a peace that came from the doing of the will of his Father. From the account he gave of the discoveries he then made, I venture to represent them in the driest and most exact form that I can find they will admit of. When I use the word *discoveries*, I need hardly say that I use it with reference to Falconer and his previous knowledge. They were these:—that Jesus taught—

First,—That a man's business is to do the will of God:

Second,—That God takes upon himself the care of the man:

Third,—Therefore, that a man must never be afraid of anything; and so,

Fourth,—be left free to love God with all his heart, and his neighbour as himself.

But one day, his thoughts having cleared themselves a little upon these points, a new set of questions arose with sudden inundation—comprised in these two :—

"How can I tell for certain that there ever was such a man? How am I to be sure that such as he says is the mind of the maker of these glaciers and butterflies?"

All this time he was in the wilderness as much as Moses at the back of Horeb, or St. Paul when he vanishes in Arabia; and he did nothing but read the four gospels and ponder over them. Therefore it is not surprising that he should have already become so familiar with the gospel story, that the moment these questions appeared, the following words should dart to the forefront of his consciousness to meet them :—

"If any man will do his will, he shall know of the doctrine, whether it be of God, or whether I speak of myself."

Here was a word of Jesus himself, announcing the one means of arriving at a conviction of the truth or falsehood of all that he said, namely, the doing of the will of God by the man who would arrive at such conviction.

The next question naturally was: What is

c 2

this will of God of which Jesus speaks? Here
he found himself in difficulty. The theology of
his grandmother rushed in upon him, threaten-
ing to overwhelm him with demands as to feeling and inward action from which his soul
turned with sickness and fainting. That they
were repulsive to him, that they appeared un-
real, and contradictory to the nature around
him, was no *proof* that they were not of God.
But on the other hand, that they demanded
what *seemed* to him unjust,—that these demands
were founded on what *seemed* to him untruth attributed to God, on ways of thinking and feeling which are certainly degrading in a man,—
these were reasons of the very highest nature
for refusing to act upon them so long as, from
whatever defects it might be in himself, they
bore to him this aspect. He saw that while
they appeared to be such, even though it might
turn out that he mistook them, to acknowledge
them would be to wrong God. But this conclusion left him in no better position for practice
than before.

When at length he did see what the will of
God was, he wondered, so simple did it appear,
that he had failed to discover it at once. Yet
not less than a fortnight had he been brooding
and pondering over the question, as he wandered up and down that burnside, or sat at the foot
of the heather-crowned stone and the silver-

barked birch, when the light began to dawn upon him. It was thus.

In trying to understand the words of Jesus by searching back, as it were, for such thoughts and feelings in him as would account for the words he spoke, the perception awoke that at least he could not have meant by the will of God any such theological utterances as those which troubled him. Next it grew plain that what he came to do, was just to lead his life. That he should do the work, such as recorded, and much besides, that the Father gave him to do—this was the will of God concerning him. With this perception arose the conviction that unto every man whom God had sent into the world, he had given a work to do in that world. He had to lead the life God meant him to lead. The will of God was to be found and done in the world. In seeking a true relation to the world, would he find his relation to God?

The time for action was come.

He rose up from the stone of his meditation, took his staff in his hand, and went down the mountain, not knowing whither he went. And these were some of his thoughts as he went:

"If it was the will of God who made me and her, my will shall not be set against his. I cannot be happy, but I will bow my head and let his waves and his billows go over me. If there is such a God, he knows what a pain I bear.

His will be done. Jesus thought it well that his will should be done to the death. Even if there be no God, it will be grand to be a disciple of such a man, to do as he says, think as he thought—perhaps come to feel as he felt."

My reader may wonder that one so young should have been able to think so practically—to the one point of action. But he was in earnest, and what lay at the root of his character, at the root of all that he did, felt, and became, was childlike simplicity and purity of nature. If the sins of his father were mercifully visited upon him, so likewise were the grace and loveliness of his mother. And between the two, Falconer had fared well.

As he descended the mountain, the one question was—his calling. With the faintest track to follow, with the clue of a spider's thread to guide him, he would have known that his business was to set out at once to find, and save his father. But never since the day when the hand of that father smote him, and Mary St. John found him bleeding on the floor, had he heard word or conjecture concerning him. If he were to set out to find him now, it would be to search the earth for one who might have vanished from it years ago. He might as well search the streets of a great city for a lost jewel. When the time came for him to find his father, if such an hour was written in the decrees of—I dare not say Fate, for Falconer hated the word—if such was the will of God, some sign would be given him—that is, some hint which he could follow with action. As he thought and thought it became gradually plainer that he must begin his obedience by getting ready for anything that God might require of him. Therefore he must go on learning till the call came.

But he shivered at the thought of returning to Aberdeen. Might he not continue his studies in Germany? Would that not be as good—possibly, from the variety of the experience, better? But how was it to be decided? By submitting the matter to the friend who made either possible. Dr. Anderson had been to him as a father: he would be guided by his pleasure.

He wrote, therefore, to Dr. Anderson, saying that he would return at once if he wished it, but that he would greatly prefer going to a German university for two years. The doctor replied that of course he would rather have him at home, but that he was confident Robert knew best what was best for himself; therefore he had only to settle where he thought proper, and the next summer he would come and see him, for he was not tied to Aberdeen any more than Robert.

CHAPTER II.

HOME AGAIN.

FOUR years passed before Falconer returned to his native country, during which period Dr. Anderson had visited him twice, and shown himself well satisfied with his condition and pursuits. The doctor had likewise visited Rothieden, and had comforted the heart of the grandmother with regard to her Robert. From what he learned upon this visit, he had arrived at a true conjecture, I believe, as to the cause of the great change which had suddenly taken place in the youth. But he never asked Robert a question leading in the direction of the grief which he saw the healthy and earnest nature of the youth gradually assimilating into his life. He had too much respect for sorrow to approach it with curiosity. He had learned to put off his shoes when he drew nigh the burning bush of human pain.

Robert had not settled at any of the universities, but had moved from one to the other as he saw fit, report guiding him to the men who spoke with authority. The time of doubt and anxious questioning was far from over, but the time was long gone by—if in his case it had ever been—when he could be like a wave of the sea, driven of the wind and tossed. He had ever one anchor of the soul, and he found that it held—the faith of Jesus (I say the faith of Jesus, not his own faith in Jesus), the truth of Jesus, the life of Jesus. However his intellect might be tossed on the waves of speculation and criticism, he found that the word the Lord had spoken remained steadfast; for in doing righteously, in loving mercy, in walking humbly, the conviction increased that Jesus knew the very secret of human life. Now and then some great vision gleamed across his soul of the working of all things towards a far-off goal of simple obedience to a law of life, which God knew, and which his son had justified through sorrow and pain. Again and again the words of the Master gave him a peep into a region where all was explicable, where all that was crooked might be made straight, where every mountain of wrong might be made low, and every valley of suffering exalted. Ever and again some one of the dark perplexities of humanity began to glimmer with light in its inmost depth. Nor was he without those moments of communion when the creature is lifted into the secret place of the Creator.

Looking back to the time when it seemed that he cried and was not heard, he saw that God had been hearing, had been answering, all the time; had been making him capable of receiving the gift for which he prayed. He saw that intellectual difficulty encompassing the highest operations of harmonizing truth, can no more affect their reality than the dulness of chaos disprove the motions of the wind of God over the face of its waters. He saw that any true revelation must come out of the unknown in God through the unknown in man. He saw that its truths must rise in the man as powers of life, and that only as that life grows and unfolds can the ever-lagging intellect gain glimpses of partial outlines fading away into the infinite —that, indeed, only in material things and the laws that belong to them, are outlines possible— even there, only in the picture of them which the mind that analyses them makes for itself, not in the things themselves.

At the close of these four years, with his spirit calm and hopeful, truth his passion, and music, which again he had resumed and diligently cultivated, his pleasure, Falconer returned to Aberdeen. He was received by Dr. Anderson as if he had in truth been his own son. In the room stood a tall figure, with its back

towards them, pocketing its handkerchief. The
next moment the figure turned, and—could it
be?—yes, it was Shargar. Doubt lingered only
until he opened his mouth, and said " Eh, Robert !" with which exclamation he threw himself
upon him, and after a very undignified fashion
began crying heartily. Tall as he was, Robert's
great black head towered above him, and his
shoulders were like a rock against which Shargar's slight figure leaned. He looked down
like a compassionate mastiff upon a distressed
Italian greyhound. His eyes shimmered with
feeling, but Robert's tears, if he ever shed any,
were kept for very solemn occasions. He was
more likely to weep for awful joy than for any
sufferings either in himself or others. " Shargar !" pronounced in a tone full of a thousand
memories, was all the greeting he returned ;
but his great manly hand pressed Shargar's delicate long-fingered one with a grasp which
must have satisfied his friend that everything
was as it had been between them, and that
their friendship from henceforth would take a
new start. For with all that Robert had seen,
thought, and learned, now that the bitterness
of loss had gone by, the old times and the old
friends were dearer. If there was any truth in
the religion of God's will, in which he was a
disciple, every moment of life's history which
had brought soul in contact with soul, must be

sacred as a voice from behind the veil. Therefore he could not now rest until he had gone to
see his grandmother.

" Will you come to Rothieden with me, Shargar? I beg your pardon—I oughtn't to keep
up an old nickname," said Robert, as they sat
that evening with the doctor, over a tumbler of
toddy.

" If you call me anything else, I'll cut my
throat, Robert, as I told you before. If anyone
else does," he added, laughing, " I'll cut his
throat."

" Can he go with me, doctor ?" asked Robert,
turning to their host.

" Certainly. He has not been to Rothieden
since he took his degree. He's an A.M. now,
and has distinguished himself besides. You'll
see him in his uniform soon, I hope. Let's drink
his health, Robert. Fill your glass."

The doctor filled his glass slowly and solemnly. He seldom drank even wine, but this was
a rare occasion. He then rose, and with equal
slowness, and a tremor in his voice which rendered it impossible to imagine the presence of
anything but seriousness, said,

" Robert, my son, let's drink the health of
George Moray, Gentleman. Stand up."

Robert rose, and in his confusion Shargar
rose too, and sat down again, blushing till his
red hair looked yellow beside his cheeks. The

men repeated the words, " George Moray, Gentleman," emptied their glasses, and resumed their seats. Shargar rose trembling, and tried in vain to speak. The reason in part was, that he sought to utter himself in English.

" Hoots ! Damn English !" he broke out at last. " Gin I be a gentleman, Dr. Anderson and Robert Falconer, it's you twa 'at's made me ane, an' God bless ye, an' I'm yer hoomble servant to a' etairnity."

So saying, Shargar resumed his seat, filled his glass with trembling hand, emptied it to hide his feelings, but without success, rose once more, and retreated to the hall for a space.

The next morning Robert and Shargar got on the coach and went to Rothieden. Robert turned his head aside as they came near the bridge and the old house of Bogbonnie. But, ashamed of his weakness, he turned again and looked at the house. There it stood, all the same, —a thing for the night winds to howl in, and follow each other in mad gambols through its long passages and rooms, so empty from the first that not even a ghost had any reason for going there—a place almost without a history—dreary emblem of so many empty souls that have hidden their talent in a napkin, and have nothing to return for it when the Master calls them. Having looked this one in the face, he felt stronger to meet those other places before

which his heart quailed yet more. He knew
that Miss St. John had left soon after Ericson's
death : whether he was sorry or glad that he
should not see her he could not tell. He thought
Rothieden would look like Pompeii, a city
buried and disinterred; but when the coach
drove into the long straggling street, he found
the old love revive, and although the blood
rushed back to his heart when Captain Forsyth's house came in view, he did not turn
away, but made his eyes, and through them his
heart, familiar with its desolation. He got down
at the corner, and leaving Shargar to go on to
The Boar's Head and look after the luggage,
walked into his grandmother's house and
straight into her little parlour. She rose with
her old stateliness when she saw a stranger enter the room, and stood waiting his address.

" Weel, grannie," said Robert, and took her
in his arms.

" The Lord's name be praised !" faltered she.
" He's ower guid to the likes o' me."

And she lifted up her voice and wept.

She had been informed of his coming, but she
had not expected him till the evening; he was
much altered, and old age is slow.

He had hardly placed her in her chair, when
Betty came in. If she had shown him respect
before, it was reverence now.

" Eh, sir !" she said, " I didna ken it was you,

or I wadna hae come into the room ohn chappit at the door. I'll awa' back to my kitchie."

So saying, she turned to leave the room.

"Hoots! Betty," cried Robert, "dinna be a gowk. Gie 's a grip o' yer han'."

Betty stood staring and irresolute, overcome at sight of the manly bulk before her.

"Gin ye dinna behave yersel', Betty, I'll jist awa' ower to Muckledrum, an' hae a caw (*drive*) throu the sessions-buik."

Betty laughed for the first time at the awful threat, and the ice once broken, things returned to somewhat of their old footing.

I must not linger on these days. The next morning Robert paid a visit to Bodyfauld, and found that time had there flowed so gently that it had left but few wrinkles and fewer grey hairs. The fields, too, had little change to show; and the hill was all the same, save that its pines had grown. His chief mission was to John Hewson and his wife. When he left for the continent, he was not so utterly absorbed in his own griefs as to forget Jessie. He told her story to Dr. Anderson, and the good man had gone to see her the same day.

In the evening, when he knew he should find them both at home, he walked into the cottage. They were seated by the fire, with the same pot hanging on the same crook for their supper. They rose, and asked him to sit down, but did

not know him. When he told them who he
was, they greeted him warmly, and John Hewson smiled something of the old smile, but only
like it, for it had no "rays proportionately delivered" from his mouth over his face.

After a little indifferent chat, Robert said:

" I came through Aberdeen yesterday, John."

At the very mention of Aberdeen, John's head
sunk. He gave no answer, but sat looking in
the fire. His wife rose and went to the other
end of the room, busying herself quietly about
the supper. Robert thought it best to plunge
into the matter at once.

" I saw Jessie last nicht," he said.

Still there was no reply. John's face had
grown hard as a stone face, but Robert thought
rather from the determination to govern his
feelings than from resentment.

" She's been doin' weel ever sin' syne," he
added.

Still no word from either; and Robert fearing some outburst of indignation ere he had
said his say, now made haste.

" She's been a servant wi' Dr. Anderson for
four year noo, an' he's sair pleased wi' her. She's
a fine woman. But her bairnie's deid, an' that
was a sair blow till her."

He heard a sob from the mother, but still
John made no sign.

" It was a bonnie bairnie as ever ye saw. It

luikit in her face, she says, as gin it kent a'
aboot it, and had only come to help her throu
the warst o' 't; for it gaed hame 'maist as sune's
ever she was richt able to thank God for sen'in'
her sic an angel to lead her to repentance."

"John," said his wife, coming behind his
chair, and laying her hand on his shoulder,
"what for dinna ye speyk? Ye hear what
Maister Faukner says.—Ye dinna think a thing's
clean useless 'cause there may be a spot upo' 't?"
she added, wiping her eyes with her apron.

"A spot upo' 't?" cried John, starting to his
feet. "What ca' ye a spot?—Wuman, dinna
drive me mad to hear ye lichtlie the glory o'
virginity."

"That's a' verra weel, John," interposed Robert quietly; "but there was ane thocht as
muckle o' 't as ye do, an' wad hae been ashamed
to hear ye speak that gait aboot yer ain dauchter."

"I dinna unnerstan' ye," returned Hewson,
looking *raised-like* at him.

"Dinna ye ken, man, that amo' them 'at kent
the Lord best whan he cam frae haiven to luik
efter his ain—to seek and to save, ye ken—
amo' them 'at cam roon aboot him to hearken
till 'im, was lasses 'at had gane the wrang gait
a'thegither,—no like your bonnie Jessie 'at fell
but ance. Man, ye're jist like Simon the Pharisee, 'at was sae scunnert at oor Lord 'cause he

loot the wuman 'at was a sinner tak her wull
o' 's feet—the feet 'at they war gaein' to tak
their wull o' efter anither fashion afore lang.
He wad hae shawn her the door—Simon wad—
like you, John; but the Lord tuik her pairt.
An' lat me tell *you*, John—an' I winna beg yer
pardon for sayin' 't, for it's God's trowth—lat
me tell *you*, 'at gin ye gang on that gait ye'll
be sidin' wi' the Pharisee, an' no wi' oor Lord.
Ye may lippen to yer wife, ay, an' to Jessie hersel', that kens better nor eyther o' ye, no to
mak little o' virginity. Faith! they think mair
o' 't than ye do, I'm thinkin', efter a'; only it's
no a thing to say muckle aboot. An' it's no to
stan' for a'thing, efter a'."

Silence followed. John sat down again, and
buried his face in his hands. At length he murmured from between them:

" The lassie's weel ?"

" Ay," answered Robert; and silence followed
again.

" What wad ye hae me do ?" asked John, lifting his head a little.

" I wad hae ye sen' a kin' word till her. The
lassie's hert's jist longin' efter ye. That's a'.
And that's no ower muckle."

" 'Deed no," assented the mother.

John said nothing. But when his visitor
rose he bade him a warm good-night.

When Robert returned to Aberdeen he was

the bearer of such a message as made poor Jessie glad at heart. This was his first experience of the sort.

When he left the cottage, he did not return to the house, but threaded the little forest of pines, climbing the hill till he came out on its bare crown, where nothing grew but heather and blaeberries. There he threw himself down, and gazed into the heavens. The sun was below the horizon; all the dazzle was gone out of the gold, and the roses were fast fading; the downy blue of the sky was trembling into stars over his head; the brown dusk was gathering in the air; and a wind full of gentleness and peace came to him from the west. He let his thoughts go where they would, and they went up into the abyss over his head.

"Lord, come to me," he cried in his heart, "for I cannot go to thee. If I were to go up and up through that awful space for ages and ages, I should never find thee. Yet there thou art. The tenderness of thy infinitude looks upon me from those heavens. Thou art in them and in me. Because thou thinkest, I think. I am thine—all thine. I abandon myself to thee. Fill me with thyself. When I am full of thee, my griefs themselves will grow golden in thy sunlight. Thou holdest them and their cause, and wilt find some nobler atonement between them than vile forgetfulness

and the death of love.   Lord, let me help those
that are wretched because they do not know
thee.   Let me tell them that thou, the Life,
must needs suffer for and with them, that they
may be partakers of thy ineffable peace.   My
life is hid in thine : take me in thy hand as
Gideon bore the pitcher to the battle.   Let me
be broken if need be, that thy light may shine
upon the lies which men tell them in thy name,
and which eat away their hearts."

Having persuaded Shargar to remain with
Mrs. Falconer for a few days, and thus remove
the feeling of offence she still cherished because
of his " munelicht flittin'," he returned to Dr.
Anderson, who now unfolded his plans for him.
These were, that he should attend the medical
classes common to the two universities, and at
the same time accompany him in his visits to
the poor.   He did not at all mean, he said, to
determine Robert's life as that of a medical man,
but from what he had learned of his feelings,
he was confident that a knowledge of medicine
would be invaluable to him.   I think the good
doctor must have foreseen the kind of life which
Falconer would at length choose to lead, and
with true and admirable wisdom, sought to prepare him for it.   However this may be, Robert
entertained the proposal gladly, went into the
scheme with his whole heart, and began to
widen that knowledge of and sympathy with

the poor which were the foundation of all his influence over them.

For a time, therefore, he gave a diligent and careful attendance upon lectures, read sufficiently, took his rounds with Dr. Anderson, and performed such duties as he delegated to his greater strength. Had the healing art been far less of an enjoyment to him than it was, he could yet hardly have failed of great progress therein; but seeing that it accorded with his best feelings, profoundest theories, and loftiest hopes, and that he received it as a work given him to do, it is not surprising that a certain faculty of cure, almost partaking of the instinctive, should have been rapidly developed in him, to the wonder and delight of his friend and master.

In this labour he again spent about four years, during which time he gathered much knowledge of human nature, learning especially to judge it from no stand-point of his own, but in every individual case to take a new position whence the nature and history of the man should appear in true relation to the yet uncompleted result. He who cannot feel the humanity of his neighbour because he is different from himself in education, habits, opinions, morals, circumstances, objects, is unfit, if not unworthy, to aid him.

Within this period Shargar had gone out to

India, where he had distinguished himself particularly on a certain harassing march. Towards the close of the four years he had leave of absence, and was on his way home. About the same time Robert, in consequence of a fever brought on by over-fatigue, was in much need of a holiday ; and Dr. Anderson proposed that he should meet Moray at Southampton.

Shargar had no expectation of seeing him, and his delight, not greater on that account, broke out more wildly. No thinnest film had grown over his heart, though in all else he was considerably changed. The army had done everything that was wanted for his outward show of man. The drawling walk had vanished, and a firm step and soldierly stride had taken its place; his bearing was free, yet dignified; his high descent came out in the ease of his carriage and manners : there could be no doubt that at last Shargar was a gentleman. His hair had changed to a kind of red chestnut. His complexion was much darkened with the Indian sun. His eyes, too, were darker, and no longer rolled slowly from one object to another, but indicated by their quick glances a mind ready to observe and as ready to resolve. His whole appearance was more than prepossessing —it was even striking.

Robert was greatly delighted with the improvement in him, and far more when he found

in, but my own shadow. In such a street as
this, however, all the shadows look as if they
belonged to another world, and had no business
here."

"I quite feel that," returned Falconer. "They
come like angels from the lovely west and the
pure air, to show that London cannot hurt
them, for it too is within the Kingdom of God
—to teach the lovers of nature, like the old or-
thodox Jew, St. Peter, that they must not call
anything common or unclean."

Shargar made no reply, and Robert glanced
round at him. He was staring with wide eyes
into, not at the crowd of vehicles that filled the
street. His face was pale, and strangely like
the Shargar of old days.

"What's the matter with you?" Robert asked
in some bewilderment.

Receiving no answer, he followed Shargar's
gaze, and saw a strange sight for London city.

In the middle of the crowd of vehicles, with
an omnibus before them, and a brewer's dray
behind them, came a line of three donkey-carts,
heaped high with bundles and articles of gipsy-
gear. The foremost was conducted by a middle-aged woman of tall, commanding aspect,
and expression both cunning and fierce. She
walked by the donkey's head carrying a short
stick, with which she struck him now and then,
but which she oftener waved over his head like

the truncheon of an excited marshal on the battle-field, accompanying its movements now with loud cries to the animal, now with loud response to the chaff of the omnibus conductor, the dray driver, and the tradesmen in carts about her. She was followed by a very handsome, olive-complexioned, wild-looking young woman, with her black hair done up in a red handkerchief, who conducted her donkey more quietly. Both seemed as much at home in the roar of Gracechurch Street as if they had been crossing a wild common. A loutish-looking young man brought up the rear with the third donkey. From the bundles on the foremost cart peeped a lovely, fair-haired, English-looking child.

Robert took all this in a moment. The same moment Shargar's spell was broken.

"Lord, it *is* my mither!" he cried, and darted under a horse's neck into the middle of the *ruck.*

He needled his way through till he reached the woman. She was swearing at a cabman whose wheel had caught the point of her donkey's shaft, and was hauling him round. Heedless of everything, Shargar threw his arms about her, crying,

"Mither! mither!"

"Nane o' yer blastit humbug!" she exclaimed, as with a vigorous throw and a wriggle, she freed herself from his embrace and pushed him away.

The moment she had him at arm's length, however, her hand closed upon his arm, and her other hand went up to her brow. From underneath it her eyes shot up and down him from head to foot, and he could feel her hand closing and relaxing and closing again, as if she were trying to force her long nails into his flesh. He stood motionless, waiting the result of her scrutiny, utterly unconscious that he caused a congestion in the veins of London, for every vehicle within sight of the pair had stopped. Falconer said a strange silence fell upon the street, as if all the things in it had been turned into shadows.

A rough voice, which sounded as if all London must have heard it, broke the silence. It was the voice of the cabman who had been in altercation with the woman. Bursting into an insulting laugh, he used words with regard to her which it is better to leave unrecorded. The same instant Shargar freed himself from her grasp, and stood by the fore wheel of the cab.

"Get down!" he said, in a voice that was not the less impressive that it was low and hoarse.

The fellow saw what he meant, and whipped his horse. Shargar sprung on the box, and dragged him down all but headlong.

"Now," he said, "beg my mother's pardon."

" Be damned if I do, &c., &c.," said the cabman.

" Then defend yourself," said Shargar. " Robert."

Falconer was watching it all, and was by his side in a moment.

"Come on, you, &c., &c.," cried the cabman, plucking up heart and putting himself in fighting shape. He looked one of those insolent fellows whom none see discomfited more gladly than the honest men of his own class. The same moment he lay between his horse's feet.

Shargar turned to Robert, and saying only, " There, Robert !" turned again towards the woman. The cabman rose bleeding, and, desiring no more of the same, climbed on his box, and went off, belabouring his horse, and pursued by a roar from the street, for the spectators were delighted at his punishment.

" Now, mother," said Shargar, panting with excitement.

" What ca' they ye ?" she asked, still doubtful, but as proud of being defended as if the coarse words of her assailant had had no truth in them. " Ye canna be my lang-leggit Geordie."

" What for no ?"

" Ye're a gentleman, faith."

" An' what for no, again ?" returned Shargar, beginning to smile.

" Weel, it's weel speired. Yer father was ane

ony gait—gin sae be 'at ye are as ye say."

Moray put his head close to hers, and whispered some words that nobody heard but herself.

"It's ower lang syne to min' upo' that," she said in reply, with a look of cunning consciousness ill settled upon her fine features. "But ye can be naebody but my Geordie. Haith, man!" she went on, regarding him once more from head to foot, "but ye're a credit to me, I maun alloo. Weel, gie me a sovereign, an' I s' never come near ye.

Poor Shargar in his despair turned half mechanically towards Robert. He felt that it was time to interfere.

"You forget, mother," said Shargar, turning again to her, and speaking English now, "it was I that claimed you, and not you that claimed me."

She seemed to have no idea of what he meant.

"Come up the road here, to oor public, an' tak a glaiss, wuman," said Falconer. "Dinna haud the fowk luikin' at ye."

The temptation of a glass of something strong, and the hope of getting money out of them, caused an instant acquiescence. She said a few words to the young woman, who proceeded at once to tie her donkey's head to the tail of the other cart.

"Shaw the gait than," said the elder, turning again to Falconer.

Shargar and he led the way to St. Paul's
Churchyard, and the woman followed faithfully.
The waiter stared when they entered.

"Bring a glass of whisky," said Falconer, as
he passed on to their private room. When the
whisky arrived, she tossed it off, and looked as
if she would like another glass.

"Yer father 'ill hae ta'en ye up, I'm thinkin',
laddie?" she said, turning to her son.

"No," answered Shargar, gloomily. "There's
the man that took me up."

"An' wha may ye be?" she asked, turning to
Falconer.

"Mr. Falconer," said Shargar.

"No a son o' Anerew Faukner?" she asked
again, with evident interest.

"The same," answered Robert.

"Weel, Geordie," she said, turning once more
to her son, "it's like mither, like father to the
twa o' ye."

"Did you know my father?" asked Robert,
eagerly.

Instead of answering him she made another
remark to her son.

"He needna be ashamed o' *your* company,
ony gait—queer kin' o' a mither 'at I am."

"He never was ashamed of my company,"
said Shargar, still gloomily.

"Ay, I kent yer father weel eneuch," she said,
now answering Robert—"mair by token 'at I

saw him last nicht. He was luikin' nae that ill."

Robert sprung from his seat, and caught her by the arm.

"Ow! ye needna gang into sic a flurry. *He* 'll no come near ye, I s' warran'."

"Tell me where he is," said Robert. "Where did you see him? I'll gie ye a' 'at I hae gin ye'll tak me till him."

"Hooly! hooly! Wha's to gang luikin' for a thrum in a hay-sow?" returned she, coolly. "I only said 'at I saw him."

"But are ye sure it was him?" asked Falconer.

"Ay, sure eneuch," she answered.

"What maks ye sae sure?"

"'Cause I never was vrang yet. Set a man ance atween my twa een, an' that 'll be twa 'at kens him whan 's ain mither 's forgotten 'im."

"Did you speak to him?"

"Maybe ay, an' maybe no. I didna come here to be hecklet afore a jury."

"Tell me what he's like," said Robert, agitated with eager hope.

"Gin ye dinna ken what he's like, what for suld ye tak the trouble to speir? But 'deed ye'll ken what he's like whan ye fa' in wi' him," she added, with a vindictive laugh—vindictive because he had given her only one glass of strong drink.

With the laugh she rose, and made for the door. They rose at the same moment to de-

tain her. Like one who knew at once to fight
and flee, she turned and stunned them as with a
blow.

" She's a fine yoong thing, yon sister o' yours,
Geordie. She'll be worth siller by the time she's
had a while at the schuil."

The men looked at each other aghast. When
they turned their eyes she had vanished. They
rushed to the door, and, parting, searched in
both directions. But they were soon satisfied
that it was of no use. Probably she had found
a back way into Paternoster Row, whence the
outlets are numerous.

CHAPTER IV.

THE DOCTOR'S DEATH.

BUT now that Falconer had a ground, even thus shadowy, for hoping—I cannot say believing—that his father might be in London, he could not return to Aberdeen. Moray, who had no heart to hunt for his mother, left the next day by the steamer. Falconer took to wandering about the labyrinthine city, and in a couple of months knew more about the metropolis—the west end excepted—than most people who had lived their lives in it. The west end is no doubt a considerable exception to make, but Falconer sought only his father, and the west end was the place where he was least likely to find him. Day and night he wandered into all sorts of places : the worse they looked the more attractive he found them. It became almost a craze with him. He could not pass a dirty court or low-browed archway. He *might* be there. Or he might have been there. Or it was such a place as he would choose for shelter.

He knew to what such a life as his must have tended.

At first he was attracted only by tall elderly men. Such a man he would sometimes follow till his following made him turn and demand his object. If there was no suspicion of Scotch in his tone, Falconer easily apologized. If there was, he made such replies as might lead to some betrayal. He could not defend the course he was adopting : it had not the shadow of probability upon its side. Still the greatest successes the world has ever beheld had been at one time the greatest improbabilities. He could not choose but go on, for as yet he could think of no other way.

Neither could a man like Falconer long confine his interest to this immediate object, especially after he had, in following it, found opportunity of being useful. While he still made it his main object to find his father, that object became a centre from which radiated a thousand influences upon those who were as sheep that had no shepherd. He fell back into his old ways at Aberdeen, only with a boundless sphere to work in, and with the hope of finding his father to hearten him. He haunted the streets at night, went into all places of entertainment, often to the disgust of senses and soul, and made his way into the lowest forms of life without introduction or protection.

There was a certain stately air of the hills about him which was often mistaken for country inexperience, and men thought in consequence to make gain or game of him. But such found their mistake, and if not soon, then the more completely. Far from provoking or even meeting hostility, he soon satisfied those that persisted, that it was dangerous. In two years he became well known to the poor of a large district, especially on both sides of Shoreditch, for whose sake he made the exercise of his profession though not an object yet a ready accident.

He lived in lodgings in John Street—the same in which I found him when I came to know him. He made few acquaintances, and they were chiefly the house-surgeons of hospitals—to which he paid frequent visits.

He always carried a book in his pocket, but did not read much. On Sundays he generally went to some one of the many lonely heaths or commons of Surrey with his New Testament. When weary in London, he would go to the reading-room of the British Museum for an hour or two. He kept up a regular correspondence with Dr. Anderson.

At length he received a letter from him, which occasioned his immediate departure for Aberdeen. Until now, his friend, who was entirely satisfied with his mode of life, and supplied him freely with money, had not even expressed a

wish to recall him, though he had often spoken of
visiting him in London.   It now appeared that,
unwilling to cause him any needless anxiety, he
had abstained from mentioning the fact that his
health had been declining. He had got suddenly worse, and Falconer hastened to obey the
summons he had sent him in consequence.

With a heavy heart he walked up to the hos-
pitable door, recalling as he ascended the steps
how he had stood there a helpless youth, in want
of a few pounds to save his hopes, when this
friend received him and bid him God-speed on
the path he desired to follow. In a moment more
he was shown into the study, and was passing
through it to go to the cottage-room, when
Johnston laid his hand on his arm.

" The maister's no up yet, sir," he said, with a
very solemn look. " He's been desperate efter
seein' ye, and I maun gang an' lat him ken 'at
ɣe're here at last, for fear it suld be ower muckle
for him, seein' ye a' at ance. But eh, sir !" he added, the tears gathering in his eyes, " ye'll
hardly ken 'im. He's that changed !"

Johnston left the study by the door to the
cottage—Falconer had never known the doctor
sleep there—and returning a moment after, invited him to enter. In the bed in the recess
—the room unchanged, with its deal table, and
its sanded floor—lay the form of his friend.
Falconer hastened to the bedside, kneeled down,

and took his hand speechless. The doctor was silent too, but a smile overspread his countenance, and revealed his inward satisfaction. Robert's heart was full, and he could only gaze on the worn face. At length he was able to speak.

"What for didna ye sen' for me," he said. "Ye never tellt me ye was ailin'."

"Because you were doing good, Robert, my boy; and I who had done so little had no right to interrupt what you were doing. I wonder if God will give me another chance. I would fain do better. I don't think I *could* sit singing psalms to all eternity," he added with a smile.

"Whatever good I may do afore my turn comes, I hae you to thank for 't. Eh, doctor, gin it hadna been for you!"

Robert's feelings overcame him. He resumed, brokenly:

"Ye gae me a man to believe in, whan my ain father had forsaken me, and my frien' was awa to God. Ye hae made me, doctor. Wi' meat an' drink an' learnin' an' siller, an' a'thing at ance, ye hae made me."

"Eh, Robert!" said the dying man, half rising on his elbow, "to think what God maks us a' to ane anither! My father did ten times for me what I hae dune for you. As I lie here thinkin' I may see him afore a week's ower, I'm jist a bairn again."

As he spoke, the polish of his speech was gone,

and the social refinement of his countenance
with it. The face of his ancestors, the noble,
sensitive, heart-full, but rugged, bucolic, and
weather-beaten through centuries of windy
ploughing, hail-stormed sheep-keeping, long-
paced seed-sowing, and multiform labour, surely
not less honourable in the sight of the working
God than the fighting of the noble, came back
in the face of the dying physician. From that
hour to his death he spoke the rugged dialect of
his fathers.

A day or two after this, Robert again sitting
by his bedside,

"I dinna ken," he said, "whether it's richt—
but I hae nae fear o' deith, an' yet I canna say
I'm sure aboot onything. I hae seen mony a
ane dee that cud hae no faith i' the Saviour; but
I never saw that fear that some gude fowk wud
hae ye believe maun come at the last. I wadna
like to tak to ony papistry; but I never cud mak
oot frae the Bible—and I read mair at it i' the
jungle than maybe ye wad think—that it 's a'
ower wi' a body at their deith. I never heard
them bring foret ony text but ane—the maist
ridiculous hash 'at ever ye heard—to justifee 't."

"I ken the text ye mean—'As the tree falleth
so it shall lie,' or something like that—'at they
say King Solomon wrote, though better scholars
say his tree had fa'en mony a lang year afore
that text saw the licht. I dinna believe sic a

read thus, one fading afternoon, the doctor broke out with:

"Eh, Robert, the patience o' him! *He* didna quench the smokin' flax. There's little fire aboot me, but surely I ken in my ain hert some o' the risin' smoke o' the sacrifice. Eh! sic words as they are! An' he was gaein' doon to the grave himsel', no half my age, as peacefu', though the road was sae rouch, as gin he had been gae-in' hame till 's father."

"Sae he was," returned Robert.

"Ay; but here am I lyin' upo' my bed, slip-pin' easy awa. An' there was he——"

The old man ceased. The sacred story was too sacred for speech. Robert sat with the New Testament open before him on the bed.

"The mair the words o' Jesus come into me," the doctor began again, "the surer I am o' see-in' my auld Brahmin frien', Robert. It's true I thought his religion not only began but end-ed inside him. It was a' a booin' doon afore and an aspirin' up into the bosom o' the infin-ite God. I dinna mean to say 'at he wasna honourable to them aboot him. And I never saw in him muckle o' that pride to the lave (*rest*) that belangs to the Brahmin. It was raither a stately kin'ness than that condescen-sion which is the vice o' Christians. But he had naething to do wi' them. The first comman'-ment was a' he kent. He loved God—nae a God

like Jesus Christ, but the God he kent—and that
was a' he could.   The second comman'ment—
that glorious recognition o' the divine in humanity makin' 't fit and needfu' to be loved, that
claim o' God upon and for his ain bairns, that love
o' the neebour as yer'sel—he didna ken.   Still
there was religion in him; and he who died
for the sins o' the whole world has surely been
revealed to him lang er' noo, and throu the
knowledge o' him, he noo dwalls in that God
efter whom he aspired."

Here was the outcome of many talks which
Robert and the doctor had had together, as they
laboured amongst the poor.

"Did ye never try," Robert asked, " to lat him
ken aboot the comin' o' God to his world in
Jesus Christ ?"

"I couldna do muckle that way honestly, my
ain faith was sae poor and sma'.   But I tellt
him what Christians believed.   I tellt him aboot
the character and history o' Christ.   But it didna
seem to tak muckle hauld o' him.   It wasna
interesstin' till him.   Just ance whan I tellt him
some things He had said aboot his relation to
God—sic as, 'I and my Father are one,'—and
aboot the relation o' a' his disciples to God and
himsel'—' I in them, and thou in me, that they
may be made perfect in one,' he said, wi' a smile,
' The man was a good Brahmin.' "

"It's little," said Robert, " the one great com-

mandment can do withoot the other. It's little
we can ken what God to love, or hoo to love
him, withoot 'thy neighbour as thyself.' Ony
ane o' them withoot the ither stan's like the ae
factor o' a multiplication, or ae wing upo' a
laverock (*lark*)."

Towards the close of the week, he grew much
feebler. Falconer scarcely left his room. He
woke one midnight, and murmured as follows,
with many pauses for breath and strength:

"Robert, my time's near, I'm thinkin'; for,
wakin' an' sleepin', I'm a bairn again. I can
hardly believe whiles 'at my father hasna a grup
o' my han'. A meenute ago I was traivellin'
throu a terrible driftin' o' snaw—eh, hoo it
whustled and sang! and the cauld o' 't was
stingin'; but my father had a grup o' me, an' I
jist despised it, an' was stampin' 't doon wi' my
wee bit feet, for I was like saven year auld or
thereaboots. An' syne I thocht I heard my
mither singin', and kent by that that the ither
was a dream. I'm thinkin' a hantle 'ill luik
dreamy afore lang. Eh! I wonner what the final
waukin' 'ill be like."

After a pause he resumed:

"Robert, my dear boy, ye 're i' the richt gait.
Haud on an' lat naething turn ye aside. Man,
it's a great comfort to me to think that ye're
my ain flesh and blude, an' nae that far aff.
My father an' your great-gran'father upo' the

gran'mither's side war ain brithers. I wonner
hoo far doon it wad gang. Ye're the only ane
upo' my father's side, you and yer father, gin he
be alive, that I hae sib to me. My will's i' the
bottom drawer upo' the left han' i' my writin'
table i' the leebrary :—I hae left ye ilka plack
'at I possess. Only there's ae thing that I want
ye to do. First o' a', ye maun gang on as yer
doin' in London for ten year mair. Gin deein'
men hae ony o' that foresicht that's been attree-
buted to them in a' ages, it's borne in upo' me
that ye *wull* see yer father again. At a' events,
ye'll be helpin' some ill-faured sowls to a clean
face and a bonny. But gin ye dinna fa' in wi'
yer father within ten year, ye maun behaud a
wee, an' jist pack up yer box, an' gang awa'
ower the sea to Calcutta, an' du what I hae tellt
ye to do i' that wull. I bind ye by nae promise,
Robert, an' I winna hae nane. Things micht
happen to put ye in a terrible difficulty wi' a
promise. I'm only tellin' ye what I wad like.
Especially gin ye hae fund yer father, ye maun
gang by yer ain jeedgment aboot it, for there 'll
be a hantle to do wi' him efter ye hae gotten a
grup o' 'im. An' noo, I maun lie still, an' may
be sleep again, for I hae spoken ower muckle."

Hoping that he would sleep and wake yet
again, Robert sat still. After an hour, he looked,
and saw that, although hitherto much oppressed,
he was now breathing like a child. There was

no sign save of past suffering : his countenance
was peaceful as if he had already entered into
his rest. Robert withdrew, and again seated
himself. And the great universe became to him
as a bird brooding over the breaking shell of the
dying man.

On either hand we behold a birth, of which,
as of the moon, we see but half. We are outside the one, waiting for a life from the unknown; we are inside the other, watching the
departure of a spirit from the womb of the
world into the unknown. To the region whither
he goes, the man enters newly born. We forget that it is a birth, and call it a death. The
body he leaves behind is but the *placenta* by
which he drew his nourishment from his mother
Earth. And as the child-bed is watched on
earth with anxious expectancy, so the couch of
the dying, as we call them, may be surrounded
by the birth-watchers of the other world, waiting like anxious servants to open the door to
which this world is but the wind-blown porch.

Extremes meet. As a man draws nigh to his
second birth, his heart looks back to his childhood. When Dr. Anderson knew that he was
dying, he retired into the *simulacrum* of his
father's *benn end*.

As Falconer sat thinking, the doctor spoke.
They were low, faint, murmurous sounds, for the
lips were nearly at rest. Wanted no more for

utterance, they were going back to the holy dust, which is God's yet.

"Father, father!" he cried quickly, in the tone and speech of a Scotch laddie, "I'm gaein' doon. Haud a grup o' my han'."

When Robert hurried to the bedside, he found that the last breath had gone in the words. The thin right hand lay partly closed, as if it had been grasping a larger hand. On the face lay confidence just ruffled with apprehension: the latter melted away, and nothing remained but that awful and beautiful peace which is the farewell of the soul to its servant.

Robert knelt and thanked God for the noble man.

CHAPTER V.

A TALK WITH GRANNIE.

DR. ANDERSON'S body was, according to the fine custom of many of the people of Aberdeen, borne to the grave by twelve stalwart men in black, with broad round *bonnets* on their heads, the one-half relieving the other—a privilege of the company of shore-porters. Their exequies are thus freed from the artificial, grotesque, and pagan horror given by obscene mutes, frightful hearse, horses, and feathers. As soon as, in the beautiful phrase of the Old Testament, John Anderson was thus gathered to his fathers, Robert went to pay a visit to his grandmother.

Dressed to a point in the same costume in which he had known her from childhood, he found her little altered in appearance. She was one of those who instead of stooping with age, settle downwards: she was still as erect as ever, though shorter. Her step was feebler, and

when she prayed, her voice quavered more.
On her face sat the same settled, almost hard
repose, as ever; but her behaviour was still
more gentle than when he had seen her
last. Notwithstanding, however, that time had
wrought so little change in her appearance,
Robert felt that somehow the mist of a separation between her world and his was gathering;
that she was, as it were, fading from his sight
and presence, like the moon towards "her interlunar cave." Her face was gradually turning
from him towards the land of light.

"I hae buried my best frien' but yersel',
granny," he said, as he took a chair close by
her side, where he used to sit when he read the
Bible and Boston to her.

"I trust he's happy. He was a douce and a
weel-behaved man; and ye hae rizzon to respec' his memory. Did he dee the deith o' the
richteous, think ye, laddie?"

"I do think that, grannie. He loved God and
his Saviour."

"The Lord be praised!" said Mrs. Falconer.
"I had guid houps o' 'im in 's latter days.
And fowk says he 's made a rich man o' ye,
Robert?"

"He 's left me ilka thing, excep' something
till 's servan's—wha hae weel deserved it."

"Eh, Robert! but it's a terrible snare. Siller 's
an awfu' thing. My puir Anerew never begud

to gang the ill gait, till he began to hae ower muckle siller. But it badena lang wi' 'im."

"But it's no an ill thing itsel', grannie; for God made siller as weel 's ither things."

"He thinksna muckle o' 't, though, or he wad gie mair o' 't to some fowk. But as ye say, it's his, and gin ye hae grace to use 't aricht, it may be made a great blessin' to yersel' and ither fowk. But eh, laddie! tak guid tent 'at ye ride upo' the tap o' 't, an' no lat it rise like a muckle jaw (*billow*) ower yer heid; for it's an awfu' thing to be droont in riches."

"Them 'at prays no to be led into temptation hae a chance—haena they, grannie?"

"That hae they, Robert. And to be plain wi' ye, I haena that muckle fear o' ye; for I hae heard the kin' o' life 'at ye hae been leadin'. God's hearkent to my prayers for you; and gin ye gang on as ye hae begun, my prayers, like them o' David the son o' Jesse, are endit. Gang on, my dear lad, gang on to pluck brands frae the burnin'. Haud oot a helpin' han' to ilka son and dauchter o' Adam 'at will tak a grip o' 't. Be a burnin' an' a shinin' licht, that men may praise, no you, for ye're but clay i' the han's o' the potter, but yer Father in heaven. Tak the drunkard frae his whusky, the deboshed frae his debosh, the sweirer frae his aiths, the leear frae his lees; and giena ony o' them ower muckle o' yer siller at ance, for fear 'at they grow fat an' kick an' defy God and you. That's my advice to ye, Robert."

"And I houp I'll be able to haud gey and near till 't, grannie, for it's o' the best. But wha tellt ye what I was aboot in Lonnon ?"

"Himsel'."

"Dr. Anderson ?"

"Ay, jist himsel'. I hae had letter upo' letter frae 'im aboot you and a' 'at ye was aboot. He keepit me acquaint wi' 't a'."

This fresh proof of his friend's affection touched Robert deeply. He had himself written often to his grandmother, but he had never entered into any detail of his doings, although the thought of her was ever at hand beside the thought of his father.

"Do ye ken, grannie, what's at the hert o' my houps i' the meesery an' degradation that I see frae mornin' to nicht, and aftener yet frae nicht to mornin' i' the back closes and wynds o' the great city ?"

"I trust it's the glory o' God, laddie."

"I houp that's no a' thegither wantin', grannie. For I love God wi' a' my hert. But I doobt it's aftener the savin' o' my earthly father nor the glory o' my heavenly ane that I'm thinkin' o'."

Mrs. Falconer heaved a deep sigh.

"God grant ye success, Robert," she said. "But that canna be richt."

"What canna be richt ?"

" No to put the glory o' God first and foremost."

" Weel, grannie; but a body canna rise to the heicht o' grace a' at ance, nor yet in ten, or twenty year. Maybe gin I do richt, I may be able to come to that or a' be dune. An' efter a', I'm sure I love God mair nor my father. But I canna help thinkin' this, that gin God heardna ae sang o' glory frae this ill-doin' earth o' his, he wadna be nane the waur; but——"

" Hoo ken ye that?" interrupted his grandmother.

" Because he wad be as gude and great and grand as ever."

" Ow ay."

" But what wad come o' my father wantin' his salvation? He can waur want that, remainin' the slave o' iniquity, than God can want his glory. Forby, ye ken there's nae glory to God like the repentin' o' a sinner, justifeein' God, an' sayin' till him—' Father, ye're a' richt, an' I'm a' wrang.' What greater glory can God hae nor that?"

" It's a' true 'at ye say. But still gin God cares for that same glory, ye oucht to think o' that first, afore even the salvation o' yer father?"

" Maybe ye're richt, grannie. An' gin it be as ye say—he's promised to lead us into a' trowth, an' he'll lead me into that trowth. But I'm thinkin' it's mair for oor sakes than his ain 'at he cares aboot his glory. I dinna believe 'at he thinks

F 2

aboot his glory excep' for the sake o' the trowth
an' men's herts deein' for want o' 't."

Mrs. Falconer thought for a moment.

" It may be 'at ye 're richt, laddie ; but ye hae
a way o' sayin' things 'at 's some fearsome."

" God 's nae like a prood man to tak offence,
grannie.   There's naething pleases him like the
trowth, an' there's naething displeases him like
leein', particularly whan it's by way o' uphaudin'
him.   He wants nae sic uphaudin.'   Noo, *ye* say
things aboot him whiles 'at soun's to me fearsome."

" What kin' o' things are they, laddie ?" asked
the old lady with offence glooming in the back-
ground.

" Sic like as whan ye speyk aboot him as gin
he was a puir prood bailey-like body, fu' o' his
ain importance, an' ready to be doon upo' onybody 'at didna ca' him by the name o' 's office—
ay think-thinkin' aboot 's ain glory ; in place
o' the quaiet, michty, gran', self-forgettin', a'-
creatin', a'-uphaudin,' eternal bein', wha took
the form o' man in Christ Jesus, jist that he
micht hae 't in 's pooer to beir and be humblet
for oor sakes.   Eh, grannie ! think o' the face o'
that man o' sorrows, that never said a hard
word till a sinfu' wuman, or a despised publican :
was he thinkin' aboot 's ain glory, think ye ?
An' we hae no richt to say we ken God save in
the face o' Christ Jesus.   Whatever 's no like
Christ is no like God."

"But, laddie, he cam to saitisfee God's justice by sufferin' the punishment due to oor sins; to turn aside his wrath an' curse; to reconcile him to us. Sae he cudna be *a'thegither* like God."

"He did naething o' the kin', grannie. It's a' a lee that. He cam to saitisfee God's justice by giein' him back his bairns; by garrin' them see that God was just; by sendin' them greetin' hame to fa' at his feet, an' grip his knees an' say, 'Father, ye 're i' the richt.' He cam to lift the weicht o' the sins that God had curst aff o' the shoothers o' them 'at did them, by makin' them turn agen them, an' be for God an' no for sin. And there isna a word o' reconceelin' God till 's in a' the Testament, for there was no need o' that: it was us that needed to be reconcilet to him. An' sae he bore oor sins and carried oor sorrows; for those sins comin' oot in the multitudes—ay and in his ain disciples as weel, caused him no en' o' grief o' mind an' pain o' body, as a'body kens. It wasna his ain sins, for he had nane, but oors, that caused him sufferin'; and he took them awa'—they're vainishin' even noo frae the earth, though it doesna luik like it in Rag-fair or Petti-coat-lane. An' for oor sorrows—they jist garred him greit. His richteousness jist annihilates oor guilt, for it's a great gulf that swallows up and destroys 't. And sae he gae his life a ransom for us: and he is the life o' the world. He took oor sins upo' him, for he cam into the middle o

them an' took them up—by no sleicht o' han',
by no quibblin' o' the lawyers, aboot imputin'
his richteousness to us, and sic like, which is no
to be found i' the Bible at a', though I dinna
say that there's no possible meanin' i' the phrase,
but he took them and took them awa'; and
here am I, grannie, growin' oot o' my sins in
consequennce, and there are ye, grannie, growin'
oot o' yours in consequennce, an, haein' nearhan'
dune wi' them a'thegither er this time."

"I wis that may be true, laddie. But I
carena hoo ye put it," returned his grandmother,
bewildered no doubt with this outburst, "sae
be that ye put him first an' last an' i' the mids'
o' a' thing, an' say wi' a' yer hert, 'His will
be dune!'"

"Wi' a' my hert, 'His will be dune,' grannie,"
responded Robert.

"Amen, amen. And noo, laddie, duv ye
think there's ony likliheid that yer father 's
still i' the body? I dream aboot him whiles sae
lifelike that I canna believe him deid. But that's
a' freits *(superstitions)*."

"Weel, grannie, I haena the least assurance.
But I hae the mair houp. Wad ye ken him
gin ye saw him?"

"Ken him!" she cried; "I wad ken him gin
he had been no to say four, but forty days i' the
sepulchre! My ain Anerew! Hoo cud ye speir
sic a queston, laddie?"

"He maun be sair changed, grannie. He maun be turnin' auld by this time."

"Auld! Sic like 's yersel, laddie.—Hoots, hoots! ye're richt. I am forgettin'. But nane-theless wad I ken him."

"I wis I kent what he was like. I saw him ance—hardly twise, but a' that I min' upo' wad stan' me in ill stead amo' the streets o' Lonnon."

"I doobt that," returned Mrs. Falconer—a form of expression rather oddly indicating sym-pathetic and somewhat regretful agreement with what has been said. "But," she went on, "I can lat ye see a pictur' o' 'im, though I doobt it winna shaw sae muckle to you as to me. He had it paintit to gie to yer mother upo' their weddin' day. Och hone! She did the like for him; but what cam o' that ane, I dinna ken."

Mrs. Falconer went into the little closet to the old bureau, and bringing out the miniature, gave it to Robert. It was the portrait of a young man in antiquated blue coat and white waistcoat, looking innocent, and, it must be confessed, dull and uninteresting. It had been painted by a travelling artist, and probably his skill did not reach to expression. It brought to Robert's mind no faintest shadow of recollec-tion. It did not correspond in the smallest de-gree to what seemed his vague memory, per-haps half imagination, of the tall worn man whom he had seen that Sunday. He could not have a

hope that this would give him the slightest aid
in finding him of whom it had once been a shadowy resemblance at least.

"Is 't like him, grannie?" he asked.

As if to satisfy herself once more ere she replied, she took the miniature, and gazed at it
for some time. Then with a deep hopeless sigh,
she answered,

"Ay, it's like him; but it's no himsel'. Eh,
the bonny broo, an' the smilin' een o' him!—
smilin' upon a'body, an' upo' her maist o' a', till
he took to the drink, and waur gin waur can
be. It was a' siller an' company—company 'at
cudna be merry ohn drunken. Verily their
lauchter was like the cracklin' o' thorns aneath
a pot. Het watter and whusky was aye the
cry efter their denner an' efter their supper, till
my puir Anerew tuik till the bare whusky i' the
mornin' to fill the ebb o' the toddy. He wad
never hae dune as he did but for the whusky.
It jist drave oot a' gude and loot in a' ill."

"Wull ye lat me tak this wi' me, grannie?"
said Robert; for though the portrait was useless for identification, it might serve a further
purpose.

"Ow, ay, tak it. I dinna want it. I can see
him weel wantin' that. But I hae nae houp left
'at ye 'll ever fa' in wi' him."

"God's aye doin' unlikly things, grannie,"
said Robert, solemnly.

"He's dune a' 'at he can for him, I doobt, already."

"Duv ye think 'at God cudna save a man gin he liket, than, grannie?"

"God can do a'thing. There's nae doobt but by the gift o' his speerit he cud save a'body."

"An' ye think he's no mercifu' eneuch to do 't?"

"It winna do to meddle wi' fowk's free wull. To gar fowk be gude wad be nae gudeness."

"But gin God could actually create the free wull, dinna ye think he cud help it to gang richt, withoot ony garrin'? We ken sae little aboot it, grannie! Hoo does his speerit help onybody? Does he *gar* them 'at accep's the offer o' salvation?"

"Na, I canna think that. But he shaws them the trowth in sic a way that they jist canna bide themsel's, but maun turn to him for verra peace an' rist."

"Weel, that's something as I think. An' until I'm sure that a man has had the trowth shawn till him in sic a way 's that, I canna alloo mysel' to think that hooever he may hae sinned, he has finally rejeckit the trowth. Gin I kent that a man had seen the trowth as I hae seen 't whiles, and had deleeberately turned his back upo' 't and said, 'I'll nane o' 't,' than I doobt I wad be maist compelled to alloo that there was nae mair salvation for him, but a cer-

tain and fearfu' luikin' for o' judgment and fiery
indignation. But I dinna believe that ever man
did sae. But even than, I dinna ken."

"I did a' for him that I kent hoo to do," said
Mrs. Falconer, reflectingly. "Nicht an' mornin' an' aften midday prayin' for an' wi' him."

"Maybe ye scunnert him at it, grannie."

She gave a stifled cry of despair.

"Dinna say that, laddie, or ye'll drive me oot
o' my min'. God forgie me, gin that be true. I
deserve hell mair nor my Anerew."

"But, ye see, grannie, supposin' it war sae,
that wadna be laid to your accoont, seein' ye
did the best ye kent. Nor wad it be forgotten
to him. It wad mak a hantle difference to his
sin; it wad be a great excuse for him. An' jist
think, gin it be fair for ae human being to influence anither a' 'at they can, and that's nae
interferin' wi' their free wull—it's impossible to
measure what God cud do wi' his speerit
winnin' at them frae a' sides, and able to put
sic thouchts an' sic pictures into them as we
canna think. It wad a' be true that he tellt
them, and the trowth can never be a meddlin'
wi' the free wull."

Mrs. Falconer made no reply, but evidently
went on thinking.

She was, though not a great reader, yet a
good reader. Any book that was devout and
thoughtful she read gladly. Through some

one or other of this sort she must have been instructed concerning free will, for I do not think such notions could have formed any portion of the religious teaching she had heard. Men in that part of Scotland then believed that the free will of man was only exercised in rejecting —never in accepting the truth; and that men were saved by the gift of the spirit, given to some and not to others, according to the free will of God, in the exercise of which no reason appreciable by men, or having anything to do with their notions of love or justice had any share. In the recognition of will and choice in the acceptance of the mercy of God, Mrs. Falconer was then in advance of her time. And it is no wonder if her notions did not all hang logically together.

"At ony rate, grannie," resumed her grandson, "*I* haena dune a' for him 'at *I* can yet; and I'm no gaein' to believe onything that wad mak me remiss in my endeavour. Houp for mysel', for my father, for a'body, is what's savin' me, an' garrin' me work. An' gin ye tell me that I'm no workin' wi' God, that God's no the best an' the greatest worker aboon a', ye tak the verra hert oot o' my breist, and I dinna believe in God nae mair, an' my han's drap doon by my sides, an' my legs winna gang. No," said Robert, rising, "God 'ill gie me my father sometime, grannie; for what man can do wantin' a father ? Human bein' canna win at the hert o' things, canna ken a' the oots an' ins, a' the sides o' love, excep' he has a father amo' the lave to love ; an' I hae had nane, grannie. An' that God kens."

She made him no answer. She dared not say that he expected too much from God. Is it likely that Jesus will say so of any man or woman when he looks for faith in the earth ?

Robert went out to see some of his old friends, and when he returned it was time for supper and *worship.* These were the same as of old : a plate of porridge, and a wooden bowl of milk for the former ; a chapter and a hymn, both read, and a prayer from grannie, and then from Robert for the latter. And so they went to bed.

But Robert could not sleep. He rose and dressed himself, went up to the empty garret, looked at the stars through the skylight, knelt and prayed for his father and for all men to the Father of all, then softly descended the stairs, and went out into the street.

CHAPTER VI.

SHARGAR'S MOTHER.

IT was a warm still night in July—moonless
but not dark. There is no night there in
the summer—only a long etherial twilight. He
walked through the sleeping town so full of
memories, all quiet in his mind now—quiet as
the air that ever broods over the house where a
friend has dwelt. He left the town behind, and
walked—through the odours of grass and of
clover and of the yellow flowers on the old
earthwalls that divided the fields—sweet scents
to which the darkness is friendly, and which,
mingling with the smell of the earth itself,
reach the founts of memory sooner than even
words or tones—down to the brink of the river
that flowed scarcely murmuring through the
night, itself dark and brown as the night, from
its far-off birthplace in the peaty hills. He
crossed the footbridge and turned into the
bleachfield. Its houses were desolate, for that
trade too had died away. The machinery stood

rotting and rusting. The wheel gave no answering motion to the flow of the water that
glided away beneath it. The thundering *beatles*
were still. The huge legs of the wauk-mill
took no more seven-leagued strides nowhither.
The rubbing-boards with their thickly-fluted
surfaces no longer frothed the soap from every
side, tormenting the web of linen into a brightness to gladden the heart of the housewife
whose hands had spun the yarn. The terrible
boiler that used to send up from its depths bubbling and boiling spouts and peaks and ridges,
lay empty and cold. The little house behind,
where its awful furnace used to glow, and
which the pungent chlorine used to fill with its
fumes, stood open to the wind and the rain : he
could see the slow river through its unglazed
window beyond. The water still went slipping
and sliding through the deserted places, a
power whose use had departed. The canal,
the delight of his childhood, was nearly choked
with weeds ; it went flowing over long grasses
that drooped into it from its edges, giving a
faint gurgle once and again in its flow, as if it
feared to speak in the presence of the stars, and
escaped silently into the river far below. The
grass was no longer mown like a lawn, but was
long and deep and thick. He climbed to the
place where he had once lain and listened to
the sounds of the belt of fir-trees behind him,

hearing the voice of Nature that whispered *God*
in his ears, and there he threw himself down
once more. All the old things, the old ways,
the old glories of childhood—were they gone ?
No. Over them all, in them all, was God still.
There is no past with him. An eternal present,
He filled his soul and all that his soul had ever
filled. His history was taken up into God : it
had not vanished : his life was hid with Christ
in God. To the God of the human heart nothing that has ever been a joy, a grief, a passing interest, can ever cease to be what it has
been ; there is no fading at the breath of time,
no passing away of fashion, no dimming of old
memories in the heart of him whose being cre-
ates time. Falconer's heart rose up to him as
to his own deeper life, his indwelling deepest
spirit—above and beyond him as the heavens
are above and beyond the earth, and yet nearer
and homelier than his own most familiar
thought. "As the light fills the earth," thought
he, "so God fills what we call life. My sorrows, O God, my hopes, my joys, the upliftings
of my life are with thee, my root, my life. Thy
comfortings, my perfect God, are strength indeed !"

He rose and looked around him. While he
lay, the waning, fading moon had risen, weak
and bleared and dull. She brightened and
brightened until at last she lighted up the night

with a wan, forgetful gleam. " So should I feel," he thought, " about the past on which I am now gazing, were it not that I believe in the God who forgets nothing. That which has been, is." His eye fell on something bright in the field beyond. He would see what it was, and crossed the earthen dyke. It shone like a little moon in the grass. By humouring the reflection he reached it. It was only a cutting of *white iron*, left by some tinker. He walked on over the field, thinking of Shargar's mother. If he could but find her! He walked on and on. He had no inclination to go home. The solitariness of the night, the *uncanniness* of the moon, prevents most people from wandering far: Robert had learned long ago to love the night, and to feel at home with every aspect of God's world. How this peace contrasted with the nights in London streets! this grass with the dark flow of the Thames! these hills and those clouds half melted into moonlight with the lanes blazing with gas! He thought of the child who, taken from London for the first time, sent home the message : " Tell mother that it's dark in the country at night." Then his thoughts turned again to Shargar's mother! Was it not possible, being a wanderer far and wide, that she might be now in Rothieden? Such people have a love for their old haunts, stronger than that of orderly members of society for their old homes. He turned back, and did not know where he was. But the lines of the hill-tops directed him. He hastened to the town, and went straight through the sleeping streets to the back wynd where he had found Shargar sitting on the doorstep. Could he believe his eyes? A feeble light was burning in the shed. Some other poverty-stricken bird of the night, however, might be there, and not she who could perhaps guide him to the goal of his earthly life. He drew near, and peeped in at the broken window. A heap of something lay in a corner, watched only by a long-snuffed candle.

The heap moved, and a voice called out querulously—

"Is that you, Shargar, ye shochlin deevil?"

Falconer's heart leaped. He hesitated no longer, but lifted the latch and entered. He took up the candle, snuffed it as he best could, and approached the woman. When the light fell on her face she sat up, staring wildly with eyes that shunned and sought it.

"Wha are ye that winna lat me dee in peace and quaietness?"

"I'm Robert Falconer."

"Come to speir efter yer ne'er-do-weel o' a father, I reckon," she said.

"Yes," he answered.

"Wha's that ahin' ye?"

"Naebody's ahin' me," answered Robert.

"Dinna lee. Wha's that ahin' the door?"

"Naebody. I never tell lees."

"Whaur's Shargar? What for doesna he come till 's mither?"

"He's hynd awa' ower the seas—a captain o' sodgers."

"It's a lee. He's an ill-faured scoonrel no to come till 's mither an' bid her gude-bye, an' her gaein' to hell."

"Gin ye speir at Christ, he'll tak ye oot o' the verra mou' o' hell, wuman."

"Christ! wha's that? Ow, ay! It's him 'at they preach aboot i' the kirks. Na, na. There's nae gude o' that. There's nae time to repent noo. I doobt sic repentance as mine wadna gang for muckle wi' the likes o' him."

"The likes o' him 's no to be gotten. He cam to save the likes o' you an' me."

"The likes o' you an' me! said ye, laddie? There's no like atween you and me. He'll hae naething to say to me, but gang to hell wi' ye for a bitch."

"He never said sic a word in 's life. He wad say, 'Poor thing! she was ill-used. Ye maunna sin ony mair. Come, and I'll help ye.' He wad say something like that. He'll save a body whan she wadna think it."

"An' I hae gien my bonnie bairn to the deevil wi' my ain han's! She'll come to hell efter me

to girn at me, an' set them on me wi' their reid
het taings, and curse me. Och hone! och hone!"

"Hearken to me," said Falconer, with as
much authority as he could assume. But she
rolled herself over again in the corner, and lay
groaning.

"Tell me whaur she is," said Falconer, "and
I'll tak her oot o' their grup, whaever they
be."

She sat up again, and stared at him for a few
moments without speaking.

"I left her wi' a wuman waur nor mysel',"
she said at length. "God forgie me."

"He will forgie ye, gin ye tell me whaur she
is."

"Do ye think he will? Eh, Maister Faukner! The wuman bides in a coort aff o' Clare
Market. I dinna min' upo' the name o' 't,
though I cud gang till 't wi' my een steekit.
Her name's Widow Walker—an auld rowdie—
damn her sowl!"

"Na, na, ye maunna say that gin ye want to
be forgien yersel'. I'll fin' her oot. An' I'm thinkin' it winna be lang or I hae a grup o' her.
I'm gaein' back to Lonnon in twa days or
three."

"Dinna gang till I'm deid. Bide an' haud
the deevil aff o' me. He has a grup o' my hert
noo, rivin' at it wi' his lang nails—as lang's
bird's nebs."

"I'll bide wi' ye till we see what can be dune for ye. What's the maitter wi' ye? I'm a doctor noo."

There was not a chair or box or stool on which to sit down. He therefore kneeled beside her. He felt her pulse, questioned her, and learned that she had long been suffering from an internal complaint, which had within the last week grown rapidly worse. He saw that there was no hope of her recovery, but while she lived he gave himself to her service as to that of a living soul capable of justice and love. The night was more than warm, but she had fits of shivering. He wrapped his coat round her, and wiped from the poor degraded face the damps of suffering. The woman-heart was alive still, for she took the hand that ministered to her and kissed it with a moan. When the morning came she fell asleep. He crept out and went to his grandmother's, where he roused Betty, and asked her to get him some peat and coals. Finding his grandmother awake, he told her all, and taking the coals and the peat, carried them to the hut, where he managed, with some difficulty, to light a fire on the hearth; after which he sat on the doorstep till Betty appeared with two men carrying a mattress and some bedding. The noise they made awoke her.

"Dinna tak me," she cried. "I winna do 't again, an' I'm deein', I tell ye I'm deein', and

that'll clear a' scores—o' this side ony gait," she
added.

They lifted her upon the mattress, and made
her more comfortable than perhaps she had ever
been in her life. But it was only her illness that
made her capable of prizing such comfort. In
health, the heather on a hill side was far more to
her taste than bed and blankets. She had a wild,
roving, savage nature, and the wind was dearer
to her than house-walls. She had come of ancestors—and it was a poor little atom of truth
that a soul bred like this woman could have
been born capable of entertaining. But she too
was eternal—and surely not to be fixed for ever
in a bewilderment of sin and ignorance—a wild-
eyed soul staring about in hell-fire for want of
something it could not understand and had
never beheld—by the changeless mandate of
the God of love! She was in less pain than
during the night, and lay quietly gazing at the
fire. Things awful to another would no doubt
cross her memory without any accompanying
sense of dismay; tender things would return
without moving her heart; but Falconer had a
hold of her now. Nothing could be done for
her body except to render its death as easy as
might be; but something might be done for
herself. He made no attempt to produce this
or that condition of mind in the poor creature.
He never made such attempts. "How can I tell

the next lesson a soul is capable of learning?" he
would say. " The Spirit of God is the teacher.
My part is to tell the good news. Let that
work as it ought, as it can, as it will." He
knew that pain is with some the only harbinger
that can prepare the way for the entrance of
kindness : it is not understood till then. In the
lulls of her pain he told her about the man
Christ Jesus—what he did for the poor creatures who came to him—how kindly he spoke
to them—how he cured them. He told her
how gentle he was with the sinning women,
how he forgave them and told them to do so no
more. He left the story without comment to
work that faith which alone can redeem from
selfishness and bring into contact with all that
is living and productive of life, for to believe in
him is to lay hold of eternal life : he is the Life
—therefore the life of men. She gave him but
little encouragement : he did not need it, for he
believed in the Life. But her outcries were no
longer accompanied with that fierce and dreadful language in which she sought relief at first.
He said to himself, " What matter if I see no
sign ? I am doing my part. Who can tell,
when the soul is free from the distress of the
body, when sights and sounds have vanished
from her, and she is silent in the eternal, with
the terrible past behind her, and clear to her
consciousness, how the words I have spoken to

her may yet live and grow in her; how the kindness God has given me to show her may help her to believe in the root of all kindness, in the everlasting love of her Father in heaven? That she can feel at all is as sure a sign of life as the adoration of an ecstatic saint."

He had no difficulty now in getting from her what information she could give him about his father. It seemed to him of the greatest import, though it amounted only to this, that when he was in London, he used to lodge at the house of an old Scotchwoman of the name of Macallister, who lived in Paradise Gardens, somewhere between Bethnal Green and Spitalfields. Whether he had been in London lately, she did not know; but if anybody could tell him where he was, it would be Mrs. Macallister.

His heart filled with gratitude and hope and the surging desire for the renewal of his London labours. But he could not leave the dying woman till she was beyond the reach of his comfort : he was her keeper now. And " he that believeth shall not make haste." Labour without perturbation, readiness without hurry, no haste, and no hesitation, was the divine law of his activity.

Shargar's mother breathed her last holding his hand. They were alone. He kneeled by the bed, and prayed to God, saying—

" Father, this woman is in thy hands. Take

thou care of her, as thou hast taken care of her hitherto. Let the light go up in her soul, that she may love and trust thee, O light, O gladness. I thank thee that thou hast blessed me with this ministration. Now lead me to my father. Thine is the kingdom, and the power, and the glory, for ever and ever. Amen."

He rose and went to his grandmother and told her all. She put her arms round his neck, and kissed him, and said,

"God bless ye, my bonny lad. And he will bless ye. He will; he will. Noo gang yer wa's, and do the wark he gies ye to do. Only min', it's no you; it's Him."

The next morning, the sweet winds of his childhood wooing him to remain yet a day among their fields, he sat on the top of the Aberdeen coach, on his way back to the horrors of court and alley in the terrible London.

CHAPTER VII.

THE SILK-WEAVER.

WHEN he arrived he made it his first business to find "Widow Walker." She was
evidently one of the worst of her class; and
could it have been accomplished without scandal,
and without interfering with the quietness upon
which he believed that the true effect of his
labours in a large measure depended, he would
not have scrupled simply to carry off the child.
With much difficulty, for the woman was suspicious, he contrived to see her, and was at once
reminded of the child he had seen in the cart on
the occasion of Shargar's recognition of his
mother. He fancied he saw in her some resemblance to his friend Shargar. The affair ended
in his paying the woman a hundred and fifty
pounds to give up the girl. Within six months
she had drunk herself to death. He took little
Nancy Kennedy home with him, and gave her
in charge to his housekeeper. She cried a good
deal at first, and wanted to go back to Mother

Walker, but he had no great trouble with her
after a time. She began to take a share in the
house-work, and at length to wait upon him. Then
Falconer began to see that he must cultivate
relations with other people in order to enlarge
his means of helping the poor. He nowise
abandoned his conviction that whatever good
he sought to do or lent himself to aid must be
effected entirely by individual influence. He
had little faith in societies, regarding them
chiefly as a wretched substitute, just better than
nothing, for that help which the neighbour is to
give to his neighbour. Finding how the unbelief of the best of the poor is occasioned by
hopelessness in privation, and the sufferings of
those dear to them, he was confident that only
the personal communion of friendship could
make it possible for them to believe in God.
Christians must be in the world as He was
in the world; and in proportion as the truth
radiated from them, the world would be able to
believe in Him. Money he saw to be worse
than useless, except as a gracious outcome of
human feelings and brotherly love. He always
insisted that the Saviour healed only those on
whom his humanity had laid hold; that he demanded faith of them in order to make them
regard him, that so his personal being might
enter into their hearts. Healing without faith
in its source would have done them harm in-

stead of good—would have been to them a windfall, not a Godsend; at best the gift of magic, even sometimes the power of Satan casting out Satan. But he must not therefore act as if he were the only one who could render this individual aid, or as if men influencing the poor individually could not aid each other in their individual labours. He soon found, I say, that there were things he could not do without help, and Nancy was his first perplexity. From this he was delivered in a wonderful way.

One afternoon he was *prowling* about Spitalfields, where he had made many acquaintances amongst the silk-weavers and their families. Hearing a loud voice as he passed down a stair from the visit he had been paying further up the house, he went into the room whence the sound came, for he knew a little of the occupant. He was one De Fleuri, or as the neighbours called him, Diffleery, in whose countenance, after generations of want and debasement, the delicate lines and noble cast of his ancient race were yet emergent. This man had lost his wife and three children, his whole family except a daughter now sick, by a slow-consuming hunger; and he did not believe there was a God that ruled in the earth. But he supported his unbelief by no other argument than a hopeless bitter glance at his empty loom. At this moment he sat silent —a rock against which the noisy waves of a

combative Bible-reader were breaking in rude
foam. His silence and apparent impassiveness
angered the irreverent little worthy. To Falconer's humour he looked a vulgar bull-terrier
barking at a noble, sad-faced staghound. His
foolish arguments against infidelity, drawn from
Paley's *Natural Theology*, and tracts about the
inspiration of the Bible, touched the sore-hearted
unbelief of the man no nearer than the clangour
of negro kettles affects the eclipse of the sun.
Falconer stood watching his opportunity. Nor
was the eager disputant long in affording him
one. Socratic fashion, Falconer asked him a
question, and was answered; followed it with
another, which, after a little hesitation, was
likewise answered; then asked a third, the
ready answer to which involved such a flagrant
contradiction of the first, that the poor sorrowful weaver burst into a laugh of delight at the
discomfiture of his tormentor. After some
stammering, and a confused attempt to recover
the line of argument, the would-be partizan of
Deity roared out, "The fool hath said in his heart
there is no God;" and with this triumphant discharge of his swivel, turned and ran down the
stairs precipitately.

Both laughed while the sound of his footsteps
lasted. Then Falconer said:

"Mr. De Fleuri, I believe in God with all my
heart, and soul, and strength, and mind; though

not in that poor creature's arguments. I don't know that your unbelief is not better than his faith."

"I am greatly obliged to you, Mr. Falconer. I haven't laughed so for years. What right has he to come pestering me?"

"None whatever. But you must forgive him, because he is well-meaning, and because his conceit has made a fool of him. They're not all like him. But how is your daughter?"

"Very poorly, sir. She's going after the rest. A Spitalfields weaver ought to be like the cats: they don't mind how many of their kittens are drowned."

"I beg your pardon. They don't like it. Only they forget it sooner than we do."

"Why do you say *we*, sir? *You* don't know anything of that sort."

"The heart knows its own bitterness, De Fleuri—and finds it enough, I daresay."

The weaver was silent for a moment. When he spoke again, there was a touch of tenderness in his respect.

"Will you go and see my poor Katey, sir?"

"Would she like to see me?"

"It does her good to see you. I never let that fellow go near her. He may worry me as he pleases; but she shall die in peace. That is all I can do for her."

"Do you still persist in refusing help—for

your daughter—I don't mean for yourself?"

Not believing in God, De Fleuri would not be obliged to his fellow. Falconer had never met with a similar instance.

"I do. I won't kill her, and I won't kill myself: I am not bound to accept charity. It's all right. I only want to leave the whole affair behind; and I sincerely hope there's nothing to come after. If I were God, I should be ashamed of such a mess of a world."

"Well, no doubt you would have made something more to your mind—and better, too, if all you see were all there is to be seen. But I didn't send that bore away to bore you myself. I'm going to see Katey."

"Very well, sir. I won't go up with you, for I won't interfere with what you think proper to say to her."

"That's rather like faith somewhere!" thought Falconer. "Could that man fail to believe in Jesus Christ if he only saw him—anything like as he is?"

Katey lay in a room overhead; for though he lacked food, this man contrived to pay for a separate room for his daughter, whom he treated with far more respect than many gentlemen treat their wives. Falconer found her lying on a wretched bed. Still it was a bed; and many in the same house had no bed to lie on. He had just come from a room overhead where lived a widow with four children. All of them lay on a floor whence issued at night, by many holes, awful rats. The children could not sleep for horror. They did not mind the little ones, they said, but when the big ones came, they were awake all night.

" Well, Katey, how are you?"

"No better, thank God."

She spoke as her father had taught her. Her face was worn and thin, but hardly death-like. Only extremes met in it—the hopelessness had turned through quietude into comfort. Her hopelessness affected him more than her father's. But there was nothing he could do for her.

There came a tap at the door.

"Come in," said Falconer, involuntarily.

A lady in the dress of a Sister of Mercy entered with a large basket on her arm. She started, and hesitated for a moment when she saw him. He rose, thinking it better to go. She advanced to the bedside. He turned at the door, and said,

" I won't say good-bye yet, Katey, for I'm going to have a chat with your father, and if you will let me, I will look in again."

As he turned he saw the lady kiss her on the forehead. At the sound of his voice she started again, left the bedside and came towards him. Whether he knew her by her face or her voice first, he could not tell.

"Robert," she said, holding out her hand.

It was Mary St. John. Their hands met, joined fast, and lingered, as they gazed each in the other's face. It was nearly fourteen years since they had parted. The freshness of youth was gone from her cheek, and the signs of middle age were present on her forehead. But she was statelier, nobler, and gentler than ever. Falconer looked at her calmly, with only a still swelling at the heart, as if they met on the threshold of heaven. All the selfishness of passion was gone, and the old earlier adoration, elevated and glorified, had returned. He was a boy once more in the presence of a woman-angel. She did not shrink from his gaze, she did not withdraw her hand from his clasp.

"I am so glad, Robert!" was all she said.

"So am I," he answered quietly. "We may meet sometimes, then?"

"Yes. Perhaps we can help each other."

"You can help me," said Falconer. "I have a girl I don't know what to do with."

"Send her to me. I will take care of her."

"I will bring her. But I must come and see you first."

"That will tell you where I live," she said, giving him a card. "Good-bye."

"Till to-morrow," said Falconer.

"*She's* not like that Bible fellow," said De Fleuri, as he entered his room again. "She don't walk into your house as if it was her own."

He was leaning against his idle loom, which, like a dead thing, filled the place with the mournfulness of death. Falconer took a broken chair, the only one, and sat down.

"I am going to take a liberty with you, Mr. De Fleuri," he said.

"As you please, Mr. Falconer."

"I want to tell you the only fault I have to you."

"Yes?"

"You don't do anything for the people in the house. Whether you believe in God or not, you ought to do what you can for your neighbour."

He held that to help a neighbour is the strongest antidote to unbelief, and an open door out of the bad air of one's own troubles, as well.

De Fleuri laughed bitterly, and rubbed his hand up and down his empty pocket. It was a pitiable action. Falconer understood it.

"There are better things than money: sympathy, for instance. You could talk to them a little."

"I have no sympathy, sir."

"You would find you had, if you would let it out."

"I should only make them more miserable. If I believed as you do, now, there might be some use."

"There's that widow with her four children in the garret. The poor little things are tormented by the rats: couldn't you nail bits of wood over their holes?"

De Fleuri laughed again.

"Where am I to get the bits of wood, except I pull down some of those laths. And they wouldn't keep them out a night."

"Couldn't you ask some carpenter?"

"I won't ask a favour."

"I shouldn't mind asking, now."

"That's because you don't know the bitterness of needing."

"Fortunately, however, there's no occasion for it. You have no right to refuse for another what you wouldn't accept for yourself. Of course I could send in a man to do it; but if you would do it, that would do her heart good. And that's what most wants doing good to—isn't it, now?"

"I believe you're right there, sir. If it wasn't for the misery of it, I shouldn't mind the hunger."

"I should like to tell you how I came to go poking my nose into other people's affairs. Would you like to hear my story now?"

"If you please, sir."

A little pallid curiosity seemed to rouse itself in the heart of the hopeless man. So Falconer began at once to tell him how he had been brought up, describing the country and their ways of life, not excluding his adventures with Shargar, until he saw that the man was thoroughly interested. Then all at once, pulling out his watch, he said:

"But it's time I had my tea, and I haven't half done yet. I am not fond of being hungry, like you, Mr. De Fleuri."

The poor fellow could only manage a very dubious smile.

"I'll tell you what," said Falconer, as if the thought had only just struck him—"come home with me, and I'll give you the rest of it at my own place."

"You must excuse me, sir."

"Bless my soul, the man's as proud as Lucifer! He wont accept a neighbour's invitation to a cup of tea—for fear it should put him under obligations, I suppose."

"It's very kind of you, sir, to put it in that way; but I don't choose to be taken in. You know very well it's not as one equal asks another you ask me. It's charity."

"Do I not behave to you as an equal?"

"But you know that don't make us equals."

"But isn't there something better than being equals? Supposing, as you will have it, that we're not equals, can't we be friends?"

"I hope so, sir."

"Do you think now, Mr. De Fleuri, if you weren't something more to me than a mere equal,

I would go telling you my own history? But I forgot: I have told you hardly anything yet. I have to tell you how much nearer I am to your level than you think. I had the design too of getting you to help me in the main object of my life. Come don't be a fool. I want you."

"I can't leave Katey," said the weaver, hesitatingly.

"Miss St. John is there still. I will ask her to stop till you come back."

Without waiting for an answer, he ran up the stairs, and had speedily arranged with Miss St. John. Then taking his consent for granted, he hurried De Fleuri away with him, and knowing how unfit a man of his trade was for walking, irrespective of feebleness from want, he called the first cab, and took him home. Here, over their tea, which he judged the safest meal for a stomach unaccustomed to food, he told him about his grandmother, and about Dr. Anderson, and how he came to give himself to the work he was at, partly for its own sake, partly in the hope of finding his father. He told him his only clue to finding him; and that he had called on Mrs. Macallister twice every week for two years, but had heard nothing of him. De Fleuri listened with what rose to great interest before the story was finished. And one of its ends at least was gained: the weaver was at home with him. The poor fellow felt that such close relation to an outcast, did indeed bring Falconer nearer to his own level.

"Do you want it kept a secret, sir ?" he asked.

"I don't want it made a matter of gossip. But I do not mind how many respectable people like yourself know of it."

He said this with a vague hope of assistance.

Before they parted, the unaccustomed tears had visited the eyes of De Fleuri, and he had consented not only to repair Mrs. Chisholm's garret-floor, but to take in hand the expenditure of a certain sum weekly, as he should judge expedient, for the people who lived in that and the neighbouring houses—in no case, however, except of sickness, or actual want of bread from want of work. Thus did Falconer appoint a sorrow-made infidel to be the almoner of his christian charity, knowing well that the nature of the Son of Man was in him, and that to get him to do as the Son of Man did, in ever so small a degree, was the readiest means of bringing his higher nature to the birth. Nor did he ever repent the choice he had made.

When he waited upon Miss St John the next day, he found her in the ordinary dress of a lady. She received him with perfect confidence and kindness, but there was no reference made to the past. She told him that she had belonged to a sisterhood, but had left it a few days before, believing she could do better without its restrictions.

" It was an act of cowardice," she said,—
" wearing the dress yesterday. I had got used
to it, and did not feel safe without it ; but I shall
not wear it any more."

" I think you are right," said Falconer. " The
nearer any friendly act is associated with the
individual heart, without intervention of class
or creed, the more the humanity, which is the
divinity of it, will appear."

He then told her about Nancy.

" I will keep her about myself for a while,"
said Miss St. John, "till I see what can be done
with her. I know a good many people who
without being prepared, or perhaps able to take
any trouble, are yet ready to do a kindness
when it is put in their way."

" I feel more and more that I ought to make
some friends," said Falconer ; "for I find my
means of help reach but a little way. What had
I better do ?   I suppose I could get some intro-
ductions.—I hardly know how."

" That will easily be managed. I will take
that in hand. If you will accept invitations, you
will soon know a good many people—of all
sorts," she added with a smile.

About this time Falconer, having often felt
the pressure of his ignorance of legal affairs, and
reflected whether it would not add to his efficiency to rescue himself from it, began such a course
of study as would fit him for the profession of

the law. Gifted with splended health, and if with a slow strength of grasping, yet with a great power of holding, he set himself to work, and regularly read for the bar.

CHAPTER VIII.

MY OWN ACQUAINTANCE.

IT was after this that my own acquaintance with Falconer commenced. I had just come out of one of the theatres in the neighbourhood of the Strand, unable to endure any longer the dreary combination of false magnanimity and real meanness, imported from Paris in the shape of a melodrama, for the delectation of the London public. I had turned northwards, and was walking up one of the streets near Covent Garden, when my attention was attracted to a woman who came out of a gin shop, carrying a baby. She went to the kennel, and bent her head over, ill with the poisonous stuff she had been drinking. And while the woman stood in this degrading posture, the poor, white, wasted baby was looking over her shoulder with the smile of a seraph, perfectly unconscious of the hell around her.

"Children *will* see things as God sees them," murmured a voice beside me.

I turned and saw a tall man with whose form I had already become a little familiar, although I knew nothing of him, standing almost at my elbow, with his eyes fixed on the woman and the child, and a strange smile of tenderness about his mouth, as if he were blessing the little creature in his heart.

He too saw the wonder of the show, typical of so much in the world, indeed of the world itself—the seemingly vile upholding and ministering to the life of the pure, the gracious, the fearless. Aware from his tone more than from his pronunciation that he was a fellow-countryman, I ventured to speak to him, and in a home-dialect.

"It's a wonnerfu' sicht. It's the cake o' Ezekiel ower again."

He looked at me sharply, thought a moment, and said,

"You were going my way when you stopped. I will walk with you, if you will."

"But what's to be done about it ?" I said.

"About what ?" he returned.

"About the child there," I answered.

"Oh ! she is its mother," he replied, walking on.

"What difference does that make ?" I said.

"All the difference in the world. If God has given her that child, what right have you or I to interfere ?"

"But I verily believe from the look of the child she gives it gin."

"God saves the world by the new blood, the children. To take her child from her, would be to do what you could to damn her."

"It doesn't look much like salvation there."

"You mustn't interfere with God's thousand years any more than his one day."

"Are you sure she is the mother?" I asked.

"Yes. I would not have left the child with her otherwise."

"What would you have done with it? Got it into some orphan asylum?—or the Foundling perhaps?"

"Never," he answered. "All those societies are wretched inventions for escape from the right way. There ought not to be an orphan asylum in the kingdom."

"What! Would you put them all down then?"

"God forbid. But I would, if I could, make them all useless."

"How could you do that?"

"I would *merely* enlighten the hearts of childless people as to their privileges."

"Which are?"

"To be fathers and mothers to the fatherless and motherless."

"I have often wondered why more of them did not adopt children. Why don't they?"

"For various reasons which a real love to child nature would blow to the winds—all comprised in this, that such a child would not be their own child. As if ever a child could be their own! That a child is God's is of rather more consequence than whether it is born of this or that couple. Their hearts would surely be glad when they went into heaven to have the angels of the little ones that always behold the face of their Father coming round them, though they were not exactly their father and mother."

"I don't know what the passage you refer to means."

"Neither do I. But it must mean something, if He said it. Are you a clergyman?"

"No. I am only a poor teacher of mathematics and poetry, shown up the back stairs into the nurseries of great houses."

"A grand chance, if I may use the word."

"I do try to wake a little enthusiasm in the sons and daughters—without much success, I fear."

"Will you come and see me?" he said.

"With much pleasure. But, as I have given you an answer, you owe me one."

"I do."

"Have you adopted a child?"

"No."

"Then you have some of your own?"

"No."

"Then, excuse me, but why the warmth of your remarks on those who——"

"I think I shall be able to satisfy you on that point, if we draw to each other. Meantime I must leave you. Could you come to-morrow evening?"

"With pleasure."

We arranged the hour and parted. I saw him walk into a low public-house, and went home.

At the time appointed, I rang the bell, and was led by an elderly woman up the stair, and shown into a large room on the first-floor—poorly furnished, and with many signs of bachelor-carelessness. Mr. Falconer rose from an old hair-covered sofa to meet me as I entered. I will first tell my reader something of his personal appearance.

He was considerably above six feet in height, square-shouldered, remarkably long in the arms, and his hands were uncommonly large and powerful. His head was large, and covered with dark wavy hair, lightly streaked with gray. His broad forehead projected over deep-sunk eyes, that shone like black fire. His features, especially his Roman nose, were large, and finely, though not delicately, modelled. His nostrils were remarkably large and flexile, with a tendency to slight motion : I found on further acquaintance that when he was excited, they expanded in a wild equine manner. The expres-

sion of his mouth was of tender power, crossed
with humour. He kept his lips a little compressed, which gave a certain sternness to his
countenance; but when this sternness dissolved
in a smile, it was something enchanting. He
was plainly, rather shabbily clothed. No one
could have guessed at his profession or social
position. He came forward and received me
cordially. After a little indifferent talk, he asked
me if I had any other engagement for the evening.

" I never have any engagements," I answered
—" at least, of a social kind. I am *burd alane.*
I know next to nobody."

" Then perhaps you would not mind going
out with me for a stroll ?"

" I shall be most happy," I answered.

There was something about the man I found
exceedingly attractive; I had very few friends;
and there was besides something odd, almost
romantic, in this beginning of an intercourse:
I would see what would come of it.

" Then we'll have some supper first," said Mr.
Falconer, and rang the bell.

While we ate our chops—

" I daresay you think it strange," my host
said, " that without the least claim on your acquaintance, I should have asked you to come
and see me, Mr.—"

He stopped, smiling.

"My name is Gordon—Archie Gordon," I said.

"Well, then, Mr. Gordon, I confess I have a design upon you. But you will remember that you addressed me first."

"You *spoke* first," I said.

"Did I?"

"I did not say you spoke to me, but you spoke.—I should not have ventured to make the remark I did make, if I had not heard your voice first. What design have you on me?"

"That will appear in due course. Now take a glass of wine, and we'll set out."

We soon found ourselves in Holborn, and my companion led the way towards the City. The evening was sultry and close.

"Nothing excites me more," said Mr. Falconer, "than a walk in the twilight through a crowded street. Do you find it affect you so?"

"I cannot speak as strongly as you do," I replied. "But I perfectly understand what you mean. Why is it, do you think?"

"Partly, I fancy, because it is like the primordial chaos, a concentrated tumult of undetermined possibilities. The germs of infinite adventure and result are floating around you like a snow-storm. You do not know what may arise in a moment and colour all your future. Out of this mass may suddenly start something marvellous, or, it may be, something you have been looking for for years."

The same moment, a fierce flash of lightning, like a blue sword-blade a thousand times shattered, quivered and palpitated about us, leaving a thick darkness on the sense. I heard my companion give a suppressed cry, and saw him run up against a heavy drayman who was on the edge of the path, guiding his horses with his long whip. He begged the man's pardon, put his hand to his head, and murmured, " I shall know him now." I was afraid for a moment that the lightning had struck him, but he assured me there was nothing amiss. He looked a little excited and confused, however.

I should have forgotten the incident, had he not told me afterwards—when I had come to know him intimately, that in the moment of that lightning flash, he had had a strange experience : he had seen the form of his father, as he had seen him that Sunday afternoon, in the midst of the surrounding light. He was as certain of the truth of the presentation as if a gradual revival of memory had brought with it the clear conviction of its own accuracy. His explanation of the phenomenon was, that, in some cases, all that prevents a vivid conception from assuming objectivity, is the self-assertion of external objects. The gradual approach of darkness cannot surprise and isolate the phantasm ; but the suddenness of the lightning could and did, obliterating everything without, and leaving that over which it had no power standing alone, and therefore visible.

"But," I ventured to ask, "whence the minuteness of detail, surpassing, you say, all that your memory could supply?"

"That I think was a quickening of the memory by the realism of the presentation. Excited by the vision, it caught at its own past, as it were, and suddenly recalled that which it had forgotten. In the rapidity of all pure mental action, this at once took its part in the apparent objectivity."

To return to the narrative of my first evening in Falconer's company.

It was strange how insensible the street population was to the grandeur of the storm. While the thunder was billowing and bellowing over and around us—

"A hundred pins for one ha'penny," bawled a man from the gutter, with the importance of a Cagliostro.

"Evening Star! Telegrauwff!" roared an ear-splitting urchin in my very face. I gave him a shove off the pavement.

"Ah! don't do that," said Falconer. "It only widens the crack between him and his fellows—not much, but a little."

"You are right," I said. "I won't do it again."

The same moment we heard a tumult in a

neighbouring street. A crowd was execrating a policeman, who had taken a woman into custody, and was treating her with unnecessary rudeness. Falconer looked on for a few moments.

"Come, policeman!" he said at length, in a tone of expostulation. "You're rather rough, are you not? She's a woman, you know."

"Hold your blasted humbug," answered the man, an exceptional specimen of the force at that time at all events, and shook the tattered wretch, as if he would shake her out of her rags.

Falconer gently parted the crowd, and stood beside the two.

"I will help you," he said, ".to take her to the station, if you like, but you must not treat her that way."

"I don't want your help," said the policeman; "I know you, and all the damned lot of you."

"Then I shall be compelled to give you a lesson," said Falconer.

The man's only answer was a shake that made the woman cry out.

"I shall get into trouble if you get off," said Falconer to her. "Will you promise me, on your word, to go with me to the station, if I rid you of the fellow?"

"I will, I will," said the woman.

"Then, look out," said Falconer to the policeman; "for I'm going to give you that lesson."

The officer let the woman go, took his baton, and made a blow at Falconer. In another moment—I could hardly see how—he lay in the street.

"Now, my poor woman, come along," said Falconer.

She obeyed, crying gently. Two other policemen came up.

"Do you want to give that woman in charge, Mr. Falconer?" asked one of them.

"I give that man in charge," cried his late antagonist, who had just scrambled to his feet. "Assaulting the police in discharge of their duty."

"Very well," said the other. "But you're in the wrong box, and that you'll find. You had better come along to the station, sir."

"Keep that fellow from getting hold of the woman—you two, and we'll go together," said Falconer.

Bewildered with the rapid sequence of events, I was following in the crowd. Falconer looked about till he saw me, and gave me a nod which meant *come along*. Before we reached Bow Street, however, the offending policeman, who had been walking a little behind in conversation with one of the others, advanced to Falconer, touched his hat, and said something, to which Falconer replied.

"Remember, I have my eye upon you," was all I heard, however, as he left the crowd and rejoined me. We turned and walked eastward again.

The storm kept on intermittently, but the streets were rather more crowded than usual notwithstanding.

"Look at that man in the woollen jacket," said Falconer. "What a beautiful outline of face! There must be something noble in that man."

"I did not see him," I answered, "I was taken up with a woman's face, like that of a beautiful corpse. It's eyes were bright. There was gin in its brain."

The streets swarmed with human faces gleaming past. It was a night of ghosts.

There stood a man who had lost one arm, earnestly pumping bilge-music out of an accordion with the other, holding it to his body with the stump. There was a woman, pale with hunger and gin, three match-boxes in one extended hand, and the other holding a baby to her breast. As we looked, the poor baby let go its hold, turned its little head, and smiled a wan, shrivelled, old-fashioned smile in our faces.

"Another happy baby, you see, Mr. Gordon," said Falconer. "A child, fresh from God, finds its heaven where no one else would. The devil could drive woman out of Paradise; but the devil himself cannot drive the Paradise out of a woman."

" What can be done for them ?" I said, and at
the moment, my eye fell upon a row of little
children, from two to five years of age, seated
upon the curb-stone.

They were chattering fast, and apparently
carrying on some game, as happy as if they had
been in the fields.

" Wouldn't you like to take all those little
grubby things, and put them in a great tub and
wash them clean ?" I said.

" They'd fight like spiders," rejoined Falconer.

" They're not fighting now."

" Then don't make them. It would be all useless.   The probability is that you would only
change the forms of the various evils, and possibly for worse.   You would buy all that man's
glue-lizards, and that man's three-foot rules, and
that man's dog-collars and chains, at three times
their value, that they might get more drink
than usual, and do nothing at all for their living
to-morrow.—What a happy London you would
make if you were Sultan Haroun ! " he added,
laughing. " You would put an end to poverty
altogether, would you not ?"

I did not reply at once.

" But I beg your pardon," he resumed ; " I am
very rude."

" Not at all," I returned.   " I was only thinking how to answer you. They would be no worse

after all than those who inherit property and lead idle lives."

" True ; but they would be no better. Would you be content that your quondam poor should be no better off than the rich ? What would be gained thereby ? Is there no truth in the words ' Blessed are the poor ?' A deeper truth than most Christians dare to see.—Did you ever observe that there is not one word about the vices of the poor in the Bible—from beginning to end ?"

" But they have their vices."

" Indubitably. I am only stating a fact. The Bible is full enough of the vices of the rich. I make no comment."

" But don't you care for their sufferings ?"

" They are of secondary importance quite. But if you had been as much amongst them as I, perhaps you would be of my opinion, that the poor are not, cannot possibly feel so wretched as they seem to us. They live in a climate, as it were, which is their own, by natural law comply with it, and find it not altogether unfriendly. The Laplander will prefer his wastes to the rich fields of England, not merely from ignorance, but for the sake of certain blessings amongst which he has been born and brought up. The blessedness of life depends far more on its interest than upon its comfort. The need of exertion and the doubt of success, renders life much more interesting to the poor than it is to those who, unblessed with anxiety for the bread that perisheth, waste their poor hearts about rank and reputation."

" I thought such anxiety was represented as an evil in the New Testament."

" Yes. But it is a still greater evil to lose it in any other way than by faith in God. You would remove the anxiety by destroying its cause : God would remove it by lifting them above it, by teaching them to trust in him, and thus making them partakers of the divine nature. Poverty is a blessing when it makes a man look up."

" But you cannot say it does so always."

" I cannot determine when, where, and how much ; but I am sure it does. And I am confident that to free those hearts from it by any deed of yours would be to do them the greatest injury you could. Probably their want of foresight would prove the natural remedy, speedily reducing them to their former condition—not however without serious loss."

" But will not this theory prove at last an anaesthetic rather than an anodyne? I mean that, although you may adopt it at first for refuge from the misery the sight of their condition occasions you, there is surely a danger of its rendering you at last indifferent to it."

" Am I indifferent? But you do not know

me yet. Pardon my egotism. There may be such danger. Every truth has its own danger or shadow. Assuredly I would have no less labour spent upon them. But there can be no *true* labour done, save in as far as we are fellow-labourers with God. We must work with him, not *against* him. Everyone who works without believing that God is doing the best, the absolute good for them, is, must be, more or less, thwarting God. He would take the poor out of God's hands. For others, as for ourselves, we must trust him. If we could thoroughly understand anything, that would be enough to prove it undivine; and that which is but one step beyond our understanding must be in some of its relations as mysterious as if it were a hundred. But through all this darkness about the poor, at least I can see wonderful veins and fields of light, and with the help of this partial vision, I trust for the rest. The only and the greatest thing man is capable of is Trust in God."

"What then is a man to do for the poor? How is he to work with God?" I asked.

"He must be a man amongst them—a man breathing the air of a higher life, and therefore in all natural ways fulfilling his endless human relations to them. Whatever you do for them, let your own being, that is you in relation to them, be the background, that so you may be a link between them and God, or rather I should say, between them and the knowledge of God."

While Falconer spoke, his face grew grander and grander, till at last it absolutely shone. I felt that I walked with a man whose faith was his genius.

"Of one thing I am pretty sure," he resumed, "that the same recipe Goethe gave for the enjoyment of life, applies equally to all work: 'Do the thing that lies next you.' That is all our business. Hurried results are worse than none. We must force nothing, but be partakers of the divine patience. How long it took to make the cradle! and we fret that the baby Humanity is not reading Euclid and Plato, even that it is not understanding the Gospel of St. John! If there is one thing evident in the world's history, it is that God hasteneth not. All haste implies weakness. Time is as cheap as space and matter. What they call the church militant is only at drill yet, and a good many of the officers too not out of the awkward squad. I am sure I, for a private, am not. In the drill a man has to conquer himself, and move with the rest by individual attention to his own duty: to what mighty battle-fields the recruit may yet be led, he does not know. Meantime he has nearly enough to do with his goose-step, while there is plenty of single combat, skirmish, and light cavalry work generally, to get him ready for whatever is to follow. I beg your pardon: I am preaching."

"Eloquently," I answered.

Of some of the places into which Falconer led me that night I will attempt no description—places blazing with lights and mirrors, crowded with dancers, billowing with music, close and hot, and full of the saddest of all sights, the uninteresting faces of commonplace women.

"There is a passion," I said, as we came out of one of these dreadful places, "that lingers about the heart like the odour of violets, like a glimmering twilight on the borders of moon-rise; and there is a passion that wraps itself in the vapours of patchouli and coffins, and streams from the eyes like gaslight from a tavern. And yet the line is ill to draw between them. It is very dreadful. These are women."

"They are in God's hands," answered Falconer. "He hasn't done with them yet. Shall it take less time to make a woman than to make a world? Is not the woman the greater? She may have her ages of chaos, her centuries of crawling slime, yet rise a woman at last."

"How much alike all those women were!"

"A family likeness, alas! which always strikes you first."

"Some of them looked quite modest."

"There are great differences. I do not know

anything more touching than to see how a woman will sometimes wrap around her the last remnants of a soiled and ragged modesty. It has moved me almost to tears to see such a one hanging her head in shame during the singing of a detestable song. That poor thing's shame was precious in the eyes of the Master, surely."

"Could nothing be done for her?"

"I contrived to let her know where she would find a friend if she wanted to be good: that is all you can do in such cases. If the horrors of their life do not drive them out at such an open door, you can do nothing else, I fear—for the time."

"Where are you going now, may I ask?"

"Into the city—on business," he added with a smile.

"There will be nobody there so late."

"Nobody! One would think you were the beadle of a city church, Mr. Gordon."

We came into a very narrow, dirty street. I do not know where it is. A slatternly woman advanced from an open door, and said,

"Mr. Falconer."

He looked at her for a moment.

"Why, Sarah, have you come to this already?" he said.

"Never mind me, sir. It's no more than you told me to expect. You knowed him better than I did. Leastways I'm an honest woman."

"Stick to that, Sarah; and be good-tempered."

"I'll have a try anyhow, sir. But there's a poor cretur a dyin' upstairs; and I'm afeard it'll go hard with her, for she throwed a bible out o' window this very morning, sir."

"Would she like to see me? I'm afraid not."

"She's got Lilywhite, what's a sort of a reader, readin' that same bible to her now."

"There can be no great harm in just looking in," he said, turning to me.

"I shall be happy to follow you—anywhere," I returned.

"She's awful ill, sir; cholerer or summat," said Sarah, as she led the way up the creaking stair.

We half entered the room softly. Two or three women sat by the chimney, and another by a low bed, covered with a torn patchwork counterpane, spelling out a chapter in the Bible. We paused for a moment to hear what she was reading. Had the book been opened by chance, or by design? It was the story of David and Bathsheba. Moans came from the bed, but the candle in a bottle, by which the woman was reading, was so placed that we could not see the sufferer.

We stood still and did not interrupt the reading.

"Ha! ha! ha!" laughed a coarse voice from the side of the chimney: "the saint you see was no better than some of the rest of us!"

"I think he was a good deal worse just then," said Falconer, stepping forward.

"Gracious! there's Mr. Falconer," said another woman, rising, and speaking in a flattering tone.

"Then," remarked the former speaker, "there's a chance for old Moll and me yet. King David was a saint, wasn't he? Ha! ha!"

"Yes, and you might be one too, if you were as sorry for your faults as he was for his."

"Sorry, indeed! I'll be damned if I be sorry. What have I to be sorry for? Where's the harm in turning an honest penny? I ha' took no man's wife, nor murdered himself neither. There's yer saints! He was a rum 'un. Ha! ha!"

Falconer approached her, bent down and whispered something no one could hear but herself. She gave a smothered cry, and was silent.

"Give me the book," he said, turning towards the bed. "I'll read you something better than that. I'll read about some one that never did anything wrong."

"I don't believe there never was no sich a man," said the previous reader, as she handed him the book, grudgingly.

"Not Jesus Christ himself?" said Falconer.

"Oh! I didn't know as you meant him."

"Of course I meant him. There never was another."

"I have heard tell—p'raps it was yourself, sir—as how he didn't come down upon us over hard after all, bless him!"

Falconer sat down on the side of the bed, and read the story of Simon the Pharisee and the woman that was a sinner. When he ceased, the silence that followed was broken by a sob from somewhere in the room. The sick woman stopped her moaning, and said,

"Turn down the leaf there, please, sir. Lily-white will read it to me when you're gone."

The some one sobbed again. It was a young slender girl, with a face disfigured by the small-pox, and, save for the tearful look it wore, poor and expressionless. Falconer said something gentle to her.

"Will he ever come again?" she sobbed.

"Who?" asked Falconer.

"Him—Jesus Christ. I've heard tell, I think, that he was to come again some day."

"Why do you ask?"

"Because—" she said, with a fresh burst of tears, which rendered the words that followed unintelligible. But she recovered herself in a few moments, and, as if finishing her sentence, put her hand up to her poor, thin, colourless hair, and said,

"*My* hair ain't long enough to wipe his feet."

"Do you know what he would say to you, my girl?" Falconer asked.

"No. What would he say to me? He would speak to me, would he?"

"He would say : Thy sins are forgiven thee."

"Would he, though? Would he?" she cried, starting up. "Take me to him—take me to him. Oh! I forgot. He's dead. But he will come again, won't he? He was crucified four times, you know, and he must ha' come four times for that. Would they crucify him again, sir?"

"No, they wouldn't crucify him now—in England at least. They would only laugh at him, shake their heads at what he told them, as much as to say it wasn't true, and sneer and mock at him in some of the newspapers."

"Oh, dear! I've been very wicked."

"But you won't be so any more."

"No, no, no. I won't, I won't, I won't."

She talked hurriedly, almost wildly. The coarse old woman tapped her forehead with her finger. Falconer took the girl's hand.

"What is your name?" he said.

"Nell."

"What more?"

"Nothing more."

"Well, Nelly," said Falconer.

"How kind of you to call me Nelly!" interrupted the poor girl. "They always calls me Nell, just."

"Nelly," repeated Falconer, "I will send a

lady here to-morrow to take you away with her, if you like, and tell you how you must do to find Jesus.—People always find him that want to find him."

The elderly woman with the rough voice, who had not spoken since he whispered to her, now interposed with a kind of cowed fierceness.

" Don't go putting humbug into my child's head now, Mr. Falconer—'ticing her away from her home. Everybody knows my Nell's been an idiot since ever she was born. Poor child !"

" I ain't your child," cried the girl, passionately. " I ain't nobody's child."

" You are God's child," said Falconer, who stood looking on with his eyes shining, but otherwise in a state of absolute composure.

" Am I? Am I? You won't forget to send for me, sir ?"

" That I won't," he answered.

She turned instantly towards the woman, and snapped her fingers in her face.

" I don't care that for you," she cried. " You dare to touch me now, and I'll bite you."

"Come, come, Nelly, you mustn't be rude," said Falconer.

" No, sir, I won't no more, leastways to nobody but she. It's she makes me do all the wicked things, it is."

She snapped her fingers in her face again, and then burst out crying.

"She will leave you alone now, I think," said Falconer. "She knows it will be quite as well for her not to cross me."

This he said very significantly, as he turned to the door, where he bade them a general good night. When we reached the street, I was too bewildered to offer any remark. Falconer was the first to speak.

"It always comes back upon me, as if I had never known it before, that women like some of those were of the first to understand our Lord."

"Some of them wouldn't have understood him any more than the Pharisee, though."

"I'm not so sure of that. Of course there are great differences. There are good and bad amongst them as in every class. But one thing is clear to me, that no indulgence of passion destroys the spiritual nature so much as respectable selfishness."

"I am afraid you will not get society to agree with you," I said, foolishly.

"I have no wish that society should agree with me; for if it did, it would be sure to do so upon the worst of principles. It is better that society should be cruel, than that it should call the horrible thing a trifle: it would know nothing between."

Through the city—though it was only when we crossed one of the main thoroughfares that I knew where we were—we came into the region of Bethnal Green. From house to house till it grew very late, Falconer went, and I went with him. I will not linger on this part of our wanderings. Where I saw only dreadful darkness, Falconer always would see some glimmer of light. All the people into whose houses we went knew him. They were all in the depths of poverty. Many of them were respectable. With some of them he had long talks in private, while I waited near. At length he said,

"I think we had better be going home, Mr. Gordon. You must be tired."

"I am, rather," I answered. "But it doesn't matter, for I have nothing to do to-morrow."

"We shall get a cab, I daresay, before we go far."

"Not for me. I am not so tired, but that I would rather walk," I said.

"Very well," he returned. "Where do you live?"

I told him.

"I will take you the nearest way."

"You know London marvellously."

"Pretty well now," he answered.

We were somewhere near Leather Lane about one o'clock. Suddenly we came upon two tiny children standing on the pavement, one on each side of the door of a public-house. They could not have been more than two and three. They were sobbing a little—not much. The tiny

VOL. III.

K

creatures stood there awfully awake in sleeping London, while even their own playmates were far off in the fairyland of dreams.

"This is the kind of thing," I said, "that makes me doubt whether there be a God in heaven."

"That is only because he is down here," answered Falconer, "taking such good care of us all that you can't see him. There is not a gin-palace, or yet lower hell in London, in which a man or woman can be out of God. The whole being love, there is nothing for you to set it against and judge it by. So you are driven to fancies."

The house was closed, but there was light above the door. We went up to the children, and spoke to them, but all we could make out was that mammie was in there. One of them could not speak at all. Falconer knocked at the door. A good-natured-looking Irishwoman opened it a little way and peeped out.

"Here are two children crying at your door, ma'am," said Falconer.

"Och, the darlin's! they want their mother."

"Do you know her, then?"

"True for you, and I do. She's a mighty dacent woman in her way when the drink's out uv her, and very kind to the childher; but oncet she smells the dhrop o' gin, her head's gone in-tirely. The purty craytures have waked up, an' she not come home, and they 've run out to look after her."

Falconer stood a moment as if thinking what would be best. The shriek of a woman rang through the night.

"There she is!" said the Irishwoman. "For God's sake don't let her get a hould o' the darlints. She's ravin' mad. I seen her try to kill them oncet."

The shrieks came nearer and nearer, and after a few moments the woman appeared in the moonlight, tossing her arms over her head, and screaming with a despair for which she yet sought a defiant expression. Her head was uncovered, and her hair flying in tangles; her sleeves were torn, and her gaunt arms looked awful in the moonlight. She stood in the middle of the street, crying again and again, with shrill laughter between, "Nobody cares for me, and I care for nobody! Ha! ha! ha!"

"Mammie! mammie!" cried the elder of the children, and ran towards her.

The woman heard, and rushed like a fury towards the child. Falconer too ran, and caught up the child. The woman gave a howl and rushed towards the other. I caught up that one. With a last shriek, she dashed her head against the wall of the public-house, dropped on the pavement, and lay still.

Falconer set the child down, lifted the wasted

form in his arms, and carried it into the house. The face was blue as that of a strangled corpse. She was dead.

"Was she a married woman?" Falconer asked.

"It's myself can't tell you, sir," the Irish-woman answered. "I never saw any boy with her."

"Do you know where she lived?"

"No, sir. Somewhere not far off, though. The children will know."

But they stood staring at their mother, and we could get nothing out of them. They would not move from the corpse.

"I think we may appropriate this treasure-trove," said Falconer, turning at last to me; and as he spoke, he took the eldest in his arms. Then, turning to the woman, he gave her a card, saying, "If any inquiry is made about them, there is my address.—Will you take the other, Mr. Gordon?"

I obeyed. The children cried no more. After traversing a few streets, we found a cab, and drove to a house in Queen Square, Blooms-bury.

Falconer got out at the door of a large house, and rung the bell; then got the children out, and dismissed the cab. There we stood in the middle of the night, in a silent, empty square, each with a child in his arms. In a few minutes we heard the bolts being withdrawn. The door opened, and a tall, graceful form wrapped in a dressing-gown, appeared.

"I have brought you two babies, Miss St. John," said Falconer. "Can you take them?"

"To be sure I can," she answered, and turned to lead the way. "Bring them in."

We followed her into a little back room. She put down her candle, and went straight to the cupboard, whence she brought a sponge-cake, from which she cut a large piece for each of the children.

"What a mercy they are, Robert,—those little gates in the face! Red Lane leads direct to the heart," she said, smiling, as if she rejoiced in the idea of taming the little wild angelets. "Don't you stop. You are tired enough, I am sure. I will wake my maid, and we'll get them washed and put to bed at once."

She was closing the door, when Falconer turned.

"Oh! Miss St. John," he said, "I was forgetting. Could you go down to No. 13 in Soap Lane—you know it, don't you?"

"Yes. Quite well."

"Ask for a girl called Nell—a plain, pockmarked young girl—and take her away with you."

"When shall I go?"

"To-morrow morning. But I shall be in. Don't go till you see me. Good-night."

We took our leave without more ado.

"What a lady-like woman to be the matron of an asylum!" I said.

Falconer gave a little laugh.

"That is no asylum. It is a private house."

"And the lady?"

"Is a lady of private means," he answered, who prefers Bloomsbury to Belgravia, because it is easier to do noble work in it. Her heaven is on the confines of hell."

"What will she do with those children?"

"Kiss them and wash them and put them to bed."

"And after that?"

"Give them bread and milk in the morning."

"And after that?"

"Oh! there's time enough. We'll see. There's only one thing she won't do."

"What is that?"

"Turn them out again."

A pause followed, I cogitating.

"Are you a society, then," I asked at length.

"No. At least we don't use the word. And certainly no other society would acknowledge us."

"What are you, then?"

"Why should we be anything, so long as we do our work?"

"Don't you think there is some affectation in refusing a name?"

"Yes, if the name belongs to you? Not otherwise."

"Do you lay claim to no epithet of any sort?"

"We are a church, if you like. There!"

"Who is your clergyman?"

"Nobody."

"Where do you meet?"

"Nowhere."

"What are your rules, then?"

"We have none."

"What makes you a church?"

"Divine Service."

"What do you mean by that?"

"The sort of thing you have seen to-night."

"What is your creed?"

"Christ Jesus."

"But what do you believe about him?"

"What we can. We count any belief *in* Him —the smallest—better than any belief about him—the greatest—or about anything else besides. But we exclude no one."

"How do you manage without?"

"By admitting no one."

"I cannot understand you."

"Well, then: we are an undefined company of people, who have grown into human relations with each other naturally, through one attractive force—love for human beings, regarding them *as* human beings only in virtue of the divine in them."

"But you must have some rules," I insisted.

"None whatever. They would cause us only trouble. We have nothing to take us from our work. Those that are most in earnest, draw most together; those that are on the outskirts have only to do nothing, and they are free of us. But we do sometimes ask people to help us—not with money."

"But who are the *we*?"

"Why *you*, if you will do anything, and I and Miss St. John, and twenty others—and a great many more I don't know, for every one is a centre to others. It is our work that binds us together."

"Then when that stops you drop to pieces."

"Yes, thank God. We shall then die. There will be no corporate body—which means a bodied body, or an unsouled body, left behind to simulate life, and corrupt, and work no end of disease. We go to ashes at once, and leave no corpse for a ghoul to inhabit and make a vampire of. When our spirit is dead, our body is vanished."

"Then you won't last long."

"Then we oughtn't to last long."

"But the work of the world could not go on so."

"We are not the life of the world. God is. And when we fail, he can and will send out more and better labourers into his harvest-field.

It is a divine accident by which we are thus associated."

"But surely the church must be otherwise constituted."

"My dear sir, you forget: I said we were *a* church, not *the* church."

"Do you belong to the Church of England?"

"Yes, some of us. Why should we not? In as much as she has faithfully preserved the holy records and traditions, our obligations to her are infinite. And to leave her would be to quarrel, and start a thousand *vermiculate* questions, as Lord Byron calls them, for which life is too serious in my eyes. I have no time for that."

"Then you count the Church of England *the* Church?"

"Of England, yes; of the universe, no: that is constituted just like ours, with the living working Lord for the heart of it."

"Will you take me for a member?"

"No."

"Will you not, if—— ?"

"You may make yourself one if you will. I will not speak a word to gain you. I have shown you work. Do something, and you are of Christ's Church."

We were almost at the door of my lodging, and I was getting very weary in body, and indeed in mind, though I hope not in heart. Before we separated, I ventured to say,

"Will you tell me why you invited me to come and see you? Forgive my presumption, but you seemed to seek acquaintance with me, although you did make me address you first.

He laughed gently, and answered in the words of the ancient mariner:—

> "The moment that his face I see,
> I know the man that must hear me:
> To him my tale I teach."

Without another word, he shook hands with me, and left me. Weary as I was, I stood in the street until I could hear his footsteps no longer.

CHAPTER IX.

THE BROTHERS.

ONE day, as Falconer sat at a late breakfast, Shargar burst into his room. Falconer had not even known that he was coming home, for he had outstripped the letter he had sent. He had his arm in a sling, which accounted for his leave.

"Shargar!" cried Falconer, starting up in delight.

"Major Shargar, if you please. Give me all my honours, Robert," said Moray, presenting his left hand.

"I congratulate you, my boy. Well, this is delightful! But you are wounded."

"Bullet—broken—that's all. It's nearly right again. I'll tell you about it by and by. I am too full of something else to talk about trifles of that sort. I want you to help me."

He then rushed into the announcement that he had fallen desperately in love with a lady who had come on board with her maid at Malta,

where she had been spending the winter. She
was not very young, about his own age, but
very beautiful, and of enchanting address.
How she could have remained so long unmar-
ried he could not think. It could not be but
that she had had many offers. She was an
heiress, too, but that Shargar felt to be a disad-
vantage for him. All the progress he could yet
boast of was that his attentions had not been,
so far as he could judge, disagreeable to her.
Robert thought even less of the latter fact than
Shargar himself, for he did not believe there
were many women to whom Shargar's attentions would be disagreeable : they must always
be simple and manly. What was more to the
point, she had given him her address in London, and he was going to call upon her the
next day. She was on a visit to Lady Janet
Gordon, an elderly spinster, who lived in Park-
street.

"Are you quite sure she's not an adventuress,
Shargar?"

"It 's o' no mainner o' use to tell ye what
I'm sure or no sure o', Robert, in sic a case.
But I'll manage, somehoo, 'at ye sall see her
yersel', an' syne I'll speir back yer ain queston
at ye."

"Weel, hae ye tauld her a' aboot yersel'?"

"No!" answered Shargar, growing suddenly
pale. "I never thocht aboot that. But I had

no richt, for a' that passed, to intrude mysel'
upo' her to that extent."

"Weel, I reckon ye're richt. Yer wounds
an' yer medals ought to weigh weel against a'
that. There's this comfort in 't, that gin she
bena richt weel worthy o' ye, auld frien', she
winna tak ye."

Shargar did not seem to see the comfort of it.
He was depressed for the remainder of the day.
In the morning he was in wild spirits again.
Just before he started, however, he said, with
an expression of tremulous anxiety—

"Oucht I to tell her a' at ance—already—
aboot—aboot my mither ?"

"I dinna say that. Maybe it wad be equally
fair to her and to yersel' to lat her ken ye a
bit better afore ye do that.—We'll think that
ower.—Whan ye gang doon the stair, ye'll see
a bit brougham at the door waitin' for ye. Gie
the coachman ony orders ye like. He's your
servant as lang 's ye're in London. Commit
yer way to the Lord, my boy."

Though Shargar did not say much, he felt
strengthened by Robert's truth to meet his fate
with something of composure. But it was not
to be decided that day. Therein lay some comfort.

He returned in high spirits still. He had
been graciously received both by Miss Hamilton
and her hostess—a kind-hearted old lady, who

spoke Scotch with the pure tone of a gentlewo-
man, he said—a treat not to be had once in a
twelvemonth. She had asked him to go to
dinner in the evening, and to bring his friend
with him. Robert, however, begged him to
make his excuse, as he had an engagement in—
a very different sort of place.

When Shargar returned, Robert had not
come in. He was too excited to go to bed, and
waited for him: It was two o'clock before he
came home. Shargar told him there was to be
a large party at Lady Patterdale's the next
evening but one, and Lady Janet had promised
to procure him an invitation.

The next morning Robert went to see Mary
St. John, and asked if she knew anything of
Lady Patterdale, and whether she could get
him an invitation. Miss St. John did not know
her, but she thought she could manage it for
him. He told her all about Shargar, for whose
sake he wished to see Miss Hamilton before
consenting to be introduced to her. Miss St.
John set out at once, and Falconer received a
card the next day. When the evening came,
he allowed Shargar to set out alone in his
brougham, and followed an hour later in a han-
som.

When he reached the house, the rooms were
tolerably filled, and as several parties had arrived just before him, he managed to enter

without being announced. After a little while
he caught sight of Shargar. He stood alone,
almost in a corner, with a strange, rather *raised*
expression in his eyes. Falconer could not see
the object to which they were directed. Certainly, their look was not that of love. He
made his way up to him and laid his hand on
his arm. Shargar betrayed no little astonishment when he saw him.

" You here, Robert !" he said.

" Yes, I'm here. Have you seen her yet ? Is
she here ?"

" Wha do ye think 's speakin' till her this
verra minute ? Look there !" Shargar said in a
low voice, suppressed yet more to hide his excitement.

Following his directions, Robert saw, amidst
a little group of gentlemen surrounding a seated lady, of whose face he could not get a peep,
a handsome elderly man, who looked more
fashionable than his years justified, and whose
countenance had an expression which he felt
repulsive. He thought he had seen him before,
but Shargar gave him no time to come to a
conclusion of himself.

" It's my brither Sandy, as sure's deith !" he
said ; " and he's been hingin' aboot her ever sin'
she cam in. But I dinna think she likes him
a'thegither by the leuk o' her."

" What for dinna ye gang up till her yersel',

man ?   I wadna stan' that gin 'twas me."

"I'm feared 'at he ken me. He's terrible
gleg. A' the Morays are gleg, and yon marquis
has an ee like a hawk."

"What does 't maitter ?   Ye hae dune naething to be ashamed o' like him."

"Ay; but it's this. I wadna hae her hear
the trowth aboot me frae that boar's mou' o' his
first. I wad hae her hear 't frae my ain, an'
syne she canna think I meant to tak her in."

At this moment there was a movement in the
group. Shargar, receiving no reply, looked
round at Robert. It was now Shargar's turn
to be surprised at his expression.

"Are ye seein' a vraith, Robert ?" he said.
"What gars ye leuk like that, man ?"

"Oh !" answered Robert, recovering himself,
"I thought I saw some one I knew. But I'm
not sure. I'll tell you afterwards. We've been
talking too earnestly. People are beginning to
look at us."

So saying, he moved away towards the group
of which the marquis still formed one. As he
drew near he saw a piano behind Miss Hamilton. A sudden impulse seized him, and he
yielded to it. He made his way to the piano,
and seating himself, began to play very softly
—so softly that the sounds could scarcely be
heard beyond the immediate neighbourhood of
the instrument. There was no change on the

storm of talk that filled the room. But in a few
minutes a face white as a shroud was turned
round upon him from the group in front, like
the moon dawning out of a cloud. He stopped
at once, saying to himself, " I was right ;" and
rising, mingled again with the crowd. A few
minutes after, he saw Shargar leading Miss
Hamilton out of the room, and Lady Janet following. He did not intend to wait his return,
but got near the door, that he might slip out
when he should re-enter. But Shargar did not
return. For, the moment she reached the fresh
air, Miss Hamilton was so much better that
Lady Janet, whose heart was as young towards young people as if she had never had the
unfortunate love affair tradition assigned her,
asked him to see them home, and he followed
them into her carriage. Falconer left a few
minutes after, anxious for quiet that he might
make up his mind as to what he ought to do.
Before he had walked home, he had resolved on
the next step. But not wishing to see Shargar
yet, and at the same time wanting to have a
night's rest, he went home only to change his
clothes, and betook himself to a hotel in Covent
Garden.

He was at Lady Janet's door by ten o'clock
the next morning, and sent in his card to Miss
Hamilton. He was shown into the drawing-
room, where she came to him.

VOL. III.

L

" May I presume on old acquaintance ?" he asked, holding out his hand.

She looked in his face quietly, took his hand, pressed it warmly, and said,

" No one has so good a right, Mr. Falconer. Do sit down."

He placed a chair for her, and obeyed.

After a moment's silence on both sides:

" Are you aware, Miss ——?" he said and hesitated.

" Miss Hamilton," she said with a smile. " I was Miss Lindsay when you knew me so many years ago. I will explain presently."

Then with an air of expectation she awaited the finish of his sentence.

" Are you aware, Miss Hamilton, that I am Major Moray's oldest friend ?"

" I am quite aware of it, and delighted to know it. He told me so last night."

Somewhat dismayed at this answer, Falconer resumed:

"Did Major Moray likewise communicate with you concerning his own history ?"

" He did. He told me all."

Falconer was again silent for some moments.

" Shall I be presuming too far if I venture to conclude that my friend will not continue his visits ?"

" On the contrary," she answered, with the same delicate blush that in old times used to

overspread the lovely whiteness of her face, " I
expect him within half an hour."

" Then there is no time to be lost," thought
Falconer.

" Without presuming to express any opinion
of my own," he said quietly, " a social code far
less severe than that which prevails in England,
would take for granted that an impassable barrier existed between Major Moray and Miss
Hamilton."

"Do not suppose, Mr. Falconer, that I could
not meet Major Moray's honesty with equal
openness on my side."

Falconer, for the first time almost in his life,
was incapable of speech from bewilderment.
But Miss Hamilton did not in the least enjoy
his perplexity, and made haste to rescue both
him and herself. With a blush that was now
deep as any rose, she resumed:

" But I owe you equal frankness, Mr. Falconer. There is no barrier between Major Moray
and myself but the foolish—no, wicked—indis-
cretion of an otherwise innocent and ignorant
girl. Listen, Mr. Falconer: under the necessity
of the circumstances you will not misjudge me
if I compel myself to speak calmly. This, I
trust, will be my final penance. I thought Lord
Rothie was going to marry me. To do him
justice, he never said so. Make what excuse for
my folly you can. I was lost in a mist of vain

imaginations. I had had no mother to teach
me anything, Mr. Falconer, and my father never
suspected the necessity of teaching me anything. I was very ill on the passage to Antwerp, and when I began to recover a little, I
found myself beginning to doubt both my own
conduct and his lordship's intentions. Possibly
the fact that he was not quite so kind to me in
my illness as I had expected, and that I felt
hurt in consequence, aided the doubt. Then
the thought of my father returning and finding
that I had left him, came and burned in my heart
like fire. But what was I to do? I had never
been out of Aberdeen before. I did not know
even a word of French. I was altogether in
Lord Rothie's power. I thought I loved him,
but it was not much of love that sea-sickness
could get the better of. With a heart full of
despair I went on shore. The captain slipped a
note into my hand. I put it in my pocket, but
pulled it out with my handkerchief in the street.
Lord Rothie picked it up. I begged him to
give it me, but he read it, and then tore it in
pieces. I entered the hotel, as wretched as girl
could well be. I began to dislike him. But
during dinner he was so kind and attentive
that I tried to persuade myself that my fears
were fanciful. After dinner he took me out.
On the stairs we met a lady whose speech was
Scotch. Her maid called her Lady Janet. She

looked kindly at me as I passed. I thought
she could read my face. I remembered afterwards that Lord Rothie turned his head away
when we met her. We went into the cathedral.
We were standing under that curious dome,
and I was looking up at its strange lights,
when down came a rain of bell-notes on the
roof over my head. Before the first tune was
over, I seemed to expect the second, and then
the third, without thinking how I could know
what was coming; but when they ended with
the ballad of the Witch Lady, and I lifted up
my head and saw that I was not by my father's
fireside, but in Antwerp Cathedral with Lord
Rothie, despair filled me with a half insane resolution. Happily Lord Rothie was at some
little distance talking to a priest about one of
Rubens's pictures. I slipped unseen behind the
nearest pillar, and then flew from the church.
How I got to the hotel I do not know, but I
did reach it. 'Lady Janet,' was all I could say.
The waiter knew the name, and led me to her
room. I threw myself on my knees, and begged
her to save me. She assured me no one should
touch me. I gasped 'Lord Rothie,' and fainted.
When I came to myself—but I need not tell
you all the particulars. Lady Janet did take
care of me. Till last night I never saw Lord
Rothie again. I did not acknowledge him, but
he persisted in talking to me, behave as I

would, and I saw well enough that he knew me."

Falconer took her hand and kissed it.

"Thank God," he said. "That spire was indeed the haunt of angels as I fancied while I played upon those bells."

"I knew it was you—that is, I was sure of it when I came to think about it; but at the time I took it for a direct message from heaven, which nobody heard but myself."

"It was such none the less that I was sent to deliver it," said Falconer. "I little thought during my imprisonment because of it, that the end of my journey was already accomplished."

Mysie put her hand in his.

"You have saved me, Mr. Falconer."

"For Ericson's sake, who was dying and could not," returned Falconer.

"Ah!" said Mysie, her large eyes opening with wonder. It was evident she had had no suspicion of his attachment to her.

"But," said Falconer, "there was another in it, without whom I could have done nothing."

"Who was that?"

"George Moray."

"Did he know me then?"

"No. Fortunately not. You would not have looked at him then. It was all done for love of me. He is the truest fellow in the world, and altogether worthy of you, Miss Hamilton. I will tell you the whole story some day, lest he should not do himself justice."

"Ah, that reminds me. Hamilton sounds strange in your voice. You suspected me of having changed my name to hide my history?"

It was so, and Falconer's silence acknowledged the fact.

"Lady Janet brought me home, and told my father all. When he died a few years after, she took me to live with her, and never rested till she had brought me acquainted with Sir John Hamilton, in favour of whom my father had renounced his claim to some disputed estates. Sir John had lost his only son, and he had no daughter. He was a kind-hearted old man, rather like my own father. He took to me, as they say, and made me change my name to his, leaving me the property that might have been my father's, on condition that whoever I married should take the same name. I don't think your friend will mind making the exchange," said Mysie in conclusion, as the door opened and Shargar came in.

"Robert, ye're a' gait (*everywhere*)!" he exclaimed as he entered. Then, stopping to ask no questions, " Ye see I'm to hae a name o' my ain efter a'," he said, with a face which looked even handsome in the light of his gladness.

Robert shook hands with him, and wished him joy heartily.

"Wha wad hae thocht it, Shargar," he added,
"that day 'at ye pat bonnets for hose upo' Black
Geordie's huves ?"

The butler announced the Marquis of Boarshead. Mysie's eyes flashed. She rose from her
seat, and advanced to meet the marquis, who
entered behind the servant. He bowed and
held out his hand. Mysie retreated one step,
and stood.

"Your lordship has no right to force yourself
upon me. You must have seen that I had no
wish to renew the acquaintance I was unhappy
enough to form—now, thank God, many years
ago."

"Forgive me, Miss Hamilton. One word
in private," said the marquis.

"Not a word," returned Mysie.

"Before these gentlemen, then, whom I have
not the honour of knowing, I offer you my
hand."

"To accept that offer would be to wrong myself even more than your lordship has done."

She went back to where Moray was standing,
and stood beside him. The evil spirit in the
marquis looked out at its windows.

"You are aware, madam," he said, "that
your reputation is in the hand I offer you?"

"The worse for it, my lord," returned Mysie,
with a scornful smile. "But your lordship's
brother will protect it."

"My brother!" said the marquis. "What do you mean? I have no brother!"

"Ye hae mair brithers than ye ken o', Lord Sandy, and I'm ane o' them," said Shargar.

"You are either a liar or a bastard, then," said the marquis, who had not been brought up in a school of which either self-restraint or respect for women were prominent characteristics.

Falconer forgot himself for a moment, and made a stride forward.

"Dinna hit him, Robert," cried Shargar. "He ance gae me a shillin', an' it helpit, as ye ken, to haud me alive to face him this day.—No liar, my lord, but a bastard, thank heaven." Then, with a laugh, he instantly added, "Gin I had been ain brither to you, my lord, God only knows what a rascal I micht hae been."

"By God, you shall answer for your damned insolence," said the marquis, and, lifting his riding-whip from the table where he had laid it, he approached his brother.

Mysie rang the bell.

"Haud yer han', Sandy," cried Shargar. "I hae faced mair fearsome foes than you. But I hae some faimily-feelin', though ye hae nane: I wadna willin'ly strike my brither."

As he spoke, he retreated a little. The marquis came on with raised whip. But Falconer stepped between, laid one of his great hands on the marquis's chest, and flung him to the other

end of the room, where he fell over an ottoman.
The same moment the servant entered.

"Ask your mistress to oblige me by coming
to the drawing-room," said Mysie.

The marquis had risen, but had not recovered
his presence of mind when Lady Janet entered. She looked inquiringly from one to the
other.

"Please, Lady Janet, will you ask the Marquis of Boarshead to leave the house," said
Mysie.

"With all my hert," answered Lady Janet;
"and the mair that he's a kin' o' a cousin o' my
ain. Gang yer wa's, Sandy. Ye 're no fit company for decent fowk; an' that ye wad ken yersel', gin ye had ony idea left o' what decency
means."

Without heeding her, the marquis went up to
Falconer.

"Your card, sir."

Lady Janet followed him.

"'Deed ye s' get nae cairds here," she said,
pushing him aside.

"So you allow your friends to insult me in
your own house as they please, cousin Janet?"
said the marquis, who probably felt her opposition the most formidable of all.

"'Deed they canna say waur o' ye nor I
think. Gang awa', an' repent. Consider yer
gray hairs, man."

This was the severest blow he had yet received. He left the room, " swearing at large."

Falconer followed him ; but what came of it nobody ever heard.

Major and Miss Hamilton were married within three months, and went out to India together, taking Nancy Kennedy with them.

CHAPTER X.

A NEOPHYTE.

BEFORE many months had passed, without the slightest approach to any formal recognition, I found myself one of the church of labour of which Falconer was clearly the bishop. As he is the subject, or rather object of my book, I will now record a fact which may serve to set forth his views more clearly. I gained a knowledge of some of the circumstances, not merely from the friendly confidences of Miss St. John and Falconer, but from being a kind of a Scotch cousin of Lady Janet Gordon, whom I had taken an opportunity of acquainting with the relation. She was old-fashioned enough to acknowledge it even with some eagerness. The ancient clan-feeling is good in this, that it opens a channel whose very existence is a justification for the flow of simply human feelings along all possible levels of social position. And I would there were more of it. Only something better is coming instead of it—a recognition of the infinite

brotherhood in Christ. All other relations, all
attempts by churches, by associations, by secret
societies—of Freemasons and others, are good
merely as they tend to destroy themselves in
the wider truth; as they teach men to be dissatisfied with their limitations. But I wander;
for I mentioned Lady Janet now, merely to account for some of the information I possess concerning Lady Georgina Betterton.

I met her once at my so-called cousin's, whom
she patronized as a dear old thing. To my
mind, she was worth twenty of her, though she
was wrinkled and Scottishly sententious. "A
sweet old bat," was another epithet of Lady
Georgina's. But she came to see her, notwithstanding, and did not refuse to share in her nice
little dinners, and least of all, when Falconer
was of the party, who had been so much taken
with Lady Janet's behaviour to the Marquis of
Boarshead, just recorded, that he positively
cultivated her acquaintance thereafter.

Lady Georgina was of an old family—an aged
family, indeed; so old, in fact, that some envi-
ous people professed to think it decrepit with
age. This, however, may well be questioned if
any argument bearing on the point may be
drawn from the person of Lady Georgina. She
was at least as tall as Mary St. John, and very
handsome—only with somewhat masculine features and expression. She had very sloping

shoulders and a long neck, which took its finest curves when she was talking to inferiors : condescension was her forte. Of the admiration of *the men*, she had had more than enough, although either they were afraid to go farther, or she was hard to please.

She had never contemplated anything admirable long enough to comprehend it; she had never looked up to man or woman with anything like reverence; she saw too quickly and too keenly into the foibles of all who came near her to care to look farther for their virtues. If she had ever been humbled, and thence taught to look up, she might by this time have been a grand woman, worthy of a great man's worship. She patronized Miss St. John, considerably to her amusement, and nothing to her indignation. Of course she could not understand her. She had a vague notion of how she spent her time; and believing a certain amount of fanaticism essential to religion, wondered how so sensible and ladylike a person as Miss St. John could *go in for* it.

Meeting Falconer at Lady Janet's, she was taken with him. Possibly she recognized in him a strength that would have made him her master, if he had cared for such a distinction; but nothing she could say attracted more than a passing attention on his part. Falconer was out of her sphere, and her influences were powerless to reach him.

At length she began to have a glimmering of the relation of labour between Miss St. John and him, and applied to the former for some enlightenment. But Miss St. John was far from explicit, for she had no desire for such assistance as Lady Georgina's. What motives next led her to seek the interview I am now about to record, I cannot satisfactorily explain, but I will hazard a conjecture or two, although I doubt if she understood them thoroughly herself.

She was, if not *blasée*, at least *ennuyée*, and began to miss excitement, and feel blindly about her for something to make life interesting. She was gifted with far more capacity than had ever been exercised, and was of a large enough nature to have grown sooner weary of trifles than most women of her class. She might have been an artist, but she drew like a young lady; she might have been a prophetess, and Byron was her greatest poet. It is no wonder that she wanted something she had not got.

Since she had been foiled in her attempt on Miss St. John, which she attributed to jealousy, she had, in quite another circle, heard strange, wonderful, even romantic stories about Falconer and his doings among the poor. A new world seemed to open before her longing gaze—a world, or a calenture, a mirage? for would she cross the " wandering fields of barren foam," to reach the green grass that did wave on the far

shore? the dewless desert to reach the fair
water that did lie leagues beyond its pictured
sweetness? But I think, mingled with whatever
motives she may have had, there must have been
some desire to be a nobler, that is a more useful
woman than she had been.

She had not any superabundance of feminine
delicacy, though she had plenty of good-breed-
ing, and she trusted to her position in society
to cover the eccentricity of her present under-
taking.

One morning after breakfast she called upon
Falconer; and accustomed to visits from all sorts
of people, Mrs. Ashton showed her into his sitting-room without even asking her name.   She
found him at his piano, apologized in her
fashionable drawl, for interrupting his music,
and accepted his offer of a chair without a shade
of embarrassment. Falconer seated himself and
sat waiting.

"I fear the step I have taken will appear
strange to you, Mr. Falconer. Indeed it appears
strange to myself.   I am afraid it may appear
stranger still."

"It is easy for me to leave all judgment in
the matter to yourself, Miss —— I beg your
pardon; I know we have met; but for the moment I cannot recall your name."

"Lady Georgina Betterton," drawled the visitor carelessly, hiding whatever annoyance she may have felt.

Falconer bowed. Lady Georgina resumed.

"Of course it only affects myself; and I am willing to take the risk, notwithstanding the natural desire to stand well in the opinion of any one with whom even *my* boldness could venture such a step."

A smile, intended to be playful, covered the retreat of the sentence. Falconer bowed again. Lady Georgina had yet again to resume.

"From the little I have seen, and the much I have heard of you—excuse me, Mr. Falconer—I cannot help thinking that you know more of the secret of life than other people—if indeed it has any secret."

"Life certainly is no burden to me," returned Falconer. "If that implies the possession of any secret which is not common property, I fear it also involves a natural doubt whether such secret be communicable."

"Of course I mean only some secret everybody ought to know."

"I do not misunderstand you."

"I want to live. You know the world, Mr. Falconer. I need not tell you what kind of life a girl like myself leads. I am not old, but the gilding is worn off. Life looks bare, ugly, uninteresting. I ask you to tell me whether there is any reality in it or not; whether its past glow was only gilt; whether the best that can be done is to get through with it as fast as possible?"

"Surely your ladyship must know some persons whose very countenances prove that they have found a reality at the heart of life."

"Yes. But none whose judgment I could trust. I cannot tell how soon they may find reason to change their minds on the subject. Their satisfaction may only be that they have not tried to rub the varnish off the gilding so much as I, and therefore the gilding itself still shines a little in their eyes."

"If it be only gilding, it is better it should be rubbed off."

"But I am unwilling to think it is. I am not willing to sign a bond of farewell to hope. Life seemed good once. It is bad enough that it seems such no longer, without consenting that it must and shall be so. Allow me to add, for my own sake, that I speak from the bitterness of no chagrin. I have had all I ever cared—or condescended to wish for. I never had anything worth the name of a disappointment in my life."

"I cannot congratulate you upon that," said Falconer, seriously. "But if there be a truth or a heart in life, assurance of the fact can only spring from harmony with that truth. It is not to be known save by absolute contact with it;

and the sole guide in the direction of it must be duty: I can imagine no other possible conductor. We must do before we can know."

"Yes, yes," replied Lady Georgina, hastily, in a tone that implied, "Of course, of course: we know all about that." But aware at once, with the fine instinct belonging to her mental organization, that she was thus shutting the door against all further communication, she added instantly: "But what *is* one's duty? There is the question."

"The thing that lies next you, of course. You are, and must remain, the sole judge of that. Another cannot help you."

"But that is just what I do not know."

I interrupt Lady Georgina to remark—for I too have been a pupil of Falconer—that I believe she must have suspected what her duty was, but would not look firmly at her own suspicion. She added:

"I want direction."

But the same moment she proceeded to indicate the direction in which she wanted to be directed; for she went on:

"You know that now-a-days there are so many modes in which to employ one's time and money that one does not know which to choose. The lower strata of society, you know, Mr. Falconer—so many channels! I want the advice of a man of experience, as to the best investment, if I may use the expression : I do not mean of money only, but of time as well."

" I am not fitted to give advice in such a matter."

" Mr. Falconer !"

" I assure you I am not. I subscribe to no society myself—not one."

" Excuse me, but I can hardly believe the rumours I hear of you—people will talk, you know—are all inventions. They say you are for ever burrowing amongst the poor. Excuse the phrase."

" I excuse or accept it, whichever you please. Whatever I do, I am my own steward."

" Then you are just the person to help me ! I have a fortune, not very limited, at my own disposal : a gentleman who is his own steward, would find his labours merely facilitated by administering for another as well—such labours, I mean."

" I must beg to be excused, Lady Georgina. I am accountable only for my own, and of that I have quite as much as I can properly manage. It is far more difficult to use money for others than to spend it for yourself."

" Ah !" said Lady Georgina, thoughtfully, and cast an involuntary glance round the untidy room, with its horse-hair furniture, its ragged array of books on the wall, its side-table littered with pamphlets he never read, with papers he never printed, with pipes he smoked by chance turns. He saw the glance and understood it.

"I am accustomed," he said, "to be in such sad places for human beings to live in, that I sometimes think even this dingy old room an absolute palace of comfort.—But," he added, checking himself, as it were, " I do not see in the least how your proposal would facilitate an answer to your question."

"You seem hardly inclined to do me justice," said Lady Georgina, with, for the first time, a perceptible, though slight shadow crossing the disc of her resolution. "I only meant it," she went on, "as a step towards a further proposal, which I think you will allow looks at least in the direction you have been indicating."

She paused.

"May I beg of you to state the proposal?" said Falconer.

But Lady Georgina was apparently in some little difficulty as to the proper form in which to express her object. At last it appeared in the cloak of a question.

"Do you require no assistance in your efforts for the elevation of the lower classes?" she asked.

"I don't make any such efforts," said Falconer.

Some of my lady-readers will probably be remarking to themselves, "How disagreeable of him! I can't endure the man." If they knew how Falconer had to beware of the forwardness and annoyance of well-meaning women, they would not dislike him so much. But Falconer could be indifferent to much dislike, and therein I know some men that envy him.

When he saw, however, that Lady Georgina was trying to swallow a lump in her throat, he hastened to add,

"I have only relations with individuals—none with classes."

Lady Georgina gathered her failing courage. "Then there is the more hope for me," she said. "Surely there are things a woman might be useful in that a man cannot do so well—especially if she would do as she was told, Mr. Falconer?"

He looked at her, inquiring of her whole person what *numen* abode in the fane. She misunderstood the look.

"I could dress very differently, you know. I will be a sister of charity, if you like."

"And wear a uniform?—as if the god of another world wanted to make proselytes or traitors in this! No, Lady Georgina, it was not of a dress so easily altered that I was thinking; it was of the *habit*, the dress of mind, of thought, of feeling. When you laid aside your beautiful dress, could you avoid putting on the garment of *condescension*, the most unchristian virtue attributed to Deity or saint? Could you—I must be plain with you, Lady Georgina, for this has nothing to do with the forms of so-called society—could your temper endure the mortifications of low opposition and misrepresentation of motive and end—which, avoid intrusion as you might, would yet force themselves on your perception? Could you be rudely, impudently thwarted by the very persons for whom you were spending your strength and means, and show no resentment? Could you make allowances for them as for your own brothers and sisters, your own children?"

Lady Georgina was silent.

"I shall seem to glorify myself, but at that risk I must put the reality before you.—Could you endure the ugliness both moral and physical which you must meet at every turn? Could you look upon loathsomeness, not merely without turning away in disgust, and thus wounding the very heart you would heal, but without losing your belief in the Fatherhood of God, by losing your faith in the actual blood-relationship to yourself of these wretched beings? Could you believe in the immortal essence hidden under all this garbage—God at the root of it all? How would the delicate senses you probably inherit receive the intrusions from which they could not protect themselves? Would you be in no danger of finding personal refuge in the horrid fancy, that these are but the slimy borders of humanity where it slides into, and is one with bestiality? I could show you one fearful baboonlike woman, whose very face makes my nerves shudder: could you believe that woman might one day become a lady, beautiful as yourself, and *therefore* minister to her? Would you not be tempted, for the sake of your own comfort, if not for the pride of your own humanity, to believe that, like untimely blossoms, these must fall from off the boughs of the tree of life, and come to nothing at all—a theory that may do for the preacher, but will not do for the worker: him it would paralyse?—or, still worse, infinitely worse, that they were doomed, from their birth, to endless ages of a damnation, filthy as that in which you now found them, and must probably leave them? If you could come to this, you had better withhold your hand; for no desire for the betterment of the masses, as they are stupidly called, can make up for a lack of faith in the individual. If you cannot hope for them in your heart, your hands cannot reach them to do them good. They will only hurt them."

Lady Georgina was still silent. Falconer's eloquence had perhaps made her ashamed.

" I want you to sit down and count the cost, before you do any mischief by beginning what you are unfit for. Last week I was compelled more than once to leave the house where my duty led me, and to sit down upon a stone in

the street, so ill that I was in danger of being
led away as intoxicated, only the policeman
happened to know me. Twice I went back to
the room I had left, crowded with human
animals, and one of them at least dying. It
was all I could do, and I have tolerable nerve
and tolerable experience."

A mist was gathering over Lady Georgina's
eyes. She confessed it afterwards to Miss St.
John. And through the mist he looked larger
than human.

"And then the time you must spend before
you can lay hold upon them at all, that is with
the personal relation which alone is of any real
influence! Our Saviour himself had to be thirty
years in the world before he had footing enough
in it to justify him in beginning to teach pub-
licly: he had been laying the needful foundations
all the time. Not under any circumstances
could I consent to make use of you before you
had brought yourself into genuine relations with
some of them first."

"Do you count societies, then, of no use whatever?" Lady Georgina asked, more to break
the awkwardness of her prolonged silence than
for any other reason.

"In as far as any of the persons they employ
fulfil the conditions of which I have spoken,
they are useful—that is, just in as far as they
come into genuine human relations with those

whom they would help. In as far as their servants are incapable of this, the societies are hurtful. The chief good which societies might effect would be the procuring of simple justice for the poor. That is what they need at the hands of the nation, and what they do not receive. But though few can have the knowledge of the poor I have, many could do something, if they would only set about it simply, and not be too anxious to convert them; if they would only be their friends after a common-sense fashion. I know, say, a hundred wretched men and women far better than a man in general knows him with whom he claims an ordinary intimacy. I know many more by sight whose names in the natural course of events I shall probably know soon. I know many of their relations to each other, and they talk about each other to me as if I were one of themselves, which I hope in God I am. I have been amongst them a good many years now, and shall probably spend my life amongst them. When I went first, I was repeatedly robbed; now I should hardly fear to carry another man's property. Two years ago I had my purse taken, but next morning it was returned, I do not know by whom: in fact it was put into my pocket again —every coin, as far as I could judge, as it left me. I seldom pretend to teach them—only now and then drop a word of advice. But possibly, before I die, I may speak to them in public. At present I avoid all attempt at organization of any sort, and as far as I see, am likely of all things to avoid it. What I want is first to be their friend, and then to be at length recognized as such. It is only in rare cases that I seek the acquaintance of any of them: I let it come naturally. I bide my time. Almost never do I offer assistance. I wait till they ask it, and then often refuse the sort they want. The worst thing you can do for them is to attempt to save them from the natural consequences of wrong: you may sometimes help them out of them. But it is right to do many things for them when you know them, which it would not be right to do for them until you know them. I am amongst them; they know me; their children know me; and something is always occurring that makes this or that one come to me. Once I have a footing, I seldom lose it. So you see, in this my labour I am content to do the thing that lies next me. I wait events. You have had no training, no blundering to fit you for such work. There are many other modes of being useful; but none in which I could undertake to direct you. I am not in the habit of talking so much about my ways—but that is of no consequence. I think I am right in doing so in this instance."

"I cannot misunderstand you," faltered Lady Georgina.

Falconer was silent. Without looking up from the floor on which her eyes had rested all the time he spoke, Lady Georgina said at last:

"Then what is *my* next duty? What is the thing that lies nearest to me?"

"That, I repeat, belongs to your every-day history. No one can answer that question but yourself. Your next duty is just to determine what your next duty is.—Is there nothing you neglect? Is there nothing you know you ought not to do?—You would know your duty, if you thought in earnest about it, and were not ambitious of great things."

"Ah then," responded Lady Georgina, with an abandoning sigh, "I suppose it is something very commonplace, which will make life more dreary than ever. That cannot help me."

"It will, if it be as dreary as reading the newspapers to an old deaf aunt. It will soon lead you to something more. Your duty will begin to comfort you at once, but will at length open the unknown fountain of life in your heart."

Lady Georgina lifted up her head in despair, looked at Falconer through eyes full of tears, and said vehemently,

"Mr. Falconer, you can have no conception how wretched a life like mine is. And the futility of everything is embittered by the consciousness that it is from no superiority to such things that I do not care for them."

"It *is* from superiority to such things that you do not care for them. You were not made for such things. They cannot fill your heart. It has whole regions with which they have no relation."

"The very thought of music makes me feel ill. I used to be passionately fond of it."

"I presume you got so far in it that you asked, 'Is there nothing more?' Concluding there was nothing more, and yet needing more, you turned from it with disappointment?"

"It is the same," she went on hurriedly, "with painting, modelling, reading—whatever I have tried. I am sick of them all. They do nothing for me."

"How can you enjoy music, Lady Georgina, if you are not in harmony with the heart and source of music?"

"How do you mean?"

"Until the human heart knows the divine heart, it must sigh and complain like a petulant child, who flings his toys from him because his mother is not at home. When his mother comes back to him he finds his toys are good still. When we find Him in our own hearts, we shall find him in everything, and music will be deep enough then, Lady Georgina. It is this that the Brahmin and the Platonist seek; it is this that the mystic and the anchorite sigh for; towards this the teaching of the greatest of men would lead us: Lord Bacon himself says, 'Nothing can fill, much less extend the soul of man, but God, and the contemplation of God.' It is Life you want. If you will look in your New Testament, and find out all that our Lord says about Life, you will find the only cure for your malady. I know what such talk looks like; but depend upon it, what I am talking about is something very different from what you fancy it. Anyhow to this you must come, one day or other."

"But how am I to. gain this indescribable good, which so many seek, and so few find?"

"Those are not my words," said Falconer emphatically. "I should have said—'which so few yet seek; but so many shall at length find.'"

"Do not quarrel with my foolish words, but tell me how I am to find it; for I suppose there must be something in what so many good people assert."

"You thought I could give you help?"

"Yes. That is why I came to you."

"Just so. I cannot give you help. Go and ask it of one who can."

"Speak more plainly."

"Well then: if there be a God, he must hear you if you call to him. If there be a father, he will listen to his child. He will teach you everything."

"But I don't know what I want."

"He does: ask him to tell you what you want. It all comes back to the old story: 'If ye then being evil, know how to give good gifts to your children, how much more will your heavenly Father give the holy Spirit to them that ask him!' But I wish you would read your New Testament—the Gospels I mean: you are not in the least fit to understand the Epistles yet. Read the story of our Saviour as if you had never read it before. He at least was a man who seemed to have that secret of life after the knowledge of which your heart is longing."

Lady Georgina rose. Her eyes were again full of tears. Falconer too was moved. She held out her hand to him, and without another word left the room. She never came there again.

Her manner towards Falconer was thereafter much altered. People said she was in love with him: if she was, it did her no harm. Her whole character certainly was changed. She sought the friendship of Miss St. John, who came at length to like her so much, that she took her with her in some of her walks among the poor. By degrees she began to do something herself after a quiet modest fashion. But within a few years, probably while so engaged, she caught a fever from which she did not recover. It was not till after her death that Falconer told any one of the interview he had had with her. And by that time I had the honour of being very intimate with him. When she knew that she was dying, she sent for him. Mary St. John was with her. She left them together. When he came out, he was weeping.

CHAPTER XI.

THE SUICIDE.

FALCONER lived on and laboured on in London. Wherever he found a man fitted for the work, he placed him in such office as De Fleuri already occupied. At the same time he went more into society, and gained the friendship of many influential people. Besides the use he made of this to carry out plans for individual rescue, it enabled him to bestir himself for the first and chief good which he believed it was in the power of the government to effect for the class amongst which he laboured. As I have shown, he did not believe in any positive good being effected save through individual contact —through faith, in a word—faith in the human helper—which might become a stepping-stone through the chaotic misery towards faith in the Lord and in his Father. All that association could do, as such, was only, in his judgment, to remove obstructions from the way of individual growth and education—to put better conditions within reach—first of all, to provide that the people should be able, if they would, to live decently. He had no notion of domestic inspection, or of offering prizes for cleanliness and order. He knew that misery and wretchedness are the right and best condition of those who live so that misery and wretchedness are the natural consequences of their life. But there ought always to be the possibility of emerging from these; and as things were, over the whole country, for many who would if they could, it was impossible to breathe fresh air, to be clean, to live like human beings. And he saw this difficulty ever on the increase, through the rapacity of the holders of small house-property, and the utter wickedness of railway companies, who pulled down every house that stood in their way, and did nothing to provide room for those who were thus ejected—most probably from a wretched place, but only to be driven into a more wretched still. To provide suitable dwellings for the poor he considered the most pressing of all necessary reforms. His own fortune was not sufficient for doing much in this way, but he set about doing what he could by purchasing houses in which the poor lived, and putting them into the hands of persons whom he could trust, and who were immediately responsible to him for their proceedings: they had to make them fit for human abodes, and let them to those who desired better accommodation, giving the preference to those already tenants, so long as they paid their reasonable rent, which he considered far more necessary for them to do than for him to have done.

One day he met by appointment the owner of a small block, of which he contemplated the purchase. They were in a dreadfully dilapidated condition, a shame that belonged more to the owner than the inhabitants. The man wanted to sell the houses, or at least was willing to sell them, but put an exorbitant price upon them. Falconer expostulated.

"I know the whole of the rent these houses could bring you in," he said, "without making any deduction for vacancies and defalcations: what you ask is twice as much as they would fetch if the full rent were certain."

The poor wretch looked up at him with the leer of a ghoul. He was dressed like a broken-down clergyman, in rusty black, with a neck-cloth of whitey-brown.

"I admit it," he said in good English, and a rather educated tone. "Your arguments are indisputable. I confess besides that so far short does the yield come of the amount on paper, that it would pay me to give them away. But it's the funerals, sir, that make it worth my while. I'm an undertaker, as you may judge from my costume. I count back-rent in the burying. People may cheat their landlord, but they can't cheat the undertaker. They *must* be buried. That's the one indispensable—ain't it, sir?"

Falconer had let him run on that he might have the measure of him. Now he was prepared with his reply.

"You've told me your profession," he said: "I'll tell you mine. I am a lawyer. If you don't let me have those houses for five hundred, which is the full market value, I'll prosecute you. It'll take a good penny from the profits of your coffins to put those houses in a state to satisfy the inspector."

The wretched creature was struck dumb. Falconer resumed.

"You're the sort of man that ought to be kept to your pound of filthy flesh. I know what I say; and I'll do it. The law costs me nothing. *You* won't find it so."

The undertaker sold the houses, and no longer in that quarter killed the people he wanted to bury.

I give this as a specimen of the kind of thing Falconer did. But he took none of the business part in his own hands, on the same principle on which Paul the Apostle said it was unmeet for him to leave the preaching of the word in order to serve tables—not that the thing was beneath him, but that it was not his work so long as he could be doing more important service still.

De Fleuri was one of his chief supports. The

whole nature of the man mellowed under the sun of Falconer, and over the work that Falconer gave him to do. His daughter recovered, and devoted herself to the same labour that had rescued her. Miss St. John was her *superior.* By degrees, without any laws or regulations, a little company was gathered, not of ladies and gentlemen, but of men and women, who aided each other, and without once meeting as a whole, laboured not the less as one body in the work of the Lord, bound in one by bonds that had nothing to do with cobweb committee meetings or public dinners, chairmen or wine-flushed subscriptions. They worked like the leaven of which the Lord spoke.

But De Fleuri, like almost every one in the community I believe, had his own private schemes subserving the general good. He knew the best men of his own class and his own trade, and with them his superior intellectual gifts gave him influence. To them he told the story of Falconer's behaviour to him, of Falconer's own need, and of his hungry-hearted search. An enthusiasm of help seized upon the men. To aid your superior is such a rousing gladness!—Was anything of this in St. Paul's mind when he spoke of our being fellow-workers with God? I only put the question.— Each one of these had his own trustworthy ac-quaintances, or neighbours, rather—for like finds out like all the world *through*, as well as *over*—and to them he told the story of Falconer and his father, so that in all that region of London it became known that the man who loved the poor was himself needy, and looked to the poor for their help. Without them he could not be made perfect.

Some of my readers may be inclined to say that it was dishonourable in Falconer to have occasioned the publishing of his father's disgrace. Such may recall to their minds that concealment is no law of the universe; that, on the contrary, the Lord of the Universe said once: "There is nothing covered that shall not be revealed." Was the disgrace of Andrew Falconer greater because a thousand men knew it, instead of forty, who could not help knowing it? Hope lies in light and knowledge. Andrew would be none the worse that honest men knew of his vice: they would be the first to honour him if he should overcome it. If he would not—the disgrace was just, and would fall upon his son only in sorrow, not in dishonour. The grace of God—the making of humanity by his beautiful hand—no, heart—is such, that disgrace clings to no man after repentance, any more than the feet defiled with the mud of the world come yet defiled from the bath. Even the things that proceed out of the man, and do terribly defile him, can be cast off

like the pollution of the leper by a grace that
goes deeper than they ; and the man who says,
" I have sinned : I will sin no more," is even by
the voice of his brothers crowned as a conquer-
or, and by their hearts loved as one who has
suffered and overcome. Blessing on the God-
born human heart ! Let the hounds of God,
not of Satan, loose upon sin ;—God only can
rule the dogs of the devil ;—let them hunt it to
the earth ; let them drag forth the demoniac to
the feet of the Man who loved the people while
he let the devil take their swine ; and do not
talk about disgrace from a thing being known,
when the disgrace is that the thing should exist.

One night I was returning home from some
poor attempts of my own. I had now been a
pupil of Falconer for a considerable time, but
having my own livelihood to make, I could not
do so much as I would.

It was late, nearly twelve o'clock, as I passed
through the region of Seven Dials. Here and
there stood three or four brutal-looking men, and
now and then a squalid woman with a starve-
ling baby in her arms, in the light of the gin-
shops. The babies were the saddest to see—
nursery-plants already in training for the places
these men and women now held, then to fill a
pauper's grave, or perhaps a perpetual cell
—say rather, for the awful spaces of silence,
where the railway director can no longer be

guilty of a worse sin than house-breaking, and his miserable brother will have no need of the shelter of which he deprived him. Now and then a flaunting woman wavered past—a *night-shade*, as our old dramatists would have called her. I could hardly keep down an evil disgust that would have conquered my pity, when a scanty white dress would stop beneath a lamp, and the gay dirty bonnet, turning round, reveal a painted face, from which shone little more than an animal intelligence, *not* brightened by the gin she had been drinking. Vague noises of strife and of drunken wrath flitted around me as I passed an alley, or an opening door let out its evil secret. Once I thought I heard the dull *thud* of a blow on the head. The noisome vapours were fit for any of Swedenborg's hells. There were few sounds, but the very quiet seemed infernal. The night was hot and sultry. A skinned cat, possibly still alive, fell on the street before me. Under one of the gas-lamps lay something long: it was a tress of dark hair, torn perhaps from some woman's head: she had beautiful hair at least. Once I heard the cry of *murder*, but where, in that chaos of humanity, right or left, before or behind me, I could not even guess. *Home* to such regions, from gorgeous stage-scenery and dresses, from splendid, mirror-beladen casinos, from singing-halls, and places of private and prolonged revelry, trail the daughters of men at all hours from midnight till morning. Next day they drink hell-fire that they may forget. Sleep brings an hour or two of oblivion, hardly of peace; but they must wake, worn and miserable, and the waking brings no hope : their only known help lies in the gin-shop. What can be done with them ? But the secrets God keeps must be as good as those he tells.

But no sights of the night ever affected me so much as walking through this same St. Giles's on a summer Sunday morning, when church-goers were in church. Oh! the faces that creep out into the sunshine then, and haunt their doors! Some of them but skins drawn over skulls, living Death's-heads, grotesque in their hideousness.

I was not very far from Falconer's abode. My mind was oppressed with sad thoughts and a sense of helplessness. I began to wonder what Falconer might at that moment be about. I had not seen him for a long time—a whole fortnight. He might be at home : I would go and see, and if there were light in his windows I would ring his bell.

I went. There was light in his windows. He opened the door himself, and welcomed me. I went up with him, and we began to talk. I told him of my sad thoughts, and my feelings of helplessness.

"He that believeth shall not make haste," he said. "There is plenty of time. You must not imagine that the result depends on you, or that a single human soul can be lost because you may fail. The question, as far as you are concerned, is, whether you are to be honoured in having a hand in the work that God is doing, and will do, whether you help him or not. Some will be honoured: shall it be me? And this honour gained excludes no one: there is work, as there is bread in his house, enough and to spare. It shows no faith in God to make frantic efforts or frantic lamentations. Besides, we ought to teach ourselves to see, as much as we may, the good that is in the condition of the poor."

"Teach me to see that, then," I said. "Show me something."

"The best thing is their kindness to each other. There is an absolute divinity in their self-denial for those who are poorer than themselves. I know one man and woman, married people, who pawned their very furniture and wearing apparel to procure cod-liver oil for a girl dying in consumption. She was not even a relative, only an acquaintance of former years. They had found her destitute and taken her to their own poor home. There are fathers and mothers who will work hard all the morning, and when dinner time comes 'don't want any,' that there may be enough for their children—or half enough, more likely. Children will take the bread out of their own mouths to put in that of their sick brother, or to stick in the fist of baby crying for a crust—giving only a queer little helpless grin, half of hungry sympathy, half of pleasure, as they see it disappear. The marvel to me is that the children turn out so well as they do; but that applies to the children in all ranks of life. Have you ever watched a group of poor children, half a dozen of them with babies in their arms?"

"I have, a little, and have seen such a strange mixture of carelessness and devotion."

"Yes. I was once stopped in the street by a child of ten, with face absolutely swollen with weeping, asking me to go and see baby who was very ill. She had dropped him four times that morning, but had no idea that could have done him any harm. The carelessness is ignorance. Their form of it is not half so shocking as that of the mother who will tremble at the slightest sign of suffering in her child, but will hear him lie against his brother without the smallest discomfort. Ah! we shall all find, I fear, some day, that we have differed from each other, where we have done best, only in mode —perhaps not even in degree. A grinding tradesman takes advantage of the over supply of labour to get his work done at starvation prices:

I owe him love, and have never thought of paying my debt except in boundless indignation."

"I wish I had your faith and courage, Mr. Falconer," I said.

"You are in a fair way of having far more," he returned. "You are not so old as I am, by a long way. But I fear you are getting out of spirits. Is to-morrow a hard day with you?"

"I have next to nothing to do to-morrow."

"Then will you come to me in the evening? We will go out together."

Of course I was only too glad to accept the proposal. But our talk did not end here. The morning began to shine before I rose to leave him; and before I reached my abode it was broad daylight. But what a different heart I carried within me! And what a different London it was outside of me! The scent of the hayfields came on the hardly-moving air. It was a strange morning—a new day of unknown history—in whose young light the very streets were transformed, looking clear and clean, and wondrously transparent in perspective, with unknown shadows lying in unexpected nooks, with projection and recess, line and bend, as I had never seen them before. The light was coming as if for the first time since the city sprang into being—as if a thousand years had rolled over it in darkness and lamplight, and now, now, after the prayers and longings of ages, the sun of God was ascending the awful east, and the spirit-voice had gone forth: "Arise, shine, for thy light is come."

It was a well-behaved, proper London through which I walked home. Here and there, it is true, a debauched-looking man, with pale face, and red sleepy eyes, or a weary, withered girl, like a half-moon in the daylight, straggled some-whither. But they looked strange to the London of the morning. They were not of it. Alas for those who creep to their dens, like the wild beasts when the sun arises, because the light has shaken them out of the world. All the horrid phantasms of the Valley of the Shadow of Death that had risen from the pit with the vaporous night had sunk to escape the arrows of the sun, once more into its bottom-less depth. If any horrid deed was doing now, how much more horrid in the awful still light of this first hour of a summer morn! How many evil passions now lay sunk under the holy waves of sleep! How many heart-aches were gnawing only in dreams, to wake with the brain, and gnaw in earnest again! And over all brooded the love of the Lord Christ, who is Lord over all blessed for ever, and shall yet cast death and hell into the lake of fire—the holy purifying Fate.

I got through my sole engagement—a very dreary one, for surely never were there stupider young people in the whole region of rank than those to whom duty and necessity sent me on the Wednesday mornings of that London season —even with some enjoyment. For the lessons Falconer had been giving me clung to me and grew on me until I said thus to myself: " Am I to believe only for the poor, and not for the rich ? Am I not to bear with conceit even, hard as it is to teach ? for is not this conceit itself the measure as the consequence of incapacity and ignorance ? They cannot help being born stupid, any more than some of those children in St. Giles's can help being born preternaturally, unhealthily clever. I am going with my friend this evening : that hope is enough to make me strong for one day at least." So I set myself to my task, and that morning wiled the first gleam of intelligent delight out of the eyes of one poor little washed-out ladyship. I could have kissed her from positive thankfulness.

The day did wear over. The evening did come. I was with my friend—for friend I could call him none the less and all the more that I worshipped him.

" I have business in Westminster," he said, " and then on the other side of the water."

" I am more and more astonished at your knowledge of London, Mr. Falconer," I said. " You must have a great faculty for places."

"I think rather the contrary," he answered. "But there is no end to the growth of a faculty, if one only uses it—especially when his whole nature is interested in its efficiency, and makes demands upon it. The will applies to the intellect; the intellect communicates its necessities to the brain; the brain bestirs itself, and grows more active; the eyes lend their aid; the memory tries not to be behind; and at length you have a man gifted in localities."

"How is it that people generally can live in such quiet ignorance of the regions that surround them, and the kind of humanity so near them?" I said after a pause.

"It does seem strange. It is as if a man should not know who were in his own house. Would-be civilization has for the very centre of its citadel, for the citizens of its innermost city, for the heart around which the gay and fashionable, the learned, the artistic, the virtuous, the religious are gathered, a people some of whom are barbarous, some cruel, many miserable, many unhappy, save for brief moments not of hope, but of defiance, distilled in the alembic of the brain from gin: what better life could steam up from such a Phlegethon! Look there: 'Cream of the Valley!' As if the mocking serpent must with sweet words of Paradise deepen the horrors of the hellish compound, to which so many of our brothers and sisters made in the image of

God, fly as to their only Saviour from the misery of feeling alive."

"How is it that the civilized people of London do not make a simultaneous inroad upon the haunts of the demons and drive them out?"

"It is a mercy they do not. They would only do infinite mischief. The best notion civilization seems to have is—not to drive out the demons, but to drive out the possessed; to take from them the poor refuges they have, and crowd them into deeper and more fetid hells—to make room for what?—more and more temples in which Mammon may be worshipped. The good people on the other hand invade them with foolish tracts, that lie against God; or give their money to build churches, where there is as yet no people that will go to them. Why, the other day, a young clergyman bored me, and would have been boring me till now, I think, if I would have let him, to part with a block of my houses, where I know every man, woman, and child, and keep them in comparative comfort and cleanliness and decency, to say no more, that he might pull them down and build a church upon the site—not quite five minutes' walk from the church where he now officiates."

It was a blowing, moon-lit night. The gaslights flickered and wavered in the gusts of wind. It was cold, very cold for the season. Even Falconer buttoned his coat over his chest.

He got a few paces in advance of me sometimes, when I saw him towering black and tall and somewhat gaunt, like a walking shadow. The wind increased in violence. It was a north-easter, laden with dust, and a sense of frozen Siberian steppes. We had to stoop and head it at the corners of streets. Not many people were out, and those who were, seemed to be hurrying home. A few little provision-shops, and a few inferior butchers' stalls were still open. Their great jets of gas, which looked as if they must poison the meat, were flaming fierce and horizontal, roaring like fiery flags, and anon dying into a blue hiss. Discordant singing, more like the howling of wild beasts, came from the corner houses, which blazed like the gates of hell. Their doors were ever on the swing, and the hot odours of death rushed out, and the cold blast of life rushed in. We paused a little before one of them—over the door, upon the sign, was in very deed the name *Death*. There were ragged women within who took their half-dead babies from their bare, cold, cheerless bosoms, and gave them of the poison of which they themselves drank renewed despair in the name of comfort. They say that most of the gin consumed in London is drunk by women. And the little clay-coloured baby-faces made a grimace or two, and sank to sleep on the thin tawny breasts of the mothers, who having ga-

thered courage from the essence of despair,
faced the scowling night once more, and with
bare necks and hopeless hearts went—whither?
Where do they all go when the gin-hells close
their yawning jaws? Where do they lie down
at night? They vanish like unlawfully risen
corpses in the graves of cellars and garrets, in
the charnel-vaults of pestiferously-crowded lodg-
ing-houses, in the prisons of police-stations,
under *dry* arches, within hoardings; or they
make vain attempts to rest the night out upon
door-steps or curbstones. All their life long
man denies them the one right in the soil which
yet is so much theirs, that once that life is over,
he can no longer deny it—the right of room to
lie down. Space itself is not allowed to be
theirs by any right of existence: the voice of
the night-guardian commanding them to move
on, is as the howling of a death-hound hunting
them out of the air into their graves.

In St. James's we came upon a group around
the gates of a great house. Visitors were coming and going, and it was a show to be had for
nothing by those who had nothing to pay. Oh!
the children with clothes too ragged to hold
pockets for their chilled hands, that stared at
the childless duchess descending from her lordly
carriage! Oh! the wan faces, once lovely as
theirs, it may be, that gazed meagre and pinched
and hungry on the young maidens in rose-

colour and blue, tripping lightly through the
avenue of their eager eyes—not yet too en-
vious of unattainable felicity to gaze with ad-
miring sympathy on those who seemed to them
the angels, the goddesses of their kind.   "Oh
God!" I thought, but dared not speak, "and
thou couldst make *all* these girls so lovely!
Thou could give them all the gracious garments
of rose and blue and white if thou wouldst!
Why should these not be like those? They are
hungry even, and wan and torn.   These too
are thy children.   There is wealth enough in
thy mines and in thy green fields, room enough
in thy starry spaces, O God!" But a voice—
the echo of Falconer's teaching, awoke in my
heart—"Because I would have these more
blessed than those, and those more blessed with
them, for they *are* all my children."

By the Mall we came into Whitehall, and so
to Westminster Bridge.   Falconer had changed
his mind, and would cross at once.   The present bridge was not then finished, and the old
bridge alongside of it was still in use for
pedestrians. We went upon it to reach the other
side.   Its centre rose high above the other, for
the line of the new bridge ran like a chord across
the arc of the old.   Through chance gaps in the
boarding between, we looked down on the new
portion which was as yet used by carriages alone.
The moon had, throughout the evening, alter-

nately shone in brilliance from amidst a lake of
blue sky, and been overwhelmed in billowy
heaps of wind-tormented clouds. As we stood
on the apex of the bridge, looking at the night,
the dark river, and the mass of human effort
about us, the clouds gathered and closed and
tumbled upon her in crowded layers. The wind
howled through the arches beneath, swept along
the boarded fences, and whistled in their holes.
The gas-lights blew hither and thither, and were
perplexed to live at all.

We were standing at a spot where some
shorter pieces had been used in the hoarding;
and, although I could not see over them, Falconer, whose head rose more than half a foot
above mine, was looking on the other bridge below.   Suddenly he grasped the top with his
great hands, and his huge frame was over it in
an instant.   I was on the top of the hoarding
the same moment, and saw him prostrate some
twelve feet below. He was up the next instant,
and running with huge paces diagonally towards
the Surrey side. He had seen the figure of a
woman come flying along from the Westminster
side, without bonnet or shawl.   When she
came under the spot where we stood, she had
turned across at an obtuse angle towards the
other side of the bridge, and Falconer, convinced
that she meant to throw herself into the river,
went over as I have related. She had all but

scrambled over the fence—for there was no parapet yet—by the help of the great beam that ran along to support it, when he caught her by her garments. So poor and thin were those garments, that if she had not been poor and thin too, she would have dropped from them into the darkness below. He took her in his arms, lifted her down upon the bridge, and stood as if protecting her from a pursuing death. I had managed to find an easier mode of descent, and now stood a little way from them.

"Poor girl! poor girl!" he said, as if to himself: "was this the only way left?"

Then he spoke tenderly to her. What he said I could not hear—I only heard the tone.

"O sir!" she cried, in piteous entreaty, "do let me go. Why should a wretched creature like me be forced to live? It's no good to you, sir. Do let me go."

"Come here," he said, drawing her close to the fence. "Stand up again on the beam. Look down."

She obeyed, in a mechanical kind of way. But as he talked, and she kept looking down on the dark mystery beneath, flowing past with every now and then a dull vengeful glitter—continuous, forceful, slow, he felt her shudder in his still clasping arm.

"Look," he said, "how it crawls along—black and slimy! how silent and yet how fierce! Is

that a nice place to go to down there? Would
there be any rest there, do you think, tumbled
about among filth and creeping things, and
slugs that feed on the dead; among drowned
women like yourself drifting by, and murdered men, and strangled babies? Is that the
door by which you would like to go out of the
world?"

" It's no worse," she faltered, "—not so bad as
what I should leave behind."

" If this were the only way out of it, I would
not keep you from it. I would say 'Poor thing!
there is no help : she must go.' But there is another way."

" There is no other way, sir—if you knew
all," she said.

" Tell me, then."

" I cannot. I dare not. Please—I would
rather go."

She looked, from the mere glimpses I could get
of her, somewhere about five and twenty, making
due allowance for the wear of suffering so evident
even in those glimpses. I think she might have
been beautiful if the waste of her history could
have been restored. That she had had at least
some advantages of education, was evident from
both her tone and her speech. But oh, the wild
eyes, and the tortured lips, drawn back from
the teeth with an agony of hopelessness, as she
struggled anew, perhaps mistrusting them, to

escape from the great arms that held her!

"But the river cannot drown *you*," Falconer said. "It can only stop your breath. It cannot stop your thinking. You will go on thinking, thinking, all the same. Drowning people remember in a moment all their past lives. All their evil deeds come up before them, as if they were doing them all over again. So they plunge back into the past and all its misery. While their bodies are drowning, their souls are coming more and more awake."

"That is dreadful," she murmured, with her great eyes fixed on his, and growing steadier in their regard. She had ceased to struggle, so he had slackened his hold of her, and she was leaning back against the fence.

"And then," he went on, "what if, instead of closing your eyes, as you expected, and going to sleep, and forgetting everything, you should find them come open all at once, in the midst of a multitude of eyes, all round about you, all looking at you, all thinking about you, all judging you? What if you should hear, not a tumult of voices and noises, from which you could hope to hide, but a solemn company talking about you—every word clear and plain, piercing your heart with what you could not deny,—and you standing naked and shivering in the midst of them?"

"It is too dreadful!" she cried, making a

movement as if the very horror of the idea had
a fascination to draw her towards the realization of it. "But," she added, yielding to Falconer's renewed grasp, "they wouldn't be so
hard upon me there. They would not be so
cruel as men are here."

"Surely not. But all men are not cruel. I
am not cruel," he added, forgetting himself for
a moment, and caressing with his huge hand
the wild pale face that glimmered upon him as
it were out of the infinite night—all but swallowed up in it.

She drew herself back, and Falconer, instantly removing his hand, said,

" Look in my face, child, and see whether you
cannot trust me."

As he uttered the words, he took off his hat,
and stood bare-headed in the moon, which now
broke out clear from the clouds. She did look
at him. His hair blew about his face. He
turned it towards the wind and the moon, and
away from her, that she might be undisturbed in
her scrutiny. But how she judged of him, I
cannot tell; for the next moment he called out
in a tone of repressed excitement:

" Gordon, Gordon, look there—above your
head, on the other bridge."

I looked and saw a gray head peering over
the same gap through which Falconer had looked a few minutes before. I knew something of

his personal quest by this time, and concluded at once that he thought it was or might be his father.

"I cannot leave the poor thing—I dare not," he said.

I understood him, and darted off at full speed for the Surrey end of the bridge. What made me choose that end, I do not know; but I was right.

I had some reason to fear that I might be stopped when I reached it, as I had no business to be upon the new bridge. I therefore managed, where the upper bridge sank again towards a level with the lower, to scramble back upon it. As I did so the tall gray-headed man passed me with an uncertain step. I did not see his face. I followed him a few yards behind. He seemed to hear and dislike the sound of my footsteps, for he quickened his pace. I let him increase the distance between us, but followed him still. He turned down the river. I followed. He began to double. I doubled after him. Not a turn could he get before me. He crossed all the main roads leading to the bridges till he came to the last—when he turned toward London Bridge. At the other end, he went down the stairs into Thames Street, and held eastward still. It was not difficult to keep up with him, for his stride though long was slow. He never looked round, and I never saw his face; but I could not help fancying that his back and his gait and his carriage were very like Falconer's.

We were now in a quarter of which I knew nothing, but as far as I can guess from after knowledge, it was one of the worse districts in London, lying to the east of Spital Square. It was late, and there were not many people about.

As I passed a court, I was accosted thus:

"'Ain't you got a glass of ale for a poor cove, gov'nor?"

"I have no coppers," I said hastily. "I am in a hurry besides," I added as I walked on.

"Come, come!" he said, getting up with me in a moment, "that ain't a civil answer to give a cove after his lush, that 'ain't got a blessed mag."

As he spoke he laid his hand rather heavily on my arm. He was a lumpy-looking individual, like a groom who had been discharged for stealing his horse's provender, and had not quite worn out the clothes he had brought with him. From the opposite side at the same moment, another man appeared, low in stature, pale, and marked with the small-pox.

He advanced upon me at right angles. I shook off the hand of the first, and I confess would have taken to my heels, for more reasons than one, but almost before I was clear of him, the other came against me, and shoved me into one of the low-browed entries which abounded.

I was so eager to follow my chase that I acted foolishly throughout. I ought to have emptied my pockets at once; but I was unwilling to lose a watch which was an old family piece, and of value besides.

"Come, come! I don't carry a barrel of ale in my pocket," I said, thinking to keep them in good-humour. I know better now. Some of these roughs will take all you have in the most good-humoured way in the world, bandying chaff with you all the time. I had got amongst another set, however.

"Leastways you've got as good," said a third, approaching from the court, as villanous looking a fellow as I have ever seen.

"This is hardly the right way to ask for it," I said, looking out for a chance of bolting, but putting my hand in my pocket at the same time. I confess again I acted very stupidly throughout the whole affair, but it was my first experience.

"It's a way we've got down here, anyhow," said the third with a brutal laugh. "Look out, Savoury Sam," he added to one of them.

"Now I don't want to hurt you," struck in the first, coming nearer, "but if you gives tongue, I'll make cold meat of you, and gouge your pockets at my leisure, before ever a blueskin can turn the corner."

Two or three more came sidling up with their hands in their pockets.

"What have you got there, Slicer?" said one of them, addressing the third, who looked like a ticket-of-leave man.

"We've cotched a pig-headed counter-jumper here, that didn't know Jim there from a man-trap, and went by him as if he'd been a bull-dog on a long chain. He wants to fight cocum. But we won't trouble him. We'll help ourselves. Shell out now."

As he spoke he made a snatch at my watch chain. I forgot myself and hit him. The same moment I received a blow on the head, and felt the blood running down my face. I did not quite lose my senses, though, for I remember seeing yet another man—a tall fellow, coming out of the gloom of the court. How it came into my mind, I do not know, and what I said I do not remember, but I must have mentioned Falconer's name somehow.

The man they called Slicer, said,

"Who's he? Don't know the ——."

Words followed which I cannot write.

"What! you devil's gossoon!" returned an Irish voice I had not heard before. "You don't know Long Bob, you gonnof!"

All that passed I heard distinctly, but I was in a half faint, I suppose, for I could no longer see.

"Now what the devil in a dice-box do you mean?" said Slicer, possessing himself of my watch. "Who is the blasted cove?—not that I care a flash of damnation."

"A man as 'll knock you down if he thinks you want it, or give you a half-a-crown if he thinks you want it—all's one to him, only he'll have the choosing which."

"What the hell's that to me? Look spry. He mustn't lie there all night. It's too near the ken. Come along, you Scotch haddock."

I was aware of a kick in the side as he spoke.

"I tell you what it is, Slicer," said one whose voice I had not yet heard, "if so be this gentleman's a friend of Long Bob, you just let him alone, *I* say."

I opened my eyes now, and saw before me a tall rather slender man in a big loose dress-coat, to whom Slicer had turned with the words:

"*You* say! Ha! ha! Well, *I* say—There's my Scotch haddock! who'll touch him?"

"I'll take him home," said the tall man advancing towards me. I made an attempt to rise. But I grew deadly ill, fell back, and remember nothing more.

When I came to myself I was lying on a bed in a miserable place. A middle-aged woman of degraded countenance but kindly eyes, was putting something to my mouth with a teaspoon: I knew it by the smell to be gin. But I could not yet move. They began to talk about me, and I lay and listened. Indeed, while I listened, I lost for a time all inclination to get up, I was so much interested in what I heard.

"He's comin' to hisself," said the woman. "He'll be all right by and by. I wonder what brings the likes of him into the likes of this place. It must look a kind of a hell to them gentle folks, though *we* manage to live and die in it."

"I suppose," said another, "he's come on some of Mr. Falconer's business."

"That's why Job's took him in charge. They say he was after somebody or other, they think. —No friend of Mr. Falconer's would be after another for any mischief," said my hostess.

"But who is this Mr. Falconer?—Is Long Bob and he both the same alias?" asked a third.

"Why, Bessy, ain't you no better than that damned Slicer, who ought to ha' been hung up to dry this many a year? But to be sure you 'aint been long in our quarter. Why, every child hereabouts knows Mr. Falconer. Ask Bobby there?"

"Who's Mr. Falconer, Bobby?"

A child's voice made reply:

"A man with a long, long beard, that goes about, and sometimes grows tired and sits on a door-step. I see him once. But he ain't Mr. Falconer, nor Long Bob neither," added Bobby in a mysterious tone. "I know who he is."

"What do you mean, Bobby? Who is he, then?"

The child answered very slowly and solemnly:

"He's Jesus Christ."

The woman burst into a rude laugh.

"Well," said Bobby in an offended tone, "Slicer's own Tom says so, and Polly too. We all says so. He allus pats me on the head, and gives me a penny."

Here Bobby began to cry, bitterly offended at the way Bessy had received his information, after considering him sufficiently important to have his opinion asked.

"True enough," said his mother. "I see him once a sittin' on a door-step, lookin' straight afore him, and worn-out like, an' a lot o' them childer standin' all about him, an' starin' at him as mum as mice, for fear of disturbin' of him. When I come near, he got up with a smile on his face, an' give each on 'em a penny all round, and walked away. Some do say he's a bit crazed like; but I never saw no sign o' that; and if any one ought to know, that one's Job's Mary; and you may believe me when I tell you that he was here night an' mornin' for a week, and after that off and on, when we was all down in the cholerer. Ne'er a one of us would ha' come through but for him."

I made an attempt to rise. The woman came to my bedside.

"How does the gentleman feel hisself now?" she asked kindly.

"Better, thank you," I said. "I am ashamed of lying like this, but I feel very queer."

"And it's no wonder, "when that devil Slicer give you one o' his even down blows on the top o' your head. Nobody knows what he carry in his sleeve that he do it with—only you've got off well, young man, and that *I* tell you, with a decent cut like that. Only don't you go tryin' to get up now. Don't be in a hurry till your blood comes back like."

I lay still again for a little. When I lifted my hand to my head, I found it was bandaged up. I tried again to rise. The woman went to the door, and called out,

"Job, the gentleman's feelin' better. He'll soon be able to move, I think. What will you do with him now?"

"I'll go and get a cab," said Job; and I heard him go down a stair.

I raised myself, and got on the floor, but found I could not stand. By the time the cab arrived, however, I was able to crawl to it. When Job came, I saw the same tall thin man in the long dress coat. His head was bound up too.

"I am sorry to see you too have been hurt—

for my sake, of course," I said. "Is it a bad blow?"

"Oh! it ain't over much. I got in with a smeller afore he came right down with his slogger. But I say, I hope as how you *are* a friend of Mr. Falconer's, for you see we can't afford the likes of this in this quarter for every chance that falls in Slicer's way. Gentlemen has no business here."

"On the contrary, I mean to come again soon, to thank you all for being so good to me."

"Well, when you comes next, you'd better come with *him*, you know."

"You mean with Mr. Falconer?"

"Yes, who else? But are you able to go now? for the sooner you're out of this the better."

"Quite able. Just give me your arm."

He offered it kindly. Taking a grateful farewell of my hostess, I put my hand in my pocket, but there was nothing there. Job led me to the mouth of the court, where a cab, evidently of a sort with the neighbourhood, was waiting for us. I got in. Job was shutting the door.

"Come along with me, Job," I said. "I'm going straight to Mr. Falconer's. He will like to see you, especially after your kindness to me."

"Well, I don't mind if I do look arter you a little longer; for to tell the truth," said Job, as he opened the door, and got in beside me, "I

VOL. III. P

don't over and above like the look of the—
horse."

"It's no use trying to rob me over again," I
said; but he gave no reply. He only shouted
to the cabman to drive to John Street, telling
him the number.

I can scarcely recall anything more till we
reached Falconer's chambers. Job got out and
rang the bell. Mrs. Ashton came down. Her
master was not come home.

"Tell Mr. Falconer," I said, "that I'm all
right, only I couldn't make anything of it."

"Tell him," growled Job, "that he's got his
head broken, and won't be out o' bed to-morrow. That's the way with them fine bred ones.
They lies a-bed when the likes o' me must go
out what they calls a custamongering, broken
head and all."

"You shall stay at home for a week if you
like, Job—that is if I've got enough to give you
a week's earnings. I'm not sure though till I
look, for I'm not a rich man any more than
yourself."

"Rubbish!" said Job as he got in again; "I
was only flummuxing the old un. Bless your
heart, sir, I wouldn't stay in—not for nothink.
Not for a bit of a pat on the crown, nohow.
Home ain't none so nice a place to go snoozing
in—nohow. Where do you go to, gov'nor?"

I told him. When I got out, and was opening the door, leaning on his arm, I said I was very glad they hadn't taken my keys.

" Slicer nor Savoury Sam neither's none the better o' you, and I hopes you're not much the worse for them," said Job, as he put into my hands my purse and watch. " Count it, gov'nor, and see if it's all right. Them pusses is mannyfactered express for the convenience o' the fakers. Take my advice, sir, and keep a yellow dump (*sovereign*) in yer coat-tails, a flatch yenork (*halfcrown*) in yer waistcoat, and yer yeneps (*pence*) in yer breeches. You won't lose much nohow then. Good night, sir, and I wish you better."

" But I must give you something for plaster," I said. " You'll take a yellow dump, at least ?"

" We'll talk about that another day," said Job; and with a second still heartier good night, he left me. I managed to crawl up to my room, and fell on my bed once more fainting. But I soon recovered sufficiently to undress and get into it. I was feverish all night and next day, but towards evening began to recover.

I kept expecting Falconer to come and inquire after me; but he never came. Nor did he appear the next day or the next, and I began to be very uneasy about him. The fourth day I sent for a cab. and drove to John Street. He was at home, but Mrs. Ashton, instead of showing me into his room, led me into her kitchen, and left me there.

A minute after, Falconer came to me. The instant I saw him I understood it all. I read it in his face: He had found his father.

CHAPTER XII.

ANDREW AT LAST.

HAVING at length persuaded the woman to go with him, Falconer made her take his arm, and led her off the bridge. In Parliament Street he was looking about for a cab as they walked on, when a man he did not know, stopped, touched his hat, and addressed him.

"I'm thinkin', sir, ye'll be sair wantit at hame the nicht. It wad be better to gang at ance, an' lat the puir fowk luik efter themsels for ae nicht."

"I'm sorry I dinna ken ye, man. Do ye ken me?"

"Fine that, Mr. Falconer. There's mony ane kens you and praises God."

"God be praised!" returned Falconer. "Why am I wanted at home?"

"'Deed I wad raither not say, sir.—Hey!"

This last exclamation was addressed to a cab just disappearing down King Street from Whitehall. The driver heard, turned, and in a moment more was by their side.

" Ye had better gang into her an' awa' hame, and lea' the poor lassie to me. I'll tak guid care o' her."

She clung to Falconer's arm. The man opened the door of the cab. Falconer put her in, told the driver to go to Queen Square, and if he could not make haste, to stop the first cab that could, got in himself, thanked his unknown friend, who did not seem quite satisfied, and drove off.

Happily Miss St. John was at home, and there was no delay. Neither was any explanation of more than six words necessary. He jumped again into the cab and drove home. Fortunately for his mood, though in fact it mattered little for any result, the horse was fresh, and both able and willing.

When he entered John Street, he came to observe before reaching his own door that a good many men were about in little quiet groups— some twenty or so, here and there. When he let himself in with his pass-key, there were two men in the entry. Without stopping to speak, he ran up to his own chambers. When he got into his sitting-room, there stood De Fleuri, who simply waved his hand towards the old sofa. On it lay an elderly man, with his eyes half open, and a look almost of idiocy upon his

pale, puffed face, which was damp and shining.
His breathing was laboured, but there was no
further sign of suffering. He lay perfectly still.
Falconer saw at once that he was under the
influence of some narcotic, probably opium; and
the same moment the all but conviction darted
into his mind that Andrew Falconer, his grandmother's son, lay there before him. That he
was his own father he had no feeling yet. He
turned to De Fleuri.

"Thank you, friend," he said. "I shall find
time to thank you."

"Are we right?" asked De Fleuri.

"I don't know. I think so," answered Falconer; and without another word the man withdrew.

His first mood was very strange. It seemed
as if all the romance had suddenly deserted his
life, and it lay bare and hopeless. He felt nothing. No tears rose to the brim of their bot-
tomless wells—the only wells that have no
bottom, for they go into the depths of the infinite soul. He sat down in his chair, stunned as
to the heart and all the finer chords of his nature.
The man on the horsehair sofa lay breathing—
that was all. The gray hair about the pale ill-
shaven face glimmered like a cloud before him.
What should he do or say when he awaked?
How approach this far-estranged soul? How
ever send the cry of *father* into that fog-filled

world? Could he ever have climbed on those
knees and kissed those lips, in the far-off days
when the sun and the wind of that northern atmosphere made his childhood blessed beyond
dreams? The actual—that is the present phase
of the everchanging—looked the ideal in the
face; and the mirror that held them both, shook
and quivered at the discord of the faces reflected. A kind of moral cold seemed to radiate
from the object before him, and chill him to the
very bones. This could not long be endured.
He fled from the actual to the source of all the
ideal—to that Saviour who, the infinite mediator,
mediates between all hopes and all positions;
between the most debased actual and the loftiest ideal; between the little scoffer of St. Giles's
and his angel that ever beholds the face of the
Father in heaven. He fell on his knees, and
spoke to God, saying that he had made this
man; that the mark of his fingers was on the
man's soul somewhere. He prayed to the making Spirit to bring the man to his right mind,
to give him once more the heart of a child, to
begin him yet again at the beginning. Then at
last, all the evil he had done and suffered would
but swell his gratitude to Him who had delivered
him from himself and his own deeds. Having
breathed this out before the God of his life, Falconer rose, strengthened to meet the honourable
debased soul when it should at length look

forth from the dull smeared windows of those ill-used eyes.

He felt his pulse. There was no danger from the narcotic. The coma would pass away. Meantime he would get him to bed. When he began to undress him a new reverence arose which overcame all disgust at the state in which he found him. At length one sad little fact about his dress, revealing the poverty-stricken attempt of a man to preserve the shadow of decency, called back the waters of the far-ebbed ocean of his feelings. At the prick of a pin the heart's blood will flow: at the sight of—a pin it was—Robert burst into tears, and wept like a child; the deadly cold was banished from his heart, and he not only loved, but knew that he loved—felt the love that was there. Everything then about the worn body and shabby garments of the man smote upon the heart of his son, and through his very poverty he was sacred in his eyes. The human heart awakened the filial—reversing thus the ordinary process of Nature, who by means of the filial, when her plans are unbroken, awakes the human; and he reproached himself bitterly for his hardness, as he now judged his late mental condition—unfairly, I think. He soon had him safe in bed, unconscious of the helping hands that had been busy about him in his heedless sleep; unconscious of the radiant planet of love that had been folding him round in its atmosphere of affection.

But while he thus ministered, a new question arose in his mind—to meet with its own new, God-given answer. What if this should not be the man after all?—if this love had been spent in mistake, and did not belong to him at all? The answer was, that he was a man. The love Robert had given he could not, would not withdraw. The man who had been for a moment as his father he could not cease to regard with devotion. At least he was a man with a divine soul. He might at least be somebody's father. Where love had found a moment's rest for the sole of its foot, there it must build its nest.

When he had got him safe in bed, he sat down beside him to think what he would do next. This sleep gave him very needful leisure to think. He could determine nothing—not even how to find out if he was indeed his father. If he approached the subject without guile, the man might be fearful and cunning—might have reasons for being so, and for striving to conceal the truth. But this was the first thing to make sure of, because, if it was he, all the hold he had upon him lay in his knowing it for certain. He could not think. He had had little sleep the night before. He must not sleep this night. He dragged his bath into his sitting-room, and refreshed his faculties with plenty of cold water, then lighted his pipe and went on thinking—not without prayer to that Power whose candle is the understanding of man. All at once he saw how to begin. He went again into the chamber, and looked at the man, and handled him, and knew by his art that a waking of some sort was nigh. Then he went to a corner of his sitting-room, and from beneath the table drew out a long box, and from the box lifted Dooble Sandy's auld wife, tuned the somewhat neglected strings, and laid the instrument on the table.

When, keeping constant watch over the sleeping man, he judged at length that his soul had come near enough to the surface of the ocean of sleep to communicate with the outer world through that bubble his body, which had floated upon its waves all the night unconscious, he put his chair just outside the chamber door, which opened from his sitting-room, and began to play gently, softly, far away. For a while he extemporized only, thinking of Rothieden, and the grandmother, and the bleach-green, and the hills, and the waste old factory, and his mother's portrait and letters. As he dreamed on, his dream got louder, and, he hoped, was waking a more and more vivid dream in the mind of the sleeper. "For who can tell," thought Falconer, "what mysterious sympathies of blood and childhood's experience there may be between me and that man?—such, it may be, that my utterance on the violin will wake in his soul the

very visions of which my soul is full while I
play, each with its own nebulous atmosphere of
dream-light around it." For music wakes its
own feeling, and feeling wakes thought, or
rather, when perfected, blossoms into thought,
thought radiant of music as those lilies that
shine phosphorescent in the July nights. He
played more and more forcefully, growing in hope.
But he had been led astray in some measure by
the fulness of his expectation. Strange to tell,
doctor as he was, he had forgotten one important
factor in his calculation: how the man would
awake from his artificial sleep. He had not reckoned of how the limbeck of his brain would be
left discoloured with vile deposit, when the fumes
of the narcotic should have settled and given up
its central spaces to the faintness of desertion.

Robert was very keen of hearing. Indeed he
possessed all his senses keener than any other
man I have known. He heard him toss on his
bed. Then he broke into a growl, and damned
the miauling, which, he said, the strings could
never have learned anywhere but in a cat's
belly. But Robert was used to bad language;
and there are some bad things, which seeing
that there they are, it is of the greatest consequence to get used to. It gave him, no doubt,
a pang of disappointment to hear such an echo
to his music from the soul which he had hoped
especially fitted to respond in harmonious unison

with the wail of his violin. But not for even
this moment did he lose his presence of mind.
He instantly moderated the tone of the instrument, and gradually drew the sound away once
more into the distance of hearing. But he did
not therefore let it die. Through various
changes it floated in the thin æther of the soul,
changes delicate as when the wind leaves the
harp of the reeds by a river's brink, and falls a
ringing at the heather bells, or playing with the
dry silvery pods of honesty that hang in the
poor man's garden, till at length it drew nearer
once more, bearing on its wings the wail of red
Flodden, *The Flowers of the Forest.* Listening
through the melody for sounds of a far different
kind, Robert was aware that those sounds had
ceased; the growling was still; he heard no
more turnings to and fro. How it was operating
he could not tell, further than that there must
be some measure of soothing in its influence.
He ceased quite, and listened again. For a few
moments there was no sound. Then he heard
the half articulate murmuring of one whose
organs have been all but overcome by the bene-
ficent paralysis of sleep, but whose feeble will
would compel them to utterance. He was
nearly asleep again. Was it a fact, or a fancy
of Robert's eager heart? Did the man really
say:

" Play that again, father. It's bonnie, that !

I aye likit the *Flooers o' the Forest.* Play awa'.
I hae had a frichtsome dream. I thocht I was
i' the ill place. I doobt I'm no weel. But yer
fiddle aye did me gude. Play awa', father?"

All the night through, till the dawn of the
gray morning, Falconer watched the sleeping
man, all but certain that he was indeed his father. Eternities of thought passed through his
mind as he watched—this time by the couch, as
he hoped, of a new birth. He was about to see
what could be done by one man, strengthened
by all the aids that love and devotion could
give, for the redemption of his fellow. As
through the darkness of the night and a slug-
gish fog to aid it, the light of a pure heaven
made its slow irresistible way, his hope grew
that athwart the fog of an evil life, the darkness
that might be telt, the light of the Spirit of God
would yet penetrate the heart of the sinner,
and shake the wickedness out of it. Deeper
and yet deeper grew his compassion and his
sympathy, in prospect of the tortures the man
must go through, before the will that he had
sunk into a deeper sleep than any into which
opium could sink his bodily being, would shake
off its deathly lethargy, and arise, torn with
struggling pain, to behold the light of a new
spiritual morning. All that he could do he was
prepared to do, regardless of entreaty, regardless of torture, anger, and hate, with the inex-

orable justice of love, the law that will not, must not, dares not yield—strong with an awful tenderness, a wisdom that cannot be turned aside, to redeem the lost soul of his father. And he strengthened his heart for the conflict by saying that if he would do thus for his father, what would not God do for his child? Had He not proved already, if there was any truth in the grand story of the world's redemption through that obedience unto the death, that his devotion was entire, and would leave nothing undone that could be done to lift this sheep out of the pit into whose darkness and filth he had fallen out of the sweet Sabbath of the universe?

He removed all his clothes, searched the pockets, found in them one poor shilling and a few coppers, a black *cutty* pipe, a box of snuff, a screw of pigtail, a knife with a buckhorn handle and one broken blade, and a pawn-ticket for a keyed flute, on the proceeds of which he was now sleeping—a sleep how dearly purchased, when he might have had it free, as the gift of God's gentle darkness! Then he destroyed the garments, committing them to the fire as the hoped farewell to the state of which they were the symbols and signs.

He found himself perplexed, however, by the absence of some of the usual symptoms of the habit of opium, and concluded that his poor father was in the habit of using stimulants as well

as narcotics, and that the action of the one interfered with the action of the other.

He called his housekeeper. She did not
know whom her master supposed his guest to
be, and regarded him only as one of the many
objects of his kindness. He told her to get
some tea ready, as the patient would most likely wake with a headache. He instructed her
to wait upon him as a matter of course, and
explain nothing. He had resolved to pass for
the doctor, as indeed he was; and he told her
that if he should be at all troublesome, he would
be with her at once. She must keep the room
dark. He would have his own breakfast now;
and if the patient remained quiet, would sleep
on the sofa.

He woke murmuring, and evidently suffered from headache and nausea. Mrs. Ashton
took him some tea. He refused it with an oath
—more of discomfort than of ill-nature, and was
too unwell to show any curiosity about the person who had offered it. Probably he was accustomed to so many changes of abode, and to
so many bewilderments of the brain, that he did
not care to inquire where he was or who waited
upon him. But happily for the heart's desire of
Falconer, the debauchery of his father had at
length reached one of many crises. He had
caught cold before De Fleuri and his comrades
found him. He was now ill—feverish and op-

pressed. Through the whole of the following week they nursed and waited upon him without his asking a single question as to where he was or who they were; during all which time Falconer saw no one but De Fleuri and the many poor fellows who called to inquire after him and the result of their supposed success. He never left the house, but either watched by the bedside, or waited in the next room. Often would the patient get out of bed, driven by the longing for drink or for opium, gnawing him through all the hallucinations of delirium ; but he was weak, and therefore manageable. If in any lucid moments he thought where he was, he no doubt supposed that he was in a hospital, and probably had sense enough to understand that it was of no use to attempt to get his own way there. He was soon much worn, and his limbs trembled greatly. It was absolutely necessary to give him stimulants, or he would have died, but Robert reduced them gradually as he recovered strength.

But there was an infinite work to be done beyond even curing him of his evil habits. To keep him from strong drink and opium, even till the craving after them was gone, would be but the capturing of the merest outwork of the enemy's castle. He must be made such that, even if the longing should return with tenfold force, and all the means for its gratification should lie within the reach of his outstretched hand, he would not touch them. God only was able to do that for him. He would do all that he knew how to do, and God would not fail of his part. For for this he had raised him up; to this he had called him; for this work he had educated him, made him a physician, given him money, time, the love and aid of his fellows, and, beyond all, a rich energy of hope and faith in his heart, emboldening him to attempt whatever his hand found to do.

CHAPTER XIII.

ANDREW REBELS.

AS Andrew Falconer grew better, the longing
of his mind after former excitement and
former oblivion, roused and kept alive the longing of his body, until at length his thoughts
dwelt upon nothing but his diseased cravings.
His whole imagination, naturally not a feeble
one, was concentrated on the delights in store
for him as soon as he was well enough to be his
own master, as he phrased it, once more. He
soon began to see that, if he was in a hospital,
it must be a private one, and at last, irresolute
as he was both from character and illness, made
up his mind to demand his liberty. He sat by
his bedroom fire one afternoon, for he needed
much artificial warmth. The shades of evening
were thickening the air. He had just had one
of his frequent meals, and was gazing, as he
often did, into the glowing coals. Robert had
come in, and after a little talk was sitting silent
at the opposite corner of the chimney-piece.

Q 2

" Doctor," said Andrew, seizing the opportunity, " you've been very kind to me, and I don't know how to thank you, but it is time I was going. I am quite well now. Would you kindly order the nurse to bring me my clothes to-morrow morning, and I will go."

This he said with the quavering voice of one who speaks because he has made up his mind to speak. A certain something, I believe a vague molluscous form of conscience, made him wriggle and shift uneasily upon his chair as he spoke.

" No, no," said Robert, " you are not fit to go. Make yourself comfortable, my dear sir. There is no reason why you should go."

" There is something I don't understand about it. I want to go."

" It would ruin my character as a professional man to let a patient in your condition leave the house. The weather is unfavourable. I cannot —I must not consent."

" Where am I? I don't understand it. I want to understand it."

" Your friends wish you to remain where you are for the present."

" I have no friends."

" You have one, at least, who puts his house here at your service."

" There's something about it I don't like. Do you suppose I am incapable of taking care of myself?"

"I do indeed," answered his son with firmness.

"Then you are quite mistaken," said Andrew, angrily. "I am quite well enough to go, and have a right to judge for myself. It is very kind of you, but I am in a free country, I believe."

"No doubt. All honest men are free in this country. But——"

He saw that his father winced, and said no more. Andrew resumed, after a pause in which he had been rousing his feeble drink-exhausted anger.

"I tell you I will not be treated like a child. I demand my clothes and my liberty."

"Do you know where you were found that night you were brought here?"

"No. But what has that to do with it? I was ill. You know that as well as I."

"You are ill now because you were lying then on the wet ground under a railway-arch—utterly incapable from the effects of opium, or drink, or both. You would have been taken to the police-station, and would probably have been dead long before now, if you had not been brought here."

He was silent for some time. Then he broke out:

"I tell you I *will* go. I do not choose to live on charity. I will *not*. I demand my clothes."

"I tell you it is of no use. When you are

well enough to go out you shall go out, but not now."

" Where am I ?   Who are you ?"

He looked at Robert with a keen, furtive glance, in which were mingled bewilderment and suspicion.

" I am your best friend at present."

He started up—fiercely and yet feebly, for a thought of terror had crossed him.

" You do not mean I am in a madhouse ?"

Robert made no reply. He left him to suppose what he pleased. Andrew took it for granted that he was in a private asylum, sank back in his chair, and from that moment was quiet as a lamb. But it was easy to see that he was constantly contriving how to escape. This mental occupation, however, was excellent for his recovery ; and Robert dropped no hint of his suspicion. Nor were many precautions necessary in consequence ; for he never left the house without having De Fleuri there, who was a man of determination, nerve, and, now that he ate and drank, of considerable strength.

As he grew better, the stimulants given him in the form of medicine at length ceased. In their place Robert substituted other restoratives, which prevented him from missing the stimulants so much, and at length got his system into a tolerably healthy condition, though at his age, and after so long indulgence, it could hardly be expected ever to recover its tone.

He did all he could to provide him with healthy amusement—played backgammon, draughts, and cribbage with him, brought him Sir Walter's and other novels to read, and often played on his violin, to which he listened with great delight. At times of depression, which of course were frequent, The Flowers of the Forest made the old man weep. Falconer put yet more soul into the sounds than he had ever put into them before. He tried to make the old man talk of his childhood, asking him about the place of his birth, the kind of country, how he had been brought up, his family, and many questions of the sort. His answers were vague, and often contradictory. Indeed, the moment the subject was approached, he looked suspicious and cunning. He said his name was John Mackinnon, and Robert, although his belief was strengthened by a hundred little circumstances, had as yet received no proof that he was Andrew Falconer. Remembering the pawn-ticket, and finding that he could play on the flute, he brought him a beautiful instrument—in fact a silver one—the sight of which made the old man's eyes sparkle. He put it to his lips with trembling hands, blew a note or two, burst into the tears of weakness, and laid it down. But he soon took it up again, and evidently found both pleasure in the tones and sadness in the memories they awakened. At length Robert brought a tailor, and had him dressed like a gentleman—a change which pleased him much. The next step was to take him out every day for a drive, upon which his health began to improve more rapidly. He ate better, grew more lively, and began to tell tales of his adventures, of the truth of which Robert was not always certain, but never showed any doubt. He knew only too well that the use of opium is especially destructive to the conscience. Some of his stories he believed more readily than others, from the fact that he suddenly stopped in them, as if they were leading him into regions of confession which must be avoided, resuming with matter that did not well connect itself with what had gone before. At length he took him out walking, and he comported himself with perfect propriety.

But one day as they were going along a quiet street, Robert met an acquaintance, and stopped to speak with him. After a few moments' chat he turned, and found that his father, whom he had supposed to be standing beside him, had vanished. A glance at the other side of the street showed the probable refuge—a public-house. Filled but not overwhelmed with dismay, although he knew that months might be lost in this one moment, Robert darted in. He was there, with a glass of whisky in his hand, trembling now more from eagerness than weakness. He struck it from his hold. But he had already swallowed one glass, and he turned in a rage. He was a tall and naturally powerful man—almost as strongly built as his son, with long arms like his, which were dangerous even yet in such a moment of factitious strength and real excitement. Robert could not lift his arm even to defend himself from his father, although, had he judged it necessary, I believe he would not, in the cause of his redemption, have hesitated to knock him down, as he had often served others whom he would rather a thousand times have borne on his shoulders. He received his father's blow on the cheek. For one moment it made him dizzy, for it was well delivered. But when the bar-keeper jumped across the counter and approached with his fist doubled, that was another matter. He measured his length on the floor, and Falconer seized his father, who was making for the street, and notwithstanding his struggles and fierce efforts to strike again, held him secure and himself scathless, and bore him out of the house.

A crowd gathers in a moment in London, speeding to a fray as the vultures to carrion. On the heels of the population of the neighbouring mews came two policemen, and at the same moment out came the barman to the assistance of Andrew. But Falconer was as well known to the police as if he had a ticket-of-leave, and a good deal better.

"Call a four-wheel cab," he said to one of them. "I'm all right."

The man started at once. Falconer turned to the other.

"Tell that man in the apron," he said, "that I'll make him all due reparation. But he oughtn't to be in such a hurry to meddle. He gave me no time but to strike hard."

"Yes, sir," answered the policeman obediently. The crowd thought he must be a great man amongst the detectives; but the bar-keeper vowed he would "summons" him for the assault.

"You may, if you like," said Falconer. "When I think of it, you shall do so. You know where I live?" he said, turning to the policeman.

"No, sir, I don't. I only know you well enough."

"Put your hand in my coat-pocket, then, and you'll find a card-case. The other. There! Help yourself."

He said this with his arms round Andrew's, who had ceased to cry out when he saw the police.

"Do you want to give this gentleman in charge, sir?"

"No. It is a little private affair of my own, this."

"Hadn't you better let him go, sir, and we'll find him for you when you want him?"

"No. He may give me in charge if he likes. Or if you should want him, you will find him at my house."

Then pinioning his prisoner still more tightly in his arms, he leaned forward, and whispered in his ear,

"Will you go home quietly, or give me in charge? There is no other way, Andrew Falconer."

He ceased struggling. Through all the flush of the contest his face grew pale. His arms dropped by his side. Robert let him go, and he stood there without offering to move. The cab came up; the policeman got out; Andrew stepped in of his own accord, and Robert followed.

"You see it's all right," he said. "Here, give the barman a sovereign. If he wants more, let me know. He deserved all he got, but I was wrong. John Street."

His father did not speak a word, or ask a question all the way home. Evidently he thought it safer to be silent. But the drink he had taken, though not enough to intoxicate him, was more than enough to bring back the old longing with redoubled force. He paced about the room the rest of the day like a wild beast in a cage, and in the middle of the night, got up and dressed, and would have crept through the room in which Robert lay, in the hope of getting out. But Robert slept too anxiously for that. The captive did not make the slightest noise, but his very presence was enough to wake his son. He started at a bound from his couch, and his father retreated in dismay to his chamber.

CHAPTER XIV.

THE BROWN LETTER.

A T length the time arrived when Robert would make a further attempt, although with a fear and trembling to quiet which he had to seek the higher aid. His father had recovered his attempt to rush anew upon destruction. He was gentler and more thoughtful, and would again sit for an hour at a time gazing into the fire. From the expression of his countenance upon such occasions, Robert hoped that his visions were not of the evil days, but of those of his innocence.

One evening when he was in one of these moods—he had just had his tea, the gas was lighted, and he was sitting as I have described —Robert began to play in the next room, hoping that the music would sink into his heart, and do something to prepare the way for what was to follow. Just as he had played over The Flowers of the Forest for the third time, his housekeeper entered the room, and receiving permission from

her master, went through into Andrew's chamber, and presented a packet, which she said, and
said truly, for she was not in the secret, had
been left for him.   He received it with evident
surprise, mingled with some consternation, looked at the address, looked at the seal, laid it on
the table, and gazed again with troubled looks
into the fire.   He had had no correspondence
for many years.   Falconer had peeped in when
the woman entered, but the moment she retired he could watch him no longer.   He went
on playing a slow, lingering voluntary, such as
the wind plays, of an amber autumn evening, on
the æolian harp of its pines.   He played so gently
that he must hear if his father should speak.

For what seemed hours, though it was but
half an hour, he went on playing.   At length
he heard a stifled sob.   He rose, and peeped
again into the room.   The gray head was bowed
between the hands, and the gaunt frame was
shaken with sobs.   On the table lay the portraits
of himself and his wife ; and the faded brown
letter, so many years folded in silence and darkness, lay open beside them.   He had known the
seal, with the bush of rushes and the Gaelic
motto.   He had gently torn the paper from
around it, and had read the letter from the grave
—no, from the land beyond, the land of light,
where human love is glorified.   Not then did
Falconer read the sacred words of his mother ;

but afterwards his father put them into his hands.
I will give them as nearly as I can remember
them, for the letter is not in my possession.

"My beloved Andrew, I can hardly write, for
I am at the point of death. I love you still—
love you as dearly as before you left me. Will
you ever see this? I will try to send it to you.
I will leave it behind me, that it may come into
your hands when and how it may please God.
You may be an old man before you read these
words, and may have almost forgotten your
young wife. Oh! if I could take your head on my
bosom where it used to lie, and without saying
a word, think all that I am thinking into your
heart. Oh! my love, my love! will you have
had enough of the world and its ways by the
time this reaches you? Or will you be dead,
like me, when this is found, and the eyes of
your son only, my darling little Robert, read
the words? O Andrew, Andrew! my heart
is bleeding, not altogether for myself, not altogether for you, but both for you and for me.
Shall I never, never be able to let out the sea of
my love that swells till my heart is like to break
with its longing after you, my own Andrew?
Shall I never, never see you again? That is the
terrible thought—the only thought almost that
makes me shrink from dying. If I should go to
sleep, as some think, and not even dream about
you, as I dream and weep every night now! If

I should only wake in the crowd of the resurrection, and not know where to find you! Oh! Andrew, I feel as if I should lose my reason when I think that you may be on the left hand of the Judge, and I can no longer say *my love*, because you do not, cannot any more love God. I will tell you the dream I had about you last night, which I think was what makes me write this letter. I was standing in a great crowd of people, and I saw the empty graves about us on every side. We were waiting for the great white throne to appear in the clouds. And as soon as I knew that, I cried, 'Andrew, Andrew!' for I could not help it. And the people did not heed me; and I cried out and ran about everywhere, looking for you. At last I came to a great gulf. When I looked down into it, I could see nothing but a blue deep, like the blue of the sky, under my feet. It was not so wide but that I could see across it, but it was oh! so terribly deep. All at once, as I stood trembling on the very edge, I saw you on the other side, looking towards me, and stretching out your arms as if you wanted me. You were old and much changed, but I knew you at once, and I gave a cry that I thought all the universe must have heard. You heard me. I could see that. And I was in a terrible agony to get to you. But there was no way, for if I fell into the gulf I should go down for ever, it was so deep. Something made me look away, and I saw a man coming quietly along the same side of the gulf, on the edge, towards me. And when he came nearer to me, I saw that he was dressed in a gown down to his feet, and that his feet were bare and had a hole in each of them. So I knew who it was, Andrew. And I fell down and kissed his feet, and lifted up my hands, and looked into his face—oh, such a face! And I tried to pray. But all I could say was, 'O Lord, Andrew, Andrew!' Then he smiled, and said, 'Daughter, be of good cheer. Do you want to go to him?' And I said, 'Yes, Lord.' Then he said, 'And so do I. Come.' And he took my hand and led me over the edge of the precipice; and I was not afraid, and I did not sink, but walked upon the air to go to you. But when I got to you, it was too much to bear; and when I thought I had you in my arms at last, I awoke, crying as I never cried before, not even when I found that you had left me to die without you. Oh, Andrew, what if the dream should come true! But if it should *not* come true! I dare not think of that, Andrew. I *couldn't* be happy in heaven without you. It may be very wicked, but I do not feel as if it were, and I can't help it if it is. But, dear husband, come to me again. Come back, like the prodigal in the New Testament. God will forgive you everything. Don't touch drink again, my dear

love. I know it was the drink that made you do
as you did. *You* could never have done it. It
was the drink that drove you to do it. You
didn't know what you were doing. And then
you were ashamed, and thought I would be
angry, and could not bear to come back to me.
Ah, if you were to come in at the door, as I
write, you would see whether or not I was proud
to have my Andrew again. But I would not be
nice for you to look at now. You used to think
me pretty—you said beautiful—so long ago.
But I am so thin now, and my face so white,
that I almost frighten myself when I look in the
glass. And before you get this I shall be all
gone to dust, either knowing nothing about
you, or trying to praise God, and always forgetting where I am in my psalm, longing so for
you to come. I am afraid I love you too much
to be fit to go to heaven. Then, perhaps, God
will send me to the other place, all for love of
you, Andrew. And I do believe I should like
that better. But I don't think he will, if he is
anything like the man I saw in my dream. But
I am growing so faint that I can hardly write.
I never felt like this before. But that dream has
given me strength to die, because I hope you will
come too. O my dear Andrew, do, do repent
and turn to God, and he will forgive you. Believe in Jesus, and he will save you, and bring
me to you across the deep place. But I must

make haste. I can hardly see. And I must not leave this letter open for anybody but you to read after I am dead. Good-bye, Andrew. I love you all the same. I am, my dearest Husband, your affectionate Wife,

" H. FALCONER."

Then followed the date. It was within a week of her death. The letter was feebly written, every stroke seeming more feeble by the contrasted strength of the words. When Falconer read it afterwards, in the midst of the emotions it aroused—the strange lovely feelings of such a bond between him and a beautiful ghost, far away somewhere in God's universe, who had carried him in her lost body, and nursed him at her breasts—in the midst of it all, he could not help wondering, he told me, to find the forms and words so like what he would have written himself. It seemed so long ago when that faded, discoloured paper, with the gilt edges, and the pale brown ink, and folded in the large sheet, and sealed with the curious wax, must have been written ; and here were its words so fresh, so new ! not withered like the rose-leaves that scented the paper from the work-box where he had found it, but as fresh as if just shaken from the rose-trees of the heart's garden. It was no wonder that Andrew Falconer should be sitting with his head in his hands when Robert looked in on him, for he had read this letter.

When Robert saw how he sat, he withdrew,
and took his violin again, and played all the
tunes of the old country he could think of, recalling Dooble Sandy's workshop, that he might
recall the music he had learnt there.

No one who understands the bit and bridle of
the association of ideas, as it is called in the
skeleton language of mental philosophy, wherewith the Father-God holds fast the souls of his
children—to the very last that we see of them,
at least, and doubtless to endless ages beyond
—will sneer at Falconer's notion of making
God's violin a ministering spirit in the process
of conversion.   There is a well-authenticated
story of a convict's having been greatly reformed
for a time, by going, in one of the colonies, into
a church, where the matting along the aisle was
of *the same pattern as that in the church to which
he had gone when a boy*—with his mother, I suppose. It was not the matting that so far converted
him : it was not to the music of his violin that
Falconer looked for aid, but to the memories of
childhood, the mysteries of the kingdom of innocence which that could recall—those memories which

> Are yet the fountain light of all our day,
> Are yet a master light of all our seeing.

For an hour he did not venture to go near

him. When he entered the room he found him
sitting in the same place, no longer weeping,
but gazing into the fire with a sad countenance,
the expression of which showed Falconer at
once that the soul had come out of its cave of
obscuration, and drawn nearer to the surface of
life. He had not seen him look so much like
one "clothed, and in his right mind," before.
He knew well that nothing could be built upon
this; that this very emotion did but expose
him the more to the besetting sin; that in this
mood he would drink, even if he knew that he
would in consequence be in danger of murder-
ing the wife whose letter had made him weep.
But it was progress, notwithstanding. He
looked up at Robert as he entered, and then
dropped his eyes again. He regarded him perhaps as a presence doubtful whether of angel or
devil, even as the demoniacs regarded the Lord
of Life who had come to set them free. Bewildered he must have been to find himself, towards the close of a long life of debauchery,
wickedness, and the growing pains of hell,
caught in a net of old times, old feelings, old
truths.

Now Robert had carefully avoided every indication that might disclose him to be a Scotch-
man even, nor was there the least sign of suspicion in Andrew's manner. The only solution
of the mystery that could have presented itself

to him was, that his friends were at the root of it—probably his son, of whom he knew absolutely nothing. His mother could not be alive still. Of his wife's relatives there had never been one who would have taken any trouble about him after her death, hardly even before it. John Lammie was the only person, except Dr. Anderson, whose friendship he could suppose capable of this development. The latter was the more likely person. But he would be too much for him yet ; he was not going to be treated like a child, he said to himself, as often as the devil got uppermost.

My reader must understand that Andrew had never been a man of resolution. He had been wilful and headstrong ; and these qualities, in children especially, are often mistaken for resolution, and generally go under the name of strength of will. There never was a greater mistake. The mistake, indeed, is only excusable from the fact that extremes meet, and that this disposition is so opposite to the other, that it looks to the careless eye most like it. He never resisted his own impulses, or the enticements of evil companions. Kept within certain bounds at home, after he had begun to go wrong, by the weight of opinion, he rushed into all excesses when abroad upon business, till at length the vessel of his fortune went to pieces, and he was a waif on the waters of the world. But in feeling he had never been vulgar, however much so in action. There was a feeble good in him that had in part been protected by its very feebleness. He could not sin so much against it as if it had been strong. For many years he had fits of shame, and of grief without repentance; for repentance is the active, the divine part—the turning again; but taking more steadily both to strong drink and opium, he was at the time when De Fleuri found him only the dull ghost of Andrew Falconer walking in a dream of its lost carcass.

CHAPTER XV.

FATHER AND SON.

ONCE more Falconer retired, but not to take his violin. He could play no more. Hope and love were swelling within him. He could not rest. Was it a sign from heaven that the hour for speech had arrived? He paced up and down the room. He kneeled and prayed for guidance and help. Something within urged him to try the rusted lock of his father's heart. Without any formed resolution, without any conscious volition, he found himself again in his room. There the old man still sat, with his back to the door, and his gaze fixed on the fire, which had sunk low in the grate. Robert went round in front of him, kneeled on the rug before him, and said the one word,

"Father!"

Andrew started violently, raised his hand, which trembled as with a palsy, to his head, and stared wildly at Robert. But he did not speak. Robert repeated the one great word. Then

Andrew spoke, and said in a trembling, hardly audible voice,

" Are you my son ?—my boy Robert, sir ?"

" I am. I am. O father, I have longed for you by day, and dreamed about you by night, ever since I saw that other boys had fathers, and I had none. Years and years of my life—I hardly know how many—have been spent in searching for you. And now I have found you!"

The great tall man, in the prime of life and strength, laid his big head down on the old man's knee, as if he had been a little child. His father said nothing, but laid his hand on the head. For some moments the two remained thus, motionless and silent. Andrew was the first to speak. And his words were the voice of the spirit that striveth with man.

" What am I to do, Robert ?"

No other words, not even those of passionate sorrow, or overflowing affection, could have been half so precious in the ears of Robert. When a man once asks what he is to do, there is hope for him. Robert answered instantly :

" You must come home to your mother."

" My mother !" Andrew exclaimed. " You don't mean to say she's alive ?"

" I heard from her yesterday—in her own hand, too," said Robert.

" I daren't. I daren't," murmured Andrew.

" You must, father," returned Robert. " It is

a long way, but I will make the journey easy
for you. She knows I have found you. She
is waiting and longing for you. She has hardly
thought of anything but you ever since she lost
you. She is only waiting to see you, and then
she will go home, she says. I wrote to her and
said, 'Grannie, I have found your Andrew.'
And she wrote back to me and said, 'God be
praised. I shall die in peace.'"

A silence followed.

"Will she forgive me?" said Andrew.

"She loves you more than her own soul,"
answered Robert. "She loves you as much as
I do. She loves you as God loves you."

"God can't love me," said Andrew, feebly.
"He would never have left me if he had loved
me."

"He has never left you from the very first.
You would not take his way, father, and he
just let you try your own. But long before
that he had begun to get me ready to go after
you. He put such love to you in my heart, and
gave me such teaching and such training, that
I have found you at last. And now I have
found you, I will hold you. You cannot escape
—you will not want to escape any more, father?"

Andrew made no reply to this appeal. It
sounded like imprisonment for life, I suppose.
But thought was moving in him. After a long
pause, during which the son's heart was hunger-

ing for a word whereon to hang a further hope, the old man spoke again, muttering as if he were only speaking his thoughts unconsciously.

"Where's the use? There's no forgiveness for me. My mother is going to heaven. I must go to hell. No. It's no good. Better leave it as it is. I daren't see her. It would kill me to see her."

"It will kill her not to see you; and that will be one sin more on your conscience, father."

Andrew got up and walked about the room. And Robert only then arose from his knees.

"And there's *my* mother," he said.

Andrew did not reply; but Robert saw when he turned next towards the light, that the sweat was standing in beads on his forehead.

"Father," he said, going up to him.

The old man stopped in his walk, turned, and faced his son.

"Father," repeated Robert, "you've got to repent; and God won't let you off; and you needn't think it. You'll have to repent some day."

"In hell, Robert," said Andrew, looking him full in the eyes, as he had never looked at him before. It seemed as if even so much acknowledgment of the truth had already made him bolder and honester.

"Yes. Either on earth or in hell. Would it not be better on earth?"

"But it will be no use in hell," he murmured.

In those few words lay the germ of the preference for hell of poor souls, enfeebled by wickedness.　They will not have to *do* anything there—only to moan and cry and suffer for ever, they think.　It is effort, the out-going of the living will that they dread.　The sorrow, the remorse of repentance, they do not so much regard: it is the action it involves; it is the having to turn, be different, and do differently, that they shrink from; and they have been taught to believe that this will not be required of them there—in that awful refuge of the will-less.　I do not say they think thus: I only say their dim, vague, feeble feelings are such as, if they grew into thought, would take this form. But tell them that the fire of God without and within them will compel them to bethink themselves; that the vision of an open door beyond the smoke and the flames will ever urge them to call up the ice-bound will, that it may obey; that the torturing spirit of God in them will keep their consciences awake, not to remind them of what they ought to have done, but to tell them what they *must* do now, and hell will no longer fascinate them.　Tell them that there is *no* refuge from the compelling Love of God, save that Love itself—that He is in hell too, and that if they make their bed in hell they shall not escape him, and then, perhaps, they will have some true presentiment of the worm that dieth not and the fire that is not quenched.

"Father, it *will* be of use in hell," said Robert. "God will give you no rest even there. You will have to repent some day, I do believe—if not now under the sunshine of heaven, then in the torture of the awful world where there is no light but that of the conscience. Would it not be better and easier to repent now, with your wife waiting for you in heaven, and your mother waiting for you on earth?"

Will it be credible to my reader?—that Andrew interrupted his son with the words,

"Robert, it is dreadful to hear you talk like that. Why, you don't believe in the Bible!"

His words will be startling to one who has never heard the lips of a hoary old sinner drivel out religion. To me they are not so startling as the words of Christian women and bishops of the Church of England, when they say that the doctrine of the everlasting happiness of the righteous stands or falls with the doctrine of the hopeless damnation of the wicked. Can it be that to such the word is everything, the spirit nothing? No. It is only that the devil is playing a very wicked prank, not with them, but in them: they are pluming themselves on being selfish after a godly sort.

"I do believe the Bible, father," returned Robert, "and have ordered my life by it. If I had

not believed the Bible, I fear I should never
have looked for you.   But I won't dispute about
it.   I only say I believe that you will be compelled to repent some day, and that now is the
best time.   Then, you will not only have to
repent, but to repent that you did not repent
now.   And I tell you, father, that you *shall* go
to my grandmother."

CHAPTER XVI.

CHANGE OF SCENE.

BUT various reasons combined to induce Falconer to postpone yet for a period their journey to the North. Not merely did his father require an unremitting watchfulness, which it would be difficult to keep up in his native place amongst old friends and acquaintances, but his health was more broken than he had at first supposed, and change of air and scene without excitement was most desirable. He was anxious too that the change his mother must see in him should be as little as possible attributable to other causes than those that years bring with them. To this was added that his own health had begun to suffer from the watching and anxiety he had gone through; and for his father's sake, as well as for the labour which yet lay before him, he would keep that as sound as he might. He wrote to his grandmother and explained the matter. She begged him to do as he thought best, for she was so happy that she did not care if she should never see Andrew in this world : it was enough to die in the hope of meeting him in the other. But she had no reason to fear that death was at hand ; for, although much more *frail*, she felt as well as ever.

By this time Falconer had introduced me to his father. I found him in some things very like his son ; in others, very different. His manners were more polished ; his pleasure in pleasing much greater : his humanity had blossomed too easily, and then *run to seed.* Alas to no seed that could bear fruit ! There was a weak expression about his mouth—a wavering interrogation : It was so different from the firmly-closed portals whence issued the golden speech of his son ! He had a sly, sidelong look at times, whether of doubt or cunning, I could not always determine. His eyes, unlike his son's, were of a light blue, and hazy both in texture and expression. His hands were long-fingered and tremulous. He gave your hand a sharp squeeze, and the same instant abandoned it with indifference. I soon began to discover in him a tendency to patronize any one who showed him a particle of respect as distinguished from common-place civility. But under all outward appearances it seemed to me that there was a change going on : at least being very willing to believe it, I found nothing to render belief impossible.

He was very fond of the flute his son had

given him, and on that sweetest and most expressionless of instruments he played exquisitely.

One evening when I called to see them, Falconer said:

"We are going out of town for a few weeks, Gordon: will you go with us?"

"I am afraid I can't."

"Why? You have no teaching at present, and your writing you can do as well in the country as in town."

"That is true; but still I don't see how I can. I am too poor for one thing."

"Between you and me that is nonsense."

"Well, I withdraw that," I said. "But there is so much to be done, especially as you will be away, and Miss St John is at the Lakes."

"That is all very true; but you need a change. I have seen for some weeks that you are failing. Mind it is our best work that He wants, not the dregs of our exhaustion. I hope you are not of the mind of our friend Mr. Watts, the curate of St. Gregory's."

"I thought you had a high opinion of Mr. Watts," I returned.

"So I have. I hope it is not necessary to agree with a man in everything before we can have a high opinion of him."

"Of course not. But what is it you hope I am not of his opinion in?"

"He seems ambitious of killing himself with

VOL. III.   S

work—of wearing himself out in the service of
his master—and as quickly as possible. A good
deal of that kind of thing is a mere holding of
the axe to the grindstone, not a lifting of it up
against thick trees. Only he won't be convinced
till it comes to the helve. I met him the other
day ; he was looking as white as his surplice.
I took upon me to read him a lecture on the
holiness of holidays. ' I can't leave my poor,' he
said. ' Do you think God can't do without you ?'
I asked. ' Is he so weak that he cannot spare
the help of a weary man ?   But I think he must
prefer quality to quantity, and for healthy work
you must be healthy yourself. How can you
be the visible sign of the Christ-present amongst
men, if you inhabit an exhausted, irritable
brain ?   Go to God's infirmary and rest a while.
Bring back health from the country to those
that cannot go to it. If on the way it be trans-
muted into spiritual forms, so much the better.
A little more of God will make up for a good
deal less of you.'"

" What did he say to that ?"

" He said our Lord died doing the will of his
Father. I told him—' Yes, when his time was
come, not sooner. Besides, he often avoided
both speech and action.' ' Yes,' he answered,
' but he could tell when, and we cannot.'
' Therefore,' I rejoined, ' you ought to accept
your exhaustion as a token that your absence

will be the best thing for your people. If there were no God, then perhaps you ought to work till you drop down dead—I don't know.'"

" Is he gone yet?"

"No. He won't go. I couldn't persuade him."

" When do you go?"

" To-morrow."

" I shall be ready, if you really mean it."

"That's an *if* worthy only of a courtier. There may be much virtue in an *if*, as Touchstone says, for the taking up of a quarrel ; but that *if* is bad enough to breed one," said Falconer laughing. "Be at the Paddington Station at noon to-morrow. To tell the whole truth, I want you to help me with my father."

This last was said at the door as he showed me out.

In the afternoon we were nearing Bristol. It was a lovely day in October. Andrew had been enjoying himself; but it was evidently rather the pleasure of travelling in a first-class carriage like a gentleman than any delight in the beauty of heaven and earth. The country was in the rich sombre dress of decay.

" Is it not remarkable," said my friend to me, " that the older I grow, I find autumn affecting me the more like spring?"

" I am thankful to say," interposed Andrew, with a smile in which was mingled a shade of superiority, "that no change of the seasons ever affects *me*."

"Are you sure you are right in being thankful for that, father?" asked his son.

His father gazed at him for a moment, seemed to bethink himself after some feeble fashion or other, and rejoined:

"Well, I must confess I did feel a touch of the rheumatism this morning."

How I pitied Falconer! Would he ever see of the travail of his soul in this man? But he only smiled a deep sweet smile, and seemed to be thinking divine things in that great head of his.

At Bristol we went on board a small steamer, and at night were landed at a little village on the coast of North Devon. The hotel to which we went was on the steep bank of a tumultuous little river, which tumbled past its foundation of rock, like a troop of watery horses galloping by with ever-dissolving limbs. The elder Falconer retired almost as soon as we had had supper. My friend and I lighted our pipes, and sat by the open window, for although the autumn was so far advanced, the air here was very mild. For some time we only listened to the sound of the waters.

"There are three things," said Falconer at last, taking his pipe out of his mouth with a smile, "that give a peculiarly perfect feeling of abandonment : the laughter of a child ; a snake lying *across* a fallen branch ; and the rush of a stream like this beneath us, whose only thought is to get to the sea."

We did not talk much that night, however, but went soon to bed. None of us slept well. We agreed in the morning that the noise of the stream had been too much for us all, and that the place felt close and torpid. Andrew complained that the ceaseless sound wearied him, and Robert that he felt the aimless end-lessness of it more than was good for him. I confess it irritated me like an anodyne unable to soothe. We were clearly all in want of something different. The air between the hills clung to them, hot and moveless. We would climb those hills, and breathe the air that flitted about over their craggy tops.

As soon as we had breakfasted, we set out. It was soon evident that Andrew could not ascend the steep road. We returned and got a carriage. When we reached the top, it was like a resurrection, like a dawning of hope out of despair. The cool friendly wind blew on our faces, and breathed strength into our frames. Before us lay the ocean, the visible type of the invisible, and the vessels with their white sails moved about over it like the thoughts of men feebly searching the unknown. Even Andrew Falconer spread out his arms to the wind, and breathed deep, filling his great chest full.

"I feel like a boy again," he said.

His son strode to his side, and laid his arm over his shoulders.

"So do I, father," he returned; "but it is because I have got you."

The old man turned and looked at him with a tenderness I had never seen on his face before. As soon as I saw that, I no longer doubted that he could be saved.

We found rooms in a farm-house on the topmost height.

"These are poor little hills, Falconer," I said. "Yet they help one like mountains."

"The whole question is," he returned, "whether they are high enough to lift you out of the dirt. Here we are in the airs of heaven—that is all we need."

"They make me think how often, amongst the country people of Scotland, I have wondered at the clay-feet upon which a golden head of wisdom stood! What poor needs, what humble aims, what a narrow basement generally, was sufficient to support the statues of pure-eyed Faith and white-handed Hope."

"Yes," said Falconer: "he who is faithful over a few things is a lord of cities. It does not matter whether you preach in Westminster Abbey, or teach a ragged class, so you be faithful. The faithfulness is all."

After an early dinner we went out for a walk, but we did not go far before we sat down upon the grass. Falconer laid himself at full length and gazed upwards.

"When I look like this into the blue sky," he said, after a moment's silence, "it seems so deep, so peaceful, so full of a mysterious tenderness, that I could lie for centuries, and wait for the dawning of the face of God out of the awful loving-kindness."

I had never heard Falconer talk of his own present feelings in this manner; but glancing at the face of his father with a sense of his unfitness to hear such a lofty utterance, I saw at once that it was for his sake that he had thus spoken. The old man had thrown himself back too, and was gazing into the sky, puzzling himself, I could see, to comprehend what his son could mean. I fear he concluded, for the time, that Robert was not gifted with the amount of common-sense belonging of right to the Falconer family, and that much religion had made him a dreamer. Still, I thought I could see a kind of awe pass like a spiritual shadow across his face as he gazed into the blue gulfs over him. No one can detect the first beginnings of any life, and those of spiritual emotion must more than any lie beyond our ken: there is infinite room for hope. Falconer said no more. We betook ourselves early within doors, and he read King Lear to us, expounding the spiritual history of the poor old king after a fashion I had never conceived—showing us how the said history was all compressed, as far as human eye could see of it, into the few months that elapsed between his abdication and his death; how in that short time he had to learn everything that he ought to have been learning all his life; and how, because he had put it off so long, the lessons that had then to be given him were awfully severe.

I thought what a change it was for the old man to lift his head into the air of thought and life, out of the sloughs of misery in which he had been wallowing for years.

CHAPTER XVII.

IN THE COUNTRY.

THE next morning Falconer, who knew the country, took us out for a drive. We passed through lanes and gates out upon an open moor, where he stopped the carriage, and led us a few yards on one side. Suddenly, hundreds of feet below us, down what seemed an almost precipitous descent, we saw the wood-embosomed, stream-trodden valley we had left the day before. Enough had been cleft and scooped seawards out of the lofty table-land to give room for a few little conical hills with curious peaks of bare rock. At the bases of these hills flowed noisily two or three streams, which joined in one, and trotted out to sea over rocks and stones. The hills and the sides of the great cleft were half of them green with grass, and half of them robed in the autumnal foliage of thick woods. By the streams and in the woods nestled pretty houses; and away at the mouth of the valley and the stream lay the village. All around, on our level, stretched farm and moorland.

When Andrew Falconer stood so unexpectedly on the verge of the steep descent, he trembled and started back with fright. His son made him sit down a little way off, where yet we could see into the valley. The sun was hot, the air clear and mild, and the sea broke its blue floor into innumerable sparkles of radiance. We sat for awhile in silence.

"Are you sure," I said, in the hope of setting my friend talking, "that there is no horrid pool down there? no half-trampled thicket, with broken pottery and shreds of tin lying about? no dead carcase, or dirty cottage, with miserable wife and greedy children? When I was a child, I knew a lovely place that I could not half enjoy, because, although hidden from my view, an ugly stagnation, half mud, half water, lay in a certain spot below me. When I had to pass it, I used to creep by with a kind of dull terror, mingled with hopeless disgust, and I have never got over the feeling."

"You remind me much of a friend of mine of whom I have spoken to you before," said Falconer, "Eric Ericson. I have shown you many of his verses, but I don't think I ever showed you one little poem containing an expression of the same feeling. I think I can repeat it.

Some men there are who cannot spare
A single tear until they feel
The last cold pressure, and the heel
Is stamped upon the outmost layer.

And, waking, some will sigh to think
The clouds have borrowed winter's wing—
Sad winter when the grasses spring
No more about the fountain's brink.

And some would call me coward-fool:
I lay a claim to better blood;
But yet a heap of idle mud
Hath power to make me sorrowful."

I sat thinking over the verses, for I found the feeling a little difficult to follow, although the last stanza was plain enough. Falconer resumed.

"I think this is as likely as any place," he said, "to be free of such physical blots. For the moral I cannot say. But I have learned, I hope, not to be too fastidious—I mean so as to be unjust to the whole because of the part. The impression made by a whole is just as true as the result of an analysis, and is greater and more valuable in every respect. If we rejoice in the beauty of the whole, the other is sufficiently forgotten. For moral ugliness, it ceases to distress in proportion as we labour to remove it, and regard it in its true relations to all that surrounds it. There is an old legend which I daresay you know. The Saviour and his disciples were walking along the way, when they came upon a dead dog. The disciples did not conceal their disgust. The Saviour said: "How white its teeth are !"

"That is very beautiful," I rejoined. "Thank God for that. It is true, whether invented or not. But," I added, "it does not quite answer to the question about which we have been talking. The Lord got rid of the pain of the ugliness by finding the beautiful in it."

"It does correspond, however, I think, in principle," returned Falconer; "only it goes much farther, making the exceptional beauty hallow the general ugliness—which is the true way, for beauty is life, and therefore infinitely deeper and more powerful than ugliness which is death. 'A dram of sweet,' says Spenser, 'is worth a pound of sour.'"

It was so delightful to hear him talk—for what he said was not only far finer than my record of it, but the whole man spoke as well as his mouth—that I sought to start him again.

"I wish," I said, "that I could see things as you do—in great masses of harmonious unity. I am only able to see a truth sparkling here and there, and to try to lay hold of it. When I aim at more, I am like Noah's dove, without a place to rest the sole of my foot."

"That is the only way to begin. Leave the large vision to itself, and look well after your sparkles. You will find them grow and gather and unite, until you are afloat on a sea of radiance—with cloud shadows no doubt."

" And yet," I resumed, " I never seem to have room."

" That is just why."

" But I feel that I cannot find it. I know that if I fly to that bounding cape on the far horizon there, I shall only find *a place*—a place to want another in. There is no fortunate island out on that sea.

" I fancy," said Falconer, " that until a man loves space, he will never be at peace in a place. At least so I have found it. I am content if you but give me room. All space to me throbs with being and life; and the loveliest spot on the earth seems but the compression of space till the meaning shines out of it, as the fire flies out of the air when you drive it close together. To seek place after place for freedom, is a constant effort to flee from space, and a vain one, for you are ever haunted by the need of it, and therefore when you seek most to escape it, fancy that you love it and want it."

" You are getting too mystical for me now," I said. " I am not able to follow you."

" I fear I was on the point of losing myself. At all events I can go no further now. And indeed I fear I have been but skirting the Limbo of Vanities."

He rose, for we could both see that this talk was not in the least interesting to our companion. We got again into the carriage, which, by Falconer's orders, was turned and driven in the opposite direction, still at no great distance from the lofty edge of the heights that rose above the shore.

We came at length to a lane bounded with stone walls, every stone of which had its moss and every chink its fern. The lane grew more and more grassy; the walls vanished; and the track faded away into a narrow winding valley, formed by the many meeting curves of opposing hills. They were green to the top with sheep-grass, and spotted here and there with patches of fern, great stones, and tall withered foxgloves. The air was sweet and healthful, and Andrew evidently enjoyed it because it reminded him again of his boyhood. The only sound we heard was the tinkle of a few tender sheep-bells, and now and then the tremulous bleating of a sheep. With a gentle winding, the valley led us into a more open portion of itself, where the old man paused with a look of astonished pleasure.

Before us, seaward, rose a rampart against the sky, like the turreted and embattled wall of a huge eastern city, built of loose stones piled high, and divided by great peaky rocks. In the centre rose above them all one solitary

curiously-shaped mass, one of the oddest peaks
of the Himmalays in miniature. From its top
on the further side was a sheer descent to the
waters far below the level of the valley from
which it immediately rose. It was altogether
a strange freaky fantastic place, not without its
grandeur. It looked like the remains of a fro-
lic of the Titans, or rather as if reared by the
boys and girls, while their fathers and mothers
" lay stretched out huge in length," and in
breadth too, upon the slopes around, and laughed thunderously at the sportive invention of
their sons and daughters. Falconer helped his
father up to the edge of the rampart that he
might look over. Again he started back, "afraid
of that which was high," for the lowly valley
was yet at a great height above the diminished
waves. On the outside of the rampart ran a
narrow path whence the green hill-side went
down steep to the sea. The gulls were screaming far below us; we could see the little flying
streaks of white. Beyond was the great ocean.
A murmurous sound came up from its shore.

We descended and seated ourselves on the
short springy grass of a little mound at the foot
of one of the hills, where it sank slowly, like the
dying gush of a wave, into the hollowest centre
of the little vale.

"Everything tends to the cone-shape here,"
said Falconer,—" the oddest and at the same

time most wonderful of mathematical figures."

" It is not strange," I said, " that oddity and wonder should come so near ? "

" They often do in the human world as well," returned he. " Therefore it is not strange that Shelley should have been so fond of this place. It is told of him that repeated sketches of the spot were found on the covers of his letters. I know nothing more like Shelley's poetry than this valley—wildly fantastic and yet beautiful —as if a huge genius were playing at grandeur, and producing little models of great things. But there is one grand thing I want to show you a little further on."

We rose, and walked out of the valley on the other side, along the lofty coast. When we reached a certain point, Falconer stood and requested us to look as far as we could, along the cliffs to the face of the last of them.

" What do you see ?" he asked.

" A perpendicular rock, going right down into the blue waters," I answered.

" Look at it : what is the outline of it like ? Whose face is it ?"

" Shakspere's, by all that is grand !" I cried. " So it is," said Andrew.

" Right. Now I'll tell you what I would do, If I were very rich, and there were no poor people in the country. I would give a commission to some great sculptor to attack that rock and

IN THE COUNTRY.

work out its suggestion. Then, if I had any money left, we should find one for Bacon, and one for Chaucer, and one for Milton; and, as we are about it, we may fancy as many more as we like; so that from the bounding rocks of our island, the memorial faces of our great brothers should look abroad over the seas into the infinite sky beyond."

" Well, now," said the elder, " I think it is grander as it is."

" You are quite right, father," said Robert. " And so with many of our fancies for perfecting God's mighty sketches, which he only can finish."

Again we seated ourselves and looked out over the waves.

" I have never yet heard," I said, " how you managed with that poor girl that wanted to drown herself—on Westminster Bridge, I mean —that night, you remember."

" Miss St. John has got her in her own house at present. She has given her those two children we picked up at the door of the public house to take care of. Poor little darlings! they are bringing back the life in her heart already. There is actually a little colour in her cheek— the dawn, I trust, of the eternal life. That is Miss St. John's way. As often as she gets hold of a poor hopeless woman, she gives her a mother- less child. It is wonderful what the childless woman and motherless child do for each other."

"I was much amused the other day with the lecture one of the police magistrates gave a poor creature who was brought before him for attempting to drown herself. He did give her a sovereign out of the poor box, though."

"Well, that might just tide her over the shoal of self-destruction," said Falconer. "But I cannot help doubting whether any one has a *right* to prevent a suicide from carrying out his purpose, who is not prepared to do a good deal more for him than that. What would you think of the man who snatched the loaf from a hungry thief, threw it back into the baker's cart, and walked away to his club-dinner? Harsh words of rebuke, and the threat of severe punishment upon a second attempt—what are they to the wretch weary of life? To some of them the *kindest* punishment would be to hang them for it. It is something else than punishment that they need. If the comfortable alderman had but 'a feeling of their afflictions,' felt in himself for a moment how miserable *he* must be, what a waste of despair must be in his heart, before he would do it himself, before the awful river would appear to him a refuge from the upper air, he would change his tone. I fear he regards suicide chiefly as a burglarious entrance into the premises of the respectable firm of Venison, Port, & Co."

" But you mustn't be too hard upon him, Falconer; for if his God is his belly, how can he regard suicide as other than the most awful sacrilege ?"

" Of course not. His well-fed divinity gives him one great commandment : ' Thou shalt love thyself with all thy heart. The great breach is to hurt thyself—worst of all to send thyself away from the land of luncheons and dinners, to the country of thought and vision.' But, alas ! he does not reflect on the fact that the god Belial does not feed all his votaries ; that he has his elect ; that the altar of his inner-temple too often smokes with no sacrifice of which his poor meagre priests may partake. They must uphold the Divinity which has been good to *them*, and not suffer his worship to fall into disrepute."

" Really, Robert," said his father, " I am afraid to think what you will come to. You will end in denying there is a God at all. You don't believe in hell, and now you justify suicide. Really—I must say—to say the least of it—I have not been accustomed to hear such things."

The poor old man looked feebly righteous at his wicked son. I verily believe he was concerned for his eternal fate. Falconer gave a pleased glance at me, and for a moment said nothing. Then he began, with a kind of logical composure :

"In the first place, father, I do not believe in such a God as some people say they believe in. Their God is but an idol of the heathen, modified with a few Christian qualities. For hell, I don't believe there is any escape from it but by leaving hellish things behind. For suicide, I do not believe it is wicked because it hurts yourself, but I do believe it is very wicked. I only want to put it on its own right footing."

"And pray what do you consider its right footing?"

"My dear father, I recognize no duty as owing to a man's self. There is and can be no such thing. I am and can be under no obligation to myself. The whole thing is a fiction, and of evil invention. It comes from the upper circles of the hell of selfishness. Or, perhaps, it may with some be merely a form of metaphysical mistake; but an untruth it is. Then for the duty we do owe to other people: how can we expect the men or women who have found life to end, as it seems to them, in a dunghill of misery —how can we expect such to understand any obligation to live for the sake of the general *others*, to no individual of whom, possibly, do they bear an endurable relation? What remains?—The grandest, noblest duty from which all other duty springs: the duty to the possible God. Mind I say *possible* God, for I judge it the first of my duties towards my neighbour to regard his duty from his position, not from mine."

"But," said I, "how would you bring that duty to bear on the mind of a suicide?"

"I think some of the tempted could understand it, though I fear not one of those could who judge them hardly, and talk sententiously of the wrong done to a society which has done next to nothing for him, by the poor, starved, refused, husband-tortured wretch perhaps, who hurries at last to the might of the filthy flowing river which, the one thread of hope in the web of despair, crawls through the city of death. What should I say to him? I should say: 'God liveth: thou art not thine own but his. Bear thy hunger, thy horror in his name. I in his name will help thee out of them, as I may. To go before he calleth thee, is to say "Thou forgettest," unto him who numbereth the hairs of thy head. Stand out in the cold and the sleet and the hail of this world, O son of man, till thy Father open the door and call thee. Yea, even if thou knowest him not, stand and wait, lest there should be, after all, such a loving and tender one, who, for the sake of a good with which thou wilt be all-content, and without which thou never couldst be content, permits thee there to stand—for a time—long to his sympathizing as well as to thy suffering heart.'"

Here Falconer paused, and when he spoke again it was from the ordinary level of conversation. Indeed I fancied that he was a little uncomfortable at the excitement into which his feelings had borne him.

" Not many of them could understand this, I daresay : but I think most of them could feel it without understanding it. Certainly the 'belly with good capon lined' will neither understand nor feel it. Suicide is a sin against God, I repeat, not a crime over which human laws have any hold. In regard to such, man has a duty alone —that, namely, of making it possible for every man to live. And where the dread of death is not sufficient to deter, what can the threat of punishment do ? Or what great thing is gained if it should succeed ? What agonies a man must have gone through in whom neither the horror of falling into such a river, nor of the knife in the flesh instinct with life, can extinguish the vague longing to wrap up his weariness in an endless sleep ! "

" But," I remarked, " you would, I fear, encourage the trade in suicide. Your kindness would be terribly abused. What would you do with the pretended suicides ?"

" Whip them, for trifling with and trading upon the feelings of their kind."

" Then you would drive them to suicide in earnest."

" Then they might be worth something, which they were not before."

" We are a great deal too humane for that now-a-days, I fear. We don't like hurting people."

" No. We are infested with a philanthropy which is the offspring of our mammon-worship. But surely our tender mercies are cruel. We don't like to hang people, however unfit they may be to live amongst their fellows. A weakling pity will petition for the life of the worst murderer—but for what? To keep him alive in a confinement as like their notion of hell as they dare to make it—namely, a place whence all the sweet visitings of the grace of God are withdrawn, and the man has not a chance, so to speak, of growing better. In this hell of theirs they will even pamper his beastly body."

" They have the chaplain to visit them."

" I pity the chaplain, cut off in his labours from all the aids which God's world alone can give for the teaching of these men. Human beings have *not* the right to inflict such cruel punishment upon their fellow man. It springs from a cowardly shrinking from responsibility, and from mistrust of the mercy of God;—perhaps first of all from an over-valuing of the mere life of the body. Hanging is tenderness itself to such a punishment."

" I think you are hardly fair, though, Falconer. It is the fear of sending them to hell that prevents them from hanging them."

" Yes. You are right, I daresay. They are not of David's mind, who would rather fall into the hands of God than of men. They think their hell is not so hard as his, and may be better for them. But I must not, as you say, forget that they do believe their everlasting fate hangs upon their hands, for if God once gets his hold of them by death, they are lost for ever."

" But the chaplain may awake them to a sense of their sins."

" I do not think it is likely that talk will do what the discipline of life has not done. It seems to me, on the contrary, that the clergyman has no commission to rouse people to a sense of their sins. That is not his work. He is far more likely to harden them by any attempt in that direction. Every man does feel his sins, though he often does not know it. To turn his attention away from what he does feel by trying to rouse in him feelings which are impossible to him in his present condition, is to do him a great wrong. The clergyman has the message of salvation, not of sin, to give. Whatever oppression is on a man, whatever trouble, whatever conscious something that comes between him and the blessedness of life, is his sin; for whatever is not of faith is sin; and from all this He came to save us. Salvation alone can rouse in us a sense of our sinfulness. One must have got on a good way before he can be sorry for his sins. There is no condition of sorrow laid down as necessary to forgiveness. Repentance does not mean sorrow: it means turning away from the sins. Every man can do that, more or less. And that every man must do. The sorrow will come afterwards, all in good time. Jesus offers to take us out of our own hands into his, if we will only obey him."

The eyes of the old man were fixed on his son as he spoke. He did seem to be thinking. I could almost fancy that a glimmer of something like hope shone in his eyes.

It was time to go home, and we were nearly silent all the way.

The next morning was so wet that we could not go out, and had to amuse ourselves as we best might in-doors. But Falconer's resources never failed. He gave us this day story after story about the poor people he had known. I could see that his object was often to get some truth into his father's mind without exposing it to rejection by addressing it directly to himself; and few subjects could be more fitted for affording such opportunity than his experiences among the poor.

The afternoon was still rainy and misty. In the evening I sought to lead the conversation towards the gospel-story; and then Falconer talked as I never heard him talk before. No little circumstance in the narratives appeared to have escaped him. He had thought about everything, as it seemed to me. He had looked under the surface everywhere, and found truth—mines of it—under all the upper soil of the story. The deeper he dug the richer seemed the ore. This was combined with the most pictorial apprehension of every outward event, which he treated as if it had been described to him by the lips of an eye-witness. The whole thing lived in his words and thoughts.

"When anything looks strange, you must look the deeper," he would say.

At the close of one of our fits of talk, he rose and went to the window.

"Come here," he said, after looking for a moment.

All day a dropping cloud had filled the space below, so that the hills on the opposite side of the valley were hidden, and the whole of the sea, near as it was. But when we went to the window we found that a great change had silently taken place. The mist continued to veil the sky, and it clung to the tops of the hills; but, like the rising curtain of a stage, it had rolled halfway up from their bases, revealing a great part of the sea and shore, and half of a cliff on the opposite side of the valley: this, in itself of a deep red, was now smitten by the rays of the setting sun, and glowed over the waters a splendour of carmine. As we gazed, the vaporous curtain sank upon the shore, and the sun sank under the waves, and the sad gray evening closed in the weeping night, and clouds and darkness swathed the weary earth. For doubtless the earth needs its night as well as the creatures that live thereon.

In the morning the rain had ceased, but the clouds remained. But they were high in the heavens now, and like a departing sorrow, revealed the outline and form which had appeared before as an enveloping vapour of universal and shapeless evil. The mist was now far enough off to be seen and thought about. It was clouds now—no longer mist and rain. And I thought how at length the evils of the world would float away, and we should see what it was that made it so hard for us to believe and be at peace.

In the afternoon the sky had partially cleared, but clouds hid the sun as he sank towards the west. We walked out. A cold autumnal wind blew, not only from the twilight of the dying day, but from the twilight of the dying season. A sorrowful hopeless wind it seemed, full of the odours of dead leaves—those memories of green woods, and of damp earth—the bare graves of the flowers. Would the summer ever come again?

We were pacing in silence along a terraced walk which overhung the shore far below.

More here than from the hill top we seemed to look immediately into space, not even a parapet intervening betwixt us and the ocean. The sound of a mournful lyric, never yet sung, was in my brain; it drew nearer to my mental grasp; but ere it alighted, its wings were gone, and it fell dead on my consciousness. Its meaning was this: "Welcome, Requiem of Nature. Let me share in thy Requiescat. Blow, wind of mournful memories. Let us moan together. No one taketh from us the joy of our sorrow. We may mourn as we will."

But while I brooded thus, behold a wonder! The mass about the sinking sun broke up, and drifted away in cloudy bergs, as if scattered on the diverging currents of solar radiance that burst from the gates of the west, and streamed east and north and south over the heavens and over the sea. To the north, these masses built a cloudy bridge across the sky from horizon to horizon, and beneath it shone the rosy-sailed ships floating stately through their triumphal arch up the channel to their home. Other clouds floated stately too in the upper sea over our heads, with dense forms, thinning into vaporous edges. Some were of a dull angry red; some of as exquisite a primrose hue as ever the flower itself bore on its bosom; and betwixt their edges beamed out the sweetest, purest, most melting, most transparent blue, the heavenly

blue which is the symbol of the spirit as red is
of the heart. I think I never saw a blue to
satisfy me before. Some of these clouds threw
shadows of many-shaded purple upon the green
sea; and from one of the shadows, so dark
and so far out upon the glooming horizon that
it looked like an island, arose as from a pier, a
wondrous structure of dim, fairy colours, a multitude of rainbow-ends, side by side, that would
have spanned the heavens with a gorgeous arch,
but failed from the very grandeur of the idea,
and grew up only a few degrees against the
clouded west. I stood rapt. The two Falconers were at some distance before me, walking
arm in arm. They stood and gazed likewise.
It was as if God had said to the heavens and
the earth and the chord of the seven colours,
"Comfort ye, comfort ye my people." And I
said to my soul : " Let the tempest rave in the
world; let sorrow wail like a sea-bird in the
midst thereof; and let thy heart respond to her
shivering cry ; but the vault of heaven incloses
the tempest and the shrieking bird and the
echoing heart; and the sun of God's countenance can with one glance from above change
the wildest winter day into a summer evening
compact of poets' dreams."

My companions were walking up over the
hill. I could see that Falconer was earnestly
speaking in his father's ear. The old man's

head was bent towards the earth. I kept away.
They made a turn from home. I still followed
at a distance. The evening began to grow
dark. The autumn wind met us again, colder,
stronger, yet more laden with the odours of
death and the frosts of the coming winter. But
it no longer blew as from the charnel-house of
the past; it blew from the stars through the
chinks of the unopened door on the other side
of the sepulchre. It was a wind of the worlds,
not a wind of the leaves. It told of the march
of the spheres, and the rest of the throne of
God. We were going on into the universe—
home to the house of our Father. Mighty adventure! Sacred repose! And as I followed
the pair, one great star throbbed and radiated
over my head.

CHAPTER XVIII.

THREE GENERATIONS.

THE next week I went back to my work, leaving the father and son alone together. Before I left, I could see plainly enough that the bonds were being drawn closer between them. A whole month passed before they returned to London. The winter then had set in with unusual severity. But it seemed to bring only health to the two men. When I saw Andrew next, there was certainly a marked change upon him. Light had banished the haziness from his eye, and his step was a good deal firmer. I can hardly speak of more than the physical improvement, for I saw very little of him now. Still I did think I could perceive more of judgment in his face, as if he sometimes weighed things in his mind. But it was plain that Robert continued very careful not to let him a moment out of his knowledge. He busied him with the various sights of London, for Andrew, although he knew all its miseries well,

had never yet been inside Westminster Abbey.
If he could only trust him enough to get him
something to do ! But what was he fit for ?
To try him, he proposed once that he should
write some account of what he had seen and
learned in his wanderings ; but the evident distress with which he shrunk from the proposal
was grateful to the eyes and heart of his son.

It was almost the end of the year when a letter arrived from John Lammie, informing Robert
that his grandmother had caught a violent cold,
and that, although the special symptoms had
disappeared, it was evident her strength was
sinking fast, and that she would not recover.

He read the letter to his father.

"We must go and see her, Robert, my boy,"
said Andrew.

It was the first time that he had shown the
smallest desire to visit her.   Falconer rose with
glad heart, and proceeded at once to make ar-
rangements for their journey.

It was a cold, powdery afternoon in January,
with the snow thick on the ground, save where
the little winds had blown the crown of the
street bare before Mrs. Falconer's house.   A
post-chaise with four horses swept wearily round
the corner, and pulled up at her door.   Betty
opened it, and revealed an old withered face
very sorrowful, and yet expectant.   Falconer's
feelings I dare not, Andrew's I cannot attempt

to describe, as they stepped from the chaise and entered. Betty led the way without a word into the little parlour. Robert went next, with long quiet strides, and Andrew followed with gray, bowed head. Grannie was not in her chair. The doors which during the day concealed the bed in which she slept, were open, and there lay the aged woman with her eyes closed. The room was as it had always been, only there seemed a filmy shadow in it that had not been there before.

"She's deein', sir," whispered Betty. "Ay is she. Och hone!"

Robert took his father's hand, and led him towards the bed. They drew nigh softly, and bent over the withered, but not even yet very wrinkled face. The smooth, white, soft hands lay on the sheet, which was folded back over her bosom. She was asleep, or rather, she slumbered.

But the soul of the child began to grow in the withered heart of the old man as he regarded his older mother, and as it grew it forced the tears to his eyes, and the word to his lips.

"Mother!" he said, and her eyelids rose at once. He stooped to kiss her, with the tears rolling down his face. The light of heaven broke and flashed from her aged countenance. She lifted her weak hands, took his head, and held it to her bosom.

"Eh! the bonnie gray heid!" she said, and burst into a passion of weeping. She had kept some tears for the last. Now she would spend all that her griefs had left her. But there came a pause in her sobs, though not in her weeping, and then she spoke.

"I kent it a' the time, O Lord. I kent it a' the time. He's come hame. My Anerew, my Anerew! I'm as happy's a bairn. O Lord! O Lord!"

And she burst again into sobs, and entered paradise in radiant weeping.

Her hands sank away from his head, and when her son gazed in her face he saw that she was dead. She had never looked at Robert.

The two men turned towards each other. Robert put out his arms. His father laid his head on his bosom, and went on weeping. Robert held him to his heart.

When shall a man dare to say that God has done all he can?

CHAPTER XIX.

THE WHOLE STORY.

THE men laid their mother's body with those of the generations that had gone before her, beneath the long grass in their country churchyard near Rothieden—a dreary place, one accustomed to trim cemeteries and sentimental wreaths would call it—to Falconer's mind so friendly to the forsaken dust, because it lapt it in sweet oblivion.

They returned to the dreary house, and after a simple meal such as both had used to partake of in their boyhood, they sat by the fire, Andrew in his mother's chair, Robert in the same chair in which he had learned his Sallust and written his versions. Andrew sat for a while gazing into the fire, and Robert sat watching his face, where in the last few months a little feeble fatherhood had begun to dawn.

"It was there, father, that grannie used to sit, every day, sometimes looking in the fire for hours, thinking about you, I know," Robert said at length.

Andrew stirred uneasily in his chair.

" How do you know that ?" he asked.

" If there was one thing I could be sure of, it was when grannie was thinking about you, father. Who wouldn't have known it, father, when her lips were pressed together, as if she had some dreadful pain to bear, and her eyes were looking away through the fire—so far away ! and I would speak to her three times before she would answer ? She lived only to think about God and you, father. God and you came very close together in her mind. Since ever I can remember, almost, the thought of you was just the one thing in this house."

Then Robert began at the beginning of his memory, and told his father all that he could remember. When he came to speak about his solitary musings in the garret, he said—and long before he reached this part, he had relapsed into his mother tongue :

" Come and luik at the place, father. I want to see 't again, mysel'."

He rose. His father yielded and followed him. Robert got a candle in the kitchen, and the two big men climbed the little narrow stair and stood in the little sky of the house, where their heads almost touched the ceiling.

" I sat upo' the flure there," said Robert, "an'

thoucht and thoucht what I wad du to get ye, father, and what I wad du wi' ye whan I had gotten ye. I wad greit whiles, 'cause ither laddies had a father an' I had nane. An' there's whaur I fand mamma's box wi' the letter in 't and her ain picter : grannie gae me that ane o' you. An' there's whaur I used to kneel doon an' pray to God. An' he's heard my prayers, and grannie's prayers, and here ye are wi' me at last. Instead o' thinkin' aboot ye, I hae yer ain sel'. Come, father, I want to say a word o' thanks to God, for hearin' my prayer."

He took the old man's hand, led him to the bedside, and kneeled with him there.

My reader can hardly avoid thinking it was a poor sad triumph that Robert had after all. How the dreams of the boy had dwindled in settling down into the reality! He had his father, it was true, but what a father! And how little he had him!

But this was not the end; and Robert always believed that the end must be the greater in proportion to the distance it was removed, to give time for its true fulfilment. And when he prayed aloud beside his father, I doubt not that his thanksgiving and his hope were equal.

The prayer over, he took his father's hand and led him down again to the little parlour, and they took their seats again by the fire ; and Robert began again and went on with his story,

not omitting the parts belonging to Mary St.
John and Eric Ericson.

When he came to tell how he had encountered him in the deserted factory :

" Luik here, father, here's the mark o' the
cut," he said, parting the thick hair on the top
of his head.

His father hid his face in his hands.

" It wasna muckle o' a blow that ye gied me,
father," he went on, " but I fell against the
grate, and that was what did it. And I never
tellt onybody, nae even Miss St. John, wha
plaistered it up, hoo I had gotten 't. And I
didna mean to say onything aboot it ; but I
wantit to tell ye a queer dream, sic a queer
dream it garred me dream the same nicht."

As he told the dream, his father suddenly
grew attentive, and before he had finished, looked almost scared ; but he said nothing. When
he came to relate his grandmother's behaviour
after having discovered that the papers re-
lating to the factory were gone, he hid his face
in his hands once more. He told him how
grannie had mourned and wept over him, from
the time when he heard her praying aloud as he
crept through her room at night to their last
talk together after Dr. Anderson's death. He
set forth, as he could, in the simplest language,
the agony of her soul over her lost son. He
told him then about Ericson, and Dr. Anderson,

and how good they had been to him, and at last of Dr. Anderson's request that he would do something for him in India.

" Will ye gang wi' me, father ?" he asked.

" I'll never leave ye again, Robert, my boy," he answered. " I have been a bad man, and a bad father, and now I gie mysel' up to you to mak the best o' me ye can. I daurna leave ye, Robert."

" Pray to God to tak care o' ye, father. He'll do a'thing for ye, gin ye'll only lat him."

"I will, Robert."

" I was mysel' dreidfu' miserable for a while," Robert resumed, " for I cudna see or hear God at a'; but God heard me, and loot me ken that he was there an' that a' was richt. It was jist like whan a bairnie waukens up an' cries oot, thinkin' it 's its lane, an' through the mirk comes the word o' the mither o' 't, sayin', ' I'm here, cratur: dinna greit.' And I cam to believe 'at he wad mak you a good man at last. O father, it's been my dream waukin' an' sleepin' to hae you back to me an' grannie, an' mamma, an' the Father o' 's a', an' Jesus Christ that's done a'thing for 's. An' noo ye maun pray to God, father. Ye *will* pray to God to haud a grip o' ye—willna ye, father ?"

"I will, I will, Robert. But I've been an awfu' sinner. I believe I was the death o' yer mother, laddie."

Some fount of memory was opened; some tide of old tenderness gushed up in his heart; at some window of the past the face of his dead wife looked in : the old man broke into a great cry, and sobbed and wept bitterly. Robert said no more, but wept with him.

Henceforward the father clung to his son like a child. The heart of Falconer turned to his Father in heaven with speechless thanksgiving. The ideal of his dreams was beginning to dawn, and his life was new-born.

For a few days Robert took Andrew about to see those of his old friends who were left, and the kindness with which they all received him, moved Andrew's heart not a little. Every one who saw him seemed to feel that he or she had a share in the redeeming duty of the son. Robert was in their eyes like a heavenly messenger, whom they were bound to aid; for here was the possessed of demons clothed and in his right mind. Therefore they overwhelmed both father and son with kindness. Especially at John Lammie's was he received with a perfection of hospitality; as if that had been the father's house to which he had returned from his prodigal wanderings.

The good old farmer begged that they would stay with him for a few days.

"I hae sae mony wee things to luik efter at Rothieden, afore we gang," said Robert.

" Weel, lea' yer father here. We s' tak guid care o' 'im, I promise ye."

"There's only ae difficulty. I believe ye are my father's frien', Mr. Lammie, as ye hae been mine, and God bless ye; sae I'll jist tell you the trowth, what for I canna lea' him. I'm no sure eneuch yet that he could withstan' temptation. It's the drink ye ken. It's months sin' he 's tasted it; but—ye ken weel eneuch—the temptation's awfu'. Sin' ever I got him back, I haena tasted ae mou'fu' o' onything that cud be ca'd strong drink mysel', an' as lang 's he lives, not ae drap shall cross my lips—no to save my life."

" Robert," said Mr. Lammie, giving him his hand with solemnity, " I sweir by God that he shanna see, smell, taste, nor touch drink in this hoose. There's but twa boatles o' whusky, i' the shape o' drink, i' the hoose; an' gin ye say 'at he sall bide, I'll gang and mak them an' the midden weel acquant."

Andrew was pleased at the proposal. Robert too was pleased that his father should be free of him for a while. It was arranged for three days. Half an hour after, Robert came upon Mr. Lammie emptying the two bottles of whisky into the dunghill in the farm-yard.

He returned with glad heart to Rothieden. It did not take him long to arrange his grandmother's little affairs. He had already made up his mind about her house and furniture.   He rang the bell one morning for Betty.

"Hae ye ony siller laid up, Betty ?"

"Ay.   I hae feifteen poun' i' the savin's' bank."

"An' what do ye think o' doin'."

"I'll get a bit roomy, an' tak in washin'."

"Weel, I'll tell ye what I wad like ye to do. Ye ken Mistress Elshender ?"

"Fine that. An' a verra dacent body she is."

"Weel, gin ye like, ye can haud this hoose, an' a' 'at's in't, jist as it is, till the day o' yer deith.   And ye'll aye keep it in order, an' the ga'le room ready for me at ony time I may happen to come in upo' ye in want o' a nicht's quarters.   But I wad like ye, gin ye hae nae objections, to tak Mistress Elshender to bide wi' ye. She's turnin' some frail noo, and I'm unner great obligation to her Sandy, ye ken."

"Ay, weel that.   He learnt ye to fiddle, Robert—I hoombly beg your pardon, sir, Mister Robert."

"Nae offence, Betty, I assure ye. Ye hae been aye gude to me, and I thank ye hertily."

Betty could not stand this.   Her apron went up to her eyes.

"Eh, sir," she sobbed, "ye was aye a gude lad."

"Excep' whan I spak o' Muckledrum, Betty." She laughed and sobbed together.

" Weel, ye'll tak Mistress Elshender in, winna ye ?"

" I'll do that, sir. And I'll try to do my best wi' her."

" She can help ye, ye ken, wi' yer washin', an' sic like."

" She's a hard-workin' wuman, sir. She wad do that weel."

" And whan ye're in ony want o' siller, jist write to me. An' gin onything suld happen to me, ye ken, write to Mr. Gordon, a frien' o' mine. There's his address in Lonnon."

" Eh, sir, but ye are kin'. God bless ye for a'."

She could bear no more, and left the room crying.

Everything settled at Rothieden, he returned to Bodyfauld. The most welcome greeting he had ever received in his life, lay in the shine of his father's eyes when he entered the room where he sat with Miss Lammie. The next day they left for London.

CHAPTER XX.

THE VANISHING.

THEY came to see me the very evening of their arrival. As to Andrew's progress there could be no longer any doubt. All that was necessary for conviction on the point was to have seen him before and to see him now. The very grasp of his hand was changed. But not yet would Robert leave him alone.

It will naturally occur to my reader that his goodness was not much yet. It was not. It may have been greater than we could be sure of, though. But if any one object that such a conversion, even if it were perfected, was poor, inasmuch as the man's free will was intromitted with, I answer: "The development of the free will was the one object. Hitherto it was not free." I ask the man who says so: "Where would your free will have been if at some period of your life you could have had everything you wanted?" If he says it is nobler in a man to do with less help, I answer, "Andrew was not

noble : was he therefore to be forsaken? The
prodigal was not left without the help of the
swine and their husks, at once to keep him alive
and disgust him with the life. Is the less help
a man has from God the better?" According to
you, the grandest thing of all would be for a
man sunk in the absolute abysses of sensuality
all at once to resolve to be pure as the empy-
rean, and be so, without help from God or man.
But is the thing possible? As well might a
hyena say: I will be a man, and become one.
That would be to create. Andrew must be
kept from the evil long enough to let him at
least see the good, before he was let alone. But
when would we be let alone? For a man to be
fit to be let alone, is for a man not to need God,
but to be able to live without him. Our hearts
cry out, "To have God is to live. We want
God. Without him no life of ours is worth living. We are not then even human, for that is but
the lower form of the divine. We are immortal,
eternal : fill us, O Father, with thyself. Then
only all is well." More: I heartily believe,
though I cannot understand the boundaries of
will and inspiration, that what God will do for
us at last is infinitely beyond any greatness we
could gain, even if we could will ourselves from
the lowest we could be, into the highest we can
imagine. It is essential divine life we want ;
and there is grand truth, however incomplete or

perverted, in the aspiration of the Brahmin. He
is wrong, but he wants something right. If the
man had the power in his pollution to will himself into the right without God, the fact that he
was in that pollution with such power, must
damn him there for ever. And if God must help
ere a man can be saved, can the help of man go
too far towards the same end? Let God solve
the mystery—for he made it. One thing is sure:
We are his, and he will do his part, which is no
part but the all in all. If man could do what in
his wildest self-worship he can imagine, the
grand result would be that he would be his own
God, which is the Hell of Hells.

For some time I had to give Falconer what
aid I could in being with his father while he arranged matters in prospect of their voyage to
India. Sometimes he took him with him when
he went amongst his people, as he called the
poor he visited. Sometimes, when he wanted
to go alone, I had to take him to Miss St. John,
who would play and sing as I had never heard
any one play or sing before. Andrew on such
occasions carried his flute with him, and the
result of the two was something exquisite.
How Miss St. John did lay herself out to please
the old man! And pleased he was. I think
her kindness did more than anything else to
make him feel like a gentleman again. And in
his condition that was much.

At length Falconer would sometimes leave him with Miss St. John, till he or I should go for him: he knew she could keep him safe. He knew that she *would* keep him if necessary.

One evening when I went to see Falconer, I found him alone. It was one of these occasions.

"I am very glad you have come, Gordon," he said. "I was wanting to see you. I have got things nearly ready now. Next month, or at latest, the one after, we shall sail; and I have some business with you which had better be arranged at once. No one knows what is going to happen. The man who believes the least in chance knows as little as the man who believes in it the most. My will is in the hands of Dobson. I have left you everything."

I was dumb.

"Have you any objection?" he said, a little anxiously.

"Am I able to fulfil the conditions?" I faltered.

"I have burdened you with no conditions," he returned. "I don't believe in conditions. I know your heart and mind now. I trust you perfectly."

"I am unworthy of it."

"That is for me to judge."

"Will you have no trustees?"

"Not one."

"What do you want me to do with your property?"

"You know well enough. Keep it going the right way."

"I will always think what you would like."

"No; do not. Think what is right; and where there is no right or wrong plain in itself, then think what is best. You may see good reason to change some of my plans. You may be wrong; but you must do what you see right —not what I see or might see right."

"But there is no need to talk so seriously about it," I said. "You will manage it yourself for many years yet. Make me your steward, if you like, during you absence: I will not object to that."

"You do not object to the other, I hope?"

"No."

"Then so let it be. The other, of course. I have, being a lawyer myself, taken good care not to trust myself only with the arranging of these matters. I think you will find them all right."

"But supposing you should not return—you have compelled me to make the supposition——"

"Of course. Go on."

"What am I to do with the money in the prospect of following you?"

"Ah! that is the one point on which I want a word, although I do not think it is necessary. I want to entail the property."

"How?"

"By word of mouth," he answered, laughing. "You must look out for a right man, as I have done, get him to know your ways and ideas, and if you find him *worthy*—that is a grand wide word—our Lord gave it to his disciples— leave it all to him in the same way I have left it to you, trusting to the spirit of truth that is in him, the spirit of God. You can copy my will —as far as it will apply, for you may have, one way or another, lost the half of it by that time. But, by word of mouth, you must make the same condition with him as I have made with you— that is, with regard to his leaving it, and the conditions on which he leaves it, adding the words, 'that it may descend thus *in perpetuum.*' And he must do the same."

He broke into a quiet laugh. I knew well enough what he meant. But he added :

"That means, of course, for as long as there is any."

"Are you sure you are doing right, Falconer?" I said.

"Quite. It is better to endow one man, who will work as the Father works, than a hundred charities. But it is time I went to fetch my father. Will you go with me ?"

This was all that passed between us on the subject, save that, on our way, he told me to move to his rooms, and occupy them until he returned.

" My papers," he added, " I commit to your discretion."

On our way back from Queen Square, he joked and talked merrily. Andrew joined in. Robert showed himself delighted with every attempt at gaiety or wit that Andrew made. When we reached the house, something that had occurred on the way made him turn to Martin Chuzzlewit, and he read Mrs. Gamp's best to our great enjoyment.

I went down with the two to Southampton, to see them on board the steamer. I staid with them there until she sailed. It was a lovely morning in the end of April, when at last I bade them farewell on the quarter-deck. My heart was full. I took his hand and kissed it. He put his arms round me, and laid his cheek to mine. I was strong to bear the parting.

The great iron steamer went down in the middle of the Atlantic, and I have not yet seen my friend again.

THE END.

LONDON : PRINTED BY MACDONALD AND TUGWELL, BLENHEIM HOUSE.